New Complete Guide to
SEWING

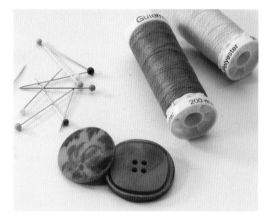

Step-by-Step Techniques for
Making Clothes and Home Accessories

New Complete Guide to
SEWING

Step-by-Step Techniques for
Making Clothes and Home Accessories

Reader's Digest

The Reader's Digest Association (Canada) Ltd. Montreal — Pleasantville, N.Y.

NEW COMPLETE GUIDE TO SEWING
Step-by-Step Techniques for Making Clothes and Home Accessories

FOR READER'S DIGEST CANADA
Project Editor: Pamela Johnson
Art Director: John McGuffie
Designer: Cecile Germain
Editorial Administrator: Elizabeth Eastman
Production Manager: Holger Lorenzen
Production Coordinator: Susan Wong
Vice President & Editorial Director: Deirdre Gilbert

FOR READER'S DIGEST UNITED STATES
Executive Editor, Trade Publishing: Dolores York
Senior Design Director: Elizabeth Tunnicliffe
Senior Designer: George McKeon
Editorial Director: Christopher Cavanaugh
Director, Trade Publishing: Christopher T. Reggio
Vice President & Publisher, Trade Publishing: Harold Clarke

FOR INTERNATIONAL BOOK PRODUCTIONS INC.
Project Editor & Art Director: Barbara Hopkinson
Editor: Judy Phillips
Designer: Dietmar Kokemohr
Consultant: Betty Ann Crosbie
Translator: Dana Selover

FOR INFORMATION ON THIS AND OTHER READER'S DIGEST
PRODUCTS, OR TO REQUEST A CATALOG:

IN THE UNITED STATES
Address any comments to:
The Reader's Digest Association, Inc., Adult Trade Publishing,
Reader's Digest Road, Pleasantville, NY 10570-7000.
You can also visit us on the World Wide Web at www.rd.com

IN CANADA
Please call our 24-hour Customer Service hotline at 1-800-465-0780.
Or visit us on the World Wide Web at www.readersdigest.ca

Library of Congress Cataloging-in-Publication Data

New complete guide to sewing : step-by-step techniques for making
clothes and home accessories / from the editors at Reader's digest
     p. cm.
   Rev. ed. of: Complete guide to sewing.
   Includes index.
   ISBN 0-7621-0420-1
   1. Sewing. 2. Dressmaking. 3. Tailoring. 4. Household linens.
I. Reader's Digest Association. II. Reader's Digest Association
(Canada). III. Complete guide to sewing.

TT705.N48 2003
646.2–dc21   2002069944

Printed in China.

02 03 04 / 5 4 3 2 1

INTRODUCTION

First published in 1976, Reader's Digest's popular COMPLETE GUIDE TO SEWING has become the standard stitch-and-seam reference book for both beginner and seasoned sewers. Its extraordinary success lies in its comprehensive step-by-step instructions, which clearly explain the techniques of sewing and tailoring.

The NEW COMPLETE GUIDE TO SEWING builds on the traditions of that classic best-seller, updating those tried-and-true step-by-step instructions. Thousands of colorful illustrations, diagrams, and photographs demonstrate exactly what to do at each stage of the sewing process. A veritable encyclopedia of sewing, this valuable guide includes detailed directions, practical advice, work-saving tips, essential techniques, and hundreds of unique creative touches to bring out the best in needlework.

Also included are 20 fun, new sewing projects for making clothes and home accessories that reflect today's styles and trends. These projects are classic in cut but easily adaptable to changes in fashion. Whether a collar is rounded or pointed, a dress long or short, or a skirt flared or pleated, sewing techniques remain the same. That's why the NEW COMPLETE GUIDE TO SEWING is an ideal book for sewers everywhere – whatever their level of skill.

Once again this indispensable reference is destined to become the authoritative sewing guide for years to come.

CONTENTS

Chapter Six

Chapter Seven

Chapter Eight

Chapter Nine

Chapter Ten

Chapter Eleven

CHAPTER 1

SEWING EQUIPMENT AND FABRICS

Sewing is easier when
you choose your sewing
supplies to suit the task at hand.
And choosing the right fabrics
guarantees better results for
all your sewing projects.

EQUIPMENT AND FABRICS

Sewing equipment

Having the right tools for the job can make sewing more successful and enjoyable. The following pages show you the basic supplies you will need.

Self-healing cutting mat
This mat is used with the rotary cutter.

Seam ripper
This tool's sharp, curved edge makes opening seams easy.

Chalk pencils
Use these pencils to make thin, accurate lines on fabrics.

Thread clipper
Fitting neatly into the palm of the hand, this tool is useful for cutting stray threads.

Fabric-marking pen
Markings made with this type of pen wash out in water or fade after a few days.

Dressmaker's shears
These are the best tool for cutting patterns since the lower blade lies flat on the fabric.

Rotary cutter
Rotary cutters are indispensible for cutting fabric. Various types of blades are available.

Tailor's chalk
Chalk wedges are ideal for marking fabric.

Adhesive tape measure
This kind of tape measure is self-adhesive and can be permanently attached to any work table.

Pinking shears
These scissors cut zigzag, fray-resistant edges. They are excellent for finishing seams and raw edges.

Square ruler
This type of ruler is especially useful for patchwork, rotary cutting, and crafts. It comes in various sizes.

Tape measure
A flexible tape measure is an absolute necessity for sewing.

Tracing wheel
This tool is used with dressmaker's tracing paper to transfer pattern markings to wrong side of fabric. Use with extra care on sheers.

Retractable tape measure
This type of tape measure is housed in a box and is sold in many sizes and lengths.

Double tracing wheel
This wheel traces patterns as does the standard tracing wheel but marks the seams at the same time.

Needle threader
This easy-to-use needle threader operates with a push button.

Needle threader
This device makes it easy to thread needles of all kinds. The wire is inserted into needle eye.

Thimble
Thimbles, used to protect the middle finger during hand sewing, come in various sizes so you should try them on for size before buying.

Leather thimble
This is designed for lighter sewing work.

Magnet
A magnet is useful for picking up needles and pins from your work surface.

Loop turner
This tool has a hook at one end and is used to turn tubing to the right side.

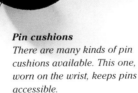

Pin cushions
There are many kinds of pin cushions available. This one, worn on the wrist, keeps pins accessible.

Magnetic pin cushion
This provides a handy and safe place to store straight pins.

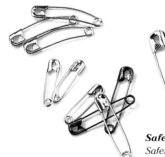

Safety pins
Safety pins are used to hold layers of fabric together. Curved safety pins are useful in quilting and patchwork.

Needles

Sewing needles (sizes 1–12)
For general sewing use medium-length needles, shorter ones for seams.

Milliners (sizes 1–10)
These long needles, also called straw needles, are very good for basting.

Leather needles (sizes 1–8)
Also called glovers needles, their triangular points pierce leather.

Tapestry needles (sizes 13–26)
Heavy and blunt, these needles are used mainly for tapestry work.

Bodkins
These are used to thread ribbon, cord, or elastic through casings.

Machine needles
These come in various sizes and should be matched to the fabric.

Twin needles
Used to sew narrow, parallel lines, or to make pin tucks.

Twin needles for stretch fabrics
A special twin needle is used for stretch fabrics, especially for jersey.

EQUIPMENT AND FABRICS

Sewing supplies

There are threads, bands, and buttons to suit every type of fabric. Choosing the right ones make sewing easier.

Basting thread
A loosely twisted cotton thread used for basting.

Button and carpet thread
Tough and thick for hand-sewing jobs requiring strong thread.

Silk thread
Fine, strong thread used for sewing wool and silk.

Polyester
An all-purpose thread, it is elastic, strong, and keeps its color.

Cotton thread
Used with light- and mediumweight cottons, rayons, and linens.

Buttonhole twist
Used for topstitching and hand-worked buttonholes.

Elastic thread
Used for ruffles and smocking.

Overlock thread
Used with an overlock machine.

Metallic thread
Used for decorative stitching.

Machine embroidery thread
Suitable for knitting and machine darning.

Twill and cotton tapes
These tapes are used to stay and strengthen seams.

Braid
One of several types of trim available ready-made.

Bias strip
These bias-cut fabric strips are used to bind curved seams and as casings.

Bias tape makers
These devices fold bias tape to the correct size for sewing.

Elastic
Elastic — single yarn, braided, or woven — comes in various thicknesses, widths, and grips.

Hook-and-loop tape (Velcro)
This type of closure is suitable for garments that need to be opened and closed quickly.

Bias tape
This tape, used to bind edges, is sold ready-made in all colors and several widths.

Buckles
Buckles come in a wide variety of colors, shapes, and sizes. Covered buckles are also available, as are buckles without prongs.

Hooks and eyes
These fasteners come in various designs and sizes to specifically suit the job at hand.

Fur clips
These sturdy fasteners are used on fur and fake fur.

Awl or stiletto
An awl is a sharp tool used to make the round holes for eyelets or key hole buttonholes.

Fastener pliers
These special pliers are used to apply no-sew snaps, studs, and eyelets simply and quickly.

Buttons
The color, size, and material from which they are made are all factors to consider when choosing buttons.

Snaps
Snaps are two-part fasteners with limited holding power. They may be sew-in or pronged.

Pressing equipment

Every seam you sew should be carefully pressed, so good pressing equipment, such as an adjustable ironing board, is essential for good sewing results.

Press mitt
A padded glovelike cushion, a press mitt is used as a pressing surface for small, curved garment areas; it is especially useful for pressing rounded sleeve caps. It can also be used over the end of a sleeve board.

Tailor's press mitt
Like the standard press mitt, the tailor's press mitt is used for ironing on curved areas. The hand, however, is more exposed.

Tailor's ham
*The ham is used for pressing shaped areas such as bust darts and curved seams. Another firmly packed cushion is the cylindrical **seam roll**, used to press long curved seams and seams in narrow areas, such as trouser legs.*

Sleeve board
This board is used for ironing seams and narrow garment sections such as sleeves and pants legs, necklines, and sleeve caps.

Iron with thermostat
Any iron you use when sewing should be equipped with a thermostat. Here are a few rules for best results when pressing:
1. Press each seam before crossing with another. First press over seamline (to embed stitches), then press open. **2.** Use a press cloth to prevent a shine on the fabric; dampen if steam is needed. See-through press cloths are useful when using iron-on products.
3. Press with a gentle up-and-down motion. **4.** Avoid pressing over pins. **5.** To finger-press, run your thumb along the opened seamline.

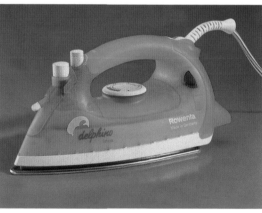

Steam iron
Pressing with steam saves you the step of dampening the fabric or pressing with a damp cloth, unless the fabric is especially sensitive. The amount of steam released and the temperature of the iron can be adjusted as needed. A "shot of steam" feature is very useful. A steam iron should be used on an ironing board that allows the steam to pass through the surface, otherwise moisture will collect underneath the garment.

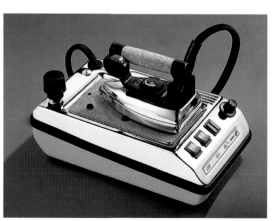

Heavy-duty steam iron
This is a steam iron attached to a container that holds a large volume of water. Steam is created under pressure in the reservoir and fed into the iron through a plastic tube. The steam immediately penetrates the fabric, smoothing it quickly. The amount of steam released and the temperature are adjustable for every kind of fabric. This type of iron also can be used as a steamer to smooth creases in garments such as suits, jackets, and blazers — just hang the garment on a sturdy hanger and steam-press.

Sewing machines

Once you decide to buy a sewing machine, take the time to carefully look over the products available on the market. There are many types of machines offered by various manufacturers. First, evaluate your sewing needs: do you plan to sew occasionally and need only a relatively simple machine or do you plan to sew a great deal and undertake complicated sewing projects? Of course, price will play a role in any decision you make.

Sewing machine sales centers provide detailed information and will explain and demonstrate the machines offered for sale. You should always try out the machines yourself. The machine should not be too complicated to operate; the buttons and levers should be well placed. Test the following: can the needle be easily threaded; does the lamp light up the work surface properly; does the machine move both light and heavy fabric evenly; does the machine stop immediately when you remove your foot from the pedal? You should also ask what extra attachments come with the machine and where it can be repaired. The instruction manual should be detailed, easily understandable, and have clear illustrations.

Choose the **sewing feet** as carefully as the machine. There are feet and attachments for hemming, edging, knitting, darning, making buttonholes, and the overlock stitch, as well as for all kinds of decorative work, such as appliqué and attaching sequins and beads.

Buy a sewing machine only once you are convinced that the manufacturer is a serious one, their customer service is efficient, and the machine is well thought-out and easy to use. For beginners and for all those who want to learn a new technique, taking a sewing course is an excellent idea. Some stores offer courses geared to a specific manufacturer's machines.

Since each manufacturer has developed its own sewing system and levers and buttons are differently located, we have only shown four general types of sewing machines as an aid to choosing the right machine for your sewing needs.

Hobby or general-purpose sewing machine
Easy to use, this type of machine offers many useful stitches, such as zigzag, stretch, and blind stitches. Many machines have a buttonhole maker and can be used to sew buttons onto garments. This machine type is an excellent beginner's machine. It is also useful for simple alterations and repairs.

Electronic sewing machine
Used mainly by the home sewer, the electronic machine has more than three times as many programs for decorating and professional finishes as the hobby machine, including stretch and overlock stitches. It also has a buttonhole maker and an automatic needle threader.

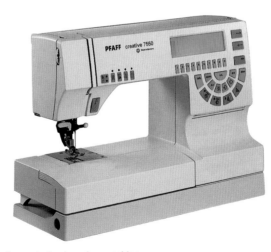

Computerized sewing machine
Along with a large selection of all-purpose stitches, the computerized sewing machine offers many kinds of embroidery stitches. Using an attachment, these machines can often be transformed into a professional embroidery machine. Some come programmed with over 170 decorative stitches. They also offer features such as an automatic needle threader.

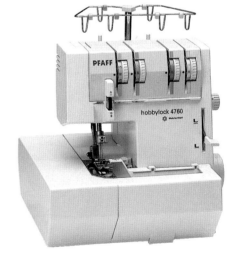

Overlock machine or serger
This piece of equipment has become extremely popular in the US and Canada. It sews a seam (sometimes at up to 1,500 stitches per minute), finishes the edge, and trims the seam allowance — all in one step. It can be used with as many as five spools of threads and can perform decorative procedures, such as a fine rolled hem. It is not a substitute for a regular sewing machine.

Fabric types

The success of a garment depends a great deal on choosing the right fabric. The fabric overview on this and the following pages will help you select the right fabric.

Acetate A cellulose-based synthetic fabric. Lustrous, moderately absorbent. Often in blends. Formal wear, linings.

Acrylic A synthetic fabric. Fluffy, wool-like. Absorbs water poorly. Sportswear, knits.

Aida cloth Basket weave construction, often of polyester and cotton, with untwisted yarns laid into the weave. Hand embroidery.

Alpaca Lightweight, soft lustrous fiber from the llama-like alpaca of South America, often blended with wool to make expensive suitings and knitwear. Suits, jackets, knits.

Angora Extremely soft hair fiber from the angora rabbit, usually blended with wool. Mainly knitwear.

Astrakhan Heavy woven fabric with tight curly pile imitating pelt of unborn lambs. Rare. Formal wear.

Barathea Fine twill-weave fabric with broken rib pattern and pebbly surface, originally wool or silk, now of various fibers. Men's and women's suits.

Batik Indonesian dyeing method in which fabric not being colored is covered with wax. Term also refers to cloth, often cotton or rayon, so dyed. Shirts, dresses, pillow covers.

Batiste Lightweight, fine, sometimes sheer fabric of cotton, or synthetic fiber in plain weave. Blouses, lingerie, linings, handkerchiefs.

Bedford cord Stout woven fabric with ribbing down the grain, made from various fibers. Pants, coats, upholstery.

Bengaline Rich fabric with strong crosswise rib, due to fine silk (or wool) warp and thick cotton weft yarns. Dresses, evening wear.

Blanket cloth Heavyweight overcoating, often napped with plaid design, mainly of wool.

Bombazine Twilled or corded fabric of cotton and worsted wool, or silk and worsted. Traditionally black for mourning clothing.

Bouclé Wool or wool blend fabric of looped or knotted yarn, giving a nubby surface. Yarn itself also called bouclé. Women's tailoring, knitwear.

Broadcloth Fine plain weave fabric. Available in cotton or cotton polyester. Multi-purpose use, including shirts. Broadcloth made from wool is a fine, lightweight fabric with a lustrous nap. Silk broadcloth is plain and low in luster.

Brocade Rich jacquard weave fabric with all-over intricate patterns and an embroidered look. Silk-type for formal wear, cotton for upholstery.

Broderie anglaise Eyelet embroidery on cotton. Available in dress and narrower widths, for trimming; also called "broderie" or "eyelet."

Buckram A stiff, open weave fabric—a form of cheesecloth with a glued finish. Used mainly for hat shaping, belt stiffening, interfacing.

Burlap or hessian. Coarse, heavy fabric made from jute, hemp, or cotton. Curtains, wall coverings, upholstery, sacks.

Calico Lightweight, plain weave cotton with small print designs. Children's clothing, quilts, home furnishings.

Cambric Fine cotton fabric with a slightly glossy surface. See **batiste, lawn.**

Camel hair Lightweight fabric, often in twill weave, derived from a camel's soft inner coat. Now usually blended with other fibers such as wool; classified for labeling as wool. "Camel" also refers to the yellowish tan color. Coats, jackets.

Candlewick Cotton fabric pierced with soft, thick, yarns that fan out to form tufts. Bedspreads, dressing gowns.

Canvas Heavy, strong, plain weave fabric usually made of cotton but sometimes from synthetic fibers or blends. Awnings, workwear, chair seats. See also **duck.**

Casement cloth Term usually limited to open weave curtain fabrics but also applied to sheer curtaining fabrics in general.

Cashmere Luxury fiber, knitted or woven. Originally hair from undercoat of Kashmir's Asiatic goat; now includes similar-quality hair from selectively bred Australian, New Zealand, and Scottish feral goats. Blended with sheep's wool or other fibers to increase wearing ability, lower cost. Tailored clothing, knitwear.

Cavalry twill Strong, twill weave cloth traditionally used for riding breeches and uniforms. Raincoats, skirts, pants.

Challis Light, supple, plain weave fabric of wool, rayon, cotton, or blends. Traditionally printed on dark background with floral or paisley design. Dresses, nightwear.

Chambray Plain weave cotton or cotton-polyester, rayon-polyester blend with dyed warp and white weft. Work clothes, sportswear, pajamas, shirts.

Chamois "Shammy." Soft yellow brushed leather, often slightly napped, originally only from chamois goat. Cloth chamois (usually polyester) has a similar napped effect. Polishing cloths, coat interlinings.

Chanel tweed Term loosely used for any tweed made from bulky yarns, thick and thin with many slubs. Popularized by French designer Coco Chanel. Suits, coats.

Cheesecloth Plain, loosely woven fabric, usually of cotton, most often for curtains, flag buntings, polishing cloths. Formerly used in cheese making.

Chenille "Caterpillar" in French. Soft yarn, with pile protruding on all sides, made from wool or other fibers. Rugs, bedspreads, dressing gowns.

Cheviot Rough-surfaced, heavily napped fabric, originally made from the wool of the Cheviot sheep. Coats.

Chiffon Originally made from silk but now often polyester. Lightweight, soft, sheer fabric, noted for its draping ability. Formal wear, scarves.

China silk Lightweight, less expensive silk used for linings and scarves. Also called **habutai.**

Chino Mediumweight, twill weave cotton or cotton-polyester with a slight sheen. Usually beige color. Sportswear, military use.

Chintz Closely woven, plain weave fabric printed with flowers, sometimes figures and birds. Usually has a glazed finish. Soft furnishings, curtains.

Chire Lightweight taffeta-like synthetic (nylon) with shiny surface. Skiwear.

Cloqué Woven fabric with blistered or puffy surface (see **matelassé**). Also used to refer to knits with a blister effect. Silk-type for apparel, wool or cotton for upholstery.

Corduroy Cotton weft-pile fabric woven and cut to produce vertical ribs. Available in various widths of ribs and in printed and plain colors. Uncut cord has all-over nap. Children's clothing, jackets, coats, pants.

Cotton Seed-pod fiber of the cotton plant. Names like Sea Island and Egyptian refer to the various qualities. Cotton is made into every known woven and knitted structure, and every weight, from the flimsiest muslin to the heaviest canvas. Often blended with other fibers.

Crash Coarse, rough-surface linen or cotton, or rayon fabric. Bookbinding, occasionally clothing, curtains.

Crepe Woven fabrics with a dull crinkled surface due to use of twisted yarns. Satin-backed crepe has satin finish on one side. Embossed crepe also available. Blouses, dresses.

Crepe de Chine Lightweight plain weave silk using fine twisted yarns for muted sheen. Now often polyester. Blouses, evening and lounge wear.

Crepon Similar to crepe but thicker and firmer, with lengthwise texture sometimes patterned with jacquard designs. Women's wear.

Cretonne Mediumweight unglazed fabric, usually cotton, in a variety of weaves and finishes. Generally printed with bright floral patterns. Curtains.

Damask Name from Damascus, where Chinese silks arrived on trade routes. Firm fabric of jacquard weave, similar to **brocade.** Most now linen, cotton, or blends. Furnishings, tablecloths.

Denim Strong, twill weave fabric traditionally made with colored warp (usually blue) and white weft. Work clothes, jeans, jackets, skirts, soft furnishings.

Dimity Fairly sheer, lightweight fabric made traditionally from cotton, now also from synthetic fibers. Has fine lengthwise ribs, stripes, checks, or very small printed patterns. Dresses, curtains.

Doeskin Fabric made from wool or synthetic fibers with a soft napped finish and a "kid glove" feel. Jackets, vests.

Dotted swiss Fine, sheer fabric of cotton or cotton blends with small fiber dots woven in, flocked, or printed on. Children's wear, curtains.

Double knit Knitted fabric with both sides identical. Has excellent body and good recovery. Men's and women's sportswear.

Douppioni Also called "douppion." Lustrous slubbed silk with weft yarns made of fibers spun from double cocoons. Synthetic versions made. Formal and bridal wear.

Drill Strong, twill weave, solid-color cotton similar to denim. Work clothes, uniforms.

Duck Heavy, tightly woven fabric of cotton or linen available in plain or ribbed weaves in various weights. The terms "duck" and "canvas" are now synonymous. Upholstery, artists' canvas, shoes.

Duffel cloth Thick, heavily napped wool fabric, much like melton. Originated in Belgium. Coats.

Eyelet See **broderie anglaise.**

Faille Closely woven fabric made from silk, cotton, wool, or synthetic fibers, with a fine, flat crosswise rib. Evening and formal wear.

Fake fur or **Fun fur** Pile fabric, usually acrylic, made to resemble various types of animal fur.

Faux leather or **Pleather** Imitation leather available by the yard (meter) in a number of finishes such as suede and chamois. Tailored coats, jackets.

Feathers Feathers from cocks, marabous, and ostriches are available in many colors either sewn onto a ½ in (12 mm) tape or with the quills overlocked onto string. Used to trim coats and formal wear or for costumes.

Felt A non-woven fabric made of wool, fur, or hair fibers meshed together by heat, moisture, and mechanical action. Increasingly being made from acrylic fibers melted together. Toy making, vests, jackets.

Flannel Plain or twill weave fabric of soft (sometimes brushed) wool or cotton. Suits, sportswear.

Flannelette Brushed cotton in plain weave, napped on one or both sides. Children's wear, sleepwear.

Fleece Thick napped wool fabric, sometimes with nylon or luxury hair fiber added. Coats.

Fleece, knit Soft, warm, napped knit. Cotton/synthetic for sweatshirts. All synthetic type is partly recycled from pop bottles, known as polar or arctic fleece. Sportswear, hats, blankets.

Foulard Lightweight plain or twill weave fabric usually of rayon or silk. Ties, scarves.

Frieze Thick, heavy fabric with rough surface of cut or uncut loops. Made from cotton or artificial fibers. Upholstery.

Gabardine Strong, hard finished, medium- to heavyweight twill weave fabric made from many different fibers or fiber blends. Raincoats, sportswear, pants.

Gauze Open weave, sheer fabric made from many different fibers. Summer apparel, bandages, curtains.

Georgette Similar to but heavier than chiffon. Made from crepe yarns, thus a matte texture. Blouses, evening wear.

Gingham Plain weave fabric formerly cotton but now often made from blends. Dyed yarns are woven in checked or striped patterns. Dresses, blouses, children's clothing.

Grosgrain Also called petersham. Heavily ribbed ribbon made with silk or rayon warp over round, firm cotton cords. Trimming, waistbands.

Habutai Also spelled habutae. Lightweight glossy fabric. Another name for china silk. Linings.

Hair cloth Also called "hair canvas." Plain weave fabric. Made from natural and synthetic fibers combined with animal hair, often goat or horse. Upholstery, interfacing for tailored garments.

Hessian See **burlap.**

Homespun Rough-surfaced, loosely spun fabric of wool, jute, linen, or cotton. Term now refers to fabrics made of almost any fiber imitating the hand-made look.

Honan Synonymous with **pongee.** A fine, crisp, plain-weave wild silk fabric with slight slub in both directions. Often dyed. Blouses, dresses.

Hopsacking Named after the sacks used for hop-gathering. Coarse fabric with rough surface made from cotton, linen, or blends. (Hopsack is also the term used for a variation of plain weave.) Upholstery, some fashion items.

Houndstooth check Small combination of twill weave and color pattern formed in warp and weft. Suits, trousers, sports jackets.

Huckaback Also called "huck." Term refers to a weave of cotton, linen, or blends principally used for hand or dish towels.

Ikat Procedure in which warp threads of a fabric are yarn dyed or printed, then woven, producing a shadowy effect. Formerly known as chine, referring to Chinese origin of the procedure. Dresses.

Interlock Fine stable weft knit once used only for underwear, now used for casual outerwear. Plain colors.

Jacquard An intricate patterned weave or knit, often with a raised surface. Damask cloths, draperies, formal wear.

Jersey Generic term for plain weft-knitted fabrics. Has extensive crosswise stretch. Cotton, synthetics, or blends. T-shirts.

Jute A natural fiber from the jute plant, used for making burlap, rug backing, trimmings, twine.

Kapok Fluffy fiber from the pods of the kapok tree, used to fill pillows, and toys. Now largely replaced by synthetic fillings.

Kersey Closely woven, compact wool fabric, diagonally twilled or ribbed, with a fine nap. In plain colors. Work clothes, uniforms.

Knit fleece See **fleece, knit.**

Lace Fabric or trimming with floral or scroll design formed without a base fabric. Now produced by machine; needlepoint lace is worked with a needle either on a core of fabric or built up entirely of looped or buttonhole stitches; bobbin lace is woven or plaited, each thread being wound on a bobbin, and has a clothlike background with a fancy filling and netlike surround. Made from a variety of fibers; some laces are washable, others require careful treatment. Available in many colors, though white and ecru predominate. With one exception, noted below, laces come in dress and trimming widths. The principal types are:
Alençon A design outlined with heavy thread (often silk) on a sheer net surround. Named after the French town of the same name. A luxury lace.
All-over A regularly repeating pattern with no surrounding net and no edging scallops.
Chantilly An elaborate design on a fine mesh surround finished with scallops at both edges. Popular for bridal wear.
Cluny A fairly heavy lace, generally of cotton, often with guipure designs but less expensive than guipure. It has no surround; the pattern sections are fixed in place by interlacing thread bars.
Guipure The pattern is embroidered on a fabric, which is later dissolved, leaving the motifs intact, joined by bars of thread. The motifs can be cut away and appliquéd as a trimming on blouses, dresses, tablecloths. The lace is thick and the designs stand up in relief.
Insertion lace Trimming lace with two straight, finished edges.
Needlerun lace Embroidered design superimposed on net.
Raschel Made on a raschel knitting machine, often imitating Chantilly designs. Its popularity owes much to its lower cost.
Ribbon lace Created by stitching ribbons in floral pattern to a net background. Requires great care in handling. Women's evening wear, bridal wear.
Valenciennes Also called "Val" and "Vals." Available in trimming widths only. A flat bobbin lace worked with one thread forming both design and background.

Lambswool Very soft wool from sheep up to seven months old. Often blended, it is generally made into sweaters.

Lamé Any woven or knitted fabric with a metallic yarn to give either the pattern or background a glittery effect. Can also be fabric embroidered with metallic thread. Evening and formal wear.

Lawn Sheer, lightweight, plain weave fabric of cotton or synthetic fiber, in plain colors and printed designs. Children's clothing, summer dresses.

Leather A number of leathers are suitable for making into coats, jackets, and skirts. Many skins are imported, so their availability can be restricted. It is usually necessary to buy complete skins or hides. The principal types of leather are:
Full grain garment leather One of the more commonly used hides. Available in fashion colors.
Garment suede split Available in fashion colors. Looks effective without the finer details of tailoring. It can be printed.
Modeling hide Heavyweight. Bags, belts, wallets.
Other hides:
Deerskin Another fine quality leather.
Kidskin Finest quality skin and versatile in use. Available in various colors.
Kip (calfskin) is available in a variety of colors.
Lambskin or sheep nappa Generally used as a trim.
Pigskin This skin is available in natural colors.

Leno Fabric produced by leno attachment on loom, giving a lacy effect. Strong, stable. Curtains.

Linen One of the world's oldest fabrics, made from fibers from the stalks of the flax plant. Now often combined with synthetic fibers to improve crease-resistance and washability. A very strong, absorbent, smooth, crisp fabric available in various weights. Tailored clothing, sportswear.

Linsey-woolsey A coarse, uncomfortable fabric made in the eighteenth century by weaving wool and linen together.

Loden cloth Wind- and water-resistant wool cloth, similar to duffel cloth but with fine nap. Originally from Austria. Coats.

Lurex Trademark of Lurex Incorporated for a metallic thread, but sometimes refers to fabric woven through with this yarn.

Madras Light cotton or cotton-blend fabric woven in soft multi-colored plaids, traditional to its native India. Shirts, shorts.

Marquisette Lightweight leno weave fabric of silk or synthetic fibers, generally used for curtains and mosquito netting.

Matelassé Luxurious, often jacquard weave, fabric with raised design giving a puckered effect. Sometimes woven through with metallic thread. Evening wear, upholstery.

Melton Tightly woven, twill weave, napped fabric, wool or wool blend. Looks like felt. Wind resistant. Coats, jackets.

Milanese Lightweight warp-knit fabric with diagonal or diamond design on the back. Run resistant. Lingerie, curtains, gloves.

Mohair Lustrous fiber of angora goat; can be straight or curly. Much is produced in the United States. Fabrics containing mohair often combined with wool. Suits, coats, wraps, throws.

Moiré Also known as watered silk, it is a silky fabric like taffeta or faille processed through heated rollers to produce a watery surface effect. Evening and bridal wear.

Moleskin Thick, heavy cotton fabric napped and shorn to produce suedelike finish. Tends to shrink but is very hard-wearing. Pants, work clothes.

Moss crepe Crepe woven with a mossy texture, giving a spongy handle. Can be made from any fiber, most often polyester. Blouses, dresses.

Mousseline de soie Silk muslin. A similar fabric made of synthetic fibers is called "mousseline." Crisp, lightweight, sheer, and similar to **organza** in appearance. Blouses, evening dresses.

Muslin Inexpensive cotton of plain weave, made in various weights. Now often a blend of cotton and polyester. True Indian muslin, often woven with gold or silver thread, is expensive. Muslin can be used to make a fitting shell before cutting an expensive fabric. Linings, shirting, sheets.

Nainsook A soft, fine, plain weave cotton or cotton blend, like **batiste** or **lawn.** Handkerchiefs, babies' dresses.

Net Open fabric, knotted in geometrically shaped holes, usually hexagonal. Made in several weights. Usually made of nylon. Curtains, mosquito nets, costumes. See also **tulle.**

Nylon Formerly a trade name, now generic term (along with polyamide) for the strongest synthetic fiber. Pure nylon fabrics are durable but non-absorbent, which may make them uncomfortable, especially in warm weather. Nylon is often blended with other fibers to increase absorbency. The durability of other fibers can be increased by blending them with nylon.

Organdy A fine, semi-sheer, loose weave of cotton or cotton blend with a crisp finish. Curtains, blouses, evening wear.

Organza Sheer, crisp silk organdy with a sheen. Also made of polyester. Bridal and evening wear.

Ottoman Heavy fabric with crosswise ribs of varying widths, originally made with a silk warp and wool weft. Once popular for evening wear, now used for coats, suits, academic gowns, upholstery.

Oxford cloth Cotton or cotton-blend basket weave shirting fabric. Men's shirts.

Peau de soie French term meaning "skin of silk." A heavy, smooth, satin weave fabric with a muted sheen. Now often polyester. Wedding dresses, evening wear.

Percale Fine, lightweight, plain weave fabric with a smooth finish, cotton or a blend of cotton and polyester. Printed or plain. Sheets.

Piqué Cotton or cotton-blend fabric woven with small, raised geometric patterns on a loom with a dobby attachment. Plain or printed. Sportswear.

Plush Thick, deep, warp-pile fabric made from silk, wool, mohair, or rayon. Pile is longer and more open than that of velvet. Coats, rugs, upholstery.

Polished cotton Also called "cotton satin." Cotton fabric to which a sheen is applied in the finishing process. Less shiny than glazed cotton. Women's wear, children's wear.

Polyester The most widely used synthetic fiber made from petroleum products. Nearly as strong as nylon, it is a chameleon that can imitate silk, serve as pillow stuffing, and blend with most other fibers. Modifications have tempered its only drawbacks — a tendency to hold oily stains and a lack of absorbency.

Pongee Lightweight plain weave silk fabric with a slight slub effect. The terms pongee and Honan are today interchangeable. Blouses, dresses.

Poodle cloth Wool or other heavy, looped fabric. Meant to resemble the coat of a poodle. Coats.

Poplin Tightly woven, hard-wearing fabric with a fine horizontal rib, usually of cotton but also cotton/synthetic blends, or of silk. Summer dresses, children's clothing.

Quilted fabric The effect is obtained by stitching (or welding) layers of fabric together in geometrical patterns, with padding between. The fabric is warm; quilted cotton is popular decorative fabric for dressing gowns, vests, upholstery, bedcovers, table mats.

Ratiné A type of looped yarn made using various fibers. Dresses.

Raw silk Silk fiber after reeling and before processing. The term is sometimes incorrectly used for wild silk.

Rayon Made from cellulose (mainly wood pulp). Rayon is inexpensive, soft, comfortable, and dyes well. Blouses, dresses, linings. Main types of rayon are:
Cuprammonium rayon Made by a process that allows very fine filament fibers to be formed, giving a finer, softer fabric than viscose rayon. Marketed as "Bemberg" for linings.
Polynosic rayon Made by a more recently developed process than viscose rayon. It is stronger and less likely to shrink or stretch. Sometimes called "Modal."
Viscose rayon Made by the most common method. Not strong, especially when wet.

Sailcloth Generic name for fabrics used for making sails. Term, when used for apparel fabrics, refers to a firmly woven canvas-style fabric now made from synthetic fibers as well as cotton. Children's clothing, sportswear.

Sari The term refers to a length of cloth, traditionally worn by South Asian women. Sari cloth usually has a border design and is sometimes made from extremely fine silk or polyester, with border designs in gold or silver thread.

Sateen Variation of satin weave with a softer sheen, in cotton or blends. Apparel, drapery lining.

Satin The term refers to a weave used for silk, cotton, and synthetic fibers. Variations include *antique satin,* reversible with a lustrous surface on one side and a slubbed effect on the other; *crepe-back satin,* also reversible; *duchesse satin,* a luxurious, heavy, and expensive fabric, often used for wedding dresses; *slipper satin,* often cotton-backed, strong and expensive; *charmeuse,* a light fluid satin.

Scrim An open, plain weave mesh fabric usually of cotton. Theatrical use, curtains, bunting.

Seersucker Lightweight fabric made of cotton or synthetic blends with a puckered look. Summer suits, casual wear.

Serge Twill weave, smooth fabric made from wool or wool blends. Uniforms, suits.

Shantung Plain weave fabric with slubs in the weft yarns producing slightly rough, nubbed surface. Silk or synthetic fibers. Formal wear.

Sharkskin Semi-crisp, hard-finish fabric with a slight sheen made of wool or wool blends. Lightweight suits.

Shetland Yarn from wool of sheep from Shetland Islands in northern Scotland. It is both coarse and soft, giving characteristic appearance, and it is very warm. Jackets, knitwear.

Shot silk Silk woven with the warp and weft in differing colors so that fabric appears to change color at different angles. Effect can also be produced using other fibers. Evening and formal wear.

Silk A natural fiber discovered in China 5,000 years ago, obtained by unwinding cocoons of the silkworm larvae. Silk fabrics are strong but have a delicate appearance, and generally have a sheen. These luxury fabrics, though not always expensive, are being replaced by synthetic fiber fabrics retaining the names previously applied to natural silk fabrics **(China silk, Honan, pongee, Shantung, crepe de Chine, surah).** Silk may be blended with other fibers to reduce its price or to achieve a particular effect.

Spandex Better known by its DuPont trade name, Lycra, it is the highly stretchable synthetic fiber that has found its way into many of today's fabrics, where tiny amounts (1–5%) vastly increase comfort. Dominates swimwear, lingerie.

Suede cloth Woven or knitted fabric of cotton, wool, synthetic fibers, or blends, usually napped to resemble suede. Sportswear.

Surah Soft silk twill fabric with a sheen, often imitated with synthetic fibers. Ties, dressing gowns.

Sweater knit A knit fabric resembling hand-knitting, achieved in various ways.

Taffeta Crisp, plain weave silk fabric with a shiny surface and great deal of scroop (rustle). Available in a variety of weights; can be silk, polyester, or acetate. Formal wear, linings.

Tarlatan Transparent, loosely woven, open mesh, cotton cheesecloth fabric, given a dressing to stiffen it. Used layer upon layer for theatrical costumes.

Tartan Twill weave wool fabric in plaid designs, each design belonging to a Scottish clan. Many imitation tartans are available.

Tencel Trade name for lyocell fiber, made from cellulose (wood pulp) by a process different from rayon. It is absorbent, stronger than rayon, often finished with a "peach skin" surface. Sportswear.

Terry cloth Cotton fabric with loop pile on one or both sides. Very absorbent. Towels, beach robes. Knit terry is often used for lounge wear and baby wear.

Thai silk A luxury wild silk fabric made in Thailand, with slight slub and in iridescent colors. In solids, woven checks, and characteristic print designs. Dresses, shirts, blouses, pillow covers.

Ticking Very strong woven fabric, usually colored stripes on white. Pillow, mattress coverings, some apparel.

Toile de Jouy Cotton or cotton-blend fabric with a sheen, printed with a pictorial design, one color on white ground. Soft furnishing, some apparel.

Tricot Fine, warp-knit fabric, usually nylon, with fine vertical ribs and zigzag effect on back. Some crosswise stretch, no vertical. Run-resistant. Lingerie, summerwear lining.

Tulle A fine net, of silk or more often nylon. Bridal and dance attire.

Tussah or **Wild silk** Silk fabric woven from silk of uncultivated silkworms, slightly coarser and stronger than that of domestic silkworms. In natural shades or dyed. Jackets, home furnishings.

Tweed Woven fabric with a hairy surface, characterized by colored slubs of yarn. Hard-wearing and warm. Some tweeds are pure wool, others are wool blends or other fiber combinations. Types include:
Donegal Hand-woven in County Donegal, Ireland. Now means any tweed with thick, colored slubs.
Harris Hand-woven from yarns spun by machine on the Outer Hebridean islands of Scotland. Very warm and tough.
Irish Distinguished by a white warp and a colored filling. (Donegal is an Irish tweed.)

Ultrasuede Trade name for luxurious, washable, non-woven fabric closely resembling suede. Made of synthetic fibers using a needling process. Apparel, trim, home furnishings.

Velour Woven or knitted fabric with a thick, short pile. Has the lustrous look of velvet or velveteen; often dyed in rich colors. Knit velour is suitable for casual and lounge wear.

Velvet Silk or synthetic silk fabric with short cut pile giving a soft texture and lustrous, rich appearance. Evening wear, tailored clothing, curtains, upholstery. Common types of velvet include:
Ciselé Satin weave fabric with a velvet pattern on a sheer ground. Similar fabrics made by flocking.
Crushed Pile is pressed flat in one or several directions to give a shimmering appearance.
Devoré Velvet pattern on sheer background achieved by "burn-out" process whereby some pile areas are dissolved chemically after weaving.
Embossed has certain areas pressed flat.
Nacré Woven with backing of one color and pile of another, giving an iridescent appearance.
Panné Pile is flattened in one direction to give a lustrous sheen.
Uncut Pile is left in loop form.

Velveteen Cotton fiber fabric produced in the same way as corduroy but with short cut pile covering entire surface. Skirts, dresses, children's clothing.

Vicuña Cloth made from the reddish-brown wool of the vicuña, a llama-like animal found in Peru. The most expensive fiber, it is soft, light, and lustrous. The vicuña is a protected animal.

Vinyl Strong woven or knit base fabric coated with polyvinyl chloride (PVC), giving a waterproof, slightly tacky surface. Also as unstructured film. Raincoats, chair coverings.

Viyella Trade name for lightweight plain weave fabric, 45% cotton, 55% wool, pre-shrunk and washable. Shirts, children's clothing.

Voile Lightweight, plain weave, crisp, sheer fabric of cotton or cotton blends. Summer wear, curtains.

Whipcord Strong, heavyweight cotton, wool, or synthetic fiber fabric with bold twill weave. Uniforms, riding clothes.

Wool Fiber from fleece of domesticated sheep. Wool fabrics are warm and resilient. Those labeled "pure wool" in Canada and the United States contain 100% virgin wool. Labeled "wool blend" if at least 55% of virgin wool is blended with one other fiber.

Woolen Type of wool yarn and fabric in which fibers are carded rather than combed to remove impurities, producing a soft and warm fabric. Jackets, sweaters.

Worsted Type of wool yarn and fabric in which the fibers are carded and combed to remove short fibers. Worsteds have a smooth surface, are harder wearing and costlier than woolens. Tailored clothing.

SEWING NEEDS AND FABRICS

Underlying fabrics

The underlying fabrics of a garment can be considered tools with which to build a better garment. Each of them — underlining, interfacing, interlining, and lining — has a specific function that influences the garment's finished appearance.

While all of the fabric types listed may not be used in a particular garment, the order of application is always underlining first, interfacing next, then interlining, and finally lining.

The more structured and detailed a design is, the greater its need for an underlining and interfacing. As well, the lighter in weight or softer the fabric is, the more support it needs. Do not over-support or undersupport any garment fabric in an attempt to achieve a certain design. Instead, choose another garment fabric more appropriate to the needs of that design.

Use your judgment when selecting a garment fabric. Some fabrics, even when supported by both underlining and interfacing, are too lightweight to sustain a very structured design. Some fabrics, on the other hand, are too heavy. When using a combination of fabrics, drape them over your hand to see and feel their combined effect.

Lining and interfacing

Purpose	Where used	Types	Selection criteria
UNDERLINING			
Give support and body to garment fabric and design	The entire garment or just sections	Fabrics sold as underlinings can be light to medium in weight, with a soft, medium, or crisp finish	Should be relatively stable and lightweight
Reinforce seams and other construction details			Color and care should be compatible with garment
Give opaqueness to garment fabric to hide inner construction		Other fabrics not specifically sold as underlinings such as China silk, organdy, organza, muslin, batiste, lightweight tricot (for knits) can be used	Underlining colors should not show through the garment fabric
Inhibit stretching, especially in areas of stress			Finish (e.g., soft, crisp) should be appropriate for desired effect
Act as a buffer layer on which to catch hems; baste facings and interfacings, fasten other inner stitching			
INTERFACING			
Support, shape, and stabilize areas, edges, and details of a garment	Entire sections of garment such as collars, cuffs, waistbands, plackets, flaps	Fusible interfacings: Woven, non-woven, weft-insertion, or knit type, with resin coating on one side. They are fused to garment fabric using an iron and steam or a damp cloth	Should give support and body without overpowering the garment fabric
Reinforce and prevent stretching	Specific garment areas such as the front, hem, neck, yoke, armholes, lapels, vents, pockets		Care and weight selected should be compatible with the rest of garment fabric. In general the interfacing should be slightly lighter than the garment fabric
Increase the life of a garment		Sew-in interfacings: Woven or non-woven, they are attached to garment fabric by basting (or gluing) when a fusible type is unsuitable	Fusible interfacings, especially firmer grades, tend to add some rigidity to fabric
		All types can be light, medium, or heavy in weight	
INTERLINING			
Provide warmth without bulk	The body of a jacket or coat, sometimes the sleeves	Lightweight, warm fabrics such as flannel, flannelette, brushed cotton, fleece	Light in weight
			Will provide warmth
			Not too bulky
			Care requirements should be compatible with rest of garment
LINING			
Cover interior construction details	Coats, jackets, dresses, skirts, and pants, in their entirety or just partially	Silky lightweight fabrics of viscose or Bemberg rayon, acetate, silk, or polyester	Should be smooth, opaque, durable
Allow garment to slide on and off easily			Weight, color, and care should be compatible with rest of garment
			An antistatic finish is desirable

Natural and man-made fibers

Fibers are the basic components of textile fabrics. Each type of fiber has unique characteristics that it imparts to fabrics made from it. Although a fiber's character can be altered by yarn structure and by fabric construction and finish, the original characteristics are still evident in the resulting fabric and are central to its use and care.

Before the twentieth century, all fibers used for cloth were from natural sources such as the cotton plant. In the twentieth century, a host of synthetic fibers appeared on the market, products of the chemical industry. The term "man-made" refers to all fibers not found naturally; it covers both synthetic fibers (made from chemicals such as petroleum) and fibers such as rayon, made in the laboratory from cellulose, a natural product. Whether a fiber is natural or man-made has some bearing on its general characteristics.

Natural fibers — plant fibers

Cotton is strong even when wet, absorbent, shrinks unless treated, creases, and is comfortable to wear. Most cottons can be laundered, colorfast ones in hot water, others in warm or cold water, and dried in the clothes dryer or ironed while damp. Cotton can be mercerized to make it smoother, shinier, and stronger. Some is pre-treated to give it easy-care qualities.

Linen, made from flax, is very strong and absorbent, creases unless treated, and is very comfortable in hot weather. It should be washed at lower temperatures to minimize shrinkage. Pre-shrunk linen can be washed in hot water. When used for tailored garments, it should be dry-cleaned.

Ramie is not as strong as linen but increases in strength when wet. It is highly absorbent and wrinkles easily. It can be dry-cleaned or laundered, depending on the care instructions. It tolerates hot water and its smooth lustrous appearance improves with washing.

Animal fibers

Wool comes from the fleece of sheep (labeled lambswool, cool wool, merino wool, pure wool) and from the hair of other animals such as camels, goats (mohair, cashmere and cashgora), alpacas, llamas and vicuñas, and angora rabbits. Wool is durable, highly absorbent, crease resistant, and holds in body heat well. Wool should be dry-cleaned or washed in cool water up to 86 °F (30 °C). Some wools can be machine-washed. Never dry in the clothes-dryer. Press at a low temperature using a damp cloth.

Silk, produced by the silk-worm, is strong, absorbent, crease resistant, and holds in body heat. It should be either dry-cleaned or washed by hand. Iron a silk garment inside-out at a low temperature setting.

Man-made fibers — cellulose and chemical fibers

Rayon or viscose is relatively weak, very absorbent, shrinks, and wrinkles unless treated. Sometimes it should be dry-cleaned, sometimes it can be machine-washed on the delicate cycle. Iron at a moderate setting using steam or a damp cloth.

Acetate is lustrous, moderately absorbent, wrinkles somewhat, holds body heat, and is heat-sensitive. Wash by hand or using the delicate cycle of the washing machine. Do not dry in the clothes-dryer. Iron all acetates at synthetic setting; they melt at high heat.

Acrylic fiber is fluffy but absorbs water poorly. Acrylic resists wrinkles, is heat-sensitive, and holds in body heat. It is popular in blends with wool and cotton. Wash at 86 °F (30 °C). Iron at a low setting.

Nylon is very strong, has a low absorbency, holds in body heat, and resists wrinkling. It does not shrink. Wash either by hand or machine-wash using the delicate cycle. Iron at a low temperature without steam.

Polyester is strong, not very absorbent, keeps its shape well, and wrinkles little. Holds creases well. Wash by machine or by hand. Spin very lightly or drip dry. May need little or no ironing; use low setting.

Microfibers (mainly polyester) are soft, strong, water-resistant, and breathe well. Machine-washable.

Care symbols

The care symbols shown at right are those commonly used on clothes labels. If you are unsure of the meaning of a symbol, consult your dry-cleaner or tailor.

Care symbols

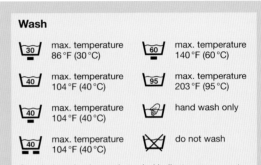

Wash

30	max. temperature 86 °F (30 °C)	60	max. temperature 140 °F (60 °C)
40	max. temperature 104 °F (40 °C)	95	max. temperature 203 °F (95 °C)
40	max. temperature 104 °F (40 °C)		hand wash only
40	max. temperature 104 °F (40 °C)		do not wash

One dash under the wash symbol indicates permanent press cycle, two dashes indicate a delicate/gentle wash.

Bleach

CL	chlorine bleach may be used	do not bleach

Iron

	hot 410 °F (210 °C)	cool 248 °F (120 °C)
	warm 320 °F (160 °C)	do not iron

Dry-clean

Ⓐ Ⓟ Ⓟ Ⓕ Ⓕ ⊗

Letters within circles indicate which solvent may or may not be used during dry-cleaning. A short line under a dry-cleaning symbol is an indication to reduce cycle, moisture, and/or heat.

do not dry-clean

Dry

medium heat	low heat	do not tumble dry

CHAPTER 2

CUTTING

A good garment fit depends on taking accurate body measurements and determining the correct pattern size. Then it is up to you to choose a pattern that suits both your style and figure.

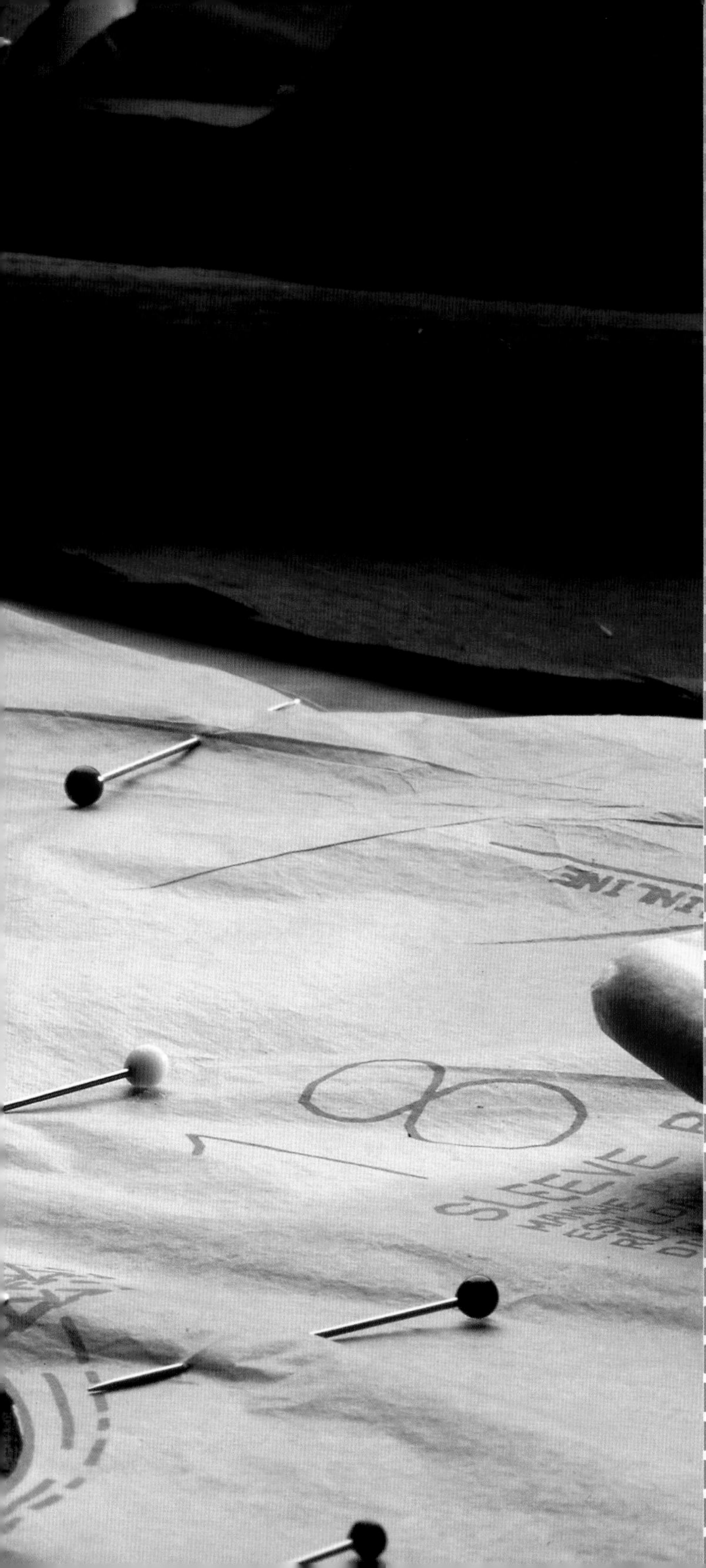

Fitting methods 36–37

Taking measurements

Measurements can be taken without assistance, but the task is easier when someone helps you. For greatest accuracy, measure over underwear. Take vertical measurements first, then those in the round. The tape should lie flat and not be too tight. Record all measurements on a chart. Select the pattern type and size with these measurements. Other measurements may be needed for garment fitting and alterations.

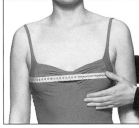
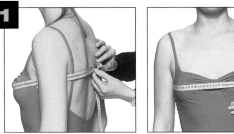

Full bust: bring the tape measure across the widest part of the back, under the arms, and across the full bustline.
High bust (not shown): bring the tape measure across the widest part of the back, under the arms, and *above* the full bustline.

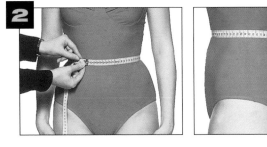

Waist: Place the tape measure horizontally and flat in the natural indentation of your waist.

Hip: Place the tape measure horizontally and flat across the fullest part of the hips (varies according to figure type).

Bustpoint: Measure the same as the bodice length (6) from the shoulder seam at the neckline to the fullest part of the bust (arrow).

Back waist length: Measure from the most prominent bone at the base of the neck along the middle of the back to the lower edge of the tape measure at the waistline (arrow).

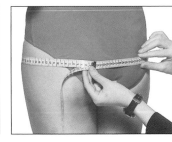

Sleeve length: Measure from the shoulder cap to the outer edge of the wrist of a slightly angled arm.

Front waist length: Measure from shoulder seam at the neckline to the lower edge of the tape measure at the waistline.

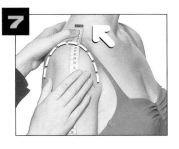

Shoulder length: Measure from the neck (arrow) to the seamline (dotted line).

Fitting methods 36–37

Sleeve width upper arm: (Also called upper arm circumference): Measure the widest part of the stronger upper arm.

Neckline: Measure from the base of the neck directly above the collar bone.

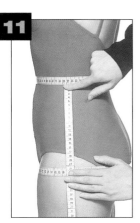

Hip height: Measure along the side seam from the lower edge of the tape measure at the waistline to the middle of the tape at the hip.

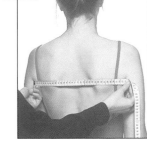

Back width: Measure across the peak of the shoulder blades from the left to right inner edge of the upper arm.

High hip: Measure parallel from the fixed waistline tape down 3 in (8 cm).

Back crotch depth: Measure from the lower edge of the fixed waistline tape in a sitting position to the seat level.

Skirt length: Measure from the desired length to the front middle of the lower edge of the fixed waistline tape. Compare this measurement with the pattern instructions.

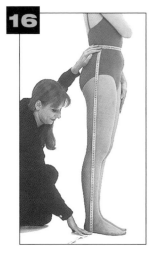

Side length: Measure along the side seam from the lower edge of the waistline tape to the floor. The normal pant length is about 3 in (7–8 cm) shorter than this measurement.

Fabric widths

Almost all pattern companies include on the backs of pattern envelopes a fabric quantity chart detailing the exact amounts of fabric needed for each style. However, usually not all widths can be listed because of space restrictions. Use the conversion chart below if the fabric you are buying is available only in a width not provided for on the pattern envelope chart.

Check the pattern envelope for advice about the use and suitability of napped fabrics for that style. The amount listed on the fabric quantity chart is usually for fabric without a nap; extra allowance must be made for "with nap" fabrics (those fabrics that have a one-way surface, such as velvet or most wools, or fabrics with a one-way print motif), as pattern pieces must be laid in one direction, usually with the nap running down. Sometimes the

amount required for certain fabric widths is the same for "with nap" fabrics as it is for "without nap" fabrics. The amounts may differ, however, for other fabric widths for the same pattern. Purchase fabric in the "with nap" amount if you are unsure whether or not your fabric has a nap.

It may be necessary to allow extra fabric for matching designs, or for other special considerations, such as an unusual garment design or particularly large pattern pieces. Add an additional $1/4$ yd (0.25 m) when there is a large difference in fabric widths, as well as for fabrics with large one-way designs and for styles with sleeves cut in one with the bodice. If pattern alterations are necessary or the fabric has a large-scale design that will need matching, you may require more; use your judgment.

To ensure that you will have enough fabric for your sewing project, do a trial layout on the fabric before it is cut. **Using the conversion chart:** The fabric width conversion chart (below) provides estimates only. To use the chart, locate the amount of fabric called for on the back of the pattern envelope in the appropriate column. Measurements located in the same row in other columns indicate the corresponding amounts needed of other fabric widths.

If, for example, the pattern envelope calls for $1^3/4$ yd (1.60 m) of 50 in (127 cm) -width fabric, locate the width of 50 in (127 cm) on the top line of the chart, then read down the column to find the amount of $1^3/4$ yd (1.60 m). Next glance across the row to the column featuring the fabric width you are planning to buy. For 58/60 in (150 cm) -width fabric, for instance, you will need $1^5/8$ yd (1.50 m).

Size range charts

Commercial patterns are sized not only for different measurements but for figure types of varying proportions. Standard pattern figure types include Misses', Miss Petite, Junior, Women's, and Women's Petite, Men's, and childrens ranges.

Figure types do not signify age groups, but they may be implied and styles designed accordingly. It is best to stay within the size range of the figure type most like yours; if you choose from another, adjust the proportions (p. 37).

Size range charts, generally consistent between North American pattern companies, are found in all pattern catalogs. European pattern companies, such as Burda, use a different sizing system (p. 31).

Maternity patterns, based on Misses' sizes, are generally calculated for the proportions of a woman five months pregnant. Styles provide ease of wear to end of term.

Fabric width conversion chart

32"	81 cm	35"/36"	90 cm	39"	100 cm	41"	104 cm	44"/45"	115 cm	50"	127 cm	52"/54"	140 cm	58"/60"	150 cm
Yard	Meter	Yard	Meter	Yard	Meter	Yard	Meter	Yard	Meter	Yard	Meter	Yard	Meter	Yard	Meter
$1^7/8$	1.70	$1^3/4$	1.60	$1^1/2$	1.40	$1^1/2$	1.40	$1^3/8$	1.30	$1^1/4$	1.10	$1^1/8$	1.00	1	0.90
$2^1/4$	2.10	2	1.80	$1^3/4$	1.60	$1^3/4$	1.60	$1^5/8$	1.50	$1^1/2$	1.40	$1^3/8$	1.30	$1^1/4$	1.10
$2^1/2$	2.30	$2^1/4$	2.10	2	1.80	2	1.80	$1^3/4$	1.60	$1^5/8$	1.50	$1^1/2$	1.40	$1^3/8$	1.30
$2^3/4$	2.50	$2^1/2$	2.30	$2^1/4$	2.10	$2^1/4$	2.10	$2^1/8$	1.90	$1^3/4$	1.60	$1^3/4$	1.60	$1^5/8$	1.50
$3^1/8$	2.90	$2^7/8$	2.60	$2^1/2$	2.30	$2^1/2$	2.30	$2^1/4$	2.10	2	1.80	$1^7/8$	1.70	$1^3/4$	1.60
$3^3/8$	3.10	$3^1/8$	2.90	$2^3/4$	2.50	$2^3/4$	2.50	$2^1/2$	2.30	$2^1/4$	2.10	2	1.80	$1^7/8$	1.70
$3^3/4$	3.40	$3^3/8$	3.10	3	2.70	$2^7/8$	2.60	$2^3/4$	2.50	$2^3/8$	2.20	$2^1/4$	2.10	2	1.80
4	3.70	$3^3/4$	3.40	$3^1/4$	3.00	$3^1/8$	2.90	$2^7/8$	2.60	$2^5/8$	2.40	$2^3/8$	2.20	$2^1/4$	2.10
$4^3/8$	4.00	$4^1/4$	3.90	$3^1/2$	3.20	$3^3/8$	3.10	$3^1/8$	2.90	$2^3/4$	2.50	$2^5/8$	2.40	$2^3/8$	2.20
$4^5/8$	4.20	$4^1/2$	4.10	$3^3/4$	3.40	$3^5/8$	3.30	$3^3/8$	3.10	3	2.70	$2^3/4$	2.50	$2^5/8$	2.40
5	4.60	$4^3/4$	4.30	4	3.70	$3^7/8$	3.50	$3^5/8$	3.30	$3^1/4$	3.00	$2^7/8$	2.60	$2^3/4$	2.50
$5^1/4$	4.80	5	4.60	$4^1/4$	3.90	$4^1/8$	3.80	$3^7/8$	3.50	$3^3/8$	3.10	$3^1/8$	2.90	$2^7/8$	2.60

Pattern size guidelines

After taking your measurements and determining the figure type most like your own (p. 37), choose a pattern size from the charts in the pattern catalogs. If your measurements do not correspond exactly to any one size, consider all pertinent factors and choose the size requiring the fewest major alterations.

Your pattern size may not be the same as your ready-to-wear size. It doesn't matter; ready-to-wear and pattern sizes do not necessarily have any relation to one another. Pattern sizes, however, *do* relate to each other — an important fact to remember. Except for Burda patterns which use European standards and are more precisely fitted, all commercial patterns are based on the same fundamental measurements, making sizing fairly consistent from brand to brand.

Differences between pattern brands are usually in shaping — variations in shoulder slope, dart contours, armhole curve, and so on. These subtle differences, which often reflect fashion trends, may cause certain pattern brands to fit some people better than others; when buying patterns, try those of different makes — in time you will know which suits your figure best.

Selecting patterns

Select dress, blouse, coat, and jacket sizes according to the full bust measurement. If your waist and/or hips do not correspond to the waist or hip allowances for this size bust, you can easily adjust the waist and hip areas in the pattern. However, if there is a difference of more than 2 in (5 cm) between the high bust and full bust measurements (see p. 28), choose the pattern size according to the high bust measurement, and adjust the bust area (see Basic pattern alterations, p. 36). Coat and jacket patterns account for wearing the garment over a dress or blouse, so buy according to your body measurements; don't be tempted to buy a larger size.

Pattern size for skirts or pants is determined by the hip measurement, even if the hips are larger, proportionately, than the waist. It is easier to take in at the waist than let out at the hip.

If you choose a pattern that includes many types of garment, such as a blouse, skirt, jacket, or pants, use your bust measurement and adjust each pattern as needed (see Basic pattern alterations, p. 36).

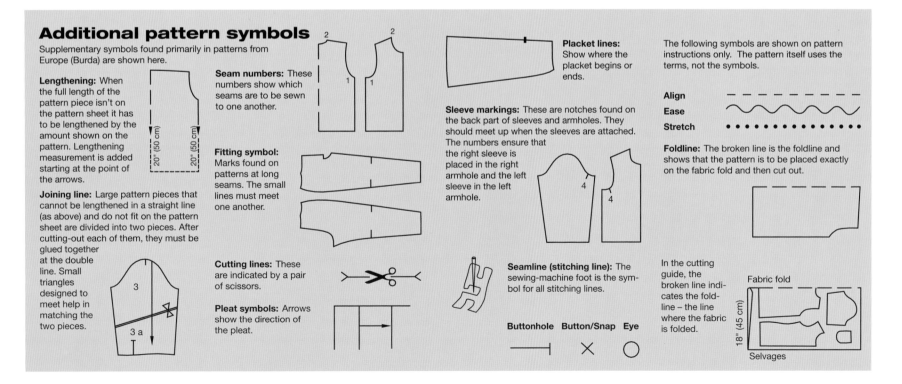

Additional pattern symbols

Supplementary symbols found primarily in patterns from Europe (Burda) are shown here.

Lengthening: When the full length of the pattern piece isn't on the pattern sheet it has to be lengthened by the amount shown on the pattern. Lengthening measurement is added starting at the point of the arrows.

Joining line: Large pattern pieces that cannot be lengthened in a straight line (as above) and do not fit on the pattern sheet are divided into two pieces. After cutting-out each of them, they must be glued together at the double line. Small triangles designed to meet help in matching the two pieces.

Seam numbers: These numbers show which seams are to be sewn to one another.

Fitting symbol: Marks found on patterns at long seams. The small lines must meet one another.

Cutting lines: These are indicated by a pair of scissors.

Pleat symbols: Arrows show the direction of the pleat.

Placket lines: Show where the placket begins or ends.

Sleeve markings: These are notches found on the back part of sleeves and armholes. They should meet up when the sleeves are attached. The numbers ensure that the right sleeve is placed in the right armhole and the left sleeve in the left armhole.

Seamline (stitching line): The sewing-machine foot is the symbol for all stitching lines.

Buttonhole   Button/Snap   Eye

The following symbols are shown on pattern instructions only. The pattern itself uses the terms, not the symbols.

Align

Ease

Stretch

Foldline: The broken line is the foldline and shows that the pattern is to be placed exactly on the fabric fold and then cut out.

In the cutting guide, the broken line indicates the foldline – the line where the fabric is folded.

Fabric fold

Selvages

Pattern catalogs

A pattern catalog is a fashion directory where you can select the latest pattern designs and find information on suitable fabrics and accessories. Catalogs are organized according to the pattern company's notion of its customers' needs, but all contain a wide variety of fashions. For women, these are grouped by style types, such as dresses, sportswear, or lingerie, and further classified by figure types. Many catalogs are divided into sections such as easy-to-make styles and designer fashions, as well as men's, children's, home furnishings, and crafts, toys, and costumes.

Information specific to each pattern may be printed alongside the illustrations. Some is pertinent to pattern selection, such as the number of views within the envelope. Back views, fabric quantity requirements, notion needs, and fabric recommendations may also be included. The latter are of special importance, particularly regarding knits and other stretchy fabrics. "Recommended for knits" means knits or woven fabrics are suitable. "For knits only" means wovens should not be used; such a style has close fit and minimum shaping, relying on the stretchy fabric to mold to the figure. Other fabric limitations also may be indicated, such as "Not suitable for plaids or stripes."

A body measurement chart for all figure types is located at the back of each catalog.

Pattern envelopes

The front of every pattern envelope bears the style number and illustrations of each fashion item and the variations on it within the envelope. Pattern price and size are usually included. Before you buy, make sure that the style and size are the ones you want. Most stores will neither exchange nor give refunds for patterns.

Selecting fabric type

Once you have decided on the view you prefer, the sketch or photo can guide you toward an appropriate fabric type. The fabric illustrated may be crisp or soft, printed or plain, depending on what best suits the fashion. If you are considering a plaid, stripe, or obvious diagonal, look for a view showing such a fabric being used. It's your best assurance that the fabric is suitable.

Pattern envelope back

The pattern envelope back supplies all the information needed at the outset of a sewing project. The arrangement of information may vary from pattern to pattern.

Look carefully at the envelope of each new pattern you buy; every part tells you something important about that particular design.

The most obvious feature, the fabric quantity chart, lists exact amounts of fabric needed for each view and every size in that pattern's range. Space does not permit the inclusion of all fabric widths; if you plan to buy fabric in a width that is not included, consult the conversion chart on page 30.

Most patterns give measurements in both metric and imperial.

Tips for shopping

1. Read the section on the pattern envelope back on suggested fabrics to learn what sort of fabrics are most suitable to the style. These are the fabrics recommended by the pattern designer.
2. Check for fabric cautions or restrictions to make sure that the fabric you have in mind is suitable.
3. Circle your size at the top of the fabric quantity chart. Run your eye down the left side until you find the view and the fabric width you have chosen; then glance across from left to right until you reach the vertical column under your size. The number you find there is the amount of fabric that you will need to buy. If you have a special fabric in mind and the width it comes in is not included in the pattern envelope list, consult the conversion chart on page 30 for the approximate amount you will need to buy.
4. Look through the rest of the fabric quantity chart for interfacing, lining, and trim requirements of your pattern.
5. Purchase all notions and trimmings specified for your view.

Pattern sheets

Some sewing magazines, published by pattern companies and available by subscription or in the crafts section of larger bookstores, contain sewing patterns. These patterns are typically of the styles featured in the magazine's editorial pages. In the Burda magazine, for instance, you will find up to 50 styles featured, all the instructions you need, and one or more pattern sheets, which are usually colored and show contour lines for various sizes. You can use this information to copy the pattern pieces onto paper. The pattern sheet shown below is from a Burda magazine; pattern sheets will vary in look from pattern company to pattern company.

Pattern number: These numbers are the same color as the cutting outline and found on the top or bottom edges (or both) of the sheet.

Trim, etc.: When copying the pattern, all lines and symbols, even those in the pattern itself, have to be duplicated.

Reference arrow: The sheet gives exact tips on its use. Here the arrow points to the reference number.

Grain of fabric: The pattern shows how the pattern should be placed on the fabric grain.

Pattern sheet: Each sheet is denoted by a different letter.

Special pattern pieces: Colors are assigned to special pattern pieces to distinguish them easily.

Cutting outlines: When a pattern encompasses several sizes, each size has its own type of line to follow in cutting.

Shoulder width: Instructions within the pattern piece such as darts, facing lines or pockets are also provided for each different size.

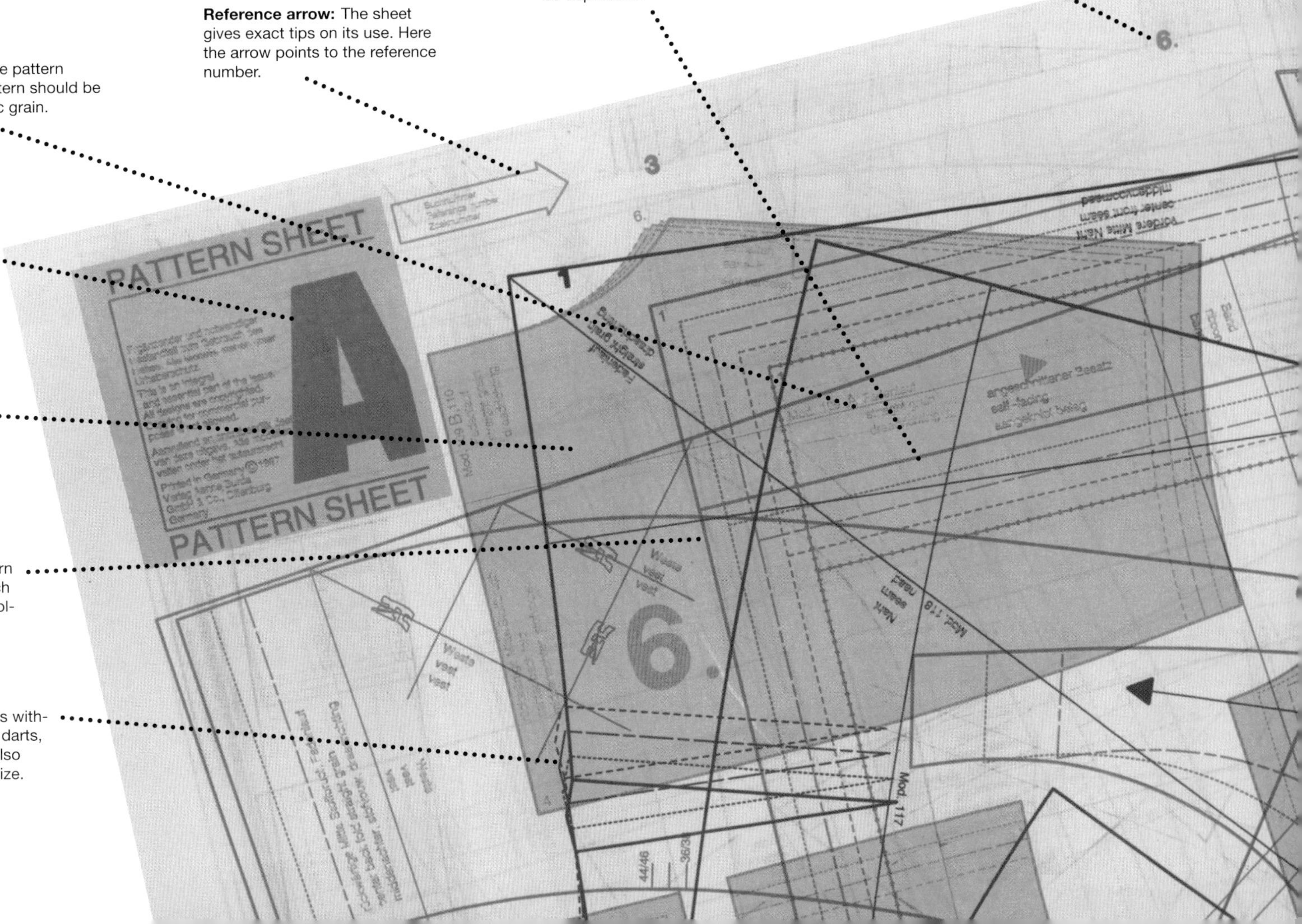

Patterns: Inside the envelope

Contents of all pattern envelopes are basically the same. The key element is the **tissue pattern,** each piece identified by name and number, and by view when pieces differ for, say, views A and B. Because garments are usually identical on right and left sides, most pattern pieces represent half a garment section and are placed on folded fabric. Turn first to the **instruction sheet,** the guide to pattern pieces needed for each view, and to cutting and sewing. Of the varied assistance it gives, the most useful parts are shown below: **1. pattern piece diagram,** for identifying pieces required for each view; **2. cutting guides,** arranged by view, fabric widths, and pattern sizes; **3. step-by-step sewing instructions**. In the pattern below, views A and B differ in sleeve length and skirt style.

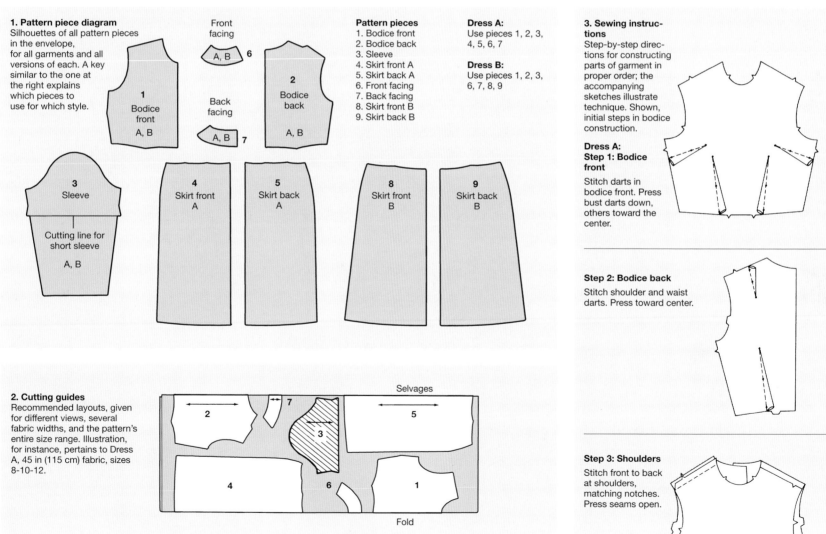

1. Pattern piece diagram
Silhouettes of all pattern pieces in the envelope, for all garments and all versions of each. A key similar to the one at the right explains which pieces to use for which style.

Front facing

A, B 6

1
Bodice front
A, B

Back facing

A, B 7

2
Bodice back
A, B

3
Sleeve

Cutting line for short sleeve
A, B

4
Skirt front A

5
Skirt back A

8
Skirt front B

9
Skirt back B

Pattern pieces
1. Bodice front
2. Bodice back
3. Sleeve
4. Skirt front A
5. Skirt back A
6. Front facing
7. Back facing
8. Skirt front B
9. Skirt back B

Dress A:
Use pieces 1, 2, 3, 4, 5, 6, 7

Dress B:
Use pieces 1, 2, 3, 6, 7, 8, 9

3. Sewing instructions
Step-by-step directions for constructing parts of garment in proper order; the accompanying sketches illustrate technique. Shown, initial steps in bodice construction.

Dress A:
Step 1: Bodice front
Stitch darts in bodice front. Press bust darts down, others toward the center.

Step 2: Bodice back
Stitch shoulder and waist darts. Press toward center.

2. Cutting guides
Recommended layouts, given for different views, several fabric widths, and the pattern's entire size range. Illustration, for instance, pertains to Dress A, 45 in (115 cm) fabric, sizes 8-10-12.

Selvages

2

7

3

5

4

6

1

Fold

Step 3: Shoulders
Stitch front to back at shoulders, matching notches. Press seams open.

What pattern markings mean

Every pattern piece bears markings that together constitute a pattern "sign language," indispensable to accuracy at every stage. Note all symbols carefully; each has special significance. Some pertain to alteration. The double line in the bodice piece below, for example, tells you to "lengthen or shorten here." Other marks are used for matching related sections. Even piece numbers are important, signifying the order in which sections are to be constructed. The markings defined below occur on most patterns.

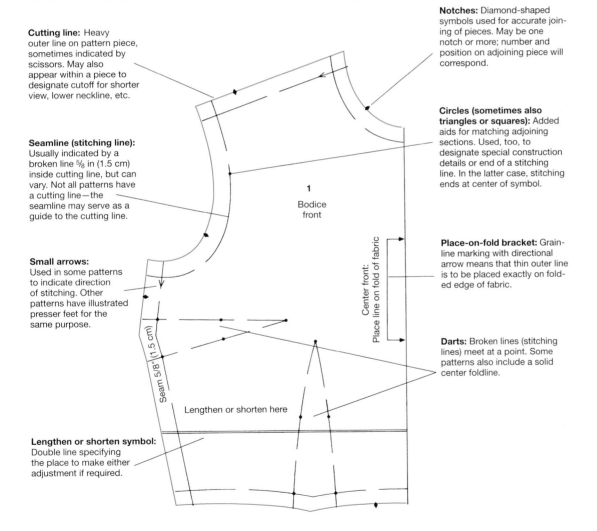

Cutting line: Heavy outer line on pattern piece, sometimes indicated by scissors. May also appear within a piece to designate cutoff for shorter view, lower neckline, etc.

Seamline (stitching line): Usually indicated by a broken line 5/8 in (1.5 cm) inside cutting line, but can vary. Not all patterns have a cutting line—the seamline may serve as a guide to the cutting line.

Small arrows: Used in some patterns to indicate direction of stitching. Other patterns have illustrated presser feet for the same purpose.

Lengthen or shorten symbol: Double line specifying the place to make either adjustment if required.

Seam 5/8" (1.5 cm)

Lengthen or shorten here

1
Bodice front

Center front:
Place line on fold of fabric

Notches: Diamond-shaped symbols used for accurate joining of pieces. May be one notch or more; number and position on adjoining piece will correspond.

Circles (sometimes also triangles or squares): Added aids for matching adjoining sections. Used, too, to designate special construction details or end of a stitching line. In the latter case, stitching ends at center of symbol.

Place-on-fold bracket: Grainline marking with directional arrow means that thin outer line is to be placed exactly on folded edge of fabric.

Darts: Broken lines (stitching lines) meet at a point. Some patterns also include a solid center foldline.

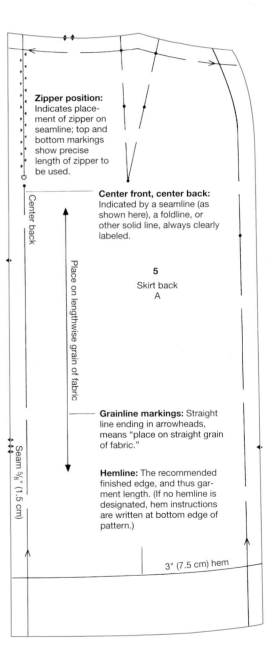

Zipper position: Indicates placement of zipper on seamline; top and bottom markings show precise length of zipper to be used.

Center back

Place on lengthwise grain of fabric

5
Skirt back
A

Seam 5/8" (1.5 cm)

Center front, center back: Indicated by a seamline (as shown here), a foldline, or other solid line, always clearly labeled.

Grainline markings: Straight line ending in arrowheads, means "place on straight grain of fabric."

Hemline: The recommended finished edge, and thus garment length. (If no hemline is designated, hem instructions are written at bottom edge of pattern.)

3" (7.5 cm) hem

Taking measurements 28–29

Basic pattern alterations

Made as they are for millions of people, patterns naturally have their limitations. The chances are that a pattern will fit you well in some places and less well in others. The trick in making clothes that fit is learning where you and the pattern part company. Once you learn what the differences are, the pattern alterations are, in fact, simple.

First of all, find out your basic measurements. Compare them with the pattern so that you know where alterations will be needed. Make any necessary alterations by following the instructions on pages 38–46.

These instructions are based on the assumption that blouse and dress patterns have been chosen according to bust size, which is a good way to choose patterns for most figures. However, if slight changes to the bust are required, you can do this quite easily by moving the darts. If your bust is disproportionately large compared with the rest of your figure, it is better to use a pattern sized to the rest of your body and then enlarge the bust section (see p. 41).

To get a good fit in pants, you usually go by the hip measurement because the waist and the length can easily be adjusted.

Make sure that you don't alter the look of the design you've chosen when you alter the pattern. If, for example, your figure size is smaller than that of the pattern you have chosen, alterations can be made quite successfully. However, never take too much width away from the pattern since this will distort the whole look of the garment.

If you find that you have to make a great many changes to the pattern it might well be that you have chosen the wrong pattern size. Most likely you would have to make fewer alterations by choosing another pattern size or by choosing the same size but one designed for another type of figure.

Getting to know your figure

If your pattern selection meant compromising on a measurement or two, as it usually does, you will need to alter the pattern accordingly. Before you think about pattern alterations, however, analyze your figure's relation to a standard pattern figure. To help you, we show below the ways people and patterns can differ: in proportion, in contours, in posture, and in symmetry. If you haven't already done so, now is the time to make an honest appraisal of your figure. The better you know your own body, the easier it will be to achieve the desired fit. It can be difficult to be honest about our own shortcomings. Remember also that your figure is not a fixed thing: the process of maturing tends to change the human form.

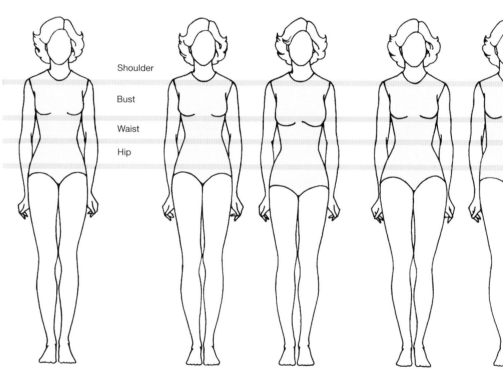

Standard pattern figure: The figure for which any pattern is sized is an imaginary one. Such a figure has perfect posture, symmetrical features, and unvarying proportions and contours. Your own figure is almost sure to differ in some way from this ideal standard.

Variations in proportion: Your key features—bust, waist, hips—may fall higher or lower along your height than those of the pattern's standard. Hem lengths are also a question of personal proportions, whatever the current fashion. Altering a pattern to suit your proportions is a simple process of taking measurements and adjusting lengths and widths.

Variations in contours: Your curves, bulges, and hollows may not only differ from the pattern's standard, but also change with time. Weight gained or lost, physical maturing, foundation garments (or their absence) all affect contours. Fitting a pattern to your personal contours may call for adjusting the darts and curved seams that shape a garment to the figure.

Comparing measurements

To decide when and where you need pattern alterations, you must compare your personal figure measurements with the corresponding measurements on the pattern. In some cases you will measure the pattern itself; in others, the relevant measurements will appear on the pattern envelope.

Remember that your measurements are not supposed to exactly match those of the paper pattern. No garment can or should fit as closely as the tape measure, for you need enough room in any garment to sit, walk, reach, and bend. The chart below gives the least amounts a pattern should measure over and above your figure in six crucial places.

This extra amount is called **wearing ease,** which should be distinguished from design ease. Design ease is the designed-in fullness that will cause some styles to measure considerably larger, overall or in particular areas, than your figure plus the applicable minimums given in the chart. You cannot know how much design ease has been included in a pattern, but you will be sure of keeping it, and therefore of retaining the style lines of the garment, if you take care to include wearing ease in your alterations.

There are exceptions to the wearing ease estimates shown below: knits and strapless styles have less, larger figures may need more.

Measurement	Yours	Plus ease: at least	Total	Pattern measure	Change + –
Bust		3" (7.5 cm)			
Waist		¾" (2 cm)			
Hip		2" (5 cm)			
Crotch depth		½" (1.25 cm)			
Front crotch length		½" (1.25 cm)			
Back crotch length		1" (2.5 cm)			

Compare bust, waist, hip, and back waist length measurements given on the pattern envelope with your own (without any allowance for wearing ease).

Measure the pattern's shoulder seam and compare it with your **shoulder length.** The two should match closely. For a dropped shoulder seam, measure pattern at shoulder markings. If the neckline is set below the neck base, the pattern will specify by how much; add this amount to the shoulder seam before making the length comparison.

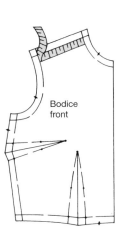

Bodice front

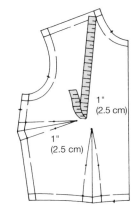

1" (2.5 cm)

1" (2.5 cm)

To check bust dart placement, measure pattern from neck seam (where it meets shoulder seam) toward the dart point to determine where pattern locates apex of bust. Then, using your body measurement, compare actual apex of bust to location on pattern. Bust darts should point toward the apex of your bust but end 1 in (2.5 cm) from it. If the neckline is set below the neck base, the pattern will tell you by how much; add this amount when measuring.

To compare sleeve lengths, measure the pattern down the center. (On fitted sleeves, this will not be a straight line.) For **elbow dart placement,** note how far from the shoulder the darts occur. This will tell you whether to alter sleeve length above or below darts, or both. The elbow dart points to the elbow when it is bent. If there are two, the elbow goes between; if three, the center one points to the elbow. If there is a cuff, allow for its finished width when comparing. Extra length must be allowed, too, for a very full sleeve.

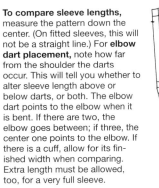

Sleeve

The finished length is usually given on the pattern envelope. Use it for comparison with the length you need or want. If it is not given, measure all patterns except pants patterns at center back, pants pattern along side seam, to determine pattern's finished length.

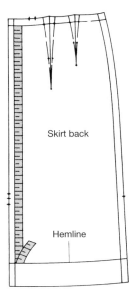

Skirt back

Hemline

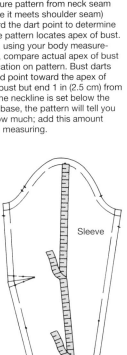

Pants back

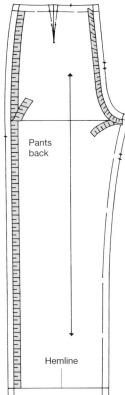

Hemline

To find crotch depth of a pants pattern, draw a line (if there is none on pattern) at right angles to the grain from the side seam to the crotch point at the inseam. Do this on front and back pattern pieces. Measure from the waist seam to this line, along the side seam, for pattern crotch depth. For **front and back crotch lengths,** measure the crotch seam on the pattern and compare result with your measurements. (The pattern should be longer for a comfortable fit.) Stand the tape measure on edge to measure accurately around curves of pattern.

Three: making the alterations

When you have compared your figure measurements with those of the pattern and decided where and how much you will need to alter, you are ready to make the basic pattern alterations. Steps for alterations are described on the following pages. To ensure accuracy in any of these alterations, follow these basic principles whenever you work with pattern pieces:

1. Press the paper pattern pieces with a warm, dry iron to remove creases before making any alterations.

2. All pattern pieces must be flat when any alteration is completed. Sometimes a pattern piece must be cut and spread; this can cause bubbles. The bubbles must be pressed flat before the pattern is laid onto the fabric for cutting.

3. Pin the alterations in first, check them with a tape measure for accuracy, then tape the change in place.

4. If it is necessary to add length or width, use tissue or regular paper to accomplish the increase.

5. Take any necessary tucks **half** the depth of the required change. Remember that the total amount that is removed by a tuck will always be twice the depth of that tuck.

6. When an alteration interrupts a cutting or stitching line, draw a new line on the pattern that is tapered gradually and smoothly into the original line. This will keep your alteration from being obvious in the finished garment.

When **several alterations** have to be made, length alterations should come first in order to make certain that any width alterations you may later make will be at the correct place on the pattern. Length alterations should be attended to in this order: above the waist, below the waist or overall length, sleeves.

When you are satisfied that your darts are pointing in the proper direction and are the correct length, you are ready to move on to any width adjustments needed. Width adjustments should be made first at the bust, then at the waist, then at the hip.

Other specialized alterations take place only after all basic length and width changes have been made.

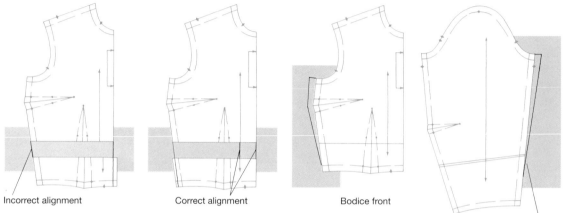

Incorrect alignment   Correct alignment   Bodice front

Front of sleeve

Grainlines and "place on the fold" lines must be straight when any alteration is completed. Note grainline indication on original pattern piece and take care to preserve it on the altered piece. To redraw a "place on the fold" line, align a ruler with the intersection of seamline and foldline at top and bottom of pattern piece; draw a new line.

Be alert to the chain effect of an alteration. Quite often, an alteration in one pattern piece calls for a corresponding alteration elsewhere, or for a matching alteration on pieces that join the changed one, so that seams will match. This is very important at the armhole. If you add to the side seam of a bodice, be aware of the effect on the sleeve seam.

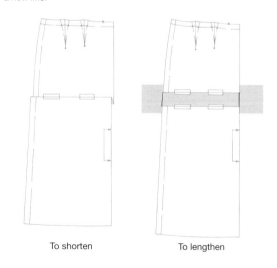

To shorten   To lengthen

For length alterations, use the printed line labeled "lengthen or shorten here" for alterations required in the body of the garment. Skirts and pants can be altered at both the alteration line and the lower edge if a large amount is being added or removed.

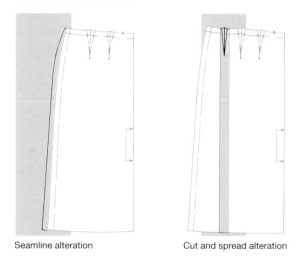

Seamline alteration   Cut and spread alteration

For width alterations, you can often add or subtract up to 2 in (5 cm) at seams. Divide required change by number of seams; add or subtract that figure at each seam. To alter more than 2 in (5 cm), use "cut and spread" technique shown to enlarge or reduce where needed.

Length alterations (increasing)

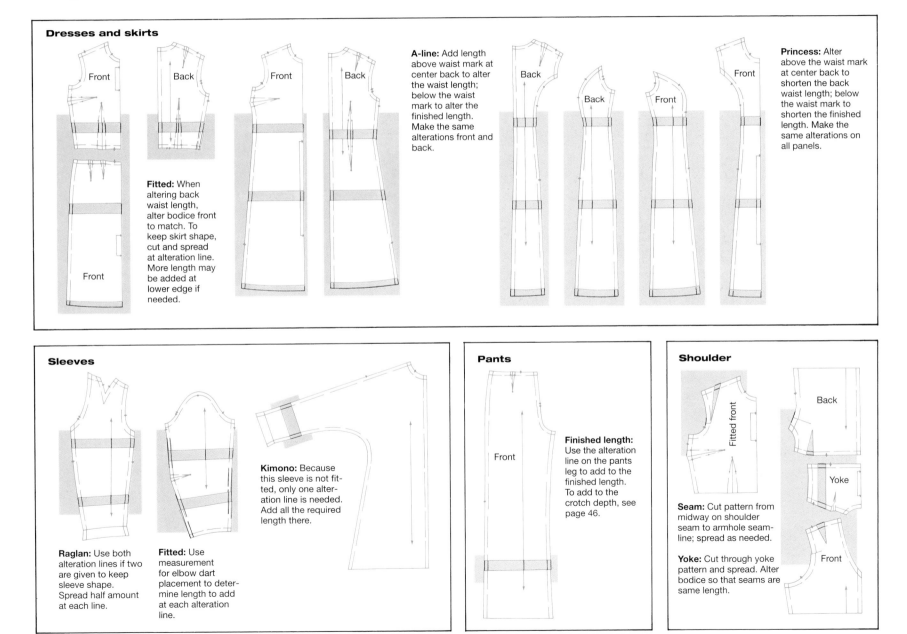

Dresses and skirts

Front **Back** **Front** **Back**

Fitted: When altering back waist length, alter bodice front to match. To keep skirt shape, cut and spread at alteration line. More length may be added at lower edge if needed.

Front

A-line: Add length above waist mark at center back to alter the waist length; below the waist mark to alter the finished length. Make the same alterations front and back.

Back **Back** **Front** **Front**

Princess: Alter above the waist mark at center back to shorten the back waist length; below the waist mark to shorten the finished length. Make the same alterations on all panels.

Sleeves

Raglan: Use both alteration lines if two are given to keep sleeve shape. Spread half amount at each line.

Fitted: Use measurement for elbow dart placement to determine length to add at each alteration line.

Kimono: Because this sleeve is not fitted, only one alteration line is needed. Add all the required length there.

Pants

Front

Finished length: Use the alteration line on the pants leg to add to the finished length. To add to the crotch depth, see page 46.

Shoulder

Fitted front **Back** **Yoke** **Front**

Seam: Cut pattern from midway on shoulder seam to armhole seamline; spread as needed.

Yoke: Cut through yoke pattern and spread. Alter bodice so that seams are same length.

Length alterations (decreasing)

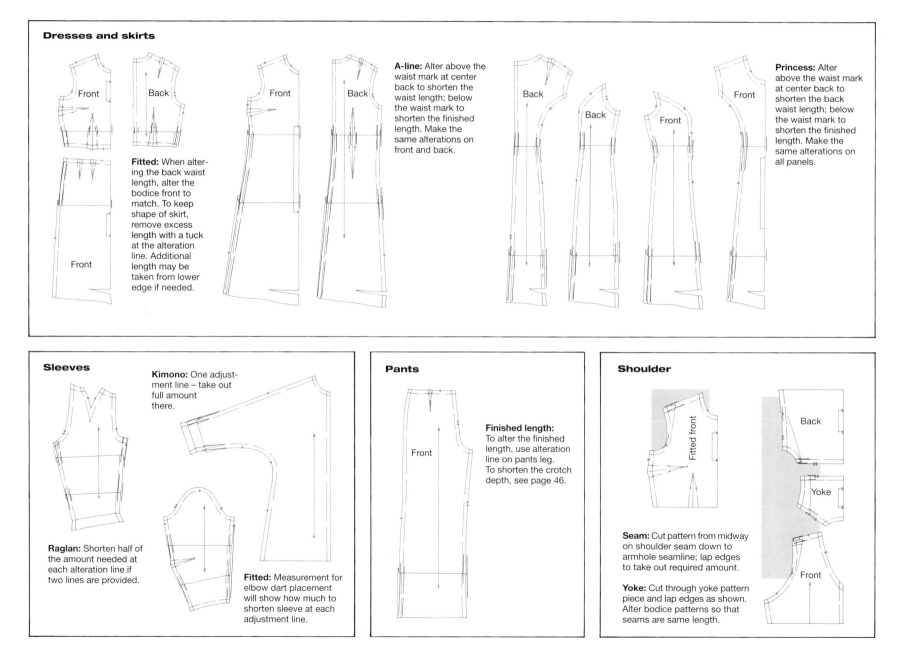

Dresses and skirts

Front Back

Front Back

A-line: Alter above the waist mark at center back to shorten the waist length; below the waist mark to shorten the finished length. Make the same alterations on front and back.

Back

Back Front

Front

Princess: Alter above the waist mark at center back to shorten the back waist length; below the waist mark to shorten the finished length. Make the same alterations on all panels.

Fitted: When altering the back waist length, alter the bodice front to match. To keep shape of skirt, remove excess length with a tuck at the alteration line. Additional length may be taken from lower edge if needed.

Front

Sleeves

Kimono: One adjustment line – take out full amount there.

Raglan: Shorten half of the amount needed at each alteration line if two lines are provided.

Fitted: Measurement for elbow dart placement will show how much to shorten sleeve at each adjustment line.

Pants

Front

Finished length: To alter the finished length, use alteration line on pants leg. To shorten the crotch depth, see page 46.

Shoulder

Fitted front

Back

Yoke

Front

Seam: Cut pattern from midway on shoulder seam down to armhole seamline; lap edges to take out required amount.

Yoke: Cut through yoke pattern piece and lap edges as shown. Alter bodice patterns so that seams are same length.

Raising bust darts

To raise bust darts slightly, mark location of new dart point above the original. Draw new dart stitching lines to new point, tapering them into original stitching lines.

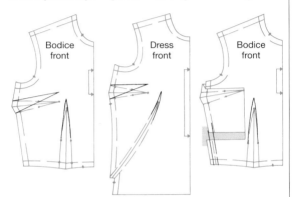

An alternative method, especially useful when an entire dart must be raised by a large amount, is to cut an "L" below and beside the dart as shown at right above. Take a tuck above the dart deep enough to raise it to the desired location.

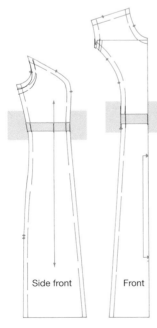

For princess styles, raise the most curved portion of the center front pattern piece by taking a tuck about halfway down armhole seam. To keep waist length equal to that of back pattern pieces, cut front pieces above the waist; spread apart by the amount bust section was raised. The underarm notches at the side seam will no longer match. You must lower the seamline and cutting line at the underarm by the amount removed in the tuck; taper into original lines.

Lowering bust darts

To lower bust darts slightly, mark location of new dart point below the original. Draw new dart stitching lines to new point, tapering them into original stitching lines.

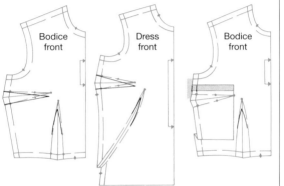

An alternative method, especially useful when the entire dart must be lowered by a large amount, is to cut an "L" above and beside the dart as shown at the right above. Take a tuck below the dart deep enough to lower it to the desired place.

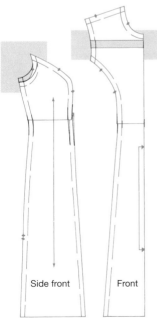

For princess styles, lower the fullest part by cutting the center front pattern piece about halfway down the armhole seam. Spread pattern the required amount. To keep the waist length equal to that of back pattern pieces, take a tuck in the altered front pattern pieces; the amount taken out by the tuck should equal amount that pattern was spread. Underarm notches at the side seam will no longer match. You must raise seamline and cutting line at underarm to equal the amount spread; taper into original lines.

Enlarging the bust area

Additions of up to 2 in (5 cm) can be made at side seams. Apportion amount equally; taper to nothing at armhole and waistline. Cut and spread larger additions as below.

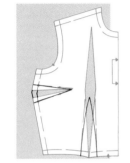

Fitted: Cut pattern from waist to shoulder seam, cutting along foldline of waist dart and through mark for bust apex. Also cut side bust dart on fold-line to within ⅛ in (3 mm) of bust point. Spread the vertical cut at the bust point by half the amount needed. (Do not spread at waist or shoulder.) This will open up the underarm cut, making bust dart deeper. Locate dart point within cuts. Redraw darts, tapering into original stitching lines.

French dart: Draw a line extending foldline of dart to center front. Cut on this line and spread pattern apart half the total amount needed. Keep neck edge on original center front. Locate dart point and redraw darts, tapering into original stitching lines. Redraw center front line.

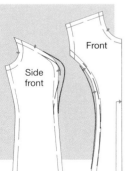

Princess seam: Up to 2 in (5 cm) can be added this way; remember that an additional 2 in (5 cm) can be added, if necessary, at side seams. Divide total inches/centimeters to be added by 4 to determine how much to add to each seam. Mark new stitching and cutting lines outside the old ones at fullest part of curve. Redraw the lines, tapering them into the original cutting and stitching lines at the armhole and waistline.

Width alterations: increasing the waist

To increase the waist, add a quarter of the total amount to each of the side seams, front and back. To make sure that you do not distort the shape, distribute some of the increase over any darts or seams that cross the waistline (except for a circular skirt).

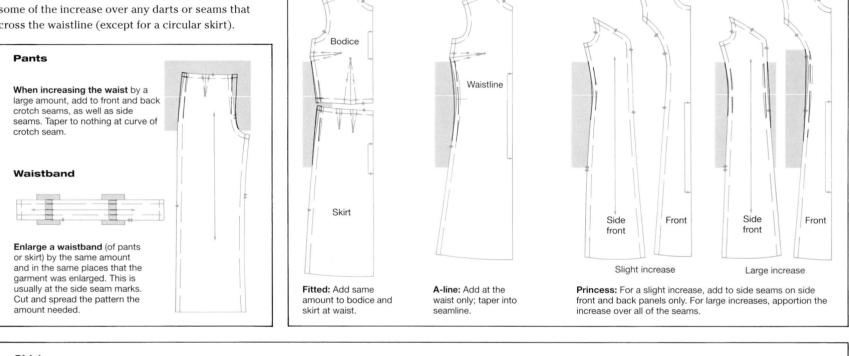

Pants

When increasing the waist by a large amount, add to front and back crotch seams, as well as side seams. Taper to nothing at curve of crotch seam.

Waistband

Enlarge a waistband (of pants or skirt) by the same amount and in the same places that the garment was enlarged. This is usually at the side seam marks. Cut and spread the pattern the amount needed.

Dresses

Bodice

Waistline

Skirt

Side front | Front | Side front | Front

Slight increase | Large increase

Fitted: Add same amount to bodice and skirt at waist.

A-line: Add at the waist only; taper into seamline.

Princess: For a slight increase, add to side seams on side front and back panels only. For large increases, apportion the increase over all of the seams.

Skirts

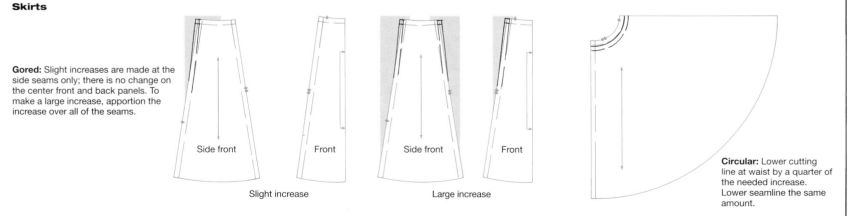

Gored: Slight increases are made at the side seams only; there is no change on the center front and back panels. To make a large increase, apportion the increase over all of the seams.

Side front | Front

Slight increase

Side front | Front

Large increase

Circular: Lower cutting line at waist by a quarter of the needed increase. Lower seamline the same amount.

Width alterations: decreasing the waist

In general, to decrease at the waist you take away a quarter of the total reduction at each of the side seams, front and back. If the reduction is large, distribute some of it over any darts or seams that cross the waistline (except for a circular skirt).

Pants

When decreasing the waist of pants by a large amount, alter front and back crotch seams. Note: Taper smoothly into original cutting line.

Waistband

Decrease a waistband (of pants or skirt) by the same amount and in the same places that the garment was decreased. This is usually at the side seam marks. Tuck out amount to be reduced.

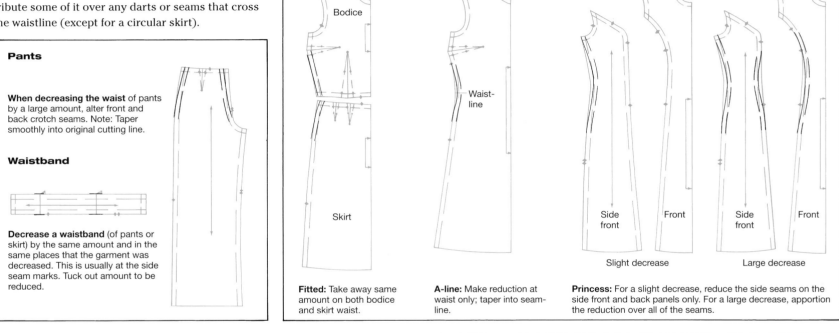

Dresses

Bodice

Waist-line

Skirt

Side front | Front | Side front | Front

Slight decrease | Large decrease

Fitted: Take away same amount on both bodice and skirt waist.

A-line: Make reduction at waist only; taper into seam-line.

Princess: For a slight decrease, reduce the side seams on the side front and back panels only. For a large decrease, apportion the reduction over all of the seams.

Skirts

Gored: Slight decreases are made at the side seams only; there is no change on the center front and back panels. For a large decrease, apportion the reduction over all of the seams.

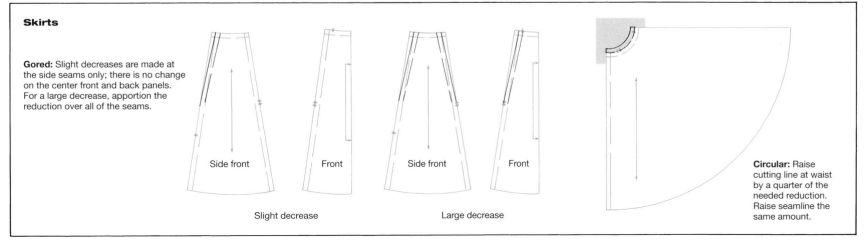

Side front | Front | Side front | Front

Slight decrease | Large decrease

Circular: Raise cutting line at waist by a quarter of the needed reduction. Raise seamline the same amount.

Width alterations: increasing the hipline

To add **2 in (5 cm) or less** to the hipline, enlarge pattern at side seams; add a quarter of the total amount needed at each side seam, front and back. To add **more than 2 in (5 cm),** distribute it more evenly over the garment as shown on this page.

Pants

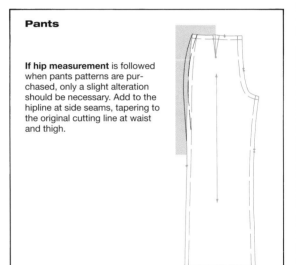

If hip measurement is followed when pants patterns are purchased, only a slight alteration should be necessary. Add to the hipline at side seams, tapering to the original cutting line at waist and thigh.

Dresses

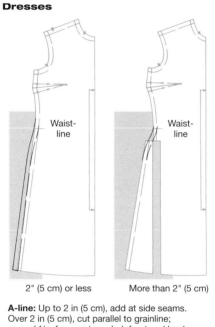

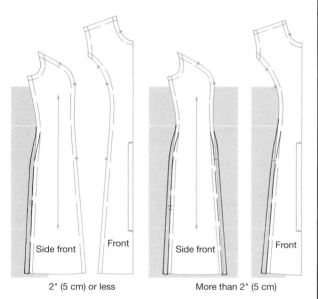

Waist-line

Waist-line

Side front

Front

Side front

Front

2" (5 cm) or less

More than 2" (5 cm)

2" (5 cm) or less

More than 2" (5 cm)

A-line: Up to 2 in (5 cm), add at side seams. Over 2 in (5 cm), cut parallel to grainline; spread ¼ of amount needed, front and back.

Princess: To add 2 in (5 cm) or less, increase at the side seams, making no change on the front and back panels. To add more than 2 in (5 cm), apportion the increase over all of the seams.

Skirts

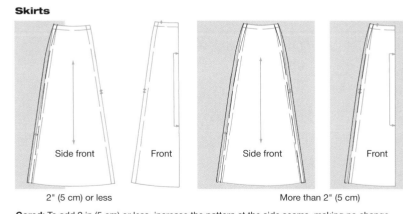

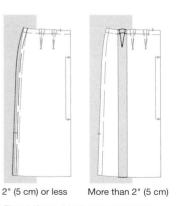

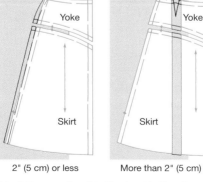

Side front

Front

Side front

Front

Yoke

Yoke

Skirt

Skirt

2" (5 cm) or less

More than 2" (5 cm)

2" (5 cm) or less

More than 2" (5 cm)

2" (5 cm) or less

More than 2" (5 cm)

Gored: To add 2 in (5 cm) or less, increase the pattern at the side seams, making no change on front and back panels. When adding more than 2 in (5 cm), apportion the increase equally over all of the seams. Taper to nothing at the waistline.

Fitted: If over 2 in (5 cm), cut parallel to grain; spread ¼ of amount needed, front and back. Add waist dart.

Yoked: For more than 2 in (5 cm), cut both patterns parallel to grainline; spread a quarter of amount needed, front and back. Add dart at waist.

Width alterations: decreasing the hipline

In most cases, to decrease at the hipline, you take away a quarter of the total reduction at each of the side seams, front and back. It is usually not wise to try to remove more than 1 in (2.5 cm) unless there are many seams, because style lines would be lost.

Pants

If the hip measurement is followed when pants patterns are purchased, only a slight alteration should be needed. Decrease the hipline at the side seams, front and back, tapering into the original cutting line at the waistline.

Dresses

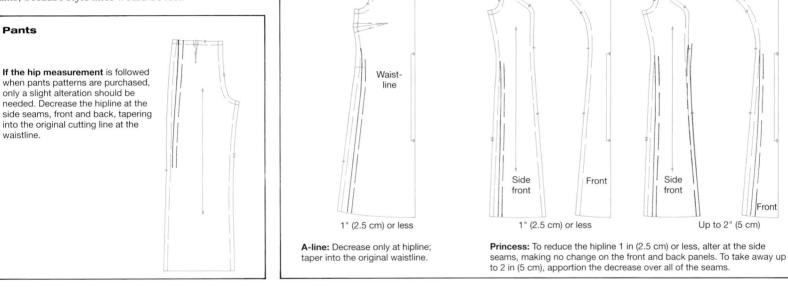

Waist-line

1" (2.5 cm) or less

1" (2.5 cm) or less

Side front

Front

Side front

Up to 2" (5 cm)

Front

A-line: Decrease only at hipline; taper into the original waistline.

Princess: To reduce the hipline 1 in (2.5 cm) or less, alter at the side seams, making no change on the front and back panels. To take away up to 2 in (5 cm), apportion the decrease over all of the seams.

Skirts

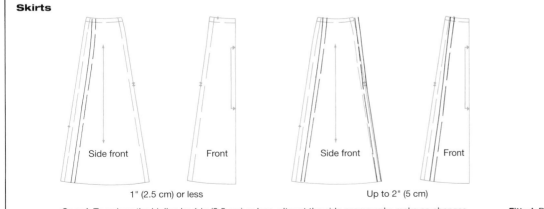

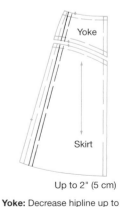

Side front

Front

1" (2.5 cm) or less

Side front

Front

Up to 2" (5 cm)

Up to 2" (5 cm)

Yoke

Skirt

Up to 2" (5 cm)

Gored: To reduce the hipline by 1 in (2.5 cm) or less, alter at the side seams only; make no changes on the front and back panels. To reduce the hipline up to but not more than 2 in (5 cm), apportion the reduction over all of the garment seams.

Fitted: Decrease hipline up to 2 in (5 cm) by taking away at side seams.

Yoke: Decrease hipline up to 2 in (5 cm) on both the yoke and the skirt at side seams.

Adjusting the pants crotch

Good fit in pants depends primarily on how the torso portion is fitted. **Width** alterations for waist and hip have been discussed on pages 42–45. The other two measurements vital to good torso fit are **crotch depth** and **crotch length.** One or both may need altering.

The crotch depth is the measurement of the distance from your waist to the bottom of your hips, taken when you are sitting. This measurement indicates whether any adjustments are needed in the area between your waist and the top of your legs. Consequently, any alterations to the crotch depth will affect both crotch seam and side seam.

The **crotch length** is the actual length of the crotch seam, taken between the legs, from waist at center front to waist at center back. This measurement takes into account any extreme stomach or hip contours, and it affects only the crotch seam — not the side seam. It is important to apportion the total crotch length into what is needed at the front and at the back. For example, if you have a protruding stomach, you should add the necessary length at the front where it is needed, and not half at the front and half at the back.

The crotch length can be altered at the **crotch point,** which is at the intersection of the crotch seam and the inseam, or it can be altered along the crotch seam.

When the length is altered at the crotch point, an additional change occurs — either an increase or a decrease in the width of the pants leg at the top of the thigh, depending on whether the crotch seam is lengthened or shortened.

Use the **crotch seam** method of altering the crotch length if only stomach or bottom is a problem. This method adds or takes away fullness exactly where it is needed at the front or back. It is possible to alter at both the point and along the seam for a very rounded or flat stomach or bottom.

When both crotch depth and crotch length alterations are needed, **alter the crotch depth first.** Then re-measure the pattern's crotch seam before determining how much if any additional altering of the crotch length is needed.

Altering crotch depth

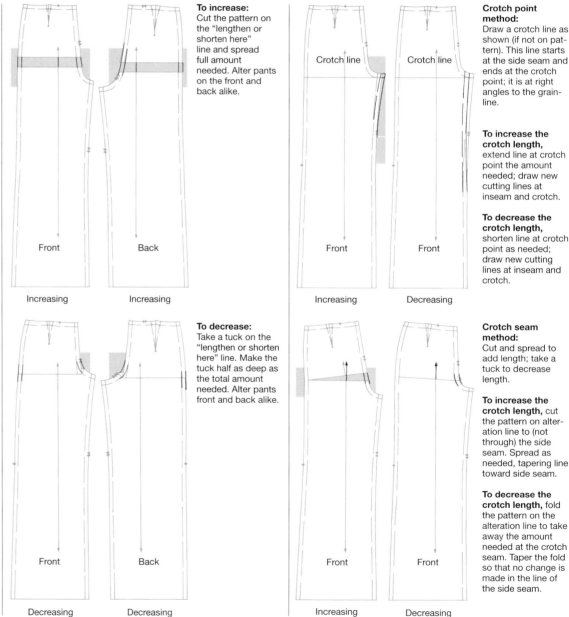

Front   Back

Increasing   Increasing

To increase:
Cut the pattern on the "lengthen or shorten here" line and spread full amount needed. Alter pants on the front and back alike.

Front   Back

Decreasing   Decreasing

To decrease:
Take a tuck on the "lengthen or shorten here" line. Make the tuck half as deep as the total amount needed. Alter pants front and back alike.

Altering crotch length

Crotch line   Crotch line

Front   Front

Increasing   Decreasing

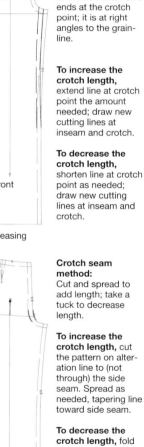

Crotch point method:
Draw a crotch line as shown (if not on pattern). This line starts at the side seam and ends at the crotch point; it is at right angles to the grainline.

To increase the crotch length, extend line at crotch point the amount needed; draw new cutting lines at inseam and crotch.

To decrease the crotch length, shorten line at crotch point as needed; draw new cutting lines at inseam and crotch.

Front   Front

Increasing   Decreasing

Crotch seam method:
Cut and spread to add length; take a tuck to decrease length.

To increase the crotch length, cut the pattern on alteration line to (not through) the side seam. Spread as needed, tapering line toward side seam.

To decrease the crotch length, fold the pattern on the alteration line to take away the amount needed at the crotch seam. Taper the fold so that no change is made in the line of the side seam.

Fitting shell and master pattern

If you need more than the basic pattern alterations, or if you want additional knowledge of fitting techniques, you will want to make a fitting shell and master pattern. A **fitting shell** is made from a basic pattern — it may be a dress, pants, or just a bodice — sewn in inexpensive fabric and used exclusively for solving fitting problems. After the shell has been altered to fit you perfectly, all the adjustments you have made are transferred to the shell's paper pattern. The adjusted shell pattern then becomes your **master pattern**.

This method takes some time and patience, but your master pattern can save considerable time and trouble whenever you sew. By using it with each new style you make, you can check for potential fitting problems before cutting the garment fabric.

Several considerations may suggest the advisability of a *test garment*. Perhaps the fabric is an expensive or unusual one, such as a beaded knit or bridal lace. Or it may require special treatment during sewing. Leathers and vinyls, for example, show pin and needle marks, which makes it impossible to fit them after cutting. Still another difficulty may be the design — a large-scale or border print, or an intricate plaid. By penciling the motif onto a test fabric, you can determine design placement before cutting the real fabric.

Sometimes the pattern itself is the problem. It may be a more intricate style than you are accustomed to, or a silhouette you have never worn. A test garment lets you practice new or complicated techniques in advance, check the suitability of the style to your figure, and make sure of the accuracy of any pattern alterations you have made.

For the test garment, choose a test fabric as close as possible in weight and draping properties to your final fabric — except if the garment is to be underlined. When this is the case, construct your mock-up of underlining fabric, make your adjustments in it, then take it apart for use as a sewing guide.

How to make the shell

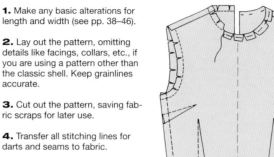

1. Make any basic alterations for length and width (see pp. 38–46).

2. Lay out the pattern, omitting details like facings, collars, etc., if you are using a pattern other than the classic shell. Keep grainlines accurate.

3. Cut out the pattern, saving fabric scraps for later use.

4. Transfer all stitching lines for darts and seams to fabric.

5. Mark center front on bodice and skirt with hand basting in a contrasting thread color.

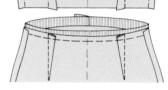

6. Sew the pieces of the shell together, following the instructions given on the pattern; use a long machine stitch for easy removal. For the dress shell, eliminate the sleeves for the first fitting — put them in after shoulders have been adjusted. Omit waistband from pants or skirt — use a length of grosgrain instead.

7. Staystitch the armholes and neckline on the stitching line; clip seam allowances and press to wrong side.

8. Baste all the hems in place.

Judging the fit

Wearing shoes and the appropriate underclothes, try on your shell, right side out. Be very critical about the fit; this is the time to settle all fitting problems, however troublesome they might be.

Track down the cause of every wrinkle and see to the adjustment that makes it disappear. Remember, too, to give your shell the comfort test: sit, reach, bend, and walk to find out whether there are any strained seams and if so, where they occur. Be sure to study your own back view as well.

To adjust the shell, first locate your fitting problems among those shown on the pages that follow. The solutions include explanations of how to adjust the shell as well as how to transfer the adjustment to the master pattern. Resolve *all* your fitting problems on the shell before putting *any* adjustments on the master pattern. This may take more than one fitting session and require taking out and restitching darts and seams. Fit your shell from the top down, because a single adjustment on top might solve the problems below. Keep a record of all the adjustments you make.

Neckline adjustments

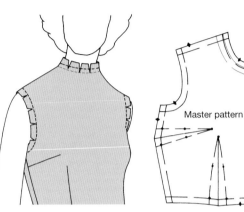

Master pattern

The neckline binds.
Solution: Lower the seamline to the neck base; clip the seam allowance until neckline feels comfortable.
Alteration: Draw cutting and stitching lines in new lowered position on the bodice front and back. Alter the neckline facings to match.

Master pattern

The neckline gapes.
Solution: Raise the seamline to the neck base with a self-fabric bias strip.
Alteration: Draw cutting and stitching lines in new raised position on the bodice front and back. Alter the neckline facings to match.

Shoulder adjustments

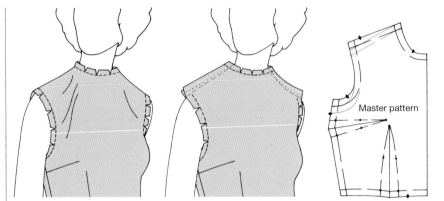

Master pattern

Shell wrinkles above the bust dart at the armhole and below the shoulder at the back. This occurs when shoulders slope more than pattern; one shoulder may slope more than the other.
Solution: Open up the shoulder seam; take out excess fabric by stitching seam deeper. Taper to original seamline at neckline. Redraw armhole to keep its shape.
Alteration: Draw new cutting and stitching lines for shoulder seams and armholes, lowering armhole at underarm by an amount equal to that removed at shoulder.

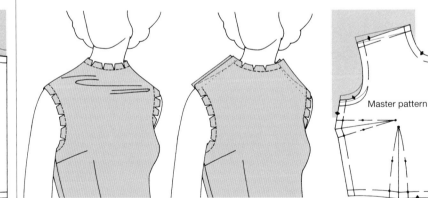

Master pattern

Shell feels tight and wrinkles across the shoulders at front and back. This occurs when shoulders slope less than pattern.
Solution: Release the shoulder seams and restitch a narrower shoulder seam to gain additional space. Taper to original seamline at neckline. Redraw the armhole to keep its original shape.
Alteration: Draw new cutting and stitching lines for shoulder seams and armholes, raising armhole at underarm by an amount equal to that added at shoulder.

Bust adjustments

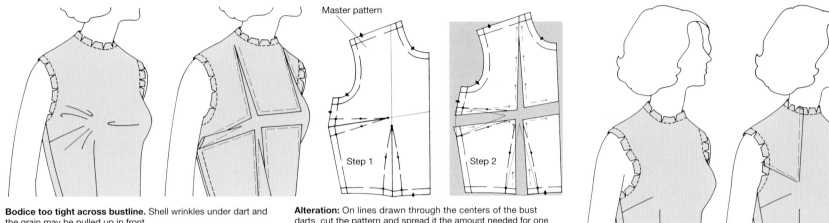

Bodice too tight across bustline. Shell wrinkles under dart and the grain may be pulled up in front.
Solution: Release bust darts, then cut fabric through center of each dart to center front and to shoulder, respectively, crossing apex of the bust. Spread each cut until bodice fits smoothly, filling in open spaces with scraps. Restitch darts, using original stitching lines.

Alteration: On lines drawn through the centers of the bust darts, cut the pattern and spread it the amount needed for one side — half the total amount. Locate the original point of dart within each slash and redraw the dart stitching lines, starting at the original stitching line at base. Restore grainline and "place on fold" line.

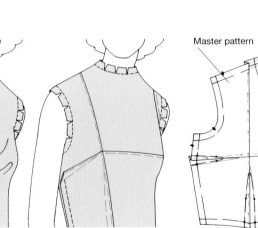

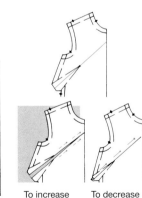

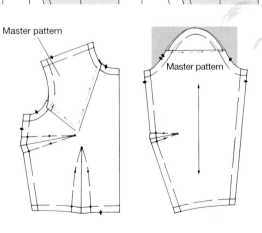

Bodice is too loose across bust. Shell caves in at bust.
Solution: Release the bust darts, then fold out excess fullness, picking up through the center of each dart. Baste folds in place, then restitch darts.
Alteration: Extend foldlines of darts to shoulder and center front; fold pattern on these lines until amount needed for one side — half the total amount — is removed. Locate original point of dart, and redraw dart stitching lines, starting at original stitching line at base. Darts become shallower.

To increase   To decrease

French dart alteration:
On a line drawn through the center of the bust dart, cut and spread (or fold out) half total amount needed. Keep neck edge on original center front.

Armholes and/or neckline gape because of full bust.
Solution: Remove excess fabric by folding out fullness from gaping area to bust point as shown above. (Since this makes the armholes smaller, you will need to remove extra ease in the sleeve cap by taking a tuck a quarter as deep as the alteration dart at the armhole.)
Alteration: Cut pattern from armhole and/or neckline to bust point, and lap the cut edges to remove excess. (Remove excess ease from the sleeve cap with a tuck as shown.)

Shoulder and back adjustments

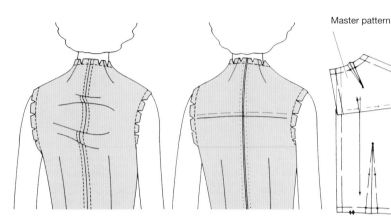

Master pattern

Shell wrinkles across shoulder blades because posture is very erect.
Solution: Baste a tuck across the shoulder blades, tapering to nothing at the armholes. (Note: This requires removal and subsequent replacement of the zipper.) Also, let out the neckline or shoulder darts, making them shorter if necessary.
Alteration: Take an identical tuck in back bodice pattern. Straighten the center back cutting line and make the neckline dart shallower (or omit it) to compensate for the amount taken away when straightening the center back line.

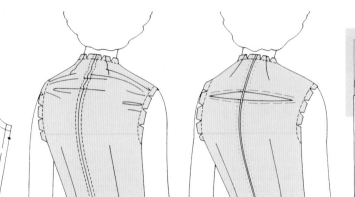

Master pattern

Shell pulls across the shoulders from slumping posture (round shoulders).
Solution: Cut shell across the back where it is strained; do not cut through armhole. Spread slash open until back fits smoothly; fill in with fabric scraps. (Note: This procedure requires removal and subsequent replacement of the zipper.)
Alteration: Cut and spread the pattern same as the shell. Straighten the center back cutting line and deepen the neckline dart (or create one) to compensate for the amount added when straightening the center back line.

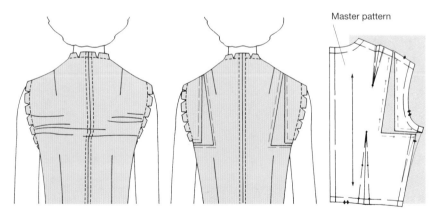

Master pattern

Bodice is too tight at armholes. Seamline may be strained to breaking point.
Solution: Relieve the strain by cutting an "L" from the side seam (do not cut through the armhole seam) to the shoulder seam. Spread slash open until back fits smoothly; fill in with fabric scraps.
Alteration: Cut and spread pattern same as shell. Deepen shoulder dart to remove any excess in shoulder seam. Redraw side seam, tapering from new position at underarm to original position at waistline. Add same amount to sleeve seams.

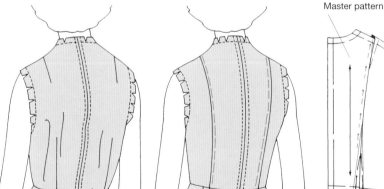

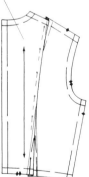

Master pattern

Bodice is too loose across back. Shoulder and waist are too big across the back.
Solution: Remove excess fabric by basting a continuous waist-to-shoulder dart.
Alteration: Take a tuck from waist to shoulder, incorporating waist and shoulder darts. This is called a fitting tuck (it will not appear on a final garment). Because waist and shoulder darts must be retained in the pattern for fitting body contours, restore the darts lost in the fitting tuck to their original position, making them shallower, if necessary, so that waist and shoulder seams will match.

Armhole adjustments

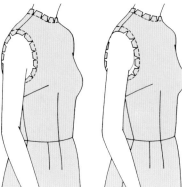
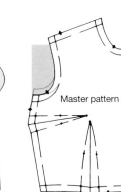

Master pattern

Armholes are too low.
Solution: Raise the underarm curve by basting in place a self-fabric bias strip.
Alteration: Draw new cutting and stitching lines to raise the underarm curve on front and back bodice patterns. Curve on sleeve at underarm must be raised by the same amount so that sleeve can be easily set into armhole.

Armholes are too high.
Solution: Relieve the strain by clipping into the seam allowance; mark a new stitching line for the armhole seam.
Alteration: Draw new cutting and stitching lines to lower the underarm curve on front and back bodice patterns. Curve on sleeve at underarm must be lowered by the same amount so that sleeve can be easily set into armhole.

Sleeves

Master pattern

Take horizontal tuck across sleeve cap ¼ as deep as total taken from fitting shell.

Sleeves are too loose.
Solution: Take a tuck down the top of the sleeve to remove the excess, tucking the entire length if the whole sleeve is too big. If it is only the upper arm that is too large, taper the tuck to nothing at the elbow.

Alteration: If you have taken in the sleeve along its entire length, take a tuck down the center of the pattern, keeping it parallel to the grainline. The tuck will remove some ease from the sleeve cap, so you must alter the armhole by raising the underarm curve (the notches on sleeve and armhole will no longer match). If only the upper arm needed adjustment, see the drawing at the far right above. Underarm curve must be raised in this situation as well.

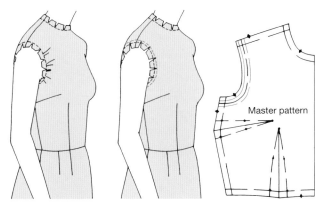
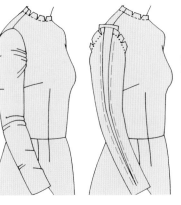

Master pattern

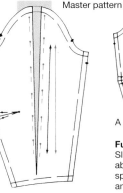

A   B

Full upper arm: Slash as shown above (A) and spread the same amount as shell.

Large elbow: Slash through dart, then up toward sleeve cap. Spread amount needed as shown above (B); redraw seam and dart.

Sleeves are too tight.
Solution: Slash shell down center of sleeve to wrist, then spread until sleeve fits smoothly. Fill in with fabric scraps. You may enlarge the entire sleeve, just the upper arm, or the elbow (see the drawing at the right).

Alteration: If entire length of sleeve needs enlarging, cut the sleeve pattern down the center to the wrist, parallel to grainline, and spread to add the needed width. This adds to the sleeve cap; to compensate, alter the armhole on front and back bodice patterns by lowering the underarm curve. The notches on sleeve and armhole will no longer match. An alteration to the armhole is required for a large upper arm alteration, but not for the elbow alteration.

Skirt or pants front adjustments

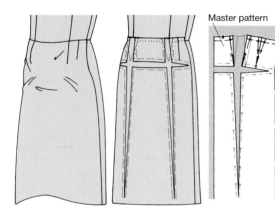

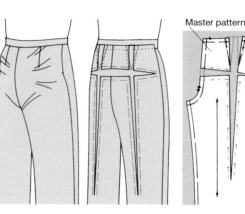

Shell is too tight across abdomen. Strain may cause skirt hem to pull up, pants to wrinkle at crotch.
Solution: Release darts nearest center front. Enlarge the area over the abdomen and make the darts deeper by cutting through the center of the released waistline darts to within 1 in (2.5 cm) of the hem edge (or to knee on pants). Cut again from side seam to side seam just below the dart points. Spread cuts the amount needed, keeping the center front line straight; fill in the spaces with fabric scraps. Pin darts back in, using the original stitching lines. If needed, make two darts out of the one.
Alteration: Carefully transfer the changes to the master pattern by cutting and spreading it to match shell.

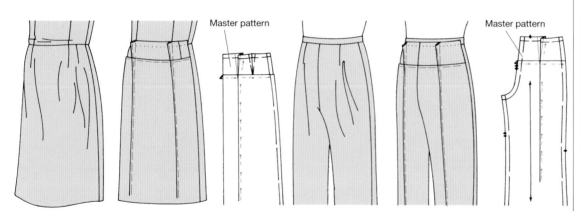

Shell caves in at abdomen. If abdomen is very flat, the skirt may droop in front, pants may wrinkle.
Solution: Release darts nearest to center front. Reduce the fabric over the abdomen and make the darts shallower by taking a tuck through the center of the dart that tapers to within 1 in (2.5 cm) of hem edge (or to knee on pants). Take another tuck from side seam to side seam, just below dart points. When satisfied that enough excess has been removed, baste the tucks in place and pin the darts back in (if they were not eliminated in tuck), using original stitching lines. Darts will be shallower.
Alteration: Carefully transfer changes by tucking pattern to match shell. Taper horizontal tuck to nothing at side seams. Redraw darts.

Side seams

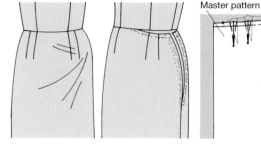

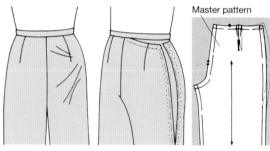

Shell pulls on one side of the body because one hip is higher or larger than the other.
Solution: For a slight adjustment, let out the waist and side seams and fit the darts to the figure contours. Do this at front and back. For a major adjustment, cut and spread the shell across the hipline as shown below. Do this in addition to the dart and seam adjustments described for slight adjustment.
Alteration: Transfer the shell changes by drawing new cutting and stitching lines. Label the alteration as for right or left side. For a major alteration, make a separate pattern piece for the affected side.

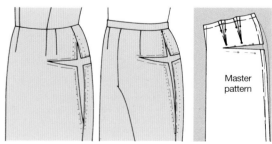

Skirt or pants back adjustments

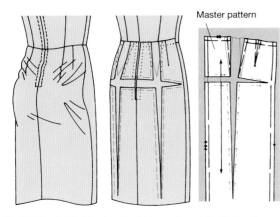

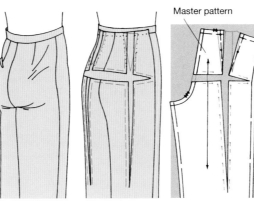

Shell is too tight at back only. Skirt may be wrinkled below the waist; pants wrinkle at the crotch.

Solution: Release the darts nearest center back. Enlarge the area over the buttocks and make the darts deeper by cutting through the center of the released waistline darts to within 1 in (2.5 cm) of the hem edge (or to knee on pants). Cut again from side seam to side seam just below the dart points. Spread cuts the amount needed, keeping center back line straight, and fill in the spaces with fabric scraps. Pin the darts back in, using the original stitching lines. If needed, make two darts out of the one.

Alteration: Carefully transfer changes to the master pattern by cutting and spreading it to match shell.

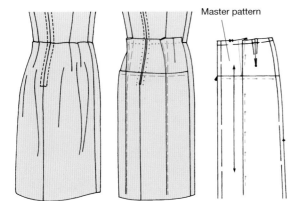

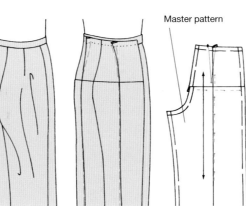

Shell is too loose at back only. Skirt will collapse in the back and the hem may droop. Pants are inclined to wrinkle from sagging at the crotch.

Solution: Release darts nearest center back. Reduce the amount of fabric over the buttocks and make the darts shallower by taking a tuck through center of dart that tapers to within 1 in (2.5 cm) of hem edge (or to knee on pants). Take another tuck from side seam to side seam, just below dart points. Baste tucks in place and pin darts back in (if not eliminated in the tuck) using original stitching lines. Darts will be much shallower.

Alteration: Carefully transfer the changes by tucking pattern to match shell. Taper horizontal tuck to nothing at side seams. Redraw darts.

Pant legs adjustments

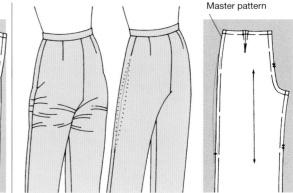

Pants legs are too tight at thigh.

Solution: Let out side seams until shell fits smoothly; taper addition to nothing at hip and knee.

Alteration: Transfer the changes made in the shell by drawing new cutting and stitching lines on the pants back and front patterns. Divide the increase equally between front and back side seams.

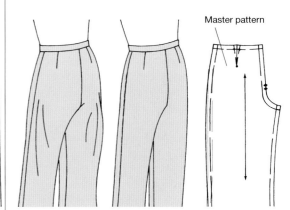

Pants legs are too loose at thigh.

Solution: Take in side seams until shell fits smoothly; taper reduction to nothing at hips and knee.

Alteration: Transfer the changes made in the shell by drawing new cutting and stitching lines on the pants back and front patterns. Divide the reduction equally between front and back side seams.

How to use the master pattern

When the shell has been adjusted to solve all fitting problems to your satisfaction, you are ready to transfer the adjustments to the pattern pieces from which the shell was made. The adjusted pieces are your master pattern. For future reference, note on this pattern each amount you have added or taken away. When adding to the master pattern, use tissue or regular paper and transparent tape.

Label any asymmetrical pattern alterations to the right or left side. Later, you can cut out on the line for the larger side and, with dressmaker's tracing paper and tracing wheel, mark the differing stitching lines for each side. If this is impractical, as it will be when, for instance, one hip is much higher than the other, make separate patterns for right and left sides and cut out the pattern pieces from single layers of fabric.

Back your altered master pattern with non-woven, iron-on interfacing; this will make it durable. Keep your fitting shell and try it on from time to time. If you find you need to make new adjustments because of figure changes, you can easily alter your master pattern.

To use the master pattern with other patterns, follow this two-step suggestion. First place the master pattern under related pieces of the new pattern and check for **length** adjustments. Align the new pattern with the master pattern at shoulders or underarm if a bodice or a dress, at waistline if a skirt or pants. Make all the needed length adjustments. Then put the new pattern over the master pattern again and match up the waistlines.

Check for **width** adjustments at the bust, waist, and hip. Also make sure that **darts** are correctly positioned. Other specialized alterations, such as high hip, gaping neckline, or armhole, should be noted at this time.

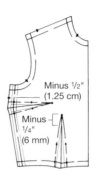

Minus 1/2" (1.25 cm)

Minus 1/4" (6 mm)

Plus 1/2" (1.25 cm) 1/4" (6 mm) 1/4" (6 mm)

Right side

Skirt front

Note on the master pattern as close to each alteration as possible the amount you have added or taken away. This will avoid any confusion about the individual alterations.

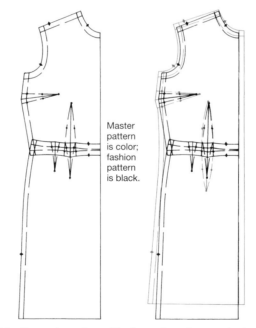

Master pattern is color; fashion pattern is black.

Using the master pattern with other patterns is a very simple procedure. Simply slip master pattern piece underneath the appropriate piece from new pattern; match up center fronts or center backs and other key points. You will be able to see clearly where the new pattern requires alteration.

The try-on fitting

It is wise to try on any garment as soon as the major seams have been stitched. Some fine adjustments can be seen only when fabric and pattern meet. This is a good time, too, to make minor seam and dart adjustments that may still be needed.

Schedule a try-on fitting when back and front have been joined at sides and shoulders, and underlining and interfacing are in place. Staystitch armholes and necklines to prevent stretching; expect these openings to be snug because of extended seam allowances. Pin up hems. Lap and pin openings.

Try on pants and skirts before the waistband is attached. Staystitch at waist to prevent stretching.

To get a clear and accurate picture of fit, wear appropriate shoes and undergarments. Remember also to try on your garment right side out.

Machine-baste sections together for this fitting; it will be easier to make changes. If your fabric is too delicate for machine stitching, pin-baste instead, placing the pins several inches/centimeters apart on the right side along the stitching lines.

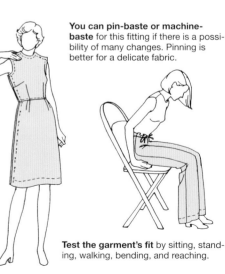

You can pin-baste or machine-baste for this fitting if there is a possibility of many changes. Pinning is better for a delicate fabric.

Test the garment's fit by sitting, standing, walking, bending, and reaching.

Advanced pattern alterations — adjusting after the try-on fitting

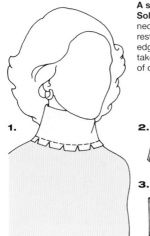

A stand-up collar is too high.
Solution: Adjust the collar, not the neckline. If the collar is shaped, restitch a deeper seam along the top edge. If collar is a folded bias band, take deeper seam at neckline edge of collar only.

1.

2.

3.

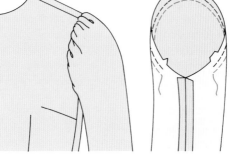

Too much ease in sleeve cap; material ripples.
Solution: Remove sleeve from garment; smooth out cap. Easestitch ⅛ in (3 mm) from seamline, within cap area (sleeve cap seam allowance is now ¾ in [2 cm]). Re-baste sleeve to armhole, aligning new ease line with armhole seam; maintain ⅝ in (1.5 cm) seam allowance between underarm notches.

A stretchy knit garment ends up too big around the middle.
Solution: Take in side seams for a closer (but not too close) fit. Remember to deepen seam allowance on sleeve underarm seams so that sleeve and bodice armholes will match.

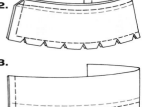

A low U-shaped or V-shaped neckline gapes.
Solution: Lift bodice front at shoulder near neck to remove excess fabric between bust apex and shoulder. Taper adjustment to nothing at the armhole. Alter the neckline facing to match.

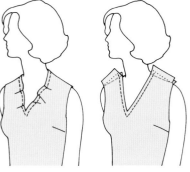

Wrinkling on either side of darts.
Solution: Darts may be too straight to conform to your figure. Restitch darts, curving them slightly inward. Taper carefully to points. Darts may need shortening.

Fabric bulges or sags below the dart.
Solution: Darts are probably too short. Restitch to a longer length, maintaining the original width. Sometimes this problem arises when dart has not been tapered smoothly to point in stitching. Restitch.

Front opening, or lapped edge on wrap skirt, sags slightly.
Solution: Re-pin the hem. If unevenness is extreme, or if back fold sags, try correcting by raising waist seamline in sagging areas. A third possibility: support the sagging edge with concealed snap fasteners (especially if fabric must be matched crosswise).

Preparing fabrics for cutting — preparing woven fabrics

Proper fabric preparation is an essential preliminary to cutting. It is helpful, before undertaking this procedure, to understand the basic facts of fabric structure. In weaving, fixed or *warp* yarns are interlaced at right angles by filler or *weft* yarns. A firmly woven strip, called the *selvage,* is formed along each lengthwise edge of the finished fabric. Grains indicate yarn direction — *lengthwise,* that of the warp; *crosswise,* that of the weft. Any diagonal intersecting these two grainlines is *bias.*

Each grain has different characteristics that affect the way a garment drapes. Lengthwise grain, for instance, has very little give or stretch. In most garments, the lengthwise grain runs vertically (that is, from shoulder to hemline). Crosswise grain has more give and thus drapes differently, giving a fuller look to a garment. As a rule, crosswise grain is used vertically only to achieve a certain design effect, as in border print placement (see Unusual prints, p. 63). Bias stretches the most. A bias-cut garment usually drapes softly. It also tends to be unstable at the hemline.

Straightening fabric ends. This first step must be taken with every fabric so that it can be folded evenly and also checked for grain alignment. *Tearing* is fastest but appropriate only for firmly woven fabrics; other types may snag or stretch. *Drawing a thread* is

slower but the most suitable for loosely woven, soft, or stretchy fabrics. *Cutting on a prominent line* is a quick, simple method for any fabric that has a strong woven linear design.

Checking fabric alignment comes next. During manufacture, the fabric may have been pulled *off-grain.* A garment made with such fabric will not hang correctly, so realignment must be done before cutting (see opposite page).

Preshrinking is advisable if shrinkage possibilities are unknown, if two or more different fabrics are being used for a washable garment, or if maximum shrinkage is expected to be more than one percent. To preshrink washable fabric, launder and dry it, following the fabric care instructions.

To preshrink dry-cleanable fabric, dampen fabric, lay on flat surface to dry (do not hang it up), and then press lightly on wrong side. One caution: This process may cause some fabrics to waterspot or become matted. It is wise to test a scrap first. Realign grain after shrinking if needed.

Press fabric that is wrinkled or has a creaseline, testing to see if the crease can be removed. If it cannot, or a faded streak shows up along the fold, this area must be avoided in layout and cutting (see Folding fabrics for cutting, p. 59).

Straightening ends

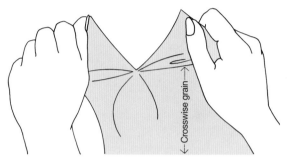

Tearing is suitable for firmly woven fabrics. First make a snip in one selvage; grasp the fabric firmly and rip across to opposite selvage. If the strip runs off to nothing on the way across, repeat, snipping selvage farther from end.

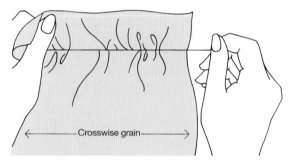

A drawn thread is better for soft, stretchy, or loose weaves. Snip selvage; grasp one or two crosswise threads and pull gently, alternately sliding thread and pushing fabric until you reach other selvage. Cut along pulled thread.

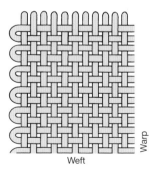

Woven fabric: Basically two sets of yarns, weft and warp, interlaced at right angles.

Selvage is formed along each lengthwise edge. **Lengthwise grain** parallels selvage; **crosswise grain** is perpendicular to it. **Bias** is any diagonal that intersects these grains; **true bias** is at a 45° angle to any straight edge when grains are perpendicular.

Cutting on a prominent fabric line is limited to fabrics with a woven stripe, plaid, check, or other linear design. For cutting printed designs, use the first or second methods (tearing or drawn thread), whichever is appropriate.

Folding a knit 59

Realigning grain

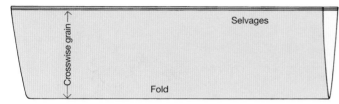

After straightening the ends, fold fabric lengthwise, bringing selvages together and matching crosswise ends. If fabric edges fail to align on three sides (as shown), or if edges align but corners do not form right angles, fabric is skewed or off-grain and must be realigned before cutting.

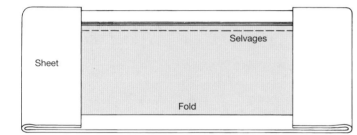

For more resistant fabrics, dampen fabric after testing to make sure water will not damage it. Fold fabric lengthwise, matching selvages and ends; baste edges together. Enclose in a damp sheet and leave several hours.

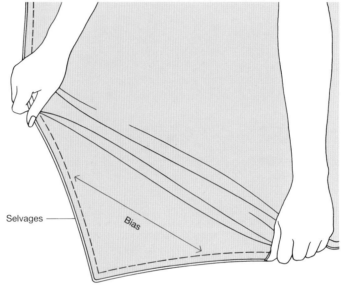

Stretch fabric on the bias. This is usually sufficient to put it back in proper shape. Pull gently, but firmly, until fabric is smooth and all corners form right angles. Use caution; too much stretching can cause further distortion. Lay fabric on a flat surface to dry, then press if necessary.

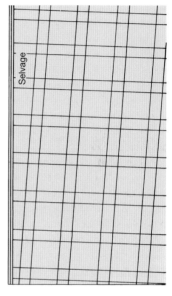

An off-grain print makes fabric seem crooked even if grainlines are true. This cannot be corrected. Avoid such fabrics by examining print before purchase.

Preparing knits for cutting

Knits are structured differently from wovens but prepared for cutting in much the same way, except for straightening of ends. Since there are no selvages, and threads cannot be pulled, you must rely on your eye to tell whether a knit is even. If the design is boldly structured, cut along a prominent line; otherwise follow the procedures below.

Knit fabrics come in two forms, *flat* and *tubular*.

Some flat knits have perforated lengthwise edges which are comparable to the selvages on wovens. These should not be used, however, as a guide for aligning fabric; they are not dependably straight.

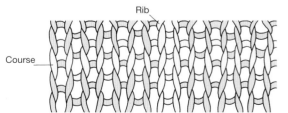

Knit fabric is formed by interlocking loops of yarn. The horizontal rows are called courses, the lengthwise rows are called ribs.

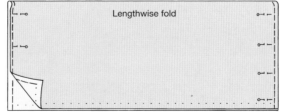

To straighten ends of a flat knit, baste with contrasting thread along one course at each end of fabric. Fold fabric in half lengthwise; align markings, and pin together.

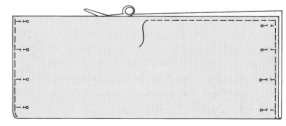

Straighten ends of a tubular knit same as flat knit, then cut open along one rib. If edges curl, press lightly, then baste together. A narrow tube (usually 18 in [45 cm] wide) is used as is.

Parts of a pattern 32–33 · Basic pattern alterations 36–46

Handling pattern pieces

1. Assemble all pieces needed for your view.

2. Return to the envelope any unneeded pattern pieces.

3. Cut apart small pieces, such as facings and pockets, if printed on one sheet of tissue.

4. *Do not trim* extra tissue margin that surrounds cutting lines; this is useful for alterations.

5. Determine how many times each piece is to be cut (such information is on the pattern itself).

6. Press pattern pieces with warm iron if exceptionally wrinkled, otherwise smooth with hands.

7. Alter pattern, if necessary (see Basic pattern alterations, pp. 38–46). Make sure that any alterations made are visible on both sides of the pattern tissue.

8. Consider possible style changes (see Cutting basic design changes, p. 64). All such remodeling must be decided upon before cutting.

Identifying right side of fabric

Right side or *face* of fabric should be identified before cutting. Often it is obvious, but sometimes careful examination is needed to tell right side from wrong. One means of identification is the way fabric is folded — cottons and linens are folded right side out, wools wrong side out. If fabric is rolled on a tube, face is usually to the inside. **Smooth fabrics** are shinier or softer on the right side. **Textured fabrics** are more distinctly so on the face; for example, slubs may be more outstanding, a twill (diagonal weave) better defined. Such fabrics often have small irregularities, such as extra thick nubs, on the wrong side. **Fancy weaves,** such as brocade, are smoother on the right side, floats usually loose and uneven on the back. **Printed designs** are sharper on the right side. Some knits roll toward the right side when stretched crosswise.

The fabric face is generally more resistant to dirt and abrasion but you can use the wrong side if you prefer its look. When there is no visible difference between sides, make one the wrong side and mark it with chalk to avoid confusion.

Selecting pattern layout

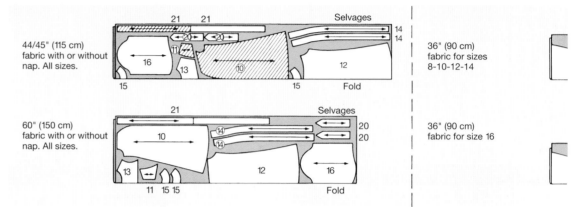

To find correct pattern layout, look for view that corresponds to your choice, then for fabric width and size that match yours. Circle this view so that you won't confuse it with other views as you work. If there is no layout for your particular fabric width, or if you are combining views, a trial layout may be necessary (see Trial layout, p. 64, for procedure).

How to interpret cutting guides

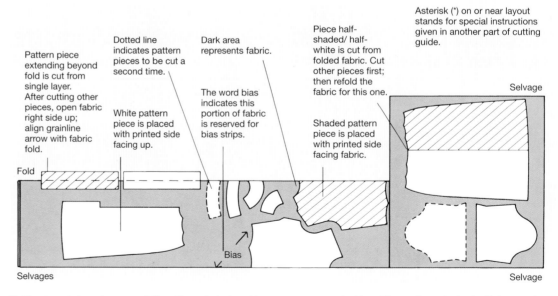

Cutting layout above is representative of types to be found in any pattern guide sheet and all possible variations are included. The average actual layout is usually much simpler. Before starting, carefully consult the instructions provided by the pattern company.

Folding fabrics for cutting

The cutting layout shows how the material should be folded. Precision is vital here. Where selvages meet, they should match exactly.

If the material was folded at the time of purchase, make sure the foldline is accurate and re-press it if necessary. Also test to see if the fold can be removed — a permanent crease must be avoided in cutting. (A double lengthwise fold, far right, is one way around the problem.) When no fold is indicated, lay fabric right side up.

Fold *right sides* together when the layout calls for partial lengthwise fold. Fold *wrong sides* together when you are working with napped fabrics, designs to be matched, prints with large motifs, non-symmetrical designs and fabric to be marked with carbon paper (see Fabric-marking methods, p. 65).

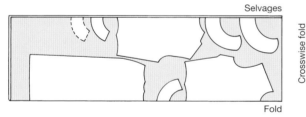

Standard lengthwise fold: Made on lengthwise grain with selvages matching along one edge (the way fabric often comes from the bolt). The fold most often encountered in layout guides, it is convenient and easy to manage.

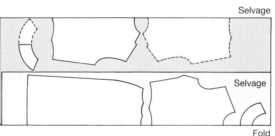

Partial lengthwise fold: Made on lengthwise grain with one selvage placed a measured distance from fold, balance of fabric is single layer. Width of double portion is determined by widest pattern piece to go in this space. Care must be taken to maintain uniform distance from selvage to fold.

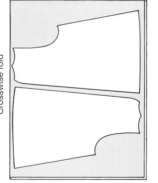

Crosswise fold: Made on crosswise grain with selvages matching along two edges. Generally used when the lengthwise fold would be wasteful of fabric, or to accommodate any unusually wide pattern pieces. Not to be used for napped or other one-way fabrics.

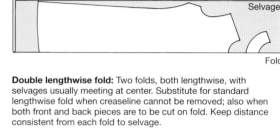

Double lengthwise fold: Two folds, both lengthwise, with selvages usually meeting at center. Substitute for standard lengthwise fold when creaseline cannot be removed; also when both front and back pieces are to be cut on fold. Keep distance consistent from each fold to selvage.

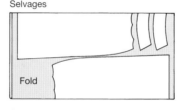

Combined folds: Fabric is folded two different ways for same layout. Most often consists of one lengthwise and one crosswise fold, though any combination is possible. Usual procedure is to lay out pattern pieces for one portion, then cut off remaining fabric and re-fold. Before dividing fabric, measure second part to make sure there is enough length.

Folding a knit

There are two ways to fold a knit accurately. You can either match the crosswise basting used for straightening ends (see Preparing knits for cutting, p. 57) or mark a lengthwise rib, as at right. Should the knit be too fine for either method, fold it as evenly as you can, making sure ribs are not twisted along foldline. If the fabric already has a crease, check it for accuracy; re-press if necessary; also make sure the crease can be removed. Special care must be taken with a knit fold as it acts as a guide for straight grain when the pattern is pinned.

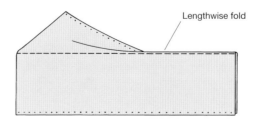

Folding lengthwise: Baste along one rib near center of fabric, using contrasting thread; fold on basted line.

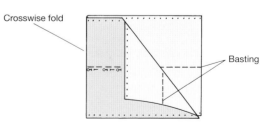

Folding crosswise: Baste first as for the lengthwise fold then fold the fabric, aligning the basting marks. Pin along the basted line.

Pinning the pattern to the fabric

For pinning pattern to fabric, the general order is *left to right* and *fold to selvages*. For each pattern piece, pin fold or grainline arrow first, then corners, and finally edges, smoothing pattern as you pin. *Place pieces as close together as possible,* overlapping tissue margins where necessary. Each layout is designed to use fabric economically. Even small changes may result in the pieces not fitting into the space apportioned to them. The efficient way to place pins is diagonally at corners and perpendicular to edges, with points toward and inside cutting lines. (On delicate fabrics, and leather and vinyl, in which pins could leave holes, pin within seam allowances.) Use pins economically — too many pins can distort fabric, making it difficult to cut accurately. Do not allow fabric to hang off the edge of the cutting surface. If it is not large enough to accommodate all fabric at once, lay out and pin one portion at a time, carefully folding up the rest.

Before starting to cut, lay out *all* illustrated pieces slowly and carefully, then re-check your placements. If underlining, lining, or interfacing are to be cut using garment pattern pieces, cut garment first; remove pattern and re-pin to each underlying fabric.

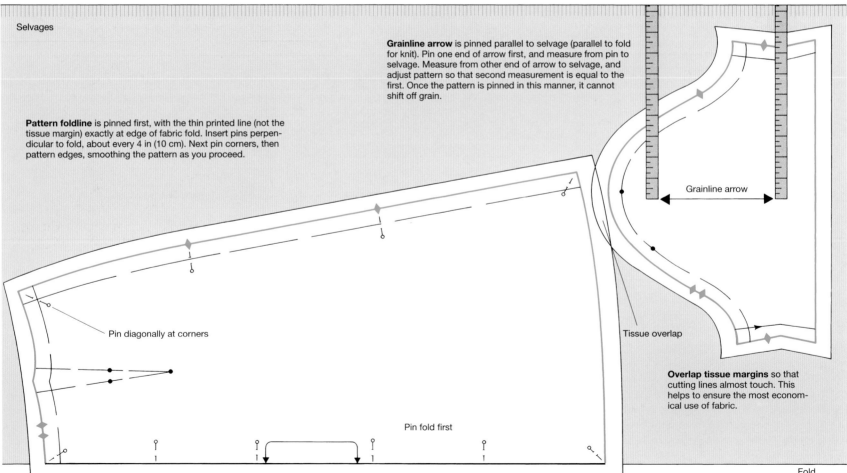

Selvages

Grainline arrow is pinned parallel to selvage (parallel to fold for knit). Pin one end of arrow first, and measure from pin to selvage. Measure from other end of arrow to selvage, and adjust pattern so that second measurement is equal to the first. Once the pattern is pinned in this manner, it cannot shift off grain.

Pattern foldline is pinned first, with the thin printed line (not the tissue margin) exactly at edge of fabric fold. Insert pins perpendicular to fold, about every 4 in (10 cm). Next pin corners, then pattern edges, smoothing the pattern as you proceed.

Grainline arrow

Pin diagonally at corners

Tissue overlap

Overlap tissue margins so that cutting lines almost touch. This helps to ensure the most economical use of fabric.

Pin fold first

Fold

Basic cutting

For accurate results when cutting, always keep fabric flat on the cutting surface, and use a rotary cutter and cutting mat, or the appropriate shears and techniques as described below. Bent-handle dressmaker's shears help keep the fabric flat. They are available in three blade types — *plain, serrated,* and *pinking.* Use only the first two types for cutting out a garment. Plain and serrated blades can be used interchangeably, but note that serrated blades are specially designed to grip knits and slippery fabrics. Pinking shears should be used *only* for seam finishing.

Make sure that the blades of any scissors you use are sharp; dull blades will chew the fabric. Never cut paper with your dressmaker's scissors; this will dull the blades. If the scissor action is stiff, adjust the blade screw slightly or apply a greaseless lubricant.

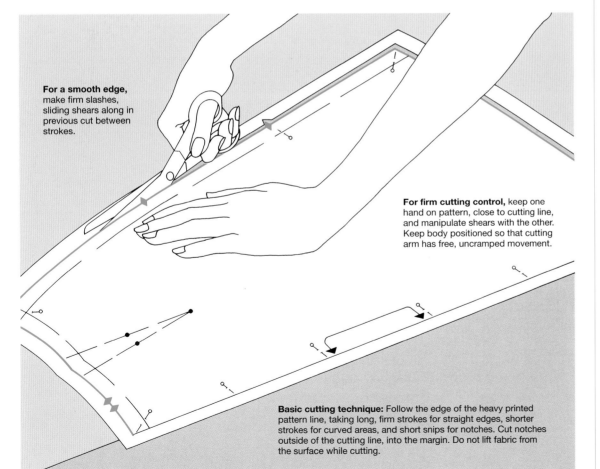

For a smooth edge, make firm slashes, sliding shears along in previous cut between strokes.

For firm cutting control, keep one hand on pattern, close to cutting line, and manipulate shears with the other. Keep body positioned so that cutting arm has free, uncramped movement.

Basic cutting technique: Follow the edge of the heavy printed pattern line, taking long, firm strokes for straight edges, shorter strokes for curved areas, and short snips for notches. Cut notches outside of the cutting line, into the margin. Do not lift fabric from the surface while cutting.

Special cutting tips

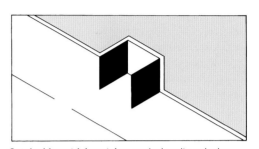

Cut double or triple notches as single units, snipping straight across from point to point — simpler and more convenient than cutting each one individually.

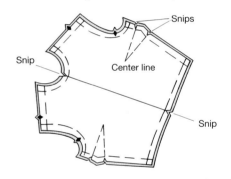

Snips

Snip

Center line

Snip

Identify garment center lines with small snip (⅛ in [3 mm]) into each seam allowance at top and bottom edges; do same for any adjoining piece, such as collar. Snips can also be useful for identifying dart lines.

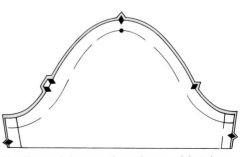

Identify top of sleeve cap by cutting a notch just above large circle on the pattern. Such a notch is easier to see when setting in the sleeve.

Cutting special fabrics

Certain fabrics involve special considerations in pattern selection and layout. A fabric can fall into one of the problem categories, or more than one. A plaid, for example, might also be a directional fabric.

Directional fabrics are so called because they must be laid in one direction for cutting; they are described as "with nap" on pattern envelope and guide sheet. Included in this category are truly napped fabrics, designs that do not reverse, and surfaces that reflect light in varying ways. To determine if a fabric is a directional type, fold it crosswise, right sides together, then fold back a part of the top layer along one selvage. If the opposing layers do not look exactly the same, the fabric is a "nap" for cutting purposes.

To test a napped fabric (one with pile or brushed surface) for direction, run a hand over it. It will feel smooth, with the nap running down and rough with the nap running up.

When deciding which direction to use, consider the following: *short naps* (such as corduroy or velvet) can be cut with nap running up for rich color tone or down for a frosty effect. The same is true of *shaded* fabrics. *Long piles* or shags should be cut with nap running down for better appearance and wear. *One-way designs* are cut according to the natural bent of the design or the effect desired.

Because all pattern pieces must be laid in one direction, a crosswise fold cannot be used. If such a fold is indicated, fold fabric as specified, with wrong sides together; cut along foldline; and, keeping wrong sides together, turn the top layer so nap faces in the same direction as it does on the layer beneath.

Plaids, most stripes, and other geometrics are, for the most part, the same for cutting purposes. What differences occur are due to proportions within the design. These fabrics are usually more effective and easier to handle in a simple style. A good pattern choice is one that shows a plaid or stripe view on the envelope. *Avoid* any pattern that is designated "not suitable for plaids or stripes."

Directional fabrics

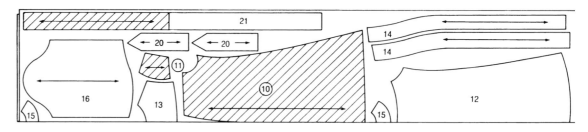

Laying out pattern on plaids and stripes

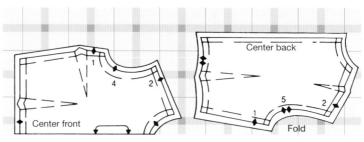

Centering is the first consideration when laying pattern on plaid, stripe, or comparable geometric design. Decide which lengthwise bar or space is to be at garment center. Fold fabric exactly in half at this point for pattern piece that is to be cut on a fold; for other sections, align point with the center seamline (or center line for piece with extended facing). Centers must be consistent for bodice and skirt, sleeve and collar—all major garment sections.

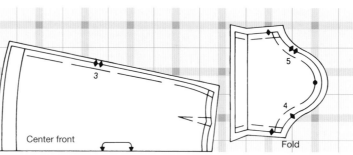

Placement of dominant crosswise bars is the second consideration when planning a layout in plaid or crosswise stripes. As a rule, the dominant stripes should be placed directly on, or as close as possible to, the garment edges, such as hemline and sleeve edge. (Exceptions are A-line or other flared shapes. In these cases, place the least dominant color section at hem edge so the curved hemline will be less conspicuous.) Avoid dominant stripes, too, at the waist and across the full part of bust or hip.

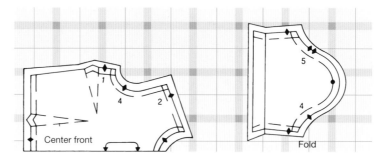

Crosswise matching of major garment sections is accomplished by placing corresponding notches on identical crossbars (lines that will be horizontal). To match sleeve and garment front, for example, place front armhole notches of both sleeve and garment on the same crossbars. Do all matching at seamlines—not at cutting lines. It may or may not be possible to match such diagonals as darts, shoulder seams, and pants inseams. This depends on angle of stitch line and particular fabric design.

Basic pattern alterations 36–46 · Boy's shirt 222–223

Even and uneven plaids

A plaid is a design of woven or printed color bars that intersect at right angles. The arrangement of these bars may be even or uneven.

A four-sided area in which the color bars form one complete design is called a *repeat*. To determine whether plaid is even or uneven, fold a repeat in half, first lengthwise, then crosswise. A plaid is *even* when color bars and intervening spaces are identical in each direction; it is *uneven* if they fail to match in one or both directions.

Stripes may also be even or uneven; each type is handled by the same methods as a corresponding plaid. The exception is a diagonal stripe.

Even plaids are the easiest to work with. An even plaid is suitable for a garment with a center opening or center seams, or for one cut on the bias.

When plaid is uneven crosswise, pattern pieces must be laid in one direction, like napped fabrics.

When plaid is uneven lengthwise, the repeats do not have a center from which the design can be balanced out. Avoid designs with center seams or kimono or raglan sleeves. An exception can be made when a plaid fabric that is uneven lengthwise is reversible. In this case, the pattern should have center seams, or they must be created (see Design changes, p. 64).

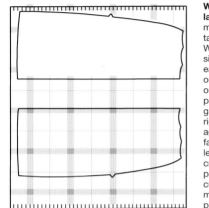

With a single layer, cutting is more accurate but takes more time. With fabric right side up, pin and cut each pattern piece once. To cut second piece, remove pattern and lay garment section right side down against remaining fabric; match bars lengthwise and crosswise; pin. For pattern piece to be cut on a fold, use method for folded plaid.

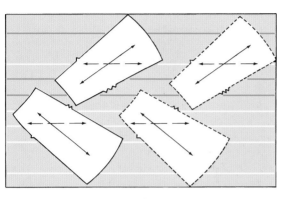

To cut stripe or plaid on the bias, draw new grainline arrows at 45° angle to original ones (unless already provided). Cut each garment section individually. See Selecting pattern layout page 58.

Diagonals

Some of the woven diagonals have barely perceptible ribs, such as gabardines; ribs of others are bold. The latter group, which also includes diagonally printed stripes, requires careful pattern selection. *Avoid* designs with center seams, long diagonal darts, gored skirt sections, the collar cut on fold, or a V-neckline. However, bold ribs that meet at the seams in V-shapes can create an attractive chevron effect.

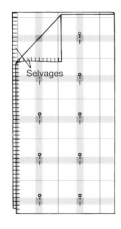

With fabric folded: Identical intersecting bars of the repeats should be pinned, through both fabric layers, every few inches/centimeters. This technique lessens the risk of the layers slipping and thus not matching.

Selvages

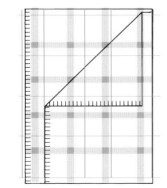

A chevron effect can be created using an obvious diagonal fabric that is reversible. Here the wrong side of the fabric is used for half the garment; diagonals are then balanced in chevron or V-shaped seams. Chevrons can also be created by cutting a plaid, stripe, or other geometric on the bias. To work this way, a design must be even lengthwise.

Unusual prints

Fabric with a large motif requires careful placement, and sometimes matching, of the design. A precise motif, such as a diamond, must be matched just like a plaid. A random motif, paisley for instance, need not be matched but should be carefully balanced.

Selvage

Hemline

Selvage   Border print fabric

Border print fabric with a marginal design running lengthwise along one edge can be used in two ways. One is to run the border vertically, placing it to each side of center front and/or center back seams. The other way is to place the border at the garment hem. For the latter, major garment sections are cut on the crosswise grain, with new grainline arrows drawn perpendicular to the original ones. If the garment being cut this way has no waistline seam, the fabric must be wider than the length of the garment. One solution is to place the hemline at the selvage, omitting the hem altogether.

Professional pinning and cutting tips

1. To keep fabric from slipping, and also protect the cutting surface, cover cutting area with felt or a folded sheet. A useful alternative is a cutting board (a sewing aid available at dressmaker's supplies stores). Fabric can be pinned directly to it to prevent slipping.

2. For better control and more comfortable cutting, have cutting surface accessible from at least three sides. If this is impossible, separate pattern sections so that you can turn pieces around if necessary.

3. For bulky fabrics, which are often difficult to pin, and delicate fabrics or leathers and vinyls which could be marred by pins, consider pin substitutes such as upholstery weights or masking tape.

4. Heavy or bulky fabric can be cut more accurately if you cut through one layer at a time.

5. When cutting from a single layer, cut each pattern piece once with printed side up, once printed side down, to obtain right and left sides for garment.

6. A very thin or slippery fabric, such as chiffon or lightweight knit, will shift less if you pin it to tissue paper (the same paper can be used later to facilitate stitching). Such fabrics are also easier to cut with serrated scissors, which grip the fabric.

7. For fewer seams to finish, place the edge of any pattern piece that corresponds to the straight grain directly on a selvage. If selvage is tight and tends to pull, clip into it every few inches/centimeters.

8. Use each pattern piece the correct number of times. Some items, such as cuffs, will often require more than two pieces.

9. Keep shears sharp by cutting nothing but fabric with them (paper dulls the blades).

10. Sharpen slightly dull scissors by cutting through fine sandpaper. Take very dull ones to a professional.

11. A rotary cutter, used with a cutting mat, provides a fast and accurate method for cutting most fabrics.

Trial layout

Should you need to establish a layout not provided in the cutting guides, the simplest approach is to choose the one closest to your requirements and make changes as needed. At first, pin only foldlines or grainline arrows, so that pieces can be shifted with minimal repinning.

If none of the layouts even approximates your needs, proceed as follows: fold fabric with standard lengthwise fold (see p. 59). Without pinning, lay out all pattern pieces, first the major garment sections, then smaller pieces. Experiment with various pattern arrangements and, if necessary, different fabric folds, until everything fits satisfactorily; then pin all pattern pieces.

Cutting basic design changes

Some characteristic of a fabric, such as its bulk or design, may suggest a change in basic pattern style. For example, a coat of heavy fabric would have sharper edges without facing seams. Or you might want to change some pattern feature, such as the location of an opening.

As a rule, seams that are added or eliminated should correspond to the fabric straight grain; if they do not, garment grainlines may be altered. Remember that a change in one section can affect the treatment of an adjoining one. Make sure that all garment sections affected are altered.

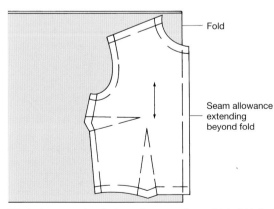

Fold

Seam allowance extending beyond fold

Eliminate a seam by placing pattern seamline on fabric fold. Such a change is recommended when fabric will be more attractive with fewer seams (for example, a plaid or large print). Method is applicable only to seams that coincide with straight grain. If zipper opening is eliminated by this step, decide where to relocate it before proceeding.

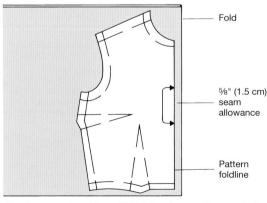

Fold

⅝" (1.5 cm) seam allowance

Pattern foldline

Create a seam by adding a ⅝ in (1.5 cm) seam allowance to the pattern foldline. This technique can be used to provide a more convenient opening, or to balance an uneven plaid or obvious diagonal when fabric is reversible. The new seam must fall on the straight grain. Pattern piece need not be cut near fabric foldline, but if it is, the fold must be slit.

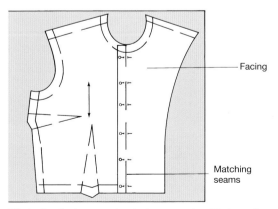

Facing

Matching seams

Eliminate a facing seam by pinning garment and facing patterns together with seamlines matching; both seams must coincide with straight grain. This produces an extended facing, as shown above, which is recommended for bulky fabric. A seam that joins two facing pieces can be eliminated in the same way (such a seam need not be on the straight grain).

Marking tacks 69 · Basting stitches 70

Marking the cut pieces — fabric-marking methods

Marking — the transfer of significant pattern notations to fabric — is done after cutting and before removing the pattern. The symbols selected for transfer are those that make clear *how* and *where* garment sections are shaped and joined and details are placed. Usually included are dart; tuck; gathering and pleat lines; large dots and squares; center front and back locations; and buttonhole and other detail placements. It is helpful to mark seamlines that are intricately shaped (or *all* seamlines, if you are inexperienced). When garment is to be underlined, usually only the underlining is marked.

Common marking methods and their typical uses are discussed below. You must decide which is most suitable for each situation. *Always test a small fabric swatch* to make sure marks show up clearly and can be removed later.

Dressmaker's tracing paper and wheel: This straightforward marking method works best on plain, opaque fabrics. It is less satisfactory for multicolored

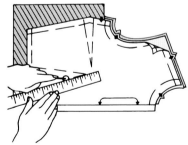

To trace marks, place waxed side of dressmaker's tracing paper against wrong side of fabric. (It may be necessary to move a few pins.) Trace markings with wheel, taking short firm strokes; use ruler as guide for straight lines.

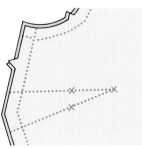

Traced marks should be precise, in a color that contrasts (but not drastically) with the fabric. Use cross hatches (Xs) to indicate pattern dots. Individual dots can also be recorded, using dull pencil or stick.

fabrics and is not recommended for sheers because marking shows through to the right side. Although it is preferred to other fabric-marking methods for its convenience, the wheel can rip tissue, thus limiting the reusability of a pattern, and also may damage the threads of the fabric if it is used too heavily. While tracing, keep a piece of cardboard under the fabric to prevent marring the work surface beneath, or use a cutting board.

When the fabric is folded wrong sides together, place tracing paper back to back between the layers. When the fabric is folded right sides together, place tracing paper against each wrong side.

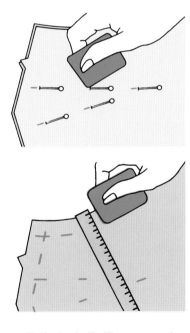

Chalk marking: First push pin through each symbol and both fabric layers, forcing pinheads through tissue. Remove pattern. Make chalk dot at each pin, on wrong side of each fabric layer.

For seamlines, remove pattern; set sewing gauge pointer for ⅝ in (1.5 cm). Then, sliding gauge along cut edge of fabric, make short lines ⅝ in (1.5 cm) from cut edge, spacing them 1 to 2 in (2.5 to 5 cm) apart.

Tailor's chalk: This is a quick marking device. Only dots are marked, but these can be connected with the chalk and a ruler after the pattern is removed. Since chalk rubs off some fabrics easily, try to sew up the garment as soon as possible after marking.

Tailor's tacks: These are time-consuming but indispensable for sheer or delicate fabrics and also for spongy or multicolored types on which neither tracing paper nor chalk make a sufficiently distinct mark. If many tacks must be made on a garment, it is helpful to use a different color thread for each pattern symbol.

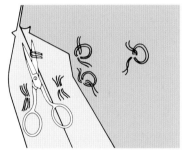

Tailor's tacks: Used to transfer individual markings to doubled fabric. When completed, tacks are cut apart between the fabric layers. (See p. 69 for detailed instructions.)

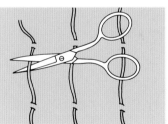

Simplified tailor's tacks: Uneven basting used to mark single fabric layer. Very useful for marking fold, center, and pleat lines. (See p. 69 for instructions.)

Thread-marking: This is a practical way to transfer markings which must show on the right side. Markings are transferred to the fabric with tracing paper, then re-traced with hand or machine basting, depending on the fabric.

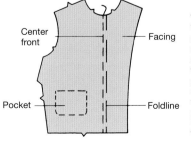

Center front — Facing
Pocket — Foldline

Thread-marking: With tracing paper and wheel, trace symbol onto wrong side of garment section. Remove pattern; go over marking with uneven basting or with straight-stitch machine basting. Use a contrasting thread color.

CHAPTER 3

STITCHES AND SEAMS

Knowing the basics of sewing means knowing how to make stitches and seams. Many of these basic construction techniques can be done using a sewing machine. Hand sewing, however, is sometimes quicker and more effective.

Hand-sewing tips

Threading: Thread the needle with thread from the spool cut at an angle. Do not tear or bite thread end.

Thread color and type: Hand-sew with a comparatively short thread. For permanent stitching, use a length of 18 to 24 in (45 to 60 cm); for basting, a longer thread. A double thread is used mainly for buttons, snaps, and hooks and eyes.

For basting and thread-marking, use white or a light-colored thread that contrasts with the fabric. Polyester thread is the easiest to use for hand

sewing, and is especially good for basting because it will not leave an impression after pressing. Cotton threads and cotton/synthetic threads are acceptable. Silk twist is used for buttonholes and buttons, and also for some decorative hand sewing.

Needle choice: Select a hand needle size suitable for the thread and fabric. A fine needle is best: use a short one for short, single stitches, such as padding stitches; a longer one for long or multiple stitches such as basting.

Twisting and knotting can be a problem in hand sewing, particularly with thread made entirely, or partly, of synthetic fibers. Use a short length of thread, and do not pull tightly on it.

Hand stitches: The most common and useful hand stitches are illustrated and described in the following pages. They are organized by use (basting stitches, hemming stitches, etc.), rather than alphabetically, so use the chart at the right as a quick-finding guide if you are interested in a particular stitch.

Securing stitching at beginning and end

Knot at beginning: Most hand stitching is secured at the beginning with a knot at the end of the thread. In basting, the knot can be visible; in permanent stitching, it should be placed out of sight.

Backstitching can also be used to secure the beginning as well as the end of a row of stitches.

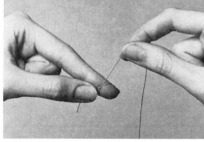

1. To tie a knot in a thread end, first hold end between thumb and index finger while bringing supply thread over and around finger.

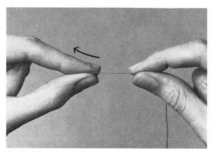

2. Holding supply thread taut, slide index finger along thumb toward palm. This will cause the thread end to twist into the loop.

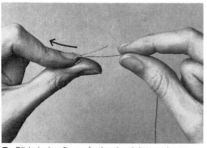

3. Slide index finger farther back into palm so that the loop will slide off finger. Hold open loop between tip of index finger and thumb.

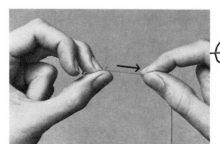

4. Bring middle finger down to rest on and hold the open loop. Pull on supply thread to make loop smaller and form the knot.

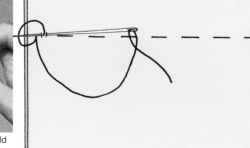

To secure thread at the end of a row of stitching, bring needle and thread to the underside. Take one small stitch behind thread, catching only a single yarn of the fabric. Pull needle and thread through, leaving a small thread loop. Take another short backstitch in the same place, but pass needle and thread through loop of first stitch. Pull both stitches close to fabric; cut thread.

Fabric-marking methods 65

Essential hand stitches — tacking

Tacks, marking

Marking tacks are used to transfer construction details and matching points from the pattern to cut fabric sections. As alternatives to chalk or dressmaker's tracing paper, they can be more time-consuming, but in certain situations, marking tacks are necessary.

Tailor's tacks are used to transfer individual pattern symbols, such as dots, to double layers of fabric.

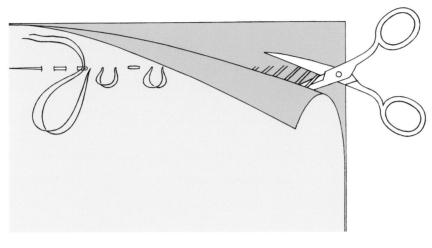

Tailor's tacks: With sharp end of needle, slit the pattern across the symbol to be marked. Using a long length of double, unknotted thread, take a small stitch through pattern and both layers of fabric at this point. Draw needle and thread through, leaving a 1 in (2.5 cm) end. Take another stitch at the same point, leaving a 1 to 2 in (2.5 to 5 cm) loop. Cut thread, leaving second 1 in (2.5 cm) end. When all symbols have been marked in this way, lift pattern off fabric carefully to avoid pulling out thread markings. Gently separate the fabric layers to the limits of the thread loops, then cut the threads.

Simplified tailor's tacks are basically uneven tacking stitches. They are best confined, as a general rule, to marking single layers of fabric; they are especially well suited to such marking as fold or center lines.

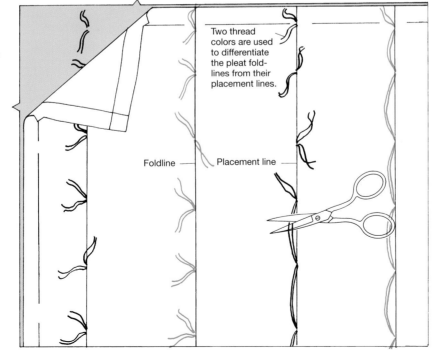

Two thread colors are used to differentiate the pleat fold-lines from their placement lines.

Foldline   Placement line

Simplified tailor's tacks: Using a long length of double, unknotted thread, take a small stitch on pattern line through pattern and fabric. Pull needle and thread through, leaving a 1 in (2.5 cm) thread end. Take similar stitches about every 2 to 3 in (5 to 7.5 cm), leaving thread slack in between. Cut threads at center points between stitches and gently lift pattern off fabric, taking care not to pull out thread markings.

Underlying fabrics 24, 326

Essential hand stitches — basting

Basting stitches

Hand basting (or tacking) is used to temporarily hold together two or more fabric layers during fitting and construction.

Even basting is used on smooth fabrics and in areas that require close control, such as curved seams, seams with ease, and set-in sleeves.

Uneven basting is used for general basting, for edges that require less control during permanent stitching, and for marking (marking stitches can be long and spaced far apart).

Diagonal basting consists of horizontal stitches taken parallel to each other, producing diagonal floats in between. It is used to hold or control fabric layers within an area during construction and pressing. Short stitches, taken close together, give more control than do longer stitches taken farther apart. The short diagonal basting is used to hold seam edges flat during stitching or pressing; long diagonal basting is used for such steps as holding underlining to garment fabric during construction.

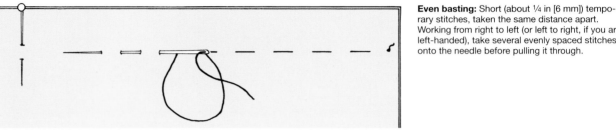

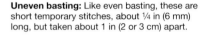

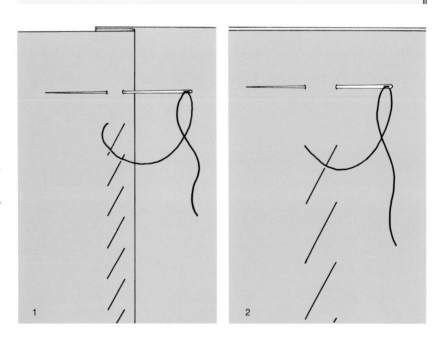

Even basting: Short (about ¼ in [6 mm]) temporary stitches, taken the same distance apart. Working from right to left (or left to right, if you are left-handed), take several evenly spaced stitches onto the needle before pulling it through.

Uneven basting: Like even basting, these are short temporary stitches, about ¼ in (6 mm) long, but taken about 1 in (2 or 3 cm) apart.

Diagonal basting: Small stitches, taken parallel to each other, producing diagonal floats in between. When making the stitches, the needle points from right to left (or left to right, for a left-hander). For greater control, take short stitches (1), spaced close together. Where less control is needed, stitches can be made longer (2), with more space in between them.

Pleating 110 · Gathering 120

Essential hand stitches — basting

Slip basting is a temporary, uneven slip-stitch that permits precise matching of plaids, stripes, and some large prints at seamlines. It is also a practical way to baste intricately curved sections, or to make fitting adjustments from the right side of the garment.

Slip basting: Crease and turn under one edge along its seamline. With right sides up, lay the folded edge in position along the seamline of the corresponding garment piece, matching the fabric design; pin. Working from right to left (or left to right, if you are left-handed) and using stitches ¼ in (6 mm) in length, take a stitch through the lower garment section, then take the next stitch through fold of upper edge. Continue to alternate stitches in this way, removing pins as you go.

Running stitch

A very short, even stitch used for fine seaming, tucking, mending, gathering, and other such delicate sewing. The running stitch is like even basting except that the stitches are smaller and usually permanent.

Running stitch: Working from right to left, weave the point of the needle in and out of the fabric several times before pulling the thread through. Keep stitches and the spaces between them small and even.

Padding stitches

These are used primarily to attach interfacing to the outer fabric. When the stitches are short and close together, they help form and control shape in garment sections such as a collar or lapel. Longer padding stitches are used just to hold interfacing in place; they are like diagonal basting except that they are permanent and the stitches shorter.

Chevron padding stitches are formed by making each row of stitches in the opposite direction from the preceding row; that is, work from top to bottom on one row, then, without turning fabric, work next row bottom to top.

Parallel padding stitches are formed by making each row of stitches in the same direction.

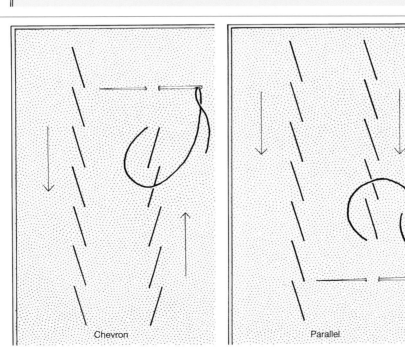

Chevron   Parallel

Chevron padding stitches: Working from top to bottom, make a row of short, even stitches from right to left, placing them parallel to each other and the same distance apart. Without turning the fabric, make the next row of stitches the same way except work them from bottom to top. Keep alternating the direction of the rows to produce the chevron effect.

Parallel padding stitches: These stitches are made the same way as the chevron padding stitches except that all rows are worked in the same direction.

Essential hand stitches — backstitching

Backstitch

One of the strongest and most versatile hand stitches, the backstitch serves to secure hand stitching and repair seams; it is also used for hand understitching, topstitching, and hand-picking zippers. Though there are several variations, each is formed by inserting the needle behind point where thread emerges from previous stitch. The beginning or end of a row of hand stitching can be secured with a backstitch. Fasten permanent stitching with a short backstitch; use a long backstitch to secure stitches that will be removed. A more secure finish combines the backstitch with a loop through which the stitch is fastened.

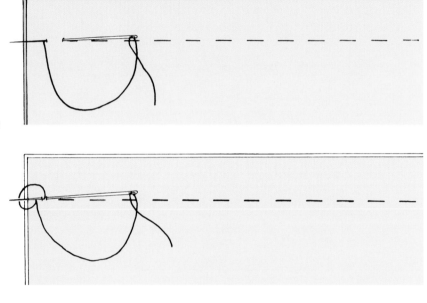

As a beginning or end in hand stitching: Bring needle and thread to underside. Insert needle through all fabric layers a stitch length *behind* and bring it up just at *back* of point where thread emerges. Pull thread through.

For a more secure finish, take a very short backstitch just behind the point where the thread emerges, but leave a thread loop by not pulling the stitch taut. Take another small backstitch on top of the first; bring the needle and thread out through the loop. Pull both stitches taut and then cut thread.

Even backstitch is the strongest of the backstitches. The stitches look much like machine stitching, as they are even in length with very little space between them. This stitch is used mainly to make and repair seams.

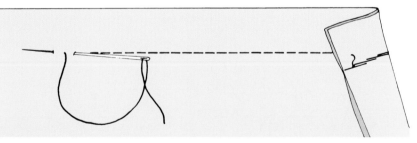

Even backstitch: Bring needle and thread to upper side. Insert needle through all fabric layers approximately 1/16 to 1/8 in (1.5 to 3 mm), or half a stitch length, behind the point where the thread emerges, and bring needle and thread out the same distance in front of that point. Continue inserting and bringing up needle and thread half a stitch length behind and in front of the thread from the previous stitch. From top side, finished stitches look similar to straight machine stitching.

Half-backstitch is similar to the even backstitch except that the length of stitches and spaces between them are equal. Although it is not as strong as the even backstitch, this stitch can also be used to repair a seam.

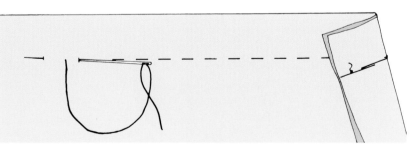

Half-backstitch: Similar to even backstitch except that, instead of finished stitches meeting on top side, there is a space between them equal to the length of the stitches. Needle is inserted through all fabric layers approximately 1/16 in (1.5 mm) behind the point where the thread emerges, but is brought out twice this distance, 1/8 in (3 mm) in front of that point.

Sewing-in zippers by hand 285, 287, 291

Essential hand stitches — backstitching / hemming and joining

Prickstitch is a much more decorative backstitch than the even or the half-backstitch. Seen from the top side, the stitches are very short, with long spaces between them. This stitch is mainly used to hand-pick a zipper.

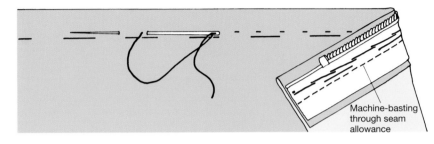

Machine-basting through seam allowance

Prickstitch: Similar to half-backstitch except that the needle is inserted through all fabric layers just a few fabric threads behind and then brought up approximately 1/8 to 1/4 in (3 to 6 mm) in front of the point where thread emerges. Finished stitches on the top side are very short, with 1/8 to 1/4 in (3 to 6 mm) space between them.

Pickstitch can look like any of the backstitches; the only difference is that the stitch is not taken through to the underlayer of fabric. Primarily a decorative backstitch, it is ideal for topstitching and hand understitching, where only the top part of the stitch should be seen.

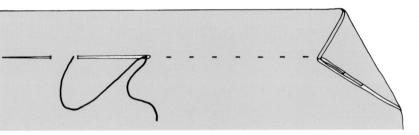

Pickstitch: Any of the backstitches but made without catching underlayer of fabric. When the underlayer is not caught, underpart of stitch becomes invisible.

Overhand stitch

These tiny, even stitches are used to topsew two finished edges as, for example, when attaching lace edging or ribbon to a garment.

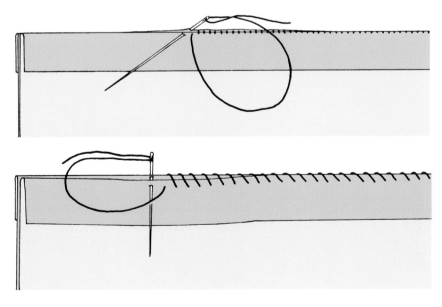

Overhand stitch: Insert needle diagonally from the back edge through to the front edge, picking up only one or two threads each time. The needle is inserted directly behind thread from previous stitch and is brought out a stitch length away. Keep the stitches uniform in both their size and spacing.

Whipstitch is a variation of the overhand stitch. The basic difference is that the needle is held straight, not diagonally, during insertion. This stitch is used either to join two finished edges or to attach an unfinished edge to a straight edge or flat surface.

Whipstitch: Working from left to right, insert the needle straight from the back edge through to the front edge, keeping as close as possible to the edge of the fabric and catching just a few fabric threads. Take small stitches and link together with a small diagonal stitch as shown.

Essential hand stitches — hemming and joining

Slipstitch

This is an almost invisible stitch formed by slipping the thread under a fold of fabric. It can be used to join two folded edges, or one folded edge to a flat surface.

Even slipstitch is used to join two folded edges. It is a fast and easy way to mend a seam from the right side, especially one difficult to reach from the inside.

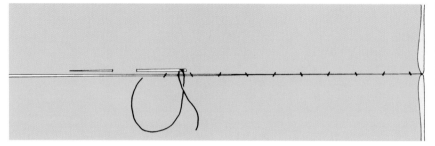

Even slipstitch: Work from right to left. Fasten thread and bring needle and thread out through one folded edge. For the first and each succeeding stitch, slip needle through fold of opposite edge for about ¼ in (6 mm); bring needle out and draw the thread through. Continue to slip the needle and thread through the opposing folded edges.

Cross-stitch

Horizontal stitches, taken parallel to each other, whose floats cross in the center to form Xs. Can be used decoratively or constructively, either in a series, as shown at the right, or as a single cross-stitch.

Cross-stitch: Working from top to bottom (1) with needle pointing left, make row of small horizontal stitches spaced as far apart as they are long. Pull the thread firmly but not taut. This produces diagonal floats between stitches. When the row is finished, reverse direction, working stitches from bottom to top (2), still with needle pointing left. Thread floats should cross in the middle, forming Xs.

Basting stitches for hemming and joining

Blanket-stitch basting is formed between two garment sections as, for example, a facing and a garment front. The blanket stitch is used, but differently from the way it is used to cover an edge. In basting applications, it catches and joins two fabric layers and there is more space (about ¾ to 2 in [2 to 5 cm]) between the stitches.

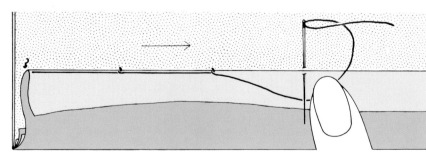

Blanket-stitch basting: Work from left to right, with facing folded back and needle pointing toward you. Fasten thread in facing. About ¾ to 2 in (2 to 5 cm) to right, with needle passing over supply end of thread, take a small vertical stitch in interfacing or underlining, then through facing. Draw needle and thread through. Repeat at ¾ to 2 in (2 to 5 cm) intervals, allowing a slight slack between stitches.

Essential hand stitches — hemming and joining

Cross-stitch basting is used to baste folds in place, such as those at the shoulder or center back of a coat. Both decorative and functional, such basting provides a degree of flexibility not possible with machine stitching.

Single cross-stitch is used in such areas as a facing edge, where only one spot needs to be basted. Usually stitched several times.

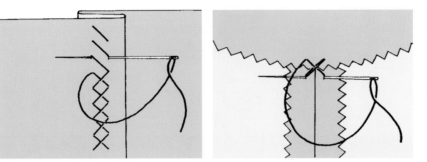

Cross-stitch basting: Pin fold in position; baste in place with a series of cross-stitches.

Single cross-stitch: Make a cross-stitch over edge to be basted (here a neck facing edge at shoulder seam), then make two or three more cross-stitches, in the same place, over the first. (For basic cross-stitch, see p. 74.)

Catchstitch basting is similar to blind-hemming using a catchstitch. When used to baste, the stitches are more widely spaced, approximately ½ to ¾ in (1.25 to 2 cm), and they are used to hold such garment sections as a facing to a front section.

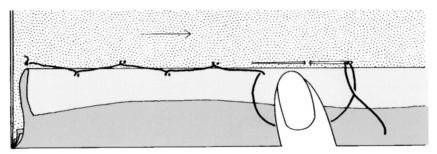

Catchstitch basting: Work from left to right, with facing folded back and needle pointing left. Fasten thread in facing. About ¾ to 2 in (2 to 5 cm) to right, take a small stitch in the interfacing or underlining. Pull needle and thread through. Take the next short stitch ½ to ¾ in (1.25 to 2 cm) to the right in the facing. Repeat sequence, allowing a slight slack between stitches.

Plain-stitch is used for basting sections of lightweight garments together. It is like the blind-hemming stitch (or blindstitch) except that the stitches are spaced farther apart.

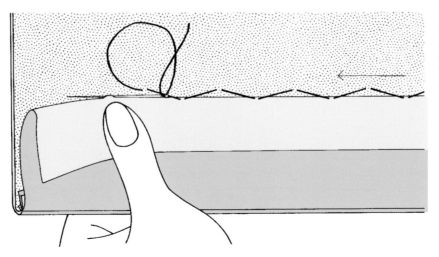

Plain-stitch basting: Work from right to left, with the facing folded back. Fasten thread in facing. Take one short horizontal stitch ½ in (1.25 cm) ahead in the interfacing or underlining; then, ½ to ¾ in (1.25 to 2 cm) ahead of this stitch, take another short horizontal stitch in facing. Pull needle and thread through and repeat. Do not pull thread taut.

Essential hand stitches — hemming and joining

Heavy-duty basting is a very sturdy stitch that is used for joining areas of a heavy garment.

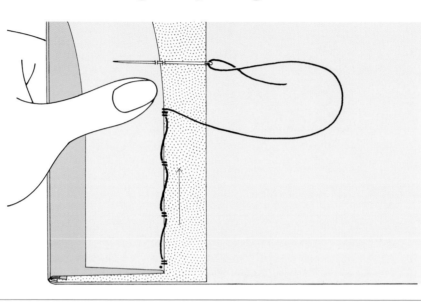

Heavy-duty basting: Work from bottom to top, with the facing folded back and the needle pointing from right to left. Fasten thread in facing. Take a short stitch, catching only a few threads of interfacing or underlining and then facing. Draw needle and thread through; take one or two more stitches above first. Do not pull thread taut. Make the next and each succeeding set of stitches ¾ to 2 in (2 to 5 cm) above the set just completed.

Tacks, construction

Construction tacks are done during construction in contrast to marking tacks (see p. 69). They are stitches used to join areas together without a seam, or as a reinforcement at points of strain.

Arrowhead tack is a triangular reinforcement tack stitched from the right side at such points of strain as pocket ends.

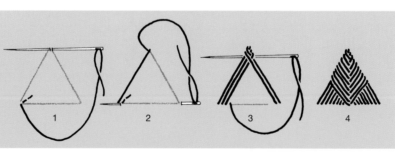

Arrowhead tack: Using chalk or thread, mark triangular arrowhead shape on right side of the garment. Take two small running stitches within triangle and bring needle and thread out at lower left corner. At upper corner, take a small stitch from right to left (1). Draw thread through and insert needle at right corner, bringing it out at left corner barely inside previous thread (2). Draw thread through and repeat, using marked lines as guides and placing threads side by side until triangle is filled (3) and (4).

Bar tack is a straight reinforcement tack used at such points of strain as the ends of a handworked buttonhole or the corners of a pocket.

Length of tack

Bar tack: Fasten thread and bring needle and thread through to right side. Take two or three long stitches (the length that the bar tack is to be) in the same place. Catching the fabric underneath, work enough closely spaced blanket stitches around the thread to cover it. (For basic blanket stitch, see p. 78.)

Essential hand stitches — hemming and joining / finishing and decorative

French tack is made similarly to the bar tack. It is used to link two separate garment sections, such as the bottom edge of a coat to the bottom edge of its lining, while still allowing a certain amount of independent movement to the two garment sections that are linked.

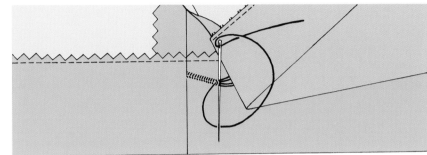

French tack: Take a small stitch through top of garment hem edge, then another small stitch directly opposite in the lining, leaving a 1 to 2 in (2.5 to 5 cm) slack in the thread between stitches. Take similar stitches several times in the same places. Then work closely spaced blanket stitches over the threads. (For basic blanket stitch, see p. 78.)

Fagoting stitch

A decorative stitch used to join two fabric sections, leaving a space in between. As a rule, fagoting should be used only in those areas where there will be little strain, such as yoke sections or bands near the bottom of a skirt or sleeve. The fabric edges must be folded back accurately to maintain the position of the original seamline, which, after fagoting, should be at the center of the space between the folded edges.

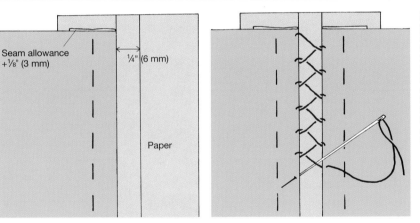

Seam allowance +⅛" (3 mm)

¼" (6 mm)

Paper

Fagoting stitch: On paper, draw parallel lines to represent width of opening between the folded-back fabric edges (usually ¼ in [6 mm]). Fold each seamline back by half this measurement, then pin and baste each edge to paper along parallel lines. Fasten thread and bring up through one folded edge. Carry thread diagonally across opening and insert needle up through opposite fold; pull thread through. Pass needle under thread, diagonally across opening, and up through opposite fold. Continue in this way along entire opening, spacing stitches evenly. When finished, remove paper and press seam.

Finishing stitches and decorative stitches

Overcast stitch

This is the usual hand stitch for finishing raw edges to prevent them from fraying. In general, the more the fabric frays, the deeper and closer together the overcast stitches should be.

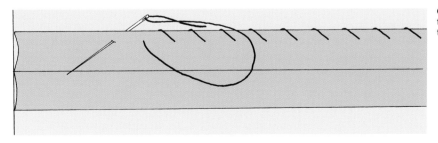

Overcast stitch: Working from either direction, take diagonal stitches over the edge, spacing them an even distance apart at a uniform depth.

Handworked buttonholes 313–314

Essential hand stitches — finishing and decorative

Blanket stitch

Traditionally an embroidery stitch, the blanket stitch can also be used in garment construction. It often serves, as in the illustration, to cover fabric edges decoratively. Another use is in construction details. A bar tack is formed, for example, by working the stitch over threads.

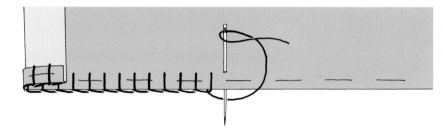

Blanket stitch: Work from left to right, with the point of the needle and the edge of the work toward you. The edge of the fabric can be folded under or left raw. Secure thread and bring out below edge. For the first and each succeeding stitch, insert needle through fabric from right side and bring out at edge. Keeping thread from previous stitch under point of needle, draw the needle and thread through, forming stitch over edge. Stitch size and spacing can be the same or varied.

Buttonhole stitch

A "covering" stitch used as a decorative finish and in the making of handworked buttonholes.

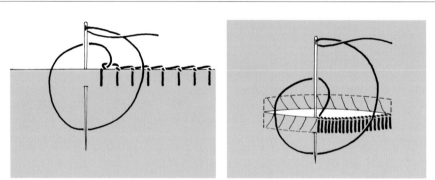

Buttonhole stitch: Work from right to left, with point of needle toward you but edge of fabric away from you. Fasten thread and bring out above the edge. For first and each succeeding stitch, loop thread from previous stitch to left, then down to right. Insert needle from underside, keeping looped thread under both point and eye of needle. Pull needle out through fabric, then away from you to place the purl of the stitch on the fabric's edge. Stitch depth and spacing can be large or small depending on fabric and circumstance.

For handworked buttonholes: Follow basic directions for buttonhole stitch; make stitches ⅛ in (3 mm) deep with no space between.

Featherstitch

Primarily decorative, featherstitch is made up of a series of stitches taken on alternate sides of a given line.

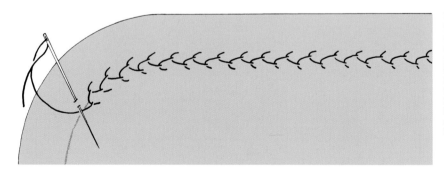

Featherstitch: Mark the line the stitching is to follow on right side of fabric. Fasten thread on underside of stitch line and bring up to right side of fabric. For first and each succeeding stitch, pass needle and thread diagonally across line to opposite side. Holding thread in place, and with needle pointing down and diagonally toward line, take a small stitch above thread, bringing point of needle out on top of thread. Draw on stitch until thread under it curves slightly. Continue making stitches on opposite sides of line, keeping stitch length, spacing, and needle slant the same.

Essential hand stitches — finishing and decorative

Saddle stitch

This is a variation of the running stitch, but the stitches and spaces between them are longer, generally ¼ to ⅜ in (6 to 10 mm). Used primarily for hand topstitching and welting, and intended to be a strong accent, the saddle stitch is usually done with buttonhole twist, embroidery thread, or tightly twisted yarn, often in a contrasting color.

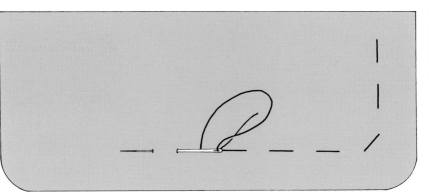

Saddle stitch: Fasten thread and bring the needle and thread through to right side of fabric. Working from right to left, take a stitch ¼ to ⅜ in (6 to 10 mm) long, leave a space the same length, then take another stitch. Continue taking stitches in this way, making them equal in length and in intervening space.

Chainstitch

A continuous series of looped stitches that form a chain. Can be used decoratively, as illustrated at right, on clothing, linens, lingerie. Takes a more functional form in the thread chain shown and described below.

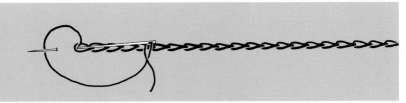

Chainstitch: Work from right to left. Fasten thread and bring up to right side. For each stitch, loop thread up and around; insert needle just behind where thread emerges and bring it up, over the looped thread, a stitch length in front of that point. Pull thread through, to the left, to form looped stitch.

A thread chain can serve as a belt carrier, thread eye, or button loop, or as an alternative to the French tack. It can be as long as needed. The chain may be fastened to lie flat against the garment, or given a looped shape by making the chain longer than the distance between the markings that indicate its beginning and end.

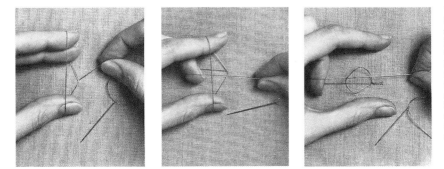

1   2   3

Thread chain: Mark on garment where chain begins and will be fastened. At the first mark take a small stitch and draw the thread through, leaving a 4 to 5 in (10 to 12 cm) loop. Hold loop open with thumb and first two fingers of left hand; hold supply thread with right thumb and index finger (1). Reach through and grasp supply thread with second finger of left hand to start new loop (2). As you pull new loop through, the first loop will slide off other fingers and become smaller as it is drawn down to fabric (3). Position new loop as in (1); continue chaining to desired length. To secure, slip needle through last loop and fasten.

Flat and blind hemming techniques 255–256

Essential hand stitches — hemming

Hemming stitches, flat

Hemming stitches are used to attach the hem to the garment fabric. Flat hemming stitches pass over the hem edge to the garment.

Slant hemming is the quickest, but least durable, because so much thread is exposed and subject to abrasion.

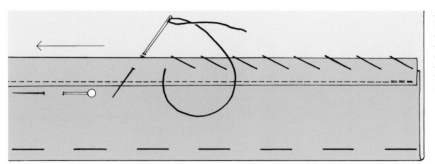

Slant hemming: Fasten thread on wrong side of hem, bringing needle and thread through hem edge. Working from right to left, take first and each succeeding stitch approximately ¼ to ⅜ in (6 to 10 mm) to the left, catching only one thread of the garment fabric and bringing the needle up through edge of hem. This method produces long, slanting floats between stitches.

Vertical hemming stitch is a durable and stable method best suited to hems whose edges are finished with woven or stretch-lace seam binding. Very little thread is exposed, reducing the risk of fraying and breaking.

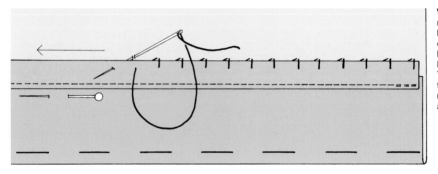

Vertical hemming: Stitches are worked from right to left. Fasten thread from wrong side of hem and bring needle and thread through hem edge. Directly opposite this point and beside the hem edge, begin first and each succeeding stitch by catching only one thread of garment fabric. Then direct the needle down diagonally to go through the hem edge approximately ¼ to ⅜ in (6 to 10 mm) to the left. Short, vertical floats will appear between the stitches.

Slipstitch

This is an almost invisible stitch formed by slipping the thread under a fold of fabric.

Even slipstitch is used to join two folded edges. It is a fast and easy way to mend a seam from the right side.

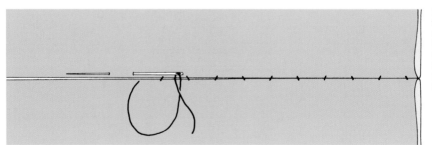

Even slipstitch: Work from right to left. Fasten thread and bring needle and thread out through one folded edge. For the first and each succeeding stitch, slip needle through fold of opposite edge for about ¼ in (6 mm); bring needle out and draw the thread through. Continue to slip the needle and thread through the opposing folded edges.

Essential hand stitches — hemming

Uneven slipstitch, also known as slip-stitch hemming, is used to join a folded edge to a flat surface. Besides being a flat hemming stitch, it is useful for attaching patch pockets, trims, and coat and jacket linings, as well as for securing the edges of a facing to zipper tapes.

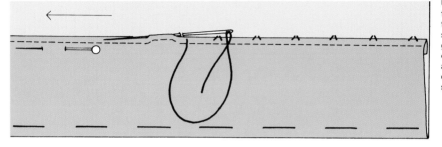

Uneven slipstitch: Work from right to left. Fasten thread and bring needle and thread out through the folded edge. Opposite, in the garment, take a small stitch, catching only a few threads of the garment fabric. Opposite this stitch, in the folded edge, insert needle and slip it through the fold for about ¼ in (6 mm), then bring the needle out and draw the thread through. Continue alternating stitches from garment to fold.

Flat catchstitch is a strong hemming stitch particularly well suited to a stitched-and-pinked hem edge. Take special note of the direction for working and of the position of the needle. Notice, too, that with each stitch, the thread crosses over itself.

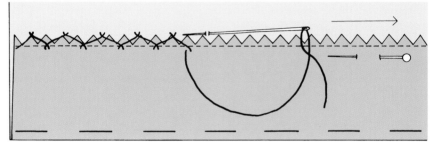

Flat catchstitch: Stitches are worked from left to right with the needle pointing left. Fasten thread from wrong side of hem and bring needle and thread through hem edge. Take a very small stitch in the garment fabric directly above the hem edge and approximately ¼ to ⅜ in (6 to 10 mm) to the right. Take the next stitch ¼ to ⅜ in (6 to 10 mm) to the right in the hem. Continue to alternate stitches, spacing them evenly. Take special care to keep the stitches small when catching the garment fabric.

Hemming stitches, blind

These stitches are taken inside, between the hem and garment. In the finished hem, no stitches are visible. The edge of the hem does not press into the garment.

Blind-hemming stitch is a quick and easy stitch that can be used on any blind hem.

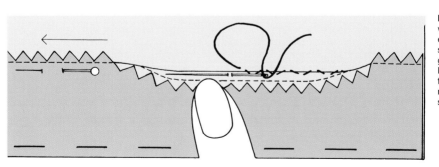

Blind-hemming stitch: Work from right to left with needle pointing left. Fold back the hem edge; fasten thread inside it. Take a very small stitch approximately ¼ in (6 mm) to the left in the garment; take the next stitch ¼ in (6 mm) to the left in the hem. Continue to alternate stitches from garment to hem, spacing them approximately ¼ in (6 mm) apart. Take care to keep stitches small, especially those taken on garment.

Flat and blind-hemming techniques 255–256

Essential hand stitches — hemming

Blind catchstitch is the same stitch as the catchstitch used for flat hemming except that it is done between the hem and the garment. This stitch is a bit more stable and secure than the blind-hemming stitch, and is particularly good for heavy fabrics.

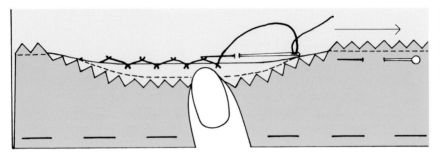

Blind catchstitch: Work from left to right with needle pointing left. Fold back the hem edge and fasten thread inside it. Take a very small stitch about ¼ in (6 mm) to the right in the garment; take the next stitch ¼ in (6 mm) to the right in the hem edge. Continue to alternate stitches from garment to hem, spacing them approximately ¼ in (6 mm) apart. Keep stitches small, especially when stitching on the garment fabric.

Hemstitching

An ornamental hem finish, traditionally used for linens and handkerchiefs. Hem edge is folded under, basted in place, then several threads are pulled from fabric directly above hem edge. The space they leave should be ⅛ to ¼ in (3 to 6 mm). Every stitch must group an equal number of lengthwise threads.

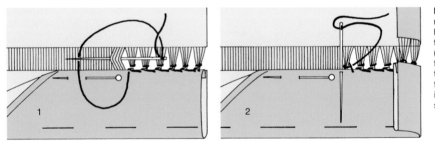

Hemstitching: Working on wrong side and from right to left, fasten thread; pull up through folded hem edge. Slide needle under several lengthwise threads; loop thread to left under point of needle (1). Pull thread through to left and draw it down firmly near the hem edge. Then take a stitch through garment and hem edge catching only a few fabric threads (2). Repeat until edge is finished. Keep the number of lengthwise yarns the same in each group.

Double hemstitching is done by applying duplicate rows of hemstitching on both sides of drawn threads. While stitching second edge, be sure to maintain the thread groupings established by the first row of stitching.

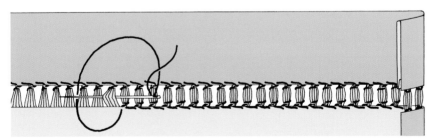

Double hemstitching: When one edge has been finished as described on the previous page, turn work and make duplicate stitches along the opposite edge of the drawn threads. Take care to retain the thread groups that were established on the first edge.

Machine stitches

With a modern sewing machine, you can create many kinds of stitches just by pushing a button. Practical stitches, produced by coordinated motions of needle and feed, can be both functional and decorative. The daisy chain stitch shown below is just one example of the numerous decorative-stitch features found on many machines. The stitches at the far right and left can be made only with a special machine called an overlock machine, also called a serger.

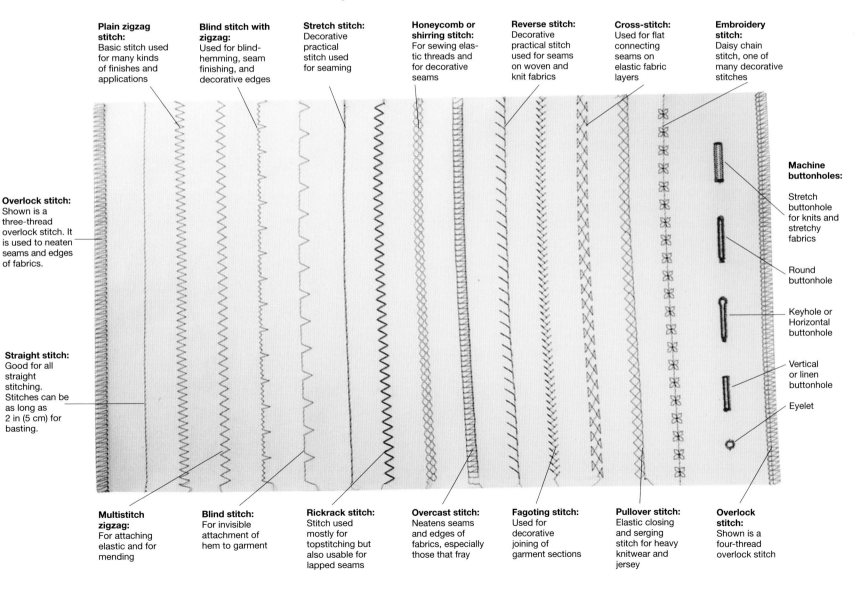

Plain zigzag stitch: Basic stitch used for many kinds of finishes and applications

Blind stitch with zigzag: Used for blind-hemming, seam finishing, and decorative edges

Stretch stitch: Decorative practical stitch used for seaming

Honeycomb or shirring stitch: For sewing elastic threads and for decorative seams

Reverse stitch: Decorative practical stitch used for seams on woven and knit fabrics

Cross-stitch: Used for flat connecting seams on elastic fabric layers

Embroidery stitch: Daisy chain stitch, one of many decorative stitches

Machine buttonholes:

Stretch buttonhole for knits and stretchy fabrics

Round buttonhole

Keyhole or Horizontal buttonhole

Vertical or linen buttonhole

Eyelet

Overlock stitch: Shown is a three-thread overlock stitch. It is used to neaten seams and edges of fabrics.

Straight stitch: Good for all straight stitching. Stitches can be as long as 2 in (5 cm) for basting.

Multistitch zigzag: For attaching elastic and for mending

Blind stitch: For invisible attachment of hem to garment

Rickrack stitch: Stitch used mostly for topstitching but also usable for lapped seams

Overcast stitch: Neatens seams and edges of fabrics, especially those that fray

Fagoting stitch: Used for decorative joining of garment sections

Pullover stitch: Elastic closing and serging stitch for heavy knitwear and jersey

Overlock stitch: Shown is a four-thread overlock stitch

Grain in fabric 56–57

Directional stitching

Directional stitching is the technique of stitching a seam or staystitching a seamline in a particular direction. Its purpose is to support the grain and to prevent the fabric from changing shape or dimension in the seam area. The need for directional stitching arises especially with curved or angled edges, or when constructing garments from loosely woven or dimensionally unstable fabrics.

Stitching should be done with the grain whenever possible. An easy way to determine the correct stitching direction is to run your finger along the cut fabric edge. The direction in which the lengthwise and crosswise fabric yarns are pushed together is **with the grain.** The direction in which they are pushed apart is **against the grain.** In general, if you stitch from the wider part of the garment to the narrower, you will be stitching with the grain. On edges where the direction of the grain changes, for example a long shaped seam, stitching should be done in the direction that stays longest with the grain. Illustrations at

With the grain   Against the grain

right show typical examples of grain direction on various garment sections. Also, stitching direction is sometimes indicated on the pattern seamline.

Necklines are treated somewhat differently from the usual because the grain, over an entire neck edge, changes direction several times. It is advisable to staystitch each neck edge in two stages, according to the changes of grain direction peculiar to each. When seaming these edges, however, it is inconvenient, and unnecessary, to change stitching direction to

follow the grain, especially if edges have been staystitched. Proper pressure and stitch tension will help to enhance the total effect of directional stitching.

Staystitching is a row of directional stitching placed just inside certain seamlines to prevent them from stretching out of shape during handling and garment construction. It also helps to support the grain at the seamline. The most important seamlines to staystitch are those that are curved or angled, as at a

neckline or armhole. When working with a loosely woven or very stretchy fabric, it is advisable to staystitch all seamlines.

Staystitching is done immediately after removing the pattern from the cut fabric sections. It is done through a single layer of fabric, using a regular stitch length and matching thread, usually ½ in (about 1.25 cm) from the cut edge. (On any placket seamlines, place staystitching ¼ in [6 mm] from cut edge.)

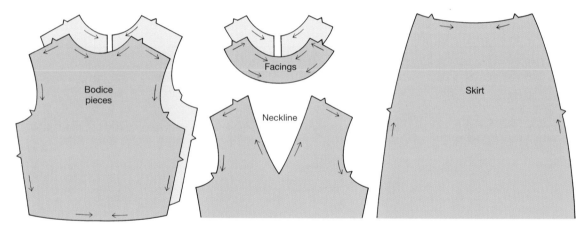

Bodice pieces

Facings

Neckline

Skirt

Staystitching for knits

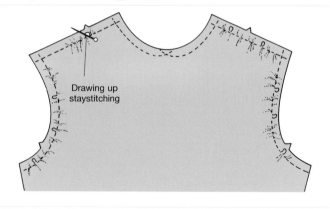

Drawing up staystitching

Staystitching for a knit is just as important as for a woven fabric, even though there is no grain direction. The principal purpose is to prevent stretching. After staystitching, lay pattern on top of each fabric section to see if it is the correct size and shape. If knit has stretched slightly, pull staystitching up gently with a pin at 2 in (5 cm) intervals until fabric shape matches pattern. If knit has been pulled in too much, clip staystitching in a few places.

Pressing equipment 14 · Hand-basting stitches 70–71 · Backstitch 72 · Knotting thread in darts 101

Seams — forming a seam

The seam is the basic structural element of any garment and so must be formed with care. The machine should be adjusted correctly to the fabric for stitch length, tension, and pressure. Thread should be properly matched to fabric. Most often, right sides of fabric are placed together; however, in some instances wrong sides are together.

Although 58 in (15 mm) is the standard seam width, always check your pattern for required width in special seaming situations. Seams should be backstitched at the beginning and end for reinforcement.

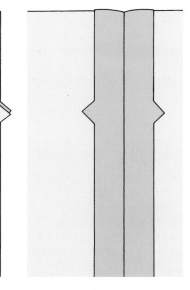

1. Pin seam at regular intervals, matching notches and other markings along seamline. Place pins perpendicular to seamline with tips just beyond seamline and heads toward seam edge.

2. Machine-baste using a long stitch on seamline, removing pins as you go. Hand-basting is an alternative for beginners, or for special situations (bias seams, velvet); with many simple seams, pinning and machining is sufficient.

3. Position needle in seamline ½ in (about 1.25 cm) from end; lower presser foot. Backstitch to end, then stitch forward on seamline, close to but not through the basting. Backstitch ½ in (about 1.25 cm) at end. Clip threads close to stitching.

4. Remove basting stitches. Unless instructions specify another pressing method, seams are first pressed flat in the same direction as stitched, then pressed open. Some seams may need to be clipped or notched before being pressed open to allow them to lie flat.

Keeping seams straight

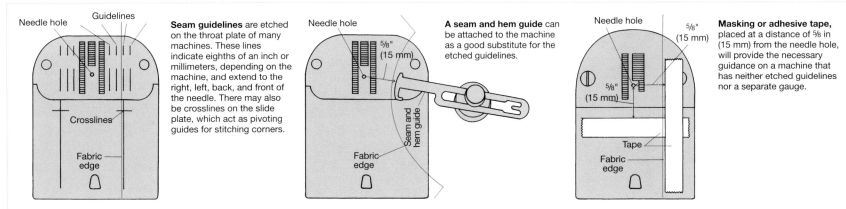

Seam guidelines are etched on the throat plate of many machines. These lines indicate eighths of an inch or millimeters, depending on the machine, and extend to the right, left, back, and front of the needle. There may also be crosslines on the slide plate, which act as pivoting guides for stitching corners.

A seam and hem guide can be attached to the machine as a good substitute for the etched guidelines.

Masking or adhesive tape, placed at a distance of ⅝ in (15 mm) from the needle hole, will provide the necessary guidance on a machine that has neither etched guidelines nor a separate gauge.

Plain seams

A straight seam is the one that occurs most often. In a well-made straight seam, the stitching is exactly the same distance from the seam edge the entire length of the seam. In most cases, a plain straight stitch is used. For stretchy fabrics, however, a tiny zigzag or special machine stretch stitch may be used.

A curved seam requires careful guiding as it passes under the needle so that the entire seamline will be the same even distance from the edge.
To achieve better control, use a shorter stitch length (15 per inch [1.5 mm]) and slower machine speed.

A cornered seam needs reinforcement at the angle to strengthen it. This is done by using small stitches (15 to 20 per inch [1 to 1.5 mm]) for 1 in (2.5 cm) on either side of the corner. It is important to pivot with accuracy (see top right). When cornered seams are enclosed, as in a collar, the corners should be blunted so that a better point results when the collar is turned.

How to make cornered seams

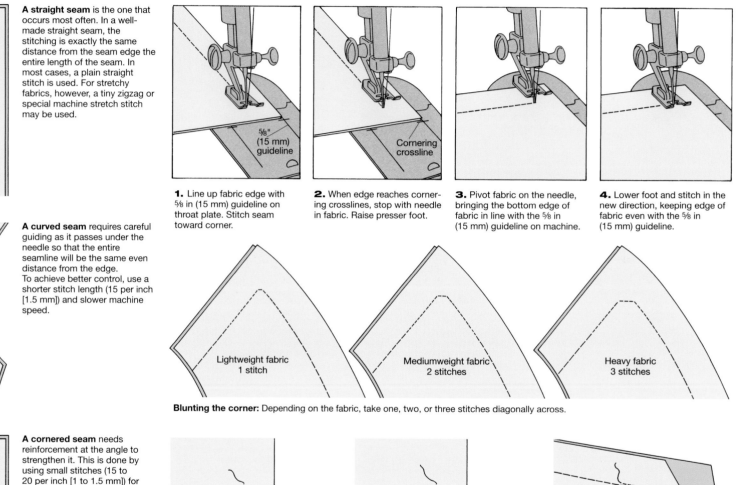

1. Line up fabric edge with ⅝ in (15 mm) guideline on throat plate. Stitch seam toward corner.

2. When edge reaches cornering crosslines, stop with needle in fabric. Raise presser foot.

3. Pivot fabric on the needle, bringing the bottom edge of fabric in line with the ⅝ in (15 mm) guideline on machine.

4. Lower foot and stitch in the new direction, keeping edge of fabric even with the ⅝ in (15 mm) guideline.

Lightweight fabric
1 stitch

Mediumweight fabric
2 stitches

Heavy fabric
3 stitches

Blunting the corner: Depending on the fabric, take one, two, or three stitches diagonally across.

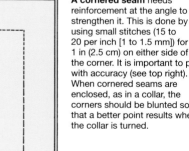

1. To join an inward with an outward corner, reinforce corner by stitching just inside seamline 1 in (2.5 cm) on either side of corner.

2. Insert a pin diagonally across the point where stitching forms the angle. Clip exactly to this point. Do not cut past the stitches.

3. Spread the clipped section to fit the other edge; pin in position. Clipped side up, stitch on the seamline, pivoting at the corner.

Pressing equipment 14 · Hand pickstitch 73 · Princess seams 100

Additional seam techniques

You may need to take additional steps, other than pressing, with some seams. Whether the steps are necessary or not depends upon the location and shape of the seam. In some situations, one extra step will suffice; in others, however, it will take several to make a seam lie flat. When more than one technique is involved, follow this order: 1. trim, 2. grade, 3. clip or notch, 4. understitch. Fabric quality plays a key role. Fabric that does not fray can be trimmed closer than one that does. Keep clipping or notching to a minimum on loosely woven fabric. The thicker the fabric, the more extra bulk has to be removed.

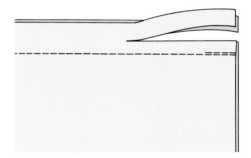

Trimming means cutting away some of the seam allowance. It is done when the full width of the seam allowances would interfere with the fit (as in an armhole) or with further construction (as in a French seam). It is the preliminary step to grading (see the next drawing); seams are first trimmed to half their width before grading them.

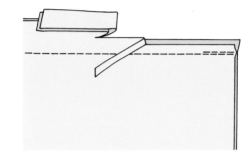

Grading (also called blending, layering, or beveling) is the cutting of seam allowances to different widths, with the seam allowance that will fall nearest the garment exterior left the widest. It is recommended that seams be graded when they form an edge or are enclosed. The result is a seam that lies flat without causing a bulky ridge.

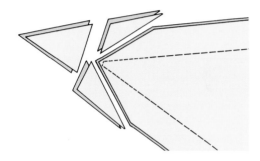

To trim a corner of an enclosed seam, first trim the seam allowances across the point close to the stitching, then taper them on either side. The more elongated the point, the farther back the seam allowance should be trimmed, so that when the point is turned, there is no danger of seam allowances overlapping and causing bulk.

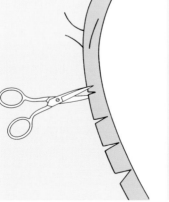

Clipping and notching are used on curved seams to allow them to lie smooth. *Clips are slits* cut into the seam allowance of concave, or *inward,* curves that permit the edges to spread. (With either technique, hold scissor points just short of seamline to avoid cutting past

stitching.) *Notches are wedges* cut from seam allowance of convex, or *outward,* curves; space opened by removal of fabric lets edge draw in. When clips and notches face one another, as in a princess seam (see next sketch), they should be staggered to avoid weakening seam.

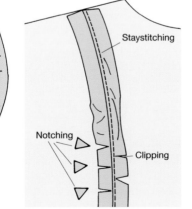

Joining inward and outward curves: This is handled in a special way. First staystitch outward curve and clip seam allowance to stitching. With clipped edge on top, stitch seam. Notch inward curve to make seam lie smooth. Press seam open over tailor's ham.

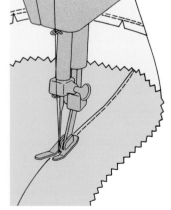

Understitching keeps a facing and its seamline from rolling to garment right side; it is done after seam allowances have been trimmed and graded, then clipped or notched. Working from the right side, stitch through facing and seam allowances, staying close to seamline.

Hand understitching is desirable on a fine fabric or when machine stitching could distort a tailored shape. Use hand pickstitch; stitch through facing and seam allowances, as with machine understitching. Advisable on tailored collar as fabric control is more precise.

Overcast stitching 77 · Zigzag stitching 83

Seam finishes

A seam finish is any technique used to make a seam edge look neater and/or keep it from fraying. Three considerations determine the seam finish decision:

1. The type and weight of fabric. Does it fray excessively, a little, or not at all?

2. The amount and kind of wear — and care — that the garment will receive. If a garment is worn often, then tossed into the washing machine, the seams need a durable finish. If the style is a passing fad, or will be worn infrequently, you may elect not to finish the seam edges.

3. Whether or not seams will be seen. An unlined jacket warrants the more elaborate bias-binding finish. A lined garment requires no finishing at all, unless the fabric frays a great deal.

   Plain straight seams are finished after they have been pressed open. Plain curved or cornered seams are seam-finished right after stitching, next clipped or notched, then pressed open.

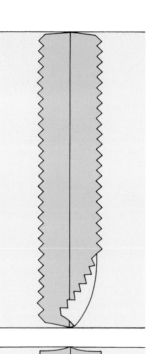

Pinked: Cut along edge of seam allowance with pinking shears. For best results, do not fully open shears or close all the way to the points. If fabric is crisp and lightweight, it is possible to trim two edges at once, before pressing seam open. Otherwise do one edge at a time. Pinking is attractive, but will not of itself prevent fraying.

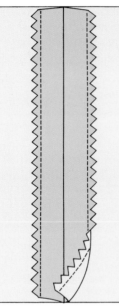

Stitched-and-pinked: Using a short stitch, place a line of stitching ¼ in (6 mm) from edge of seam allowance, then pink edge. This finish can be used where pinking is desired, and it will minimize fraying.

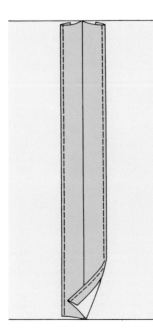

Turned-and-stitched (also called clean-finished): Turn under edge of seam allowance ⅛ in (3 mm) (¼ in [6 mm] if fabric frays easily); press. Stitch along edge of fold. It may be helpful, on difficult fabrics or curved edges, to place a row of stitching at the ⅛ or ¼ in (3 or 6 mm) foldline to help turn edge under. This is a neat, tailored finish for lightweight to mediumweight fabrics and is suitable for an unlined jacket.

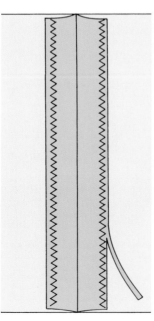

Hand-overcast: Using single thread, make overcast stitches at edge of each seam allowance slightly more than ⅛ in (3 mm) in depth and spaced ¼ in (6 mm) apart. Do not pull thread too tight. Use this method when a machine finish is impractical or a hand finish is preferred.

Zigzagged: Set stitch for medium width and short length (about 15 per inch [1.5 mm]). Stitch on edge of seam allowance without exceeding it and then trim the excess fabric to the edge of the seam allowance. This is one of the quickest and most effective ways to finish a fabric that frays. A zigzagged finish can be used on a knit, but care must be taken not to stretch the seam edge or it will ripple.

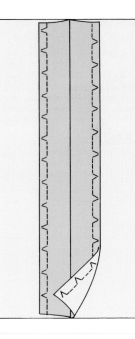

Machine-overedged:
Done with overedge or blindstitch setting (special stitch pattern of 4–6 straight stitches and 1 zigzag) using a regular sewing machine. Point of zigzag should fall on edge of fabric. If using over-edge, position fabric to right of the needle; for blindstitch, to the left. This method is an alternative to the regular zigzag. Done with an overlock stitch if using a serger (see p. 15 and p. 83).

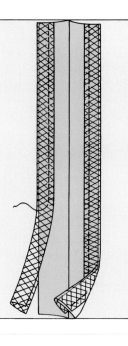

Bias-bound: Trim notches from seam edge; wrap bias tape around it. (Use ready-made tape, or cut your own from lining or underlining fabric.) Stitch close to edge of top fold, catching underneath fold in stitching. Bias tape is especially good for finishing seams in an unlined jacket or coat.

Net-bound: Cut ½ in (1.25 cm) -wide strips of nylon net or tulle; fold in half lengthwise, slightly off center. Trim notches from seam edge and wrap net around edge with wider side underneath. From top, edgestitch narrow half of binding, catching wider side underneath in the stitching. This is an inconspicuous and appropriate finish for delicate fabrics, such as velvet or chiffon.

Hong Kong:
This is an alternative to the bias-bound finish and is especially suitable for heavy fabrics.
1. Cut 1½ in (4 cm) -wide bias strips from lightweight fabric that matches the garment fabric, or use purchased bias tape and press it open.

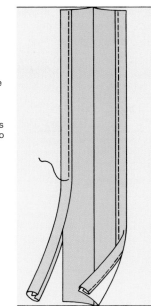

2. With right sides together stitch the bias strip to seam allowance, ¼ in (6 mm) from the edge.

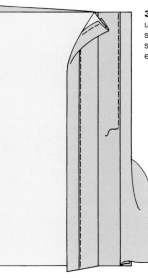

3. Turn bias over the edge to the underside and press. From right side, stitch in crevice of the first stitching. Trim the unfinished edge of the bias.

Pressing equipment 14

Self-enclosed seams

Self-enclosed seams are those in which all seam allowances are contained within the finished seam, and a separate seam finish is avoided. They are most appropriate for visible seams, which occur with sheer fabrics and in unlined jackets. Also, they are ideally suited to garments that will receive rugged treatment. Proper trimming and pressing are important if the resulting seams are to be sharp and flat rather than lumpy and uneven. Precise stitching is essential, too.

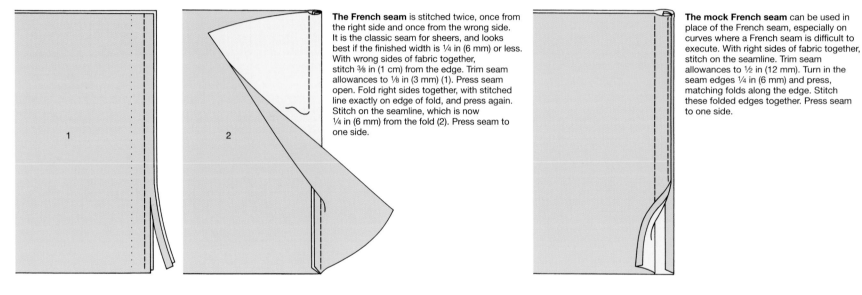

The French seam is stitched twice, once from the right side and once from the wrong side. It is the classic seam for sheers, and looks best if the finished width is ¼ in (6 mm) or less. With wrong sides of fabric together, stitch ⅜ in (1 cm) from the edge. Trim seam allowances to ⅛ in (3 mm) (1). Press seam open. Fold right sides together, with stitched line exactly on edge of fold, and press again. Stitch on the seamline, which is now ¼ in (6 mm) from the fold (2). Press seam to one side.

The mock French seam can be used in place of the French seam, especially on curves where a French seam is difficult to execute. With right sides of fabric together, stitch on the seamline. Trim seam allowances to ½ in (12 mm). Turn in the seam edges ¼ in (6 mm) and press, matching folds along the edge. Stitch these folded edges together. Press seam to one side.

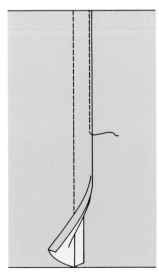

The flat-felled seam is very sturdy and so is often used for sports clothing and children's wear. Since it is formed on the right side, it is also decorative, and care must be taken to keep widths uniform, within a seam and from one seam to another. With wrong sides of fabric together, stitch on the seamline. Press seam open, then to one side. Trim the inner seam allowance to ⅛ in (3 mm). Press under the edge of outer seam allowance ¼ in (6 mm). Stitch this folded edge to the garment. Be careful to press like seams in the same direction (e.g., both shoulder seams to the front). A felling foot or jeans foot is available for some machines. This foot rolls the fabric under as it stitches.

The self-bound seam works best on light-weight fabrics that do not fray easily. Stitch a plain seam. Trim one seam allowance to ⅛ in (3 mm). Turn under the edge of the other seam allowance ⅛ in (3 mm) and press (1). Turn and press again, bringing the folded edge to the seamline, so that the trimmed edge is now enclosed. Stitch close to fold as shown in (2), as near as possible to first line of stitching.

Overlock machine 15 · Zigzag stitching 83 · Overlock stitching 83

Overedge seams

Overedge seams are very narrow, never more than ¼ in (6 mm) wide, and are used when a seam should be flexible or have minimum bulk. Seam allowances are either finished by the seam stitches themselves when the seam is stitched, or later with another row of stitches. Overedge seams, including hairline seams, are usually made using a zigzag stitch. Some seams are trimmed to the finished width before they are constructed, some during and some after.

The hairline seam can be used for collars, cuffs, and facings in sheer fabrics. This seam is stitched with a narrow zigzag, then trimmed close to the stitching so that no seam allowances show through. To give it more weight, filler cord may be added during the stitching. Set machine for narrow and short zigzag stitch. Unwind enough cord to ensure that there will be no strain on it. Lead the cord under the stitching (consult machine manual for exact instructions). Stitch along the seamline, covering cord in the process. Trim seam allowances. Turn to right side. Work seam to the edge and press.

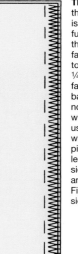

The zigzag seam is similar to the hairline seam, but the stitch is wider. Its principal use is with fur and fake fur fabrics, where the stitch will disappear into the fabric. Trim seam allowances to ⅛ in (3 mm) for short pile, ¼ in (6 mm) for a long pile fabric. (Cut through the skin or backing only, not the fur.) Mark notches on new seam edges with chalk. Baste seam. Stitch, using a plain zigzag (medium width and short length for short pile; wide width and regular length for longer pile). From right side, with a pin, gently pull free any hairs caught in the stitching. Finger-press the seam to one side.

A double-stitched seam is especially good for knits, such as tricot or soft jersey, where edges tend to curl. Stitch a plain seam with straight or straight reverse stitch. Machine-stitch a second row ⅛ in (3 mm) from the first, using one of the following: a straight stitch (1), a zigzag (2), a blindstitch or other overedge stitch (3). Trim seam allowances close to the stitching. Press seam to one side.

The overlock stitch seam is done by using a special stitch pattern that is a combination of straight and zigzag stitches, or by using an overlock machine, or serger, that combines sewing and oversewing in one operation. The three-, four-, or five-thread machine loops threads as it trims and sews to make a narrow seam and trim the edge (see p. 83). These seams are suitable for knit or stretch fabric or fine woven fabrics. Start with a ¼ in (6 mm) seam allowance. Baste and then stitch seam.

1

2

3

Evening blouse

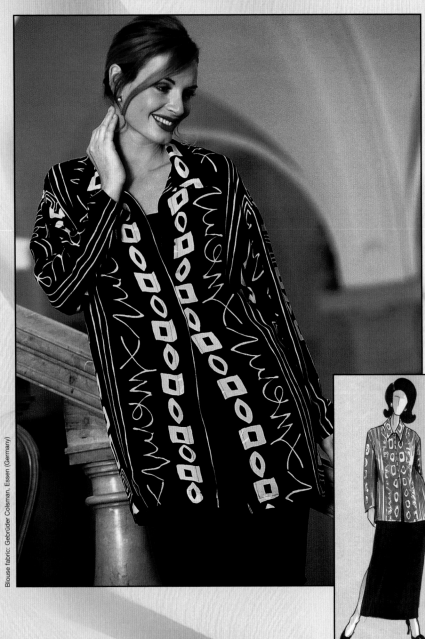

Blouse fabric: Gebrüder Colsman, Essen (Germany)

Fabrics
Sheer or semi-sheer fabrics like georgette, voile, or chiffon made from viscose or silk

Amount
For size 12: 1⅝ yd (1.50 m) of 58/60 in (150 cm) -width fabric

Notions
4 covered shank buttons, ⅝ in (1.5 cm)

Pattern pieces ▶▶▶▶▶▶▶▶▶▶▶▶▶
1 Front – cut 2
2 Back – cut 2 on fold
3 Collar – cut 3
4 Sleeves – cut 2

Burda pattern 3129 was modified for this blouse. It does not have a yoke as does the original.

The buttons can be made at home according to the directions or you can have them covered.

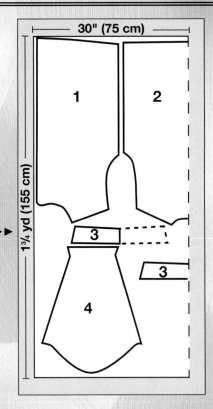

It is best to use French seams when working with sheer fabrics. Thin fabrics tend to fray easily and the seams are difficult to finish in any other way. Since seams in sheer fabrics tend to pucker, it is important to hold the fabric taut while sewing.

In this project, three collar pieces are cut. The third piece is used in place of interfacing since interfacing would show through the fabric.

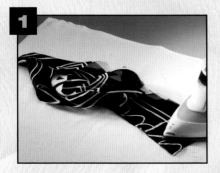

Sewing instructions
● **Collar:** Lay the three collar pieces together with two pieces facing right sides together and the third against one of the wrong sides.
● Stitch the collar pieces together, except for the neck edge.
● Trim the seam allowances and trim the corners diagonally.

● Turn the collar right side out with the pieces that were facing right sides together facing out. Press (Fig. 1).

● **Shoulder seam:** To make French seams, lay the front and back pieces together with wrong sides together. Stitch at $1/4$ in (6 mm); press flat and then to one side.
● Turn the fabric right sides together and stitch the shoulder seam along the original seam line. The unfinished edges are now enclosed within the second seam. Press to the back of the garment.

● Staystitch neck edge of blouse.
● **Attach collar:** Turn under seam allowance on neck edge of the top collar layer and press.
● Baste the two lower layers to the blouse neck edge, right sides together, and stitch. Trim.
● Pin the top collar over the neck seam and stitch the pressed seam allowance (Fig. 3) to the neck edge by hand or machine.
● **Sew sleeves:** Attach the sleeves to armhole edges, matching markings, using French seams.
● Press seam allowances toward the sleeve.

● **Close sleeves and side seams:** Complete the side seams and sleeve seams as one, using French seams.
● Press the sleeve and side seam allowances toward the back.
● **Hem:** Fold the front edge, blouse, and sleeve hems 1 in (2.5 cm) twice, pin, and press.

● Stitch the hems close to the folded edge.
● **Buttonholes:** Work the buttonholes by machine or by hand on the marked positions. First, make a test buttonhole on a piece of leftover fabric.
● **Buttons:** Make the fabric-covered buttons according to the instructions on the package of button forms.
● To check the position markings for the buttons, lay the front edges of the blouse together and place a pin through each buttonhole.
● Sew the buttons onto the marked spots.

Basting stitch 70–71

Decorative seams and special seams — topstitching

Seams are topstitched from the right side, with usually one or more seam allowances caught into the stitching. Topstitching is an excellent way to emphasize a construction detail, to hold seam allowances flat, or to add interest to plain fabric.

There are two main considerations when topstitching. The first is that normal stitching guides will not, as a rule, be visible, so new ones need to be established. A row of basting stitches or tape, applied just next to the topstitching line, can help.

The other factor to consider with topstitching is keeping the underlayers flat and secure. *Even* basting will hold pressed-open seam allowances; *diagonal* basting will hold those that are enclosed or pressed to one side.

A long stitch length is best. Use special topstitching thread (a polyester type widely available) or single or double strands of regular thread. Adjust needle and tension accordingly.

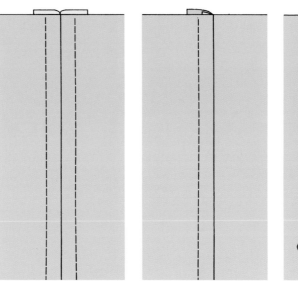

Double-topstitched seam   Welt seam   Tucked seam

Double-topstitched seam: Press plain seam open. Topstitch an equal distance from each side of seamline, catching seam allowances into stitching.

Welt seam: Stitch a plain seam and press both seam allowances to one side; trim inside seam allowance to ¼ in (6 mm). Topstitch, catching wider seam allowance.

Tucked seam: Fold under one seam allowance; press. With folded edge on top, match seamlines and baste through all thicknesses. Stitch ¼ to ⅜ in (6 to 10 mm) from fold. If seam is curved, first staystitch top seam allowance; clip or notch; press to wrong side. Baste in position; topstitch close to fold.

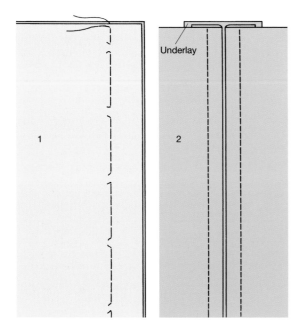

Slot seam: Machine baste on the seamline, leaving long threads at each end. Clip bobbin thread every fifth stitch (1). Press seam open. Cut a 1½ in (4 cm) -wide underlay of same or contrasting fabric. Center it under seam and baste. Topstitch an equal distance from the center on each side. Pull out basting threads (2).

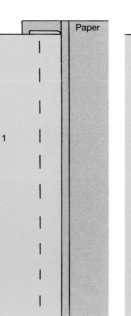

Fagoted seam: Machine version of openwork consists of two folded edges, positioned parallel and apart, with each edge caught by the outer points of a multistitch zigzag. First make a test stitch to determine width of opening. Divide this width in half; fold each seamline back by this halved amount. On paper, draw parallel lines to represent width between folded edges. Pin refolded fabric to paper along parallel lines. Baste (1). Stitch, centering opening under foot and making sure that each edge is caught in stitching (2).

Making piping and cording 264

Seaming interfacings

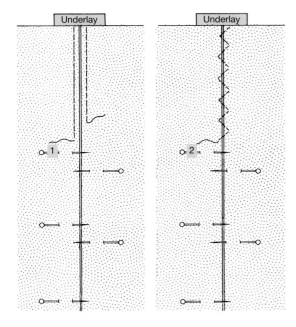

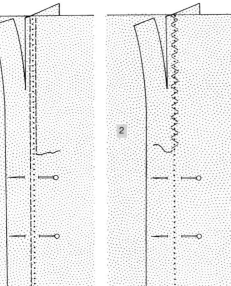

Abutted seams are one way of eliminating bulk from interfacing seams. Trim off seam allowances, bring two edges together, and pin or baste them to an underlay of seam binding or cotton tape cut slightly longer than seams. With a short stitch length, stitch (1) ⅛ in (3 mm) from each edge with straight stitches, or (2) through center of seam with multi-stitch zigzag. For zigzag, abutted edges should be aligned with center of presser foot so that stitches catch both sides equally.

Lapped seams are also used to eliminate bulk, especially on interfacing and interlining. Mark seamlines. Lap one edge over the other with seamlines meeting in the center. Place a row of straight stitching on either side of seamline (1), or stitch with wide zigzag through center (2). Trim both seam allowances close to stitching.

Corded seams

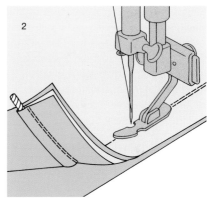

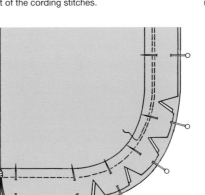

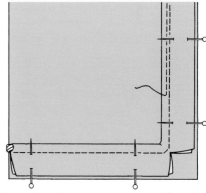

A corded seam is used in both dressmaking and home decorating. You can buy covered cording or make your own. To insert cording in a seam:
1. Pin or baste cording to right side of one seam allowance, aligning cording stitch line with seamline, and having raw edge of cording toward raw edge of garment seam. With zipper foot to right of needle, stitch, placing the stitching just to the left of the cording stitches.

2. Place seam allowances with right sides together and cording in between. Using the original line of stitching as a guide, stitch through all layers, crowding stitches between cord and first stitching. Press; trim and grade seam as necessary. When stitching corded seams, it is important that each successive row of stitching be placed slightly closer to the cording. In this way, no stitching will show on the right side.

To apply cording to a curved seam: Pin cording to right side of one seam allowance, matching cording stitch line and seamline. Around curve, clip or notch seam allowance of cording almost to stitching. Stitch as in Step 1 above, using a shorter stitch length around curve. Stitch seam as in Step 2 above. Trim cording seam allowance to ⅛ in (3 mm); trim, grade, and clip remaining seam allowances. Press. Turn right side out.

To apply cording to a square corner: Pin cording to right side of one seam allowance, matching cording stitch line and seamline. At corner, clip seam allowance of cording almost to stitching. Stitch as in Step 1 above, using a short stitch length at corner. Stitch seam as in Step 2 above. Cut diagonally across corner close to stitching. Trim cording seam allowance to ⅛ in (3 mm); trim and grade the remaining seam allowances.

Thread 12 · Grain in fabric 56–57 · Gathering 120–121

Cross seams

Seams that cross should be pressed and then seam-finished before they are joined. To make sure that the seamlines of cross seams will align exactly after they are joined, pin through both seamlines with a fine needle; then pin through both seam allowances on each side of the matched seamlines. When the seam is stitched, trim all the seam allowances diagonally, as shown, to reduce bulk.

Bias edge to bias edge

When joining two bias edges, first baste and then stitch, being careful not to stretch the fabric. To reduce the risk of the stitches breaking under strain during wear, use a shorter than usual stitch length and a thread with give. If it is a lengthwise seam, fasten basting with a long backstitch and cut, leaving a good length of thread. Allow the basted piece to hang overnight so that it can stretch before seaming.

Bias edge to straight edge

When joining a bias edge to a straight edge, take special care not to stretch the edge that is bias, or the seam will not lie smooth (that is, it will ripple). Handling the bias edge carefully, pin it to the straight edge, placing pins perpendicular to the seamline at intervals of approximately 3 to 4 in (7.5 to 10 cm). Stitch the seam with the bias edge on top, removing the pins as you stitch.

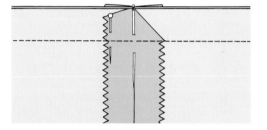 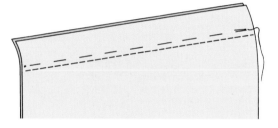 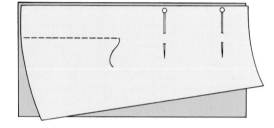

Seams with fullness

When two seams to be joined are uneven in length, the longer edge must be drawn in to fit the shorter. This is done by either easing or gathering: easing for slight to moderate fullness; gathering for a larger amount. When finished, an eased seam has subtle shaping but is smooth and unpuckered. It may or may not call for control stitching. A gathered seam requires control stitching and retains more fullness. For both, the key to success is even distribution of fullness.

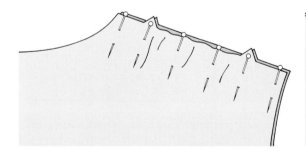  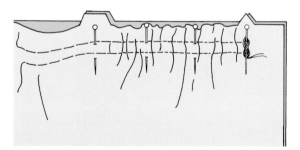

Slight ease, of the kind that might be needed along the back side of a shoulder seam, requires minimal control; pinning is often sufficient. (Pins hold the fabric layers together more tightly than basting stitches, keeping fullness from slipping during stitching.) Working from the longer side, pin seam at ends and notches; between notches, distribute the fullness evenly, pinning where necessary to hold it in place. Remove the pins as you stitch. If easing falls on both sides of the garment center, each side must be stitched in the same direction.

Moderate ease is controlled by machine-basting, then pinning. Test stitch length on single layer of fabric. Stitch should be long enough to allow fullness to be drawn up easily on the bobbin thread, but not too long or it will not control the fullness evenly. Machine-baste a thread's width from the seamline in area of longer piece to be eased in; pin seam at ends and notches. Draw fabric up on easestitching, distributing fullness evenly. Pin as needed to hold fullness. With seam still pinned, baste. Stitch, eased side up, removing pins as you stitch.

Gathering is the process of drawing fullness into a much smaller area using two rows of machine-basting. From the right side, stitch one basting line just next to the seamline; stitch the second ¼ in (6 mm) away in seam allowance. (See Gathering pages for details.) If seams intersect gathered area, begin and end gathering stitches at seamlines. Pin seam edges together at matching points, such as notches. Draw up bobbin threads, distributing fullness evenly. Wind drawn threads around a pin to secure gathers. Pin and stitch seam gathered side up.

Unusual seams — taped seams

Tape is sometimes added to a seam to keep it from stretching, or to strengthen it. This is called staying. Tapes or stays can be made of cotton or bias tape, ribbon seam binding, fusible stay tape, or a length of fabric selvage. The type used depends on the type of seam and the fabric. While the seams most often taped are those at waistline, shoulder, and neckline, taping is advisable for any seam where there is likely to be strain during wear, such as the underarm curve of a kimono sleeve. When very little give is wanted in the seam, use firm tape, such as cotton tape. If a seam should have give yet hold its shape, use bias tape. All tapes should be preshrunk. Tape should not extend into cross seams. Whenever possible, stitch tape side up to ensure tape is caught in the seam.

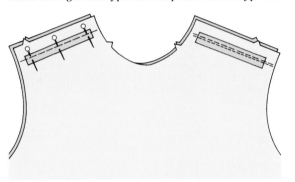

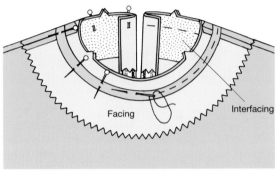

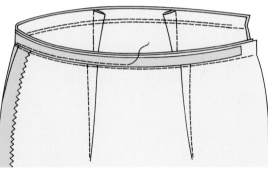

Tape at shoulder (or other straight seam) should be attached to one side of the seam only, usually the back. Using pattern as a guide, cut cotton tape (¼, ⅜, or ½ in [6, 10, or 12 mm] width) just long enough to fit between neck and armhole seams. Baste tape to seamline, positioning it ⅛ in (3 mm) into seam allowance. Stitch tape side up.

Tape at neckline (or any curved area) is easier to apply if preshaped into a curve (see How to preshape binding). Use ¼ in (6 mm) cotton tape; it shapes more easily than other firm types. Baste interfacing and facing to neck. Center tape over the neck seamline, on top of the facing. With tape side up, baste then stitch through all layers.

Tape at waistline is applied to the skirt, after waist seam is stitched. Position tape close to seamline; stitch along edge closest to the seamline. Trim seam allowances even with outer edge of tape. Here tape serves three purposes: it keeps the waist from stretching, strengthens the seam, and minimizes fraying of seam allowances.

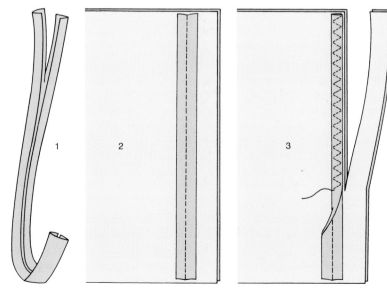

Taping with bias is advisable for raschel and other open-structured or stretchy knits. Use nylon bias tape, cut in half lengthwise (1). Place the fold exactly on the seamline. Open the tape, baste and stitch through crease and seamline (2). If the seam is to be overedged, refold tape and zigzag or overedge stitch through tape and both seam allowances. Trim seam allowances close to the stitching (3).

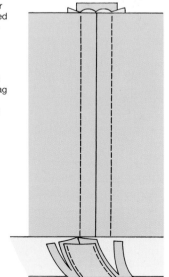

Tape under a topstitched seam, especially when garment is a knit, will contribute stability and support. Use cotton tape, here ¾ in (2 cm) wide. Center it over the seam on the wrong side. Baste each edge of the tape through both the seam allowance and garment. Topstitch ¼ in (6 mm) to each side of the seam. Tape will be caught in the stitching. Trim seam allowances even with the tape.

Seams for special fabrics — sheers, knits, and vinyls

Sheers and laces

Because construction details in sheers and laces show through, seams in these fabrics should be narrow and inconspicuous. The traditional seams for these fabrics are the French and the mock French seams, but double-stitched seams are a good choice for a very textured sheer, such as heavy lace; hairline

seams are appropriate for collars, cuffs, and similar garment parts.

Pin, or hand-baste with polyester thread, in the seam allowance only. Use the straight stitch throat plate if possible; it has a small hole and fabric is less likely to be dragged into it. Pressure and tension should generally be decreased slightly and a shorter stitch

used. Roller and no-snag feet prevent fabric from being caught or snagged.

Knits

Seam choice for a knit fabric is based on the amount of stretch in the fabric.

Generally, seams in knits should be constructed with give so that the stitching will not break when the fabric is stretched. Polyester thread is very strong and elastic, and is thus an excellent choice for knits and other stretchy fabrics. A ball-point needle, which goes between yarns instead of cutting through them, reduces the risk of damage.

The stitch pattern is determined by the machine; study your instruction manual for special stretch stitches and uses. A straight stitch works perfectly well even on stretchy knits if the proper thread is used and the fabric is stretched a little during stitching in the following way: hold the fabric in front of the presser foot with one hand and, with the other hand behind the presser foot, gently stretch the fabric as it passes under the needle. First test the seam on a scrap of fabric. The seam should be smooth and even.

Vinyls and smooth leathers

These fabrics show puncture marks from pins and needles. To avoid blemishing the finished garment, pin or baste only in seam allowances or hold edges together with paper clips; stitch only after fit of garment is satisfactory.

Specially coated or specially designed presser feet are available that prevent these fabrics from sticking

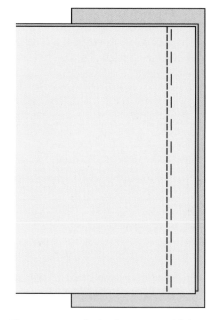

Tissue paper under hard-to-manage fabrics can be an aid to stitching. It assists the fabric to feed through the machine and prevents the fabric from being damaged by the feed dog. Baste a strip of the paper to one side of the seam. With the paper next to the feed dog, stitch the seam. To remove paper, pull it away first from one side of stitching, then from the other.

when stitched. Or you can coat the sewing surface of the fabric with baby oil, talcum powder, or cornstarch. Test on a fabric scrap first to make sure that whatever you use will come off easily.

Wedge-shaped needles make it easier to sew vinyls and leather. The stitch length should not be too short. Tie off the thread ends instead of backstitching. Flatten seams open with a mallet, and use rubber cement to hold seam allowances flat, or topstitch on either side of seams.

Hand-basting 70–71

Seaming pile fabrics

Pile fabrics encompass short-to-long pile lengths and sparse-to-dense pile coverage; the backing fabric may be woven or knitted. In most cases, the pile, rather than the backing fabric, is the major concern when stitching.

To avoid distorting the pile, stitch seams in the direction of the pile. Most piles slip and feed unevenly, so take care to exert the proper amount of pressure on fabric while stitching. Basting and top feed attachments will also help the layers feed evenly.

The longer or denser the pile, the greater the need to reduce bulk from seams. To do this, shave pile from seam allowances or narrow the seam allowance and use an overedge seam.

If fabric is a knit, some give should be built into the seam; use a zigzag stitch or stretch the fabric slightly while using a straight stitch. Finish all seam edges. Avoid forward-reverse stitches, as these can distort the pile and its direction.

Short pile can be trimmed from the seam allowances before seaming. Be sure to fit the garment first, as seamlines cannot be let out once pile has been shaved off. To shave pile, hold scissors close to and parallel to backing fabric. Cut with short and even strokes. Take care not to shave pile past ⅛ in (3 mm) inside the seamline.

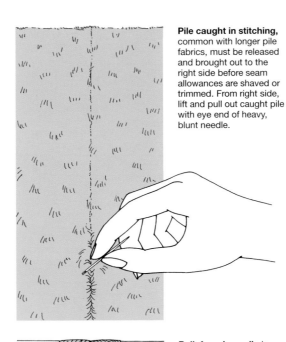

Pile caught in stitching, common with longer pile fabrics, must be released and brought out to the right side before seam allowances are shaved or trimmed. From right side, lift and pull out caught pile with eye end of heavy, blunt needle.

Bulk from long pile is removed after seaming and releasing pile caught in the stitching. Finger-press seam open before shaving pile from seam allowances. Be sure of your seamlines; they are difficult to let out after the pile has been shaved off.

Joining unlike fabrics

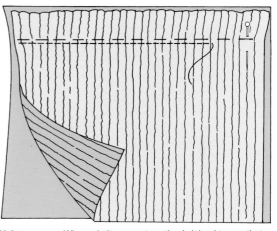

Knit to woven: When a knit garment section is joined to one that is woven, the knit section will usually be smaller than the woven. To ensure balanced distribution of the two in relation to each other, divide and pin-mark both edges into eighths. Then with right sides together, match sections at pin marks and baste the two together. Stitch with knit side uppermost, stretching the knit to fit the woven.

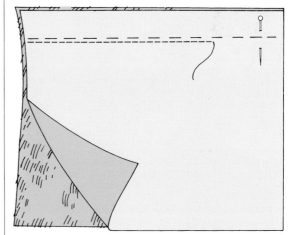

Pile to smooth: There may be difficulty, when stitching a pile fabric to one with a smooth surface, in getting the two surfaces to feed evenly with each other. This slipping can be minimized by hand-basting the two edges together with short, even stitches. Then, exerting appropriate pressure on the fabrics, stitch in the direction of the pile, the smooth-surfaced fabric uppermost as you stitch.

Pressing equipment 14 · Clipping and notching 87

Princess seams

Princess seams are shaped seams designed to fit the body's contours. Beginning at the shoulder or armhole, front or back, and running lengthwise, they may go just to the waistline seam or extend to the hem of a jacket or dress. A typical princess seam will curve *outward* to accommodate the fullest part of the bust or back, then inward to conform to the waist, and finally *outward* again to fit over the hips.

Extreme care must be taken during fitting, adjusting the pattern, and transferring the markings, as well as while sewing, if the curves of the seam are to follow the contours of the body.

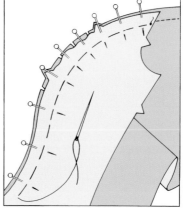

1. Place a row of reinforcement stitches just inside the seamlines of the center panel, from the top edge to just below the bottom notch. Clip between notches.

2. With side panel on top, match and pin the seamline, spreading the clipped edge to fit. Make additional clips if necessary. Baste in place.

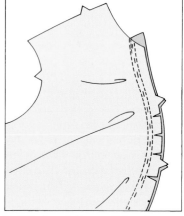

3. With clipped side up, stitch on the seamline, beyond the ends of the clips, being careful to keep the underside smooth. Backstitch at both ends of seam.

Every princess seam consists of two separate edges curved in a precise relationship to each other. When joined, the seam shapes itself around the contours of the body. An entire dress front, as illustrated above and at left, will have a center panel and two identical side panels, together producing a princess seam on each side of the garment front. Transfer all markings carefully to fabric before removing pattern.

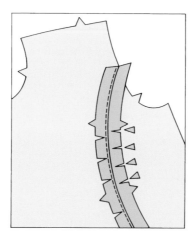

4. Remove basting; finger-press seam open. Notch out fullness from inward curve. Try to stagger the positioning of clips and notches.

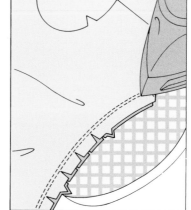

5. Close seam and place over tailor's ham. Press flat with iron tip. Do not press into body of the garment, especially in curved areas.

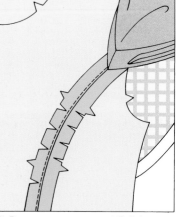

6. Press seam open over a tailor's ham. Reposition seam as necessary to keep curve of ham matched to curve of seam.

Seams as a way of shaping / Darts — forming plain darts

Darts are one of the most basic structural elements in dressmaking. They are used to build into a flat piece of fabric a definite shape that will allow the fabric to conform to a particular body contour or curve. Darts occur most often at the bust, the waist, and the hips; accuracy in their position and fit is important if they are to gracefully emphasize the lines in these areas.

Precise marking of construction symbols is also important. Choose a marking method suitable for the fabric. Stitching direction is from the wide end to the point. Backstitching can be used as a reinforcement at the wide end but should not be used at the point.

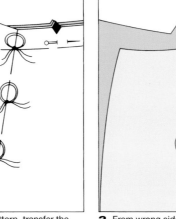

1. Before removing pattern, transfer the markings to wrong side of fabric. Tailor's tacks are shown here, but the method will depend on fabric being marked.

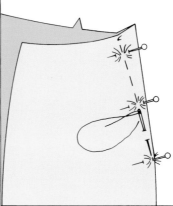

2. From wrong side, fold dart through center; match and pin corresponding tailor's tacks (or other markings). Baste, then remove tailor's tacks.

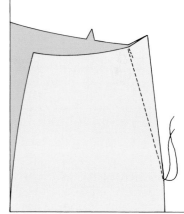

3. Starting from wide end of dart, stitch toward point, taking last few stitches parallel to and a thread's width from the fold. Cut the thread, leaving 4 in (10 cm) ends.

Darts are formed from triangular shapes marked on the pattern and consisting of stitching lines on each side of a center line. These lines meet at the point of the dart. During construction, the dart shape is folded (or in some instances cut) along the center line so that the stitching lines can be matched and stitched. After stitching, darts should be pressed. Press vertical darts toward center front or center back and horizontal darts downward. Unusually deep or bulky darts are often trimmed or slashed and pressed open. A finished dart should point toward the fullest part of the body contour to which it is conforming.

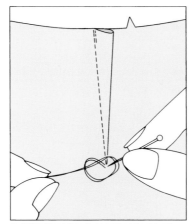

4. With thread ends together, form knot. Insert pin through knot into point of dart. Tighten knot, letting pin guide it to dart point.

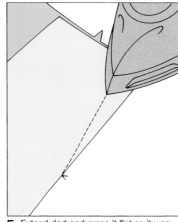

5. Extend dart and press it flat as it was stitched. Press toward the point, being careful not to go beyond it.

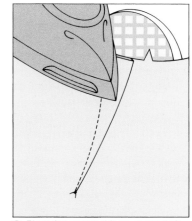

6. Place dart, wrong side up, over tailor's ham. Press according to direction it will take in finished garment.

Pressing equipment 14 · Fabric-marking methods 65

Contour dart and French dart

A contour dart is a long, single dart that fits at the waistline and then tapers off in two opposite directions to fit either both the bust and hip (known as a front contour dart) or the fullest part of both the back and the hip (known as a back contour dart). In effect, it takes the place of two separate waistline darts, one of them tapering toward the bust or back and the other toward the hip.

A **French dart** extends diagonally from the side seam in the hip area to the bust. The diagonal line can be straight or slightly curved. French darts are found on the front of a garment, never the back.

Although both types of darts are constructed in different ways (see illustrations right and p. 103), all the stitching, fold, or slash lines, as well as all matching points, should be clearly marked. Because their lines are usually more complex than those of the simple dart, they are best marked with a tracing wheel and dressmaker's tracing paper. If you must mark some other way, make sure that the shape of the lines is clearly indicated.

Clipping is another essential in these darts. It will relieve strain at the waist and other curved sections, permitting the dart to lie smooth.

Constructing a contour dart

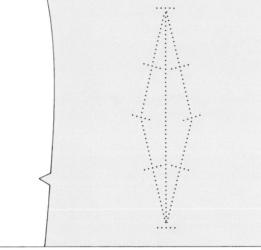

1. Transfer construction symbols to wrong side of fabric. A tracing wheel is good for this purpose, but test it first for legibility of markings and effect on fabric. Mark the stitching lines, center line, and all matching points.

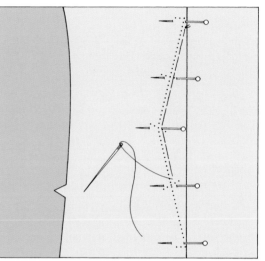

2. Working from wrong side, fold dart along center line. Match and pin stitching lines, first at the waist, then at both points, then at other matching points in between. Baste just inside the stitching line; remove pins after basting.

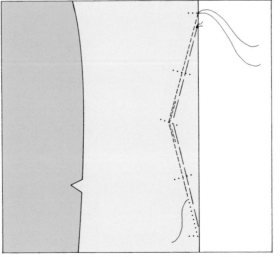

3. A contour dart is stitched in two steps; each begins at the waist, stitching toward the point. Instead of backstitching, overlap stitching at waist. Tie thread ends at both points of dart (see p. 101).

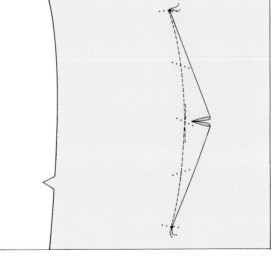

4. Remove basting. At waistline, clip to within 1/8 in (3 mm) of stitching to relieve strain and allow dart to curve smoothly past waist. Press dart flat as it was stitched; then press it toward center of garment.

Easing seams with fullness 96

Constructing a French dart

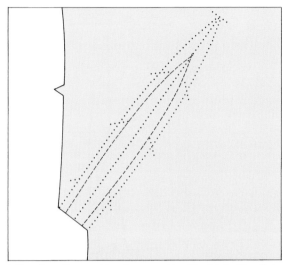

1. Transfer pattern markings to wrong side of the fabric. Staystitch ⅛ in (3 mm) inside each stitching line. Start each line of staystitching from the seamline end of dart and taper both to meet approximately 1 in (2.5 cm) from point of dart.

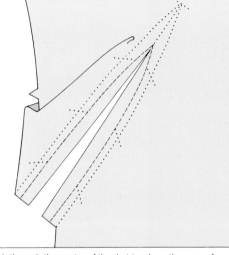

2. Slash through the center of the dart to where the rows of staystitching intersect. (This will not be necessary on those French darts in which part or all of the center portion is removed when the garment section is cut out.)

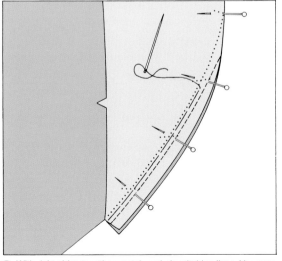

3. With right sides together, match and pin stitching lines. You may need to ease the lower edge to the upper edge to get the points to match accurately. Baste along the stitching line, then remove pins.

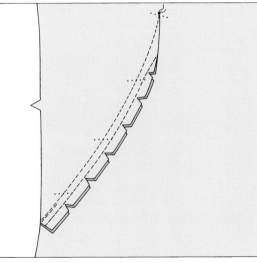

4. Stitch dart from end to point, knotting thread (see p. 101). Remove basting and clip seam allowances to relieve strain, letting dart curve smoothly. Press flat, then downward over tailor's ham.

Continuous-thread darts

A continuous-thread dart is one that is stitched in a way that leaves no thread ends to be tied at the point. Stitching direction is from the point to the end, the opposite of the usual way. This type of dart is used mainly where a thread knot would detract from the look of a garment; for example, when sheer fabrics are used or when the dart fold is to be on the outside of the garment.

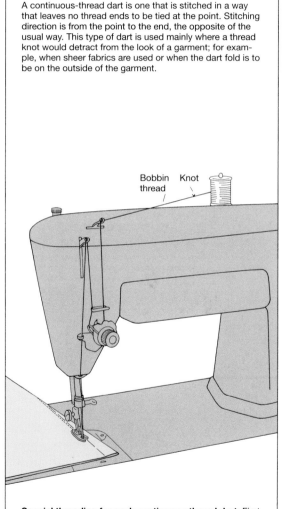

Bobbin thread   Knot

Special threading for each continuous-thread dart: First, thread machine as usual and pull bobbin thread up through throat plate. Then unthread needle and pass bobbin thread through needle eye in direction opposite to way needle was originally threaded. Tie bobbin and upper threads together with as small a knot as possible. Rewind top thread back onto spool, allowing knot, and enough bobbin thread to stitch one full dart, to pass through top threading points.

Dress pants

Pants fabric: Drews, Krefeld (Germany)

Fabrics
Firm yet fluid natural or synthetic fabrics, such as fine gabardine, crepe, or satin

Amount
For size 12: $1^3/_8$ yd (1.3 m) of 58/60 in (150 cm) -width fabric

Notions
Fusible interfacing, $8 \times 23^1/_2$ in (20×60 cm)
1 zipper, 7 in (18 cm)

Pattern pieces ▶▶▶▶▶▶▶▶▶▶▶▶▶▶▶▶
1 Pants front – cut 2
2 Pants back – cut 2
3 Front facing – cut 2
4 Back facing – cut 2
5 Pockets – cut 4 of fashion or lining fabric

Burda pattern 8903 was used for this project. In the original pattern, the zipper is sewn into the side seam. In our version, pockets are added and sewn into the side seams and the zipper placed in the center back seam. The upper edge is faced.

This is a classic design especially suitable for dressy occasions. The trousers have a smoothly fitted torso and flared legs.

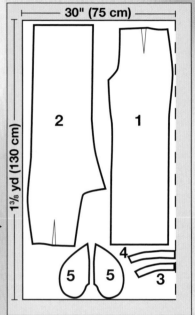

These dress pants go well with the tailored jacket, page 164, and the lace blouse, page 278.

Cutting

● **Fabric:** Fold the fabric in half with right sides together. Lay all pattern pieces on the fabric with the grainlines parallel to the selvage edge, and pin in place. Cut using shears or a rotary cutter.

● **Interfacing:** Cut the interfacing from the facing pattern pieces, then cut away all seam allowances. Fuse interfacing to wrong side of facing pieces.

Sewing instructions

● **Seam finishes:** Finish seam and hem edges on front and back pant pieces, with a zigzag stitch or with a serger (overlock machine).

● **Darts:** Baste the darts on the pants front and back, starting at the wide end and tapering to a fine point.

● **Pockets:** Match each pocket section to the markings on the side seam of pants fronts and backs, right sides together. Pin and stitch using a seam allowance of 1/4 in (6 mm). Press the seams toward the pocket sections and understitch (Fig. 3).

● **Basting seams:** With right sides together, pin and baste the center front seam and the back seam below the mark for the zipper opening. Pin and baste the inseams, matching the crotch point. Pin and baste the side seams. Try on to check fit and adjust if necessary.

● **Stitching seams:** After adjusting the fit, permanently stitch the darts, fastening the thread ends at the dart tips. Permanently stitch the front and back seams and the inseams.

● Permanently stitch the side seams and the matched pocket sections (Fig. 4). Stitch long seams from the lower edge up. Remove basting where necessary.

● **Pressing seams:** Press seams as stitched to set the stitches and then press open. Turn the pocket bags toward the pants front; to allow them to lie flat it is necessary to clip the seams at the top and base of each pocket. Finish the pocket seam allowances.

● **Zipper:** Open zipper, place the right chain on the right seam allowance, right sides together. The zipper teeth should be concealed. Baste.

● Close the zipper and place on the left seam allowance. Baste.

● Turn the pants to the right side and stitch through all layers — fabric, seam allowance, and zipper

tape. Remove basting threads.

● **Waist facing:** Assemble the facing by joining backs to front at the side seams, right sides together. Press seams open and trim. Finish the lower edge of the facing.

● Pin the facing to the top edge of the pants, matching side seams. Turn back the ends of the facing at the

zipper placket to align with the pant edges. Stitch the facing to the pants at the waist edge.

● Flip up the facing and understitch close to the seam through the facing and both seam allowances. Trim and grade the seam allowance.

● Press the facing to the inside of the pants and, if desired, stitch again close to the fold.

● Hand sew the facing to the zipper placket and tack to the side seams of the pants. Sew a hook and eye to the top of the zipper opening.

● **Hem:** Turn up the hem to the correct length and hand-sew to the pants legs. Press.

Pressing equipment 14 · Fabric-marking methods 65 · Flat catchstitch 81

Darts in interfacing and underlined garments

Abutted dart

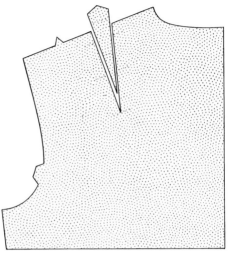

1. An abutted dart is a special type of dart that is used in such fabrics as interfacing to eliminate unnecessary bulk. The first step is to mark the stitching lines and matching points of the dart. Then cut out center of dart along both stitching lines.

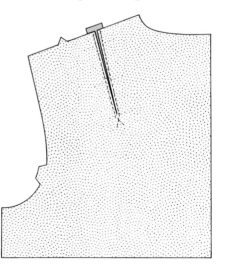

2. Bring cut edges together and baste in place to an underlay of cotton tape or a 1 in (2.5 cm) -wide strip of lightweight fabric. With straight stitching, stitch ⅛ in (3 mm) to each side of abutted line; if using zigzag stitch, center over the abutted line. Press.

Lapped dart

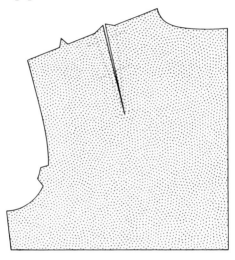

1. A lapped dart is another special dart type used to eliminate unnecessary bulk from interfacing. Mark the matching points and the center and stitching lines. Slash along center of dart to the point, being careful not to cut beyond the point.

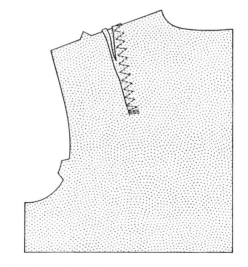

2. Lap edges so the stitching lines meet; baste in place. Center the presser foot over the stitching line and stitch, using a short, wide multistitch zigzag or plain zigzag stitch. Trim the excess fabric and press.

Catchstitched dart

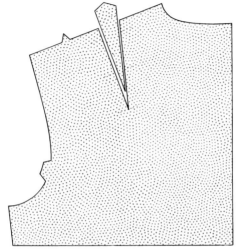

1. A catchstitched dart is an effective way to eliminate the bulk of an interfacing dart that is aligned with a dart in the garment. Using tracing wheel and dressmaker's tracing paper, mark the dart stitching lines and matching points. Cut along both stitching lines to remove center portion of dart.

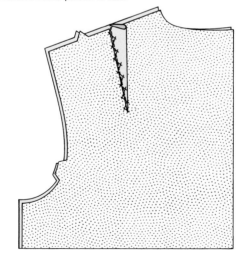

2. Position the open interfacing dart over the stitched garment dart and pull dart up through the two cut edges. Pin edges of interfacing alongside the stitching lines of the dart. Catch each edge to the dart over its stitching line with catchstitches. Press.

Darts in underlined garments

Darts in underlined garments can be handled by either constructing each dart through both garment and underlining fabrics as if the two fabrics were one or by stitching the garment darts and the underlining darts separately. The former method, stitching both darts as one, is most often used. It is especially recommended for sheer fabrics because the dart does not show through to the outside. The latter, stitching darts separately, is suitable for very heavy or bulky fabrics. Whichever method is used, each dart is constructed according to its type.

There is one slight difference in French dart construction when the dart is to be underlined as one with the garment fabric. The two rows of staystitching for the French dart, if stitched from point of intersection to end of dart, will hold fabrics together in this area; a row of machine-basting from point of dart to staystitching intersection will secure the center (see right).

Darts stitched through two layers

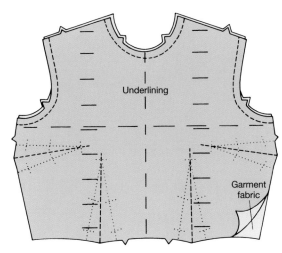

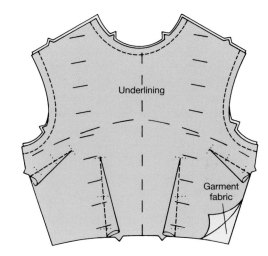

1. Transfer pattern markings to right side of underlining. Wrong sides together, baste underlining to garment fabric (see Underlining). Where needed, staystitch through both layers. Starting just beyond point, machine-baste down center of darts.

2. Match, baste, and stitch each dart. Remove machine-basting beyond point. Press darts flat and then in correct wearing direction. Basting that is holding layers together should remain in place during further garment construction.

Darts stitched separately

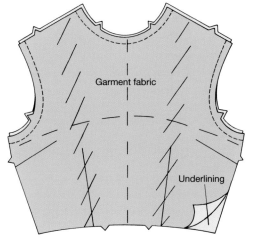

1. When stitching underlining and garment darts, mark both fabrics on wrong side and staystitch each layer individually. Stitch all darts; press flat as stitched. Then press each garment dart in its correct direction; press corresponding underlining dart in opposite direction.

2. With wrong sides together, baste underlining to garment fabric (see Underlining). Because of shaping built in by darts, it may be necessary to place the layers over a tailor's ham for basting. When layers are joined, continue garment construction, handling both layers as one.

Pressing equipment 14 · Grain in fabric 56–57 · Fabric-marking methods 65

Tucks — plain tucks

A tuck is a stitched fold of fabric that is most often decorative, but it can also be a shaping device. Each tuck is formed from two stitching lines that are matched and stitched; the fold of the tuck is produced when the lines come together.

A tuck's width is the distance from the fold to the matched lines. Tucks that meet are **blind tucks;** those with space between them are **spaced tucks.** A very narrow tuck is a **pin tuck.** Most tucks are stitched on the straight grain, parallel to the fold, and are uniform in width. Curved dart tucks are an exception (see p. 109).

Blind tucks

Spaced tucks

Pin tucks

How to make a plain tuck

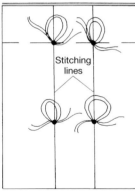

1. Mark the stitching lines of each tuck. If a tuck is to be made on the outside of garment, mark the right side of fabric; if on the inside, mark on wrong side. Use marking method suitable for fabric and for tuck location (see Marking methods). Width of tuck is one-half the distance between its stitching lines.

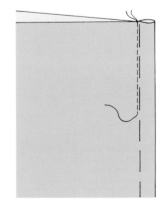

2. Remove pattern. Fold tuck to inside or outside of the garment, according to design, and crease with a warm iron. Stitch tuck on stitching line.

Useful gauges

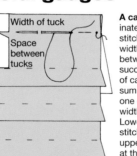

A cardboard gauge can eliminate the need for marking stitching lines. First determine width of tuck and space between stitching lines of successive tucks. Cut a piece of cardboard as long as the sum of these two widths; from one end mark off the tuck width and make a notch. Lower edge is placed along stitching line of previous tuck; upper edge is at fold; notch is at the stitching line of tuck being formed.

Throat plate markings on the machine are helpful gauges for precise stitching of tucks that range from ⅜ to ⅝ in (10 to 15 mm) and sometimes ¾ in (2 cm) in width. For instance, you can stitch a ⅜ in (10 mm) tuck by keeping the fold of the tuck on the ⅜/10 mark. Other aids to stitching to a precise width are the edge of the presser foot (for narrow tucks), a separate seam gauge, or a quilter guide-bar (for wider tucks).

Pressing tucks

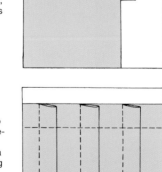

1. Press each tuck flat as it was stitched. If pressing from right side, use a press cloth to avoid marring the fabric.

2. Press all tucks in the direction in which they will be worn. To ensure that the ends of all tucks will stay in position during the balance of garment construction, staystitch across them as they were pressed.

Zigzag stitching 83 · Overhand stitch 73

Special tucks

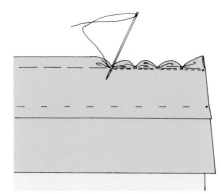

Hand shell tuck: Baste a narrow tuck. With threaded needle, do a few stitches every ½ in (about every 1.25 cm) to scallop the tuck, passing needle through tuck between scallops.

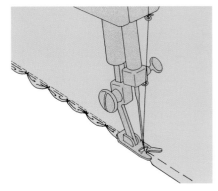

Machine shell tuck: Baste a ⅛ in (3 mm) tuck. Set machine for the blindstitch. Place tuck under foot with fold to left of needle so that the zigzag stitch will form over the fold and scallop the tuck.

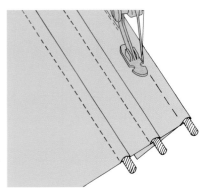

Corded, or piped, tuck: Fold the tuck, positioning cord inside along the fold. Baste. Using a zipper foot, stitch close to cord. Make sure that the size of the cord is right for the width of the tuck.

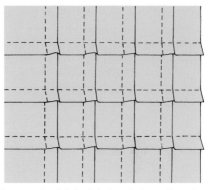

Cross tucks: Stitch all the lengthwise tucks and press them in one direction. Then stitch the crossing set of tucks at right angles to the first, keeping the first set of tucks facing downward.

Adding tucks to plain garments

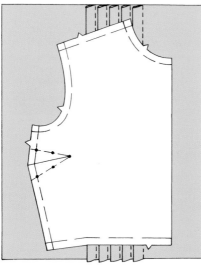

Tucks can be added to any plain garment before it is cut. Tuck fabric first, then strategically position pattern over tucks and cut out section. The required extra fabric width is equal to twice the width of a tuck times the total number of tucks being added to the garment piece.

Adding material: When the fabric is not wide enough to allow you to turn over the edge, pin a fold so that ½ in (1.25 cm) seam allowance remains. Lay the fold with the stitching line ½ in (1.25 cm) over the edge of the second layer of fabric. Pin and stitch.

Dart or released tucks

Dart tucks, sometimes also called released tucks, are used to control fullness and then release it at a desired point, such as the bust or hips. They can be formed on the inside or outside of the garment; fullness can be released at either or both ends. Sometimes the tuck is stitched across the bottom. Dart tucks may be stitched on the straight grain, or, in some instances, the stitching lines may be curved to build in a certain amount of shaping. Care must be taken, especially when stitching lines are curved, to match them accurately. Reinforce the stitches by tying threads or backstitching. Press carefully to avoid creasing folds.

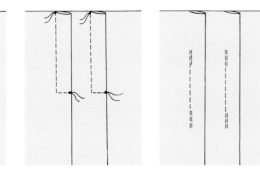

Pressing equipment 14 · Grain in fabric 56–57 · Simplified tailor's tacks 69

Pleats — pleating methods

Pleats are folds in fabric that provide controlled fullness. Pleating may occur as a single pleat, as a cluster, or around an entire garment section. Each pleat is folded along a specified line, usually referred to on patterns as the **foldline,** and the fold aligned with another line, the **placement** line.

If the fabric has a definite motif, mark and form the pleats from the right side. If the pleat is a type that is to be stitched on the inside from the hip to the waist, it will be easier to mark and form the pleats from the wrong side.

Some patterns may also require matching and stitching the pleats from the wrong side, for example, when you are constructing a pleat with a separate underlay.

In pressing pleats, press lightly if at all for soft pleats. For sharp pleats, use steam and, if necessary, a press cloth to help set the creases. To help maintain folds during further construction, do not remove the basting stitches holding the pleats until necessary.

Pleats formed from the right side

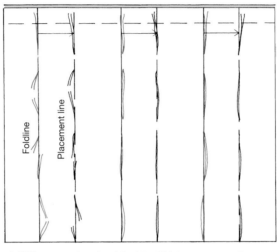

1. With pattern pinned to right side of fabric and using different colored threads, mark each fold and placement line with simplified tailor's tacks. Before removing pattern, clip thread between stitches.

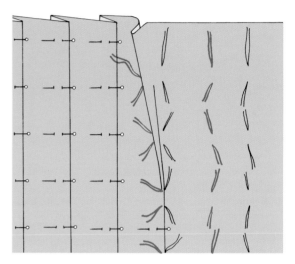

2. Remove pattern carefully. Working from right side, fold fabric along a foldline; bring fold to its placement line. Pin pleat through all thicknesses in the direction it will be worn. Do the same for each pleat, removing thread markings as you pin.

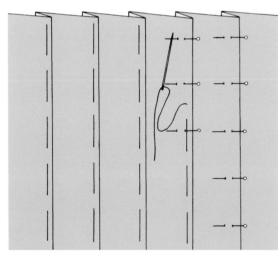

3. Baste each pleat close to foldline through all thicknesses. Remove pins as you baste. Baste with spun polyester thread; it leaves the fewest indentations in the fabric after pressing. Retain this basting as far into further garment construction as possible.

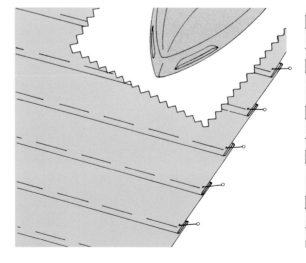

4. With fabric right side up, position a group of pleats over ironing board. Using a press cloth, press each pleat. For soft pleats, press lightly; for extra sharp pleats, dampen the press cloth and let pleats dry before moving them.

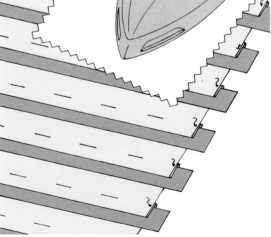

5. With garment wrong side up, press pleats again, using press cloth. If backfolds leave ridges during pressing, remove them by first gently pressing beneath each fold; then insert strips of heavy paper beneath folds and press again.

Pressing equipment 14 · Fabric-marking methods 65

Pleats formed from the wrong side

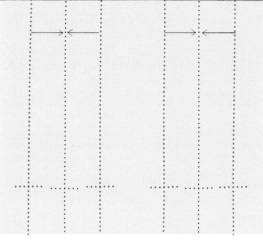

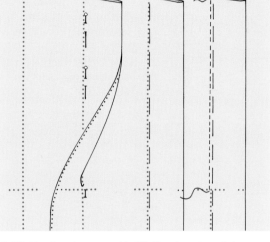

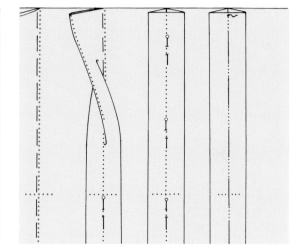

1. Before removing pattern, mark, on the wrong side of fabric, all foldlines and placement lines. Choose a method of marking that will show on but not mar the fabric. Use one color (thread or tracing paper) to mark foldlines; another to mark placement lines.

2. Working from the wrong side, if knife or box pleats, bring together and match each foldline to its placement line; if pleats are inverted (shown), bring together and match each set of foldlines. Pin and baste through both thicknesses. If pleats will be stitched, as from hip to waist, do this now.

3. Position inverted pleats in the direction they are to be worn. This is done by spreading open the underfold of each pleat and aligning placement line to matched foldlines. Pin, then baste in place through all thicknesses for the entire length of each pleat.

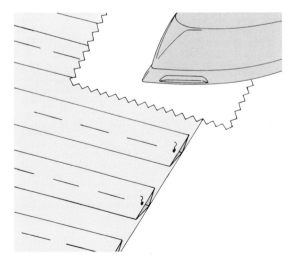

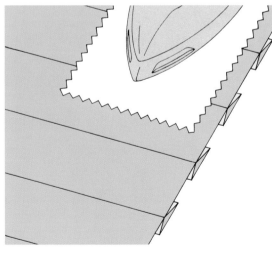

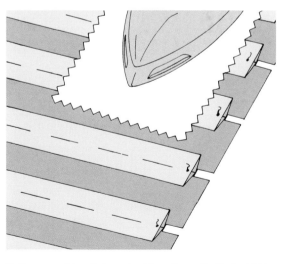

4. With wrong side up, press all of the pleats in the direction they will be worn. When they are knife pleats, all of the backfolds should be turned in one direction; the backfolds of box pleats will be facing each other; inverted pleats are pressed as shown above.

5. Turn garment to right side and press again. Be sure that all the pleats are facing in the direction that they will be worn. The basting that is holding the pleats in position should be left in place as long as possible during the rest of garment construction.

6. To remove ridges that may have been formed by the backfolds, turn garment to wrong side and press again gently under each fold. Then insert strips of heavy paper under the folds and press again. These procedures can also be used on right side.

Pressing equipment 14 · Whipstitch 73 · Tying thread ends 101 · Hemming 254–257

Pleat with separate underlay

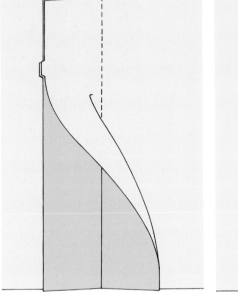

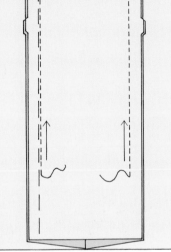

1. To form a pleat with a separate underlay, first bring together and match foldlines. Baste. If fold-lines are to be partially stitched together, do this step next; then remove basting from stitched area only. Press pleat extensions open along foldlines.

2. With right sides together, lay pleat underlay over the pleat extensions, matching markings; baste along each seam. Beginning 6 in (15 cm) up from the hem edge, stitch each side of the pleat underlay to each pleat extension.

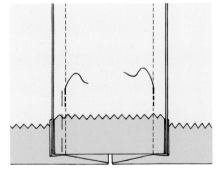

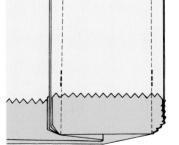

3. Remove basting, holding foldlines together. Hem skirt and pleat extensions separately from underlay. Then match, baste, and stitch unstitch-ed part of the underlay to the pleat extensions. Stitch from hem edge up to previous stitching.

4. Press seams flat as stitched. Finish seam allowances of underlay and extension so their edges will not show beyond hem edge: first trim diagonally across the corners of all seam allow-ances; then whipstitch together each set of seam allowances within the hem area.

Topstitching and edgestitching pleats

Pleats lie and hang well when they are topstitched and edgestitched. **Top-stitching** serves also to hold pleats in place in the hip-to-waist area. It is done through all thicknesses of the pleat. **Edgestitching** is applied along the fold of a pleat after the hem is finished in order to give a sharper crease.

In both cases, stitch from the bot-tom of the garment up toward the top. When applying both techniques to the same pleat, edgestitch first.

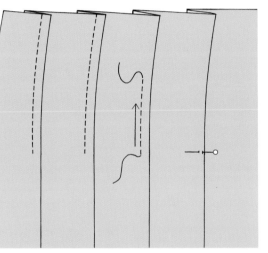

To topstitch knife pleats in the hip-to-waist area, first pin-mark each pleat at the point where the topstitching will begin. Then, with the garment right side up, stitch through all thicknesses, along the fold, from the pin to the top of pleat. Bring thread ends to underside and tie.

Topstitch inverted pleats on both sides of the matched foldlines. Pin-mark each pleat where the topstitching will begin. With garment right side up, insert needle between foldlines at marked point. Take two or three stitches across the pleat, pivot, then stitch along foldline to waist. Beginning again at the mark, stitch across pleat in opposite direction, pivot, then stitch to the waist. Bring all threads through to the underside and tie.

Turned-and-stitched seam finish 88 · Tying thread ends 101

Staying pleats

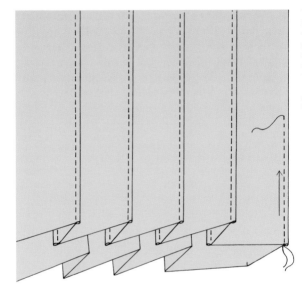

To edgestitch pleat folds:
Extend the pleat and stitch, through the two thicknesses, as close to the fold as possible. Stitch from the finished hem edge up. Bring thread ends through to underside and tie. Both folds can be edgestitched, as shown, or just outer or inner folds if that is more suitable.

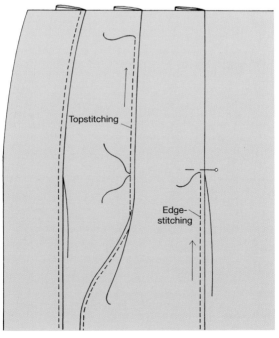

To edgestitch *and* topstitch:
Folds are first edgestitched up to the point where the top-stitching will begin. If pleat has already been stitched together in the hip-to-waist area, remove a few stitches so that the edge-stitching can extend to exact hip point where the topstitching will begin. Starting at that point precisely, topstitch from hip to waist through all thicknesses. Bring all thread ends to under-side and tie.

Topstitching

Edge-
stitching

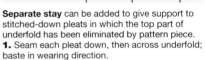

Separate stay can be added to give support to stitched-down pleats in which the top part of underfold has been eliminated by pattern piece.
1. Seam each pleat down, then across underfold; baste in wearing direction.

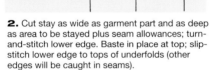

2. Cut stay as wide as garment part and as deep as area to be stayed plus seam allowances; turn-and-stitch lower edge. Baste in place at top; slip-stitch lower edge to tops of underfolds (other edges will be caught in seams).

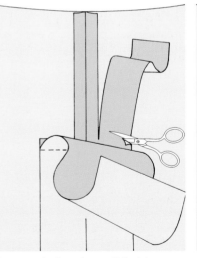

Self-stay can be formed on a stitched-down inverted pleat. First stitch down pleat. Then, in two steps, stitch across both sides of underfold.
1. Slit along backfolds to stitching; trim fabric behind to ⅝ in (15 mm) from stitching.

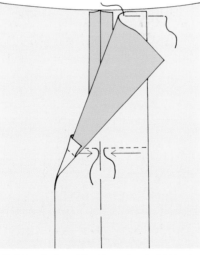

2. Bring the top of the trimmed underfold back up to top edge of garment. Carefully align this self-stay with the rest of the pleat and baste it in place along top. This top edge will be caught into the seam.

Whipstitch 73 · Finishing seams 88–89 · Hemming 254–257

Hemming pleated garments

Depending on the type of pleats, the hem in a pleated garment is sewn sometimes before and sometimes after pleats are formed. **Hemming before pleating** is easier but is appropriate only when the pleats are all-around and straight, when the hem must follow a line in a plaid, or when the top portion does not require seaming or extensive fitting. **Hemming after pleating** is more usual and is necessary when there is only a single pleat or cluster; when the pleat is formed with a separate underlay; or when, on an all-round-pleated garment, the pleats are seamed or fitted at the top. It may be helpful, especially with heavier fabrics, to press in the pleat folds to within 8 in (20 cm) of the hem edge, complete hem, then press in the rest of the pleat folds.

Seams within a hem are treated in different ways according to where the seam is and whether the seam is stitched before or after hemming. Most seams are stitched before hemming, but, in some cases, such as a garment that is hemmed before pleating, or a pleat formed with a separate underlay, there will be one or two seams to be stitched after hemming.

Handling seam allowances in hem area

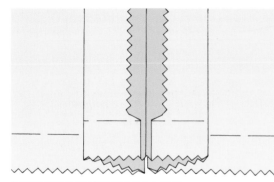

A seam that is at a flat part of the pleat:
1. Press open and trim to half its width from the hem edge to the hemline. This is a grading technique to eliminate bulk from the hem.

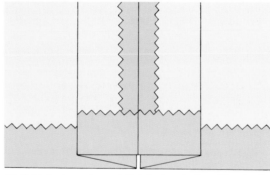

2. Finish the hem edge and stitch the hem in place. When turning up hem, make certain that seamlines are matched and seam allowances are in the pressed-open position.

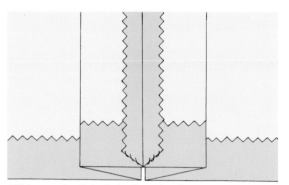

If this seam is stitched after hemming, first press seam open, then trim diagonally across each corner at the bottom of the seam allowances. Whipstitch these trimmed edges flat to the hem.

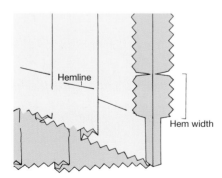

A seam that is at the backfold of a pleat:
1. The seam is also first pressed open and trimmed to half its width from hem edge to hemline. Then, so that seam allowances can turn in different directions, clip into them a hem width above hemline.

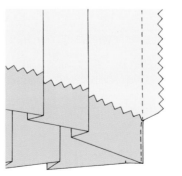

2. Finish the hem edge and stitch hem in place, using a suitable hemming method. To keep backfold creased, edgestitch close to the fold, from the hemline up, to meet the seam at the point where it was clipped. Secure thread ends.

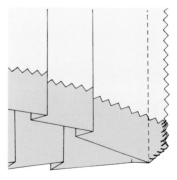

If this seam is stitched after hemming, first press seam flat as stitched. Then trim diagonally across both corners at bottom of seam allowances. Whipstitch together the trimmed edges, then the rest of hem area seam allowances.

Invisible zipper 286–287

Adjusting fullness within hem

The amount of fullness in a pleated hem can be reduced or increased by restitching the seam.

To reduce fullness, restitch a deeper seam, wider at hem edge and meeting original seam at hemline. Remove original stitches from the old seam; press; trim new seam allowances.

To increase fullness, restitch a shallower seam, narrower at hem edge and meeting original seam at hemline. Remove original stitches from the old seam; press; trim new seam allowances.

In either case, do not alter the original seamline so much that you distort the shape and hang of the hem.

To reduce fullness, stitch a deeper seam.

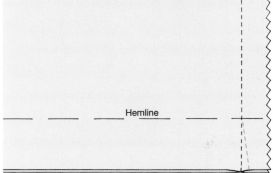

To increase fullness, stitch a narrower seam.

Plackets in pleated garments

The placket seam is usually the last seam to be formed in a pleated garment. It is at this point that the zipper is sewn in. The pleats around the zipper can then be formed. If the pleats are **box or inverted,** try to position the placket seam down the center of the pleat underfold; then install the zipper by either the centered or invisible zipper method. If the garment is **knife pleated,** try to position the placket seam where the pleat backfold will fall.

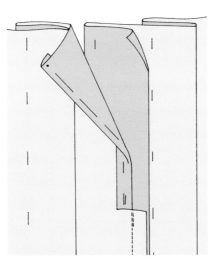

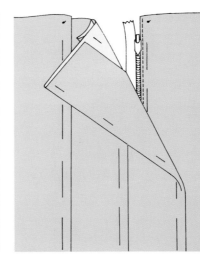

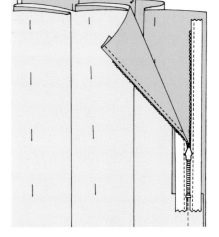

For box or inverted pleats, position the final seam down center of underfold and use either the centered or invisible zipper application. With inverted pleats, the folds will conceal the zipper placket; box pleats may not.

For knife pleats:
1. Stitch the final seam at the pleat backfold, leaving the top part open for the zipper. Clip into the left seam allowance; turn it to wrong side of garment and baste in place, as shown.

2. Turn garment to right side; position closed zipper under basted seam allowance with the folded edge close to the teeth and top stop just below top seamline. Baste. Then, using a zipper foot, stitch close to fold.

3. Turn garment to wrong side; extend unclipped seam allowance. Place other half of zipper face down on the seam allowance with the teeth 1/8 in (3 mm) beyond the seamline. Baste, then open zipper and stitch to seam allowance.

Selecting the correct pattern size 37

Altering pleated garments

Alterations in a pleated garment will be fewer, and
easier to make, if the pattern is selected by hip measurement. Overall width or length adjustments are
best made in the pattern before the garment is cut
out. Slight fitting modifications are taken care of in
the garment itself after a test-fitting.

Width alteration in a garment with all-around
pleats must be divided and applied equally to each of
the pleats. With knife or box pleats, this involves
moving both the fold and placement lines; with inverted pleats, only the foldlines. For a garment with a single pleat or a cluster, it is easier to alter the unpleated
part.

So that pleats hang properly, grainline must be
maintained from at least the hip down. (It is often
impossible to keep the grain perfect above the hip
because of the shaping involved.) If the fabric you are
using has a definite vertical design, it is necessary to
position width alterations to conform to it.

Length adjustments

Length alterations are best made on the pattern,
along the lengthening/shortening line specified on the
pattern piece. The length can also be adjusted at the
hemline during hemming. After hemming, the length
can be changed slightly by lowering or raising the
garment at the top seamline.

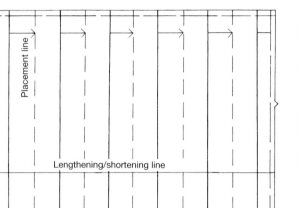

To lengthen, cut pattern along the lengthening/
shortening line. Tape tissue paper to one edge, then
spread the two cut pattern edges apart the amount
that the pattern is to be lengthened. Tape in place.
Redraw all the pleat, seam, and cutting lines affected
by the alteration.

To shorten, measure up from the lengthening/
shortening line the amount the pattern is to
be shortened. Draw a line across the pattern parallel
to, and the measured distance from, the adjustment
line. Fold pattern on adjustment line. Bring fold to the
drawn line and tape in place. Redraw the pleat, seam,
and cutting lines that were affected by the alteration.

Width adjustments in pattern

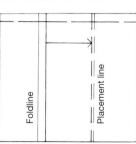

Knife pleats are altered by
repositioning both the fold
and the placement lines.

To increase garment
width, redraw both lines so
pleat is narrower.

To decrease garment
width, redraw both lines so
the pleat is wider.

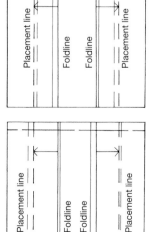

Box pleats are altered by
repositioning both foldlines
and both placement lines.

To increase garment width,
redraw the lines so the
pleat is narrower.

To decrease garment
width, redraw a wider pleat.

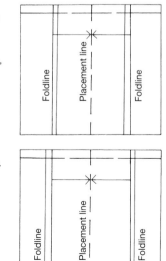

Inverted pleats are altered
by repositioning the foldlines only.

To increase garment
width, redraw each foldline
inside the original.

To decrease garment
width, redraw each foldline
outside the original.

Width adjustments in hip-to-waist area

To find out how much adjustment a pleated garment needs in the hip-to-waist area, try on the garment after the pleats have been basted. Then remove the garment and release basting in hip-to-waist area. Divide total amount of alteration by the number of pleats and alter each pleat by the fractional amount.

Correcting the hang

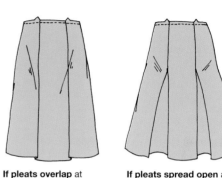

If pleats overlap at bottom, lower skirt from top (no more than half the seam allowance). Re-fit pleats at top if necessary; mark new top seam. If pleats still overlap, overall width must be adjusted (see below).

If pleats spread open at the bottom edge, raise garment from top to correct the hang. Re-fit the pleats at the top if necessary; mark new seamline. If this proves inadequate, readjust overall garment width (see below).

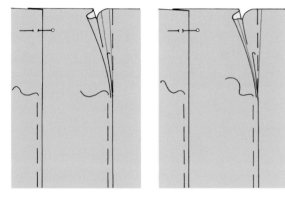

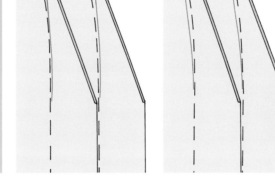

Pleats only folded: Refold all pleats by the same amount, narrower to increase and deeper to decrease garment width.

Pleats to be seamed: Reposition all seams equally inside originals to increase and outside to decrease garment width.

Adjusting overall garment width in fabric

Overall garment width can be adjusted in the fabric after all pleats have been basted in place. The technique is similar to width adjustment in patterns. It differs in that, along with a uniform width adjustment from the hip down, the garment can be tapered through the hip-to-waist area. For knife or box pleats, adjustment is made equally on fold and placement lines. With inverted pleats, only foldlines are altered. Maintain the original grainline from the hip down.

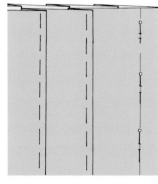

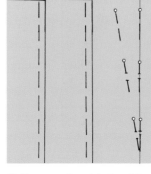

1. Release one pleat. Re-pin this pleat on marked lines but extend it out from the garment.

2. Try garment on; take in or let out extended pleat at hip, tapering to waist, until garment fits comfortably.

3. Pin-mark both new pleat lines; release pleat. Measure distance between old and new lines at a few points and double measurement.

4. Divide amount of total change at each point by the number of pleat lines to be changed. Alter each line by that amount at the same points. From hip down, the new line should remain parallel to the original.

Pleated skirt

Skirt fabric: Colsman, Essen (Germany).

Fabrics
Light worsted wool or polyester twill

Amount
For size 12: 1 yd (0.9 m) of 58/60 in (150 cm) -width fabric or more fabric for a longer skirt

Notions
Fusible interfacing
1 zipper, 9 in (24 cm)

Pattern pieces ▶▶▶▶▶▶▶▶▶▶▶▶▶▶
1 Waistband front – cut 2
2 Waistband back – cut 4
3 Skirt panel – cut 2 on fold
This pleated skirt features a wide contoured waistband/hip yoke. Fusible interfacing is applied to the wrong side of the band to give it stability.

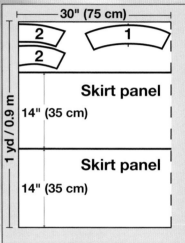

There are two ways to create pleats:
1. Fold the fabric into pleats as desired, pin the pleats, baste into position, and press.
2. Have the fabric permanently pleated by a professional. Some dry-cleaning businesses provide pleating services. However, professional pleating is not possible with natural fibers; it can be done only with fabrics made of synthetic fibers.

Cutting

Cut the front and back skirt panels to the desired length using the entire width of the fabric, adding an upper seam allowance and enough for a narrow hem. Cut the back skirt section in half down the fabric fold.

Cut waistband sections as shown, one set for the outer waistband and another for the waistband facing. (For a pattern, use the top area of a fitted skirt pattern, closing the darts first.) Cut interfacing pieces (without

seam allowances) for waistband. Fuse to the wrong side of outer waistband pieces.

Sewing instructions

● **Preparation:** Iron the fusible interfacing to the wrong side of one set of waistband pieces (three pieces).
● **Finishing:** Finish top and bottom edges of skirt sections.
Skirt seams: With right sides together, pin and stitch back skirt sections to each side of front skirt. Finish seam allowances together and press to one side.

Hem: Turn lower edge of skirt to inside ¼ in (6 mm) and press. Turn

again to form hem and press. Stitch close to folded edge (Fig. 1).

● **Pleating:** Take the full hip measurement and use it to calculate the size and number of pleats. Take the skirt to a professional pleating service or pin and press the pleats into position using plenty of steam. Be sure to conceal each side seam within a pleat. Baste along upper edge to hold the pleats in position (Fig. 2).

● **Waistband:** Assemble the waistband by joining the fused sections at the side seams. Press seam allowances open and trim. Check that it fits the upper hip area before continuing. Repeat with the waistband facing pieces.
● With right sides together, join the two waistband layers along the waist edge. Fold the waistband facing up and understitch through it and the two seam allowances close to waist seam. Trim and clip seam. Press facing to inside (Fig. 3).
● Pin outer waistband to pleated skirt edge, right sides together, making sure that the edges of skirt and waistband match exactly

at the center back. Baste, then stitch with pleat side up, making sure that the pleats stay in position (Fig. 4).
● Trim and finish seam, then press upward.

● Press under the seam allowance on the waistband facing.
● **Zipper:** Press back the seam allowances along the zipper area of skirt and waistband.
● Working with the zipper open, attach first to the right side and then repeat for the left side (Fig. 5).
● Pin turned-in lower edge of waistband facing in place over waistband seam. Handsew or topstitch from right side, catching in facing edge.
● **Back seam:** Finally, complete the center back seam and finish seam allowances together. Make sure that the seam is concealed in a pleat.

Grain in fabric 56–57 · Seam finishes 88–89

Gathering

Gathering is the process of drawing a given amount of fabric into a predetermined, smaller area, along one or several basting lines, to create soft, even folds. Fabric is usually gathered to one-half or one-third the original width.

Gathering most often occurs in a garment at waistline, cuffs, or yoke, or as ruffles. Gathering is done after construction seams have been stitched, seam-finished, and pressed. Because gathers fall best on the lengthwise

grain, the rows of basting should run *across* the grain.

Suitable stitch lengths for gathering vary from 6 to 12 stitches per inch (2 mm to 4 mm), shorter for sheer or light fabrics, longer for thick, heavy materials. The

shorter the stitch length, the more control you have over the gathers, no matter what the fabric. Loosening the upper thread tension will make it easier to draw up the gather. For extensive gathering, use extra-strength thread in the bobbin.

How to gather fabric

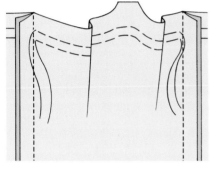

1. Working on the right side of the fabric, stitch two parallel rows in seam allowance, one a thread width above seamline, the other ¼ in (6 mm) higher. Leave long thread ends. Break stitching at the seams.

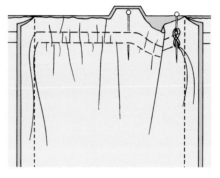

2. Pin stitched edge to corresponding straight edge, right sides together, matching notches, center lines, and seams. Anchor bobbin threads (now facing you) at one end by twisting in figure 8 around pins. Excess material is now ready to gather.

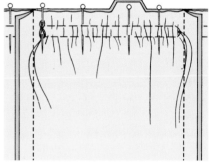

3. Gently pull on the bobbin threads while you slide, with the other hand, the fabric along the thread to create uniform gathers. When this first gathered section fits the adjoining edge, secure thread ends by winding them around a pin.

4. To draw up the ungathered portion, untie the bobbin threads and repeat the process from the other end. Fasten the thread end. Adjust gathers uniformly and pin at frequent intervals to hold folds in place.

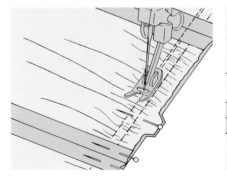

5. Before seaming gathered section, set machine to a suitable stitch length and tension. With gathered side up, stitch seam on seamline, holding fabric on either side of needle so that gathers will not be stitched into little pleats.

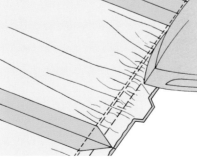

6. Trim any seam allowances that are caught into the gathered seam. Press seam as stitched, in the seam allowances, using just the tip of the iron. Seam-finish the edge with a zigzag or over-lock stitch, or apply a stay (see p. 121).

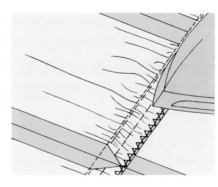

7. Open garment section out flat and press seam as it should go in finished garment — toward bodice if a waistline seam, toward shoulder if a yoke seam, toward wrist if a cuff.

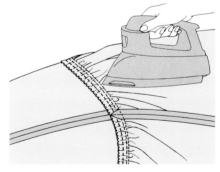

8. Press the gathers by working the point of the iron into the gathers toward the seam. Press from the wrong side of the fabric, lifting the iron as you reach the seam. Do not press across the gathers; this will flatten and cause them to go limp.

Zigzag stitch 83 · Basting stitch 70 · Running stitch 71

Further gathering methods

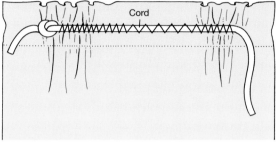

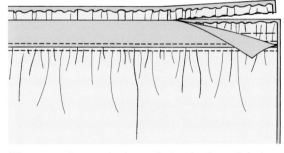

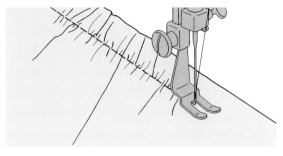

Zigzag stitching over a cord or heavy thread is useful if gathering a long strip or bulky fabric. Place cord ¼ in (6 mm) above seamline; use widest zigzag stitch over cord. Pull on cord to form gathers.

Hand stitching can be used to gather small areas or very delicate fabrics. Using small, even running stitches, hand-sew at least two rows. To gather, gently pull unknotted ends of threads.

A gathering foot automatically gathers. The longer the stitch, the more closely the fabric will be gathered. Determine the amount of fabric needed by measuring a sample before and after gathering.

Staying a gathered seam

A gathered seam often needs a stay to prevent stretching or fraying, to reinforce, or to add comfort. Stay can be woven seam binding, cotton tape, or narrow grosgrain ribbon. With gathered edge of seam up, place stay on seam allowances so that one edge is right next to permanent stitching.

Straight-stitch close to lower edge, through all thicknesses. Trim seam allowances even with the top edge of the stay. If fabric frays readily, zigzag-stitch or serge seam allowances to the stay. Press in correct direction.

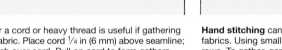

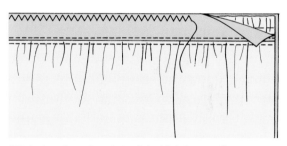

Trim seam to be stayed only once the tape has been stitched on.

Stitch along top edge of stay if the fabric frays easily.

Joining one gathered edge to another

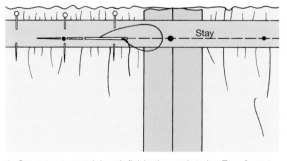

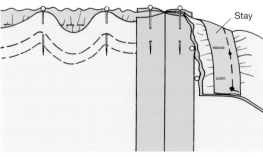

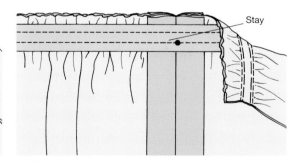

1. Cut a stay to match length finished seam is to be. Transfer pattern markings to stay and pin to wrong side of one section, matching markings. Gather section and baste to tape.

2. Pin ungathered section to section gathered in Step 1, right sides together, matching all markings. Gather second section to fit first one, and baste in place.

3. Stitch through all layers, including stay tape, on seamline. Stitch a second row ¼ in (6 mm) into seam allowances. Press seam allowances in one direction with stay uppermost.

Shirring

Shirring is formed with multiple rows of gathering and is primarily a decorative way of controlling fullness. In contrast to gathering, in which fullness is controlled within a seam, the fullness in shirring is controlled over a comparatively wide span.

Lightweight fabrics and easy-care fabrics are the most appropriate for shirring. Voiles, batistes, crepes, and jerseys are excellent choices.

Your pattern should specify the areas to be shirred; these can range from a small part to an entire

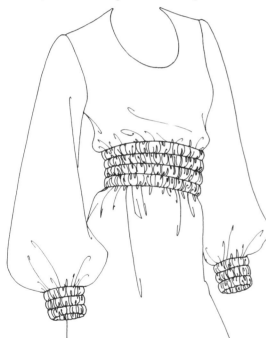

A shirred waist and shirred cuffs give a special flair to an otherwise simple dress.

garment section. Rows of shirring must be straight, parallel, and equidistant. They may be as close together as ¼ in (6 mm) or as far apart as an inch or so (2 or 3 cm), depending on personal preference and pattern specifications. Width to be shirred is set by the pattern.

How to shirr fabric

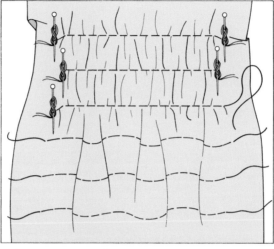

1. Stitch repeated rows of gathering stitches over section to be shirred, spacing rows an equal distance apart. Gather each row separately by pulling on bobbin thread. Measure first row when shirred. Make sure to gather all further rows to the same length.

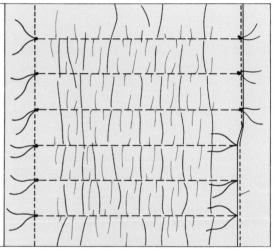

2. Secure rows, after all have been gathered, by tying the thread ends on each row; then place a line of machine stitching across the ends of all rows. If ends of shirred area will not be stitched into a seam, enclose the thread ends in a small pin tuck.

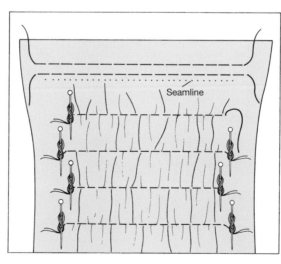

If shirring is to be joined to a flat piece, first place gathering stitches in seam allowance, one row just inside seamline and a second ¼ in (6 mm) above. Stitch rows for shirring, and shirr to desired width. Gather and attach seam as specified in basic procedure for gathering (p. 120).

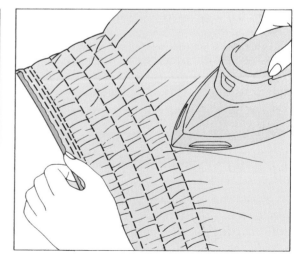

3. The fullness produced by shirring should be pressed with great care; if it is not, the weight of the iron will flatten the folds and ruin the intended effect. Press on the wrong side, into the fullness, with just the point of the iron. Do not press into the shirred area itself.

Uneven slipstitch 81

Staying a shirred area

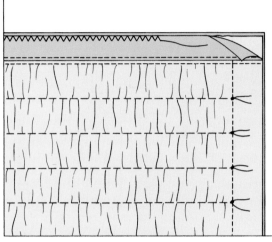

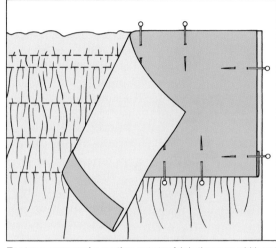

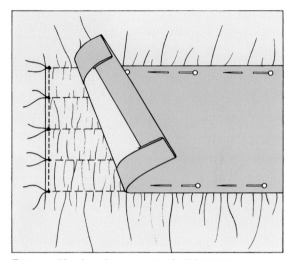

To stay a seam only, the procedure is exactly like that for a gathered seam (p. 121). Position stay tape over shirred side of untrimmed seam allowance, keeping edge just next to seamline. Stitch lower edge of tape; trim seam allowance even with top edge, then zigzag through all layers.

To stay a seam and a section, cut stay fabric the same width and ½ in (1.25 cm) deeper than shirred section. Pin stay to wrong side of shirred area, turning under lower edge and keeping seam edges even; baste. Stitch stay into seams when garment sections are joined; secure lower edge to last row of gathering.

To stay a shirred section, cut a strip of self-fabric 1 in (2.5 cm) wider and deeper than shirring. Turn in raw edges ½ in (1.25 cm) on all sides; pin in place to the wrong side of shirred area. Hand-sew the stay in place with small, invisible stitches. A stay will protect the shirred area from strain.

Elasticized shirring

This stretchy, flexible form of shirring, which hugs the body neatly, is easily done by using elastic thread in the bobbin and regular thread in the needle. Wind the elastic thread on the bobbin, stretching it slightly, until the bobbin is almost full.

Set the machine to a 6-7 stitch length (4 mm), and test the results on a scrap of your fabric. Adjust stitch length and tension if necessary. To get the desired fullness, the bobbin (elastic) thread may have to be pulled after stitching, as in gathering.

Mark the rows of shirring on the right side of the garment. As you sew, hold the fabric taut and flat by stretching the fabric in previous rows to its original size. To secure ends, draw the needle thread through to the underside and tie. Run a line of machine stitching across all the knots or hold them with a narrow pin tuck at each end of the shirred section.

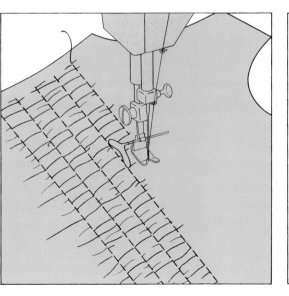

Shirring with cord

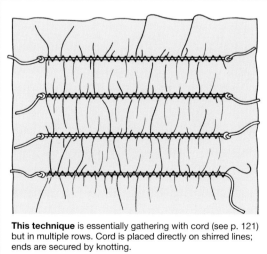

This technique is essentially gathering with cord (see p. 121) but in multiple rows. Cord is placed directly on shirred lines; ends are secured by knotting.

Christening dress

Fabrics: Rocle, Tartare (France)

Fabrics

Lightweight cotton or cotton blend such as batiste, lawn, voile. A woven stripe in overskirt fabric adds contrast and facilitates smocking.

Amount

For size 3 mos:
Plain fabric: 1 yd (0.9 m) of 58-60 in (150 cm) -width fabric
striped fabric: 1 yd (0.9 m) of 58-60 in (150 cm) -width fabric

Notions

⅜ yd (35 cm) fine elastic, ⅜ in (1 cm) width
6 buttons
Embroidery thread for smocking

Pattern pieces ▶▶▶▶▶▶▶▶▶▶▶▶▶▶▶

Plain fabric:
1 Sleeve – cut 2
2 Bow ties – cut 4
3 Front skirt panel – cut 1 on fold
4 Back skirt panel – cut 2
Striped fabric:
5 Bodice center front – cut 1 on fold
6 Bodice side front – cut 2
7 Bodice back – cut 2
8 Collar – cut 6
9 Overskirt panel – cut 1 on fold
Burda pattern 3039 was modified for this project into a one-piece dress with smocked center front bodice section and an overskirt 4 in (10 cm) shorter than the dress. It closes with buttons down the back.

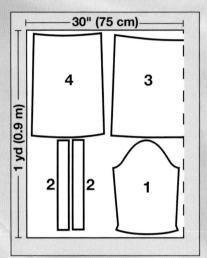

30" (75 cm)

1 yd (0.9 m)

4   3

2 2   1

Plain fabric

30" (75 cm)

1 yd (0.9 m)

9

7   6   8   8

5

Striped fabric

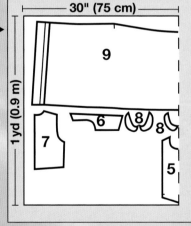

Smocking is an especially appealing way to embellish clothing. Popular areas for this type of decorative stitching include yokes, bodices, and cuffs — always before the garment is constructed.

Cutting

From folded fabric, cut a rectangle three times the width and as long as pattern piece no. 5 for the smocking piece.

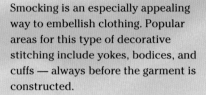

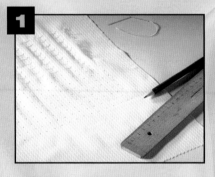

Smocking

● There are many ways to mark fabric with dots for smocking: with graph paper, ruler and pencil, transfer paper, or a pleating machine; by counting threads; or by using lines or squares in the fabric. Mark entire bodice piece with dots $\frac{3}{8}$ in (1 cm) apart.

● **Gauging (advance gathering):** Begin on the top row of dots. Secure the thread. Taking small stitches under dots, baste along each row. Draw up two rows at a time to make tiny pleats (Fig. 2; see also pp. 126–127).

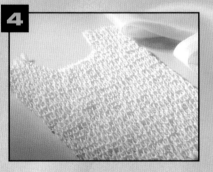

● Working from left to right, connect two folds at the dots using two backstitches. Take the next stitch at the next dot in the row below and connect these two folds again with two backstitches. Continue at the next dot over in the row above.

● Smock the entire bodice in this way (Fig. 3). Do not pull the threads

in the folds too tight otherwise the smocked bodice will not stretch.

● Place the pattern piece for the center front on the smocked fabric and cut (Fig. 4).

Sewing instructions

● **Bodice:** Pin and stitch bodice side fronts to smocked front. Finish seams and press toward smocking.

● Make French seams to join the bodice front to backs at shoulders.

● Turn in center back bodice edges $1\frac{1}{4}$ in (3 cm) twice to inside and press. Staystitch neck edge.

● **Collar:** The two-part collar has three fabric layers, with one acting as interfacing. Pin layers together (two facing up, one down) and stitch around collar edges. Trim, notch, turn (two right sides out), and press collars. Join the two halves with a hand stitch on seam line at center front.

● Pin collar to neckline with ends even with back edges of bodice. Stitch to bodice and finish with a strip of bias fabric as a binding.

● Make French seams at bodice sides.

● **Skirts:** Sew seams of skirt and overskirt using French seams. Finish hem edges with narrow double-turned stitched hems.

● Gather (separately) the upper edge of the skirt and the overskirt using double rows of machine basting. Draw up bobbin threads to gather.

● Right sides together, pin overskirt waist edge to bodice waist edge

matching centers and adjusting gathers. Pin waist of main skirt on top, adjusting its gathers. Stitch through all three layers. Trim and finish seam; press seam up.

● **Sleeves:** Baste two gathering rows around each sleeve cap. Stitch the long sleeve seams closed. Pin sleeves into armholes, adjusting gathers. Stitch and finish.

● Turn under raw edge of sleeve ends, then press under 2 in (5 cm) to form the wrist ruffle. Stitch $1\frac{1}{2}$ in (4 cm) from the edge and again almost 2 in (5 cm) from the edge, catching turned-in edge and leaving gap for inserting elastic.

● **Closing:** Make buttonholes in back overlap and sew buttons to underlap.

Grain in fabric 56–57

Smocking

Smocking consists of fabric folds that are decoratively stitched together at regular intervals to create a patterned effect. The folds may be pulled in as the stitching is done, or the fabric may be first gathered into folds and then smocked (see **Gauging,** below). You can also use a pleating machine to prepare the fabric for smocking. Lightweight and crisp fabrics are best, but almost any fabric can be smocked. You will need two and one-half to three times the desired finished width; patterns specify fabric required.

Smocking is done before the garment is constructed. Popular areas for smocking are yokes, bodices, pockets, sleeves, and waistlines. Smocking is based on a grid of evenly spaced dots (see **Stitching guide,** below); stitch variety is achieved by joining dots at differing points. If a fabric like gingham is used, its pattern can serve as a guide in place of the grid.

A decorative thread such as six-strand embroidery cotton is best for smocking; the colors can match or complement the fabric. Smocking can be simulated using decorative stitches provided by sewing machines.

Stitching guide

The stitching guide or pattern may be purchased as an iron-on transfer, or you can make your own. Rows of dots should align with the fabric grain.

Typical use of smocking shows decorative effect.

Gauging (advance gathering)

Taking small stitches under dots, baste along each row. Leave one end loose; draw up two rows at a time to desired width. Dots will appear at tops of folds.

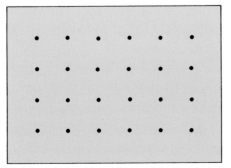

Mark the dots to guide stitching on right side of fabric.

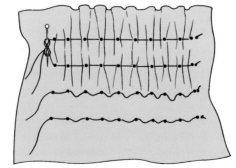

Smock at dots; when finished, remove gathering stitches.

Cable stitch

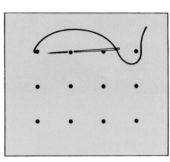

1. Bring the needle up from underside at first dot. Keeping thread above the needle, take a short stitch through fabric under second dot and draw fabric up.

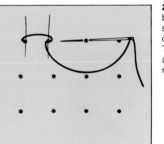

2. Keeping thread below needle, take a short stitch under third dot. Draw up fabric. To keep folds even, always pull thread at right angle to stitch.

3. On fourth dot, keep thread above needle. Alternate in this way until the row is finished. Try to keep folds even when drawing up stitch.

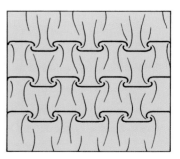

4. Repeat the same procedure for each subsequent row, alternating thread above and below needle in matching pattern dots. This will make rows exact duplicates, as this pattern requires.

Honeycomb stitch

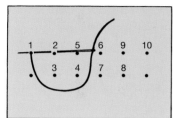

1. Work from left to right with needle pointing left. Bring the needle out at dot (1), then take a small stitch at dot (2), and another at dot (1); pull thread taut.

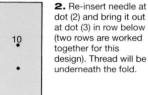

2. Re-insert needle at dot (2) and bring it out at dot (3) in row below (two rows are worked together for this design). Thread will be underneath the fold.

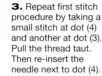

3. Repeat first stitch procedure by taking a small stitch at dot (4) and another at dot (3). Pull the thread taut. Then re-insert the needle next to dot (4).

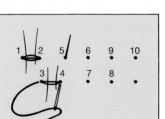

4. Pass the needle up from dot (4) to dot (5) in the upper row, and continue to repeat the pattern until the whole row is finished. End stitching in the bottom row.

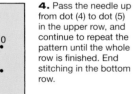

5. This stitch produces long floats on wrong side. A stay will prevent snagging of the floats during wear. Apply the stay the same as for a shirred section (see p. 123).

Wave stitch

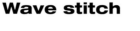

1. Bring the needle up from the underside at dot (1). Keeping thread above the needle, take a stitch at dot (2). Pull thread tight to complete stitch.

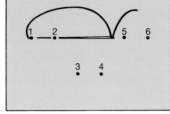

2. Take next stitch at dot (3) in second row (in this design, two rows are worked together); draw the thread through.

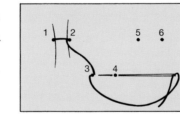

3. Keeping the thread below needle, take a stitch under dot (4) and draw stitches together by pulling thread up. The thread emerges from inside the stitch.

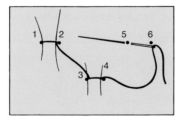

4. Return to first row by taking complete stitch at dot (5). Keep thread above needle when picking up dot (6). Draw stitches together. Continue to end of that row.

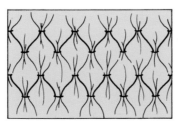

5. Repeat for all pairs of rows, with thread above the needle on upper rows and below needle on lower rows.

Smocked effect by machine

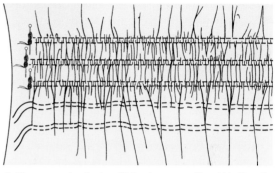

1. Place rows of gathering stitches in groups of two ¼ in (6 mm) apart. Repeat paired rows as required by size of smocked area, spacing them ¾ in (2 cm) apart. Gather each group.

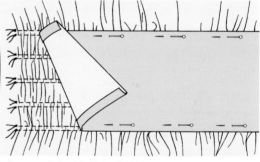

2. Cut an underlay 1 in (2.5 cm) wider than the shirred area; fold under long raw edges ½ in (1.25 cm) and pin or baste it to the wrong side.

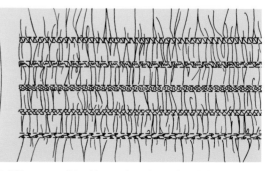

3. With garment right side up, place decorative stitching between the ¼ in (6 mm) rows of shirring. Striking effects can be created using different patterns and thread colors.

Grain in fabrics 56–57 · Cutting and joining bias strips 262–263

Ruffles and flounces — types of ruffle

A ruffle is a strip of fabric cut or handled in such a way as to produce fullness. Ruffles are of two types, **straight** and **circular.** The straight ruffle is cut as a strip of fabric; the circular ruffle is cut from a circle. With the straight ruffle, both edges are the same length and the fullness is produced through gathering or pleating. For the circular ruffle, a small circle is cut

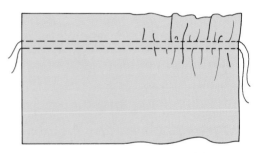

Straight ruffles are gathered to produce fullness.

from the center of a larger one and the inner edge forced to lie straight, producing fullness on the outer, longer edge. Soft, lightweight fabrics ruffle best.

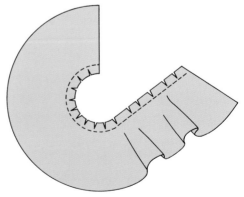

Circular ruffles are specially cut to produce fullness.

A general rule for deciding the proper relation between ruffle width and fullness: the wider the ruffle (or the sheerer the fabric), the fuller the ruffle should be.

Straight ruffles

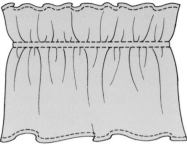

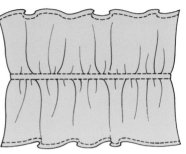

A plain ruffle has one finished edge (usually a small hem); the other edge is gathered to size and then sewn into a seam or onto another unfinished edge.

A ruffle with a heading has both edges finished or hemmed. It is gathered at a specified distance from the top edge to give a gracefully balanced proportion.

A double ruffle is gathered in the center, halfway between the two finished edges. It is then topstitched through the center to the garment section.

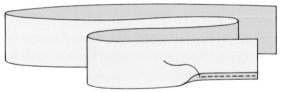

Single-layer ruffles are made from one layer of fabric and the edges finished with either a narrow machine or hand-rolled hem.

A self-faced ruffle is a single layer of fabric folded back on itself. It is used when both sides of a ruffle will be visible, or to give added body to sheer or flimsy fabrics.

Determining length

Finished length

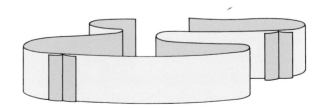

To determine length of fabric which will be needed for a ruffle, allow about three times the finished length for a fully gathered ruffle, twice the length for a ruffle that is slightly gathered. Straight ruffles are usually cut on either the crosswise or the bias grain.

Piecing of fabric strips is frequently necessary to achieve required length. Seam strips with right sides together, making sure sections match in pattern and direction of grain. On ruffles for sheer curtains, strips can be cut along the selvage to get maximum length without piecing and to avoid the necessity of hemming.

Single-layer straight ruffles

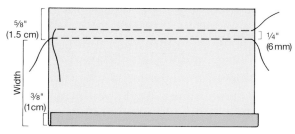

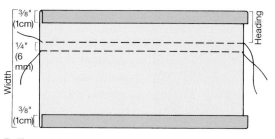

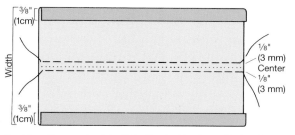

Plain ruffles can be any width. Cut strip to finished width plus 1 in (2.5 cm). This allows for ⅝ in (1.5 cm) seam allowance and ⅜ in (1 cm) hem. Make hem first (see Hemming, below). Then place two rows of gathering stitches ¼ in (6 mm) apart, inside seam allowance. Pull bobbin threads to gather.

Ruffles with headings require a fabric strip ¾ in (2 cm) wider (for hems) than the finished width. Make a ⅜ in (1 cm) hem on each edge (see Hemming, below). Determine width of heading; place first gathering row that distance from one edge. The second row is placed ¼ in (6 mm) below. Gather to size.

Double ruffles require strips ¾ in (2 cm) wider than ruffle is to be. Make a ⅜ in (1 cm) hem on each edge (see Hemming, below). Place gathering rows at the center of the strip, one ⅛ in (3 mm) below and the other ⅛ in (3 mm) above the center line. Stitch so bobbin thread is on right side of ruffle.

Hemming single-layer ruffles

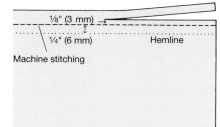

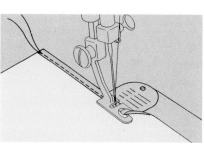

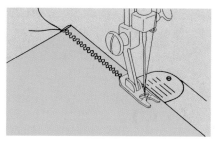

To hem edge by hand: 1. First machine-stitch ¼ in (6 mm) above marked hemline. Trim hem allowance to ¼ in (6 mm). Fold hem to wrong side, so that the stitch line shows.

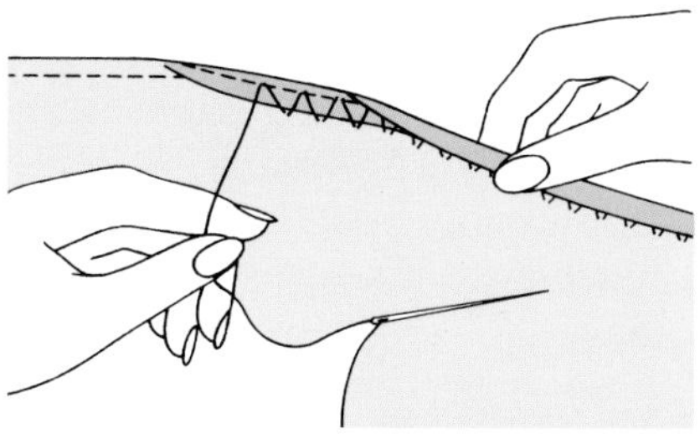

2. Working right to left, take small stitch through fold; then, ⅛ in (3 mm) below and beyond that stitch, catch a few threads of ruffle. Pull thread to roll hem to wrong side.

Machine hems can be made to look very much like hand-rolled hems with the help of a hemmer foot attachment. Check machine instruction manual for specific directions.

Decorative machine stitching can be placed on a turned-back hem edge to both hold and finish it, or it can be applied along a raw, unturned edge using an overlock machine.

Self-faced ruffles

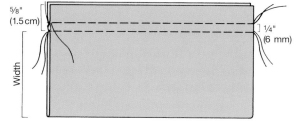

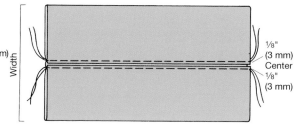

Plain self-faced ruffles: Fold a double width of fabric in half, wrong sides together. Cut strip twice as wide as ruffle is to be, plus 1¼ in (3 cm) (⅝ in [1.5 cm] seam allowance on each layer). After folding strip, stitch gathering rows and pull threads.

Ruffles with headings: Fold a fabric strip double the intended width with wrong sides together, so edges meet on underside at desired depth of heading. Where edges meet, sew two rows of stitches, ¼ in (6 mm) apart, each holding a raw edge in place.

Double ruffles to be self-faced require strips exactly twice desired finished width. Fold fabric, wrong sides together, so edges meet at center line. Pin. Stitch gathering rows ¼ in (6 mm) apart (⅛ in [3 mm] from each edge). Have bobbin thread on right side; it aids gathering.

Curtains

Fabrics
Cotton or cotton blends

Amount
For a pair of curtain panels with a finished length of 3 yd (2.7 m) including a self-faced ruffle 12 in (30 cm) deep: 7³/₄ yd (7.1 m) of 58/60 in (150 cm) -width fabric, for a curtain length of 6 ft 6 in (2 m) and a ruffle length of 27¹/₂ in (70 cm)

Notions
10 ft (3 m) curtain gathering tape
Curtain hooks and runners

Pattern pieces
1 Curtain – cut 2 lengths of 2³/₄ yd (2.55 m)
2 Ruffles – cut 3 lengths of 25¹/₂ in (65 cm)
These curtains are hung on a traverse rod. Hooks are fastened directly to curtain tape and then into runners.

Ruffles are a popular decoration on clothing and home textiles alike. These curtains are made with self-faced ruffles. The length of the ruffle is adjustable; in this project, they have a finished length of 12 in (30 cm).

Estimating fabric needs

Two measurements are especially important for estimating fabric needs for window coverings: the finished length and the finished width. To calculate the finished length, measure from the top of the rod or track to the level where the hem will fall. Standard choices are to the sill, base of window trim, or to the floor. Then add the hem and heading allowances. The curtains shown here touch the floor.

Narrow windows will require only single panels as shown here, whereas wider windows will need two or more panels joined by a self-enclosed seam.

To determine the width, measure the entire span of the rod or track. To ensure that your curtain has enough fullness, double the finished width figure. Then add the side hem and panel seam allowances.

This curtain project adds 1¼ in (3 cm) for each side seam, 4 in (10 cm) for the heading, and 1 in (2.5 cm) for the hem.

In this project, the ruffle width before gathering is 1.5 times the curtain width. Cut three strips across the fabric, each 25½ in (65 cm) long. Cut one in half; use one and a half strips for each ruffle.

Sewing instructions

● **Side hems:** Fold in the side edges of the curtain twice, ⅝ in (1.5 cm) each time. Press and stitch close to inner fold (Fig. 1).

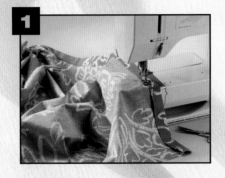

● **Ruffles:** With right sides together, use a self-enclosed seam to join the two parts. Finish the side hems as shown above.

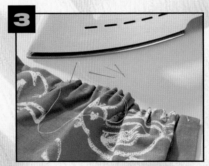

● With right sides together, fold each ruffle strip in half down its length.
● Stitch the long edge together (Fig. 2).
● Turn the ruffle right side out and press stitched edge.

● Machine baste two rows of gathering stitches close together about ⅜ in (1 cm) from seamed edge. Draw up the pair of threads from each end to form gathers.
● Finish the lower edge of the curtain with a narrow hem.
● Lap the gathered ruffle on the lower edge of the curtain ⅜ in (1 cm) from the bottom edge, and pin, adjusting gathers. Stitch the ruffle at

⅜ in (1 cm), making sure that the gathers are evenly distributed.

Remove pins and re-check length before completing top of curtain.

● **Heading:** Fold under the upper edge of the curtain at 4 in (10 cm) and press.
● Turn in the raw edge 1 in (2.5 cm) and stitch close to this fold.
● Cut the gathering tape the width of the curtain adding 1¼ in (3 cm) to each side. Pull out the gathering cord at each end. Fold under the tape ends even with curtain edges.
● Pin the cord tape about 1¼ in (3 cm) from the upper edge of the heading on the wrong side of the curtain.
● Stitch the cord tape close to both edges, making sure that the cord remains free on the ends. Pull the cords on both sides until the curtain has the desired width (Fig. 5).

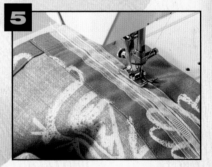

● Knot the cord tape ends together and tuck the rest of the cord tape inside the casing. Attach curtain hooks into tape at regular intervals.

Gathering 120–121 · Collars 162

Plain ruffles and flounces — stitching a plain ruffle into a seam

To sew a ruffle into a seam, first hem or face the ruffle strip; next pin the ungathered strip to one garment section; then gather the ruffle to fit and permanently stitch in place. The adjoining garment section is then sewn on over the ruffle.

Special care must be taken with the ruffle seam allowance so that its extra fullness does not cause bulk in the completed seam. Before attaching the second garment section, press the seam allowance flat. After attaching, the seam should be carefully graded, clipped, and notched.

The finished seam should be pressed so that the seam allowance of the ruffle is not pressed back onto the ruffle, where it would distort the ruffle's hang.

Stitching a ruffle to curves or corners

Ruffles must frequently be sewn into curved seams or sharp corners. In such cases, the ungathered ruffle must be pinned to the garment piece with extra fullness provided at the curve or corner. This allows for the greater distance that the ruffle's outer edge must span. After stitching, the fullness within the seam allowance should be carefully graded and notched out.

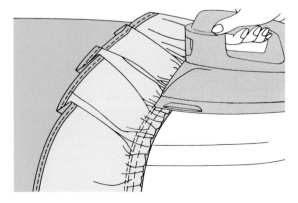

1. Pin-mark the prepared ruffle strip and the garment edge to which it will be joined into an equal number of parts. Right sides together, match and pin ruffle to garment at markings. Gather ruffle to fit edge, distributing fullness evenly.

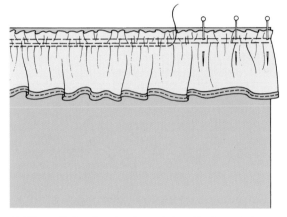

2. When ruffle is gathered to size and pinned in place, stitch it to garment section on seamline. Stitch with ruffle up and hold work in such a way that the gathers are not sewn into little pleats.

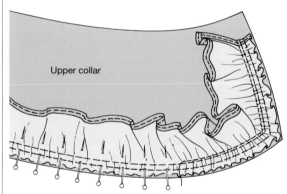

1. When attaching a hemmed ruffle, remember that the right side of the ruffle must show on the completed garment. If the garment piece is a collar, have right side of ruffle against right side of upper collar as you stitch.

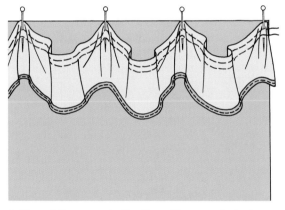

3. Press seam before joining to the second garment section to prevent lumps or uneven stitching. Using just the point of the iron, press ruffle edge flat. Do not let the iron go beyond the stitch line.

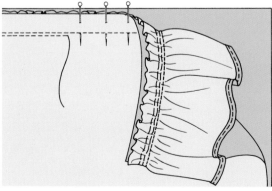

4. Pin edge with ruffle attached to second seam edge, right sides together, so ruffle is between the two garment sections. Stitch a thread width from first seam.

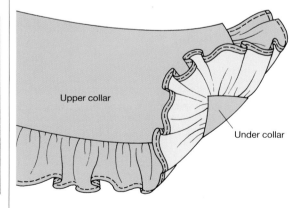

2. As the under and upper collar are being joined, the ruffle will be between the two garment sections. The final stitching should be done slightly outside any other stitching.

Slipstitch 74, 80 · Reducing seam bulk 87 · Bias strips 262–263

Stitching a plain ruffle to an edge

Attaching headed or double ruffles

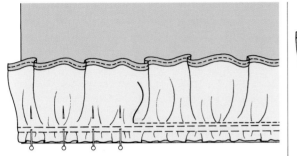

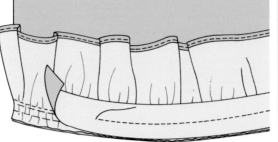

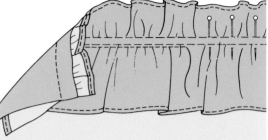

To attach a ruffle to a straight edge: 1. Pin the ungathered strip to the straight edge, gather it to fit, then permanently stitch in place. Trim the seam allowance of the ruffle only to ⅛ in (3 mm), leaving other seam allowances intact.

To stitch a ruffle to a curved edge: 1. Proceed as for gathering ruffle to edge; baste in place. Place right side of a 1¼ in (3 cm) -wide bias strip to wrong side of ruffle, raw edges even. Stitch through all thicknesses on seamline.

If ruffle is at an edge: 1. Place wrong side of ungathered ruffle against wrong side of garment, matching bottom row of gathering stitches to seamline on garment. Gather ruffle to fit; stitch, with the ruffle up, along the seamline.

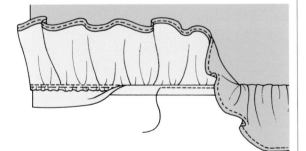

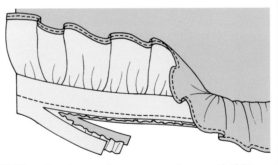

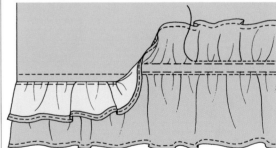

2. Fold untrimmed seam allowance under ⅛ in (3 mm), then fold again so that cut edge of ruffle is enclosed and inside fold of seam allowance is on seamline. Pin in place and topstitch along edge at stitch line through seam allowances only.

2. Trim and grade seam allowances, removing as much of the bulk of the ruffle seam allowance as possible. Bias strips are recommended here because they shape around curves better than the straight seam allowance could.

2. Trim seam allowance of garment to ⅛ in (3 mm). Turn ruffle to outside of garment and topstitch in place along top row of gathering stitches. The seam allowance will be completely enclosed by the second line of stitching.

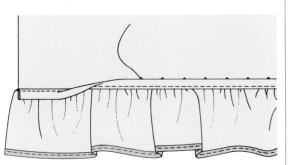

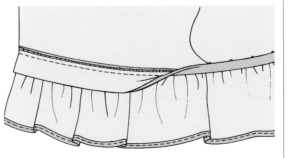

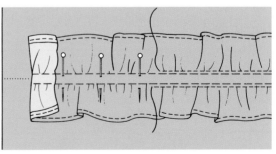

3. Turn ruffle away from straight edge and press the finished seam allowance toward garment. To be sure seam allowance will stay in that position, slipstitch the finished edge to the garment.

3. Turn ruffle away from edge toward garment and press the seam allowance flat. Turn under remaining raw edge of bias strip ¼ in (6 mm) and slipstitch to garment.

If ruffle is not at an edge, first mark desired location for ruffle on right side. Pin ungathered ruffle to garment, gather to fit, and topstitch to garment. Stitch just alongside the gathering stitches.

STITCHES AND SEAMS

Grain in fabric 56–57

Circular ruffles

The deep fullness and the fluid look of circular ruffles are created by the way the fabric is cut, not by means of gathering stitches. They are especially effective at necklines and when made of sheer, filmy fabrics. To make circular ruffles, a paper pattern is essential. Measure the length of the edge to which ruffle will be attached; this will be the circumference of the inner circle. Next, decide the width of the ruffle; this will be the distance between the inner and outer circles.

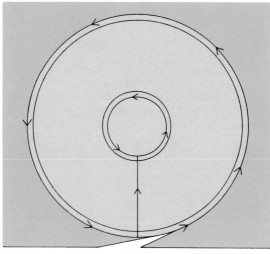

On paper, draw the inner circle first. Draw outer circle at width of ruffle. Add ⅝ in (1.5 cm) at edge of each circle.

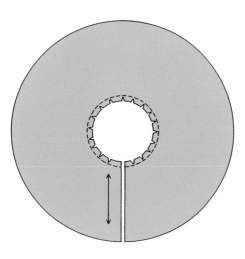

Cut fabric along the outermost circle first. Then cut on grainline to the innermost circle and cut it out.

Staystitch the inner circle on seamline. Clip the seam allowance repeatedly until the inner edge can be pulled out straight.

Piecing to achieve length

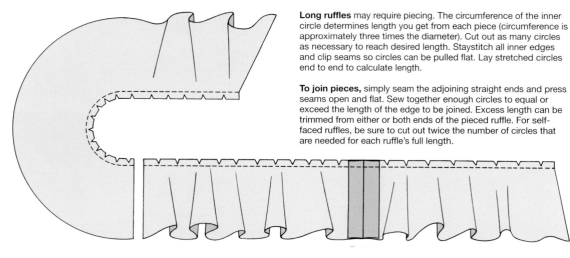

Long ruffles may require piecing. The circumference of the inner circle determines length you get from each piece (circumference is approximately three times the diameter). Cut out as many circles as necessary to reach desired length. Staystitch all inner edges and clip seams so circles can be pulled flat. Lay stretched circles end to end to calculate length.

To join pieces, simply seam the adjoining straight ends and press seams open and flat. Sew together enough circles to equal or exceed the length of the edge to be joined. Excess length can be trimmed from either or both ends of the pieced ruffle. For self-faced ruffles, be sure to cut out twice the number of circles that are needed for each ruffle's full length.

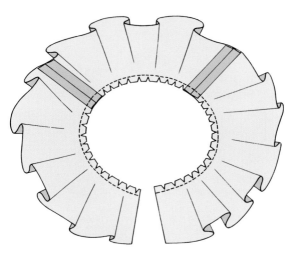

Understitching 87 · Neckline finishes 139–141

Finishing the outer edge

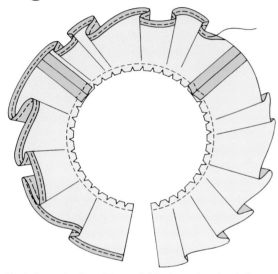

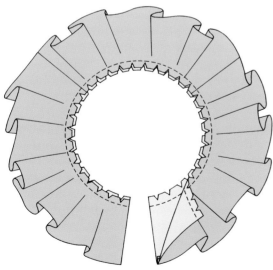

Single-layer circular ruffles are finished on outer edge, before attaching, with a narrow machine hem or serger blind hem. This creates a definite "right" and "wrong" side.

Self-faced circular ruffles require duplicate circles, or two identical pieced strips. With right sides together, stitch along outer edge. Trim seam and turn to right side.

Attaching to a garment

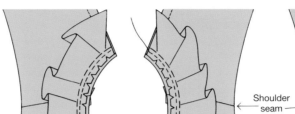

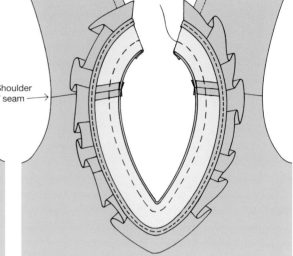

Shoulder seam

1. Place wrong side of ruffle against right side of garment with the ruffle seam allowance flat and smooth (additional clips may be required). Baste layers together.

2. Join facing sections and seam-finish outer edge. Match facing to garment edge, seams and notches aligned. Baste, then stitch, reinforcing point with short stitches.

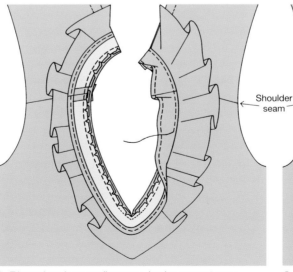

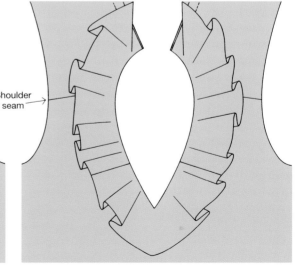

Shoulder seam

3. Trim and grade seam allowances, leaving garment seam allowance the widest. Clip seam allowances to stitching. Understitch to keep facing from rolling to right side.

4. Turn facing to inside, finish ends, and baste to zipper. Turn the ruffle away from garment when pressing neckline seam; do not press ruffle flat onto the garment.

CHAPTER 4

NECKLINE FINISHES AND COLLARS

A neckline finish or collar is a focus point for your garment and calls for special care in sewing. There are many ways to finish necklines and many different types of collars — from a simple facing to a standing collar.

Neckline facings

A facing is the fabric used to finish raw edges of a garment at such locations as neck, armhole, and front and back openings. There are three categories: shaped facings, extended facings (essentially shaped facings), and bias facings.

A facing is shaped to fit the edge it will finish either during cutting or just before application. A **shaped facing** is cut out, using a pattern, to the same shape and on the same grain as the edge it will finish. A **bias facing** is a strip of fabric cut on the bias so that it can be shaped to match the curve of the edge it will be applied to. After a facing is attached to the garment's edge, it is turned to the inside of the garment and should not show on the outside.

To reduce bulk, shaped and bias facings can be cut from a fabric lighter in weight than the garment fabric. The extended facing is cut as one with the garment and so garment and facing fabric are always the same.

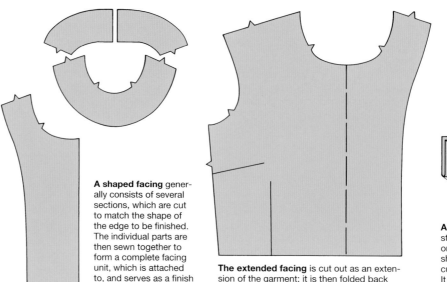

A shaped facing generally consists of several sections, which are cut to match the shape of the edge to be finished. The individual parts are then sewn together to form a complete facing unit, which is attached to, and serves as a finish for, the raw edge.

The extended facing is cut out as an extension of the garment; it is then folded back along the edge it finishes.

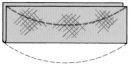

A bias facing is a narrow strip of lightweight fabric cut on the bias so that it can be shaped to conform to the curve of the edge it will finish. It is less bulky and conspicuous than a shaped facing.

Interfacing necklines

Depending on pattern and fabric, it may be necessary or desirable to interface a garment neckline before applying the facing. Interfacing will help to define, support, and reinforce the shape of the neck.

The quickest method is to apply fusible interfacing to the neckline interfacing. The more traditional method involves applying interfacing directly to the garment neckline (shown below). If the pattern does not include separate pattern pieces for cutting out the interfacing, use the facing pattern pieces but trim away ½ in (1.25 cm) from the outer edges of the interfacing. When it is an extended facing, the inner edge of the interfacing may either meet the garment foldline or may extend ½ in (1.25 cm) beyond it into the facing portion. If edge and foldline meet, catch-stitch the edge to the foldline; if the edge extends, match the garment and interfacing foldlines and stitch the two together along the fold, using very short stitches approximately ½ in (1.25 cm) apart. If a zipper is to be inserted, reduce bulk of interfacing by trimming it away at the placket seamline.

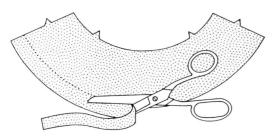

If the facing pattern was used to cut out interfacing pieces, trim ½ in (1.25 cm) from the outer edge of each.

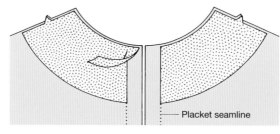

If zipper has not been applied to the garment, trim away the unnecessary interfacing along the placket seamline.

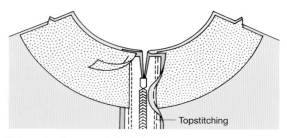

If zipper has been applied, trim interfacing along placket topstitching; position cut edges under seam allowances.

Pressing equipment 14 · Staystitching 84 · Seam finishes 88–89

Construction of shaped neckline facings

Shown and explained below are the three most typical examples of shaped neckline facings. Although they look different, they are similarly constructed. If any alterations have been made to the garment that affect the edges to be faced, be sure to alter facing and interfacing accordingly.

3. Keeping seam allowances open, apply a finish suitable to the fabric along the outer, unnotched edge of the facing unit. Some of the possible finishes are shown below. (Also see Seam finishes.)

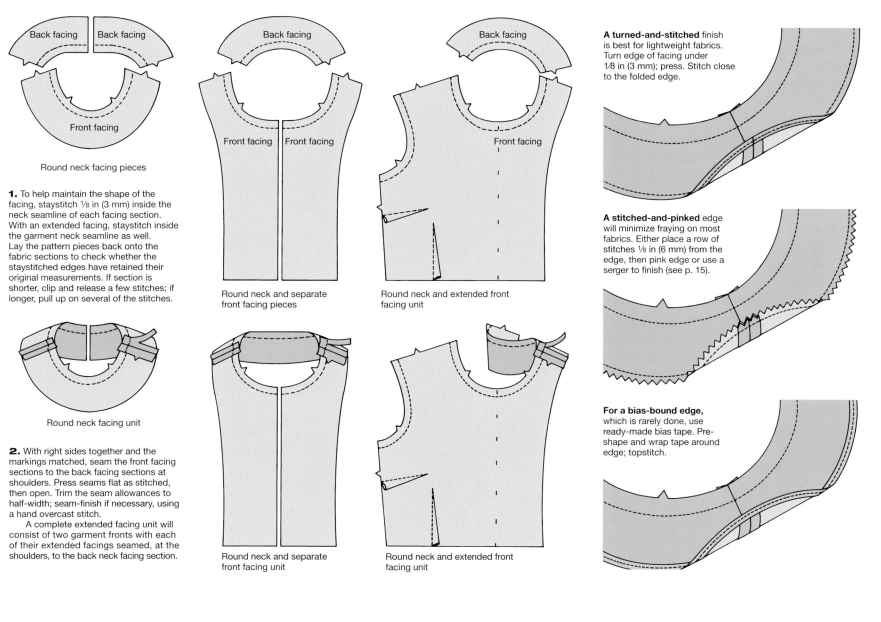

Round neck facing pieces

1. To help maintain the shape of the facing, staystitch ⅛ in (3 mm) inside the neck seamline of each facing section. With an extended facing, staystitch inside the garment neck seamline as well. Lay the pattern pieces back onto the fabric sections to check whether the staystitched edges have retained their original measurements. If section is shorter, clip and release a few stitches; if longer, pull up on several of the stitches.

Round neck facing unit

2. With right sides together and the markings matched, seam the front facing sections to the back facing sections at shoulders. Press seams flat as stitched, then open. Trim the seam allowances to half-width; seam-finish if necessary, using a hand overcast stitch.

A complete extended facing unit will consist of two garment fronts with each of their extended facings seamed, at the shoulders, to the back neck facing section.

Round neck and separate front facing pieces

Round neck and separate front facing unit

Round neck and extended front facing unit

Round neck and extended front facing unit

A turned-and-stitched finish is best for lightweight fabrics. Turn edge of facing under ⅛ in (3 mm); press. Stitch close to the folded edge.

A stitched-and-pinked edge will minimize fraying on most fabrics. Either place a row of stitches ⅛ in (6 mm) from the edge, then pink edge or use a serger to finish (see p. 15).

For a bias-bound edge, which is rarely done, use ready-made bias tape. Pre-shape and wrap tape around edge; topstitch.

Pressing equipment 14 · Reducing seam bulk 87 · Centered zippers 286–287 · Invisible zippers 290–291

Shaped neckline facings — applying shaped facing to neckline with zipper

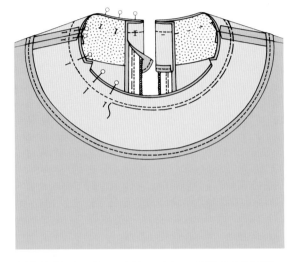

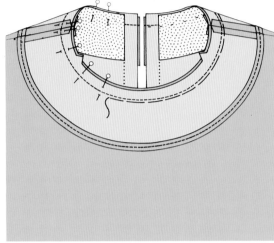

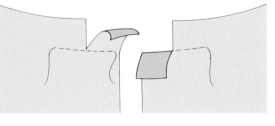

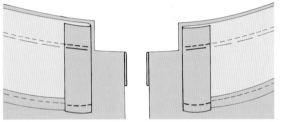

1. Right sides together, matching notches, markings, and seamlines, pin facing to neck. **If zipper has been inserted,** open zipper and wrap ends of facing to inside around each zipper half. Baste facing to garment along neck seamline.

If zipper has not been inserted, facing ends can be handled in two ways. To use the **first method,** shown above, keep center back seam allowances of both facing and garment extended; then pin and baste them together in this position.

In second method, reinforce neck seamline for ½ in (1.25 cm) on each side of center back seam. Clip seam allowance along center seamline to reinforcement stitches; fold ends down to inside of garment. Fold facing seam allowances back; baste.

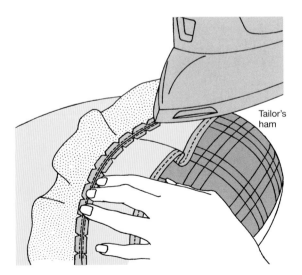

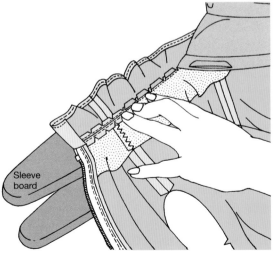

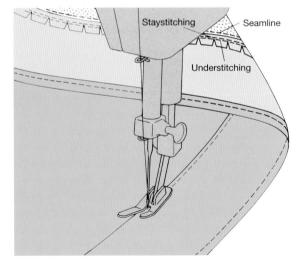

4. Place seam, wrong side up, over a tailor's ham. Using the tip of the iron, press seam open. Press carefully to prevent the seam edges from making an imprint on right side of garment.

5. From the wrong side, with facing extended away from the garment, place seam over a sleeve board and press all seam allowances toward facing. Steps 4 and 5 can be replaced by Step 6.

6. To keep facing from rolling to outside of garment, extend facing and seam allowances away from garment, stitch from right side close to neck seamline, through facing and seam allowances.

Whipstitch 73 · Cross-stitch basting (single) 75 · Uneven slipstitch 81 · Hook and eye fasteners 320

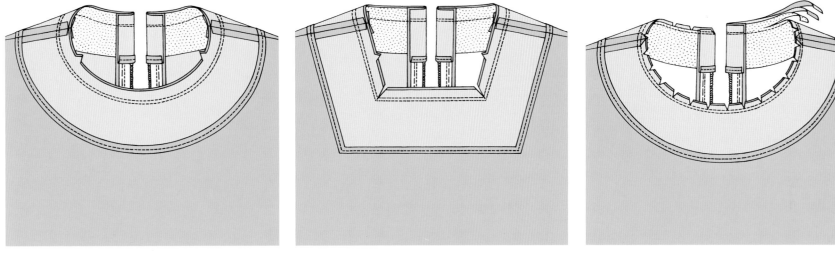

2. With facing side up, stitch facing to garment along the neck seamline; secure stitching at both ends. Check to be sure that the neck seamlines will align with each other when the zipper is closed. Remove basting. Press seam flat.

If it is a square neckline, apply the facing in the same way but reinforce the corners by using short stitches for 1 in (2.5 cm) on both sides of each corner. To relieve strain when facing is turned to inside of garment, clip into the corners.

3. Trim and grade seam allowances, making garment seam allowance the widest. Trim diagonally across center back seam allowances and cross-seam allowances at shoulders. Clip curved seam allowances. If not already in, insert zipper.

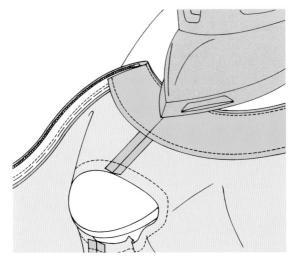

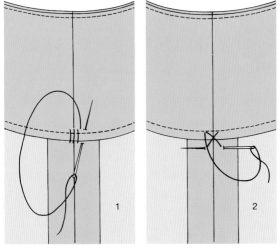

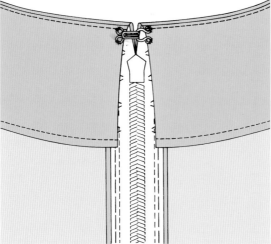

7. Turn facing to inside of garment, allowing seamline to roll inside slightly. Align facing and garment seamlines and center markings, then press along neck edge.

8. With facing and garment seamlines aligned at shoulders, baste facing in place. Use either whipstitches (1) or a cross-stitch tack (2), catching only facing edge and seam allowances of garment.

9. With ends folded under, pin facing to zipper tape. Open zipper and slipstitch facing to zipper tape. Close the zipper and attach the fastener at the top of the placket.

Pressing equipment 14 · Grain in fabric 56–57 · Separating zippers 291 · Bound buttonholes 300–311

Applying shaped facing to neckline and garment opening

The facing used for the opening may be a separate piece or an extended facing. Buttonholes are the usual closure. Bound buttonholes are constructed *before* facing is applied, machine buttonholes *after*.

Neck and separate front facing

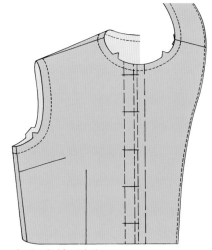

Neck and extended front facing

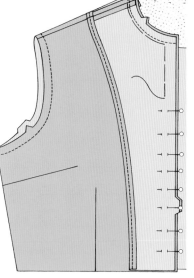

Neck and separate front facing

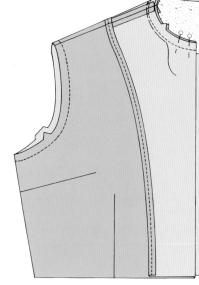

Neck and extended front facing

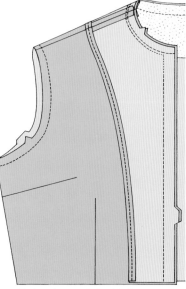

Neck and separate front facing

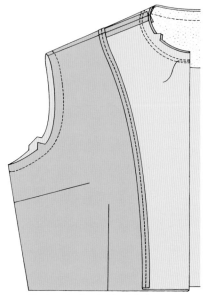

Neck and extended front facing

1. With right sides together, matching markings and notches, pin and baste the facing to the garment along the neck seamline. When it is a **separate front facing,** pin and baste down the opening edge. With an **extended facing,** the facing has been folded back onto the garment, producing a fold rather than a seam. In this situation, there is no need to match, pin, and baste.

2. Stitch facing to garment along the seamline. With the **separate front facing,** it may be advisable to stitch directionally, starting at center back and stitching to lower edge of front facing on each side. Reinforce corners formed by the neckline and opening edge seamlines, by taking small stitches for 1 in (2.5 cm) on both sides of each corner. With the **extended facing,** just the neck seamline is stitched; backstitch at both ends to secure stitching. After appropriate stitching, remove basting and press the seam flat as stitched. Do not press the fold of an extended facing.

Whipstitch 73 · Cross-stitch basting (single) 75 · Separating zippers 291 · Bound buttonholes 300–311

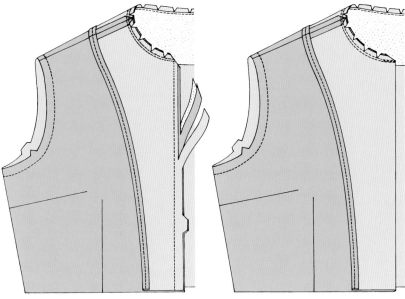

Neck and separate front facing   Neck and extended front facing

3. Trim, grade, and clip seam allowances, making garment seam allowance the widest. Trim diagonally across the seam allowances at the corners and cross-seams.

4. Place curved part of seam over a tailor's ham or a seam roll; for corners and straight part of seam, use a sleeve board. With tip of iron, press seam open.

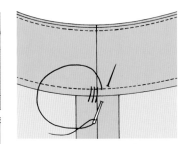

Tailor's ham

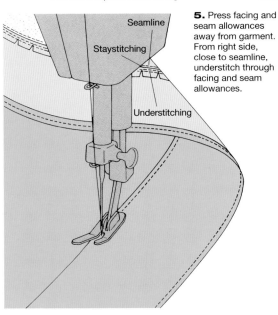

Seamline

Staystitching

Understitching

5. Press facing and seam allowances away from garment. From right side, close to seamline, understitch through facing and seam allowances.

6. Turn facing to the inside; align center markings and seamlines. Diagonal-baste along neck, if needed, to hold layers together; press.

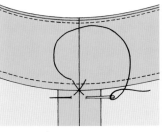

Basting with whipstitches

Cross-stitch tack

7. With seamlines and center markings aligned, baste facing to garment at shoulders, using either a whipstitch or a cross-stitch tack. Catch only the facing and the seam allowances of the garment. Finish the backs of bound buttonholes with the facing, or make machine buttonholes through garment and facing.

Pressing equipment 14 · Whipstitch 73 · Cross-stitch basting (single) 75 · Uneven Slipstitch 81 · Reducing seam bulk 87

Combination facings and bias facings

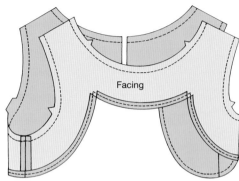

Facing

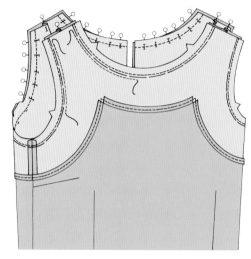

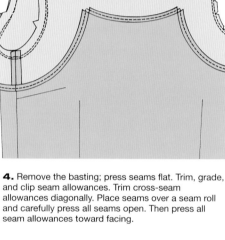

1. A combination facing is a shaped facing in which both the neck and armholes are finished by the same facing unit. Staystitch neck and armholes of both facing and garment. Construct facing unit and garment, leaving all the shoulder seams open. Zipper may be inserted before or after the facing is applied.

Garment

2. Pin a narrow tuck in fronts and backs of garment shoulders. This tuck will be released later.

3. Right sides together, pin and baste facing to garment along the neck and armhole seamlines of the facing. (For facing treatment at zipper placket, see p. 140.) Facing side up, stitch facing to garment, starting at shoulder seamlines.

4. Remove the basting; press seams flat. Trim, grade, and clip seam allowances. Trim cross-seam allowances diagonally. Place seams over a seam roll and carefully press all seams open. Then press all seam allowances toward facing.

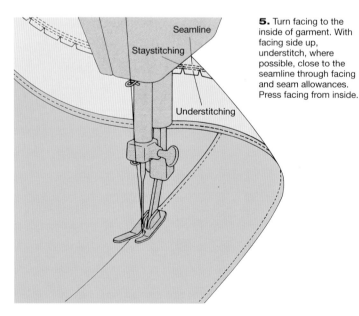

Seamline

Staystitching

Understitching

5. Turn facing to the inside of garment. With facing side up, understitch, where possible, close to the seamline through facing and seam allowances. Press facing from inside.

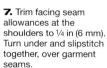

Garment

Facing

6. Release tucks at shoulders. With neck and armhole seam allowances folded back and the facing out of the way, baste then stitch the garment shoulder seams. Tie thread ends. Press seams flat, then open; push through opening.

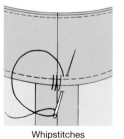

Whipstitches

8. Press facing at shoulder seams. With side seams aligned, baste the facing to garment seam allowances, using either a whipstitch or a cross-stitch tack. At zipper placket, slipstitch the turned-under facing ends to the zipper tapes. Attach fastener at top of placket.

7. Trim facing seam allowances at the shoulders to ¼ in (6 mm). Turn under and slipstitch together, over garment seams.

Cross-stitch tack

Constructing and applying a bias facing

A bias facing is a narrow rectangular strip of light-weight fabric, cut on the bias so that it can be shaped to conform to the curve of the edge it will be sewn to and finished. This shaping is done with a steam iron.

The bias facing is often used instead of a shaped facing on garments made of sheer or bulky fabrics or on knit garments. A conventional shaped facing, because of its width, might be too conspicuous on a garment made from sheer fabric; a shaped facing cut from garment fabric might be too bulky when the fabric is thick or heavy.

The finished width of a bias facing is generally from ½ to 1 in (1.25 to 2.5 cm). The *cut* width of the strip, however, must be twice the finished width plus two seam allowances. (The strip is folded in half lengthwise. The folding automatically gives the facing one finished edge.) The total length needed equals the length of the seamline of the edge being faced plus 2 in (5 cm) for ease and finishing.

Always insert the zipper before applying a bias facing.

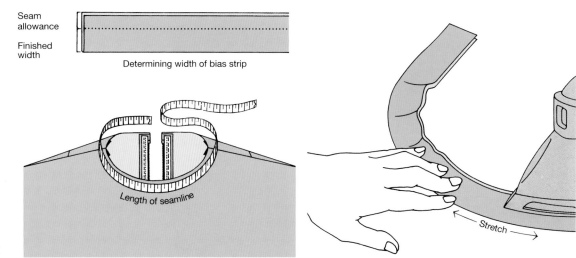

Seam allowance

Finished width

Determining width of bias strip

Length of seamline

Determining length of bias strip

Length and width. Bias strip should be twice the desired finished width plus two seam allowances, each the same width as the garment seam allowance. Length equals length of edge being faced plus 2 in (5 cm) for ease and finishing.

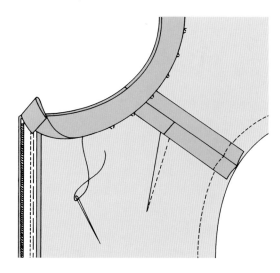

1. Cut out strip; fold it in half lengthwise. Using a steam iron, press strip flat. Shape by pressing again, stretching and curving folded edge to mold raw edges into curve that matches edge being faced. Keep raw edges even.

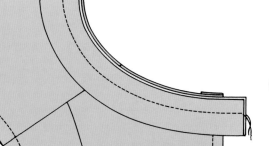

2. With all edges even, pin and baste facing to right side of garment. If edges of facing are slightly uneven from the shaping, trim and even them first. Stitch along seamline.

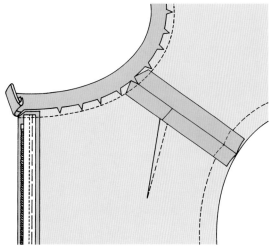

3. Trim and grade seam allowances. Clip seam; trim ends of bias to ¼ in (6 mm). Extend facing up and away from garment and press along seamline. Fold ends of facing to inside.

4. Turn the facing to inside of garment, letting the seamline roll slightly beyond the edge. Pin in place along folded edge. Slipstitch edge and ends of facing to inside of garment.

Summer dress

Dress fabric: Drews, Bad Säckingen (Germany).

Fabrics

Linen or cotton, viscose, silk

Amount

For size 12: $1^5/_8$ yd (1.5 m) of 58/60 in (150 cm) -width fabric without nap or one-way design

Notions

$1^1/_8$ yd (1.0 m) lightweight fusible interfacing, $23^1/_2$ (60 cm) width
1 zipper, 22 in (55 cm)
6 buttons, $^3/_4$ in (2 cm) diameter

Pattern pieces ▶▶▶▶▶▶▶▶▶▶▶▶▶

1 Bodice front – cut 1 on fold
2 Bodice back – cut 2
3 Front skirt panel – cut 2
4 Back skirt panel – cut 2
5 Front facing – cut 1 on fold
6 Back facing – cut 2
7 Sleeves – cut 2

Burda pattern 2933 has been modified to create this dress. Underarm darts are used instead of waist darts. An extension of 2 in (5 cm) has been added to the skirt center front pattern for facings. The front skirt is closed with six buttons and has no darts. The pattern can be altered further to include in-seam pockets (see p. 244).

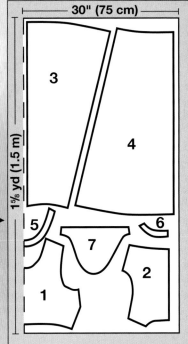

30" (75 cm)

$1^5/_8$ yd (1.5 m)

This dress has a mock button closing that gives a vertical line to the skirt front. It closes with a back zipper. The neckline is finished with shaped facings.

● **Preparing pattern pieces:** Cut interfacing to fit all neckline facings. Fuse to wrong side of each piece (Fig. 1). Cut strips of interfacing 2 in (5 cm) wide and long enough for skirt fronts.

Sewing instructions

● Finish the edges of all pattern pieces. Staystitch neck edge.
● **Facings:** Stitch together the shoulder seams of the neckline facings.
● Fold over facing on front edges of front skirt panels 2 in (5 cm), and press.
● **Skirt:** Lay the back skirt panels right sides together. Stitch the back center seam up to the zipper placket marking. Press the seam allowances open.
● Make the buttonholes on the right front skirt panel. For the correct buttonhole size, add ⅛ in (3 mm) to the button size.
● Mark the button positions on the

left side of the front skirt panel and sew on the buttons.
● Button up the front skirt panel. Stitch lapped edges together at top.
● Place the front and back skirt panels right sides together. Baste and stitch the side seams. Remove the basting. Press seam allowances open.
● **Front top:** Stitch the darts on the front top. Press downward (Fig. 2).
● Lay the back top on the front top, right sides together. Stitch shoulder seams. Press seam allowances open.
● Pin the shaped facing onto the neckline with right sides together, making sure to match the shoulder seams. Stitch the facing to the neckline while folding the seam allowances at the ends of the facing inward to allow for the zipper placket (Fig. 3). Clip the curves on the neckline seam.

● Turn the seam allowances toward the facing and understitch through all three layers close to seam. Grade the seam allowance. Press and tack to shoulder seams. Secure the facing on shoulder seams (Fig. 4).

● **Sleeves:** To gather the sleeve cap, stitch two closely spaced lines of machine basting on the upper sleeve edge. Pull the bobbin threads slightly to gather. The sleeves are attached using the shirt-sleeve method in which the open sleeve is sewn into the armhole before the garment side seams are stitched. Apply sleeves to armholes right sides together, matching notches and shoulder points. Stitch with bodice on top. Trim seams and finish edges together.

Turn seams toward sleeves. Stitch the side seams of sleeve and top in one continuous seam.
● Baste the top to the skirt, matching the side seams. Stitch. Remove basting threads, then press the seam

allowances upward. Press seam allowances of zipper placket to the inside.
● **Hem:** Fold the bottom skirt edge at 1½ in (3.5 cm) and finish the hem by hand using hemstitching (p. 82). Secure front edges to hem. Remove the basting.
● Fold the sleeve hems at ¾ in (2 cm) and baste. Stitch at approximately ⅝ in (1.5 cm) from the edge. Remove the basting.
● **Zipper:** Using a zipper foot, insert zipper in back opening so that top

end is ⅜ in (1 cm) below neck edge. Hand sew facing edges to zipper tape.

Corded seams 95 · Cutting and joining bias strips 262–263 · How to make piping and cording 264

Neckline finishes with cording

The application of cording, made from self- or contrasting fabric, gives a decorative finish to a neckline or other edges. There are two application methods for cording. The more common method is to stitch the cording to the garment and then apply a separate facing. The second requires a specially constructed cording made with knit fabric and is a combination cording and facing. The way the ends are finished depends on whether or not the neckline has a placket opening. If cording is applied to a neckline that does not have a placket, the finished neckline must be large enough to slip easily over the head.

Narrow or wide cord may be used as a filler for the cording. If a woven fabric is used to cover the cord, cut it on the bias; knit fabric can be cut on the cross or bias. If applying to a *neckline that will be*

faced, cut fabric for cording wide enough to encase the cord plus two seam allowances.

When using the *special knit combination* cording and facing, cut the fabric wide enough to encase the cord plus 1 in (2.5 cm). The length of cording needed for any application is the length of the neck seamline plus 1¼ in (3 cm). Before applying any cording, finish all garment details at the neck seamline.

Application of cording to faced neckline

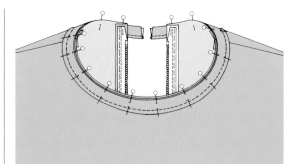

1. With zipper open, pin the cording to right side of garment, with cord just outside seamline and the cording stitch line just inside seamline. Leave excess cording at ends.

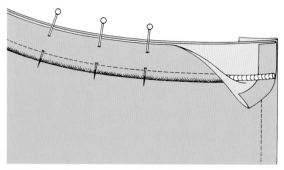

2. At ends, release enough of stitching holding cord to open fabric, then cut cord even with placket edges. Trim fabric ends to ¼ in (6 mm); fold in, even with cord; re-wrap around cord.

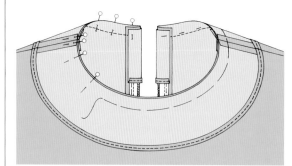

4. Construct facing unit (see p. 139). With right sides together, pin and baste facing to garment. Wrap ends of facing around zipper halves to inside of garment.

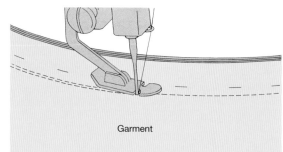

5. With wrong side of garment up, stitch facing to garment along seamline. Crowd stitching between cord and the row of stitching from Step 3. Secure thread ends. Remove basting.

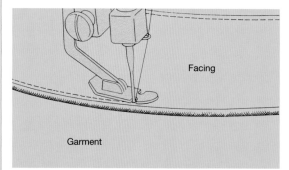

7. Extending facing and seam allowances away from garment, understitch along neck seamline. Use zipper foot; stitch from right side of facing, through all seam allowances.

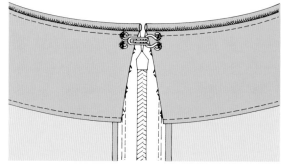

8. Turn facing to inside and press. Tack facing to garment at shoulders. Close ends of cording with hand stitches. Slipstitch facing ends to zipper tapes. Attach fastener at top.

Uneven slipstitch 81 · Trimming and grading seams 87 · Seam finishes 88–89 · Snap fasteners 322

Application of knit combination cording and facing

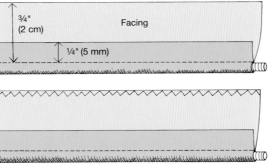

1. Wrap strip around cord as shown. Using a zipper foot, stitch close to cord. Seam-finish "facing" edge. Trim garment seam allowance to ¼ in (6 mm).

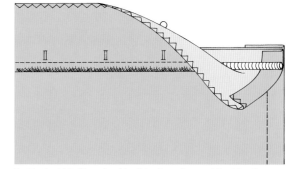

2. Pin the ¼ in (6 mm) -wide side of cording to right side of garment, aligning its edge with garment edge, its stitch line along garment seamline. Treat ends as on page 148, Step 2.

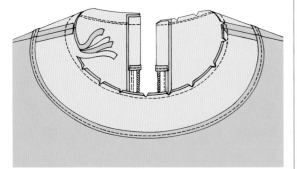

3. Baste cording to garment; remove pins. Using a zipper foot adjusted to right of needle, stitch cording to garment. Stitch between cord and the stitching encasing the cord.

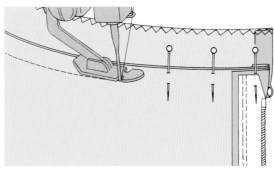

3. With wrong side of garment up, and the zipper foot adjusted to right of needle, stitch cording to garment on the ¼ in (6 mm) seamline. Remove pins as you stitch.

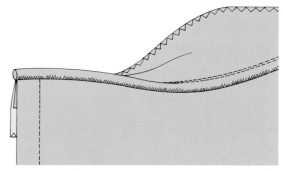

4. Turn cording to inside of garment; press. Sew fabric closed at ends of cording. Tack cording to garment at shoulders and zipper, attach fastener.

6. Press seam flat. Trim, grade, and clip the seam allowances. Trim diagonally at cross seams and corners. Press seam open, then press facing and seam allowances away from garment.

Cording necklines without plackets

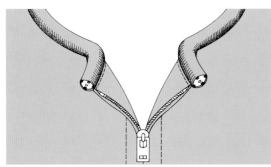

If heavy cord has been used, instead of sewing the fabric closed at ends, attach a large snap to ends of cording. This will serve as a finish and as a fastener for the neckline as well.

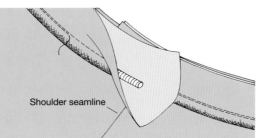

To cord a neckline with no placket opening, apply cording as required by its type, but allow the ends to overlap at a shoulder seamline. Release the stitching at each end and trim cord to

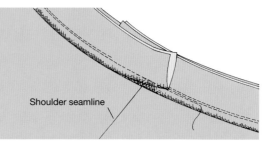

shoulder seamline. Overlap ends, easing empty part of casing away from seamline. Stitch across ends through all layers. Turn cording to inside and baste.

Bound and banded necklines

The illustrations below are designed to show how finished bound and banded necklines differ from each other and from a plain faced neckline.

If all four necklines were based on the simple jewel neckline, as these are, the uppermost edge of the **faced, bound,** and **shaped-band** necklines would be at the same level; the seamline of the **strip band** would be at this level, but its uppermost edge would be above this level.

With a plain **faced** neckline, the facing is stitched to the neck seamline, which becomes the finished edge when the facing is turned to the inside. With a **bound** neckline, the original seam allowance is trimmed from the garment, and the upper edge of the binding ultimately falls where the original seamline was.

A **shaped band** is an additional, but integral, part of the garment; its upper edge forms the finished neckline edge without changing the location. A **knit band** is an extension above the original neckline. See p. 154 for further information on the shaped band and knit band neckline.

Faced neckline

Bound neckline

Shaped-band neckline

Strip-band neckline

Bound necklines

A neck edge can be finished by binding it with a strip of self- or contrasting fabric. The finished width of the binding is usually between ½ in (1.25 cm) and 1 in (2.5 cm).

If your pattern is not designed for binding, cut away the original seam allowance so that the top edge of the bound neckline finish will fall along the original seamline. The actual width of the strip will depend on whether it is to be a single-layer binding or a double-layer binding. The **length needed** is the length of the neck seamline plus 2 in (5 cm). Cut the strip on the grain with the most stretch (see p. 56).

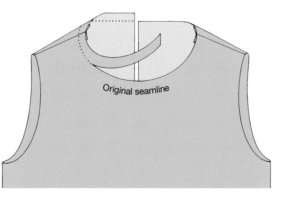

Original seamline

If your pattern is not designed for a bound neckline finish, trim away the seam allowance. This permits the top edge of the finished neckline to fall along the original seamline.

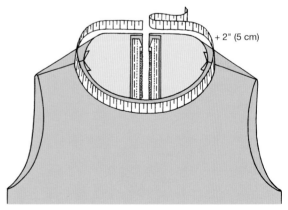

+ 2" (5 cm)

The length of the binding strip equals the length of the neck seamline plus 2 in (5 cm) for ease and finishing the ends. Take this measurement after the zipper has been inserted.

Uneven slipstitch 81 · Hook and eye fasteners 320–321

Applying bindings — a single-layer binding

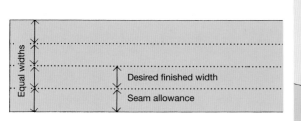

Equal widths

Desired finished width

Seam allowance

1. For a single-layer binding, cut a strip four times the desired finished width and length of the neck seamline plus 2 in (5 cm). Make seam allowance widths the same as finished width.

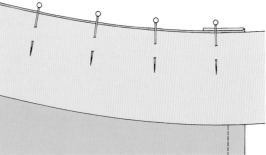

2. Open the zipper. With right sides together and edges even, pin the binding to the garment along the seamline. Stretch binding if necessary to fit smoothly around curves.

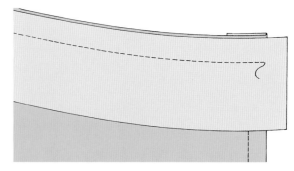

3. With binding up, stitch to garment along the seamline, removing pins as you stitch. Secure thread ends. Press flat. Trim excess binding at ends to ½ in (1.25 cm).

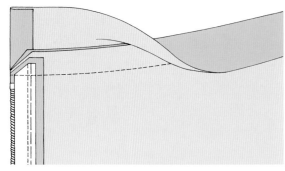

4. Fold ends of binding back, even with placket edges. Trim across corners and cross-seam allowances. Bring binding up over the seam allowances to inside of garment. Press.

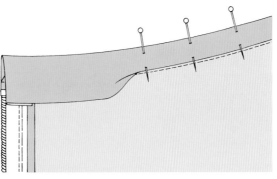

5. If binding strip is made of a **woven** fabric, turn under the raw edge along the seamline. Press with fingers to shape the binding to the curve; pin in place.

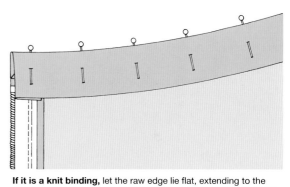

If it is a knit binding, let the raw edge lie flat, extending to the inside of the garment. Pin binding in place, but from the right side, through all thicknesses, along seamline.

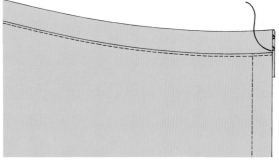

6. With **bindings of woven fabric,** slipstitch ends of binding closed. Slipstitch folded edge to garment along the entire neck seamline. Stitches should not show on right side.

On knit bindings, slipstitch ends closed (see Step 6). Then, from right side of garment, stitch in seam groove through all the thicknesses, removing pins as you stitch. Trim off excess binding.

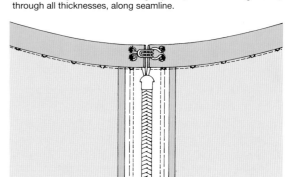

7. From inside, press the neck edge. Close zipper and attach a hook and round eye to binding ends. The ends of the binding should meet when hook and eye are fastened.

Pressing equipment 14 · Uneven slipstitch 81 · Hook and eye fasteners 320–321

Applying a double-layer binding

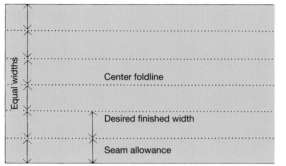

1. For a double-layer binding, cut the strip six times the desired finished width and the length of neck seamline plus 2 in (5 cm). Have seam allowance widths the same as finished width.

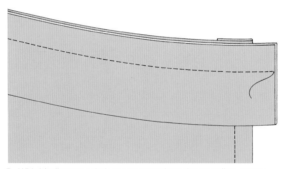

3. With binding up, stitch to garment along the seamline, removing pins as you stitch. Secure thread ends. Press flat. Trim excess binding at ends to ½ in (1.25 cm).

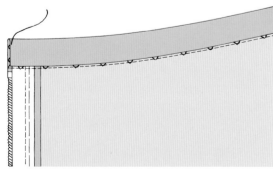

5. Slipstitch ends of binding closed. Then slipstitch the folded edge of binding to garment along the entire neck seamline. The stitches should not show on right side of garment.

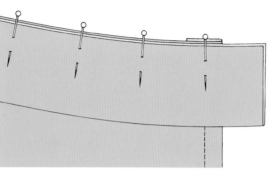

2. Open zipper. Wrong sides together, fold binding strip in half lengthwise. Keeping all edges even, pin to garment along seamline. Stretch binding to fit around curves.

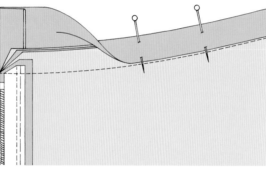

4. Fold ends of binding back, even with placket edges. Trim across corners and cross-seam allowances. Bring binding up over seam allowances to inside of garment. Pin in place.

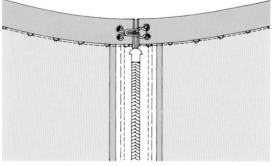

6. From the inside, press the neck edge. Close zipper and attach a hook and round eye to binding ends. The ends of the binding should meet when hook and eye are fastened.

Binding a neckline without placket

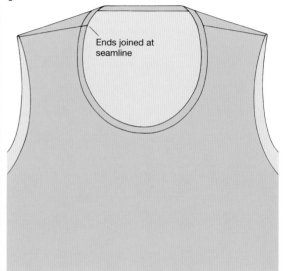

Ends joined at seamline

Single- or double-layer binding may be used. The only difference from the basic applications is in the handling of the ends and that they should be joined at a garment seamline.

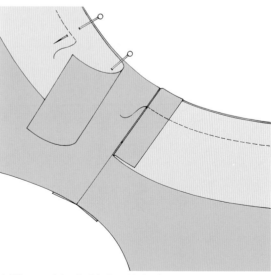

1. When applying the binding, fold back the starting end ½ in (1.25 cm) and align fold with garment seamline. Pin binding in place and stitch to within 3 in (7.5 cm) of starting point.

Ready-made binding

Single- or double-fold bias tape and fold-over braid can both be used to bind necklines. Most are already folded off-center; if they are not, press the off-center fold first to ensure that when the tapes are positioned properly both edges will be caught in the same stitching. These tapes can also be preshaped to match the curve they will be applied to. Other tapes can also be used, provided they have finished edges and can be shaped.

To shape tape to fit an inward curve, stretch the open edges while easing in the folded edge. To shape tape to fit an outward curve stretch the fold while easing in the open edges.

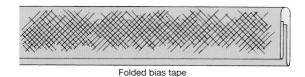

Folded bias tape

Fold-over band

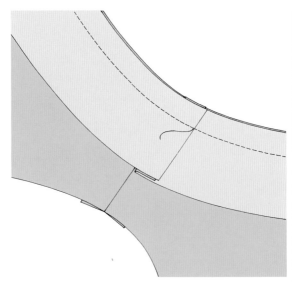

2. Trim away excess binding at this end to ½ in (1.25 cm) beyond fold of starting end. Lap this end over the beginning fold and stitch the rest of the way across, through all thicknesses.

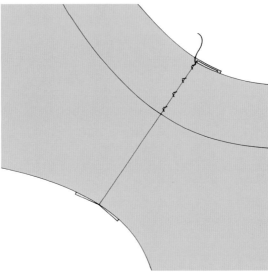

3. When the binding is turned up, the end folded first will be on top. Slipstitch ends together as they lie. Finish according to binding type (single-layer or double-layer).

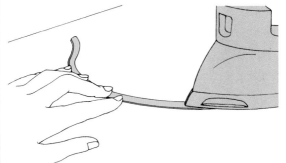

1. These bindings should be shaped to match the curve of the neck edge before application to garment. With your hand and a steam iron, mold the binding into the proper curve.

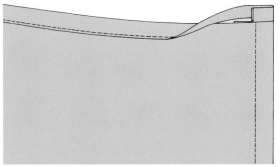

If neckline has a placket opening, fold ends back even with edges of placket. Then topstitch binding to neckline and attach fastener at ends (see Step 6, opposite page).

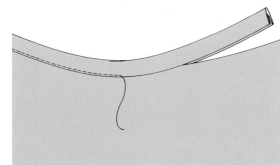

2. Wrap shaped binding around neck edge with wider half to inside of garment and the fold along the neck edge. Topstitch along outer edge of narrower half, handling ends as below.

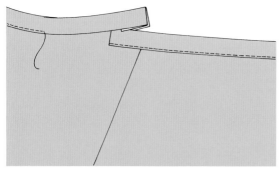

If there is no placket, place starting end ½ in (1.25 cm) ahead of a garment seamline. Stitch to within 3 in (7.5 cm) of start. Fold second end under to align with seam; complete stitching.

Shaped bands and placket bands — shaped and knit

Another way to finish a neckline is with a separate fabric band. The two basic types are the **shaped band** and the **knit band.** The shaped band, which is cut to a precise shape according to a pattern, has two main parts: the band and its facing (sometimes an extended facing).

The knit band is a strip of knitted fabric which is folded in half lengthwise; it is shaped to conform to the neckline curve before or during application.

Shaped-band neckline finish

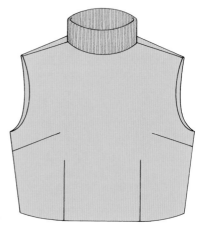

Knit-band neckline finish

Shaped-band neckline finish

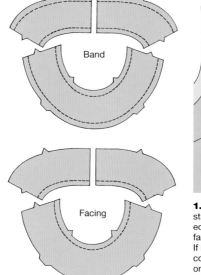

Band

Facing

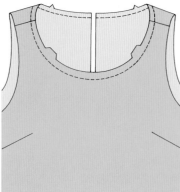

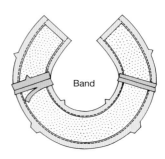

Band

1. To help maintain their shapes, apply staystitching along the neck and outer edges of the band, the neck edge of the facing, and the top edge of the garment. If neckline is a V or square, reinforce the corners with short stitches for 1 in (2.5 cm) on both sides of corners, then clip into the corners. Do not insert zipper.

2. Select an interfacing appropriate to the garment fabric and apply it to the band. Interfacing illustrated is iron-on type. With right sides together, match and then seam the band sections to form complete band. Press seams flat, then open. Trim seam allowances to half-width. Construct facing unit as described on page 139.

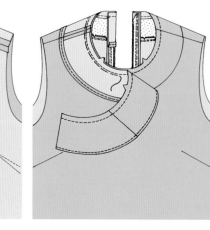

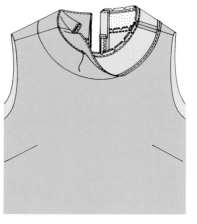

3. With right sides together, matching all markings, notches, and cross-seamlines, pin and baste the band to the garment. Stitch along seamline. Remove the basting and press seam flat. Trim, grade, and notch the seam allowances. Press the seam open; then press the seam allowances and the band up, away from the rest of the garment.

4. Insert the zipper, positioning the top stop ½ in (1.25 cm) below neck seamline, being sure to match the cross-seams within the placket. Open zipper. With right sides together, and matching all markings, notches, and seamlines, pin and baste the facing to the band along neck edge. Stitch. Remove basting and press the seam flat.

5. Trim, grade, and clip the seam allowances. With facing right side up, understitch along seamline through all layers. Turn the facing to inside; secure it to garment at shoulder seams and slipstitch the ends of the facing to the zipper tapes. Attach the fastener at top.

Bound buttonholes 300–311 · Attaching buttons 318

Placket bands

The **placket band** is a variation of the shaped band in that it is cut from a pattern and applied in a similar way. Both a type of garment opening and its finish as well, it is most often straight, which permits both the band and its facing to be cut out as one piece. Such a facing is an extended facing.

Sometimes the unit will be a **combination neck and placket band.** This is applied by a combination of techniques from those used for the neckline shaped band (see p. 154), and the placket band (see right).

Straight placket band

Combination neck and placket band

Straight placket bands

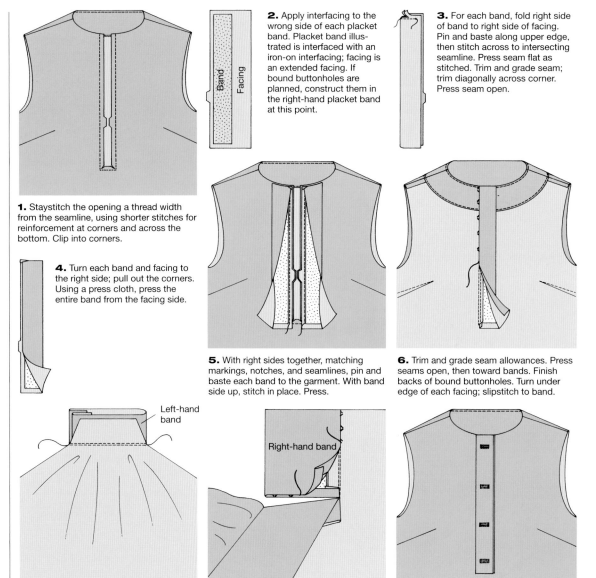

2. Apply interfacing to the wrong side of each placket band. Placket band illustrated is interfaced with an iron-on interfacing; facing is an extended facing. If bound buttonholes are planned, construct them in the right-hand placket band at this point.

3. For each band, fold right side of band to right side of facing. Pin and baste along upper edge, then stitch across to intersecting seamline. Press seam flat as stitched. Trim and grade seam; trim diagonally across corner. Press seam open.

1. Staystitch the opening a thread width from the seamline, using shorter stitches for reinforcement at corners and across the bottom. Clip into corners.

4. Turn each band and facing to the right side; pull out the corners. Using a press cloth, press the entire band from the facing side.

5. With right sides together, matching markings, notches, and seamlines, pin and baste each band to the garment. With band side up, stitch in place. Press.

6. Trim and grade seam allowances. Press seams open, then toward bands. Finish backs of bound buttonholes. Turn under edge of each facing; slipstitch to band.

7. Right sides together, match, pin, and stitch lower edge of left-hand band to end of placket. Press seam flat, then downward.

8. At lower end of right-hand band, trim and turn in seam allowances; slipstitch them together. Press flat.

9. Match center lines and lap right-hand band over left. Sew buttons to left band.

Grain in fabric 56–57 · Overedge seams 91 · Hairline seams and double-stitched seams 91

Knit bands

Knit bands are a suitable neckline finish for knit and woven fabrics. Two application techniques have been devised. The first is for knits with **limited stretch,** e.g., for most double knits, and woven fabrics; the second is for **very stretchy** knits, such as sweater knits. Bands that are cut from slightly stretchy (limited stretch) knits are shaped to match the curve of the neck before being applied.

If the neckline is high, it may be necessary to insert a zipper (see pp. 158–159). If it is a wide or low neckline, such as shown right, a zipper is not needed. Stretchy knit bands, which are ideal for higher necklines, are shaped to the neck edge during application, and a zipper is optional.

Neckline finished with a slightly stretchy band

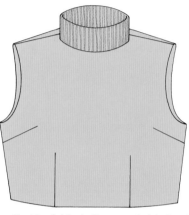

Neckline finished with a very stretchy band

Applying a limited-stretch knit band

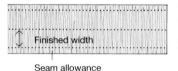

Finished width

Seam allowance

1. Cut strip twice the desired finished width plus two seam allowances. Length is equal to the length of neckline seam plus two seam allowances. Cut on crosswise grain.

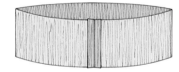

2. Form a closed circle by seaming ends of band together. Trim and press open. An overedge seam can also be used. Form all bodice seams that intersect the neckline.

3. Fold strip in half lengthwise, with its wrong sides together and edges even. Baste edges together. Pin-mark center back (the seam) and center front (at opposite halfway point in band).

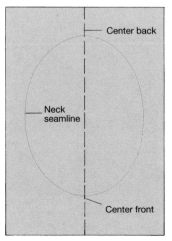

Center back

Neck seamline

Center front

4. On a piece of muslin or heavy paper, draw the exact shape of the entire neckline seam. Mark on it center front and center back. Place this guide on the ironing board.

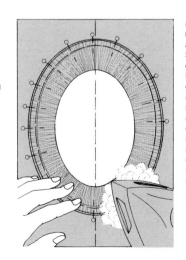

5. Pin band to guide, matching center front and back markings. Shape band so that curve of its neck seamline matches drawn guideline. Shape with the aid of a steam iron, stretching the cut edges and allowing the folded edge to ease itself into shape. Pin in place while shaping. Allow band to dry before removing it. If shine develops on top surface, use this side as underside. Remove basting stitches.

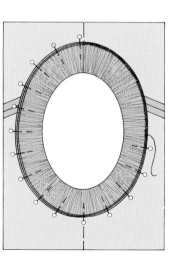

6. Turn the garment inside out. Pin band to right side of garment, matching seamlines and center markings. With band side up, stitch to garment, using an overedge or double-stitched seam (see Seams). Remove pins as you stitch. Press seam allowances toward the garment; band extends away from the garment.

Overedge seams 91 · Hairline seams and double-stitched seams 91

Stretchy knit bands

A stretchy knit band can be cut from the same fabric as the garment or cut from a purchased banding called ribbing. Ribbing is a stretchy knit fabric sold by the yard/meter, cut and finished to a specific width. Whether you use the garment fabric or a bought ribbing, the knit should be stretchy but have the ability to recover.

The most typical necklines to which stretchy bands can be applied successfully are the **crew neck,** the **mock turtleneck,** and the **turtleneck.** The width of the band will be determined by the neckline type. Examples of suitable finished widths are 1 in (2.5 cm) for a crew neck, 2 in (5 cm) for a mock turtleneck, and 4 in (10 cm) or more for a turtleneck (2 in [5 cm] when

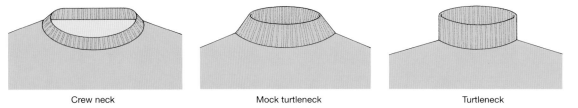

Crew neck · Mock turtleneck · Turtleneck

it is turned back on itself). All purchased ribbings are a precise width and can be used only at that width. If you are cutting the band yourself, cut it twice the finished width plus two seam allowances. Fold it in half lengthwise, producing one finished edge.

The length of the band is determined by **1.** the stretch and recovery capabilities of the knit; **2.** measure-

ments at the parts of the body it must first pass over and then fit snugly (that is, the head and neck); **3.** tension required for close fit during wear. Generally such a band is cut from 2 to 4 in (5 to 10 cm) shorter than the neck seamline. If the neckline has a zipper opening, the band can be very nearly the same length as the neckline because it will only have to hug the neck.

Applying a stretchy knit band or strip band

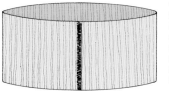

1. With right sides together, seam ends of band to form a closed circle. Use overedge or double-stitched seam. Form bodice seams that intersect neck seamline.

2. Fold band in half lengthwise, wrong sides together and edges even. Divide the band into four equal parts; mark with pins. One pin is placed in the center back seam.

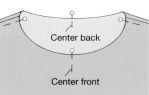

Center back

Center front

3. To ensure equal distribution of the band over garment edge, divide the garment's neckline into four equal parts. Two marks are at center front and back, others are halfway between.

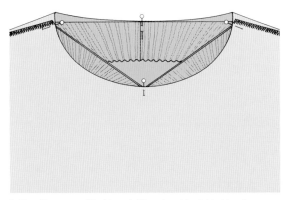

4. Turn the garment inside out. Place band to right side of garment, matching pin marks and neck seams. Stretch band to fit garment neckline; pin in place. Take care to keep raw edges of band and garment even.

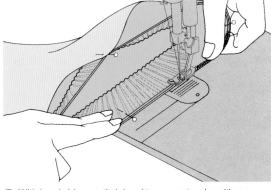

5. With band side up, stitch band to garment, using either an overedge or double-stitched seam. Stretch the band so that it lies flat against the garment's edge; do not stretch the garment. Remove pins as you stitch.

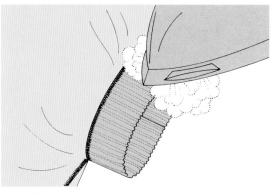

6. Holding the iron above the seam, allow the steam to return the seam and band to their unstretched state. Then press the seam allowances toward the garment. Let the band dry thoroughly before handling so that it will not stretch out of shape.

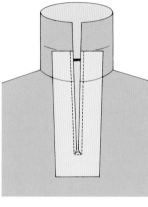

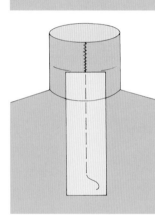

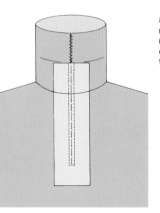

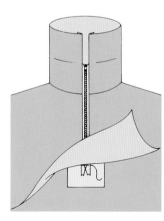

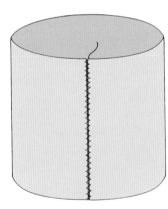

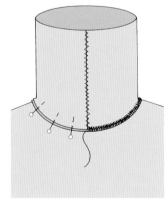

Zippers in knit band necklines

If necessary, a zipper can be added to a knit band neckline. This is done by applying the band to the garment, according to the type of fabric it is cut from, while making allowances for the insertion of the zipper. The techniques described here place the zipper between the two layers of the band.

If you use a single-layer ready-made ribbing, the top of the zipper is finished differently. Use the exposed zipper method if garment has no placket seam, the centered zipper method if there is a seam.

Exposed zipper

1. Cut band according to type of neckline and fabric (see pp. 156 and 157). Temporarily seam band into closed circle, using an abutted seam, as follows: trim away seam allowances, then abut seamlines and join with a zigzag stitch, catching both of the edges in the stitching.

2. Apply band to garment, using appropriate method (see p. 156 or 157), except stitch only one band edge, the one facing the right side of garment. Press seam up toward band.

3. To locate center of placket, lightly press a crease, from the right side, along the center front or back of the garment. To determine how long placket opening should be, place zipper along crease, with top stop just below the fold-line of band (the top of the placket), and insert a pin just below the bottom stop to mark bottom of placket.

Top of placket

Bottom of placket

4. Cut a piece of stay fabric 3 in (7.5 cm) wide and 2 in (5 cm) longer than placket opening. Draw a line or press a crease in stay fabric the length of the placket opening. Center this line over crease in garment; pin and baste in place along line.

5. Sew stay fabric to garment by stitching ⅛ in (3 mm) from both sides of centered lines and across the bottom of the placket.

6. Slash through and remove stitching of the abutted seam in the band and cut along the centered lines to within ½ in (1.25 cm) from end of placket. Then cut to the stitching at each corner, forming a wedge at bottom.

7. Turn all the stay fabric to inside of garment; press so that none of it shows on the right side of the garment.

8. Position zipper under opening with top stop at fold of band and bottom stop at the end of placket of opening; pin. Slip-baste zipper to edges of opening. Lift garment up to expose the wedge and bottom of zipper. Using a zipper foot, stitch across base of wedge, through the wedge, stay fabric, and zipper tapes.

Catchstitch (flat and blind) 81–82 · Centered zipper application 286–287

Centered zipper in a seam

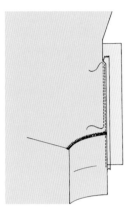

9. With zipper closed, fold back one side of garment to expose zipper and stitching from Step 5. Using a zipper foot, sew zipper to garment by stitching, from bottom to top, along the stitching line. Fold back other side of garment and stitch other zipper tape to garment in the same way. Trim away the excess stay fabric.

10. Trim excess zipper tape at top of placket. Open the zipper and extend one tape, its seam allowance, and stay fabric. Fold free half of band down to right side of band, matching the ends. Pin in place and stitch along zipper stitching line. Repeat process for other half of zipper.

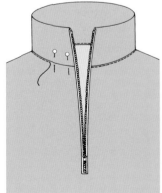

11. Turn band to inside of garment and match neck seamlines of band and garment; pin in place from right side. Stitch from the right side, in the seam groove, removing pins as you stitch. Use a straight stitch for this, stretching the fabric, if necessary, as you stitch.

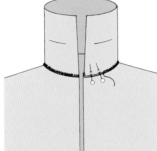

1. Cut band according to type of neckline and fabric (see p. 156 or 157). Apply band to garment according to the appropriate method chosen, except do not sew band into a circle, and sew only one of its edges — the one closest to the garment's right side — to the garment. Press the seam up toward the band.

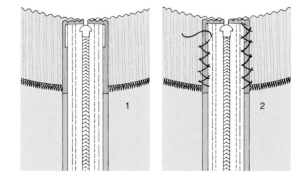

3. Open zipper and fold free half of band to inside of garment. Match the neck seamlines of band and garment; pin in place from right side. Fold under edges of band at each zipper tape and slipstitch them to the tapes.

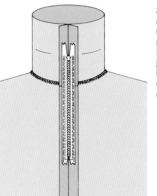

2. With band extended away from the garment, machine-baste the entire placket seam closed. Positioning the top stop just below the fold of band, insert the zipper, using the centered zipper application.

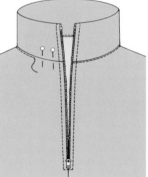

4. Stitch from the right side, in the seam groove, through all layers; remove pins as you stitch. Use a straight stitch for this, stretching the fabric, if necessary, as you stitch.

Ready-made ribbing

Since ready-made ribbing usually comes in only one layer, the part of the zipper that extends into the band cannot be stitched between layers.

When positioning a zipper for a neckline that has a single-layer band, place its top stop at the top edge of the band and turn under the upper ends of the tapes. Then apply the zipper, catching the turned-under tapes in the stitching (1). To finish the zipper within the band area, and ensure that it will lie flat against the band, sew the edges of the zipper tape to the band with catchstitches (2).

NECKLINE FINISHES

Types of collars

Though they come in many shapes and sizes, all collars are basically one of three types: **flat, standing,** or **rolled.** And different as they may be in other respects, each has a top and bottom portion, usually called the *upper* and *under* collar, sometimes the *collar* and *collar facing.* It does not matter how the outer edge of a collar is shaped. The curve of the inner edge, however, is important. It is the relation of the curve at this edge to the neckline curve that determines the collar's type. The more alike the two curves are, the less the collar will stand up from the neck edge (flat collar). The more these curves differ, the more the collar will stand up (standing collar). If the curves differ slightly, the collar will stand up to some extent, then fall (rolled collar).

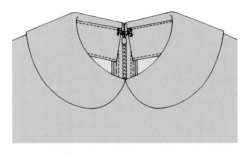

A flat collar emerges from the neck seamline to lie flat against the garment, rising only slightly above the neck edge. Examples are Peter Pan and sailor collars. Flat collars occur most often in untailored garments, such as blouses, and in children's wear.

A complete flat collar may consist of two separate units or one continuous unit. When a collar has two units, one is intended for the right-hand portion of the neck, the other for the left-hand portion. (See pp. 162–163.)

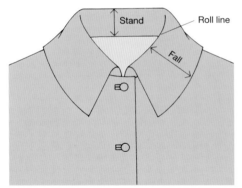

A rolled collar first stands up from the neck edge, then falls down to rest on the garment. The line at which the collar begins to fall is called the roll line. The positioning of this line determines the extent of the stand, and thus the fall, of the collar. Examples of the rolled collar, other than the one shown, are the notched and the shawl collars.

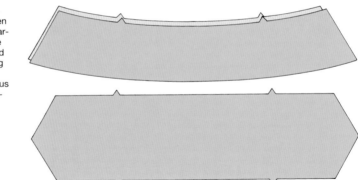

Rolled collars are usually constructed from separate upper and under collars. Some, however, are constructed from one piece, which, when folded back onto itself, forms the entire collar. Either type may or may not have a seam at the center back. Construction and application methods for the rolled collar are on pages 168–175.

A standing collar extends above the neck seamline of the garment either as a narrow, single-width band or as a wider, double-width band that will fold back down onto itself. Most standing collars are straight, but they can be curved so that they stand up at a slight angle. A shirt collar with a stand is a variation of the standing collar.

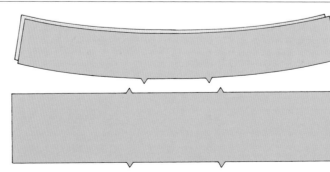

A standing collar may be either rectangular or slightly curved in shape. Some have a separate upper and under collar; others are formed from one piece that folds back on itself to form the entire collar. (See pp. 179–181.)

Fabric-marking methods 65 · Tailoring 333–338

Collar interfacings

Interfacing is an important part of any collar because it helps to define and support the collar's shape. On collars that are not tailored, any type of interfacing can be used, so long as its weight is compatible with that of the garment fabric. Interfacing can be woven, knit or non-woven, either fusible or sew-in. It is applied before pattern markings are transferred. If a collar is to be tailored, the best interfacing choice is the appropriate weight of an iron-on interfacing or a hair canvas which add firmness but relatively little shape to the collar.

This section deals only with those collars that will not be tailored. For a more tailored collar, see the instructions in the Tailoring section. The basic methods of applying interfacing to an under collar are given below.

Where to apply the interfacing

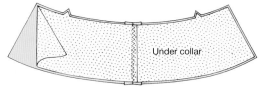

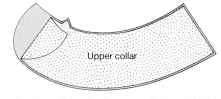

Interfacing is generally applied to the wrong side of the under collar. Some exceptions to this rule are discussed in connection with the adjoining three illustrations.

If constructing a flat collar from a very lightweight fabric, apply interfacing to wrong side of upper collar. This prevents seams from showing through to the finished side.

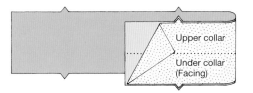

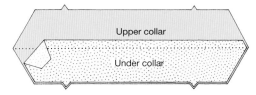

If constructing a standing collar in which both parts of the collar are one piece, interfacing can be applied to wrong side of entire piece if garment fabric is not too bulky.

With a one-piece rolled collar, interfacing is applied to wrong side of the under collar area but, if you prefer, it can extend ½ in (1.25 cm) beyond foldline into the upper collar.

Interfacing applications

The method chosen for the application of interfacing depends upon the type of interfacing being used. Some general rules, however, apply to them all.

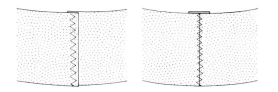

Lapped seam   Abutted seam

1. Transfer all pattern markings to the interfacings.
2. If there is a center back seam, and the interfacing is a sew-on, join the interfacing, before application, with either a lapped or an abutted seam.
3. Reduce bulk at corners by trimming across them ¹⁄₁₆ in (2 mm) inside the seamline. On collars that are to be tailored, the interfaced under collar requires pad-stitching (see Padding stitches, p. 71).

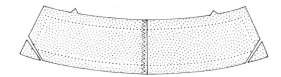

Lighter-weight sew-in interfacings: Transfer markings. Form seam if necessary. Trim across corners ¹⁄₁₆ in (2 mm) inside the

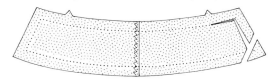

Heavy sew-in interfacings: Transfer markings. Form seam if necessary. Trim away all seam allowances and across corners. Match

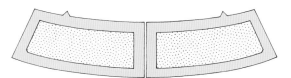

Fusible interfacings: Transfer markings. Trim all seam allowances and corners. Iron onto wrong side of under collar. If necessary,

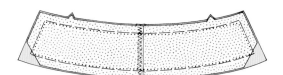

seamline. With the interfacing to the wrong side of the under collar, match, pin, and baste inside the seamline.

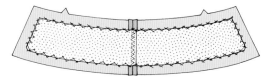

and baste the interfacing to wrong side of under collar. Catchstitch to under collar over all the seamlines. Mainly done by tailors.

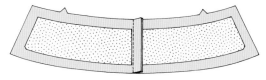

form center back seam in garment fabric (do not catch interfacing in seam). Press seam flat, then open.

Pressing equipment 14 · Diagonal basting 70 · Seams 86–87

Flat collars

Flat collars are the easiest type to construct and apply. The most familiar form, used primarily on children's garments, is the Peter Pan collar, shown on these two pages. It consists of two collar units, one applied to the left side of the neck, the other to the right side.

If the garment closes with a zipper, which is the usual closure for flat collars, insert the zipper before applying the collar. If instead the garment has a button closure, make the buttonholes after the collar construction is complete.

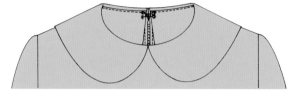

Construction of a flat collar

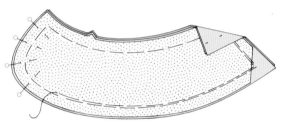

1. Apply interfacing to wrong side of each under collar. Right sides together, match, pin, and baste each upper collar to each under collar, leaving neck edges open.

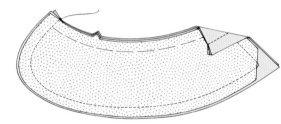

2. Stitch each unit along outer seamline, again leaving neck edges open. Use short reinforcement stitches at corners; stitch across corners to blunt them (see Seams). Press.

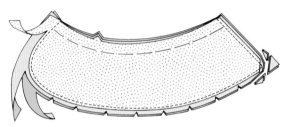

3. Trim and grade seam allowances; trim across corners and taper seam allowances on both sides of each; notch or clip the curved seam allowances.

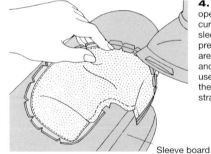

4. Press all seams open. Use the curved section of a sleeve board to press the curved areas of the seams and the corners; use the flat part of the board for the straight portions.

Sleeve board

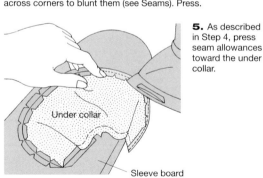

5. As described in Step 4, press seam allowances toward the under collar.

Under collar

Sleeve board

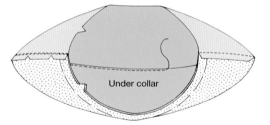

Under collar

6. If desired, understitch the outer edge of each collar unit. With under collar right side up, understitch along the seamline, catching the seam allowances underneath.

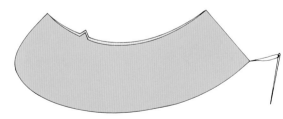

7. Turn collar units right side out. To pull out corners, push a needle, threaded with a double, knotted length of thread, out through corner point. Pull on thread.

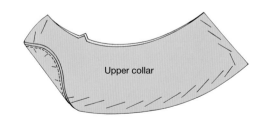

Upper collar

8. With the fingertips, work each outer seamline slightly toward the under collar side; hold edges in place with diagonal basting. Using a press cloth, press collar.

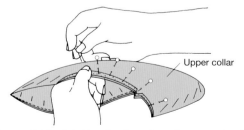

Upper collar

To form a slight roll, hold each collar unit, as shown, over hand, upper collar on top. Pin neck edges together as they fall; baste together along seamline of under collar.

Applying a flat collar

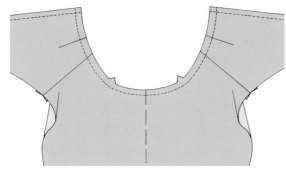

1. Before applying the collar, staystitch the neckline and form all seams and darts that intersect the neck seamline. Apply interfacing to the garment if necessary.

2. If collar consists of two units, as this Peter Pan flat collar does, align and join the two with hand stitches where their neck seamlines meet (seam allowances may overlap).

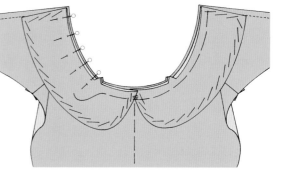

3. Match, pin, and baste the collar to the garment along the neck seamline. Be sure that the point at which the two units are joined falls at the garment center.

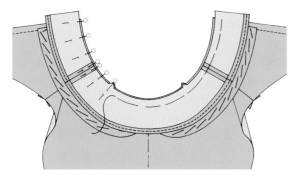

4. Form facing unit (see p. 139). With the right side of facing toward upper collar, match, pin, and baste unit to collar and garment at neck seamline (ends will extend at placket).

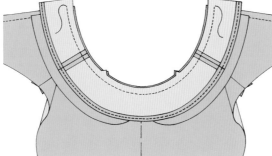

5. Facing side up, stitch facing and collar to garment at neck seamline; secure stitching. Be sure ends of seamline align when zipper is closed. Remove basting; press.

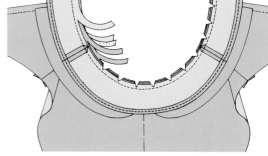

6. Trim and grade the seam allowances, making the garment seam allowance the widest. Trim diagonally across the cross-seam allowances. Clip the seam allowances.

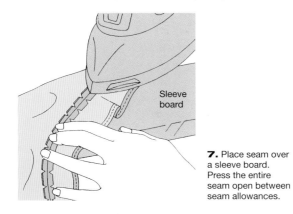

Sleeve board

7. Place seam over a sleeve board. Press the entire seam open between seam allowances.

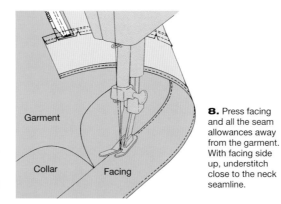

Garment

Collar   Facing

8. Press facing and all the seam allowances away from the garment. With facing side up, understitch close to the neck seamline.

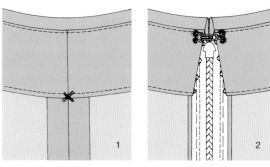

1   2

9. Press facing to inside of garment. Cross-stitch tack facing edge in place at shoulder seamlines (1). Turn facing ends under at zipper and slipstitch in place; attach fastener (2).

Tailored jacket

Fabrics

Lightweight wool, linen, heavy silk, synthetic blends
For the lining: Bemberg, acetate

Amount

For size 12: 2 yd (1.9 m) of 58/60 (150 cm) -width fabric
Lining: $1^1/_2$ yd (1.4 m) of 54/56 in (140 cm) -width fabric

Notions

1 yd (0.90 m) lightweight fusible interfacing, ⅝ yd (60 cm) width
2 buttons, 2¾ in (2 cm) diameter
2 thin shoulder pads

Pattern pieces ▶▶▶▶▶▶▶▶▶▶▶▶▶▶▶▶▶▶▶▶▶

Garment fabric:
 1 Jacket front – cut 2
 2 Jacket side front – cut 2
 3 Jacket center back – cut 2
 4 Jacket side back – cut 2
 5 Pocket flap – cut 2
 6 Pocket piping – cut 4
 7 Pocket – cut 2
 8 Under collar – cut 1 on fold
 9 Upper collar – cut 1 on fold
10 Front facing – cut 2
11 Back neck facing – cut 1 on fold
12 Upper sleeve – cut 2
13 Under sleeve – cut 2
Lining:
 2 Side front – cut 2
 4 Side back – cut 2
 5 Pocket flap – cut 2
 7 Pocket – cut 2
12 Upper sleeve – cut 2
13 Under sleeve – cut 2
14 Lining front – cut 2
15 Lining back – cut 1

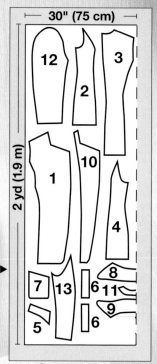

Garment fabric

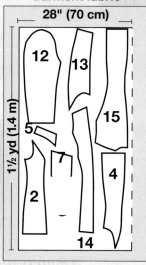

Lining

This project illustrates an approach to sewing tailoring garments that is somewhat different to the classic tailoring methods covered by this book. The jacket was made from a Burda pattern whose assembly was modified to demonstrate methods used by the modern garment industry, including the lining technique known as "bagging," which is done entirely by machine.

Whether traditional or industrial methods are followed, classic features of fine tailoring include the notched collar with lapels and slash pockets with flaps and these two features are included here. Both are considered challenging to sew but can be mastered with careful attention to the instructions. The double-breasted jacket goes well with the pleated skirt on page 118, the dress pants on page 104, and the shirt blouse on page 172.

Pattern alterations

Before cutting, compare the measurements of the main pattern pieces of a jacket pattern with your own and make any alterations necessary. In order to apply the assembly methods shown here, it is useful to sew a test jacket or "muslin" from inexpensive fabric before cutting into your fashion fabric. Make any fitting adjustments to the muslin and transfer them back onto the pattern. A muslin consists of the jacket body, under-collar, and one sleeve.

Cutting

● Fold fabric right sides in. Lay out and cut all jacket pieces in the same direction, respecting the nap or one-way effect of most fabrics.
● Cut interfacing pieces, without seam allowance, for the following: nos. 1 and 2 (front and side front), nos. 5 and 6 (pocket flap and piping), nos. 8 and 9 (under and upper collar), and nos. 10 and 11 (front facing and back neck facing).
● Cut strips of fusible interfacing ³⁄₄ in (2 cm) wide to reinforce the

following edges: lapel and front edges, sleeve caps, hems, and top edges of pockets.

Preparation

Fuse the interfacing to the wrong sides of all pieces. Fuse reinforcement strips to all edges mentioned above (Fig. 1).

Assembling lining

● Stitch darts in lining front and press down.

● Match backs at center back seam and stitch. Press in a pleat 1¼ in (3 cm) wide at center back. Hold in place with basting stitches at the top and bottom. This will provide ease of movement during wear.
● Match the side back pieces to the back, right sides together, and stitch.
● Match the side front pieces to the fronts, right sides together, and stitch, easing fullness at the bust curve. Notch the seam allowance at the curve.
● Join the lining fronts to the back at the shoulders.
● Join side seams. Press all the seams open.
● Match the upper and under sleeve sections, right sides together, and stitch both seams, leaving an 8 in (20 cm) opening in one seam of one sleeve for turning the garment right side out later. Press seams open.
● Pin the lining sleeves into the armholes, matching the notches. Baste and stitch, easing the sleeve to fit the armhole.
● Turn under the hem edges of lining and sleeves 1¼ in (3 cm) and press.

● Attaching jacket facings to lining

In this industry method of assembly, the jacket facings are joined to the finished lining to form a unit. Join the front and back neck facings of the jacket at the shoulders. Press the seams open and trim. Pin the lining

to the facing edges, right sides together, matching the shoulder seams. Stitch from one lower edge around to the other; press the seam allowance toward lining. Press the entire lining/facing unit well, as it cannot be pressed once it is in the jacket.

Assembling the jacket

● Stitch the darts in the jacket front and press downward.
● Join the side front to fronts, right sides together. Notch the seam allowance at the curve and press seam open. Make pockets in fronts.
● **Pockets:** Pocket placement markings, consisting of two lines ½ in (1.25 cm) apart and the length of the

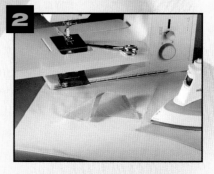

finished flap, and a shorter slash line between them, can be traced onto the interfaced side of the jacket front from the pattern. Transfer these markings, including the center slash line, to the right side of the garment with basting stitches in contrasting thread.

● To make the flaps, trim a tiny amount off the edges of the under

flaps (cut from lining) first to make it slightly smaller than the upper flap, ensuring that the finished seam will be hidden. Pin the upper and under flaps together, matching edges, and then stitch around three sides, leaving the top edge open. Turn right side out and press flat, allowing seam to roll slightly toward the under side (Fig. 2).

● **Piping:** On all four piping strips, press under ½ in (1.25 cm) on one long edge, then fold in another ½ in (1.25 cm) and press (Fig. 3).

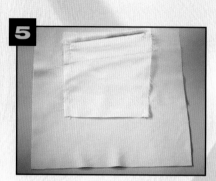

● For upper piping, lap the open edge of pocket flap (lining side up) onto the ½ in (1.25 cm) fold of a piping strip and baste down center (Fig. 4).

● Place this basted line on the upper pocket marking line (with flap turned upward) and stitch on top of basting, stopping exactly at the ends of the flap.

● Place a folded piping strip (without a flap) so the mid-line of the ½ in (1.25 cm) fold is on the lower pocket line. Stitch down center of fold, stopping exactly even with first strip at each end. Secure all thread ends.

● Separate the piping fabric and slash through the jacket along the slash line, snipping diagonally all the way into each corner. This leaves small triangles of cloth at each end.

● Turn the piping and triangles to the inside. Flip up the jacket front and stitch across the piping and triangles at each end to hold them together securely.

● Stitch the lining pocket pieces to the free edges of the piping strips, with the one cut from lining sewn to the lower piping (Fig. 5).

● Bring the pocket pieces to meet and sew them together to form the pocket bag. Press pockets gently from the outside over a tailor's ham using a press cloth.

● Draw the pocket opening together with loose temporary hand basting.

● **Body seams:** Join the center back seam of the jacket, right sides together. Clip the curve and press open. Join side back seams in a similar way and press open.

● Join the jacket front and back at the side seams, right sides together. Clip the curve near the waist and press open.

● Join the shoulder seams, right sides together, easing the back to fit the front. Press all seams open well.

● **Sleeve:** Join the upper and lower sleeve seams, right sides together. Press the seams open.

● **Hems:** Press up 1½ in (3 cm) at jacket hem and sleeve edges.

● **Collar:** Pin the upper collar to the under collar, right sides together and stretching the under collar to fit.

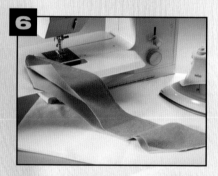

Stitch the long back edge of the collar layers together. Grade the seam allowance (Fig. 6).

● Pin the neck edge of the upper collar to the neck edge of the facing/lining unit, matching the notches. Stitch, press open, and trim, clipping the curve.

● Match the slanted end seams of the upper and under collars and stitch, starting at the notch of the lapel and ending at the collar points. Press seams open on a point presser. Turn collar right side out and press from the under side, making sure that the collar seams show on the under side all round.

● Pin the front and lapel seam edges of the jacket and facing/lining units together for stitching.

● Stitch from collar notch to lapel point. Keep seam allowances of neck seam free while stitching.

● Stitch each front edge from lower edge up to lapel point (Fig. 7).

● Press open all seams on a point presser board. Grade seams to different widths, leaving the side that will be toward the jacket exterior the widest. Trim lapel points well to remove all bulk.

● Turn the jacket right side out and poke out the corners of the lapels with care. Press the jacket front and lapel edges firmly, rolling the seam slightly to the underside of the lapels and to the interior of the lower jacket fronts.

● Join undercollar neck edge to jacket neck. Trim. Press open.

● Diagonal-baste the collar layers together, shaping the collar into the turned-down position it will take around the neck. Pin the two collar attachment seams together from the inside and join them together with loose hand backstitching.

● **Sleeves:** Slide the lining sleeves into the jacket sleeves, right sides together, matching the vertical seams to avoid twisting. Stitch the hem edges together.

● Turn the jacket inside out, ready for attaching sleeves.

● Fit sleeves into the armholes matching all notches and markings. Industry methods do not use the easing threads familiar to home sewers. However, industry patterns (those used in garment factories) have less shoulder ease than most home-sewing patterns. If the sleeves will not fit without easing lines, add lines of machine basting on and just inside the sleeve seam line. Draw the basting up gently and distribute any fullness.

● Baste armhole seams. Check for fit, then stitch. Turn seam allowance toward the sleeve but do not press. Trim underarm portion of seam to ¼ in (6 mm).

● At the underarm point, bring together the side seam of the jacket and lining and secure by stitching the seam allowances together for a short distance. This keeps the lining in place when taking off the jacket.

● Pin shoulder pads into place, with longer part to the back. Hand-sew loosely to shoulder and armhole seam allowances. Add sleeve headers to the sleeve caps if required.

● **Hems:** Fold down the creased-up hem edges of jacket and lining.

● Pin the jacket and lining hem edges together, right sides together and matching all seams. Stitch across the hem, meeting the existing stitching at each end.

● Turn the jacket right side out by pulling it through the opening in the sleeve lining. Close this opening by bringing the turned-in edges together and stitching.

● Give the jacket a final pressing, mainly around lapels and hems. The

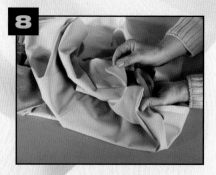

points where the collar joins the lapels should lie flat with no puckering. If slight puckering exists, pull the area gently to release (Fig. 8). If a small hole exists at the lapel/collar join, it can be closed with a loose hand-stitch.

● **Closings:** Mark the position of the buttonholes on the right front of the jacket. Work the buttonholes by machine or hand ⅛ in (3 mm) larger than the buttons.

● Place the right front over the left front and mark the position for the buttons with pins. Sew on the buttons, making thread shanks long enough to allow smooth closing.

Pressing equipment 14 · Uneven Slipstitch 81 · Seam allowance 87

Rolled collars

Rolled collars are differentiated from flat collars by a **roll line** that breaks the collar into **stand** and **fall** areas. The position of the roll line determines the location and size of both stand and fall. Typical examples of rolled collars are illustrated below, the second being the classic notched collar.

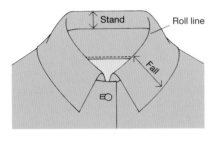

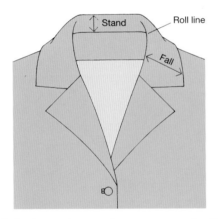

Methods are given on these two pages for the construction of both the two-piece form of the rolled collar (upper and under collars separate) and the one-piece (upper and under collars set apart by a fold). Methods of application are on pages 170–175; the choice of method depends upon the weight of the garment fabric and whether there is a back neck facing.

On tailored garments, a collar may be interfaced with hair canvas or fusible interfacing. Padding stitches will give firmness and some shape.

Construction of a two-piece rolled collar

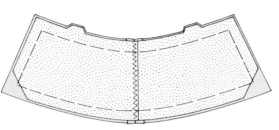

1. Apply interfacing to wrong side of the under collar. If there is a center back seam: for the garment fabric, use a plain seam trimmed to half-width and pressed open; for the interfacing, use a lapped or an abutted seam. Trim almost all the ½ in (1.25 cm) seam allowance from fusible interfacing before application.

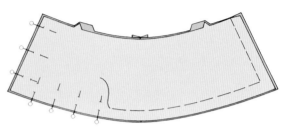

2. Right sides together, match, pin, and then baste the upper collar to the under collar along the outer seamline, leaving the neck edges open. If necessary, slightly stretch the under collar to fit the upper collar.

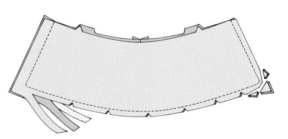

4. Trim and grade the seam allowances, making the seam allowance nearest the upper collar the widest. Trim across corners and taper seam allowances on both sides of corners. Notch or clip curved seam allowances.

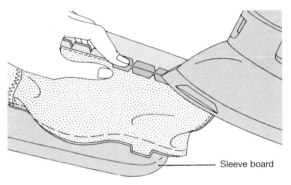

Sleeve board

5. Carefully press the entire seam open. Use a sleeve board for the curved areas of the seam and for the corners; use the ironing board for the straight portions of the seam. Try not to press a crease into the collar itself.

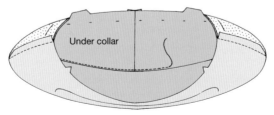

Under collar

7. Understitch the outer seamline. With the under collar side up, understitch close to the seamline, catching all of the seam allowances underneath. Then turn collar right side out; to pull out corners, see Step 7, page 162.

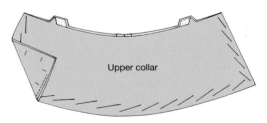

Upper collar

8. Work the outer seamline slightly toward the under collar side so that it will not show from the upper side. Hold the outer edges in place with diagonal basting (see p. 70), leaving the neck edges open. Using a press cloth, press the collar.

Pressing equipment 14 · Diagonal basting 70 · Seams 86–87

Construction of a one-piece rolled collar

In one-piece rolled collars, the upper and the under collars are areas defined at their outer edges by a fold rather than separate pieces joined by a seam. One half of the collar piece is designated the upper collar, the other half the under collar. (There are some one-piece collars that begin, literally, as two pieces because of a center back seam; when it is sewn, the two form one piece.)

The fold between the upper collar and under collar areas makes the construction of a one-piece rolled collar different from that of the two-piece version, the one-piece collar being formed when the two halves are folded together and seamed at the sides. The application of both collars, however, is the same (see pp. 170–175).

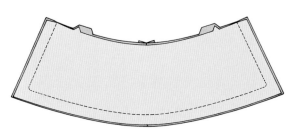

3. Stitch upper collar to under collar along outer seamline, leaving neck edges open. Use short reinforcement stitches at corners; stitch across corners to blunt them. Remove basting from outer seamline; press.

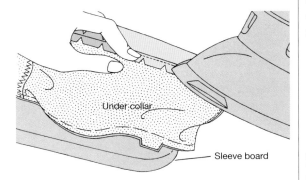

Sleeve board

6. Press all seam allowances toward under collar, again placing the curved, straight, and cornered parts of seam over sleeve board or ironing board. Take care not to crease the rest of the collar.

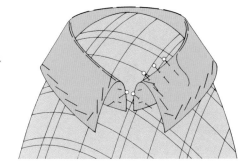

9. Mold collar over tailor's ham into shape. Pin and baste through all layers along roll line. Steam collar; let dry. Remove from ham; pin and baste neck edges together as they fall. Remove basting.

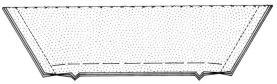

2. Fold collar in half along the foldline so that the right sides of the upper and under collars are facing. Match, pin, and baste along the side seams; stitch along the seamlines and secure stitching at ends. Remove basting from side seams.

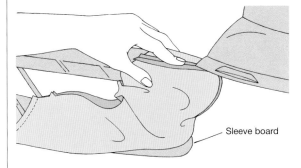

Sleeve board

4. Using a sleeve board, press seams open, then press all seam allowances toward the under collar. Turn the collar right side out; to pull out corners (p. 162). Using a press cloth, press the collar.

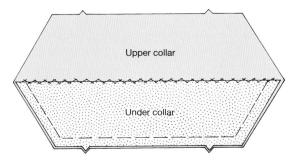

Upper collar

Under collar

1. Apply interfacing to the under collar area. If edge of interfacing meets the foldline, catchstitch in place over the foldline; if edge extends beyond the foldline, hold in place along foldline with small stitches spaced ½ in (1.25 cm) apart. If you are using fusible interfacing, trim almost all the ½ in (1.25 cm) seam allowance from the fusible interfacing before application.

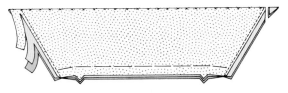

3. Press the seam flat as stitched. Trim and grade the seam allowances, making the one nearest the upper collar the widest. Taper the seam allowances at the corners, being careful not to cut into the stitching.

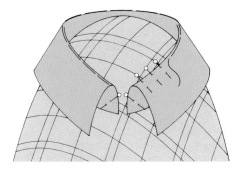

5. Mold collar over tailor's ham into shape intended by pattern. Pin and baste through all layers along roll line. Steam collar; let dry. Remove from ham; pin and baste neck edges together as they fall.

Pressing equipment 14 · **Directional stitching 84** · **Seams 86–87**

Applying a rolled collar (lightweight to mediumweight fabrics)

This method of collar application can be used if the garment fabric is light to medium in weight. Both the upper and under collars are sewn to the garment at the same time that the facing is being attached to the garment. If garment needs interfacing, apply it before attaching collar. If bound buttonholes are being used, construct them before applying collar; finish their backs (or construct machine buttonholes) after collar and facing have been applied to the garment.

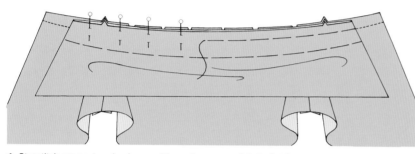

1. Staystitch garment neck edges and form all seams and darts that intersect neck seamline. With under collar toward right side of garment, match, pin, and baste collar to garment, clipping garment seam allowance, if necessary, so collar will fit easily.

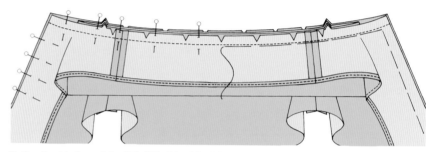

2. Construct facing unit (p. 139). With right side of facing toward right side of garment and upper collar, match, pin, and baste facing through collar and garment at neck and garment opening. Clip facing seam allowance at neck, if necessary, so facing fits easily.

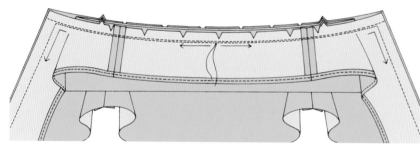

3. Facing side up, stitch facing and collar to garment. Stitch each side directionally, from center back to the bottom of the garment opening. Use shorter reinforcement stitches for 1 in (2.5 cm) on both sides of each corner. Remove basting. Press seam flat as stitched.

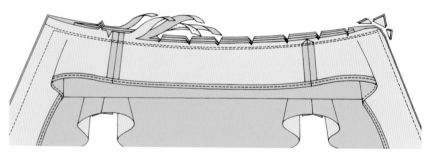

4. Trim and grade the seam allowances, making the one nearest the garment the widest. Trim diagonally across the cross-seam allowances and corners; taper the seam allowances on both sides of each corner. Notch or clip the curved seam allowances.

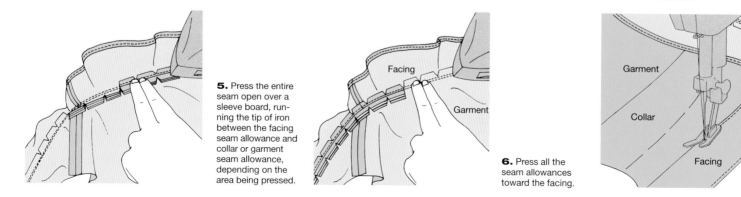

5. Press the entire seam open over a sleeve board, running the tip of iron between the facing seam allowance and collar or garment seam allowance, depending on the area being pressed.

6. Press all the seam allowances toward the facing.

7. Understitch the neck and garment opening seamlines where necessary. Facing side up, stitch close to seamline, through all the seam allowances. Press facing to inside of garment; attach to shoulder seams with a single tack.

Plain-stitch basting 75 · Bound and worked buttonholes 300–314

Applying a rolled collar (heavy or bulky fabrics)

If garment fabric is bulky or heavy, the under collar is sewn to the garment and the upper collar to the facing. Seams are pressed open and allowed to fall onto each other as they will. In this way, the bulk at the neckline is divided between the two seams. If necessary, interface the garment before attaching collar. If using bound buttonholes, construct them before applying collar. Make machine buttonholes after applying collar and facing.

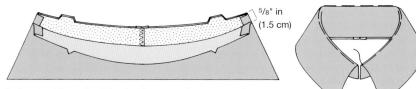

1. Construct the collar, following the appropriate construction method from pages 166–167, but ending stitching at the sides ⁵/₈ in (1.5 cm) from the neck edge.

⁵/₈" in (1.5 cm)

2. Mold the collar as shown in Step 5 or 9, pages 168–169, but do not baste neck edges together.

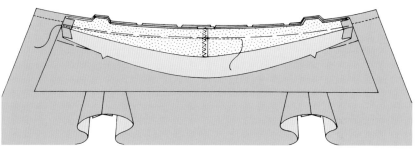

3. Staystitch garment neck edge; form all seams and darts that intersect neck seamline. Right sides together, match, pin, and baste under collar to garment; clip garment seam allowance if necessary for collar to fit. Stitch along seamline; secure stitching. Press.

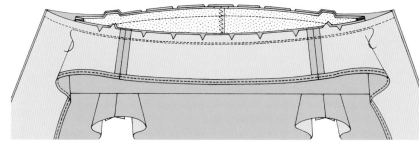

4. Construct facing unit (p. 139). With right sides together, match, pin, and baste facing to upper collar only; clip facing seam allowance if necessary for facing to fit. Upper collar side up, stitch facing to upper collar; secure stitching. Remove basting stitches.

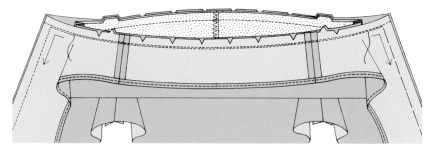

5. Match, pin, and baste remaining portions of facing to garment. Directionally stitch each side; starting at a collar end, stitch to bottom of garment opening; secure stitching. Use short reinforcement stitches at corners. Remove basting stitches.

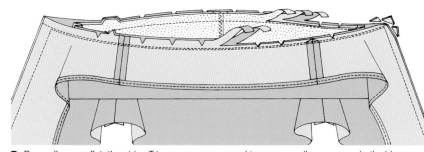

6. Press all seams flat, then trim. Trim across corners and taper seam allowances on both sides of each corner. Grade seam allowances beyond the collar ends to the bottom of each opening side. Notch or clip all seam allowances.

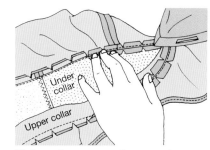

Under collar

Upper collar

7. Press all seams open; then press the seams beyond collar and along garment opening toward facing.

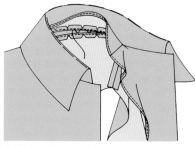

8. Turn facing to inside. Allow neck seamlines of collar to fall as they may; pin, then baste in place with plain-stitch.

Shirt blouse

Fabrics

Cotton, viscose, silk

Amount

For size 12: 1⅝ (1.4 m) of
54/56 in (140 cm) -width fabric

Notions

10 in (25 cm) lightweight fusible
interfacing
9 buttons, ⅝ in (1.5 cm) diameter

Pattern pieces ▶▶▶▶▶▶▶▶▶▶▶▶▶▶

1 Blouse front – cut 2
2 Yoke – cut 2
3 Blouse back – cut 1 on fold
4 Collar – cut 2 on fold
5 Collar band – cut 2 on fold
6 Sleeve – cut 2
7 Cuff – cut 2
8 Cuff placket underlap – cut 2
9 Template and cuff placket
   overlap – cut 2

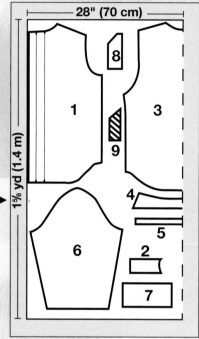

Burda pattern 3716 was modified for
this blouse. The side seams are
2¾ in (7 cm) shorter and the hem is
rounded. A tailored sleeve placket
has been added.

Blouse sizes are based on bust
measurements. Be sure to compare
your measurements with the pattern
catalog's size chart.

The template for the binding on
the sleeve placket (the striped piece
on the layout, right) is made of cardboard.

The shirt blouse has a shirt collar with a separate stand and one-piece lapped button cuffs with a shirt cuff placket.

● **Preparing pattern pieces:** Cut interfacing for the upper collar, upper collar band, and the cuffs without the seam allowances, and iron to wrong sides. Interface cuffs to center line only.

Sewing instructions

● **Collar:** Lay collar pieces together, right sides facing. Stitch unnotched edges together.

● Trim seam allowances, then trim corners diagonally. Clip curves and press seam open.

● Turn collar right side out, press, and topstitch close to the edges.

● Turn the long-edge seam allowance of the upper collar band with interfacing to inside, and press.

● Lay the collar, right sides facing, on the under collar band and pin. Then pin the upper collar band to the right side of the collar. Baste all layers together. Remove pins. Stitch seam. Remove basting. Trim seam (Fig. 1).

● Turn collar band right side out. Press seam allowances and collar band down.

● **Facing:** Turn in the facing on the right front edge 1½ in (4 cm) twice, press, and stitch almost 1½ in (4 cm) from the front edge, catching the fold in stitching (Fig. 2).

● Turn the facing on the left front edge to inside and stitch same as right side.

● **Yoke:** Stitch yokes to blouse fronts and back.

● Finish seam allowances together and press toward yokes.

● Staystitch neck edge.

● **Attach collar:** Baste the lower collar band to neck edge, right sides facing. Stitch, then press seam allowances toward collar band. Trim seam to reduce bulk (Fig. 3).

● Lap and pin the upper collar band to the attachment seam. Working from the right side of the blouse, topstitch

close to all edges of collar band.

● **Sleeve plackets:** Slash lower edge of sleeve at placket slash mark. Lay pleats in lower edge of sleeve in direction of placket and baste across lower edge.

● Turn underlap piece in 3/16 in (5 mm) on both sides, and stitch to the placket back.

● To construct the overlap, place the cardboard template on the wrong side of the facing piece and fold the seam allowances over the template edges. Press from the right side.

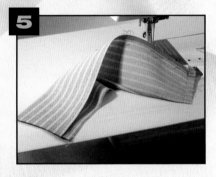

● Fold facing lengthwise in half. Fold the tip to a triangle and press.

● Slide the overlap facing into placket edge and secure with pins. Stitch overlap edges and tip. Remove pins (Fig. 4).

● **Seams:** Pin sleeve to armhole edge, right sides together. Stitch with body of blouse on top. Trim and finish seam allowances together and press toward the body of the blouse. Topstitch close to original seam from the right side.

● Baste sleeve and side seams. Try on the shirt to check fit and sleeve length, then stitch permanently.

Finish seam allowances together and press toward the back.

● **Cuff:** Fold in seam allowance on the long edge of the interfaced side of cuff, and press. Fold the cuff down the center along the interfacing edge, right sides facing, and press. Stitch seams at ends of cuffs.

● Press cuff seams open and trim seams and corners. Turn cuff right side out and press (Fig. 5).

● Match the right side of the extending cuff edge to the wrong side of lower sleeve edge, pin, and stitch. Fold the cuff down. Press seam toward cuff.

● Lap turned-in cuff edge over seam, pin, and stitch close to fold. Stitch around cuff close to edges.

● **Hem:** Turn up hem ¼ in (7 mm), and press. Turn again ¼ in (7 mm) and stitch hem close to the edge.

● Work buttonholes in cuff overlap and blouse right front edges ⅛ in (3 mm) larger than the buttons.

● Mark positions and sew the buttons on the blouse left front and cuff underlap.

Reducing seam bulk 87

Applying a rolled collar to garment without back neck facing

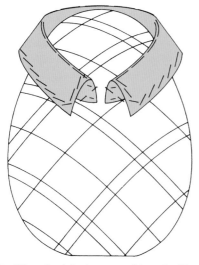

1. Construct the collar, following appropriate method from pages 168–169. Mold the collar over a tailor's ham as in either Step 5 or Step 9 on pages 168 and 169. Remove collar from ham as directed but do not baste neck edges together.

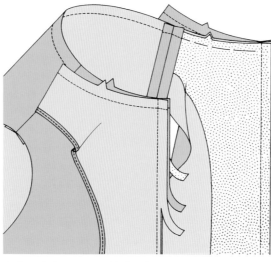

2. Staystitch garment and facing; form all seams and darts that intersect garment neck seam. Interface garment; construct bound buttonholes. Sew facing to garment at opening edges. Press seams flat; trim and grade; press seams open.

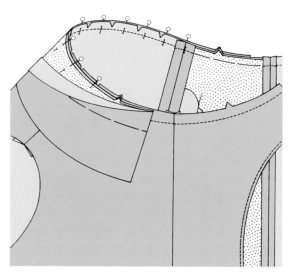

3. Right sides together, match and pin the under collar to the garment neck seamline from one shoulder to the other, clipping the seam allowance of the garment where necessary so that the collar will fit smoothly.

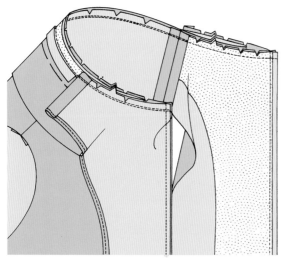

7. Keeping the upper collar seam allowance free across the back, stitch the facing and collar to the garment along the neck seamline. Secure stitching at both ends. Remove all of the basting stitches; press the seam flat.

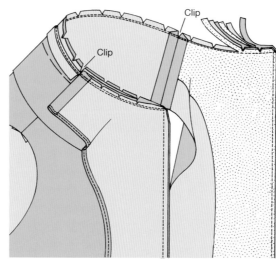

8. Trim and grade seam allowances, making seam allowance of garment the widest. Trim across corners and taper seam allowances on both sides of each corner; at both shoulders, clip into all seam allowances. Clip curved areas.

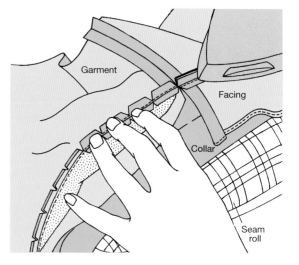

9. Using a seam roll, press the entire seam open, pressing between the facing and the collar or garment from each shoulder to front edge; between under collar and garment across the back neck from shoulder to shoulder.

Pressing equipment 14 · Uneven slipstitch 81 · Buttonholes 300–314

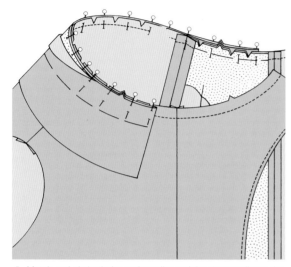

4. Match and pin both the under collar and the upper collar to the garment neck seamline from each shoulder to corresponding end of collar. Clip the garment seam allowance if this is necessary for the collar to fit.

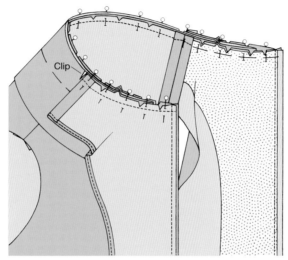

5. At both shoulders, clip upper collar to seamline. Right sides together, match and pin facing to garment and collar along neck seamline, clipping facing seam allowance if necessary. Fold back facing ends at shoulder seamlines.

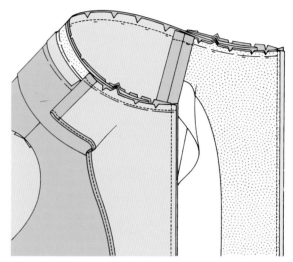

6. Fold back the free portion of the upper collar seam allowance. Baste through all layers along the neck seamline, taking care to keep the upper collar seam allowance free along the entire back neck edge. Remove all pins.

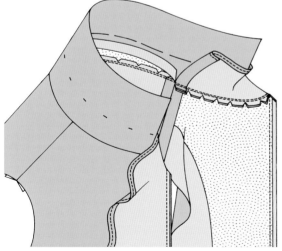

10. Place seam over a seam roll and press the front parts of the seam down, toward the garment, the back portion of the seam up, toward the collar. Press seams at opening edges toward facing; turn facing to inside of garment.

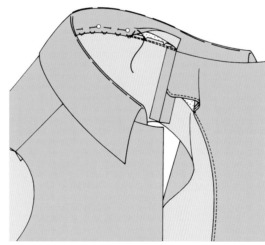

11. Let the collar fall into position along its roll line; smooth the upper collar over the under collar. Turn under the free upper collar seam allowance; pin, then slipstitch in place along the garment neck seamline. Press.

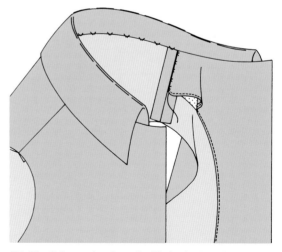

12. Slipstitch turned-under ends of facing in place along garment shoulder seamlines; press. Remove basting stitches from collar at roll line.

Pressing equipment 14 · Staystitching 84

Shawl collar

The shawl collar is like the standard notched collar in that the completion of both these collar styles involves the formation of lapels (see illustration below and on p. 168). The shawl is different from the notched collar in that its upper collar and lapels are cut from a single pattern piece. The outer edge of a shawl collar is usually an unbroken line, but on some

Constructing and applying a shawl collar

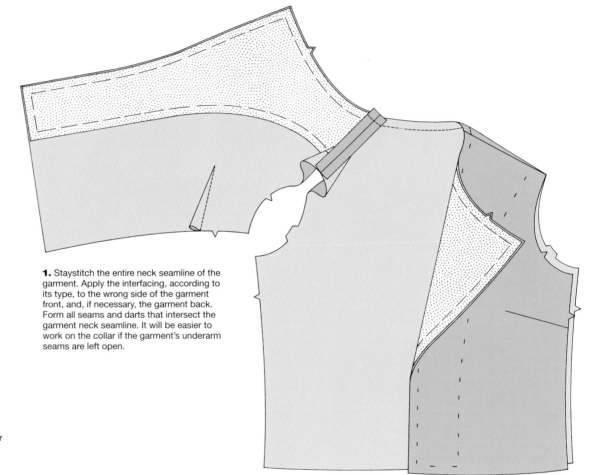

1. Staystitch the entire neck seamline of the garment. Apply the interfacing, according to its type, to the wrong side of the garment front, and, if necessary, the garment back. Form all seams and darts that intersect the garment neck seamline. It will be easier to work on the collar if the garment's underarm seams are left open.

Under collar

Collar/ lapel/ front facing

Back neck facing

Pattern pieces for a typical shawl collar are shown here. Notice that the upper collar, lapels, and front facing are cut from the same pattern piece. The under collar and back neck facing are separate pattern pieces.

patterns this edge will be scalloped or notched to give the impression of a notched collar.

The shawl collar can be attached to a wrapped-front garment that is held together by a tie belt. When used on garments such as jackets or blouses, buttons or some other kind of fastener will be used.

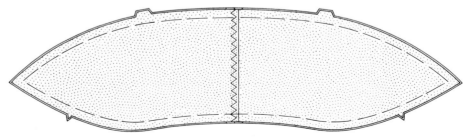

2. Form the center back seam in the under collar. Press seam flat, trim to half-width, then press open. Apply interfacing to wrong side of under collar (see p. 161).

Slipstitch 74, 80 · Seams 86–87 · Seam finishes 88–89

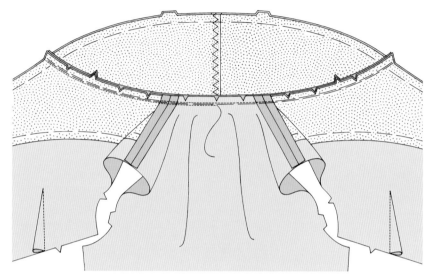

3. Right sides together, match and pin under collar to garment along neck seamline; clip garment seam allowance if necessary for collar to fit smoothly. Baste along neck seamline. Garment side up, stitch under collar to garment. Remove basting; press seam flat.

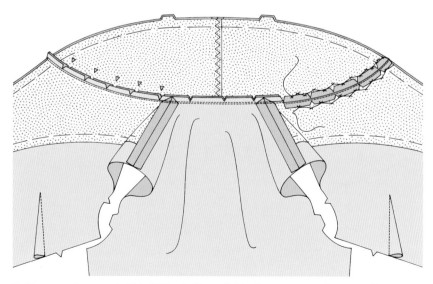

4. Trim seam allowances to ½ in (1.25 cm); diagonally trim the cross-seam allowances. Finger-press seam open; clip garment seam allowance and notch under collar seam allowance until they both lie flat. Press seam open; catchstitch over both edges to hold seam open.

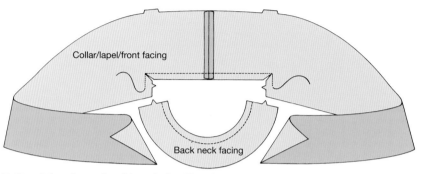

Collar/lapel/front facing

Back neck facing

5. Staystitch neck seamline of the collar/lapel/front facing pieces and reinforce corners with short stitches. Seam the two pieces together. Press seam open, then flat; trim to half-width. Clip into both corners. Staystitch neck seamline of back neck facing piece.

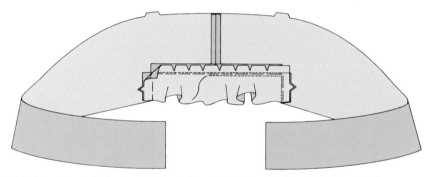

6. Match and baste the back neck facing to the collar/lapel/front facing; clip back neck facing seam allowance where necessary and spread collar/lapel/front facing at corners. Collar/lapel/front facing side up, stitch the seam, reinforcing and pivoting at corners.

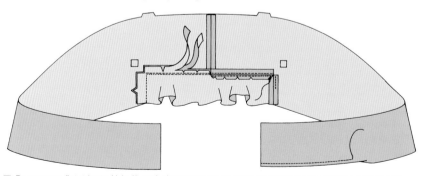

7. Press seam flat, trim to ¼ in (6 mm), then press seam open. Notch out both corners of the back neck facing seam allowance; slipstitch these edges together. If necessary, apply a seam finish to the outer, unnotched edge of the entire unit. (Continued page 178)

Constructing and applying a shawl collar (continued)

8. With right sides together, match and baste the collar/lapel/facing unit to the under collar. Stitch the seam directionally, from center back down on each half. Press seam flat; trim. Clip into seam at both ends of lapel roll line. Grade seam above the clips, making seam allowance of collar/lapel/facing unit the widest; grade seam below clips so that the garment seam allowance is the widest. Notch the seam; press open. Press seam above clips at roll line toward the under collar; press the seam below these clips toward the facing.

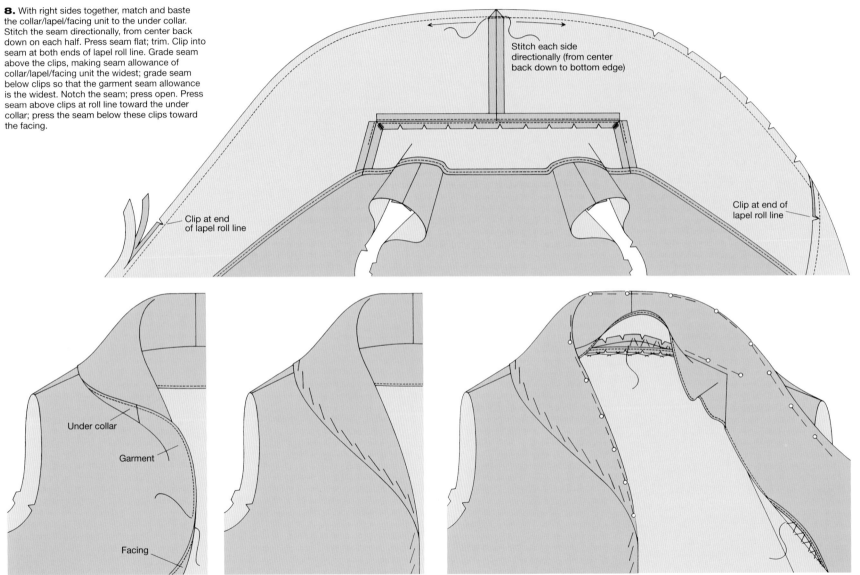

Stitch each side directionally (from center back down to bottom edge)

Clip at end of lapel roll line

Clip at end of lapel roll line

Under collar

Garment

Facing

9. With under collar and garment side up, understitch outer edge of collar and lapels. With facing side up, understitch each edge of garment opening below the lapels.

10. Turn collar/lapel/facing unit to right side. Roll outer edge of collar and lapels toward under collar; roll edges of garment opening toward facing. Diagonal-baste along edges (optional).

11. Allow collar, lapels, and the facing unit to fall smoothly into place. Pin through all layers along the roll line and just above the back neck seamline. Lift up back neck facing and, using hand basting, stitch facing and garment neck seamlines together as they fall. Remove pins. Attach lower edges of facing to garment with tacks.

Pressing equipment 14 · Stitching cornered seams 86 · Reducing seam bulk 87

Standing collars

Standing collars extend up from the neck seamline and are of two types: the **plain standing collar,** also called the band or mandarin collar; and the **turn-down standing collar,** sometimes known as the turtleneck or roll-over collar. The basic difference is their initial width; the turn-down collar is twice as wide as the band style so that it can turn back down onto itself.

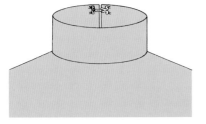

Plain standing collar

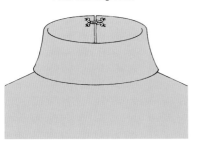

Turn-down standing collar

Rectangular standing collars, either plain or turn-down, can be constructed from either one or two pieces. A curved standing collar (plain type only) must consist of two pieces. Names given to the parts of a standing collar vary. The parts of the collars shown on the next few pages have been identified as either *collar* or *facing*. Sometimes only the collar is interfaced; if it is a one-piece unit, secure interfacing at foldline. Both collar and facing can be interfaced if desired, depending on the weight of the garment fabric. For a variation of the standing collar, a shirt collar with a stand, see page 181.

Constructing a one-piece standing collar

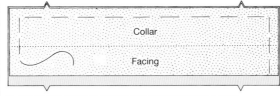

1. Interfacing for plain band collar is trimmed along neck seamline of facing, then applied to wrong side of collar and facing. (If garment fabric is bulky, interface collar only.)

3. Fold section along its foldline with right sides of collar and facing together. Match and stitch together along side seams. Press flat; trim and grade seam allowances.

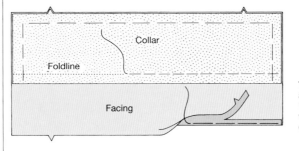

Turn-down collar is cut twice as wide as it would be if it were a plain band collar. Apply interfacing to the collar portion and ½ in (1.25 cm) into the facing area. Hold in place at the foldline with short stitches, spaced ½ in (1.25 cm) apart. Proceed with construction, following Steps 2, 3, and 4 above.

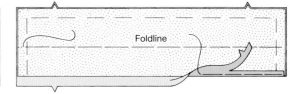

2. If necessary, baste interfacing in place along foldline. Fold up facing edge along its neck seamline; baste in place along seamline. Press; then trim to ¼ in (6 mm).

4. Press the seam open, then toward the facing. Turn collar right side out. Using a press cloth, press the collar. Remove basting stitches at foldline.

Constructing a two-piece standing collar

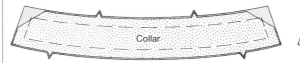

Construction of the two-piece collar is the same as for a rectangular collar. **1.** Apply interfacing to the wrong side of the collar.

3. With right sides together, match, baste, and stitch collar to facing along the side and upper seamlines. Press seams flat. Trim, grade, and notch or clip seam allowances.

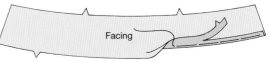

2. Fold up edge of facing along its neck seamline and toward its wrong side. Baste in place near fold. Trim to ¼ in (6 mm).

4. Press seams open, then toward the facing. Understitch the upper seamline if necessary. Turn collar right side out. Using a press cloth, press the collar.

Pressing equipment 14 · Uneven slipstitch 81 · Reducing seam bulk 87 · Hook and eye fasteners 320

Applying a standing collar to a garment

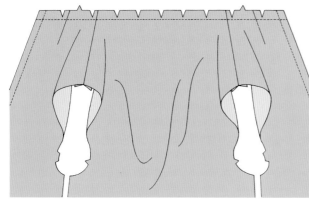

1. Staystitch the neck seamline of the garment. Form all seams and darts that intersect the neck seamline. Insert the zipper. Clip into the neck seam allowance at 1 in (2.5 cm) intervals; this will permit the collar to fit smoothly onto the garment.

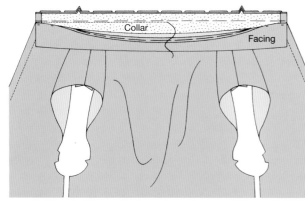

2. With right sides together, match, pin, and baste the edge of the collar to the garment along the neck seamline. Stitch the seam and secure stitching at both ends.

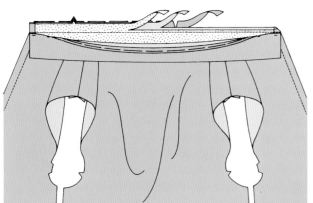

3. Press seam flat. Trim and grade seam allowances, making the collar seam allowance the widest. Trim diagonally across the corners and cross-seam allowances.

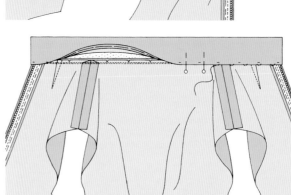

4. Using the rounded edge of a sleeve board, press the seam open, then press it up, toward the collar.

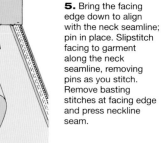

5. Bring the facing edge down to align with the neck seamline; pin in place. Slipstitch facing to garment along the neck seamline, removing pins as you stitch. Remove basting stitches at facing edge and press neckline seam.

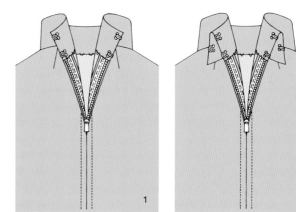

6. Attach fasteners so that the ends of collar meet when fastened. With a plain standing collar (1), sew two sets to the inside of collar, placing one set at neck, the other at the top of collar. For a turn-down collar (2), attach two sets as for the plain collar but sew another set to the center of the turned-down portion.

Pressing equipment 14 · Stitching cornered seams 86 · Reducing seam bulk 87 · Topstitching 94 · Shirt blouse 172–173 · Boy's shirt 222–223

Shirt collar with a stand

A shirt collar with a stand is commonly found on men's shirts but can also be used for jackets and women's wear. This type of collar has two sections: the collar area and the stand area. Regardless of whether the stand is cut as a separate piece or is an extension of the collar, the collar unit is applied to the garment the same way. As a rule, it is the under collar that is interfaced, but if the fabric is very lightweight or sheer, interfacing can be applied to the upper collar. It is always advisable to interface the stand. If the stand area is an extension of the collar, the interfacing is applied to both the under collar and the stand in a single piece.

A buttonhole, which is the usual closure, is generally constructed in the collar stand after the stand has been applied to the garment. Topstitching of the collar and stand is optional, but it is usually necessary if the placket of the garment has been topstitched.

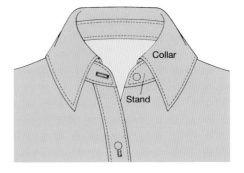

Constructing a shirt collar with a separate stand

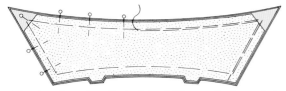

1. Interface the under collar (and stand, if it was cut out as part of under collar). Baste upper collar to under collar along side and upper seamlines. (If stand's facing was cut out as part of upper collar, handle neck edge as in Step 5.)

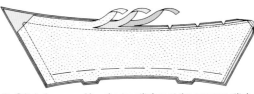

2. Stitch the seam. Use shorter stitches at the corners; stitch across corners to blunt them. Press seam flat. Trim, grade, and clip the seam allowances. Trim across corners and taper seam allowances on both sides of the corners.

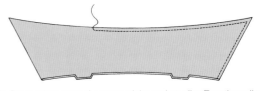

3. Press seam open, then toward the under collar. Turn the collar to the right side; pull out the corners (see Step 7, p. 162). Press collar from the under collar side. If desired, topstitch along the outer finished edges.

4. Apply the interfacing to the wrong side of the collar stand. (If collar stand was cut out as a continuation of the collar, stand was interfaced in Step 1 when interfacing was applied to under collar.)

5. Fold up the stand's facing edge along its neck seamline and toward wrong side of facing. Pin, then baste in place close to fold. Remove pins. Press; then trim the seam allowance to ¼ in (6 mm).

6. With right side of the under collar toward right side of the stand, match and pin the collar to the stand along the lower edge of the collar. The stand will extend beyond the ends of the collar.

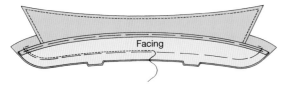

7. With right side of upper collar toward right side of the stand's facing, match and pin facing to collar and stand. Baste through all thicknesses along seamline, stitch seam. Remove basting.

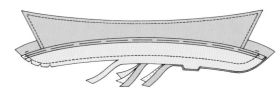

8. Press seam flat. Trim and grade the seam, making the facing seam allowance the widest. Notch and clip the curved seam allowances. Press the seam open.

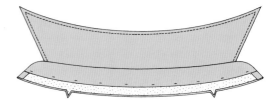

9. Turn stand and facing to the right side. Press the seam, facing and stand down, away from the collar. Fold collar down over stand into wearing position.

CHAPTER 5

WAISTLINES AND BELTS

Waistline seams, stays, and casings are sewn using various techniques demonstrated in this chapter. Whether you are joining a bodice to a skirt, making a casing or a decorative fabric belt, your garment will reflect the time and care you take.

Fitting methods 36–37 · Gathering 120–121

Waistline joinings

Waistline seams that join the top and bottom of a garment may be located almost anywhere on the body between the hip and bust. A garment waistline may fall at the natural waistline, but it may also lie just underneath the bust, as in an Empire style, or be placed on the hips, as in a dropped-waist style. The waistline may be either closely or loosely fitted.

Some waistlines are formed with a casing or an insert of fabric or ribbing. The basic procedure for constructing a joining, insert, or casing remains the same regardless of location or fit.

Waistline seams are not always straight horizontal seams; they may be curved or angled sharply toward the bust or hips. Fit the bodice and skirt individually to the body before joining them with the waist seam.

Preparation

Before sewing waistline seam, 1. staystitch waistline edges on bodice and skirt; 2. make all darts, tucks, or pleats; 3. stitch, seam-finish, and press open all vertical seams; 4. easestitch skirt waistline seam. Easestitch from right side of skirt waist seamline, breaking stitching at side seams and leaving 3 in (7.5 cm) thread ends. For bodice ease, follow pattern. Insert a zipper intersecting waistline after forming the waist seam.

Joining a bodice to a fitted skirt

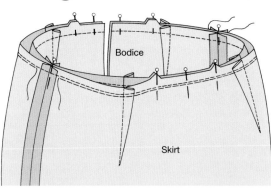

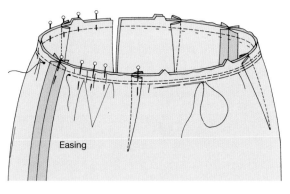

1. Turn the skirt to the wrong side and the bodice to the right side. Slip the bodice into the skirt. (Work is done with bodice inside skirt, their right sides together.) Align and pin cut edges, being careful to match side seams, center front and back, and all notches. The skirt may be slightly larger than the bodice, but easestitching will correct this.

2. Pull on bobbin threads of easestitching until each skirt section exactly fits corresponding bodice section. Secure ease threads by knotting. Distribute fullness evenly, avoiding gathers, tucks, or any fullness within 2 in (5 cm) of either side of center front and back. Pin at frequent intervals, then baste. Try on garment and make any necessary adjustments.

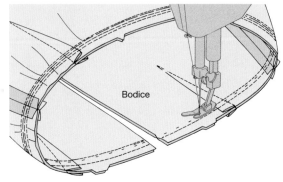

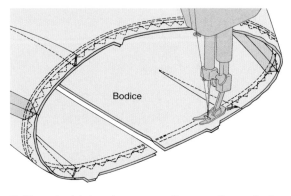

3. Stitch the waistline seam from placket edge to placket edge. Reinforce the seam by beginning and ending it with backstitching. Stitch the seam from the inside, along the bodice seamline.

4. Trim ends of darts and cross-seam allowances. Remove basting. Press seam as stitched. Finish seam either by stitching seam allowances together with a zigzag or overlock stitch; or by applying a waistline stay. Pull bodice out of skirt and press seam again, with both seam allowances directed toward the bodice.

Gathering 120–121

Joining a bodice to a gathered skirt

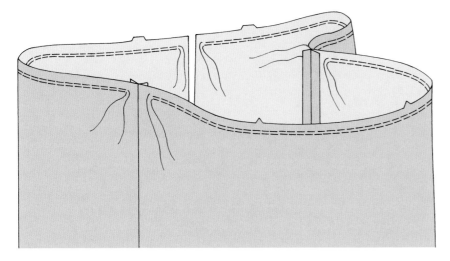

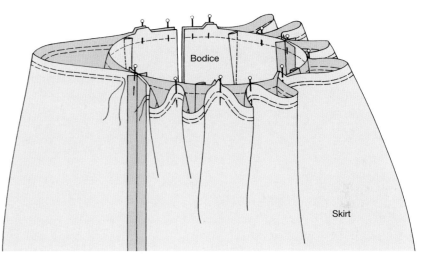

1. To prepare skirt for gathering, first machine-baste on right side along waist seamline. Section stitch so that it begins and ends at the center back and side seams, at least ⅝ in (1.5 cm) away from the vertical seamlines. This ensures that the bulk of vertical seam allowances will not be caught in the gathers. Leave thread ends at least 3 in (7.5 cm) long. Place second row of gathering stitches ¼ in (6 mm) away from the first, inside the seam allowance.

2. Turn skirt to the wrong side and bodice to the right side. Slip bodice into the skirt so that their right sides are together. With raw edges even, pin the two sections at center front and back, side seams, and notches. Pin again at points midway between those already pinned, carefully apportioning the fabric. If the skirt has a great deal of fullness, the fabric may need further dividing and pinning.

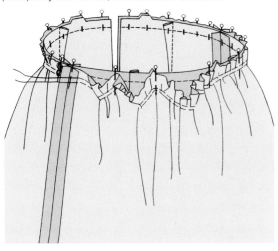

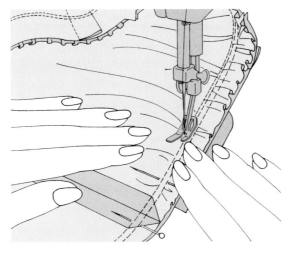

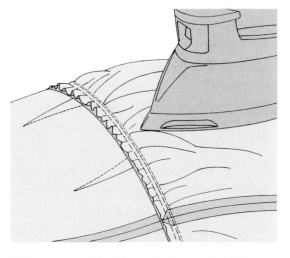

3. Pull on bobbin threads until each skirt section lies flat against corresponding bodice section. Knot threads or wrap them around vertically placed pins to secure. Distribute fullness evenly. Pin at frequent intervals. If desired, baste the waistline seam and try on garment for final fitting before stitching.

4. Stitch waistline on skirt side, from opening to opening. This is easiest to do with the skirt inside the bodice. Work slowly, feeding fabric through machine carefully and keeping any folds of fabric from being caught in the seam. Trim darts and cross-seam allowances. Remove any gathering threads visible on the right side.

5. Press seam as stitched, then pull bodice up out of skirt. To avoid flattening gathers, press up into them with the tip of the iron. Press seam allowances flat from bodice end, taking care to touch iron to seam edge only. To finish seam, stitch raw edges together with the zigzag or overlock stitch, or apply a waistline stay.

WAISTLINES

Seam finishes 88–89

Applying a waistline stay

Many waistline seams should be stayed to prevent stretching. The stay may be applied before or after zipper insertion. A stay applied *before* zipper insertion is machine-stitched to the skirt seam allowances, the ends caught into the zipper seam. A stay applied

after zipper insertion is basted to darts and seams by hand and fastens separately behind the zipper. It is particularly useful for delicate or stretchy fabrics and dresses that have no separate waistline seam or whose skirt fabric is heavier than that of the bodice.

The stay should be made of firmly woven tape or grosgrain ribbon. Width can vary from ½ to 1 in (1.25 to 2.5 cm); the greater width is recommended for the stay that fastens separately. It will be necessary to preshrink whatever material is to be used as a stay.

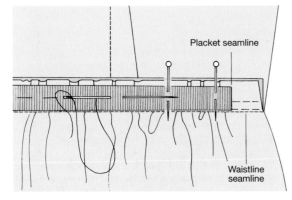

To stay a waistline before inserting a zipper:
1. Measure the garment's waistline from placket seamline to placket seamline; cut stay to this measurement. Pin and baste it to the seam allowances on the skirt side, with ends at placket seamlines and the edge along the waist seamline.

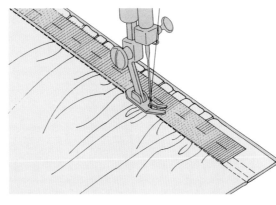

2. Holding the stay and the seam allowances together, let the bodice fall inside the skirt so that the right sides of the bodice and skirt are together. With the garment in this position, machine-stitch the stay, through both of the seam-allowance layers, just above the stitched seam.

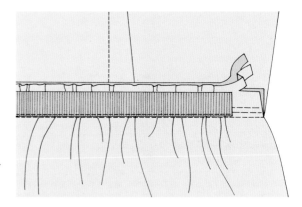

3. Trim seam allowances to the width of the stay, taking care not to cut the stay. If the fabric is bulky, trim the skirt seam allowance narrower than that of the bodice. If the fabric frays easily, apply a suitable seam finish through the stay and both of the seam allowances. Press toward bodice.

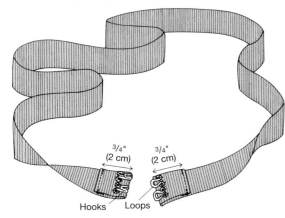

To apply a waistline stay after zipper insertion: 1. Cut grosgrain ribbon length of waistline seam plus 2 in (5 cm). Fold ends back 1 in (2.5 cm); turn raw edges under ¼ in (6 mm); machine-stitch in place. Sew hooks and round eyes to ends, loops extending beyond edge.

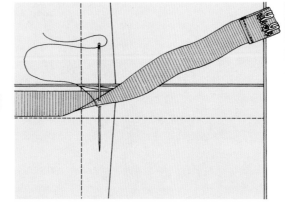
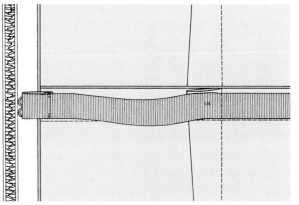

2. Position stay over waistline seam and pin its center to seam allowance at center front. With this as the starting point, pin stay to side seams and darts. Tack the stay securely at these points. Make sure the stitches go through both waistline seam allowances, as well as darts or vertical seam allowances, but do not show on the right side, as illustrated above right. If garment has no center front seam, tack stay to just the waist seam allowances at these points. Leave at least 2 in (5 cm) of stay free at each side of the zipper for easy fastening before the zipper is closed.

Knits seaming 98

Inset waistlines

A waistline inset can be made of fabric or ribbed stretch banding. On a fabric inset, there are two waistline seams to sew; each should be stayed, or the inset faced, with the facing serving as a stay. Ribbed stretch banding (ribbing) pulls the waistline to size while providing comfortable fit. The amount of ribbing depends on its stretchability and whether the garment has a zipper.

To estimate the amount needed to encircle the waist, allow ½ in (1.25 cm) for joining seams, and 1¼ in (3 cm) for seam allowances if there will be a zipper.

For a garment with no zipper, seam ribbing into a circle. Right sides together, join ends with a ¼ in (6 mm) seam. If the ribbing is to be used double, seam, press open; fold ribbing with seam allowances inside.

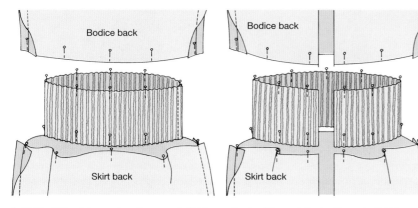

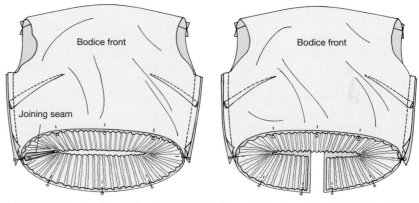

1. Divide ribbing into equal sections; mark divisions with pins. Pin-mark the bodice and skirt into eighths also. For accuracy, pin-mark first at the side seams, center fronts and backs, then halfway between these points. **If a zipper is to be inserted,** leave the ⅝ in (1.5 cm) seam allowances out of sectioning; place a pin ⅝ in (1.5 cm) from each end of ribbing, then divide the area between the two pins into eight equal sections.

2. With right sides together, pin the ribbing to the bodice, matching pin markings. If ribbing has been sewn into a circle, match the joining seam to a bodice construction seam (either the left side seam or center back seam). **If there is to be a zipper,** pin free ends of ribbing to placket openings, with raw edges of ribbing matched to raw edges of bodice. Ribbing may have to be stretched slightly.

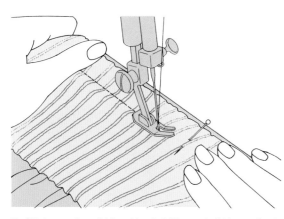

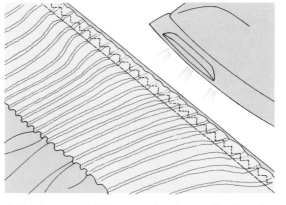

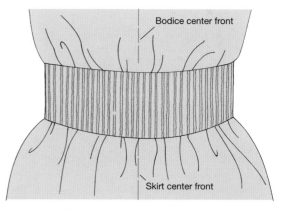

3. Stitch seam from ribbing side, stretching each ribbing section to fit corresponding bodice section. Finish seam with a second row of stitching or a zigzag stitch, ¼ in (6 mm) from first row of stitching, within seam allowance. Trim seam close to second stitching.

4. To help seam and ribbing recover from the stretching done when the seam was stitched, steam the seam from both the ribbing and bodice sides. Hold iron above fabric and allow the steam to penetrate the seam for a few seconds. Let area cool before continuing.

5. To attach ribbing to skirt, repeat Steps 2 to 4. Pin carefully so that the ribs of the insert run vertically. This is easily done by following one rib down from bodice center front to skirt center front. **If a zipper is to be inserted,** carefully match cross-seams of inset.

Waistline casings

A casing is a fabric "tunnel" enclosing elastic or a drawstring. When the elastic or drawstring is drawn in, the effect is similar to that of a conventional waistline joining or waistband, but far easier to construct. Waistline casings are practical because they can be adjusted easily to changes in waist measurement. Replacement of drawstring or elastic is equally simple.

All casings should be at least ¼ in (6 mm) wider than the elastic or drawstring they are to enclose. There are two types of casing: fold-down and applied.

A **fold-down casing** is formed by turning an extension at the garment edge to the inside and stitching it in place. This casing is ideal for pull-on pants and skirts, especially those made of knit fabrics. An **applied casing** consists of a separate strip of fabric stitched to the area to be drawn up, on either the outside or inside of the garment. If the casing is inside but the drawstring is to be tied on the outside, provision must be made to lead the drawstring outside. This can be done with buttonholes or with openings

Applied casing at an edge Applied casing in place of waistline seam Fold-down casing

in the garment seam; either must be planned and constructed before the casing is applied.

A *heading* can be formed on either type of casing, provided it occurs at an edge. Simply allow extra width for the desired heading, stitch the casing as directed,

then stitch a second row at the proper depth for the casing. When the casing is drawn up, it will gather the heading automatically. For a *shirred effect,* stitch several additional rows on an extra-wide casing and thread elastic or drawstrings through each of the channels.

Fold-down casings

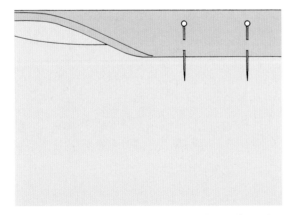

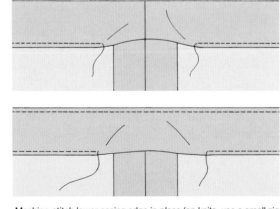

A fold-down casing is best for straight edges but can be used on a curved edge if kept very narrow. It is mainly used at the waistline of skirts and pants. To make casing, turn garment edge under ¼ in (6 mm); press. Turn casing to wrong side to desired depth; pin in place.

Machine-stitch lower casing edge in place (on knits, use a small zig-zag stitch for elasticity). If a closed casing, leave a small opening for threading elastic or drawstring (not needed if ends are open). If casing will have no heading, place second row of stitching near top fold.

For a casing with a heading, follow preceding steps, but make casing wider and omit edgestitching along top fold. Measure up from lower stitching the desired width of casing; machine-stitch second row (no opening needed). Backstitch (or overlap) ends to secure.

Diagonal crosswise grain 56

Applied casings

An applied casing may be sewn onto a one-piece garment that has no waistline seam, or as a facing for the top edge of pants and skirts and the lower edge of blouses and jackets.

It may be sewn to either the inside or the outside of a garment. If it is sewn outside, the casing may be made from garment fabric or from a contrasting trim. A casing sewn inside is usually made of a lightweight lining fabric or a ready-made bias tape. If an inside casing has a drawstring that is to be led to the out-

side, it is necessary to provide buttonhole or in-seam openings. An applied casing is most easily shaped to a garment if casing is cut on the bias.

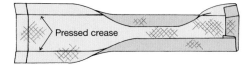

To prepare casing from fabric, first determine the width of the finished casing. It must equal the width

of the elastic or drawstring plus ¼ in (6 mm) ease. In addition, allow an extra ½ in (1.25 cm) in your width calculation for the edges. Length is determined by the circumference of the garment where the casing will be applied plus ½ in (1.25 cm) for finishing ends.

Determine the true bias of the fabric, then chalk the dimensions of the casing onto the fabric. After cutting, fold under and press ¼ in (6 mm) to the wrong side on all edges. Press the ends under before pressing down the sides.

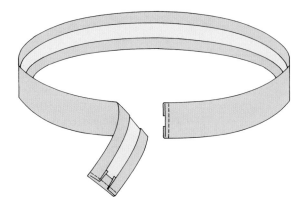

If casing is to be sewn to a one-piece garment, edgestitch both ends (turned under in preparation described above).

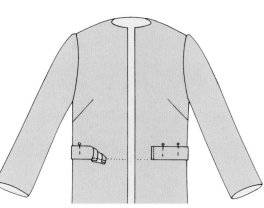

Pin casing to garment with lower edge on waistline marking on inside or outside of garment as pattern instructs.

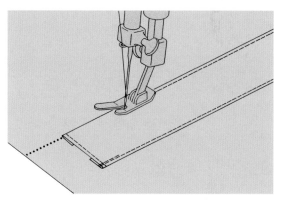

Edgestitch casing to garment on long sides. Backstitch at both ends of stitch lines to strengthen. Press casing flat.

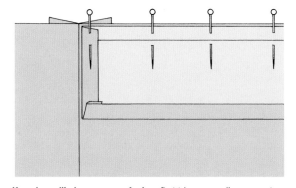

If casing will also serve as facing, first trim seam allowance at garment edge to ¼ in (6 mm). With right sides together and starting at a vertical seam, pin casing to garment.

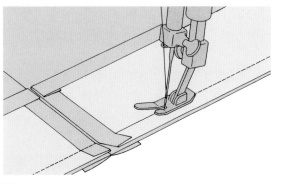

With ends of casing turned back as shown, machine-stitch along pressed crease of casing, which is ¼ in (6 mm) from cut edge. Overlap the stitching at ends for reinforcement.

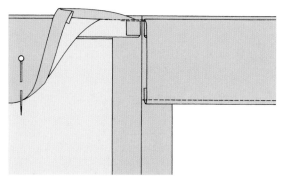

Turn casing to wrong side of garment, letting garment edge roll slightly inside. Pin casing in place. Edgestitch along lower edge, again overlapping stitching. Press flat.

Flat catchstitch 81 · Uneven slipstitch 81 · In-seam buttonholes 307 · Worked buttonholes 312–313

Threading elastic and drawstrings

Casings are threaded with elastic or drawstrings that, when drawn or tied, fit snugly around the body. Elastic for this purpose should be a firm, flat type or non-roll waistband elastic.

The length depends upon the elastic's stretchability, but it should be slightly less than the measurement of the body at the casing position plus ½ in (1.25 cm) for lapping. Drawstrings may be cord, fabric tubing, braid, leather strips, ribbons, even scarves. Elastic can be combined with fabric or ribbon tie ends to give comfort and a pretty finish; the length of the ribbon ends depends upon the type of tie you have in mind.

Finishing a full casing

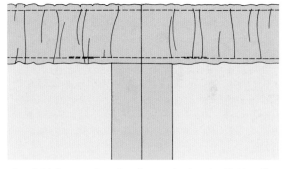

On a fold-down casing, close the opening by edgestitching. Keep area flat by stretching the elastic slightly as you sew. Take care not to catch the elastic in the stitching along the bottom edge.

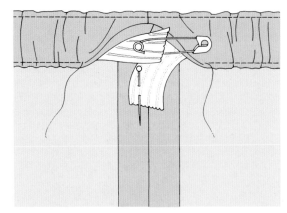

To insert elastic into a casing, attach a safety pin to one end of the elastic; secure other end to garment so it will not be pulled through the casing as the pin is worked around the waistline. Take care not to twist the elastic.

To join ends of elastic, first overlap them ½ in (1.25 cm) and pin. Stitch a square on the overlapped area, crisscrossing it for strength. Or make several rows of zigzag stitching. Pull joined ends inside casing.

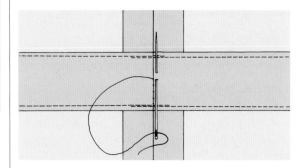

To finish an inside applied casing, slipstitch the ends of the casing together by hand. Make certain that the drawstring or elastic is not caught in the stitching.

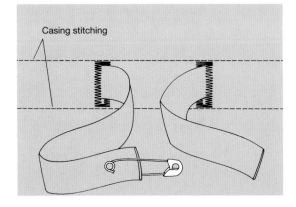

A drawstring can be threaded through a casing with a safety pin. If it is an inside casing, the drawstring can be led in and out through two vertical buttonholes, worked on garment before casing is applied.

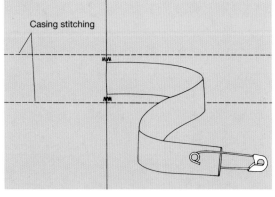

A drawstring can also be led through an inside casing by way of in-seam openings. Leave openings in seams the width of drawstring; reinforce with bar tacks at ends.

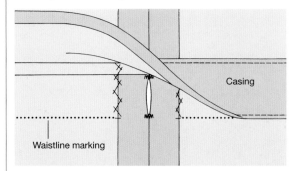

To hold seam allowances flat in an in-seam opening, catch-stitch them to garment. Be sure to do this before the casing is applied, taking care that the stitches do not show on outside of garment.

Whipstitch 73 · Invisible zipper 284 · Centered zipper 286

Finishing a partial casing

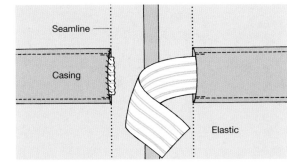

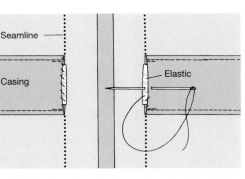

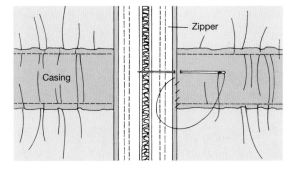

1. If a centered zipper is used with a casing, casing should stop at zipper seamlines. Apply casing; insert elastic or drawstring; whipstitch ends of elastic to ends of casing.

2. If an invisible zipper is used with a casing, extend the casing ¼ in (6 mm) beyond zipper seamlines as it is applied. Sew ends of elastic or drawstring to ends of casing.

3. Insertion of either zipper will secure ends of casing and elastic or drawstring. To finish, press zipper seam allowances flat over casing; whipstitch to casing as shown.

Mock casings

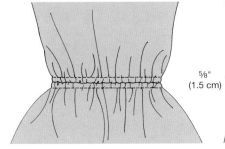

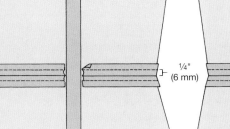

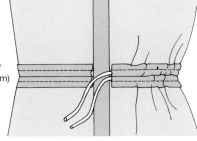

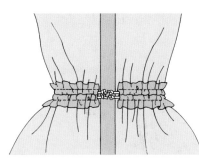

Plain seams, threaded with round elastic or fine strong cord, can substitute for conventional casing. The effect resembles shirring.

1. Stitch waistline seam; press open. Form "casings" by stitching seam allowances to garment ¼ in (6 mm) on each side of seamline.

2. Using a tapestry needle, thread cord or elastic through the casings. Adjust the shirring to the desired waist measurement.

3. Knot the ends of the cord or elastic, then stitch over them when inserting the zipper or closing the center back seam.

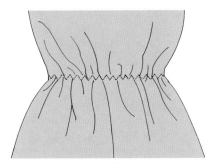

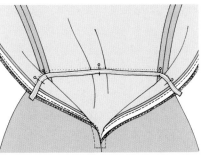

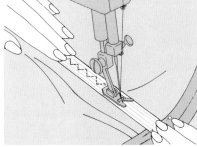

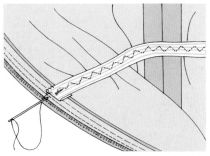

Narrow elastic can be stitched to the wrong side of a garment that has no waist seam. The result is very similar to that of a casing.

1. Cut elastic to desired length plus 1 in (2.5 cm); divide it and waistline into eighths. Pin elastic in place, with ½ in (1.25 cm) ends at openings.

2. Stretch the elastic between pins as you stitch. Use either a narrow multistitch zigzag or two rows of straight stitching.

3. Turn the loose ends of the elastic under ½ in (1.25 cm) and whipstitch them securely to the seam allowances or zipper tapes.

Sheer curtains

Fabric: Rocle, Tarare (France)

Fabrics

Sheer cotton or synthetic curtain fabric

Amount

For a 48 in (120 cm) -wide window, two lengths of 58/60 in (150 cm) -width fabric, approximately 6 yd (5.5 m) wide.

See "Cutting," next page, for details on how to determine the amount of fabric you will need for the curtains.

Notions

Fishing line to weigh down the hem (available where fishing supplies are sold)

Pattern pieces

1 Curtain panel – cut 2

Cutting

These sheer curtains have a casing with a ¾ in (2 cm) heading above the casing. They are slipped over a curtain rod and the fabric is distributed evenly along the rod. Measure the casing generously so that it slips easily over the curtain rod and still fits after possible shrinkage during laundering. The casing allowance includes the following: the diameter of the rod, double the heading height, ⅜ in (1 cm) seam allowance, and, depending on fabric thickness, an extra ⅜ to ¾ in (1 to 2 cm) to ensure an easy fit over the curtain rod. You can also simply pin the fabric over the rod for an exact fit.

Add 4 to 6 in (10 to 15 cm) to the length (floor to window top) so that the curtains drape generously on the floor if desired with a narrow hem or hang just to the floor with a wider hem.

The curtain width is determined by the width of the curtain rod and the desired fullness. The standard width is usually double to triple the rod size. The side hems are folded twice and require an additional 3 in (8 cm). If the fabric width is not sufficient, you will need to join one or more fabric panels with a simple seam. Make certain that any possible cut edges are placed on the left or right outer edges of the finished curtains. When using a fabric with a printed motif, be careful to match the design. If the motifs need to be cut apart, make sure to use the full motif at the opposite end.

Sewing instructions

● **Side hems:** Turn in the edges about ¾ in (2 cm), and press (Fig. 1).

● Fold the side edges once again at the same width, and press. Stitch close to second fold (Fig. 2).

● **Casing:** Fold the upper edges of the fabric ¾ in (2 cm), and press. Then fold the fabric once again at 2½ in (6 cm), and press (Fig. 3).
● Stitch the casing close to the lower folded edge (Fig. 4).

● Mark the heading about ¾ in (2 cm) from the upper edge with pins placed parallel to heading. Slide the curtain rod through the casing to make certain it fits before stitching and make adjustments if necessary.
● Stitch the heading seam along this marking, removing the pins as you go.
● **Hem:** Fold the lower hem narrowly twice, and press. Stitch close to fold.
● Using a bodkin, pull the fishing line through the hem to provide the weighting.

● Tie a loop at each end of the line and secure them to the hem with a few hand stitches (Fig. 5).
● For floor-length curtains, turn up and stitch a wider double hem.

Hanging the curtains

● Slide the curtain rod through the casing.
● Distribute the fabric evenly on the rod.

Grain in fabric 56–57 · Uneven slipstitch 81

Straight waistbands — waistline formed as it is applied

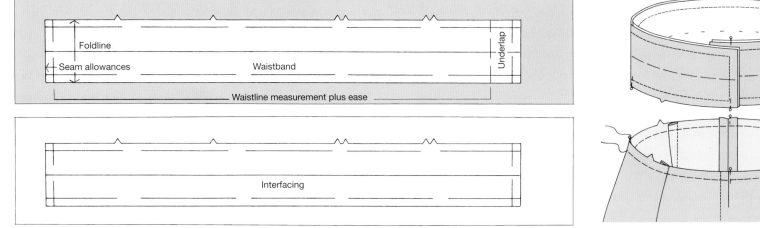

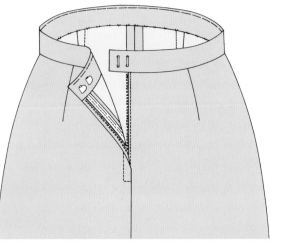

This is perhaps the most basic and traditional of all the waistband techniques. The waistband for this method is cut with an extended (self) facing and then applied to the garment as a flat piece. The ends are formed and finished while it is being applied to the garment. If the waistband is to be cut without a pattern, determine the correct

length and width plus underlap. The length of the waistband should be placed on the lengthwise grain of fabric for greatest stability. Cut and apply interfacing according to type of interfacing and number of layers being used. Mark the foldline of waistband by hand-basting through all thicknesses.

1. Pin-mark waistband and garment into sections (mark edge of waistband to be sewn to the garment). Place one pin at beginning of overlap or seam allowance and one at beginning of underlap. Divide remainder of band into quarters. Pin-mark garment waistline also into four equal parts, using zipper opening as the starting point.

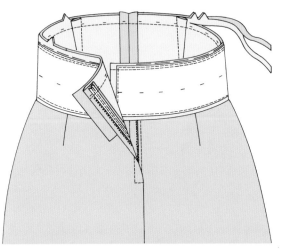

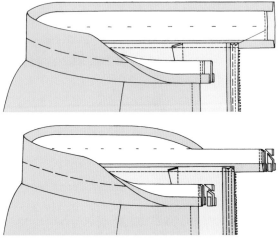

2. With right sides together, pin waistband to garment, matching pin marks and notches. Draw up the ease thread on garment between pins so that the fullness is evenly distributed and the garment lies flat against the waistband. Baste, then stitch, on the seamline. Press seam flat. Grade the seam allowances. Press the waistband and seam up.

3. Turn the ⅝ in (1.5 cm) seam allowance on the long unstitched edge of the waistband to the wrong side and press. To finish the ends, fold the waistband along the foldline so that the waistband is wrong side out, with right sides together. Pin at each end and stitch on the ⅝ in (1.5 cm) seamline. Trim both seams and corners and turn waistband right side out.

4. Pull corners out so that they are square. Press the waistband facing to the inside of the garment along the foldline, keeping the turned-under seam allowance intact. Pin the turned-under seam allowance to the garment. Slipstitch folded edge to the seamline, making certain that no stitches show through to the outside. Attach suitable fasteners to ends of waistband.

Cornered seams 86 · Reducing seam bulk 87 · Seams with fullness 96

Straight waistband made before application

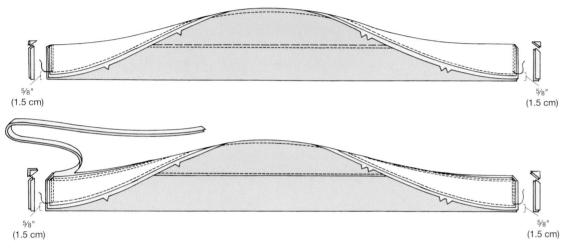

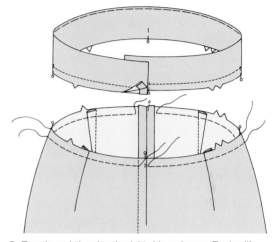

1. This waistband may be cut with an **extended facing,** as in the method shown opposite, or with a **separate facing.** Apply the interfacing according to type and the number of layers being used, making sure it is attached to the side that will be outermost in the finished garment. To construct the waistband with an extended facing, fold the waistband in half lengthwise, right sides together,

and stitch across each end from the fold to within ⅝ in (1.5 cm) of the opposite edge. Secure the stitching. If the band has a separate facing, place right sides of facing and waistband together and stitch across ends and top. Stop and secure stitching ⅝ in (1.5 cm) from lower edge on ends. Press the seams flat, then grade seams and trim corners.

2. Turn the waistband to the right side and press. To simplify matching waistband to garment, pin-mark both into four equal sections. On the waistband, first place a pin at the beginning of the underlap, then divide remainder of band into quarters. Pin-mark the garment seamline evenly into quarters as well, starting at the actual opening of the zipper.

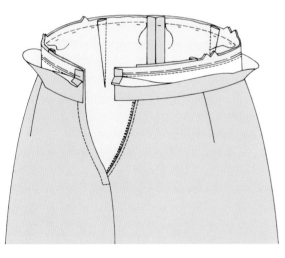

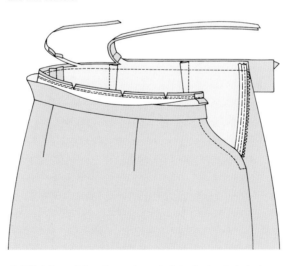

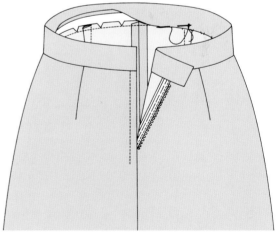

3. With right sides together, pin the waistband to garment edge. Carefully match all notches and pin marks, making sure finished edge of waistband overlap is flush with edge of zipper closing. Pull up the ease thread and adjust fullness evenly between pins so the skirt lies flat against the waistband. Baste along seamline.

4. Stitch the waistband seam from placket edge to placket edge. Be careful that no tucks are formed in garment ease and caught in the stitching. Press the seam as stitched, then grade seam allowances. Clip seam allowances so they will lie flat when encased in waistband. Remove any basting that might show from right side.

5. Turn waistband right side out. Press along foldline and ends. Turn under ⅝ in (1.5 cm) along unstitched edge and pin to garment. Slipstitch fold of seam allowance to garment around waist seamline and underlap. Sew carefully so no stitches are visible on right side of garment. Attach suitable fasteners to ends of waistband.

Slipstitch (uneven) 81 · Seams with fullness 96

Straight waistband with professional waistbanding

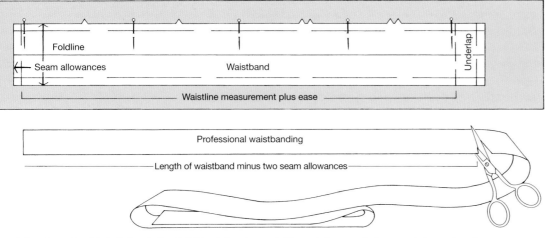

Foldline

Seam allowances   Waistband   Underlap

Waistline measurement plus ease

Professional waistbanding

Length of waistband minus two seam allowances

The waistband used for this technique is the straight waistband with self-facing. Cut the waistband twice the width of the professional waistbanding plus two seam allowances. The length of the waistband equals the body waist measurement, plus ease allowance, plus two seam allowances, and at least 1¼ in (3 cm) for underlap (allow extra length for an overlap).

1. Pin-mark the areas between underlap and overlap or seam allowance into quarters. Cut waistbanding (which has been purchased in the exact width the finished waistband is to be) the length of the waistband minus two seam allowances; extend waistbanding through underlap and overlap but not into seams at ends.

2. Pin-mark garment waistline into quarters. Pin waistband to garment, matching all marks. Place beginning of the underlap to the back edge of the zipper opening, and overlap or seam allowance to front edge of zipper opening. Distribute garment ease evenly; baste and stitch seam. Press as stitched, then press seam and waistband up. **Do not grade seam.**

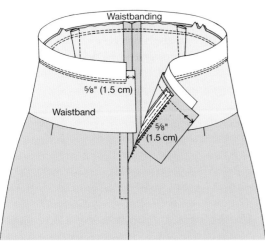

Waistbanding

⅝" (1.5 cm)

Waistband

⅝" (1.5 cm)

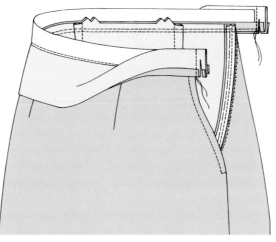

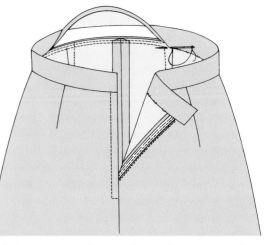

3. With waistband down over garment, lap the waistbanding over seam allowances. Place so that the width of the waistbanding is away from the garment, one edge is aligned exactly to the seamline, and the ends are ⅝ in (1.5 cm) away from the ends of the waistband. Sew along edge of banding, through both seam allowances. Grade now if desired.

4. To form the ends of the waistband, fold band along the center foldline so that right sides are together. Pin once at each end to hold the fold in place. Stitch along each end of the waistband as close as possible to the waistbanding without actually stitching through it. Trim seams and corners. Turn the waistband right side out, over banding.

5. Pull corners square, then press the waistband down over the banding. Turn under the ⅝ in (1.5 cm) seam allowance along the unstitched edge and press in place. Pin the folded edge to the waistband; slipstitch this fold to the waistband seam or just above it. Stitching should not show on the right side of the fabric. Finish the ends by attaching fasteners.

Grain in fabric 56–57 · Hand stitches 73, 81, 82 · Reducing seam bulk 87 · Zippers with underlay 299

Straight ribbon-faced waistband

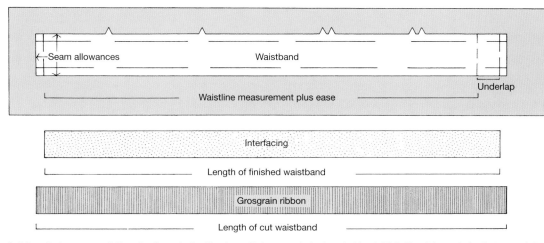

Seam allowances · Waistband · Underlap

Waistline measurement plus ease

Interfacing

Length of finished waistband

Grosgrain ribbon

Length of cut waistband

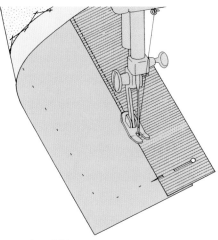

A ribbon facing on a waistband reduces bulk without sacrificing stability, making it a practical choice for nubby or heavy fabrics. Cut waistband on lengthwise grain of fabric. Width should equal that of finished waistband plus two seam allowances. Length should total waist measurement, plus ease, two seam allowances, overlap if

desired, and at least 1¼ in (3 cm) for underlap (or to equal zipper underlay if there is one — see Step 4). Purchase straight grosgrain ribbon for the facing the width of *finished* waistband and length of *cut* waistband. Cut interfacing the width and length of finished waistband. Catchstitch or iron to wrong side of waistband.

1. Lap one edge of ribbon over the right side of waistband upper seam allowance. Align edge of ribbon with seamline and match the cut ends of ribbon with ends of the waistband. For accuracy in stitching, it is best to pin or baste the ribbon in place. Stitch as close to the edge of the ribbon as possible, using a short stitch.

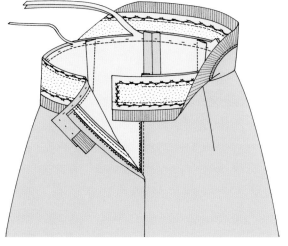
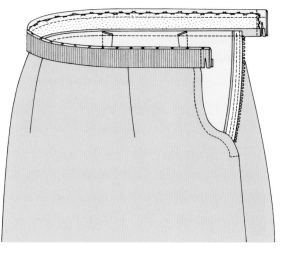
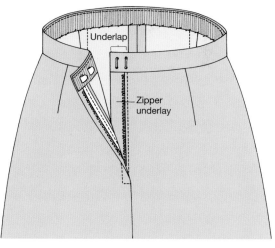

2. Pin-mark the waistband and garment into four equal sections, as described on page 194. Pin waistband to garment, right sides together, matching pin marks and notches. Draw up the ease thread so garment lies flat against waistband; keep ease evenly distributed. Baste and stitch the seam. Press seam as stitched; grade the seam allowances.

3. Press waistband and seam allowances up. To finish ends, fold right sides of the waistband together along the edge of the ribbon. Pin ends in place and stitch across them on the seamlines. Trim seams and corners; turn waistband to the right side. Press ribbon facing to the wrong side along the folded edge. Pin the free edge of ribbon to waist seam.

4. Slipstitch the free edge of the ribbon to the waistband seam; attach fasteners. The zipper underlay illustrated here is used for fine tailored garments, often in conjunction with a ribbon-faced waistband. If this is the zipper application you are using, allow for an underlap equal to the zipper underlay when cutting the waistband, ribbon, and interfacing.

Bermuda shorts

Shorts fabric: Roole, Tarare (France)

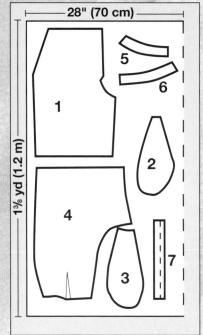

28" (70 cm)

1³⁄₈ yd (1.2 m)

Fabrics

Cotton or cotton-blend sportswear fabrics, linen, microfiber

Amount

For size 12: 1³⁄₈ yd (1.2 m) of 54/56 in (140 cm) -width fabric

Notions

½ yd (45 cm) fusible interfacing, 24 in (60 cm) width
1 zipper, 7 in (18 cm)
2 buttons, ⁵⁄₈ in (1.5 cm) diameter

Pattern pieces ▶▶▶▶▶▶▶▶▶▶▶▶▶▶

1 Shorts front – cut 2
2 Pocket front – cut 2
3 Pocket back – cut 2
4 Shorts back – cut 2
5 Front facing – cut 2
6 Back facing – cut 2
7 Belt carriers – cut 1

Burda pattern 3098 was modified for this project. In our version, the shorts have pleats in front instead of darts, and the zipper fly facings are cut as part of the front pattern pieces.

Pleats, which are in effect unfinished darts, provide comfort and create a graceful effect when used in pants and shorts. If you wish, you can use darts instead in this project.

The Bermuda shorts go well with the safari jacket, page 240.

Sewing instructions
● **Darts and pleats:** Stitch the darts on the shorts back pieces. Press darts toward back center.
● Lay the pleats according to the dart notches, pin, and secure by stitching ⅜ in (1 cm) from the upper edge (Fig. 1).
● Finish all side seam and hem edges.
● **Pockets:** Cut a ¾ in (2 cm) -wide strip of interfacing shaped to follow the opening edge of the pocket front, and fuse to shorts front piece. Lay pocket fronts on shorts front, right sides facing, and stitch. Trim seam allowances. Turn pocket to inside, and press. Topstitch close to pocket edge at ¼ in (7 mm) (Fig. 2).

● Lap shorts fronts onto pocket back pieces, matching notches at top and side. Stitch raw edges of pocket bag together. Baste side and upper edges of pocket to shorts front.
● **Belt carriers:** Press long edges of strip for belt carriers ⅜ in (1 cm) under. Fold strip in half and press. Topstitch close to long edges. Cut into 8 pieces, each 2½ in (6 cm) long.

Position carriers on waist edge at darts and pleats. Baste to waist edge.
● **Closing center seams:** Stitch back and front center seams to marking for zipper placket (Fig. 3).
● **Waistline finished with shaped facing:** Cut the interfacing for the waistline facing and fuse to facing. Join facing center back seam. Finish all lower edges. Stitch each part of waist facing to corresponding section of pants (Fig. 4).

● **Side seams:** Lay shorts front and back together and stitch side seams, including facing. Press seams open.
● Turn waistline facing into place, press, and topstitch from garment right side at ³⁄₁₆ in (5 mm) and 2¾ in (7 cm).
● **Zipper:** Press zipper placket to inside along center front of right side and ¾ in (2 cm) from center toward

cut edge for left side. Place zipper under the left side fold, with excess length at top. Stitch close to fold. Pin fly closed, matching center fronts. Baste right zipper tape to underlap and stitch. Topstitch the right zipper placket from outside (Fig. 5).
● **Finishing waist:** Turn under the unfinished ends of the belt carriers and pin them into position on the waistband. Make sure to allow ample

width for inserting the belt. Stitch to the topstitch lines. Fasten waist facing to inside at zipper and side seams by hand.
● **Hem:** Check the length of the shorts. For the hem, turn hem edge under ¼ in (7 mm), and press. Turn again 1¼ in (3 cm), and press. Topstitch close to fold.

● **Buttons and buttonholes:** Work the two buttonholes in right front edge, ⅝ in (1.5 cm) and 1½ in (4 cm) from upper edge.
● Sew the buttons to placket.

Topstitching 94 · Reducing seam bulk 87 · Seams with fullness 96

Topstitched straight waistband

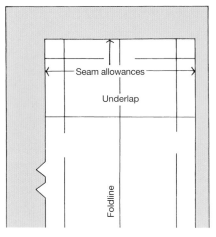

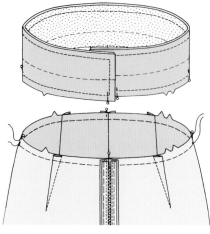

1. This quick and secure waistband is suitable for casual garments. Cut the waistband length to equal the waist measurement, plus ease, seam allowance, underlap, and overlap if desired. Width is twice the finished width plus seam allowances. Apply interfacing.

2. Divide waistband and garment into sections. On the waistband, place a pin at beginning of underlap and another pin at overlap or seam allowance; pin-mark the space between the pins into quarters. Pin-mark the garment waistline into quarters, starting at the zipper.

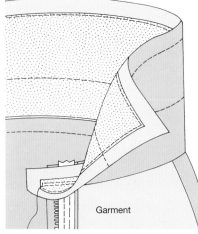

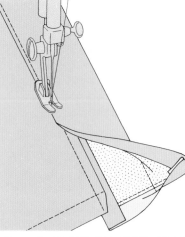

3. Pin the *right* side of the waistband to the *wrong* side of the garment, matching all pin marks and notches. Draw up ease thread and distribute any fullness evenly. Stitch the seam. Press as stitched, then press both seam and waistband up. Grade seam; trim corners.

4. Turn under seam allowance on free edge and ends of waistband; press. Turn waistband down to *right* side on the foldline and pin turned-under edge over waistline seam, covering first stitching. Topstitch close to the edge through all the thicknesses. Attach fasteners.

Straight waistband formed with selvage

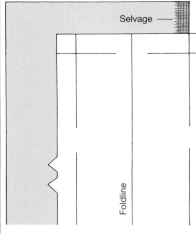

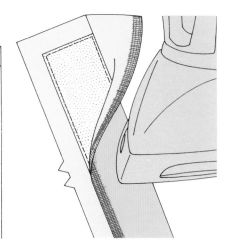

1. Not merely quick, this waistband technique helps to reduce bulk by eliminating a seam allowance. Determine the size of the waistband, then cut the waistband so that the *seamline* of one long edge falls on the selvage. This provides one finished edge.

2. Fold the waistband lengthwise along foldline, wrong sides together (the long raw edge should extend ⅝ in [1.5 cm] below the selvage); press. Interface the half of the waistband that has the raw edge. Interfacing should not extend into any seam allowances.

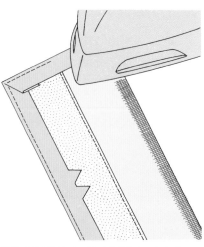

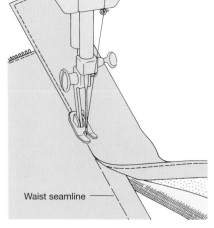

3. Turn the long raw edge and the ends to the wrong side on the seamlines and press. Make certain that the pressed-under-edge does not extend below selvage edge when waistband is folded in half. Pin-mark waistband and garment into quarters as directed on page 195.

4. To enclose the garment edge within the waistband, place selvage to the inside and fold along waist seamline. Match all pin marks; pin if desired. Topstitch close to fold, from end to end, catching selvage in stitching. Press waistband flat. Attach fasteners.

Basting stitches 70 · Hemming stitches 81

Contour waistbands — construction and application

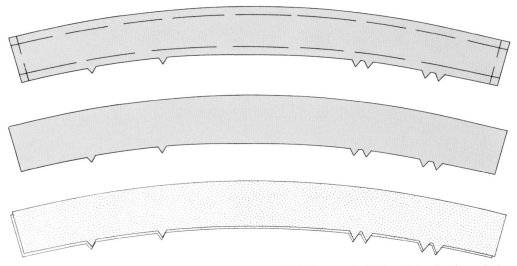

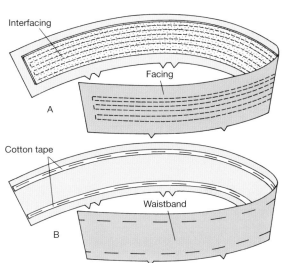

A contour waistband is at least 2 in (5 cm) wide and is formed to fit the body's curves; it is often decoratively shaped along the top edge as well. The width and shape of this waistband requires a separate facing as well as a double layer of firm interfacing. The interfacing is not applied to the waistband, as is usually done, but instead to the waistband facing. This is done by padstitching the facing, which builds in and holds a permanent shape. (See Padding stitches, p.71.)

1. Apply the two layers of interfacing to wrong side of waistband facing and padstitch through all layers by machine (A). To prevent stretching of the long edges, baste ¼ in (6 mm) cotton tape over seamline on wrong side of waistband (B) (optional).

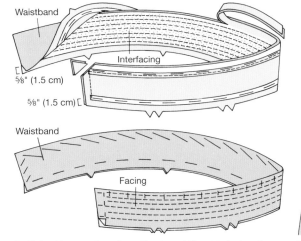

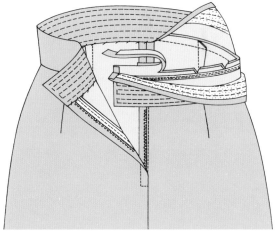

2. Right sides together, pin and baste waistband to facing along ends and upper edge. Starting and ending ⅝ in (1.5 cm) from lower edge, stitch as basted, pivoting at corners and stitching through center of cotton tape. Press seam flat. Trim and grade seam allowances. Turn the waistband right side out; diagonal-baste around all three finished edges and press.

3. Pin-mark waistband and garment waistline into quarters; on waistband, place a pin at beginning of the underlap, then divide remainder of band into quarters. Pin waistband to garment, right sides together, matching all markings and the finished end of waistband to front edge of zipper opening. Adjust ease as needed; baste, then stitch seam.

4. Trim and grade the waistline seam; press it and waistband away from garment. Turn under seam allowance on lower edge of the facing and slipstitch the fold to the waistline seam and underlap. Remove all basting. Press the finished waistband. Apply fasteners; the width of the waistband determines the number of sets and their placement.

Uneven slipstitch 81 · Staystitching 84 · Seam finishes 88–89 · Fasteners 320–322

Waistbands with facing — waistline finished with shaped facing

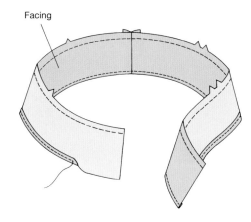

Facing

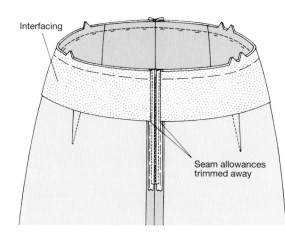

Interfacing

Seam allowances trimmed away

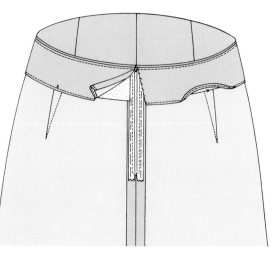

Facing

Interfacing

1. Cut facing from garment fabric; if this fabric is heavy, facing may be cut from a sturdy lighter-weight fabric to reduce bulk. Staystitch facing sections ⅛ in (3 mm) inside waist seamline. Stitch sections together, leaving open the seam that corresponds to the placket opening. Apply appropriate seam finish to the outer edge of the facing.

2. For medium to lightweight fabrics, apply a fusible interfacing or, if you wish to use a more traditional method, apply one layer of interfacing to garment. Seam interfacing the same as facing; trim away ½ in (1.25 cm) from outer edge and all of seam allowances at ends. Baste wrong side of interfacing to wrong side of garment, matching markings and positioning ends over zipper tapes.

If fabric is heavy, the combination of two layers of interfacing plus padding stitches will support the waistline area and reduce wrinkling during wear. Cut the interfacing from facing pattern minus waistline seam allowance; trim lower edge of interfacing to same width as facing. Stitch interfacing seams and apply to wrong side of facing; padstitch. (See Padding stitches, p. 71.)

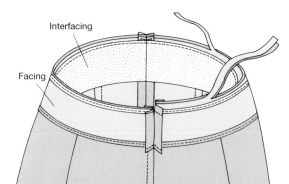

Interfacing

Facing

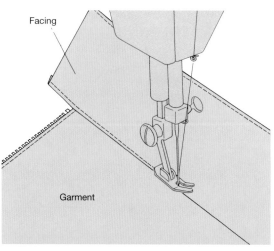

Facing

Garment

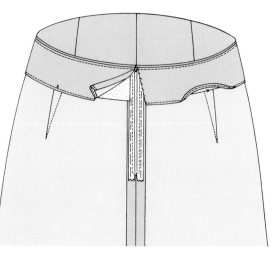

3. To apply facing, first pin facing to garment, right sides together, matching all seams and notches. Match seam allowances at ends of facing to edges of placket opening. Pin ½ in (6 mm) -wide cotton tape over waist seamline. Baste through all thicknesses. Stitch seam and press flat. Then trim, grade, and clip along the seam allowances.

4. From the wrong side, with the facing extended away from the garment, press all seam allowances toward the facing. Understitch the seam to keep facing from rolling to the outside of the garment. With facing and seam allowance extended away from garment, stitch from right side close to waist seamline, through facing and seam allowances.

5. Turn facing to inside of garment, allowing seamline to roll inside slightly. Press along waist edge. Baste facing to garment at seams and darts. Turn seam allowances of facing ends to wrong side, making sure facing is turned in such a way that it will not catch in zipper, slipstitch to zipper tape. Attach a hook and eye or hanging snap fastener at top of placket.

Slipstitch 74, 80 · Seam finishes 88–89 · Shaping bias 263 · Snap fasteners 322

Waistline finished with ribbon facing

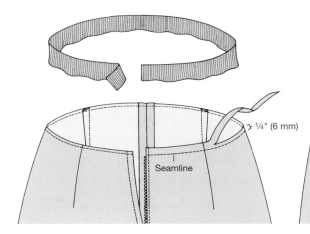

1. Use 1 in (2.5 cm) -wide grosgrain ribbon available by the yard/ meter or in prepackaged quantities. Cut it to a length equal to the garment waistline measurement plus 1¼ in (3 cm). Staystitch the garment waistline on the seamline and trim the seam allowance to ¼ in (6 mm).

2. Place a pin ⅝ in (1.5 cm) from each end of ribbon. Lap wrong side of ribbon over right side of garment waistline so that the edge of the *inside* curve of the ribbon is over the staystitched seamline. Match pins at ribbon ends to placket edges. Baste in place. Stitch close to edge of ribbon.

3. Turn the ribbon to inside of garment, allowing garment edge to roll in slightly. Fold under ribbon ends on ⅝ in (1.5 cm) mark so that they clear zipper, and press entire edge of ribbon. Baste ribbon to garment at all seams and darts; whipstitch (see p. 73) ends to zipper tape. Attach fasteners.

Waistline finished with extended facing

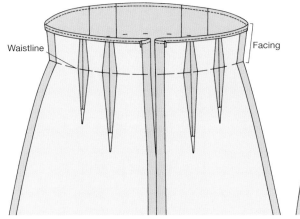

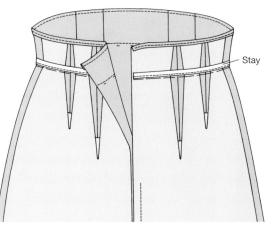

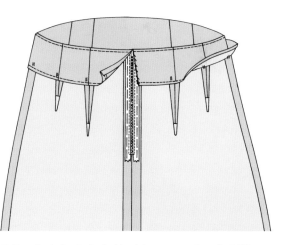

Some patterns are designed with an extended (self) waistline facing. Garment darts extend through the waistline into the facing; pattern foldline marks finished waistline edge.
1. Stitch darts and seams on both the garment and facing. Press the seams open; slash and press open the darts. Finish facing edge as required for fabric.

2. No interfacing is used; instead, a stay is applied to the waistline. Measure the garment along the foldline from edge to edge, cut a length of seam binding or cotton tape to that measurement. With width of tape on facing, pin the stay along the foldline; have ends of stay even with open edges. Stitch through stay and garment ⅛ in (3 mm) from foldline.

3. Turn the facing to the inside of the garment along the foldline; press. Insert the zipper as recommended by the pattern. Turn in the ends of the facing, being sure to clear the zipper; slipstitch (see p. 80) them to the zipper tape. Baste the facing to the garment at all seams and darts. Finish top of closure with a hook and eye or a hanging snap fastener.

Skirt

Skirt fabric: Rocle, Tarare (France)

Fabrics
Stretch gabardine, synthetic blends
   Caution: Stretch fabrics can shrink. Press the fabric with a damp cloth or with a steam iron or pre-wash before cutting.

Amount
For size 12: ³/₄ yd (0.7 m) of 58/60 in (150 cm) -width fabric. Lining: ⁵/₈ yd (0.6 m) of 54/56 in (140 cm)-width lining.

Notions
8 in (20 cm) mediumweight inter-facing, 24 in (60 cm) width
1 zipper, 7 in (18 cm)

Pattern piece
1 Skirt front – cut 1 on fold
2 Skirt back – cut 2
3 Front facing – cut 1 on fold
4 Back facing – cut 2
Lining – cut using pattern pieces 1 and 2
Burda pattern 2541 was used for this skirt. However, this project uses only one dart in the skirt front, not two as in the original pattern. Waist facings have been added as well.
   The skirt length is 21 in (52 cm). If your measurements are different, adjust accordingly.

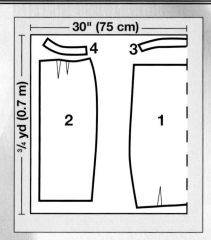

30" (75 cm)

³/₄ yd (0.7 m)

4   3

2   1

This basic skirt is a minimalist design, with tapered side seams, a back slit for movement, and shaped waist facings onto which the lining is attached.

This skirt goes well with the safari jacket on page 240.

Tips for stretch fabrics: To build stretch into seams, stitch using a very narrow zigzag stitch or a stretch stitch.

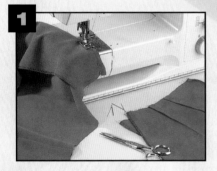

Sewing instructions

● Staystitch waist edges.
● **Darts:** Baste and stitch the darts on the front and back skirt panels. Press darts toward the center front or center back (Fig. 1).
● Finish the seam and hem edges of the garment.
● Pin skirt backs with right sides together. Baste center back seam including the placket and the skirt slit. Then, machine stitch between the placket marks and the top of the slit.
● Press seam open. Remove basting at placket and skirt slit.

● Lay skirt front on skirt back, right sides together. Baste side seams, try skirt on, and stitch permanently.
● Press seams open (Fig. 2).

● **Lining and facing:** Do not stitch the darts on the lining. Instead, fold and press.
● Finish all seam and hem edges of the lining.
● Cut the interfacing for the facing pieces. Fuse to wrong side of facings.
● Join facings to corresponding lining sections (Fig. 3). Press the seam allowances toward the lining. Stitch the back center seam of lining

between the slit and zipper placket. Stitch the side seams. Press seams open. Finish slit edges of lining with narrow hem.
● Match the waist edges of skirt and facing, right sides together. Baste and stitch.
● Understitch the waist seam close to original seam through facing and seam allowances. Turn lining to inside and press (Fig. 4).

● **Zipper:** Baste the zipper to the skirt fabric under the edges of the placket so that the zipper teeth are covered. Stitch zipper in place by machine, using the zipper foot (Fig. 5).
● Fasten the turned-in ends of facing to the zipper tapes. Leave edges of lining free.

● **Hem:** Check skirt length. Shorten if necessary, leaving 1½ in (4 cm) for the hem. Turn up hem and press. Press slit edges back over hem. Topstitch hem and slit from right side or hand-finish, depending on the fabric. The lining can be hand-sewn to slit edges if desired.
● Turn the lining under ⅜ in (1 cm) twice at the lower edge and stitch. The lining should be ¾ in (2 cm) shorter than the skirt.

Elastic waistbands — applied elastic waistband (self-band)

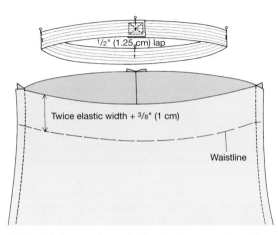

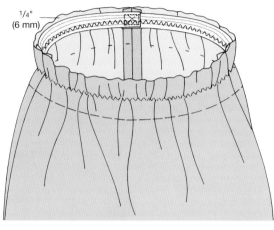

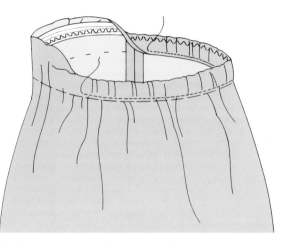

1. This technique can be used only when the garment has not been dart-fitted at waistline. Cut garment with an extension above waistline that is twice the width of the elastic plus 3/8 in (1 cm). Mark waistline with basting stitches. Cut a length of elastic to fit snugly around waist plus 3/8 in (1 cm). Overlap ends and stitch securely; pin-mark elastic into quarters.

2. Pin elastic to the inside of extension, matching each pin mark to a side seam, center back, or center front. Place top edge of elastic 1/4 in (6 mm) down from top edge of the extension. Stitch along the lower edge of the elastic, stretching it between the pins as you stitch to fit the fabric. A wide zigzag stitch is best but a short straight stitch may be used.

3. Turn the elastic and fabric to inside of the garment along stitched edge of elastic. The elastic will be completely covered. If fabric does not fray, raw edge may be left as it is. If fabric frays, turn under 1/4 in (6 mm) on raw edge. Stitch along the waistline marking through the waistband, elastic, and garment, stretching the elastic during stitching.

Applied elastic waistband (separate band)

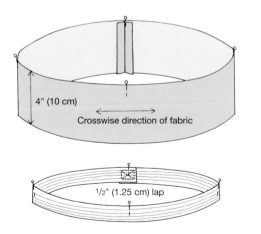

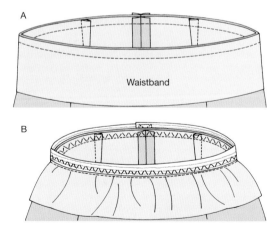

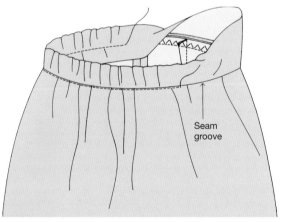

1. This method is suitable only for stretchy knits. Cut waistband on crosswise grain of fabric, 4 in (10 cm) wide and same length as *garment* waist measurement plus seam allowances. Join ends with a 5/8 in (1.5 cm) seam. Cut 1 in (2.5 cm) -wide elastic to fit *body* waist snugly plus 1/2 in (1.25 cm). Overlap 1/2 in (1.25 cm) at ends; stitch securely. Pin-mark waistband, elastic, and waistline into quarters.

2. Matching pin marks and seams, pin waistband to skirt with right sides together. Stitch a 5/8 in (1.5 cm) seam, stretching both pieces of fabric as you sew (A). Press seam as stitched. Lap elastic over waistline seam allowance with the bottom edge of elastic just above first row of stitching. Using a zigzag stitch, sew elastic to seam allowance, stretching it to fit between pins (B) as you stitch.

3. Fold waistband over elastic to the inside of garment. Working from the outside, pin the waistband in place, inserting pins just below the seamline so the excess length of the waistband, on the inside, is caught in the pinning. Stitch from right side in the seam groove, stretching elastic so waistband is flat. Trim away excess seam allowance from lower edge of waistband inside the garment.

Decorative stretch waistbands

Decorative stretch waistbands are available in solid colors, plaids, or stripes. Variously woven, braided, or shirred, they come in several different widths. Choose an elastic similar in weight to the fabric.

Woven elastics are called webbings, and their stretchability varies from limited to moderate. Webbings are quite firm and will not roll over during wear. Limited-stretch webbing should be used only when the garment has a placket opening. **Braided elastics** have a moderate amount of stretch and can often be used without a placket opening. **Shirred bandings** are any fabric stitched with elastic thread.

On some products, both **edges are finished**; on others, only one. This determines how banding is applied. On unfinished edges, stitching lines often are indicated.

Attaching decorative elastic

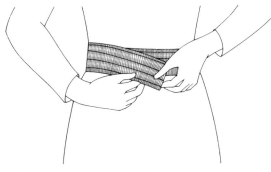

1. Purchase decorative elastic or shirred banding in a length to fit around the waistline snugly, allowing an additional 2 in (5 cm) for finishing ends. Width choice depends on the effect desired. To avoid fraying during construction, always cut straight across the elastic. As an extra precaution, stitch across cut ends with a straight or zigzag stitch.

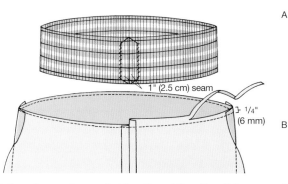

2. Sew all garment seams that form the waistline. Staystitch on garment waistline seam and trim seam allowance to 1/4 in (6 mm). If no closure is being used, seam ends of elastic or banding by placing right sides together and stitching a 1 in (2.5 cm) seam. Press open. Turn top edges of seam allowance in diagonally and baste seam allowances to waistband.

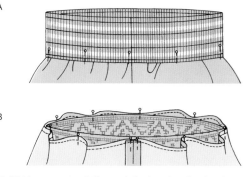

3. Divide garment waistline and elastic or banding into four or eight equal parts; pin-mark. If both edges of elastic are finished, lap wrong side of elastic over right side of garment. Place waistband seam at center back and match pins (A). If one edge is unfinished, place elastic inside garment, right sides together, matching pins and stitch lines (B).

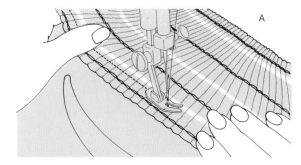

4. Stitch elastic with either a straight stitch set at 12–14 (2 mm) stitch length or a zigzag stitch of medium length and width. For a lapped waistline seam (A), stitch just inside the first elastic thread if sewing banding, but close to the finished edge if elastic webbing is being used. If the elastic has one unfinished edge, sew along indicated line (B). Sew between elastic threads if possible. With

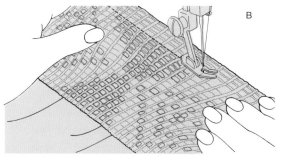

one hand behind presser foot, the other in front, carefully stretch elastic between pins as you stitch, to fit garment. Make certain stitch line of elastic remains aligned with seamline of skirt. Remove pins as you reach them; do not stitch over them. Overlap stitching at ends. Press seam carefully as it was stitched; test iron temperature first on a scrap to make sure the heat will not damage elastic.

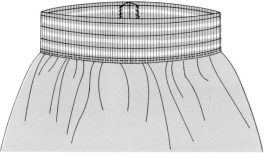

5. Press waistband up. The finished waistband pulls the garment into size by forming soft gathers; the number of gathers depends on size difference between waistline of garment and waistband. If a closure is included in garment, finish the ends of the elastic by turning them under the desired amount and tacking down. Underlap should extend under overlap enough to allow for fasteners.

Girl's skirt

Fabrics
Cotton, cotton jersey

Amount
For size 6: 18 in (0.5 m) of
54/56 in (140 cm) -width fabric

Notions
18 in (0.5 m) ribbed stretch banding

Layout ▶▶▶▶▶▶▶▶▶▶▶▶▶▶▶▶▶▶▶▶
1 Skirt
No pattern is needed for this skirt.
Simply measure the desired length, in
this example, 14½ in (37 cm).

When using knits, it is not
necessary to finish the seams.

This project is ideal for a novice
or young sewer.

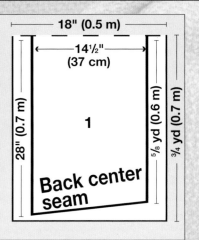

18" (0.5 m)
14½"
(37 cm)
28" (0.7 m)
⅝ yd (0.6 m)
¾ yd (0.7 m)
1
Back center seam

Skirt fabric: Rocle, Tarare (France)

This easy-to-sew skirt is gathered at the waist and made with commercially available elasticized ribbing. See page 207 for a description of attaching this type of waistband.

In order to save sewing time, buy only ribbing that is finished on both edges.

The project calls for basting before stitching, as it is aimed at the beginner sewer.

Cutting

Measure the desired length of the skirt and add ⅜ in (1 cm) for the upper seam allowance and 1¼ in (4 cm) for the hem. When using a very light fabric add more to the hem and turn the edge three times instead of two. Cut the fabric double, using its full width.

Sewing instructions

● **Back center seam:** With the right sides together, match the edges, pin, and baste. Stitch the seam. Remove pins and basting threads. Finish the seams and press open (Fig. 1).

● Finish the hem edge.

● **Ribbing:** Try on the ribbing at its stretched-out width; cut to size, allowing 1¼ in (3 cm) for the seam.

● Make the ribbing into a ring using an enclosed seam. With wrong sides together, stitch seam, using ⅜ in (1 cm) seam allowances. Trim and turn right sides together; stitch enclosing first seam (Fig. 2).

● Divide the ribbing into four equal quarters with pin or pencil markings along one edge. One marking should be on the seam (Fig. 3).

● Mark the upper edge of the skirt in a similar fashion with pins or small snips in the cloth.

● Place two rows of gathering stitches on the upper edge of the skirt. Leave the threads long.

● Pull gently on the bobbin threads from each end to gather the edge (Fig. 4).

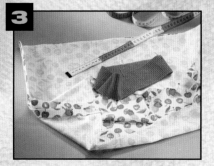

● Matching skirt and waistband seams and all other pin or snip markings, lay wrong side of waistband over gathered skirt edge so it covers the gathering threads. Pin at right angles to the edges, stretching to distribute the gathers. Baste close to waistband edge, stretching gently as you sew (Fig. 5). Stitch permanently.

● Remove the pins and basting threads.

● Remove any visible gathering threads.

● **Hem:** Fold the hem twice and stitch close to upper fold.

Even slipstitch 74, 80

Belts — tie belts

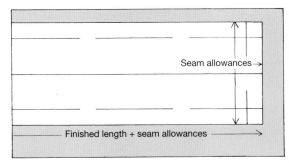

Seam allowances →

Finished length + seam allowances →

1. Belt may be cut on either the bias or straight grain. Cut it twice the desired finished *width* plus seam allowances, and the necessary *length* plus seam allowances. Length should equal waist circumference plus enough extra to tie ends.

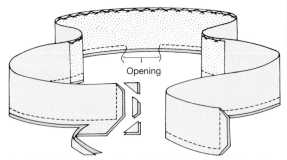

Opening

2. If belt is to be interfaced, apply interfacing only to portion that encircles waist. Fold belt in half lengthwise, right sides together. Stitch ends and long edge, leaving an opening for turning. Trim and grade seams and corners.

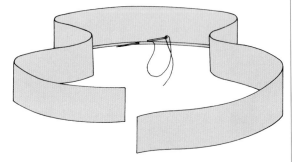

3. Turn belt to the right side through the opening. Pull corners out so that they are square, and press edges carefully. Press in the seam allowances at opening and slipstitch opening closed. Give finished belt a final pressing.

Reinforced belts

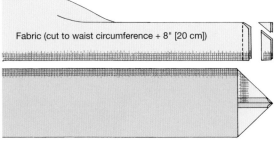

Fabric (cut to waist circumference + 8" [20 cm])

To hand-finish: 1. Cut fabric for belt twice the width of belting plus ½ in (1.25 cm), with one long edge on the selvage. To form a point at one end, fold fabric in half lengthwise and stitch end with ½ in (1.25 cm) seam. Press seam open.

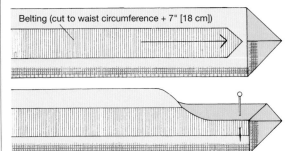

Belting (cut to waist circumference + 7" [18 cm])

2. Turn finished end right side out. Cut belting so one end has the same point as the fabric. Insert pointed end of the belting into fabric point. Press flat. With belting centered on fabric, pin raw edge of fabric over belting.

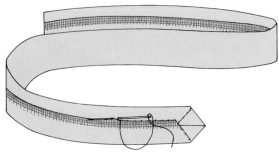

3. Pin selvage edge over raw edge, pulling the fabric taut around belting. Slipstitch at point, then along selvage edge. Finish the belt by attaching buckle to unfinished end. If a prong buckle will be used, insert eyelets.

Belting

To machine-finish: 1. Cut fabric twice width of belting plus 1¼ in (3 cm). Shape one end of belting. Fold fabric over belting, wrong side out. Stitch close to belting, using a zipper foot. Trim seam allowances to ¼ in (6 mm); center seam.

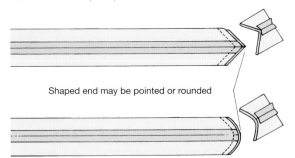

Shaped end may be pointed or rounded

2. Press the seam open with the tip of the iron. Pull shaped end of belting into position inside stitched fabric tube. Carefully stitch close to, but not through, the belting. Trim seam. A closely fitted cover for the belting has now been made.

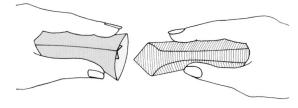

3. Remove the belting and turn the fabric tube right side out. Do not press. Cup belting and slip it into belt, shaped end first. Attach buckle to unfinished end. If a prong buckle will be used, insert eyelets in shaped end of belt.

Uneven slipstitch 81

Contour belts

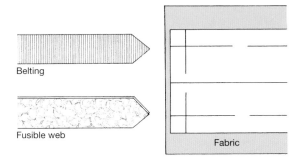

Belting

Fusible web

Fabric

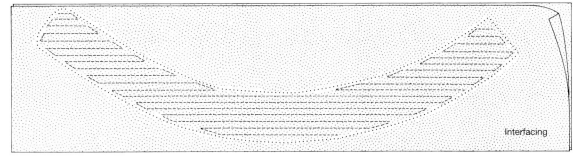

Interfacing

To fuse: 1. Cut belting and two strips of fusible web the length and width that the finished belt is to be. Shape one end of each of the strips into a point. Cut the belt fabric the length and twice the width of the belting.

Because a contour belt is shaped to fit the curve of the body, regular straight belting cannot be used for backing. Use two layers of a sturdy interfacing, such as hair cloth or firm-grade iron-on. A separate shaped facing is required.

1. Cut all layers of the belt on the lengthwise grain. If *sew-on interfacing* is being used, pin the two layers together and trace shape of finished belt onto one. Make rows of machine stitching within outline on lengthwise grain.

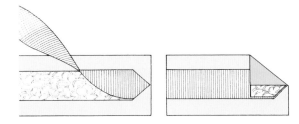

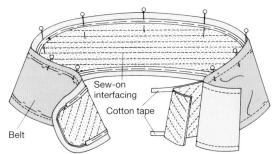

Sew-on interfacing

Cotton tape

Belt

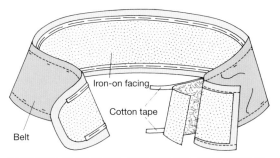

Iron-on facing

Cotton tape

Belt

2. Center a strip of fusible web, then the belting, on the wrong side of fabric. Follow manufacturer's directions to fuse layers. Cut a triangular piece of fusible web and place on belting point. Fold fabric over point and fuse point only.

2. Cut the interfacing along the outline. Staystitch the belt along all outer edges. Center the padstitched interfacing on the belt, leaving a ⅝ in (1.5 cm) margin on all sides; baste in place. Center and baste ⅛ in (3 mm) cotton tape over seamlines.

If using iron-on interfacing, cut two layers to shape of finished belt. Center one layer at a time on the wrong side of the belt, leaving ⅝ in (1.5 cm) on all sides. Fuse in place. Center and baste ⅛ in (3 mm) -wide cotton tape over seamlines.

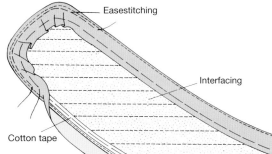

Easestitching

Interfacing

Cotton tape

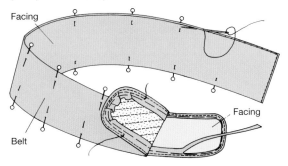

Facing

Facing

Belt

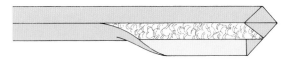

3. Fold the long edges of the fabric over belting and press. Insert fusible web and then cut away any web not covered by fabric at the point. Fuse the fabric in place. Attach buckle; insert eyelets for a prong buckle.

3. Apply a row of easestitching on seamline at curved end of belt. Press seam allowances to wrong side, over interfacing, drawing up easestitching as needed so seam allowances lie flat. Hand-baste to interfacing with long stitches.

4. Staystitch belt facing and turn all edges in ¾ in (2 cm); baste in place. Trim seam allowances to ½ in (1.25 cm). Pin facing to belt and slipstitch into place along all edges. Remove basting. Attach buckle; insert eyelets for a prong buckle.

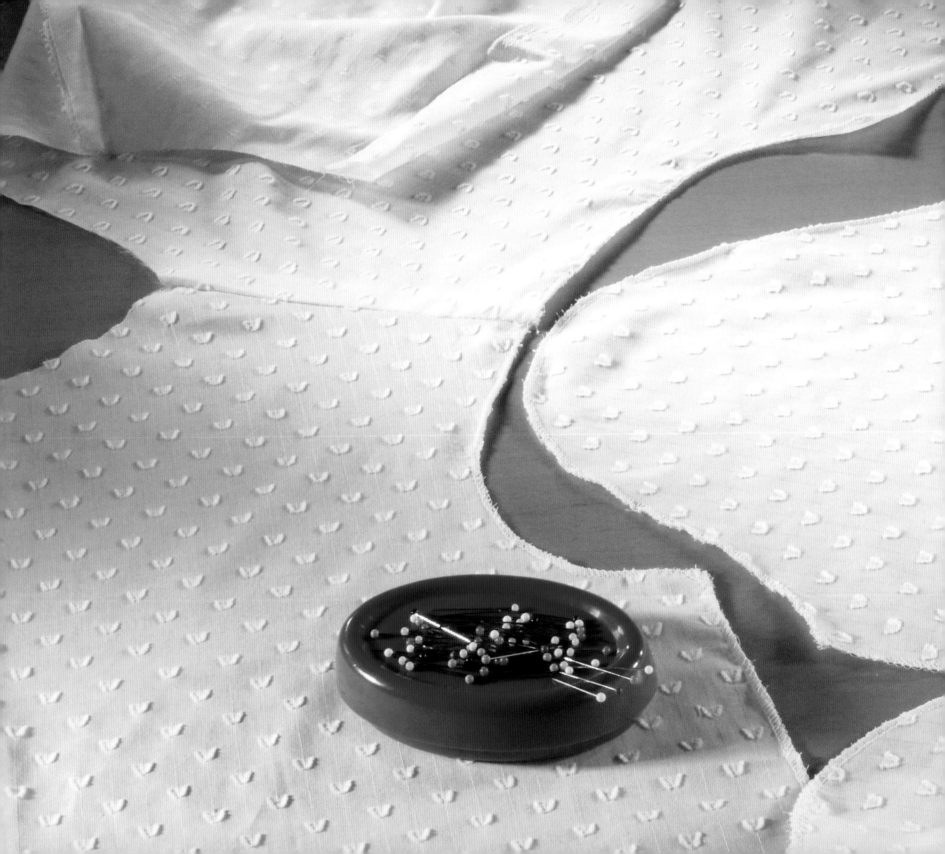

CHAPTER 6

SLEEVES AND SLEEVE FINISHES

Dresses, blouses, and jackets are always finished using specific types of sleeves or sleeve finishes. Whether a garment has set-in sleeves or a sleeveless finish, the secret to success always depends on an exact fit.

Basic sleeve types

There are many types of sleeves. A garment may have armholes that are merely finished, producing a **sleeveless** look; or it may have sleeves, either **set-in** or **raglan,** that are separately made and attached to the garment. Still another possibility, **kimono** sleeves, are cut as extensions of the main bodice.

Armholes on most sleeveless garments are cut to comfortably encircle the arm, with upper edge resting at shoulder point. There are many variations of the sleeveless look. Garments are sometimes designed with wider-than-usual shoulder widths that drop over the shoulders to create a little cap. Whatever an armhole's shape, it is usually finished with a facing unit cut to the same shape.

Set-in sleeves are the most widely used type. The top edge or *cap* can be slightly rounded or fully gathered, the length long or short, the bottom tapered, flared, or gathered. Armholes can vary from the standard round armhole to more deeply cut styles.

Most set-in sleeves have a slightly rounded cap; the cap should meet the shoulder edge with no dimples or puckers (see p. 216). The raglan sleeve is joined to the garment in one continuous seam running diagonally from the front neckline to the underarm and up to the back neckline (see p. 218). The kimono sleeve is one of the easiest types to construct because it is merely an extension of the bodice. The kimono sleeve is usually loose fitting, but in garments where it is cut for a closer fit, it will require an underarm gusset (see pp. 220–221).

Set-in sleeve   *Sleeveless*   *Raglan sleeve*   *Kimono sleeve*

Hand-basting stitches 70 · Understitching 87 · Reducing seam bulk 87

Proper sleeve fit

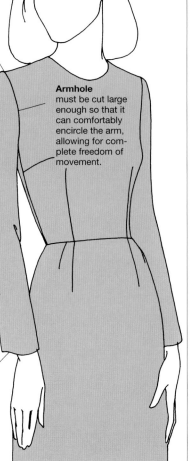

Shoulder point, an important matching point for sleeves, should sit exactly on top of shoulder, dividing front and back portions of body.

Upper arm of sleeve must have sufficient ease around it to enable the sleeve to hang smoothly from shoulder, and arm to move freely.

Armhole must be cut large enough so that it can comfortably encircle the arm, allowing for complete freedom of movement.

Lower arm section of sleeve should fit comfortably without being too tight. Darts or easestitching along elbow area can help to provide shaping for more comfort and freer arm movement.

Sleeve length should be appropriate for design of garment as well as for individual figure proportions.

Sleeveless finish

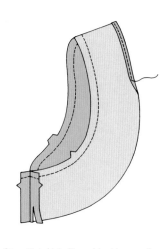

1. Staystitch ⅛ in (3 mm) inside seamline of the garment armhole and facing unit. With right sides together, match and seam facing ends together. Press seam flat, then open. Trim seam allowance to half-width. Finish free edges.

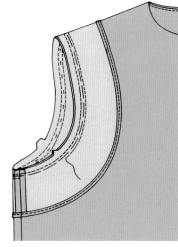

2. With the right sides together, pin and baste facing to garment armhole, matching the underarm seams, notches, and shoulder points. Start at underarm and, with facing side up, stitch the armhole seamline, overlapping a few stitches.

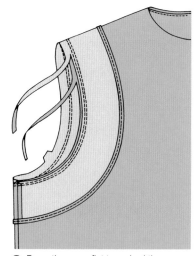

3. Press the seam flat to embed the stitches. To help reduce bulk around the armhole, trim and grade the seam allowances, making the garment seam allowance the widest. Trim across the underarm seam allowance diagonally.

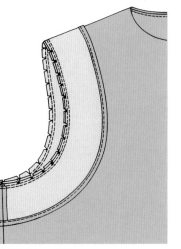

4. Clip into and, if necessary, notch out fullness from seam allowances; this will enable armhole facing to lie flat when it is turned to the inside.

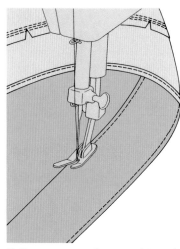

5. Press seam open, then press it toward the facing. Extend facing and seam allowances; from right side, understitch close to seamline.

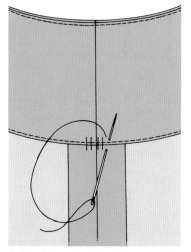

6. Turn facing to inside; roll seamline slightly inside. Align underarm seams and press. Tack facing to garment seam allowances at underarm and shoulder.

Gathering 120 · Tailored sleeves 345

Set-in sleeves

Though set-in sleeves occur in a variety of garments and in many design variations, all are inserted by a method much like the one described at right. Depending on the curve of the sleeve edge, a sleeve cap can be either slightly rounded or full and gathered. If a

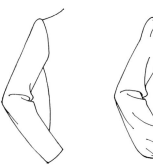

Standard set-in sleeve   Gathered set-in sleeve

sleeve is to have a nicely rounded cap, it must be carefully manipulated when it is eased into the armhole to avoid puckers and dimples along the seamline. If the sleeve is to have a gathered cap, the shirring must be evenly distributed along the upper

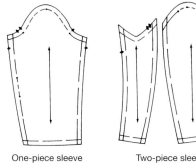

One-piece sleeve   Two-piece sleeve

curve. The set-in sleeve used most often is cut from a one-piece pattern. A two-piece sleeve is common in tailored garments. Another available type has a two-piece look but is actually cut as one and the seam positioned at the back of the arm.

Set-in sleeve method

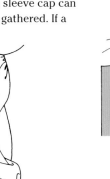
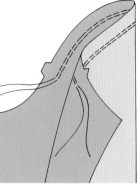

1. The curved edge on most set-in sleeves measures more than the armhole circumference; thus easing along cap is needed to fit the sleeve into the armhole. To provide ease control between sleeve cap notches, place two rows of easestitching within the seam allowance, the first a thread's width from seamline, the second ⅛ in (3 mm) from first.

2. With right sides together, match, pin, and baste underarm seam of sleeve. (For long sleeve requiring elbow ease, follow one of the methods on the opposite page.) Stitch as basted. Press seam flat, then press open.

3. Insert sleeve into armhole with right sides together; pin at all matched markings. To draw up sleeve fullness, pull the bobbin thread ends from easestitching line as a pair; distribute eased fullness evenly along cap. (For a gathered cap, use easestitching threads to gather excess fullness.) Hold sleeve in position by pinning on seamline at ½ in (1.25 cm) intervals; take small "pin bites." Baste in place, using small stitches.

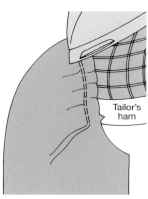

Tailor's ham

4. Check sleeve from right side; cap should be rounded and smooth. If there are puckers or dimples along seamline, secure easestitching thread ends; remove basted-in sleeve. With right side out, drape sleeve over press mitt or tailor's ham; steam-press along the cap, "shrinking out" as much of the puckering as possible. Re-baste sleeve into the armhole.

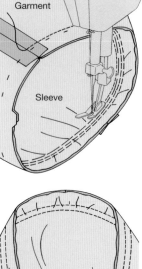

Garment

Sleeve

5. Start at underarm seam and, with the sleeve side up, stitch along seamline; use fingers to control eased-in fullness as you stitch. Overlap a few stitches at end.

6. Diagonally trim cross-seam allowances at the shoulder and underarm. Place another row of stitches (either straight or narrow zigzag) within the seam allowance, ¼ in (6 mm) from first row. Trim seam allowances close to second row of stitching. To help maintain rounded cap, turn seam allowances toward the sleeve; do not press seams.

Shirt sleeves

One form of the set-in sleeve is attached by the shirt-sleeve method, which permits the sleeve to be sewn into the armhole before the garment side and sleeve seams are stitched.

Sleeves eligible for this method are less rounded than usual along the shoulder line because the cap is not so steeply curved; there is less difference

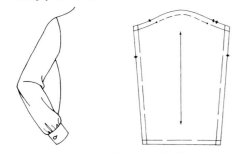

Sleeve cap is less rounded because of shallower curve.

between the measurement of the armhole and the upper sleeve curve, and easestitching along that curve is usually not necessary. Flat-felled seams are often used in this method. Because of the armhole curve, they should be narrow and made on the wrong rather than the right side. A popular method for men's shirts, the easy shirt-sleeve technique is widely used for children's and casual clothing, and most knits.

Shirt-sleeve method

1. With right sides together, match and pin sleeve to armhole; ease in sleeve's slight fullness as it is being pinned (underarm seam and side seam are still open). Baste as pinned, and stitch with garment side up, stretching gently to fit.

2. Diagonally trim cross-seam allowances at shoulder. If a flat-felled seam is desired, construct at this time. For regular seam finish, place another row of stitches (straight or zigzag) within seam allowance ¼ in (6 mm) from the first row. Trim the seam allowance close to the second row of stitching. Alternatively, serge, narrowing seam to half its width.

3. With right sides facing, match, pin, and baste underarm seams (turn armhole seam allowances toward sleeve). Stitch in one continuous seam from bottom of garment to bottom of sleeve.

4. Diagonally trim cross-seam allowances. If a flat-felled seam is desired, construct at this time. For regular seam finish, place another row of stitches (straight or zigzag) within seam allowance close to second row of stitching ¼ in (6 mm) from first row. Trim seam allowance. Alternatively, serge, narrowing seam to half its width.

Elbow shaping

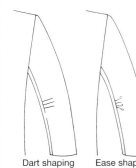

Dart shaping   Ease shaping

A close-fitting sleeve that extends beyond the elbow usually requires darts or easestitching along the sleeve seam to give the shaping and ease necessary for the elbow to bend comfortably.

Sleeves with elbow darts: With right sides together, form each elbow dart, stitching from the wide end to the point; leave 4 in (10 cm) thread ends and tie knot at each point (see Darts). Extend each dart and press flat as stitched. With wrong side up, place darts over tailor's ham and press them toward the sleeve bottom. With the right sides together, match, pin, and baste sleeve seam.

Sleeves with easestitching: Between designated markings on back seamline of sleeve, place a row of easestitching within seam allowance, a thread's width from seamline. Pin sleeve seams together, right sides facing, at all matched markings. Pull bobbin thread ends of easestitching line to draw up fullness along back seam; distribute fullness evenly. Pin in place and baste.

Pressing equipment 14 · Darts 101

Raglan sleeves

A raglan sleeve is attached to the garment by a seam that runs diagonally down from the front neckline to the underarm, and up to the back neckline. This sleeve covers the entire shoulder. To make it conform to the shoulder's shape, a dart that extends from

neckline to shoulder edge is required when the sleeve pattern is one piece. When the sleeve is made from two pieces, a shaped seam that runs from the neckline over the shoulder to the sleeve bottom is used.

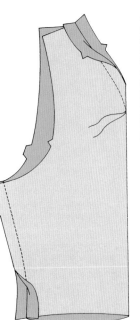

1. With right sides facing, match, pin, and stitch shoulder darts from wide end to point; leave 4 in (10 cm) thread ends. Knot thread ends. Press dart flat. Slash darts if necessary and press open over a tailor's ham. Match, pin, and stitch underarm seams, right sides together. Press flat, then press open.

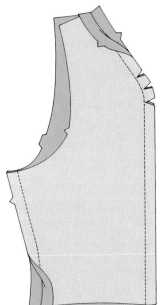

For a two-piece sleeve, place front and back together, right sides facing. Match, pin, and stitch the shoulder seam. Press the seam flat to embed stitches, then finger-press open. Notch out fullness from seam allowance along shoulder curve. Press seam open over a tailor's ham. With right sides together, match, pin, and stitch the underarm seams. Press flat, then open.

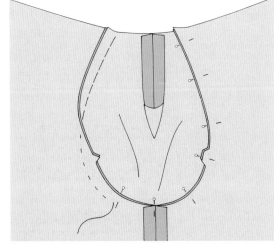

2. Garment side seams should be already finished. With right sides together, pin sleeve to armhole, aligning underarm seams, and matching all markings; work with wrong side of sleeve toward you. Baste as pinned.

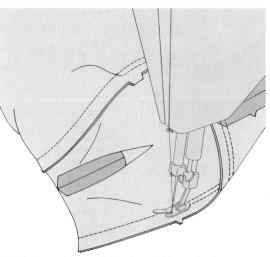

3. With sleeve side up, stitch as basted. Diagonally trim cross-seam allowances at underarm seams. Between front and back notches of underarm curve, place another row of stitching (either straight or zigzag) ¼ in (6 mm) from first row.

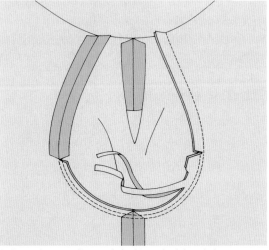

4. Press the seam flat as stitched to embed the stitches. Clip into the seam allowances at the point of each notch. Trim underarm seam allowances close to the second row of stitching. Press seams open above the clips.

Kimono sleeves

A kimono sleeve is cut as an extension of the main bodice piece and can be either loose or close fitting. If the sleeve fit is very close, a gusset is usually necessary (see pp. 220–221). To construct a kimono sleeve

without a gusset, follow one of the methods shown here for reinforcement under the arm. Method 1 uses regular seam binding, Method 2 uses ½ in (1.25 cm) cotton tape.

Method 1

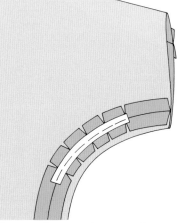

1. Complete shoulder seam; press open. Match and pin front to back at underarm seamline, right sides facing. Center and pin a 4 to 5 in (10 to 12 cm) piece of tape over curved underarm seamline, on back garment section. Baste entire seam, catching in tape.

2. Stitch the underarm seam as basted, shortening the stitches slightly along the length of the tape. Press the seam flat. Clip seam allowance along the curve, being careful not to cut tape. Press seam open over a seam roll.

Method 2

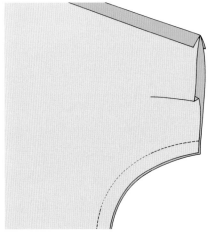

1. Complete shoulder seam and press open. With right sides facing, match, pin, and baste front to back at underarm seamline. Stitch, shortening stitches along curve. Press flat.

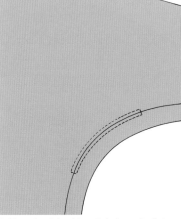

2. Clip seam allowances along curve. Press open. Center, pin, and baste a 4 to 5 in (10 to 12 cm) piece of reinforcing tape along curved seamline. Make sure stitches go to right side.

3. From the right side, stitch through all the thicknesses, approximately ⅛ in (3 mm) on each side of basted line. Secure thread ends on wrong side. Remove basting and press.

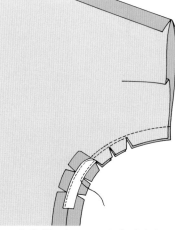

If exposed stitching is not wanted, stitch the tape from wrong side, catching the *tape and seam allowance only* on each side of basted line. Remove basting and press.

Fabric-marking methods 65 · Staystitching 84

Gussets

A gusset is a small fabric piece inserted into a slashed opening, usually under the arm of a close-fitting kimono sleeve, to provide ease for a comfortable fit.

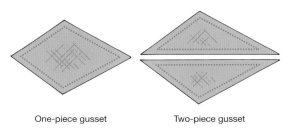

One-piece gusset   Two-piece gusset

Although gusset shapes vary, there are two basic gusset types: **one-piece** and **two-piece.** The one-piece type is the more difficult of the two types to insert because the entire gusset must be sewn into an enclosed slashed opening after the underarm and side seams have been stitched. With the two-piece gusset, each piece is separately inserted into a slashed opening on each bodice piece; the underarm, both gusset sections, and the side seams are then stitched in one seam. Because a two-piece gusset is easier to insert, you may want to convert a one-piece to that type (see p. 221).

For maximum ease of movement, cut the gusset so that its length is on the bias. Transfer all pattern markings, especially at gusset corners and garment slash points. Reinforce point at marked gusset opening before slashing. For lightweight fabrics or those fabrics that fray, use a bias square or seam binding. A lightweight iron-on interfacing can also be used. If the fabric is firm, staystitching is usually sufficient reinforcement.

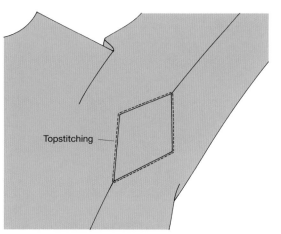

Topstitching

In a well-constructed gusset, all points are precisely related to shape of slashed opening; joining is accurate and smooth. For greater strength, topstitching may be added.

Reinforcing point of slash opening

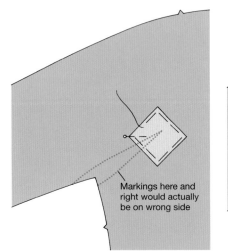

Markings here and right would actually be on wrong side

1. To reinforce point of slash opening, cut a 2 in (5 cm) square of bias. On *right* side of garment, position the center of the fabric square over the slash point; pin and baste patch in place.

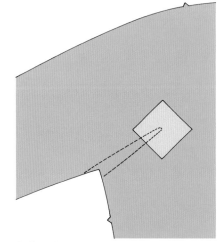

A 4 in (10 cm) piece of regular seam binding can be used in place of bias square; fold tape into a V. Position and pin tape to right side of garment; baste.

2. Staystitch a thread's width from marked stitching line. Start at wide end, stitch up one side to point, pivot, take one stitch across point, pivot again, stitch down other side.

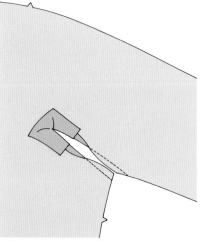

3. Press the staystitched area flat. Slash through center of opening (between stitching lines) up to reinforced point; cut through fabric square as well. Turn square to wrong side; press lightly.

Inserting a one-piece gusset

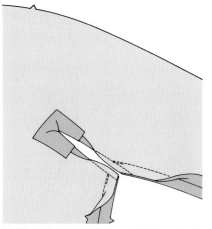

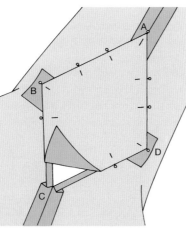

1. With right sides together, match, pin, and baste garment front to back at underarm seams and side seams. Stitch from sleeve bottom to intersecting lines of gusset opening; secure stitches. Stitch from lower edge of bodice to intersecting lines of gusset opening; secure stitches. Press seams flat, then open.

2. Position gusset over slashed opening so marked points of gusset (designated here as A, B, C, D) match corresponding markings of opening. With right sides together, pin the gusset into the slashed opening; match all points accurately and align stitching line of opening to gusset seamline.

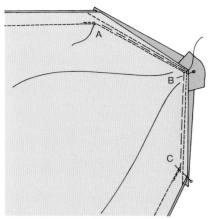

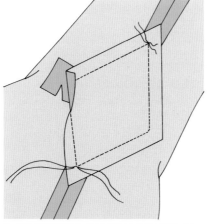

3. Baste, but do not remove pins from corners. Garment side up, stitch from point A to B; pivot, take one stitch across point, pivot again, and stitch to point C. Leave 4 in (10 cm) thread ends at beginning and end. Stitch other side of gusset (C to D to A) the same way.

4. Pull all thread ends to wrong side of gusset and knot. Press seams toward garment. Trim the edges of fabric squares to ½ in (1.25 cm), re-press seams toward garment. If desired, topstitch close to seamline on right side of garment (see p. 220); pull threads to wrong side and knot.

Inserting a two-piece gusset

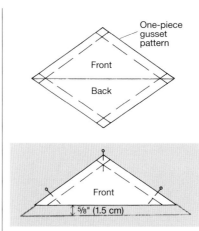

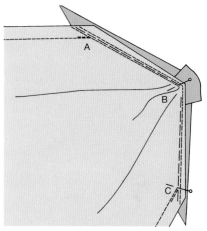

1. To convert a one-piece gusset into a two-piece, determine which halves of gusset pattern correspond to front and back bodice pieces; divide with a line; cut in half. Pin triangular pattern pieces to fabric; add ⅝ in (1.5 cm) to cut edge (for underarm seam allowance). Cut out pieces and transfer markings.

2. With right sides together, match and pin gusset to slashed opening of front bodice; align seamlines of opening and gusset. Baste, but do not remove pins from corners. Garment side up, stitch from edge A to B (shorten stitches around B); pivot, take one stitch across point, pivot, stitch to edge C.

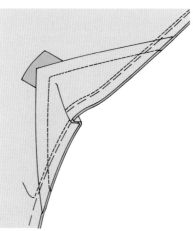

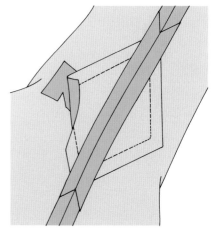

3. Press the seams toward the garment. Insert the other triangular gusset piece into slashed opening of back bodice in same way as for the front bodice. With the right sides together, pin the garment back to front at underarm seam. Baste and then stitch.

4. Press seam flat to embed stitches, then press seam open. Trim extending edges of fabric squares at gusset points to ½ in (1.25 cm); re-press seams toward garment. If desired, topstitch close to seamline on right side of garment (see p. 220); pull threads to wrong side and knot.

Boy's shirt

Shirt fabric: Bennet, Bad Säckingen (Germany).

Fabrics

Cotton, cotton blends

Amount

For size 6: $1^3/_8$ yd (1.3 m) of
54/56 in (140 cm) -width fabric.
If you use a plaid, you will need a bit
more fabric.

Notions

10 in (25 cm) fusible interfacing
6 buttons, $^3/_8$ in (1 cm) diameter

Pattern pieces ▶▶▶▶▶▶▶▶▶▶▶▶▶

1 Front – cut 2
2 Back – cut 1 on fold
3 Yoke – cut 2
4 Collar – cut 2
5 Collar band – cut 2
6 Sleeve – cut 2

Burda pattern 2753 was modified for
the shirt. The yoke is cut on the bias
to highlight the plaid. There is no
pocket. When sewing for children, it
is advisable to stitch wide seam
allowances and cut patterns a bit
longer. This allows for growth spurts
(see also Alterations on pp. 354–355).

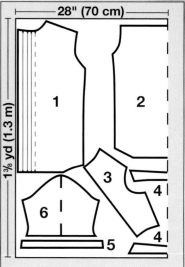

This project employs a hem tuck technique on the shirt sleeves — a type of sleeve finish different from those shown on the following pages. It is a fast finish and looks like a turned-up cuff.

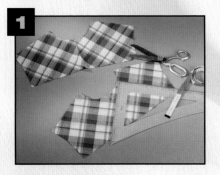

Cutting plaids

If sewing with plaids, be sure to match the bars. Fold the fabric so that the identical bars overlap, and pin along the repeats to avoid slipping during cutting. Place the pattern pieces on the fabric so that the plaid bars match. Cut the yoke on the bias. Pay special attention to the distribution of colors with plaids (Fig. 1).

Sewing instructions

Collar preparation: Cut interfacing for the upper collar and collar band. Fuse to the wrong side of fabric.
● Lay collar pieces together, right sides facing. Stitch all edges except neck edge. Trim seam allowances and trim the corners diagonally.
● Turn collar right side out. Press and topstitch the seam edges at ¼ in (6 mm).

● Baste raw edges together.
● Turn seam allowance of collar band with interfacing ⅜ in (1 cm) to inside, press, and stitch at ¼ in (6 mm) (Fig. 2).

● Turn under seam allowance at the attachment edge of the collar band piece without interfacing and press. Pin this collar band piece to interfaced side of collar and pin interfaced collar band piece to other side of collar.
● Stitch collar band pieces together, catching collar. Trim seam allowances and clip curves. Turn collar band right side out.
Shirt front and back pieces: Fold front edges to inside twice at 1½ in (4 cm), and press. Stitch close to fold and then topstitch close to the front edge (Fig. 3).

● Make the fitting pleats at the center back by folding on lines marked. Baste.
● Lay the shirt back piece between the two yoke pieces, pin, and stitch. Press both yokes up (Fig. 4).

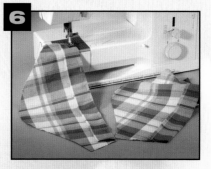

● Match shoulder edges of inner yoke to fronts, right side of yoke to wrong side of fronts. Stitch seams, trim, and press toward yoke.
● Press under seam allowance on outer yoke, and lap edges over shoulder seams. Pin and topstitch near fold (Fig. 5).

Attach collar: Baste and stitch the outer collar band to neck edge, right

sides facing. Trim, clip, and press seam toward collar.

● Lap the folded edge of inner band over the neck seam. Pin and topstitch near fold.
Sleeves: Turn sleeve hem to inside twice at 1½ in (4 cm) and press, concealing raw edges. Topstitch at ¼ in (7 mm) from lower fold. Then fold down the hem and press (Fig. 6).
● Attach the sleeves to the open armholes, matching notches. Stitch, with shirt on top, sleeve beneath. Finish seam allowances together with zigzag stitch or serger.
● Stitch sleeve and side seams in a continuous seam. Finish edges together. Press
Hem: Turn shirt hem under twice at ¼ in (6 mm) and press. Stitch at ³⁄₁₆ in (5 mm).
● Work a horizontal buttonhole into the left collar band and 5 vertical buttonholes into the left front edge by machine or hand.
● On the right side of fabric, mark the positions for buttons with pins. Sew on the buttons.

Pressing equipment 14 · Diagonal basting 70 · Reducing seam bulk 87 · Hems 255–256 · Interfacing hems 257

Sleeve finishes

The finishing of a sleeve edge usually depends on pattern design. It may be a simple **self-hem** or **faced finish,** or decorative **double binding** of self- or contrasting fabric. The finish is sometimes a design feature such as a **casing** (pp. 226–227) or a **cuff** (pp. 228–229) would be. For successful completion of any sleeve, follow these guidelines: 1. Mark the hemline to length to suit the wearer; sleeve length helps to determine total garment silhouette and can add to or detract from it; 2. Use proper pressing techniques throughout; 3. Reduce bulk wherever possible.

A self-hemmed edge can also be faced.

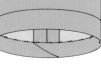

A double-fold binding is sewn at the sleeve edge.

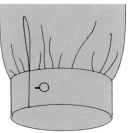

Applied casing is sewn at the sleeve edge.

A cuff can have a placket opening or have no opening.

Self-hem

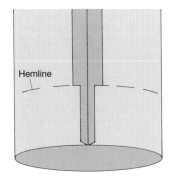

1. Mark sleeve hemline. To reduce bulk at seamline within hem width, trim seam allowance below marked hemline to half-width.

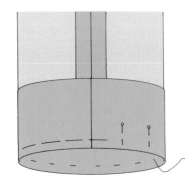

2. If interfacing is desired, apply it now (see Hems). Turn hem to wrong side along marked hemline; pin and baste near fold.

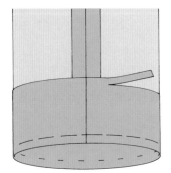

3. To even hem allowance, measure from fold to desired width, and mark that distance around entire hem. Trim along marked line.

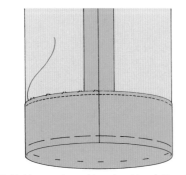

4. Finish raw edges of hem (see Hems). Pin edge to sleeve and secure, using appropriate hemming stitch. Remove basting. Press.

Shaped facing

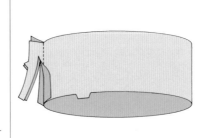

1. With right sides together, match, pin, and stitch facing ends. Press flat, then open. Trim seam allowances to half-width.

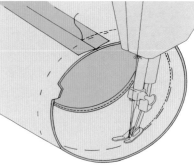

2. Finish unnotched facing edge. With right sides together, match, pin, and baste facing to sleeve edge. Stitch with facing side up.

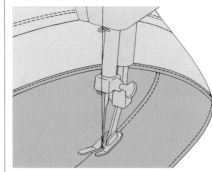

3. Press seam flat. Trim and grade seam allowances; clip if needed. Extend facing and seam allowances; understitch along facing.

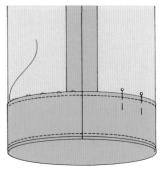

4. Turn the facing to wrong side; roll edges in slightly. Press. Pin in place and secure with suitable hemming stitch.

Hemming stitches 80 · Cutting bias strips 262–263

Bias facing

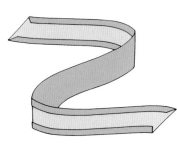

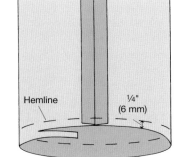

1. Cut a strip of 1½ in (4 cm) bias to sleeve circumference plus 2 in (5 cm). Press under long edges ¼ in (6 mm).

2. Mark hemline along bottom edge of sleeve. To facilitate application of bias facing, trim hem allowance to ¼ in (6 mm) width.

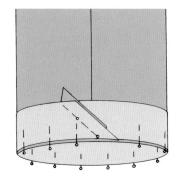

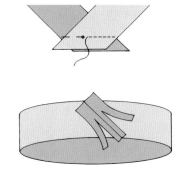

3. Open folded edges and pin facing to sleeve edge, right sides together; pin ends together in diagonal seam (straight grain).

4. Remove facing; keep ends pinned. Stitch the ends along straight grain. Trim seam allowances to ¼ in (6 mm) and press open.

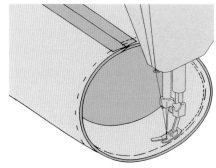

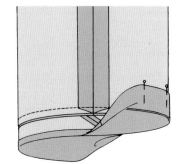

5. Re-pin facing to sleeve, raw edges even. Baste in place; stitch ¼ in (6 mm) from raw edge, using foldline as guide. Press flat.

6. Turn facing to wrong side; roll edges in slightly and press. Pin folded edge of facing to sleeve and slipstitch in place.

Bias binding

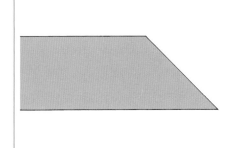

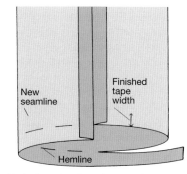

1. Cut a strip of self-fabric bias equal in *length* to the sleeve edge circumference plus 2 in (5 cm), in *width* to six times the finished width.

2. Mark sleeve hemline, trim away hem allowance. Mark new seamline a distance from cut edge equal to the finished tape width.

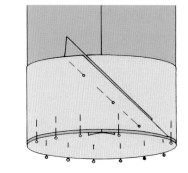

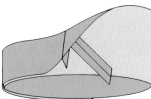

3. With right sides together, pin tape to sleeve, raw edges even. Pin the tape ends together in diagonal seam (straight grain).

4. Remove tape; keep ends pinned. Stitch. Trim seam allowances to ¼ in (6 mm); press open. Fold tape in half, wrong sides together.

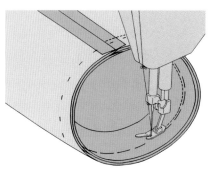

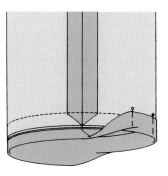

5. Pin tape to right side of sleeve, raw edges even; baste in place along new sleeve seamline. Stitch with tape side up.

6. Press seam flat. Extend tape up and press; turn to wrong side so fold meets the stitching line. Pin and slipstitch in place.

Sewing equipment 10–11

Casings

A casing is a fabric tunnel through which elastic or drawstring can be passed; either will draw up sleeve fullness, creating a puffed effect. There are two types of casing. The first is a **self-faced casing,** in which the tunnel is created by turning the sleeve edge to the inside. Some self-faced casings are positioned above the sleeve edge so that a gathered flounce, known as a *heading,* will hang below. To construct a self-faced casing, enough fabric allowance must be provided

below the hemline. The second type, the **applied casing,** is a separate bias strip sewn to the sleeve edge to form the tunnel. An applied casing is used when there is not enough hem allowance for a self-faced casing or when fabric bulk makes a casing of thinner fabric desirable. Ready-made bias tape can be used; select the width closest to but slightly wider than the elastic. For both casing types, select a narrow elastic (⅛ to ½ in [3 to 12 mm]).

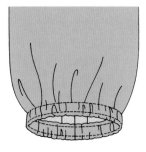
Casing

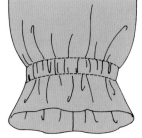
Casing with heading

Self-faced casing

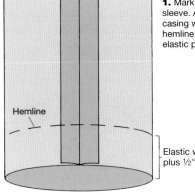

1. Mark hemline on sleeve. Allow enough casing width below hemline to equal width of elastic plus ½ in (1.25 cm).

Hemline

Elastic width plus ½" (1.25 cm)

2. Along the raw edges of the sleeves, turn a scant ⅛ in (3 mm) to the wrong side and press.

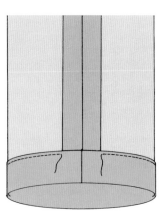

3. Turn casing width to wrong side along marked hemline; pin and baste close to free edge. Stitch along the basted line, leaving a small opening at the sleeve hemline.

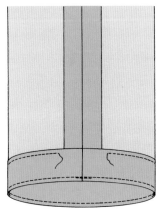

4. Stitch close to fold on lower edge of sleeve, overlapping for a few stitches. Fit the elastic around arm where the casing will be worn; add ½ in (1.25 cm) and cut.

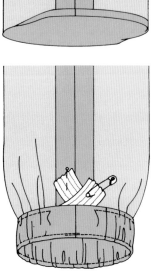

5. Attach a safety pin to one end of elastic and insert into casing. Pin other end to sleeve to keep that end from slipping through. Work safety pin around entire casing; avoid twisting the elastic.

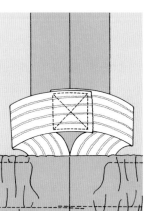

6. Unpin both elastic ends; overlap them ½ in (1.25 cm) and pin together. Stitch a square on overlapped area, crisscrossing it for strength. Pull joined ends inside the casing. Edgestitch opening to close it, stretching elastic slightly as you sew.

Cutting bias strips 262–263

Self-faced casing with heading

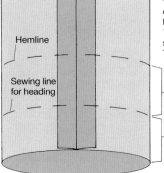

Hemline

Sewing line for heading

Heading width

Elastic width plus ½" (1.25 cm)

1. Mark hemline, with enough width below it for heading and elastic plus ½ in (1.25 cm). Mark sewing line for heading. Thread-mark traced lines.

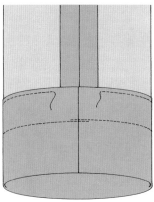

2. Turn ¼ in (6 mm) to wrong side and press. Turn heading and elastic-band width to wrong side along marked hemline; pin and baste close to free edge. Stitch along the basted line, leaving a small opening at the sleeve hemline. Then stitch close to header seam, overlapping for a few stitches to reinforce.

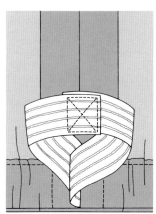

3. Fit the elastic around arm where casing will be worn; add ½ in (1.25 cm) and cut. (See Steps 5 and 6 on page 226.)

Applied casing

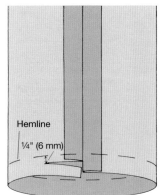

1. To make casing, cut a strip of bias equal in length to circumference of sleeve edge plus 1 in (2.5 cm) and equal to the elastic width plus 1 in (2.5 cm). If using ready-made bias, select one slightly wider than the elastic. Turn under ½ in (1.25 cm) on both ends of the bias strip and stitch across. Press under ¼ in (6 mm) on both long edges.

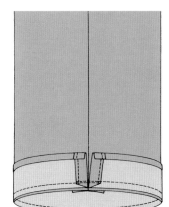

Hemline

¼" (6 mm)

2. Mark hemline on sleeve and trim the hem allowance to ¼ in (6 mm).

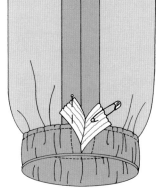

3. Open out one folded edge of casing. Starting at sleeve seam, pin casing to sleeve edge, right sides together and raw edges even; casing ends should meet. Baste and stitch along pressed crease of casing; overlap stitches at ends to reinforce.

4. Turn casing to wrong side; roll sleeve edge slightly inside. Press. Pin the folded inner edge of casing in place and baste; edgestitch along fold, overlapping stitches at end. Fit elastic around arm where casing will be worn; add ½ in (1.25 cm) and cut.

5. Attach a safety pin to one end of elastic and insert into casing. Pin other end to sleeve to keep that end from slipping through. Work safety pin around entire casing; avoid twisting the elastic.

6. Unpin both elastic ends; overlap them ½ in (1.25 cm) and pin together. Stitch a square on overlapped area, crisscrossing it for strength. Pull joined ends inside the casing. Edgestitch opening to close it, stretching elastic slightly as you sew.

Uneven slipstitch 81 · Seam finishes 88–89

Cuffs — cuffs with plackets

Cuffs are fabric bands at the bottom of straight, gathered, or pleated sleeve edges. Cuffs will basically be one of two general types. The first type can be used on both long and short sleeves, and is made large enough around for the hand or arm to slip in and out easily. The second type of cuff is generally attached to a full-length sleeve and requires a cuff-and-placket opening fastened snugly around the wrist. Of this cuff type, the three most popular styles are the **lapped cuff, shirt cuff,** and **French cuff.** Each is constructed and applied to the sleeve (see pp. 230–231) after the placket opening is made at the sleeve edge.

The three most commonly used plackets are the **faced placket, continuous bound placket,** and **shirt placket.** Note that edges of the faced placket meet at the opening, while edges of the other two plackets lap. The continuous bound placket is finished with a single fabric strip to create a narrow lap; the shirt placket is finished with two separate pieces to create a wider lap.

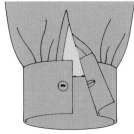

The **lapped cuff,** here with a continuous bound placket, has one end projecting from the placket edge. The **shirt cuff** is sewn with its ends aligned to the underlap and overlap edges of the shirt placket. The **French cuff,** here with a faced placket, is sewn to the placket edges so cuff ends meet rather than lap; the cuff is cut wide to double back onto itself.

Lapped cuff

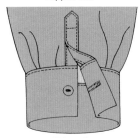

Shirt cuff

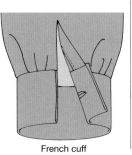

French cuff

Faced cuff plackets

1. Cut a rectangular facing that is 2½ in (6.5 cm) wide and as long as the length of the slash plus 1 in (2.5 cm). If garment fabric is heavy, use lining for facing. Apply a seam finish to the raw edges of the facing except on the bottom edge.

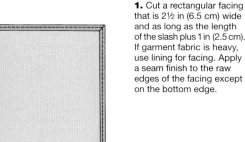

2. Center facing over marked opening, right sides together and raw edges even. Pin at each corner. From the wrong side of sleeve, stitch along the marked lines; start from one edge, stitch to point (shorten stitches for about 1 in [2.5 cm] on either side of point), pivot, and stitch down to other edge. Press flat.

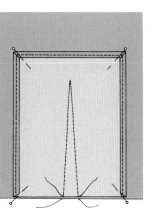

3. Slash to point; be sure not to clip stitching. Press seam open, then toward facing. Turn facing to wrong side of sleeve; roll edges slightly inside. Press. Slipstitch or tack top edge of facing to sleeve.

Continuous bound cuff plackets

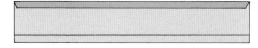

1. Cut binding from self-fabric to measure 1¼ in (3 cm) wide and twice the length of the marked slash. Along one long edge of cut binding, press under ¼ in (6 mm) to wrong side. Mark ¼ in (6 mm) seam allowance along the other long binding edge.

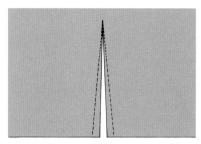

2. Reinforce stitching line of placket opening: Within a thread's width of seamline, stitch to point (shorten stitches for about 1 in [2.5 cm] on either side of point), pivot, and stitch down. Press flat. Slash to point; take care not to clip threads.

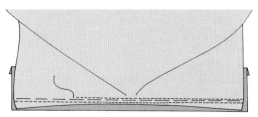

3. Spread slash and pin to unfolded edge of binding, right sides together. Align reinforced stitching line to marked ¼ in (6 mm) seamline on binding. Baste, then stitch with sleeve side up. Press seam flat to embed stitches.

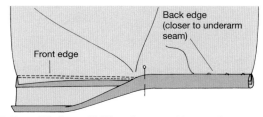

Back edge (closer to underarm seam)

Front edge

4. Extend binding and fold it to the wrong side, encasing raw edges; folded edge of binding should meet stitching line. Pin in place and secure with slipstitching. Turn front edge of binding to wrong side of sleeve and press.

Reducing seam bulk 87 · Shirt blouse 172–173

Shirt cuff plackets

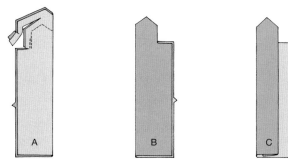

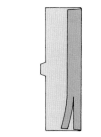

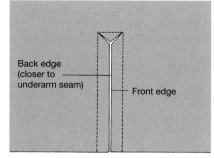

1. **To construct overlap,** fold in half, right sides together; pin and stitch around top edge to matching point at side. Press seam flat. Clip seam allowance at matching point; trim and grade; taper corners and point (A). Turn right side out; pull out corners and points. Press flat (B). Press under the seam allowance along the unnotched edge (C).

2. **To prepare underlap** piece, simply press seam allowance to the wrong side along unnotched edge. Trim this pressed-under seam allowance to about half-width.

3. Place reinforcing stitches within placket seamline. Slash to within ½ in (1.25 cm) of placket top, then to corners. Determine front and back edges of opening.

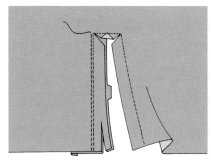

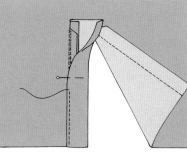

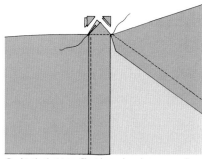

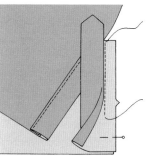

4. With seamlines aligned, pin and stitch right side of underlap raw edge to wrong side of the back placket edge; secure stitches at top corner of placket. Press flat; trim.

5. Press seam allowance toward underlap. Fold underlap to right side; pin its folded edge over stitch line. Edgestitch through all thicknesses; stop at corner; secure stitches.

6. At placket top, flip triangular piece up and pin to underlap. Stitch across base of triangle, securing stitches at beginning and end. Taper square corners of underlap.

7. Pin right side of overlap's extended edge to wrong side of remaining (front) placket edge, align seamlines, and keep raw edges at bottom even. Stitch; secure stitches at top.

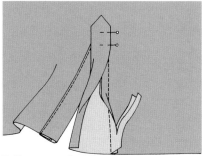

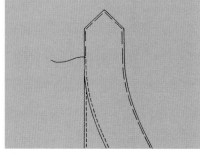

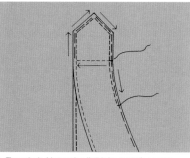

8. Press seam flat. Trim seam allowance to about half-width and press toward overlap. Bring the folded edge of overlap to stitching line and pin it in place.

9. Pin the top portion of overlap to sleeve, completely covering the top portion of underlap; pin down as far as placket corner. Baste along all pinned edges.

10. Topstitch along the basted fold of overlap (make sure not to catch any part of underlap in stitching); pull threads to wrong side at stopping point and knot.

11. Topstitch (through all thicknesses) across the overlap and around basted edges; follow direction of arrows. Secure stitches at beginning. Remove basting; press.

Pressing equipment 14 · Uneven basting stitch 70 · Reducing seam bulk 87

Construction of cuffs with plackets

Cuffs consist of a cuff and a facing section, cut all-in-one or as two pieces. Buttonholes should be made after cuff is constructed.

Before starting cuff application, complete underarm sleeve seams. Note the placement of cuff end to placket edge. A **lapped cuff** will have one end flush

with and one end projecting from the placket edges; both ends of the **shirt cuff** and the **French cuff** will be flush with the placket edges.

One-piece and two-piece cuff construction

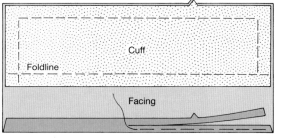

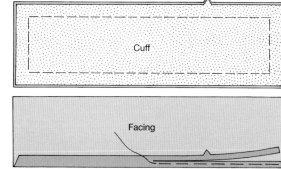

For one-piece cuff, apply interfacing to cuff section. Interfacing can come to foldline or, for a softer fold, extend ½ in (1.25 cm) beyond it into facing section (see Interfacing). Turn and press seam allowance to wrong side along facing edge and trim to ½ in (1.25 cm); uneven-baste along folded edge.

For two-piece cuff, apply interfacing to wrong side of cuff section. Turn, trim, baste notched edge of facing section.

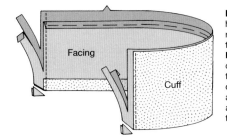

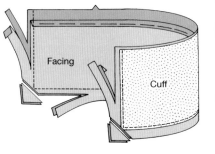

For one-piece cuff, left, fold in half along marked foldline with right sides together and pin the two ends.
For two-piece cuff, right, pin cuff to facing, right sides together, leaving notched edge open. Baste either one as pinned, and stitch. Press seam flat. Trim and grade seam allowances; taper corners.

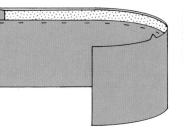

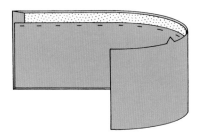

For both one-piece and two-piece cuffs, press seam allowances open, then toward facing. Turn cuffs right side out; pull out the corners. Roll facing edges slightly under, and press.

Shirt and French cuff construction

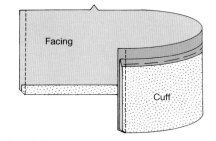

A shirt cuff differs slightly from the cuff constructed at left. Because of the shirt cuff application method (see p. 231), the edge of the *cuff* section rather than the facing section is turned under and basted. Before turning the interfaced cuff edge under, trim away the interfacing seam allowance along that edge. Complete cuff construction as directed at left.

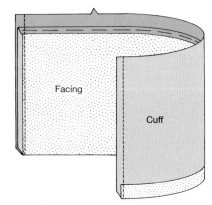

A French cuff is cut double the width of a standard cuff so that it can fold back onto itself. This turnback action exposes the facing, and so the *facing* section, rather than the cuff section (as described at left), is interfaced. Before turning the facing edge under, trim away the interfacing seam allowance along that edge. Complete construction of the cuff as directed at left.

Uneven slipstitch 81 · Seams with fullness 96 · Bound buttonholes 300–311 · Worked buttonholes 312–314

Lapped cuff application

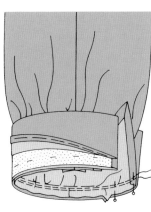

1. Pin cuff to sleeve at all matched markings, right sides together. Cuff end at back placket edge (edge closest to underarm seam) should project out to create underlap; other end should be flush with remaining placket edge. Pull gathering threads (if any) to ease in fullness of sleeve; distribute gathers evenly while pinning. Baste in place.

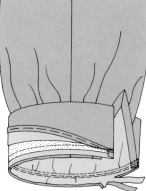

2. Stitch as basted; secure thread ends at beginning and end. Press the seam flat. Trim the cross-seam allowances diagonally. Trim and grade seam allowances so widest is next to cuff.

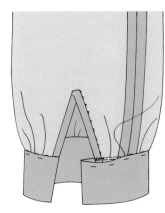

3. Pull cuff down; press seam allowances toward cuff. Bring folded edge of facing to stitching line on wrong side of sleeve; pin and slipstitch entire folded edge to sleeve. Remove basting and press. Complete the underside of the bound buttonholes or make worked buttonholes. Topstitch if desired.

Shirt cuff application

1. Pin right side of cuff facing to *wrong* side of sleeve at all matched markings. Cuff ends should be flush with the underlap and overlap edges of the shirt placket. Pull gathering threads (if any) to ease in fullness of sleeve; distribute the gathers evenly while pinning. Baste in place.

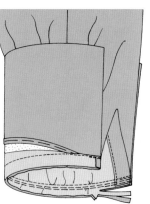

2. Stitch as basted; secure thread ends at beginning and end. Press the seam flat. Trim cross-seam allowances diagonally. Trim and grade seam allowances so widest is next to cuff.

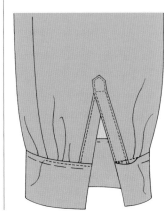

3. Pull cuff down; press seam allowances toward cuff. Bring folded edge of cuff just over stitching line on right side of sleeve; pin and baste in place. Edge-stitch along basted edge; continue stitching around entire cuff if desired; secure thread ends. Remove basting and press. Make buttonholes. Topstitch if desired.

French cuff application

1. Pin cuff to sleeve at all matched markings, right sides together; cuff ends should be flush with both edges of the placket. Pull gathering threads (if any) to ease in fullness of sleeve; distribute the gathers evenly while pinning. Baste in place.

2. Stitch as basted; secure thread ends at beginning and end. Press the seam flat. Trim cross-seam allowances diagonally. Trim and grade seam allowances so widest is next to cuff.

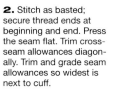

3. Pull cuff down; press seam toward cuff. Bring folded edge of cuff facing to stitching line on wrong side of sleeve; pin and slipstitch folded edge to sleeve. Remove basting and press. Complete underside of bound buttonholes or make worked buttonholes. Fold cuff in half and press lightly.

CHAPTER 7

POCKETS

Pockets can be functional
or decorative and are
sometimes both at the
same time, but they
always reflect the
quality of a garment.
When sewing pockets, great
attention to detail is
essential for perfect results.

Types of pockets

There are two general pocket classifications for women's wear: patch pockets and inside pockets.

Patch pockets appear on the outside of the garment. They are made from the fashion fabric, can be lined or unlined, and may be attached by machine or by hand. They can be square, curved, rectangular, or pointed and may be decorated with topstitching, lace or braid trims, or construction details such as tucks.

Inside pockets are usually made from a lining fabric; they are kept on the inside of the garment, and the opening to the pocket can be either invisible or decorative. There are three types of inside pockets: the **in-seam** pocket, which is sewn to an opening in a seam; the **front-hip** or **front curved** pocket, which is attached to the garment at the waist and side seams; and the **slashed** pocket, which is identified by a slit in the garment, variously finished with the pocket itself, or with a welt, a flap, or a combination of both the welt and the flap.

In-seam pockets are most common in side seams but are also found in side-front seams and even in horizontal seams occasionally.

Placement of the pocket on the garment depends on whether the pocket is functional or strictly decorative. A pocket to be used should be located at a level that is comfortable for the hand to reach. If a pocket is to serve a decorative purpose only, as pockets above the waist usually do, it should be placed where it will be most flattering.

A special kind of in-seam pocket is the watch or small-change pocket. It isn't actually sewn in the side seam but directly under the trouser waistband in the waistline seam. The sewing method is the same.

In-seam pockets

Front-hip or front curved pockets

Slashed pockets with flaps

Patch pockets

Patch pockets

Patch pockets are shaped pieces of fabric finished on all sides, then attached to the garment. They may be lined or unlined, and may be decorated in any of several ways before being attached.

If pockets are to be used in pairs, take care that the finished pockets are the same size and shape; a cardboard template cut to that size is helpful for guiding stitching and pressing.

If a plaid, stripe, or print is to be matched, the pocket must be cut so this is possible; a striped or plaid pocket may be cut on opposite grain from the garment or on the bias for added contrast.

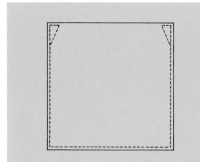

Plain patch pocket, attached with topstitching

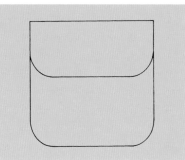

Patch pocket with flap, attached by hand

Unlined patch pockets

Unlined patch pockets are most often used on casual clothes, such as jeans, shirts, and aprons. Edges are finished by turning facing at top and seam allowances at sides and bottom to wrong side. If lower corners are rounded, extra fullness in seam allowance must be notched out to avoid bulky overlapping of fabric. Square lower corners must be mitered.

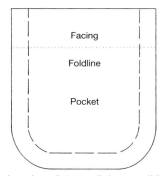

Unlined patch pockets usually have a self-facing at the opening edge, which is turned to the inside during construction.

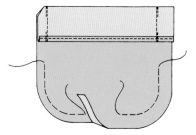

3. Trim entire pocket seam allowance to ½ in (1.25 cm) and cut across each corner at top. Turn facing to wrong side; pull corners out.

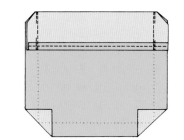

To miter a square corner, first make a diagonal fold to the right side across the junction of the seamlines. Press to crease.

1. Turn under raw edge of pocket facing and edgestitch. Fold facing to the right side along foldline and stitch each side on seamline.

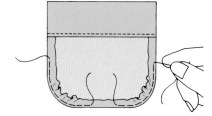

4. Press top edge. Pull easestitching at corners to draw in seam allowance and shape pocket curve. Notch out excess fabric.

Open the fold and place the *right* sides of the seam allowances together. Stitch on the crease from raw edge to corner. Trim.

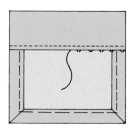

2. If pocket has rounded corners, easestitch at each corner a thread's width into the seam allowance from the seamline.

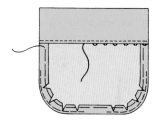

5. Press pocket seam allowances and facing flat. Hand-baste around entire pocket edge and topstitch or slipstitch facing to pocket.

Turn corners and facing to wrong side and press entire pocket flat. Hand-baste around all edges and topstitch or slipstitch facing to pocket.

Uneven slipstitch 81 · Reducing seam bulk 87 · Lining fabrics 346–351

Lined patch pockets

Lining will give patch pockets a neat custom finish. As well, it will add body and opaqueness to loosely woven or sheer fabrics.

A patch pocket can be self-lined or lined with matching lining fabric. It may also require partial or complete interfacing. The lining may extend to all edges or, if the pocket has a facing, it may extend only to the facing.

Important: Use this trick to ensure that no lining shows at pocket edges. First, cut the lining slightly smaller than the pocket by trimming ⅛ in (3 mm) from all its cut edges. Next, pin the lining to the pocket so edges correspond, and stitch on the seamline. When the pocket is turned, the lining will pull the finished edge slightly to the wrong side. Press, remembering that the objective is crisp, sharp pocket edges with no lining visible on the right side.

Patch pocket lined entirely to edge

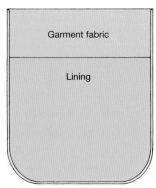

Patch pocket lined to edge of facing

Lining entire pocket

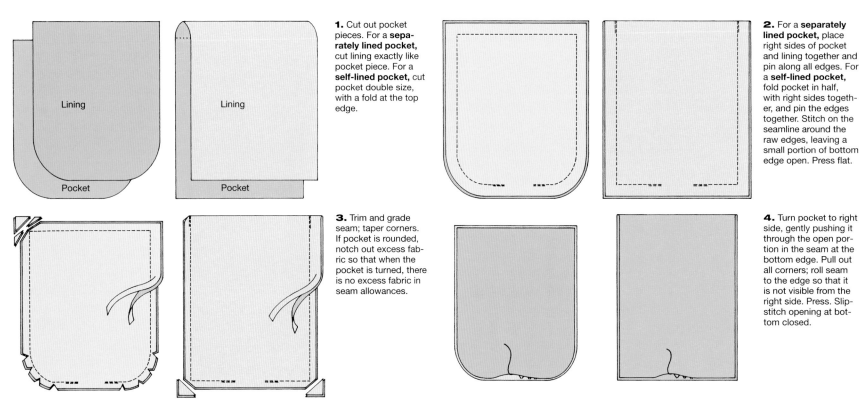

1. Cut out pocket pieces. For a **separately lined pocket,** cut lining exactly like pocket piece. For a **self-lined pocket,** cut pocket double size, with a fold at the top edge.

2. For a **separately lined pocket,** place right sides of pocket and lining together and pin along all edges. For a **self-lined pocket,** fold pocket in half, with right sides together, and pin the edges together. Stitch on the seamline around the raw edges, leaving a small portion of bottom edge open. Press flat.

3. Trim and grade seam; taper corners. If pocket is rounded, notch out excess fabric so that when the pocket is turned, there is no excess fabric in seam allowances.

4. Turn pocket to right side, gently pushing it through the open portion in the seam at the bottom edge. Pull out all corners; roll seam to the edge so that it is not visible from the right side. Press. Slipstitch opening at bottom closed.

Separate lining applied to facing

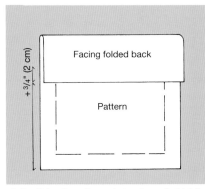

1. Cut lining from the pocket pattern, first folding the facing down out of the way along the foldline. Add ³/₄ in (2 cm) to lining piece at folded edge of the pattern.

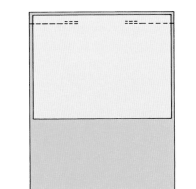

2. Pin top of lining to pocket facing, right sides together. Stitch a ¹/₂ in (1.25 cm) seam, leaving a small opening in the center of the seam for turning. Press seam toward lining.

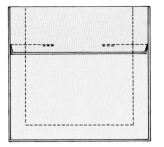

3. With right sides still together, match bottom and side edges of lining and pocket. Pin, then stitch around the marked seamline. Press flat to embed the stitches.

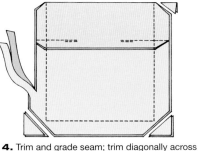

4. Trim and grade seam; trim diagonally across corners at top of pocket and at lower edges so that seam allowances in the corners will not be folded back on themselves.

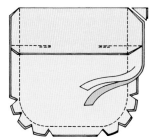

5. If pocket has rounded corners, first trim and grade the seam. Then trim diagonally across the corners at the top and notch out excess fabric in lower rounded corners.

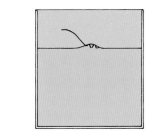

6. Gently turn pocket to right side through opening in facing/lining seam. Press, rolling seam to underside so it will not show on right side. Slipstitch opening closed.

Adding details

Trimming details, such as topstitching, piping, braid, or lace, may be added to pockets during their construction. Topstitching is the most popular addition.

Topstitching is most successful when done before pocket is applied to the garment (as compared with using topstitching as both a decorative measure and a means of attaching pocket). Use a longer stitch length (8 stitches

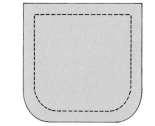

Patch pocket decorated with topstitching

Make tucks before pocket is constructed

per inch [3 mm]) when topstitching.

A patch pocket can also be trimmed with buttons and buttonholes, or with appliqués. Studs on jeans and denim skirts contribute both decoration and reinforcement. Decorate pocket before applying it to garment. Form construction details, such as tucks and pleats, before the pocket is constructed.

Applying patch pockets

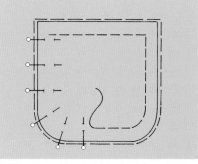

1. Pin and hand-baste finished patch pocket to the right side of the garment, carefully matching it to traced markings.

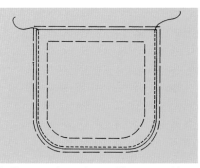

2. To sew pocket on **by machine,** set machine for a regular stitch length; stitch as close as possible to edge of pocket.

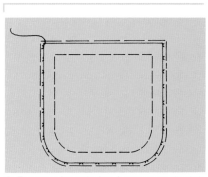

3. To sew pocket on **by hand,** use uneven slipstitch. Do not pull stitches too tight or pocket will pucker.

POCKETS

Slipstitches 74 · Bar tacks 76

Corner reinforcement

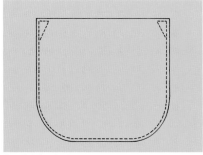

Small, identical triangles stitched at each top corner. This is the pocket reinforcement seen most frequently on shirts.

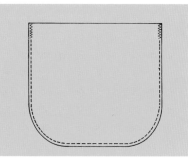

A zigzag stitch ⅛ in (3 mm) wide and closely spaced, run down ½ in (1.25 cm) from the top of each side. Good for children's clothes.

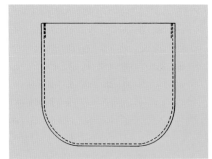

A backstitch for ½ in (1.25 cm) on each side of the pocket's opening edge, with thread ends tied. This method is often used on blouses.

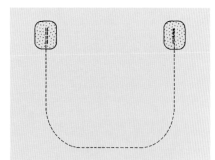

A patch of fabric or iron-on interfacing, placed on the wrong side of the garment under reinforcement stitching, adds strength.

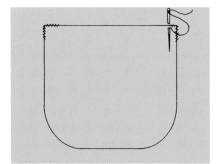

Hand reinforcement may be preferable. One method is to **slipstitch** invisibly for ¼ in (6 mm) on each side of top corners.

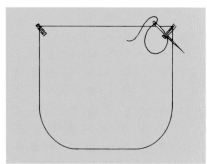

Another hand method is a **bar tack** — ¼ in (6 mm) -long straight stitches diagonally across corner with blanket stitches worked over them.

Patch pockets with flaps

Patch pockets can also be varied by means of flaps. These are finished, sometimes intricately shaped, free-hanging additions located at the top of the pocket. There are two methods for constructing a flap. One is to cut an extra-deep pocket facing, which is turned back over itself to the right side to create a self-flap; the opening of the pocket is above the flap. In the second method, a flap is attached to the garment above the pocket opening, then pressed down over the opening.

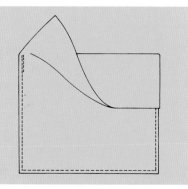

Patch pocket with self-flap

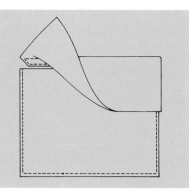

Patch pocket with separate flap

Patch pocket with self-flap

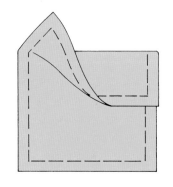

Flap foldline

1. Using pattern, cut out pocket and construct as for any lined or unlined patch pocket with facing. Fold the pocket top down to the right side along line marking depth of flap; press.

2. Attach pocket to the garment and reinforce corners as for a regular patch pocket, keeping flap up out of the way. Start and end stitching at the flap foldline. Remove all basting; give pocket a final pressing.

Fabric-marking methods 65 · Uneven slipstitch 81 · Reducing seam bulk 87

Patch pocket with separate flap

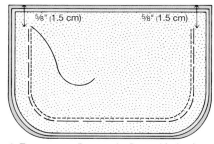

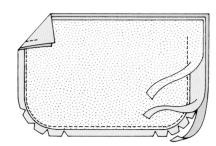

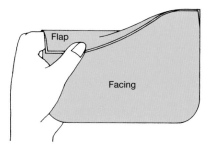

1. To construct flap, cut the flap and facing from same pattern; interface flap. Pin flap to facing, right sides together, and stitch on the seamline, starting and ending ⅝ in (1.5 cm) from base of flap. Press to embed stitching.

2. Trim and grade seams; clip or notch curves if the flap has shaped or rounded corners. Interfacing should be trimmed away completely to the seamline; the seam allowance of the flap should be left widest.

3. Turn flap right side out, easing the seamed edge slightly to facing side so that the seam will not show on finished flap. **If the fabric is bulky,** roll the seam allowances at top edge over your finger, with the flap side up, to get additional

width from the flap seam allowance. This will help the flap to lie flat and prevent curling on lower edge. Pin, then hand-baste, across the opening a scant ⅝ in (1.5 cm) away from the raw edges. Carefully press the flap flat.

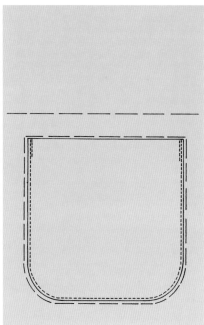

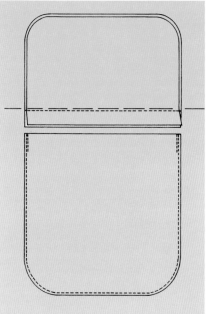

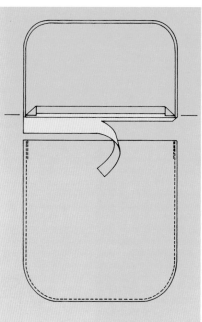

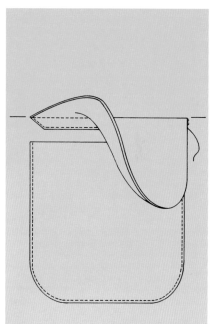

4. To attach pocket and flap to garment, pin finished pocket onto garment within basted markings and sew in place, using any of the methods on page 237. Reinforce top edges of pocket. Press pocket. Mark flap seamline with basting ⅝ in (1.5 cm) above top of pocket.

5. Pin flap to garment, right sides together, with flap extended away from pocket. Edge of seam allowances should be aligned with top of pocket; seamline of flap should be on marking. Stitch on flap seamline. Pull thread ends to wrong side of garment and tie.

6. With the uppermost seam allowance of the flap held out of the way, carefully trim the lower seam allowance close to the stitching. Fold under ¼ in (6 mm) on the long edge of upper seam allowance and fold in the ends diagonally to eliminate all raw edges in finished flap.

7. Pin upper seam allowance over the trimmed seam allowance and edgestitch around the ends and along the long side. Fold flap down over pocket and press. If necessary to hold flap flat, slipstitch the upper corners of the flap to the garment.

Safari jacket

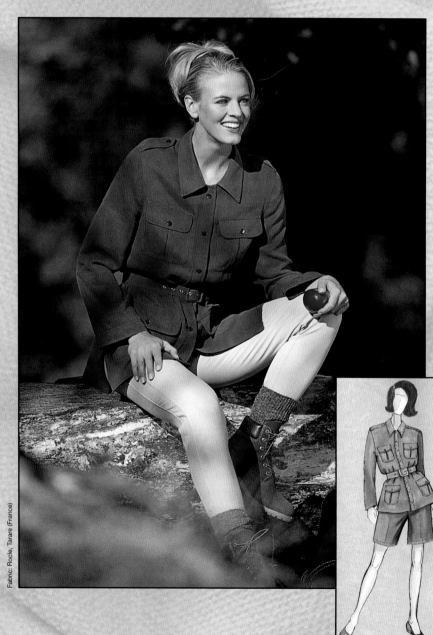

Fabric: Rocle, Tarare (France)

Fabrics

Lightweight wool, rayon, microfiber fabrics

Amount

For size 12: 1⅞ yd (1.7 m) of 54/56 in (140 cm) -width fabric

Notions

1 yd (0.95 m) lightweight fusible interfacing
11 colored snap fasteners
5 belt eyelets
1 belt buckle

Pattern pieces ▶▶▶▶▶▶▶▶▶▶▶▶▶▶▶▶▶

 1 Front – cut 2
 2 Upper pocket – cut 2
 3 Upper pocket flap – cut 4
 4 Pocket – cut 2
 5 Pocket flap – cut 4
 6 Back – cut 1 on fold
 7 Yoke – cut 2 on fold
 8 Collar – cut 2
 9 Sleeve – cut 2
10 Cuffs – cut 2
11 Epaulette – cut 4
12 Belt carriers – cut 1
13 Belt – cut 2

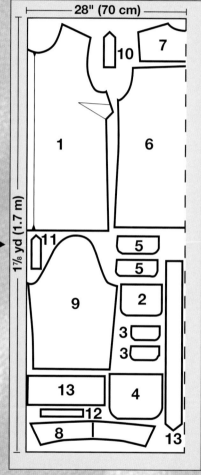

This jacket has patch pockets with topstitched inverted pleats and separate flaps. The front edges have a cut-on facing. The topstitched inverted pleat on the back piece allows for more freedom of movement.

The jacket goes well with the Bermuda shorts on page 198 and the skirt on page 118.

Preparing pattern pieces

Cut interfacing for the upper collar, pocket flaps, epaulettes, and belt without seam allowances and fuse to wrong sides of corresponding garment pieces.

Sewing instructions

● **Darts:** Stitch the bust darts on the markings, and press downward.
● **Belt carriers:** Fold the belt carriers pieces for the side seams lengthwise, right sides together. Stitch lengthwise edges together.
● Turn carriers right side out and press. Cut in half.
● **Belt:** Place the belt pieces right sides together. Stitch around edges, leaving straight end open. Trim seam allowances and cut corners diagonally.
● Turn the belt right side out, press, and topstitch close to the edge.

● Cover the belt buckle with fabric. Sew to the open end of the belt.
● **Epaulettes:** Place the two epaulette pieces right sides together. Stitch the edges together, leaving the straight ends open. Trim seam allowances.
● Turn epaulettes right sides out, press, and topstitch close to the edge and then at ¼ in (7 mm).
● **Front edges:** On the right front edge of the jacket, fold the facing in 1½ in (4 cm) twice to the outside, and press (Fig. 1).
● Turn right front edge back so that right sides are together. Stitch the upper neckline edge between the front edge and the collar attachment point and clip (Fig. 2). Turn the corner out again and press (Fig. 3).

● Topstitch the front edge at ¼ in (7 mm) on the inner and outer edges, leaving the hem edges open (Fig. 4).
● On the left front edge of the jacket, fold the attached facing to the outside in the same manner and press.
● Turn the left front edge back so that right sides are together. Stitch

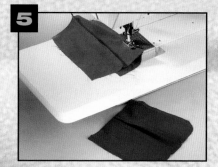

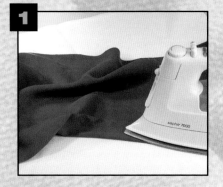

the upper neckline edge between the front edge and the collar attachment point and clip.
● Turn the front edge right side out again and press.
● Topstitch same as right side.

● **Pockets:** The small pockets attach to the upper bodice front, and the larger pockets below the waist.
● Sew inverted pleats into the pockets as follows:
● Fold the pockets lengthwise, right sides together.
● Baste on pleat marking line. Press inverted pleat open. Remove basting.
● Topstitch the fold lines close to the edge and again at ¼ in (7 mm) (Fig. 5). Secure the pleat on the upper and lower edges with basting.
● To make pockets, cut pressing templates the size of the pockets out of thick white cardboard.

Project 14

● Place the template on the wrong side of the pocket. Press the top edge over the template 1½ in (4 cm), and

press the seam allowances over the template. The creases should be sharp (Fig. 6).
● Fold the top edge first at ⅜ in (1 cm), then at 1¼ in (3 cm), and press. Topstitch close to the edge

and then at 1¼ in (3 cm) (Fig. 7).
● Pin the pockets onto the fronts. Topstitch close to the edge and then at ¼ in (7 mm), leaving the top edge open. Secure the seams on the upper edges with extra backstitching (Fig. 8).

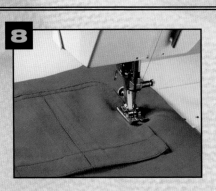

● **Pocket flaps:** Match two layers of each flap (one interfaced, one not) right sides together.
● Stitch, leaving the straight edge open.
● Trim the seam allowances and notch the rounded edges.
● Turn right side out and press (Fig. 9).
● Topstitch the flap close to the edge and then at ¼ in (7 mm) (Fig.10). Stitch top of flap closed close to raw edge.
● Place the flap above the corresponding top pocket edge with flap extended away from the pocket, and stitch.

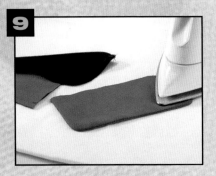

● Fold flap down over pocket, and press. Topstitch close to the edge and then at ¼ in (7 mm) (Fig. 11).
● **Front and back sections:** Form an inverted pleat in the upper edge of the back piece by folding the pleat in

the center of the back from the wrong side at 1 in (2.5 cm) width and basting down from the top about 4 in (10 cm). Then press apart to create an inverted pleat. Remove basting.
● Topstitch each crease for about 1½ in (4 cm) down, stitching close to edge and at ¼ in (7 mm) from edge.
● **Yoke:** To join to back, match one yoke to back edge, right sides together. Match other yoke to wrong side.

Stitch through three layers, turn, and press toward yoke.
● Topstitch the yoke seam close to the seam on the right side, and then at ¼ in (7 mm) in from seam.
● Stitch the shoulder seams of the front pieces to the inner yoke section. Press toward yoke. Press under the seam allowances of the outer yoke. Lap fold over yoke seam and topstitch near edge and at ¼ in (7 mm).
● Stitch the epaulettes in place at armhole edges.

● **Collar:** Place the two collars right sides together.

● Stitch together, leaving the neck edges open. Use smaller stitches near the corners.
● Trim the seam allowances, cutting the corners diagonally. Clip the curved areas (Fig. 12).

● Press collar seam open using a point presser. Press collar flat.
● Turn under the neck edge seam allowance of the upper collar and press (Fig. 13).

● Pin the under collar to the neckline edge, right sides together, being careful to match notches and ends.
● Stitch the under collar to the neck edge, making certain that the upper collar is not caught (Fig. 14).

● Trim seam and press toward the under collar. Lap folded edge of top collar over seam. Pin and stitch near fold (Fig. 15).
● Topstitch the collar outer edges close to the edge and then at ¼ in (7 mm).

● **Sleeves:** Place two rows of gathering stitches on the sleeve caps between the markings and gently gather to ease. Pin the sleeve caps to open the armholes, catching the epaulettes, and stitch with the garment on top, sleeve beneath.
● Finish the seam allowances and press toward the garment. Topstitch close to the edge and then at ¼ in (7 mm).
● **Side seams:** Stitch the side seams in a continuous seam from the jacket slit to the bottom of the sleeve.
● Finish the seam allowances down to the bottom of the jacket. Press open.
● **Slit:** Press under the seam allowance of the slit and topstitch at ¼ in (7 mm).
● **Cuffs:** The cuffs here are finished without interfacing. When using interfacing to support flimsy fabric, cut the interfacing half the width of the cuff without seam allowances and fuse to the wrong side.
● Pin cuff pieces to sleeve edges, matching markings. Stitch and press toward cuffs.
● Turn the seam allowances under on the long edges and press. Fold wrong sides together and press the center creases. Join cuff ends, right sides together. Press cuff seams open, then restore creases.
● Lap folded edge over cuff seam and pin. Baste. Topstitch cuffs close to all edges, then at ¼ in (7 mm).
● Turn the jacket hem under ³⁄₁₆ in (5 mm), baste, and stitch.
● **Belt:** Pin the belt carriers to the side seams, allowing room for the belt to pass through. Stitch on.

● Insert eyelets into pointed end of belt.
● **Snap fasteners:** Mark the positions of the snap fasteners on the front edges, epaulettes, and pockets on both sides of the fabric.
● Attach the snaps according to the directions on the package. Use either the tool included in the kit or pliers to set the snaps.
● Be careful to position the snap caps on the right front edge.

Reducing seam bulk 87 · Seam finishes 88–89

Inside pockets — all-in-one in-seam pocket

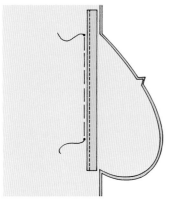

1. Reinforce garment front along pocket opening using non-stretch tape or seam binding. With right sides together and markings matched, pin together the front and back sections along the pocket opening. Baste by hand along pocket opening (optional).

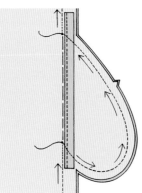

2. Pin and baste the remaining part of the seam together. Stitch the pocket and seam in one continuous stitching, reinforcing corners of pocket with small stitches. Press flat to embed the stitches. Clip the seam allowance of the back section of the garment at the corners and press open the garment seam allowances above and below the pocket.

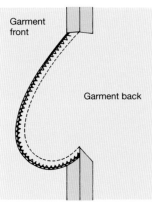

Garment front

Garment back

3. Finish and then reinforce raw edges of pocket with an overedge stitch, catching in garment front seam allowance at the top and bottom. Press the pocket toward the garment front and remove basting at opening.

Separate in-seam pocket

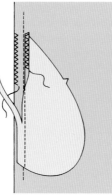

1. Reinforce garment front. Pin one pocket section to front garment piece, right sides together, matching markings. Stitch a scant ⅝ in (1.5 cm) seam. Grade the *front* pocket seam allowance only and finish each seam edge separately. Pin, stitch, and seam-finish the other pocket section and back garment piece in same way, but do not trim seam allowance.

2. With right sides together and pockets extended, match markings and pin front and back sections together along pocket opening. Hand-baste across opening (optional). Pin and stitch side seams above and below pocket opening; reinforce with backstitches at pocket markings. Press flat.

3. Press back pocket seams open and front pocket seams toward pocket. Pin pocket sections together, matching raw edges, and stitch around pocket, backstitching at pocket markings and catching front seam in stitching. Press flat.

4. Seam-finish edges of pocket together, using the same stitch as on seam allowances. Catch front seam allowance into the seam-finishing at top and bottom of pocket. Press pocket toward garment front and remove basting from opening. Trim off point of the pocket at the top.

Adding a facing of garment fabric to the opening edge of the pocket will keep any of the pocket fabric from showing if the pocket gapes open.

+ 3" (7.5 cm)

Length of pocket opening

2" (5 cm)

1. Cut two strips of garment fabric on straight grain, each measuring 2 in (5 cm) wide by the length of pocket opening plus 3 in (7.5 cm). Turn under and press ¼ in (6 mm) to wrong side on one long edge of each facing strip.

2. Apply facing to pocket before sewing pocket into garment. Place wrong side of each facing on right side of each pocket piece, with the raw edges even at opening. Edgestitch along pressed-under edge, then stitch other long edge of pocket facing to pocket ½ in (1.25 cm) from raw edge. Trim away excess facing fabric at top and bottom of pocket.

Cornered seams 86 · Seam finishes 88–89

Extension in-seam pocket

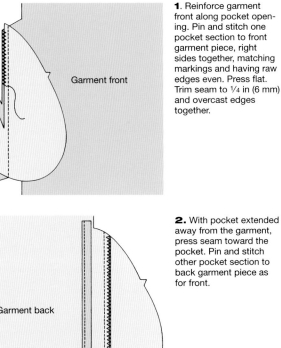

1. Reinforce garment front along pocket opening. Pin and stitch one pocket section to front garment piece, right sides together, matching markings and having raw edges even. Press flat. Trim seam to 1/4 in (6 mm) and overcast edges together.

2. With pocket extended away from the garment, press seam toward the pocket. Pin and stitch other pocket section to back garment piece as for front.

3. With right sides together and all markings matched, pin the front and back sections together along pocket opening. Hand-baste across opening (optional).

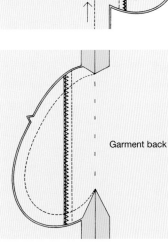

4. Pin and baste remainder of side and pocket seam together and stitch in one continuous seam, reinforcing the corners with small stitches.

5. Press flat to embed stitches. Clip seam allowance of back garment section to corner and press seam open above and below the pocket.

6. Seam-finish edges of the pocket together, using the same stitch as on the pocket seam allowance edges. Catch in garment front seam allowance at the top and bottom. Press the pocket toward the garment front and remove the basting at the opening.

Front-hip pockets

Front-hip pockets are attached to the garment at the waist and side seams and must be included in waist or hip alterations made in the garment.

All hip pockets consist of two pattern pieces: a pocket piece and a facing piece. The shapes of the two are never the same, because the facing piece finishes off the pocket opening, while the pocket piece becomes part of the main garment at the waistline. The pocket piece must be cut from garment fabric, but lining fabric may be used for facing. See next page.

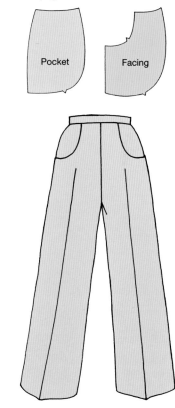

Reducing seam bulk 87 · Seam finishes 88–89

Construction of front-hip pocket

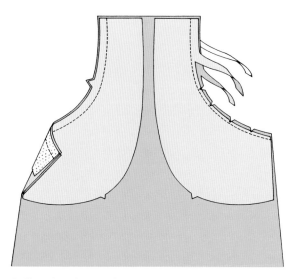

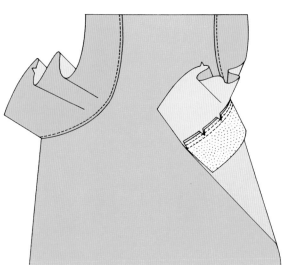

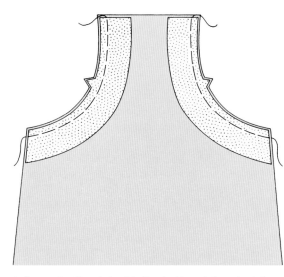

1. Cut a strip of interfacing 2 in (5 cm) wide and shaped to follow the opening edge of pocket. Baste to wrong side of garment at opening edge of pocket. Alternatively, baste stay-tape to pocket opening seamline.

2. Pin and stitch pocket facing to the garment, right sides together, along opening edge of pocket. Press flat to embed stitches. Trim and grade the seam, leaving garment seam allowance the widest. Clip or notch curves.

3. Press seam open, then press both seam allowances toward facing. Understitch the facing to keep it from rolling to the right side: with garment right side up, stitch close to seamline through facing and seam allowances.

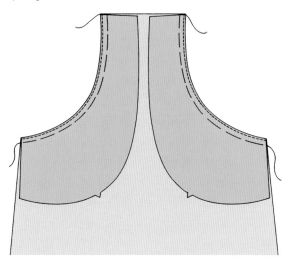

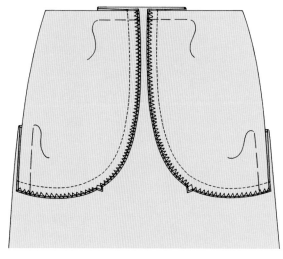

4. Turn the facings to inside along the seamline and press. Baste around the curved edge. If topstitching is desired for a decorative effect, apply it now.

5. Pin pocket to facing, right sides together, and stitch as pinned around seamline to the side of the garment. Press. Seam-finish raw edges. Baste side edges of pocket to side seam of garment and top edge of pocket to waistline.

6. Pin together and stitch side seams of garment, catching in pocket and facing seams. Press seams flat, then open. Treat the upper part of the pocket as part of the waistline seam when applying bodice or waistband.

Slashed pockets

The three types of slashed pocket differ only in the way the pocket opening is finished. When the pocket acts as a finish, the result is a **bound** pocket, which looks like a large bound buttonhole. A second method is with a **flap,** which covers the pocket after insertion into the upper edge of the slash. Flaps are usually, but not necessarily, rectangular. The third finish, a **welt,** is a rectangular piece, cut separately or as a part of the pocket, that fits over the pocket opening and is sewn into the lower edge of the slash. (A variation is a double welt — one at each edge of the slash.)

Bound pocket

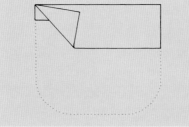

Pocket with flap on top edge

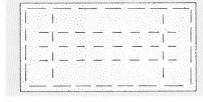

Single welt pocket

Marking and cutting slashed pockets

Slashed pockets, thought to be difficult to construct, are actually only a matter of precise marking and exact stitching, along with very careful cutting. Construction is very much like that of a bound buttonhole, although the finished result is much larger. The pocket back and front are not joined until they have been attached to the opening edge, which is the slash in the garment.

Carefully thread-mark the opening for pocket on right side of garment, using a small hand stitch. Be sure markings are exactly on grain (unless pockets are diagonally placed) and that center and stitching lines are exactly parallel. Do all permanent machine stitching with a very short stitch. Press carefully at each step of construction; a final pressing by itself is not sufficient to set sharp edges.

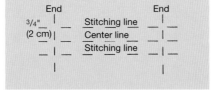

Baste across ends to mark *width* of opening, then through center line and on parallel stitching lines to mark *depth* of opening; extend marks about ¾ in (2 cm) beyond the actual limits. Be sure lines are on-grain and parallel.

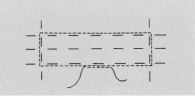

Stitch rectangle precisely for any type of slashed pocket. Begin stitching at center of one side; pivot at corners. Take same number of stitches across each end; overlap stitches at starting point to secure.

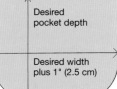

If garment fabric is lightweight or loosely woven, add a stay of lightweight interfacing for stability and crispness. Cut it about 4 in (10 cm) long and 2 in (5 cm) wider than opening: center it behind pocket opening and baste or fuse in place.

Curve pocket corners if they are square on the pattern, to prevent any lint buildup in the pocket from wear and washing. Instead of pivoting then stitching the pocket, simply round the corners off.

Bound pockets

Bound pockets are those in which the pockets themselves are used to finish off, or bind, the edges of the pocket slashes in the garment. From the right side of the garment, a bound pocket looks like a large bound buttonhole. Because the pocket fabric will show on the outside of the garment, use the garment fabric or contrast trim, rather than the lining fabric.

Check any pattern you plan to use to be sure that the pocket pieces meet the specifications below. If they do not, you will need to alter them to conform.

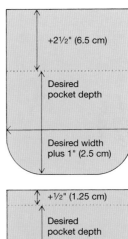

Pieces for bound pocket: The first pocket piece should measure desired pocket depth plus 2½ in (6.5 cm); the second, depth plus ½ in (1.25 cm). Cutting width (both): desired width plus 1 in (2.5 cm).

Hand basting 70–71 · Whipstitch 73 · Seam finishes 88–89

Constructing bound pockets

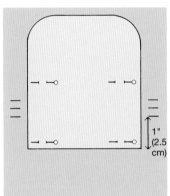

1. With right sides together, pin the long pocket section over pocket markings on garment, with straight (top) edge of pocket 1 in (2.5 cm) below the lower marked stitching line.

1" (2.5 cm)

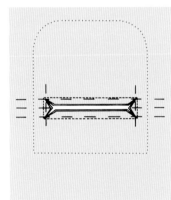

2. Turn garment side up for stitching. Following basted markings, stitch a rectangle as shown on preceding page. Slash through all thicknesses between stitching lines; stop ½ in (1.25 cm) before ends and slash diagonally into the four corners.

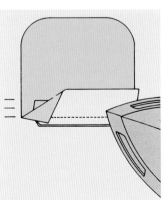

3. Gently push pocket section through slash to the wrong side of the garment. Pull on the small triangles at each end to square the corners of the rectangular opening. Press triangular ends and seam allowances away from the opening. Press straight end of pocket up over the opening.

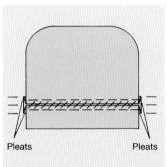

Pleats   Pleats

4. Fold pocket to form even pleats that meet in the center of opening. Check from the right side to make sure that the pleats (or "lips") are equal in depth to one another across entire width of the pocket. Baste through folded edges and whipstitch lips together. Remove the basted markings from garment.

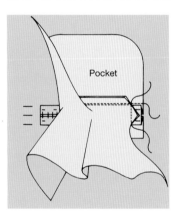

Pocket

5. Turn garment right side up and flip back garment so that the side edge of pocket is exposed. Stitch over the triangle and the ends of the lips at each side of pocket. Fold the garment down so that top seam allowance of opening shows. Stitch through the seam allowances and the pocket, as close as possible to the first stitching.

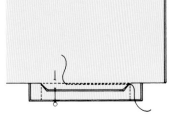

6. Slip the remaining pocket section under one sewn to garment and pin along outer edges. Flip garment up so that bottom seam allowance of opening is exposed and stitch through seam allowance and both pocket sections.

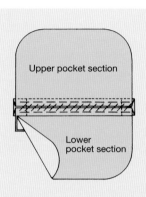

Upper pocket section

Lower pocket section

7. Turn garment to wrong side. Unpin pocket edges and turn lower pocket section down. Press in place.

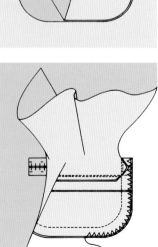

8. Turn upper pocket section down; bottom raw edges of both sections should be even. If they are not, trim them to the same length. Pin sections together.

9. Turn garment to right side again and fold garment in such a way that side of pocket is exposed. Stitch around pinned pocket on the seamline, starting at the top and stitching across triangular ends as close as possible to original stitching. Backstitch at beginning and ends. Press flat. Seam-finish outer raw edges. Remove all basting.

Flap and separate welt pockets

In these two types of pockets, either a flap or a welt is completely constructed then attached to one of the seam allowances of the pocket opening. The **flap** is attached to the top seam allowance, the **welt** to the bottom one.

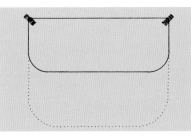

Inside pocket with flap

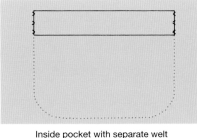

Inside pocket with separate welt

Making the flap or welt

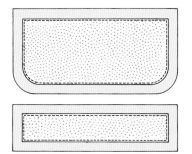

1. Cut welt or flap and its facing from pattern and interface wrong side of welt or flap. Trim interfacing seam allowance.

2. Pin welt or flap to facing, right sides together, and stitch around marked seamline, leaving base edge open. Press flat.

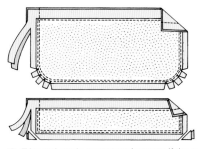

3. Trim and grade seam; notch curves if the corners are rounded. Turn and press, easing facing under slightly.

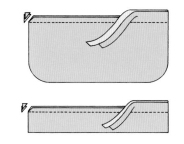

4. Trim base edge to ¼ in (6 mm). Machine-stitch ¼ in (6 mm) from raw edge to hold layers together. Trim across corners diagonally.

Making the pocket

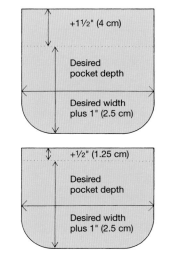

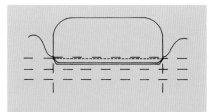

1. Cut two pocket sections, one to desired pocket depth plus 1½ in (4 cm), the other to desired depth plus ½ in (1.25 cm). Both pocket sections should be the desired pocket width plus 1 in (2.5 cm) for side seam allowances.

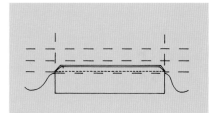

2. Baste right side of welt or flap to right side of garment over pocket markings. If a flap is being used, the seamline of flap should align with *upper* stitch line; if a welt is used, match its seamline to the *lower* stitch line.

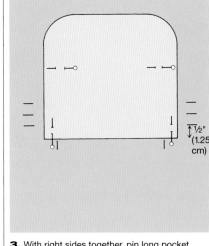

3. With right sides together, pin long pocket section over pocket markings, extending edge ½ in (1.25 cm) below lower marked stitching line. (Note: the flap or welt will be between the pocket and the garment at this step.)

4. Turn the garment section to the wrong side. Following basted marking precisely, stitch a perfect rectangle, pivoting at the corners and overlapping stitching on one long side. Remove all basting stitches.   (Continues on next page.)

POCKETS

Hand bar tacks 76 · Uneven slipstitch 81 · Reducing seam bulk 87

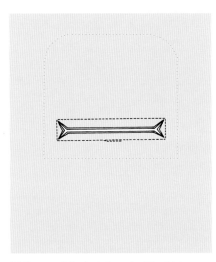

5. Very carefully slash through all the thicknesses at center of rectangle; stop ½ in (1.25 cm) before ends and cut diagonally into the four corners, forming small triangles at each end. Do not cut into stitching.

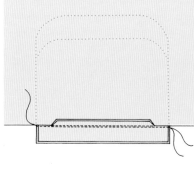

6. Gently push pocket through slash to wrong side. Turn a flap *down* over opening; turn a welt *up*. Pull on small triangles to square corners of opening. Press triangles and seam allowances away from opening.

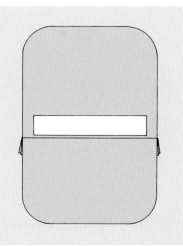

7. With garment right side up, flip up garment to expose pocket edge. Slip the remaining pocket section under opening, right side up, matching raw edges of pocket sections; pin. Stitch, as shown, on first stitch line.

8. Press seam allowance of the opening back away from opening, then turn the garment to the wrong side and bring down the lower pocket section. Press flat. One edge of the pocket is now completely finished.

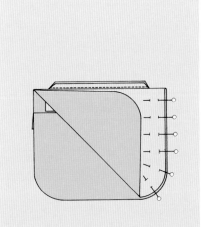

9. Turn upper pocket section down over opening. Bottom raw edge of both pocket sections should be even. If they are not, trim to same length. Pin sections together, taking care not to catch garment.

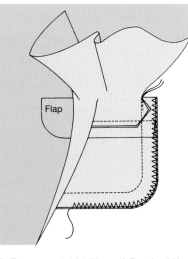

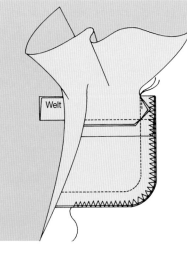

10. Turn garment right side up. A **flap** should be in a downward position, pocket opening completely covered. A **welt** will point upward and cover pocket opening. Flip garment back so pocket is

exposed. Stitch around pinned pocket, starting at top. Stitch across triangle ends as close as possible to original stitching; back-stitch at beginning and end. Press flat. Seam-finish pocket outer edge.

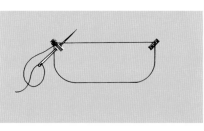

11. To finish off the **welt** pocket (top), slipstitch ends of the welt invisibly to garment. This will hold welt in an upright position. To finish the **flap,** make a tiny bar tack by hand to hold flap down.

Whipstitch 73 · Seam finishes 88–89

Easy self-welt pocket

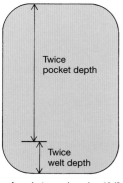

Twice pocket depth

Twice welt depth

Width of pocket opening plus 1" (2.5 cm)

1. Cut pocket from garment fabric on the lengthwise grain. The pocket length should be twice the desired pocket depth plus twice desired depth of the welt; pocket width should equal that of the pocket opening plus 1 in (2.5 cm) for side seam allowances.

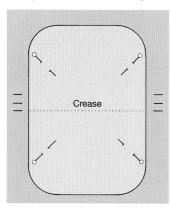

Crease

2. Fold pocket in half horizontally and press in a crease at the fold. With right sides together, pin the pocket section to the garment, aligning crease with marked lower stitching line.

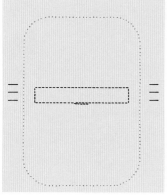

3. Turn garment to the wrong side. Following basted guidelines, stitch around pocket, forming a perfect rectangle (see p. 247). Remove basting stitches.

4. Carefully cut through garment and pocket at center of rectangle; stop ½ in (1.25 cm) before ends and cut diagonally into the four corners, forming a small triangle at each end of opening.

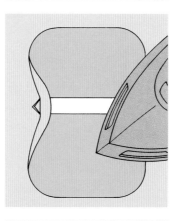

5. Gently push pocket through slash to wrong side. Pull on the small triangular ends to square the corners of the opening. Press triangular ends and pocket opening seam allowances away from the opening.

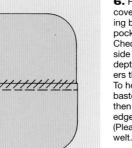

6. Form a pleat to cover the pocket opening by folding lower pocket section up. Check from the right side to see that pleat depth is even and covers the entire opening. To hold pleat in place, baste through the fold, then whipstitch folded edge to top of opening. (Pleat becomes the welt.)

7. Turn garment right side up. Flip up bottom portion of the garment to expose the lower seam allowances of the opening. Stitch through seam allowances and pocket.

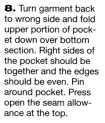

8. Turn garment back to wrong side and fold upper portion of pocket down over bottom section. Right sides of the pocket should be together and the edges should be even. Pin around pocket. Press open the seam allowance at the top.

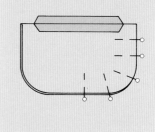

9. Turn the garment right side up again and flip it out of the way to expose the pocket. Stitch around the pinned pocket, starting at the top and stitching across triangular ends as close as possible to original stitching; backstitch at beginning and end. Press flat. Seam-finish outer raw edges of pocket. Remove all basting.

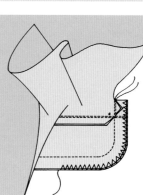

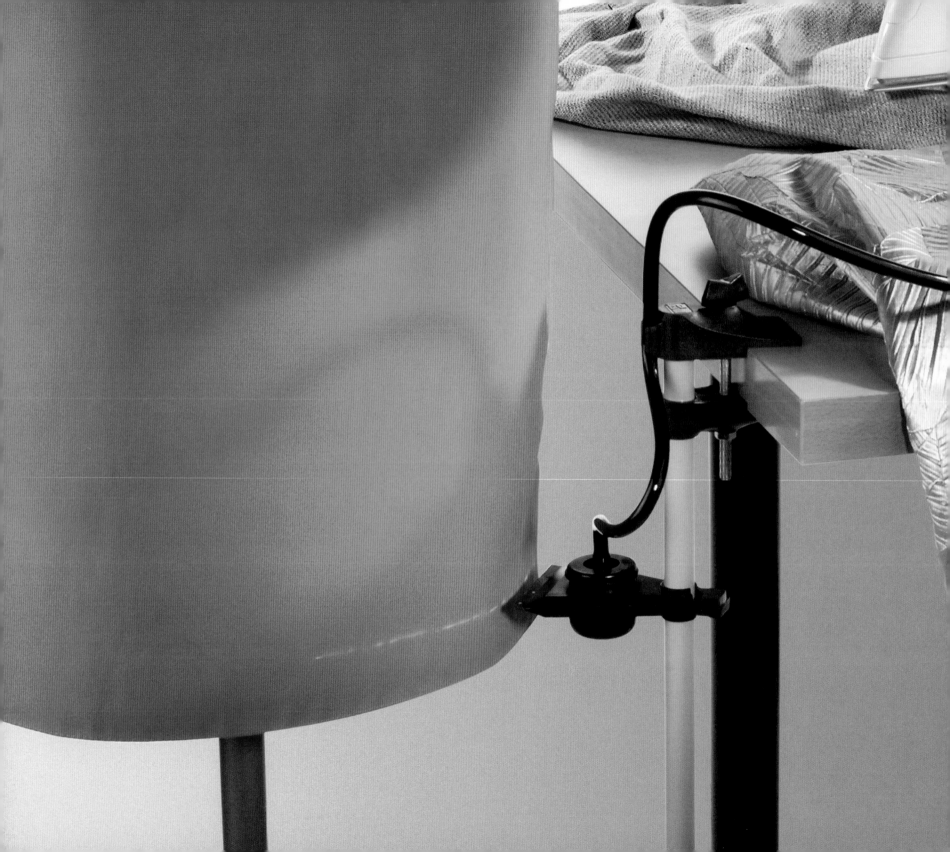

CHAPTER 8

HEMS

Some hems are made
by simply turning up an
edge, others are made
using a seam binding
or bias tape as finishing.
Whatever type of hem
you make, it is often
the last major step
in sewing your garment.

Measuring devices 10 · What pattern markings mean 35

Turned-up hems

In a standard turned-up hem, the **hem allowance** is folded inside the garment, then secured by hand, machine, or fusing. This is the hem type usually provided for in pattern designs, with the amount of turn-up indicated on the pattern by a line or written instructions. It is wise to check this allowance before cutting out the garment, should a change be desirable.

The hem's shape, straight or curved, generally determines how much should be turned up. As a rule, the straighter the edge, the deeper the hem allowance; the more it curves, the shallower the allowance. Exceptions are sheer fabrics, in which a very deep or a narrow rolled hem may be preferable, and soft knits, where a narrow turn-up will minimize sagging.

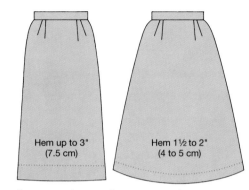

Hem up to 3" (7.5 cm)

Hem 1½ to 2" (4 to 5 cm)

Hem allowance varies according to garment shape. Up to 3 in (7.5 cm) is usually allowed for a straight garment, 1½ to 2 in (4 to 5 cm) for a flared one.

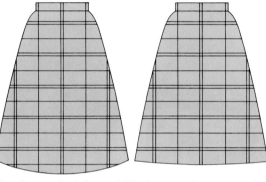

A hemline may look distorted if the hem curve is too extreme for, or does not align with, the fabric design. A slight adjustment may be necessary for a better effect.

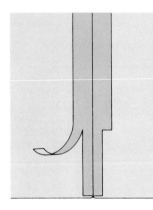

1. Before turning up the hem, reduce bulk within the hem allowance by trimming seam allowances to half their original widths. This will make hem smoother at the seamlines.

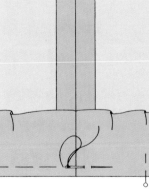

2. With wrong side facing you, fold hem on the hem line, placing pins at right angles to the fold. Try on garment; make adjustments if necessary. After removing the garment, baste close to the folded edge or simply crease with warm iron.

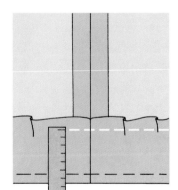

3. Make the hem allowance an even width all around by measuring the desired distance from the fold then marking with chalk. The ironing board is an ideal place to work, as it lets you deal with a small part of the hem at a time. A sewing gauge is the easiest measuring device to use.

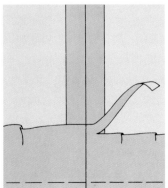

4. Trim excess hem allowance along the marks. At this stage, you can see whether or not the hem edge lies smoothly against the garment. If the hem ripples, control the fullness by easing, a step that is usually necessary with gored skirts and other flared styles.

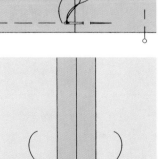

5. Ease the hem by machine-basting ¼ in (6 mm) from the edge, beginning and ending stitches at each seam. Draw up fabric on easestitching until each section of the hem edge corresponds with that part of garment. Take care not to draw the edge in too much, or it will pull against the garment when finished.

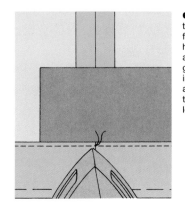

6. Press the hem lightly to shrink out excess fullness, keeping the hem allowance grainlines aligned with those of the garment. Heavy paper inserted between hem and garment will prevent the hem edge from leaving a ridge.

Hand-sewing tips 68 · Overhand stitch 73 · Hemming stitches 80–82 · Seam finishes 88–89

Sewing hems by hand

While overlock machines, or sergers, can be used to finish seam edges and sew seams quickly, it is important to be able to secure hems by hand. First, the raw edge should be neatly finished according to fabric characteristics and garment style. The edge can be left uncovered on fabric that does not fray, and also where a lining covers the hem.

There are two basic hand-hemming methods — *flat,* where stitches pass over the hem edge to the garment, and *blind,* where stitches are taken inside, between hem and garment. Blind hems are best for heavier fabrics and knits because the hem edge is not pressed into the garment.

Uncovered hem edges

A turned-and-stitched edge is suitable for all lightweight fabrics, especially crisp sheers; an excellent, durable finish for washable garments.

A stitched-and-pinked edge is a quick hem finish for fabrics that fray little or not at all; it is a particularly good choice for knits.

A stitched-and-overcasted edge is more time-consuming than the zigzagged edge. It is most often used for medium-heavy to heavy fabrics that fray.

A zigzagged edge is a fast and relatively neat finish usable for any fabric that frays; it is also suitable for knits (care must be taken to not stretch the edge).

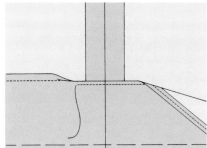

1. Turn the hem edge under ¼ in (6 mm); press. (If using an easestitch, turn edge under along stitching line.) Topstitch ⅛ in (3 mm) from fold.

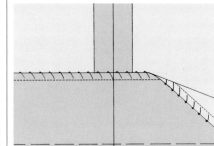

1. Stitch ¼ in (6 mm) from the hem edge, using regular stitching or easestitching (see p. 254). Trim edge with pinking shears.

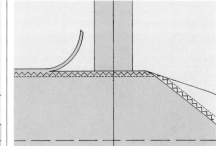

1. Stitch ¼ in (6 mm) from the hem edge using an easestitch if necessary. Using the stitching line as a guide, overcast the raw edge of the fabric.

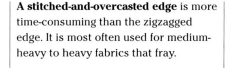

1. Stitch close to hem edge with a zigzag of medium width and length. If necessary, easestitch just below zigzag. Trim excess fabric.

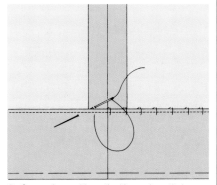

2. Secure hem with vertical hemming stitches, or use uneven slipstitches, spacing the stitches ⅜ in (1 cm) apart. Do not pull thread taut.

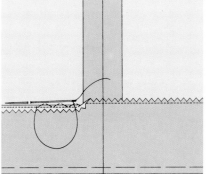

2. Turn hem edge back ¼ in (6 mm); secure with a blind-hemming stitch, as shown, or with a blind catchstitch (for a heavy fabric).

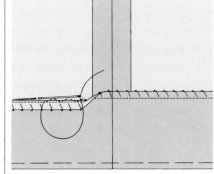

2. The hem edge should be turned back ¼ in (6 mm) and secured with a blind-hemming stitch, as shown, or with a blind catchstitch.

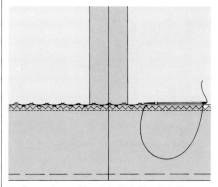

2. Secure hem with catchstitch if material is lightweight or tends to curl. For heavier fabric, use a blind-hemming stitch.

Tapes 12 · Cutting and joining bias strips 262–263

Covered hem edges

Double-stitched hem

Seam binding provides a clean finish for fabric that frays. Use the woven-edge type for a straight-edge hem, a stretchy lace for a curved shape and for knit or other stretch fabric.

Bias tape is a neat hem finish for garments with a flared shape — the bias adjusts to curves. Use the ½ in (12 mm) width, in matching color if available, otherwise a neutral shade.

Hong Kong finish is suitable for any garment style or fabric, but especially good for heavy or bulky fabrics; recommended also for velvet or satin, using net in place of a bias strip.

This technique is recommended for very heavy fabrics, as in coats, since it gives better support. The edge is left uncovered as a rule, but a Hong Kong finish is also appropriate.

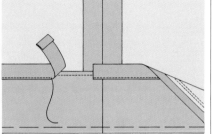

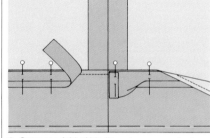

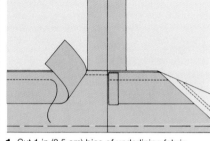

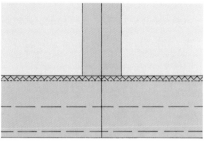

Lay seam binding on right side of hem, lapping it ¼ in (6 mm) over the edge. Edgestitch, overlapping ends at a seam, as shown.

1. Open one fold of binding; place crease just below easestitching on right side of hem. Fold end back ¼ in (6 mm); align with a seam; pin.

1. Cut 1 in (2.5 cm) bias of underlining fabric, or use packaged ½ in (12 mm) width. Stitch to the hem, ¼ in (6 mm) from edge, lapping ends.

1. After finishing the hem edge, place a row of basting stitches halfway between the edge and the fold at the hemline.

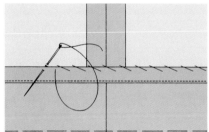

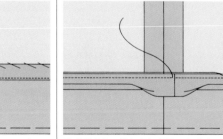

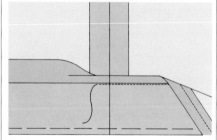

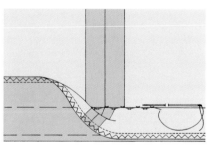

For light- to mediumweight fabric, secure hem with one of the flat hemming stitches — slant (shown), vertical, or catchstitch.

2. Stitch to within 3 in (7.5 cm) of starting point. Trim tape to lap ¼ in (6 mm) beyond fold of starting end; stitch the rest of the way across.

2. Wrap bias over the raw edge and press. From the right side, stitch in the groove formed by the first row of stitching.

2. Fold the hem back along the basting and secure the fold with a blind catchstitch, spacing the stitches ½ in (1.25 cm) apart.

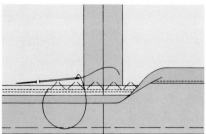

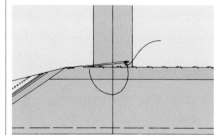

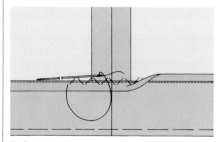

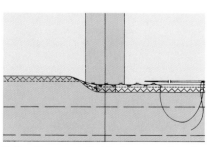

For bulky fabric, fold back tape and hem edge; blindstitch, as shown, catching the stitches through the hem edge only.

3. Secure hem edge with uneven slipstitches, as shown, or use either vertical or slant hemming stitches to secure it.

3. Secure the hem with blind-hemming stitch, or use a blind catchstitch. Be careful not to pull thread too tight.

3. Turn the upper half of the hem up again and secure the edge with a blind catchstitch. Do not pull the thread too tight.

Facing and underlining fabrics 24 · Hand-sewing tips 68 · Hemming stitches 80–82

Fusing a hem

A fast and inconspicuous way to secure a hem is to bond it with fusible web (a sheer non-woven material that melts with application of heat and moisture). This web is available in packaged pre-cut strips, suitable for most hem jobs, and also in larger sheets, from which you can cut strips. A hem can be fused on any fabric that can be steam-pressed, but pressing time varies with different fabrics, so a test is essential.

Check on a scrap to see if the bond is secure and the appearance satisfactory.

If properly done, fusing lasts through normal washing and dry-cleaning procedures. Removal is possible, but messy, so adjust your hem carefully before application. The following additional precautions are necessary: 1. Avoid stretching a fusible web during application; 2. Do not let it touch the iron; 3. Do not glide the iron over the fabric.

Stiffened hemlines for tailored garments

Interfacing adds body and support to a hem, and can also serve as a cushion to keep the edge from being pressed sharply against the garment. Hem interfacing is cut on the bias (see pp. 262–263) from underlining fabric or from a fairly heavy grade of good quality cotton interfacing.

You can interface the hem of a lined or an unlined garment. In a lined, tailored garment, the interfacing can be cut very

wide even if the hem allowance is narrow, as the lining will cover the part of the interfacing above the hem edge. The interfacing extends below the hemline before it is folded. This method is also suitable for velvet or satin garments, as the hemline has a rolled or padded look. In an unlined garment, the hem allowance must be deep enough to enclose the interfacing. Cut the interfacing the depth of hem allowance minus ½ in (1.25 cm).

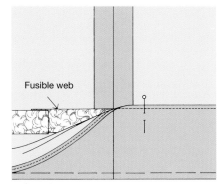

1. Slip a ¾ in (2 cm) strip of fusible web between hem allowance and garment, placing top edge of strip just below hem edge; pin.

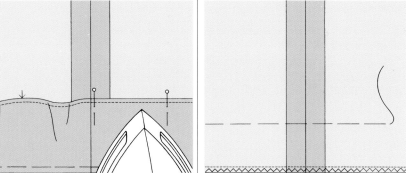

2. With iron at steam setting, fuse the hem lightly in place by pressing between pins with the tip of the iron. Remove pins.

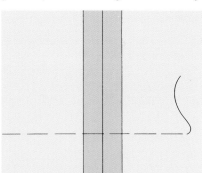

1. Baste hemline with contrasting thread. Make the hem allowance even; finish the edge. Lay garment with wrong side toward you.

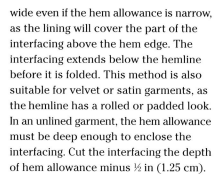

Interfacing cut 2" (5 cm) wider than hem allowance

2. Pin interfacing with lower edge extending ¾ in (2 cm) below hemline. Catchstitch both edges. Overlap ends where they meet.

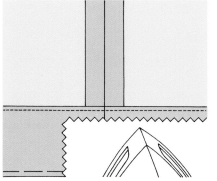

3. Cover hem with damp press cloth. Press a section at a time, holding iron on cloth until dry. Let fabric cool before handling.

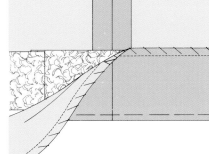

To fuse heavy fabric, use 2 in (5 cm) strip of fusible web to support extra weight. This may take extra pressing time, especially at seams.

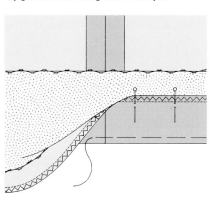

3. Turn hem up along basted line and pin, then baste close to the fold. (Interfacing will extend above the hem edge about ¾ in [2 cm].)

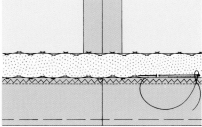

4. Secure hem edge with catchstitches, as shown, taking the stitch that is above the hem edge through interfacing only.

Pressing equipment 14 · Hand-sewing tips 68 · Whipstitch 73 · Hemming stitches 80–82

Hemming a faced opening

There are two ways to finish the hem edge of a faced opening. One is to hem the facing itself, then fold and secure it inside the garment. This is appropriate for all light- to mediumweight fabrics, and permits later lengthening of the hem.

In the second method, the hem allowance is trimmed at the facing and the part of the garment that is covered by it. The bottom of the facing is then sewn to the garment. This technique is

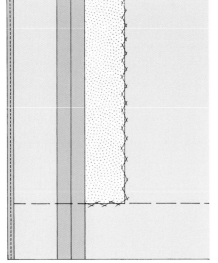

suitable for any fabric but is especially good for a heavy one. It does not, however, permit the hem to be lengthened.

Whichever of the two methods you choose, the lower edge of the completed facing should be smooth and lie flat. The easiest way to achieve this is to trim the interfacing at the hemline and sew it in place with a flat catchstitch, as shown in the diagram above.

Method 1

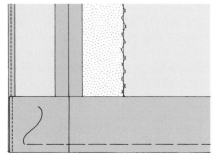

1. After marking the garment hemline, make sure faced edges are the same length. Press facing seam open; fold and baste hemline.

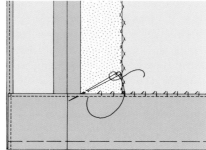

2. Ease the hem if necessary (see p. 254). Finish and secure hem edge in appropriate way (see pp. 255–256), hemming to the edge of the facing.

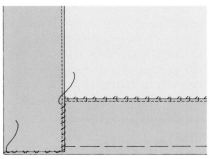

3. Fold facing inside the garment and press. Slipstitch bottom edge of facing to hemline. Whipstitch free edge of facing to hem.

Method 2

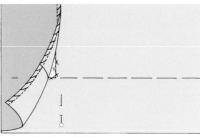

1. Mark hemline with thread; make sure the faced edges are the same length. On the hem allowance, pin-mark where facing ends.

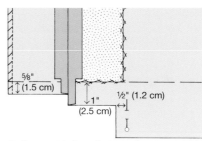

2. Open out facing; trim hem allowance to ⅝ in (1.5 cm), of garment to 1 in (2.5 cm); end ½ in (1.25 cm) from pin. Trim seam allowances.

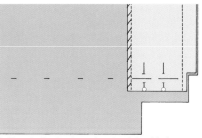

3. Turn facing back so that the right side is toward the garment. Pin and baste the bottom edge, aligning traced hemlines.

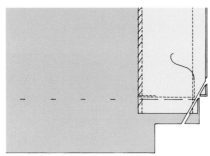

4. Stitch from inner edge of facing to seam at garment edge; pivot, and stitch up seam for ¾ in (2 cm). Trim corners diagonally.

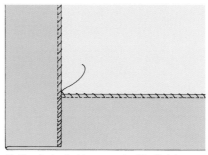

5. Turn facing inside garment; whipstitch inner facing edge to hem allowance. Secure hem with appropriate stitch.

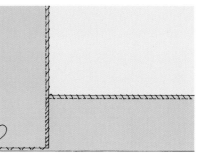

If preferred, omit the stitching in Step 4, and slipstitch the lower edge. On a very heavy fabric, this edge can be left open.

Hand-sewing tips 68 · French tack 77 · Hemming stitches 80–82

Hemming a lining

There are two ways to handle a lining hem: 1. Sew it to the garment, providing extra length for easy movement; 2. Hem the lining separately, securing it to the garment with French tacks. The first is appropriate for a jacket, vest, or a sleeve lining; the second, for a garment that extends below the hips. Before a

lining is hemmed, garment hem should be finished and lining sewn in place except for 6 in (15 cm) at the lower edge.

To adjust lining length, put garment on wrong side out and have someone pin lining to garment all around, about 6 in (15 cm) above hemline. If there is no one to help, drape garment on a

dressmaker's form or the ironing board, pin it first at the seams, then at intervals in between. When the lining is anchored, trim excess fabric. For an attached hem, trim lining to ⅝ in (1.5 cm) below garment hemline; for a free-hanging style, the amount left should equal the lining hem allowance minus 1 in (2.5 cm).

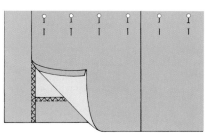

Hem of lining attached to garment

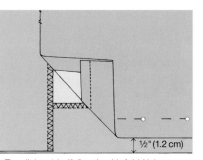

1. Trim lining to ⅝ in (1.5 cm) below finished garment edge. If hem must be eased, sew easestitching ½ in (1.25 cm) from hem edge.

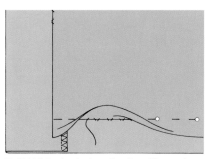

2. Turn lining 1 in (2.5 cm), with fold ½ in (1.25 cm) from garment edge. Pin lining to the garment, placing pins ½ in (1.25 cm) above fold.

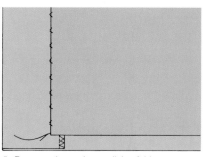

3. Fold lining back along the pinned line and slipstitch it to the garment hem, taking care to catch underlayer of lining only.

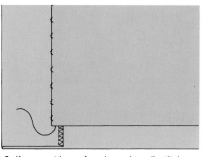

4. Remove pins and press lining fold lightly. If garment has a faced opening, slipstitch remaining lining edges to the facing.

Hem of free-hanging lining

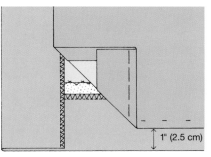

1. Turn under the lining, so that fold is 1 in (2.5 cm) from garment hemline; baste close to fold. Make the hem allowance an even width.

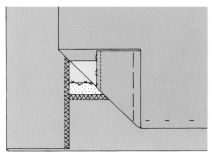

2. Ease the hem edge if necessary (see p. 254); finish and secure the hem by an appropriate method (see pp. 255–256 for the choices).

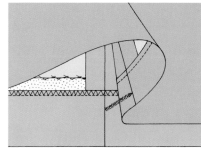

3. Attach the lining to the garment with French tacks ¾ in (2 cm) long, placing one at each seam (see Hand sewing for details of the method).

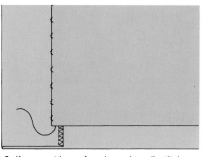

4. If garment has a faced opening, slipstitch remaining lining edge to the facing. Lining is now secured, yet moves freely.

Pillow cover

Pillow fabric: Texo Print, Enschedde (Netherlands)

Fabrics

Cotton, linen, silk

Amount

For one pillow cover, $15^3/_4 \times 15^3/_4$ in
(40×40 cm):
$^1/_2$ yd (0.5 m) of all fabric widths over
36 in (90 cm)
12 in (30 cm) of plain-colored fabric
for trim

Notions

1 pillow form, 16 in (40 cm) square
1 zipper, 14 in (35 cm)

Pattern pieces

1 Front panel – cut 1
2 Back panel – cut 1
3 Border strips – cut 2
When choosing fabric, consider how
its color, design, and texture will blend
with your room. Bring along samples
of fabric already in the room when
shopping for new fabric. Or, buy a
swatch of the fabric you are considering, to test at home first. This is also a
good precaution as the store lighting
may differ from that of your room.

This pillow cover is made with a 1½ in (4 cm) mitered border of contrast fabric, and a zipper in the center of the back panel. You can sew your own pillow form to any size and shape, and purchase a suitable filling at any fabric store.

Cutting

● The most common throw pillow size was chosen for this project. Cut one front panel, 17¼ × 17¼ in (44 × 44 cm) and two back panels, 17¼ × 9½ in (44 × 24 cm).

● For larger covers, measure the pillow size and add ½ in (1.5 cm) for seam allowances on all edges of the front and back panels.

● Cut two strips of border fabric 33 in (84 cm) long and 4 in (10 cm) wide, piecing as required.

● If you are using a light or flimsy fabric for the decorative bias strip, it is advisable to use a double layer of fabric (Fig. 1).

Sewing instructions

● **Borders:** Fold the strips lengthwise down the center, with wrong sides together.

● To form a mitered corner, fold a strip in half lengthwise. Then fold one half back, forming a 90° angle, with folded edge outward. Press flat (Fig. 2).

● Unfold the strip and turn right sides in. Pin the diagonal creases

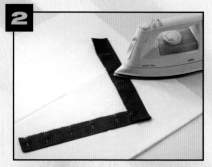

together through the two layers. Stitch on crease line, forming a right angle at center. Trim seam allowance to ¼ in (6 mm) (Fig. 3).

● Repeat with the second strip.

● Press corner seams open. Turn the strips to the right side and press the corners flat (Fig. 4). Unfold the strips again, and stitch the raw ends with the right sides together, using a ½ in (1.25 cm) seam allowance. Complete

the two remaining corners as described above. Baste raw edges of trim together near edge.

● Match the completed square border strip to the right side of the front panel, matching corners and edges. Pin.

● Baste, making sure the corners are sewn precisely. Sew up to the corner, leave the needle in the fabric, and then raise the presser foot and turn the fabric at a right angle. Lower the foot once again and continue stitching. Trim the corners (Fig. 5).

● **Zipper:** Press back the seam allowances for the zipper on the two back sections. Open the zipper, place

the zipper face down on the right side of the zipper placket seam allowance, baste so that the zipper chain aligns with the fabric edge, and stitch. Close the zipper and lay it onto the other seam allowance. Attach as above. Open zipper slightly before final step.

● Match back to front, right sides together. Pin and stitch around all four sides very close to the basting. Turn to right side through zipper opening. Press cover flat.

Sewing equipment 10 · Grain in fabric 56–57 · Hand-sewing stitches 68 · Hemming stitches 80–82

Faced hems

In a faced hem, most of the hem allowance is eliminated; a band of lightweight fabric is then stitched to the hem and turned inside so it does not show. There are two basic facing forms: **shaped** (cut with grainlines and shape conforming to hem) and **bias** (cut as a bias strip, then shaped to fit). You can buy bias hem facing ready-made in various colors.

A shaped facing is applied, as a rule, where a hem shape is unusual, as in the wrap skirt, shown at right. Its use is limited to a hem with minimal flare.

A bias hem facing is recommended in place of a turned-up hem when there is not enough hem allowance to turn up, the fabric is exceptionally bulky, or a skirt is circular in style.

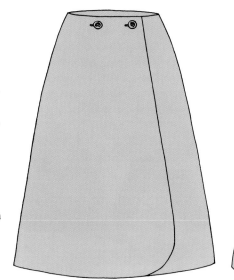

Shaped facing for hems with unusual shapes

Bias facing for widely flared skirts

Shaped hem facing

1. Cut facings to fit the hem. If there are no patterns, make your own, tracing the hemline from garment pieces. Cut them 2½ in (6 cm) wide.

2. Join the facing sections and press the seams open. Trim the seam allowances to half of their original width.

3. Finish the inner facing edge (the smaller curve), using one of the methods for an uncovered hem edge described on page 255.

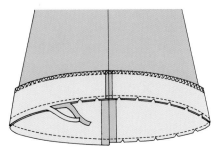

4. Before attaching facing, mark hemline; trim allowance to ⅝ in (1.5 cm). Right sides together, sew facing to garment with ½ in (1.25 cm) seam. Trim, grade, and notch seam allowances.

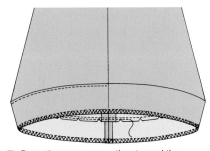

5. Press the seams open, then toward the facing. With the facing pulled out flat, stitch facing close to the seam edge (see p. 147), through all of the seam allowances.

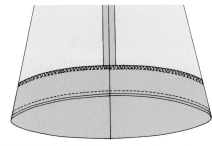

6. Turn facing inside the garment and press the hemline (seam should be ⅛ in [3 mm] from fold). Secure free edge of facing to garment with an appropriate hem stitch (see p. 255).

Cutting bias strips

Bias strips are bands of fabric cut on the true bias (that is, any diagonal at a 45° angle to the lengthwise or crosswise grain). They have many uses, ranging from hem facings to piping and covered cording, bandings and bindings, neckline facings, casings, and ruffles.

When more than one strip is required, joining is done on the straight grain, either individually (two to four sections) or continuously (several strips at once). These methods are shown on opposite page. When bias is attached to a garment, the final seam is sometimes joined on the bias and aligned with a garment seam for a neat effect (see pp. 265–267, for examples).

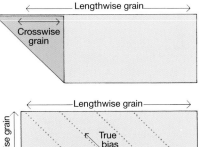

To cut the needed pieces, first locate the true bias by folding fabric diagonally so that a straight edge on the crosswise grain is parallel to the lengthwise grain (selvage). Press fabric along the diagonal fold; open it out and, using the crease as a guide, mark parallel lines, spacing them the width of one strip.

Purchased bias can be used if width, color, and fabric are suitable.

Lengthwise grain 56 · Clipping seams 87

Joining bias strips

1. To join bias strips individually, first cut on marked lines; make sure all ends are on straight grain. Mark ¼ in (6 mm) seam allowances.

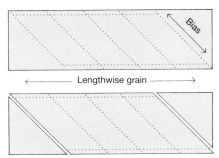

1. To join several bias strips, mark all strips but do not cut them apart — just trim excess fabric. Mark ¼ in (6 mm) seam allowance on lengthwise grain along each edge.

2. Right sides together, pin two strips with seamlines matching. The strips should form a "V" exactly as shown, with seam ends aligned.

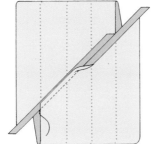

2. Fold fabric into a tube, right sides together; align the seams and the marks, having one strip width extending beyond the edge on each side. Stitch; press seam open.

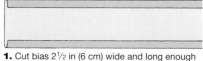

3. Stitch; press seam open. Trim protruding corners of seam allowances to align with edge of strip. Join as many strips as needed.

3. Beginning at one end, cut along the marked line, cutting continuously until you reach the edge of the strip at the opposite end. Trim protruding corners at each end.

Shaping bias

When a bias strip is to be stitched to a curved edge such as a hem, application will be easier and the finished edge smoother if you shape the strip first to conform to the curve.

The shaping method shown at right can be used for hem facings, either with your own bias strips or packaged hem facing. It can also be used to shape bias strips that will become binding or banding.

Before applying shaped bias, determine how its edges should relate to the garment curves. With a hem facing, for instance, the stretched edge would be stitched to the hemline.

To shape bias, set the iron for steam; using the tip of the iron to hold bias in position on one edge, stretch and mold the opposite edge into a curve. After each section is shaped, press it gently to set the curve. When bias is to be used for a banding or binding, fold strip in half before shaping it.

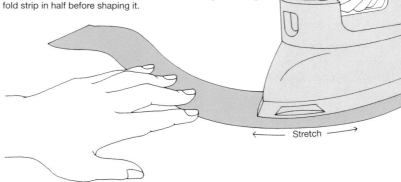

Stretch

Bias hem facing

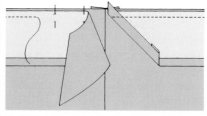

1. Cut bias 2½ in (6 cm) wide and long enough to span hem edge plus 3 in (7.5 cm). Join and shape strips if necessary. Press under ¼ in (6 mm) along each edge. Trim garment hem allowance to ½ in (1.25 cm).

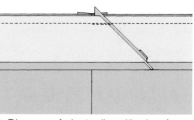

2. Open out one folded edge of bias; fold the end back ¼ in (6 mm). Beginning at a garment seam, pin bias to hem, right sides together and raw edges aligned. Stitch along the creaseline to within 3 in (7.5 cm) of starting point.

3. Trim excess facing to align with edge of starting end. Lap this end over the first one; stitch the rest of the way across.

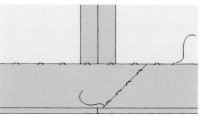

4. Press the seam open, clipping where necessary. Fold bias inside garment along the hemline; press. Secure bias to garment; finish the ends with a slipstitch.

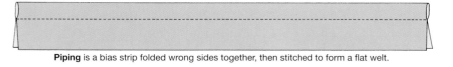

Decorative hem finishes — faced hem with decorative insert

One way to accent a hemline is with a decorative insert. Many ready-made trims, such as lace and ruffled eyelet, will serve this purpose. Each such trim has a plain or unfinished edge meant to be caught between facing and hem edge.

Two popular insert trims are **piping** and **cording,** both made with bias strips, folded and stitched. Piping is flat,

and cording is filled with a length of cable cord. Ready-made piping and cording are available in a limited range of fabrics, widths, and colors, so it may be necessary or preferable to make your own.

Inserted edging adds body and often stiffness to a hem, causing it to stand away from the figure; consider how this will affect your garment style.

Piping is a bias strip folded wrong sides together, then stitched to form a flat welt.

Cording is a bias strip wrapped around cable cord and stitched to hold the cord in place.

How to make piping and cording

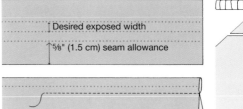

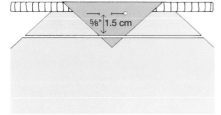

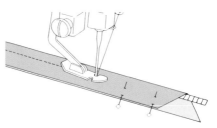

To make piping: Cut bias twice the exposed width plus 1¼ in (3 cm) for the seam allowances. Fold strip in half lengthwise, wrong sides together, stitch ½ in (1.25 cm) from raw edges.

To make cording: 1. Select a cable cord thickness; fold a corner of fabric (or tissue paper) over it and pin, encasing cord snugly; measure ⅝ in (1.5 cm) out from pin and cut.

2. Use measured piece as a pattern for marking the width of the bias strips. Join cut strips individually or continuously (see pp. 262–263 for cutting and joining bias).

3. Wrap bias around cord with right side of fabric out, seam edges even; pin. With zipper foot to left of needle, stitch close to cord, but do not crowd stitching against it.

Applying piping or cording to a hemline

The application of piping or cording is done in two stages. It is stitched first to the garment, then to the facing, with each successive line of stitching placed

closer to the trim. When completed, no stitching should show on the right side of the garment. Any inserted trim can be applied in the same way.

Before proceeding, mark the hemline and trim hem allowance to ⅝ in (1.5 cm). If the exposed portion of the trim is more than ¼ in (6 mm) wide, adjust the

hemline to allow for the amount that will show. For example, if the trim is 1 in (2.5 cm) after insertion, raise the hemline 1 in (2.5 cm).

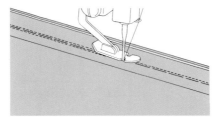

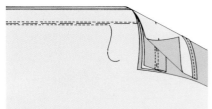

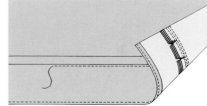

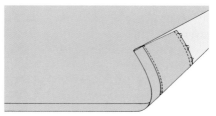

1. Baste piping to right side of hem, aligning piping seam and hemline. With zipper foot to right of needle, stitch left of piping stitches.

2. Baste facing to hem with right sides together, raw edges even. Stitch on the hem, crowding stitches between piping and first stitching.

3. Trim, grade, and notch seam allowances. Press seams open, then toward facing. Understitch the facing, using a zipper foot.

4. Press facing inside garment so that piping falls at the hem edge; secure facing with appropriate hemming stitch (see p. 255).

Slipstitch 80–81 · Shaped-band neckline finish 154

Enclosing a hem edge

For an enclosed hem edge, the hem allowance is eliminated and the raw edge encased by either a **banding** or **binding.** These two finishes are prepared and applied in a similar way but, when finished, banding becomes an extension of the hem and binding wraps around it.

Which type should be used depends on garment style and fabric. A banding would be the choice if a garment needs lengthening (a child's dress, for example) or when a wide edging is desired. A binding is used for reversible styles and for garments made from sheer fabrics.

When preparing your own banding or

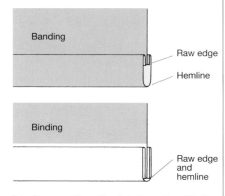

binding, cut it on the fabric grain with the greatest stretch: bias for a woven, crosswise grain for a knit. The natural flexibility of these grains makes application smoother, especially on curved edges.

Bias strips are usually joined on the straight grain, but another method is used for banding and binding. Here, the ends of the strip are squared off, joined on the bias, and the juncture is aligned with a garment seam. Take care not to stretch the fabric when joining.

Banding

Banding is an extension of a garment edge. It can be cut the same shape as the edge, as for a neckline finish, or on the bias. Since it is ideal for adding

1. Cut strip to fit hem plus 1¼ in (3 cm). Press in half lengthwise, wrong sides together. Open strip; press edges under ¼ in (6 mm).

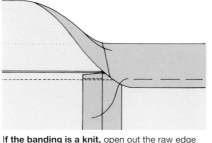

If **the banding is a knit,** open out the raw edge and finger-press it flat. Baste in place with raw edge extending ¼ in (6 mm) beyond seamline.

length, a bias cut is the usual approach for a hem banding. To prepare the hem for banding, mark the hemline at the desired length. Then, measure up from

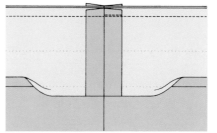

2. Open out folds; stitch ends and press seam open. Right sides together and seams aligned, stitch band to garment ¼ in (6 mm) from edge.

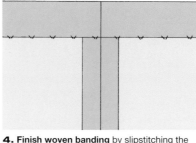

4. Finish woven banding by slipstitching the folded edge to the seamline. Stitches should not show on the right side of the garment.

the hemline a distance equal to the finished banding width. Finally, mark a new line and trim all but ¼ in (6 mm) of fabric below it.

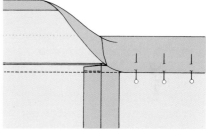

3. Press seam allowances toward the banding. Fold banding in half. If the banding is **woven,** bring folded edge to meet the seamline; pin.

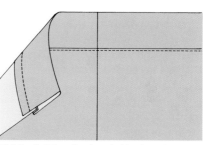

Finish a knit banding by stitching from the right side in the seam groove. Leave inside edge as is, overlock, or trim with pinking shears.

Quick application method for knit banding

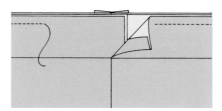

1. Fold strip in half, wrong sides together; press. Fold one end under ½ in (1.25 cm). Pin band to garment, folded end at seam.

2. Stitch ¼ in (6 mm) from edge; begin ¾ in (2 cm) from folded end and stop 3 in (7.5 cm) before end. Slip end between folds. Continue sewing.

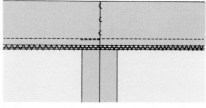

3. Zigzag edges together. Press band away from garment, seam allowances toward garment. Slipstitch ends of band where they overlap.

Sewing equipment 10 · Slipstitch 80–81

Hems with bound edges — binding

Binding is a strip of fabric that encloses a hem or other garment edge. It is a neat and practical finish for the hem of a reversible garment, and can also be an attractive trim, especially when in a contrasting color or texture.

The strip used for binding can be woven fabric cut on the bias, or knit cut on the crosswise grain. It might also be a folded braid, bias tape, or grosgrain ribbon (the most difficult to apply).

There are two basic binding types: **single** and **double.** Single binding is suitable for any fabric; double binding is most appropriate for sheers.

To prepare hem for binding, mark hemline, then trim away all hem allowance (binding fold should be at hem edge when completed). Cut strips with seam allowances same width as finished binding. Completed width should be narrow.

A single binding can be applied in two stages or in a single stage. The latter requires careful pressing to make one side slightly wider.

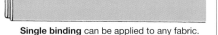

Single binding can be applied to any fabric.

Double binding is most appropriate for sheers.

Preparation of a single binding

1. Cut bias strips four times the finished *width* of the binding, and the *length* of the edge to be bound plus 2 in (5 cm) for ease and joining.

2. Fold the strip in half lengthwise, with wrong sides together. Press it lightly, taking care not to stretch the fabric.

3. Open out binding and fold edges to meet at the center crease; press. Shape the binding if necessary (see p. 263 for method).

Applying a single binding

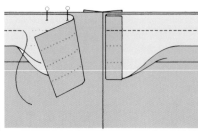

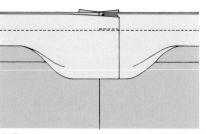

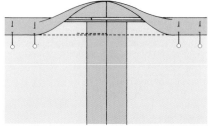

1. Open out one fold of binding; pin it to the hem edge, right sides together and raw edges aligned. Turn back starting end ½ in (1.25 cm) and align the fold with a garment seam; stitch to within 3 in (7.5 cm) of the starting point.

2. Trim away excess binding at this end so that it laps ½ in (1.25 cm) beyond the fold of the starting end. Lap the second end over the first one and stitch the rest of the way across, through all of the thicknesses.

3. Press seam allowances toward the binding. Fold binding in half on the pressed line. If the binding fabric is **woven,** bring the turned-under edge to meet the seamline; pin in place, taking care not to stretch the fabric.

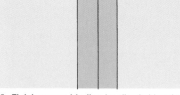

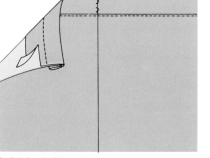

If binding is a knit, open the raw edge and finger-press it flat. Baste in place, matching the binding crease and garment seamline.

4. Finish woven binding by slipstitching the folded edge to the seamline. Slipstitch binding ends where they overlap.

To finish a knit binding, stitch on right side in the seam groove. Slipstitch binding ends. Trim excess binding inside garment.

Slipstitch 80–81

Preparing single binding for topstitching

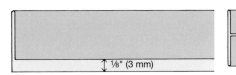

1. Fold bias strip lengthwise, a little off-center, so that one side is ⅛ in (3 mm) wider than the other; press the strip lightly.

2. Open out strip and fold cut edges to meet at pressed crease; press folds lightly. Shape if necessary (see p. 263 for method).

Topstitch application of single binding

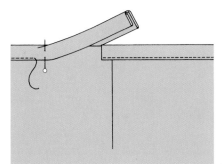

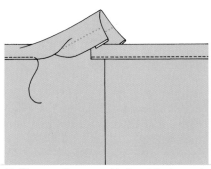

1. With garment right side up, wrap binding over the hem edge with wider side beneath. Pin binding, positioning the starting edge to extend ½ in (1.25 cm) beyond a garment seam. Stitch to within 3 in (7.5 cm) of starting point.

2. Trim away the excess binding at the free end so that it laps the starting end by 1 in (2.5 cm). Fold the second end under ½ in (1.25 cm) and lap it over the first one, aligning the second fold with the garment seam.

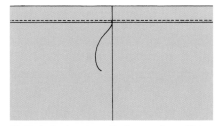

3. Tuck all edges in neatly, then continue stitching, ending at the garment seam (do not reverse stitch at end). Remove pins.

4. Pull threads to the wrong side and tie a knot. Slipstitch the folded edge where binding overlaps. Press binding lightly.

Preparing a double binding

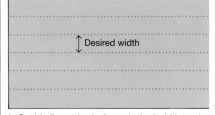

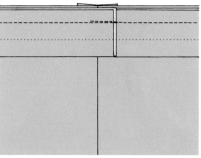

1. Cut binding strip six times desired width, and the length of edge to be bound plus 2 in (5 cm). (Seam allowances equal finished width.)

Fold the strip in half lengthwise, wrong sides together, press. Fold the halved strip in thirds; press. Shape if necessary (p. 263).

Applying a double binding

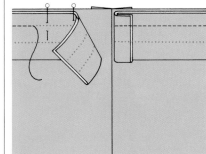

1. Lay the binding on right side of hem with raw edges aligned. Turn back the starting end ½ in (1.25 cm) and align the fold with a garment seam; pin. Stitch, in binding crease nearest the edge, to within 3 in (7.5 cm) of starting point.

2. Trim away the excess binding at the free end so that it laps ½ in (1.25 cm) beyond the fold of the starting end. Lap the second end over the first and stitch the rest of the way across, through all thicknesses.

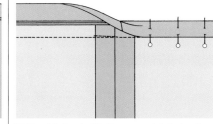

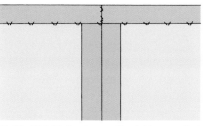

3. Turn binding inside the garment, bringing the long folded edge just to the stitching line. The folded end will be on top.

4. Slipstitch binding to seamline, taking care that stitches do not show on right side. Slipstitch the binding ends where they overlap.

Beach towel

Fabrics
Terry cloth
For the appliqué: cotton, linen

Amount
Terry cloth: 1½ yd (1.35 m) of 39 in
(100 cm) -width fabric (or bath towel)
Cotton: 1⅛ yd (1 m) of 54/56 in
(140 cm) -width fabric.

Notions
Fusible web with paper on one side

Pattern pieces
Terry cloth:
1 Cut to neat rectangle
Cotton:
1 Border strips
2 Appliqué – cut 3
3 Appliqué – cut 5
4 Appliqué – cut 1
Create an original design for the
appliqué and make your own unique
beach towel.

This beach towel is embellished with appliqué and border trim. The mitering technique is used.

In this project we describe how to apply appliqués with the help of fusible web. This method is most suitable for larger appliqués.

You can use various fabrics to make appliqués. Fabric leftovers are often sufficient for smaller projects.

If you are using a colored fabric, pre-wash it first to make sure the color won't bleed.

Press all fabrics before starting. The appliqués are stitched in place with all-purpose thread.

Essential tools for completing this project include a pair of sharp scissors, a pencil for marking, a ruler, and paper.

Appliqués

● Draw a design for the appliqué on paper. You can find ideas for designs in books and magazines. You can also cut motifs from printed fabrics for the appliqués (Fig. 1).

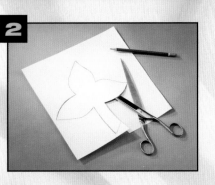

● Make a template for each motif. If you prefer, you can buy stencils and templates in specialty stores (Fig. 2).
● Match fusible web, paper side up, to the wrong side of a piece of appliqué fabric and iron on.
● Trace the template onto the paper side of the fusible web (Fig. 3).
● Cut out the motif (Fig. 4).

● Repeat for all the designs.
● Arrange motifs on terry cloth as a test. Remove.
● Lay out all motifs with paper side

up and iron gently to warm them. Peel off paper and arrange motifs on terry cloth. Press firmly in place with steam iron (Fig. 5).

Sewing instructions

● Stitch along the edges of the motif pieces using a short zigzag or satin stitch. Use a stitch width suitable to the motif. Position the needle on the right-hand side for the outer corners and on the left-hand side for the inner corners (Fig 6).

Trim: Press long raw edges of trim to wrong side. Fold the fabric strips in the middle lengthwise with wrong sides and edges together, and press.

● Pin the trim onto the edges of the towel while leaving an inch or two (a few centimeters) open at the corners; baste.
● Arrange the corners into mitered folds by pressing. See page 261 for further details on applying mitered trim.
● Stitch the trim through all layers to the towel. Stitch miters closed at corners.

Finishing corners — mitering

Corners that occur at garment edges can be satisfactorily finished in any hem style (turned-up, faced, bound, etc.) by means of a technique called **mitering**. Mitering is the diagonal joining of two edges at the corner. The join may be stitched or just folded in place. The key to successful mitering is the accurate pressing of folds at the corner, with the mitered piece always at a right angle to the corner's sides. These pressed lines sometimes act as stitching guides for the miter.

Mitered corners basically consist of two distinct types, **outward** and **inward**

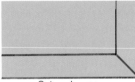

Outward corner

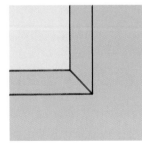

Inward corner

(see illustrations above); mitering techniques will differ for each.

If the mitered piece (e.g., binding) goes around the corner, it is an outward corner; if the mitered piece lies within the corner, it is an inward corner.

Mitering turned-up hems

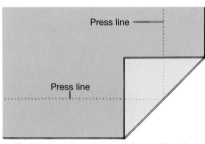

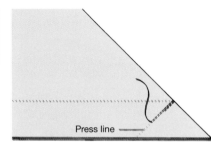

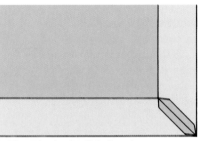

1. Fold on seamlines on crosswise and length-wise edges; press. Open out edges. Fold corner up, aligning creased lines; press.

2. Open out corner. Fold garment diagonally (on bias), right sides together and raw edges even. Stitch on diagonal press line.

3. Trim point, leaving ¼ in (6 mm) seam allowance. Taper seam allowance at corner; press seam open. Turn corner right side out; press.

Mitering a flat trim

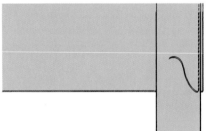

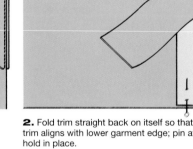

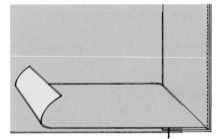

1. Pin the trim to finished edge of garment. Stitch along outer edge of trim; stop at corner; pull threads to wrong side and knot.

2. Fold trim straight back on itself so that fold of trim aligns with lower garment edge; pin at fold to hold in place.

3. Fold trim down, creasing a diagonal fold at corner and aligning outer edge of trim with lower edge of garment. Press diagonal fold.

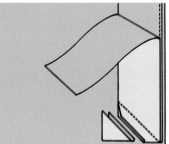

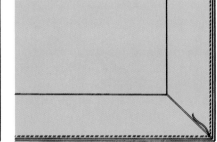

4. Lift up trim at corner and stitch on diagonal press line through all thicknesses. Trim the corner to reduce bulk.

5. Fold trim back, aligning its lower edge with garment edge. Starting in last stitch at corner, stitch along outer edge of trim.

6. Pull threads at corner to wrong side and knot. Then stitch along inner edge of trim. Press entire trim and garment.

Square neckline finish 141

Mitering a bias facing

When applying a bias facing to a garment edge with corners, make sure that the facing is turned inside and lies flat at each corner. Before starting, trim the seam allowances to ¼ in (6 mm) along the edge to be faced. Use prepackaged

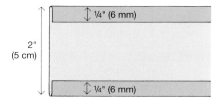

bias hem facing or cut facing from a lightweight underlining as shown above. Cut a bias strip (see pp. 262–263) 2½ in (6 cm) wide, and press both long edges ¼ in (6 mm) to the wrong side. Follow the instructions at right for mitering at an outward corner. To miter an inward corner, follow the steps illustrated below; this technique enables you to change a straight bias piece into a shaped facing. Trim carefully during construction to help eliminate bulk.

Mitering a bias facing (outward corner)

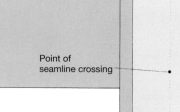

1. Open out one folded edge of bias facing; pin to garment edge, right sides together. Mark facing at point of seamline crossing.

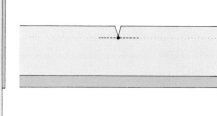

2. Place a short row of stitches within foldline in area of marked point. Clip seam allowance to point; avoid cutting threads.

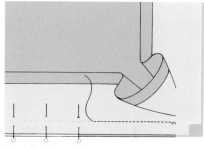

3. Pin facing to garment as before; at the slash point, bring facing around corner. Stitch along foldline, pivoting at corner.

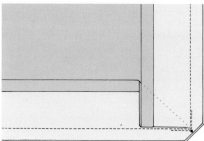

4. Trim off seam allowances at the corner. Carefully fold the facing so it is at right angles to itself. Press lightly.

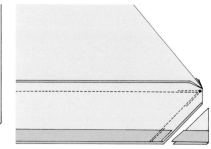

5. Fold garment, right sides together, so facing edges are even. Stitch on diagonal press line. Trim point; leave ¼ in (6 mm) seam allowance.

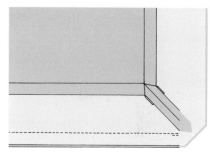

6. Clip seam allowance at corner; press mitered seam open. Press open seam allowances at edges; turn facing to wrong side; press.

Mitering a bias facing (inward corner)

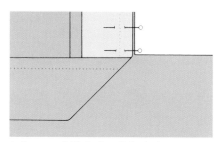

1. Open one folded edge of bias facing; pin to garment edge, right sides together. Diagonally fold facing at corner edge; press.

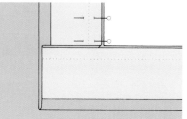

2. Fold facing straight back toward the corner, aligning fold with the outer edge of facing; press lightly. Remove facing.

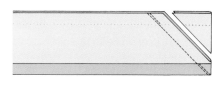

3. Fold facing along press line, right sides together. Stitch on the diagonal press line. Trim corner point, leaving ¼ in (6 mm) seam allowance.

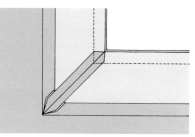

4. Clip seam allowance at point; press open. Treat mitered facing as a shaped facing and apply to garment (see Neckline facing, p. 142).

Slipstitch 80–81

Mitering banding (outward corner)

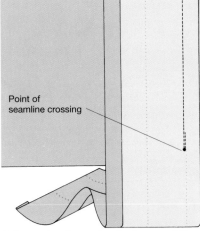

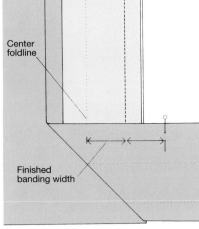

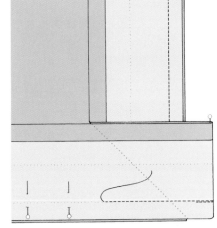

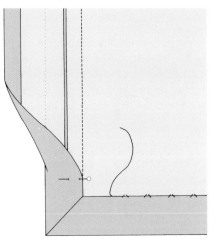

Point of seamline crossing

Center foldline

Finished banding width

1. Prepare banding as described on page 265. Open out one folded edge. With the right sides together, pin banding to garment edge; stitch along the banding foldline; stop and secure stitches at seamline crossing.

2. Diagonally fold banding away from garment; press lightly. From the center foldline of the banding, measure a distance equal to twice the width of the finished banding, and mark that point with a pin.

3. Fold the banding straight back from the pin mark, and pin banding edge to the adjoining garment edge. Stitch along the banding foldline, securing stitches at the beginning. Then press the seam flat.

4. Form a neat miter on right side of garment; fold banding over edges to wrong side and form miter on that side. Bring folded edge of banding to stitching line; pin and slipstitch banding edge and mitered fold in place.

Mitering banding (inward corner)

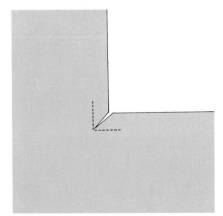

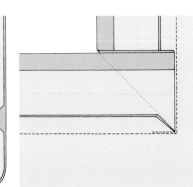

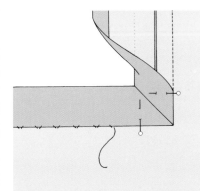

1. Reinforce inner garment corner with small stitches: stitch within a thread's width of the seamline for ¾ in (2 cm) on either side of the corner. Clip into the corner, being careful not to cut threads of reinforcement stitches.

2. Prepare banding (see p. 265). Open out one folded edge. Spread the slashed corner and pin edge to banding, right sides together; keep banding foldline aligned with garment seamline. Stitch from the garment side.

3. Carefully fold banding to form miter on the right side. Illustration above shows folds from the wrong side; note straight fold of mitered banding is placed between edges of clip. Keep edges at right angles to one another.

4. Turn banding down over seam allowances, forming miter on the wrong side; folded edge of banding should come to the stitching line. Pin and slipstitch the banding edge and mitered fold in place.

Whipstitch 73

Mitering knit banding (outward corner)

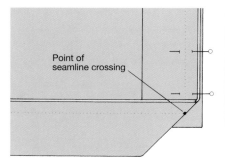

Point of seamline crossing

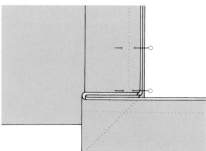

1. Prepare banding (see p. 265). Open folded edges, then fold banding along center foldline. Pin to garment; stop at seamline crossing; fold banding diagonally toward garment.

2. Fold the banding straight back toward the corner so that the fold is aligned with the banding edge; press lightly. Remove banding, and open it out completely.

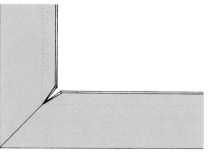

3. Fold the banding along the horizontal press line, right sides facing. Stitch along the press lines that form a "pyramid"; start and stop ¼ in (6 mm) from edges; secure stitches.

4. Trim excess at corners, leaving a ¼ in (6 mm) seam allowance on each side; clip to point. Press seam allowances open, and turn mitered banding right side out. Press.

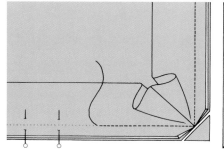

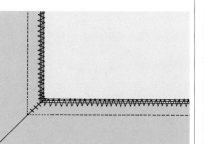

5. Pin banding onto garment as before, bringing it around corner. Stitch along banding foldline; shorten stitches around corner. Trim off garment seam allowance at corner.

6. Place another row of stitches (zigzag, overlock, or straight) within the seam allowance. Press flat, then press banding away from garment. Whipstitch corners together.

Mitering knit banding (inward corner)

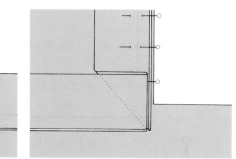

Point of seamline crossing

1. Prepare banding (see p. 265). Open folded edges, then fold banding on center foldline. Pin to garment; stop at seamline crossing. Fold banding diagonally away from corner.

2. Fold banding straight back toward the garment so that the fold is aligned with the raw edge of the banding; press lightly. Remove banding, and open it out completely.

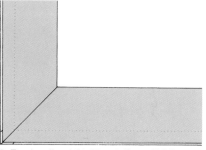

3. Fold banding along horizontal press line, right sides facing. Stitch press lines that form "inverted pyramid." Trim triangular piece; leave ¼ in (6 mm) seam allowances; clip; press open.

4. Turn banding right side out. Press. Reinforce inner garment corner with small stitches: stitch within a thread's width of seamline for ¾ in (2 cm) on either side of corner.

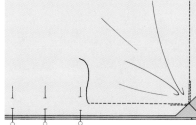

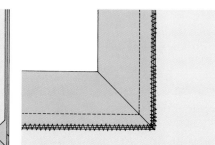

5. Clip into corner. Spread sides of slashed corner, and pin banding to right side of garment, foldline and seamline aligned. Stitch from garment side, pivoting at corner.

6. Sew another row of stitches (zigzag or straight) within the seam allowance. Press flat to embed the stitches. Press the banding away from the garment.

Slipstitch 80–81

Mitering bindings

Methods of constructing and applying single and double bindings are discussed earlier in this chapter. Though these differ according to type of binding, mitering techniques for both single and double binding are similar for outward and inward corners. The illustrations below show mitering of a single binding; note that one folded edge is opened before application begins. When mitering a double binding, keep binding folded in half, and proceed as directed below.

Mitering single or double binding (outward corner)

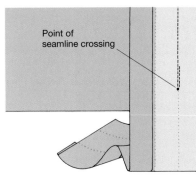

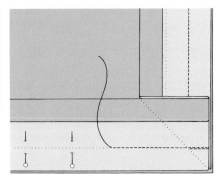

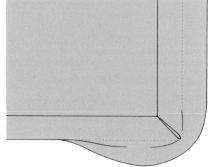

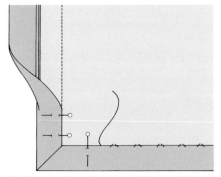

1. Prepare the single or double binding (see pp. 266–267). With right sides together, pin binding to garment, aligning foldline and seamline. Stitch along the binding foldline; stop and secure stitches at seamline crossing.

2. Diagonally fold binding away from garment; press. Fold banding straight back toward garment so that the fold is aligned with the binding edge. Stitch along the binding foldline, securing stitches at the beginning.

3. Press the seam flat to embed the stitches. Fold the binding over raw edges to the wrong side; at the same time, carefully form a neat miter on the right side of the garment. Keep the mitered corner squared.

4. Form a miter on the wrong side as well; bring the folded edges of the binding to the stitching line; pin and slipstitch the edge of the binding and the fold of the miter in place. Press the entire binding.

Mitering single or double binding (inward corner)

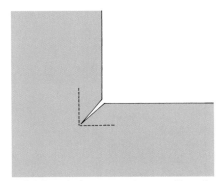

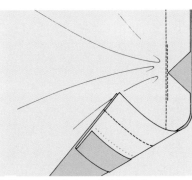

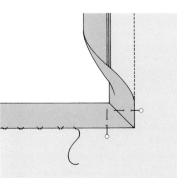

1. Reinforce the inner garment corner with small stitches. Stitch within a thread's width of the seamline for ¾ in (2 cm) on either side of the corner. Clip into the corner, being careful not to cut the reinforcing stitches.

2. Prepare the single or double binding (see pp. 266–267). Spread the slashed corner, and pin edge to binding, right sides together; keep binding foldline aligned with garment seamline. Stitch from the garment side.

3. Carefully fold binding to form miter on right side. Illustration above shows folds from wrong side; note straight fold of mitered binding is placed between edges of clip. Keep edges at right angles to one another.

4. Turn the binding down over the seam allowances, forming a miter on the wrong side; the folded edge of the binding should come to the stitching line. Pin and slipstitch the binding edge and mitered fold in place.

Mitering topstitched binding (outward corner)

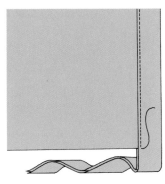

1. Prepare binding for topstitching application (see p. 267). Insert one garment edge into the fold of the binding; pin and stitch along inner edge of binding; stop at the bottom of the garment.

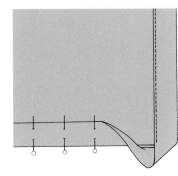

2. Bring binding around the corner, encasing bottom raw edge of garment; pin in place, forming miter around corner.

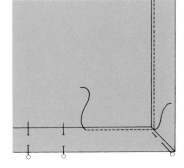

3. Pin mitered fold in place. Resume stitching at last stitch in inner corner. Pull threads through at starting point and knot. Slipstitch mitered fold if necessary.

Mitering topstitched binding (inward corner)

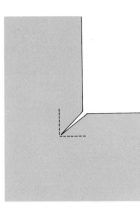

1. Reinforce the inner garment corner with small stitches: stitch within a thread's width of the seamline for ¾ in (2 cm) on either side of the corner. Clip into the corner, being careful not to cut threads.

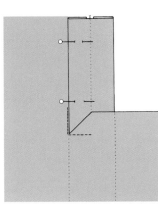

2. Prepare binding for topstitching application (see p. 267). Open out center fold and pin binding to one side of corner, smooth side out, aligning center fold with raw edge.

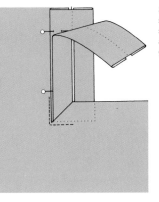

3. Fold the binding straight back on itself so that the fold is aligned with the garment's stitching line.

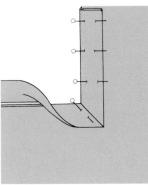

4. Then fold binding diagonally; press lightly. Pin the diagonal fold to hold it in place.

5. Fold binding over raw edge, mitering corner on the wrong side of the garment; pin in place.

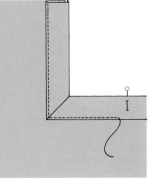

6. From the right side, stitch along binding edge through all thicknesses. Slipstitch mitered fold in place if necessary.

Pattern alterations 36–46, 52–53 · French tack 77

Special hemming techniques — problem hems

Special techniques are required on some garments to achieve a satisfactory hem finish. An even, smooth hem on pants cuffs, for example (see right), demands careful handling of the lines that form the cuff and hem. A long evening gown may need help to hold its hemline flare; a good quality interfacing added to the hem fortifies it (see opposite page).

Hems in standard garments may need special handling because of unusual fabric characteristics, mainly texture or structure. Suggestions for techniques for such fabrics as lace, fake fur, leather, velvet, stretchy knits, and sheers are on pages 280–281. Hard-to-ease fabrics,

such as permanent press and tightly woven fabrics, can be treated normally except for minor special considerations at the hemline. When a garment made of such fabric has a shaped hem, keep the hem allowance narrow; it will be far easier to control the excess fullness. Brocade and fabrics like it can quickly become worn-looking; as a preventive measure, use a light touch when pressing the hem fold. Some such fabrics may waterspot; to avoid this, press with a dry iron set low. To retain reversibility of garments made from double-faced fabrics, hems can be either banded or bound (see pp. 265–267).

Adding cuffs to an uncuffed pants pattern

To make cuffed pants using a pants pattern not designed for cuffs:

1. Make all pattern alterations in waist-to-hip area (waist, crotch) and width of leg.
2. Determine finished pants length from the waistline; measure along your side, or take the side seam measurement from another pair of pants that fits well.
3. Measure this same distance down from the waistline marking on pattern pieces and mark them.
4. Decide on the cuff depth; double this measurement, add to pattern (tape tissue paper to bottom for added length).
5. To this amount, add another 1¼ in (3 cm) for a hem allowance.
6. Mark and identify each line.
7. Cut out pants; thread-mark hem, fold-lines, and turn-up lines.
8. Construct and hem the cuff as directed above right.

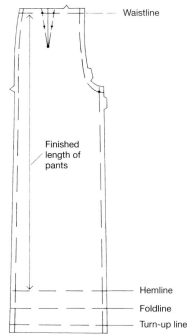

Waistline

Finished length of pants

Hemline
Foldline
Turn-up line

Hemming pants cuffs

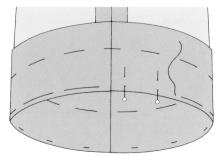

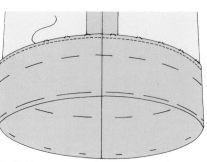

1. Complete pants construction. Press seams open. Turn hem allowance to wrong side along foldline; pin, then baste close to fold.

2. Finish raw edge, and secure to pants leg; if desired, machine-stitch in place (stitching will not show when cuff is turned).

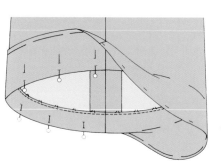

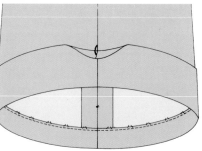

3. Turn cuff up to the right side along turn-up line; pin in place. Baste close to fold, through all thicknesses. Press gently.

4. To keep the cuff from falling, sew a short French tack at seams, ½ in (1.25 cm) below top edge of cuff. Remove all basting; press.

Adding cuffs to shaped pants

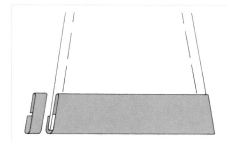

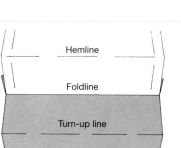

Hemline

Foldline

Turn-up line

To add cuffs to a shaped pants pattern, add length to pattern as explained at left; fold pattern according to the line indications;

make cutting edges at bottom continuous with those above. Open out pattern piece; use to cut and mark pants.

Whipstitch 73 · Cross-stitch basting 75 · Uneven slipstitch 81

Stiffening hemlines using tape

Tape used to stiffen hemlines is made from synthetic material, usually nylon. It is primarily applied to the hems of garments in order to add body and support and give hems an elegant flare.

Nylon tape is available in various widths. The narrower width is used mainly for lighter fabrics, the wider width for mediumweight fabrics. Wide tape is easier to apply to a flared hem

when you run a gathering stitch along one of the edges of the tape, as illustrated in the diagrams below.

Before attaching the tape to the garment, remove all creases and folds

from the tape with a steam iron. When applying the tape, make sure that it is not pulled or stretched in any way. Narrow and wide tape is sewn to the hem in the same way (see below).

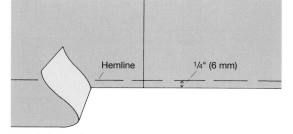

1. Mark the hemline on the edge of the garment. Trim seam to within ¼ in (6 mm) of the hem allowance.

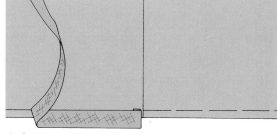

2. Starting at a seam, and working on the right side, place the top edge of the tape along the hemline, turning in the tape edge.

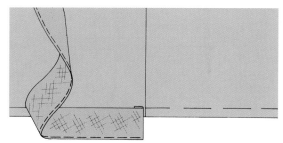

Wide tape is first sewn along one edge using a gathering stitch. Place the other tape edge along the marked hemline.

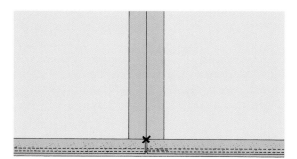

3. Closely stich the tape along the edge of the hem. Trim tape where both ends meet at the seam and turn the edges in.

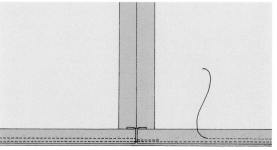

4. Fold tape inside garment along the hemline. Stich along the fold through all fabric layers.

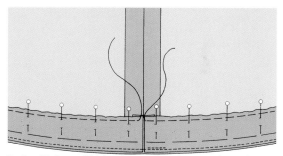

Baste wide tape which has been gathered at one edge to the foldline. Gather thread, press, and pin.

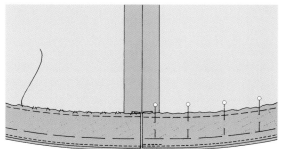

5. Turn under the open edges of the band at the seam and tack to the garment, as shown above, using cross-stich basting.

Attach wide tape which has been gathered at one edge by sewing the open edges of the tape to the garment with an uneven slipstitch.

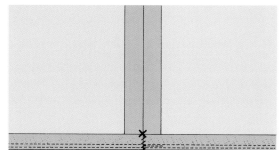

6. Close the tape edges at the seam using a whipstitch. Remove all basting threads and press.

Lace blouse

Fabrics
Cotton or synthetic lace with scalloped border on two edges

Amount
For size 12 (38): 1¹/₈ yd (1.1 m) of 48 in (122 cm) -width fabric

Notions
1³/₈ yd (1.3 m) satin bias tape

Pattern pieces ▶▶▶▶▶▶▶▶▶▶▶▶▶▶
1 Front – cut 1
2 Back – cut 1
3 Sleeves – cut 2
Take a basic T-shirt or overblouse pattern and modify it for a scoop neck and a length ending just at the hip. Holding the pattern in place on the body, select desired length and cut or fold away extra pattern.

Shorten sleeves in the same way. The length from the sleeve cap to the hem is about 11 in (28 cm).

Enlarge the neckline, making it wider at each shoulder seam and lower at center front. Mark the new neckline on the pattern piece and cut out. The neckline is finished with satin bias tape.

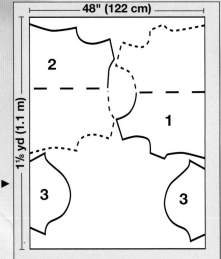

This top demonstrates using scalloped edges to make a hem and also how to make a French seam.

Tips for working with lace

Lace has no grainlines and thus layout and fabric amounts are variable. Be sure to take along the pattern when purchasing fabric. The motifs must be accurately positioned and should match across seams as well as possible. Some lace fabrics have scalloped edges that can be used for sleeve, hem, and neckline finishes or finishes for the front edges.

The lace fabric used here has two scalloped edges instead of selvages.

These edges are used as hem decoration. For this, the pattern pieces are placed horizontally on the fabric.

The sleeve pattern piece is cut singly, one on each scalloped edge. Be sure that the center of the sleeve is placed on the middle of a scallop. Before cutting the front and back pieces, fold fabric so that the center lines are on the middle of a scallop (Fig. 1).

Because construction details show through in laces, seams should be narrow and inconspicuous. The seam traditionally used for lightweight laces is the French seam, for heavier laces, the double-stitched seam or serged finish.

Sewing instructions

● **Darts:** Mark the underarm darts on the front piece with contrasting thread. Baste and stitch darts. Press darts down (Fig. 2).

● **Shoulder seam:** Place the blouse front on back, right sides together. Baste the shoulder seams and stitch. Finish seams.

● **Neck edge:** If you cannot buy suitable folded bias tape, you can make your own using bias strips cut from satin fabric and a bias tape maker.

● Shape the bias tape into a curve using the iron before applying it to lace neck edge. Enclose the neck edge with the folded bias tape, and pin. Place the join at one shoulder. Stitch close to edge of tape from outside of blouse, stretching gently to create a curved neck edge (Fig. 3).

● **Sleeves:** Pin sleeves to armhole edge, right sides together. Baste and stitch. Finish and press seams toward sleeves.

● **Side seams:** Lay top front and back right sides together, folding sleeves lengthwise. Stitch in one continuous seam.

● Finish seam allowances. Press seam.

● **Alternative method for shoulder and side seams:** French seams. With wrong sides together, stitch seams ⅜ in (1 cm) from the edge. Trim seam allowances to ⅛ in (3 mm). Press seam open. Fold right sides together with stitched line exactly on fold

edge and press again. Stitch along the seamline, which is now ¼ in (6 mm) from the fold. Press seams to back.

● **Tip:** A sequined and beaded lace fabric was used for this top. To prevent the needle from breaking if it hits a bead or sequin, remove all the beads and sequins on the seamline and in the seam allowance before stitching. Baste and stitch directly on the seamline. Secure any loose beads with a few hand stitches.

● Avoid pressing fabrics that have sequins or beads.

Whipstitch 73 · Uneven slipstitch 81 · Flat catchstitch 81

Hemming special fabrics — hemming laces

Lace fabrics range from lightweight to heavy, and are available in a variety of patterns with straight or scalloped edges. The hemming method you use depends upon the type of lace chosen. Laces that are backed can be finished by one of the various turned-up hem methods described on pages 255–256; hems for heavy laces can be faced (see pp. 262–263). For lightweight laces, a rolled hem is recommended; an alternative to this is a lace trim appliquéd to the hemline (see below). If the lace is already scalloped, the finished edge can be used as the hemline (see below) and left as it is.

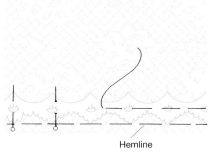

Hemline

To appliqué a lace trim to the edge: 1. Mark hemline. Place trim on right side of garment, aligning lower edge with garment hemline. Pin, then baste through center of trim.

2. Stitch trim to garment by the appliqué method (whipstitch along inner edge of trim's motif, or use a narrow machine zigzag). Cut away hem allowance underneath the lace trim.

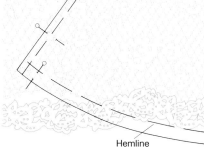

Hemline

To use scalloped edge as hem: 1. Pin pattern to fabric; align hemline with bottom edge of scallop motif. Cut above scallop to separate part of motif that falls below hemline curve.

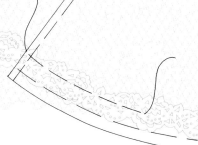

2. Reposition separated portion of scallop to follow hemline curve; pin and baste. Cut out garment. Secure repositioned part of scallop with whipstitching or machine zigzag.

Hemming fake furs

Difficulties which arise when hemming fake fur are usually caused by the bulk and weight of the fur's long hairs. When a fake fur has short hairs, as many do, it can be handled like a mediumweight fabric. A turned-up hem is the finish to use; the raw edge is covered with seam binding and the hem then secured with double stitching (see p. 256). Garments that are made of exceptionally heavy or dense fake fur require a bias hem facing, either the packaged type or one made from the lining fabric, as described on page 263. The facing method for such fake furs (see below) is similar to the standard facing technique.

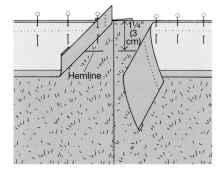

Hemline

1. Mark hemline. Trim hem allowance to 1¼ in (3 cm). Open one folded edge of facing; fold end back ¼ in (6 mm). Starting at garment seam, pin facing to hem, right sides together.

2. Stitch on crease of fold to within 3 in (7.5 cm) of the starting point, removing pins as you go. Cut excess facing to overlap the first end, and continue stitching across. Press flat.

3. Turn hem up to wrong side along marked hemline on garment; pin and baste through hem fold to hold in place. Catchstitch raw edges of fabric and facing to the garment.

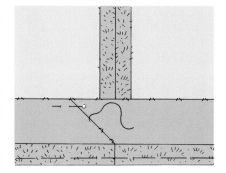

4. Press facing up, and pin to back of fur fabric; secure. Slipstitch lapped ends in place. Remove all basting stitches. If necessary, steam-press gently, using a press cloth.

Hemming leathers

Precautions must be taken when hemming leather and some leatherlike fabrics because they tend to retain surface pin marks and tear easily. Avoid pins entirely by using chalk to mark the hemline and paper clips to hold the hem in place.

To avoid tearing, hems can be either topstitched or glued. **Topstitching** is the easier of the two techniques; use a wedge-shaped needle and a fairly long stitch. **Gluing** must be done with meticulous care. Apply a thin coat of rubber cement over the appropriate area; take care not to use too much.

To reduce hem bulk, trim seam allowance below hemline to half-width. If the leather is very firm and heavy, you can just mark and trim off the hem allowance.

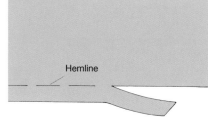

Hemline

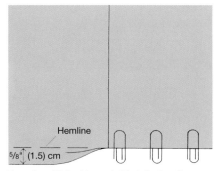

Hemline

5/8" (1.5) cm

For a topstitched hem: 1. Mark the hemline, and trim the hem allowance to 5/8 in (1.5 cm). Turn hem to wrong side along marked hemline; hold hem in place with paper clips.

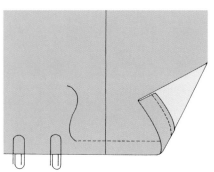

2. From right side of garment, topstitch (6 to 8 stitches per inch / 3 to 4 mm) 1/2 in (1.25 cm) from folded edge; use sewing machine gauge or a length of masking tape for guidance.

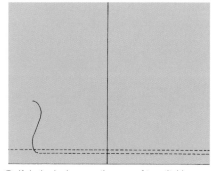

3. If desired, place another row of topstitching 1/8 in (3 mm) below the first row. With a press cloth beneath the iron, press the hem with the iron set at low temperature.

Hemming velvets

Velvet is a lush and elegant pile fabric. The pile creates a definite "up" and "down" nap that must be carefully considered when a garment is cut. Because velvets tend to mar easily, hems on velvet demand special care and techniques. Such pile fabrics as corduroy and velveteen also have naps, but they are less susceptible to marring and can generally be handled like any ordinary mediumweight fabric.

A recommended hem treatment for velvets is the Hong Kong finish (p. 256) with, as shown below, a strip of nylon net used to encase the raw edge. Often a soft roll is desired at the bottom edge of a velvet garment; to obtain a soft roll and to keep the shape of the hemline, the hem is interfaced. If the velvet garment has a circular skirt, the finish can also be a hand-rolled hem.

It is best to use polyester thread to hand-stitch velvet hems. Press velvet on the wrong side, without steam, on a velvet board or thick towel.

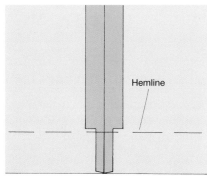

Hemline

For a glued hem: 1. Mark hemline; trim hem allowance to 2 in (5 cm) or less. Spread rubber cement over wrong side of hem, where garment hem will cover it, and under seams.

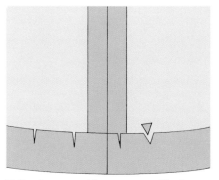

2. Turn hem up and finger-press, working from center toward side seams. If hem is curved, snip small wedges from the full areas of the hem and bring their cut edges together.

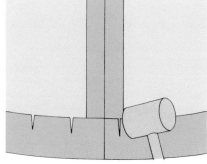

3. When entire hem is complete, gently pound the glued portion of the hem from the inside with a mallet. Let the glue dry completely before handling the garment again.

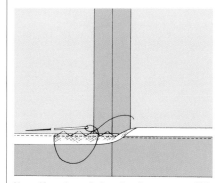

Hong Kong hem: Follow directions on page 256, using a strip of nylon net to cover raw edge of velvet; loosely blindstitch edge in place, basting securely every 4 to 5 in (10 to 12 cm).

CHAPTER 9

FASTENINGS

The invention of the
zipper revolutionized the
way clothes, as well as other
items such as sleeping bags
and tents, are fastened.
Zippers are simple to use and
extremely durable.
Sometimes, however, buttons
are the better choice, especially
when a decorative effect
is desired.

Types of zippers

All zippers consist of a chain of metal or plastic teeth, or a synthetic filament formed into a ladder or coil sewn to fabric tapes. Zippers open and close by means of a slider with a tab that moves it up and down. Top and bottom stops keep the slider from running off the zipper.

Zippers are made in many weights and sizes, heavier ones being stronger. Since metal and nylon zippers are about equal in strength and performance, the choice is largely a matter of personal preference. However, nylon zippers are lighter and usually more flexible than metal zippers.

All modern sewing machines come equipped with a zipper sewing foot. This foot is asymmetrical so that it can run alongside the teeth or coil of the zipper.

Metal chain zipper
Metal zippers are used for heavy-duty fabrics such as denim but also as ornamentation.

Pant or trouser zipper
Specially designed for pants, this zipper has a hook under the zipper tab to prevent the zipper from opening by itself.

Invisible zipper
The invisible zipper has spiral teeth. It is constructed so that it disappears into a seam; it has one closed end.

Conventional zipper
A conventional zipper has plastic teeth, comes in many colors, and is used in a wide variety of garments.

Dual separating zipper
Separating zippers are open at both ends and are sewn into a seam that will open completely.

Whipstitch 73 · Staystitching 84 · Seam finishes 88–89 · Machine buttonholes 83

Types of application

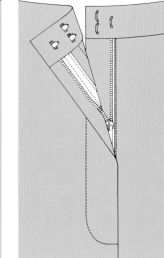
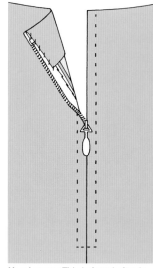
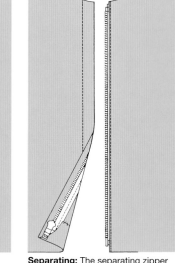

Centered: Application involving a conventional zipper. Used at the center front or back of garment, at edges of sleeves, and in home decorating.

Lapped: This application, too, takes a conventional zipper. Most often used at the left side seam of pants, skirts, and dresses.

Fly-front: This traditional pants application is used on men's pants and on women's pants and skirts. Requires a pants zipper or a conventional zipper.

Hand-sewn: This is found often in hand-tailored dresses and skirts using an invisible zipper and, using a conventional zipper, in delicate fabrics.

Separating: The separating zipper may be sewn in with a centered or lapped application. Used for jackets, tracksuit tops, vests, or skirts.

Installation tips

Before any zipper is sewn into a garment, the placket seam should be **seam-finished** and then, in most cases, basted shut and pressed open. **Staystitch** any curved or bias placket seamlines about ¼ in (6 mm) from the cut edge to prevent possible stretching.

It is not generally necessary to preshrink zippers as the garment fabric and the zipper tape will shrink in unison when laundered. But if you are using a **stretch fabric** that is washed before stitching, preshrink zipper by immersing it in hot tap water for a few minutes; roll it in a towel to absorb excess moisture, air-dry.

Double-sided basting tape can be used instead of pins to position a zipper.

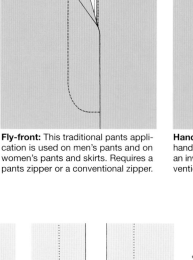
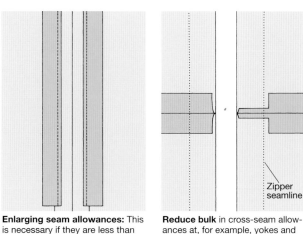
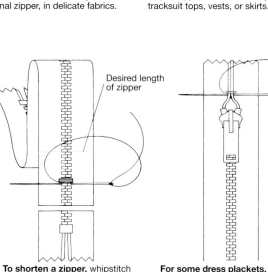

Enlarging seam allowances: This is necessary if they are less than ⅝ in (1.5 cm) wide. Edgestitch woven seam binding to edge of seam allowances only.

Reduce bulk in cross-seam allowances at, for example, yokes and waistlines. Trim seam allowances slightly past zipper seamline as shown, and press open.

To shorten a zipper, whipstitch several times over ladder or chain as shown, ¾ in (2 cm) below desired new length, then cut off the excess zipper and tapes.

For some dress plackets, a zipper must be closed above the top stop. Whipstitch edges of tapes together ¼ in (6 mm) above top stop, or attach a straight-eye fastener.

Hand-basting stitches 70–71 · Machine-basting stitches 83 · Seam finishes 88–89

Centered zippers

The method for applying a centered zipper is the same regardless of garment type; the only variable is in the placement of the zipper below the top edge of the garment. Where it is placed depends on how this edge will be finished. If a facing is to be used, place the top stop of the zipper ½ in (1.25 cm) below seamline of garment. This allows extra space for turning down the facing and for attaching a hook and eye. If the finish does not require seam allowances to be turned down, for instance at a waistband or on a standing collar, place the top stop *just below* the seamline (¼ in [6 mm]).

All work is done on *inside* of garment except topstitching. **Work from bottom to top** of placket, in both preliminary basting and topstitching. Keep zipper closed, except in Step 3, and slider tab up.

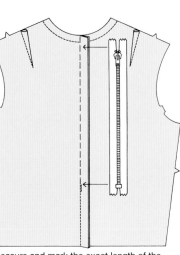

1. Measure and mark the exact length of the placket opening, using the zipper as a guide. Close the seam with machine stitching: stitch up to the mark for bottom of the zipper with a regular stitch length, backstitch, then change to machine basting for placket seam.

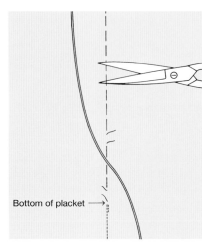

Bottom of placket →

2. Clip both of the machine-basting threads at the bottom of the placket; then clip only the bobbin thread at ½ in (1.25 cm) intervals — this will make removal of basting easier. Press the seam open and, if necessary, seam-finish the edges with a finish suitable for the fabric.

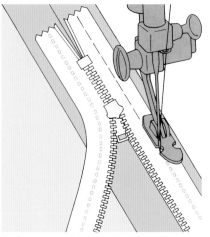

3. Extend the right-hand seam allowance and place zipper face down, with the top stop at mark and the edge of the opened chain or spiral along the seamline; pin in place. Using a zipper foot, machine-baste along stitching guideline on the zipper tape.

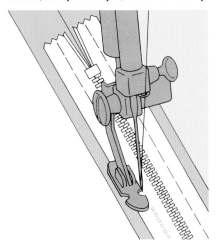

4. Close the zipper and keep the slider tab up. Extend the remaining seam allowance. Position zipper foot to the left of the needle and machine-baste the unstitched zipper tape, from bottom to top, to the seam allowance, following the guideline on the tape.

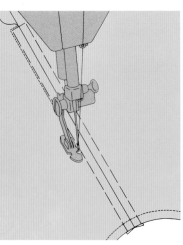

5. Turn the garment right side up and spread it as flat as possible. Starting at the center seam, hand-baste across the bottom and up one side, ¼ in (6 mm) from the seamline, catching the garment seam allowance and zipper tape in basting. Repeat for the other side.

6. Change to a regular stitch length. Begin at bottom of the placket, just outside the basting, and topstitch through all three layers: garment, seam allowance, and tape. Take two or three stitches across bottom of placket, pivot, and stitch to top.

7. Position the zipper foot to the right side of the needle and topstitch the remaining side in same way, taking the same number of stitches across bottom of placket. Pull thread ends to wrong side and tie. Remove the hand-basted stitches and open the placket.

Prickstitch 73 · Uneven slipstich 81 · Blind hemming stitch (machine) 83 · Neckline finishes 138–163 · Waistline finishes 188–207

Zipper sewing techniques

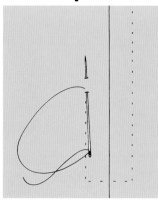

Hand-finishing gives a custom look to a garment. Follow basic procedure through to Step 5. Then remove machine basting to open placket seam. See Prickstitch for formation of stitch. Work from center seam across bottom of zipper, then up one side; repeat for other side. If fabric is heavy, work second set of stitches, placing them between first stitches for strength.

Machine blindstitching is a quick, durable way to simulate hand stitching. Follow basic procedure through to Step 5. See Machine blindstitch (p. 83). In this method, the action of the zigzag stitch requires that you stitch from bottom to top on one side of the zipper and from top to bottom on the other.

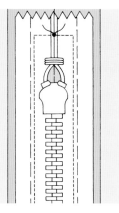

In some dresses, for example, both ends of the zipper placket are closed. The zipper must therefore be closed at the top by basting the tapes together before inserting the zipper. Follow the basic procedure with one exception: when doing final stitching, continue across top of zipper placket to vertical seam. Pull thread ends to wrong side and tie.

Centered application of separating zipper

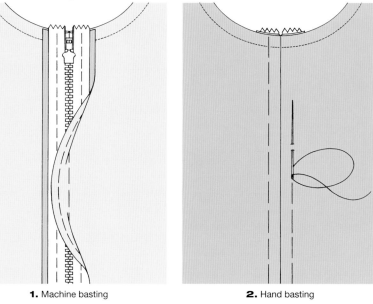

1. Machine basting

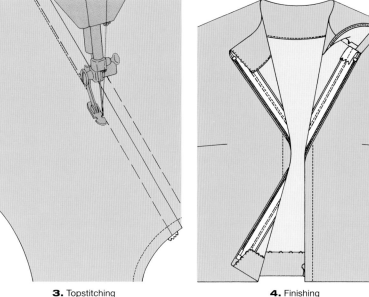

3. Topstitching

2. Hand basting

4. Finishing

A separating zipper is best sewn in before any facings or hems are in place.

1. First **machine-baste** opening closed. Press seam open; finish if necessary. Position the closed zipper face down on the seam allowances, centering zipper teeth over seam. Extend seam allowance and tape; machine-baste down center of tape. Keeping slider tab turned up, machine-baste free side of tape in the same way.

2. Next, **hand-baste** the seam allowances and the zipper to the garment from right side, ¼ in (6 mm) on either side of seamline (½ in [1.25 cm] from seamline for the heavy, large-toothed jacket zippers). Do not stitch across the bottom.

3. **Topstitch** each side of the zipper, stitching slightly outside the hand basting and from the bottom up. Keep the stitching straight and the same distance from center seam the entire length of the seam. Pull the thread ends to wrong side of garment; tie. Remove the hand basting, then open the center seam.

4. If the facing and the hem are in place, as they would be when replacing a zipper, release the hem, but not the facing. Push facing out of the way during zipper application. Turn top tape ends under at a slight slant so that they will not be caught in the teeth. After application, turn under and slipstitch facing or hem edges to the zipper tapes.

Uneven basting 70 · Slip basting 71

Exposed zippers

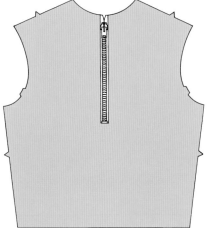

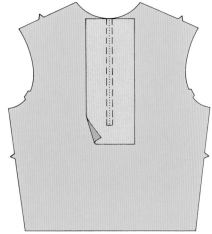

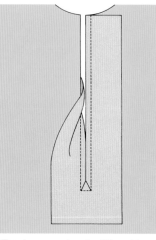

The exposed zipper can be applied only where there is no seam. Although it can be used on woven fabrics, it is most often seen on sweater knits. Before installation of the zipper, a stay is sewn to the placket area, which prevents sagging and stretching.

1. Cut a stay 3 in (7.5 cm) wide and 2 in (5 cm) longer than the zipper from woven lining fabric. Mark opening down center of garment and stay to equal the length of zipper ladder or chain plus ⅝ in (1.5 cm). Right sides together, match markings and baste stay to garment.

2. The zipper opening should be wide enough to expose only the zipper ladder or chain. Stitch ⅛ in (3 mm) on each side of the center line and across bottom at end of center marking. Remove basting. Slash down center line to within ½ in (1.25 cm) of bottom; cut into corners.

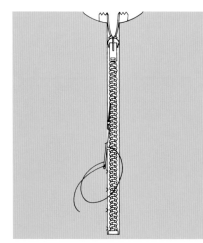

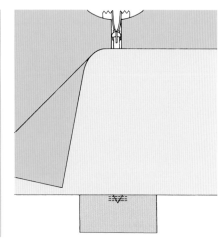

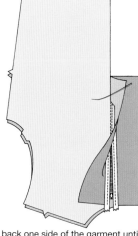

3. Turn stay to inside and press, making sure that none of the stay shows on the right side of the garment. Center zipper under opening with bottom stop of zipper at bottom end of opening. Slip-baste zipper to garment along the folds on each side and at bottom of zipper.

4. Lift the bottom part of the garment to expose the ends of the zipper tape and the triangle of garment and stay fabric at the bottom of the opening. Using a zipper foot, stitch across the base of the triangle to secure it to the zipper tapes and stay.

5. Fold back one side of the garment until the original stitching line is visible. Working from bottom to top, stitch the garment to the zipper tape along this stitching line. Repeat for the other side of the zipper. Remove the slip basting that held zipper in position.

Enclosed exposed zipper

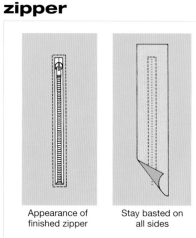

Appearance of finished zipper · Stay basted on all sides

If both ends of zipper opening are closed, as in a pocket or pillow cover, follow procedure opposite, with these exceptions: **Cut the stay** 3 in (7.5 cm) wide and 4 in (10 cm) longer than opening. Center stay over mark for opening. Stitch across ends when sewing stay onto fabric.

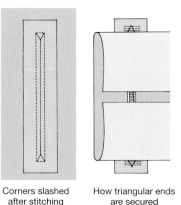

Corners slashed after stitching · How triangular ends are secured

Slash after stitching as in Step 2, but cut into corners at both ends.
Close the zipper tapes above top stop with a bar tack. Baste the zipper into finished opening as in Step 3, basting top as well as bottom.
Stitch triangles at both top and bottom to zipper tape (see Step 4).

Decorative exposed zipper

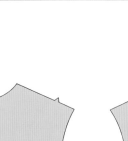

1. Length of opening equals length of the zipper ladder (plus ⅝ in [1.5 cm] if facing has not been applied). Mark opening down center of garment. Stitch around opening ⅛ in (3 mm) from center mark on both sides and at bottom.

2. Cut carefully along center line to within ½ in (1.25 cm) of the bottom, then cut diagonally into each corner. This will form a ⅛ in (3 mm) seam allowance on each of the long sides of the opening and a small triangle at the bottom.

3. Turn the ⅛ in (3 mm) seam allowance on the long sides to right side of garment. Baste seam allowances in place and press opening flat. When application is completed, seam allowances will be covered by the decorative trim.

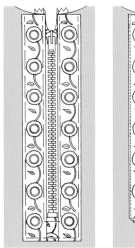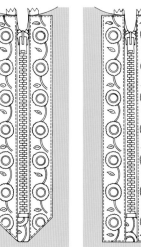

4. Center the zipper under the opening with the bottom stop at bottom end of opening and top stop at finished edge (⅝ in [1.5 cm] from upper edge if facing has not been applied). Using a zipper foot, edgestitch zipper from garment side through all thicknesses.

5. Trim should be at least ¼ in (6 mm) wide to cover seam allowances. Position the trim around the zipper; miter trim to make a square or pointed end, as you prefer. Try, if possible, to match the design horizontally across zipper. Baste trim in place by hand.

6. Using the zipper foot, topstitch the trim to the zipper, first next to the ladder or chain, then on the outer edge. (If the trim contrasts in color with the garment, choose thread and zipper colors to match the trim.) If the facing is not already in place, apply it now.

Mitering the trim

For mitering purposes, trim should be twice the length of the zipper tape plus whatever extra is required to match a design. Some additional length is also needed for finishing the ends: **twice** the width of the trim for a pointed end; **four times** the width of the trim for a square end.

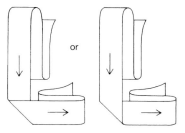

For a point, first fold the trim straight across itself, making a 45° angle.

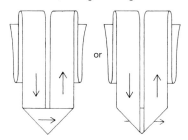

Then fold again, forming an opposite 45° angle, to complete the miter.

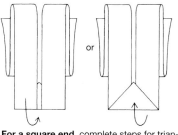

For a square end, complete steps for triangular miter; then fold point either under or back onto trim.

Even basting stitch 70 · Whipstitch 73 · Machine-basting stitches 83

Lapped zippers

A lapped zipper is applied the same way regardless of garment type; the only variable is in the placement of the zipper in relation to the garment edge. If there will be a facing finish, place the top stop ½ in (1.25 cm) below the seamline. If the garment will have a waistband or standing collar, place the top stop *just below* the seamline. Do all work on inside of the garment, except topstitching; keep the zipper closed throughout application. **Work from the bottom to the top** on all steps; this will ensure that the lap goes in the proper direction on the garment.

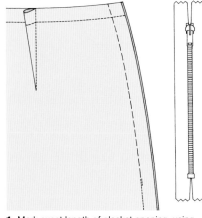

1. Mark exact length of placket opening, using the zipper as a guide. Stitch seam up to bottom of zipper placket with a regular stitch length, backstitch, then change to machine basting for placket. Clip basting thread at intervals. Press seam open; seam-finish.

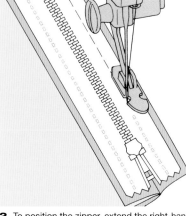

2. To position the zipper, extend the right-hand seam allowance and place the zipper on it face down, with top stop at mark and edge of ladder or chain along the seamline; pin in place. Using a zipper foot, positioned to the right of needle, machine-baste on stitching guideline.

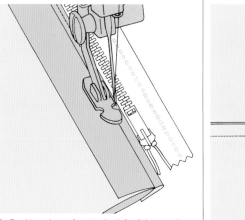

3. Position zipper foot to the left of the needle. Turn the zipper face up, forming a fold in the seam allowance. Bring the fold close to, but not over, the zipper ladder or chain; pin if necessary. Stitch along the edge of fold through all of the thicknesses.

Enclosed lapped application

Before beginning the basic application, whipstitch zipper tapes together above top stop. The length of placket should be the distance from bottom stop to whipstitches.

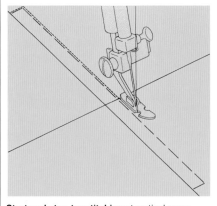

If placket intersects a cross-seam, such as a waistline, make sure the seam is matched perfectly before basting the placket opening. Trim cross-seam allowances as shown to reduce unnecessary bulk. Stitch from bottom of seam to bottom of placket using a regular stitch length, backstitch, then change to machine basting and stitch to top of placket. At the top of placket, return the stitch length to normal, backstitch two stitches, and complete the seam. Then press the seam open.

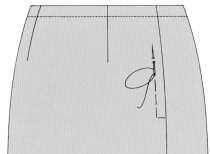

4. Turn garment to right side; spread fabric as flat as possible over the unstitched zipper tape. Hand-baste across bottom of zipper, then up along the side, about ½ in (1.25 cm) from seamline. This should place basting close to stitching guideline on zipper tape.

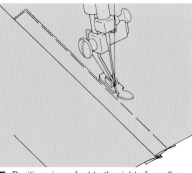

5. Position zipper foot to the right of needle. Topstitch close to the basting across bottom of the zipper and up along the side, pivoting at the corner. Take care not to stitch over the basting. Bring thread ends to underside and tie. Remove basting stitches.

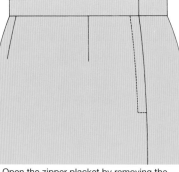

6. Open the zipper placket by removing the machine basting in the placket seam. Tweezers are helpful for getting out any stubborn thread ends. Finish top edge of garment with appropriate finish — facing, collar, or waistband — as pattern directs.

Start and stop topstitching at vertical seam. Stitch from seam across bottom of zipper, up along the side, then back across the top. Pull thread ends to wrong side and tie.

Prickstitch 73 · Blind hemming stitch (machine) 83 · Neckline finishes 139–163 · Waistline finishes 188–207

Finishing lapped application

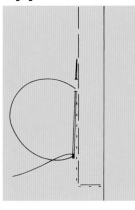

Hand finishing is a sign of careful work. Follow basic instructions to Step 5. See Prickstitch for formation of the hand stitch. Work from the bottom to top of zipper. For extra strength, turn garment to inside and machine-stitch the edge of front *seam allowance* to zipper tape.

Machine blindstitching gives the appearance of hand finishing but is more durable.

1. Allow ⅞ in (2.25 cm) seam allowances when cutting out garment. Follow instructions for basic application up to Step 3. Baste free zipper tape to the remaining seam allowance through center of tape.

2. Set the sewing machine for a short narrow blindstitch. Keep foot to right of needle. Fold back garment on basting line and, with bottom of placket away from you, position zipper tape over machine feed. With zipper foot on seam allowance, blind-stitch full length of placket, closely following fold. Prickstitch by hand across bottom. Remove basting.

Lapped application of separating zipper

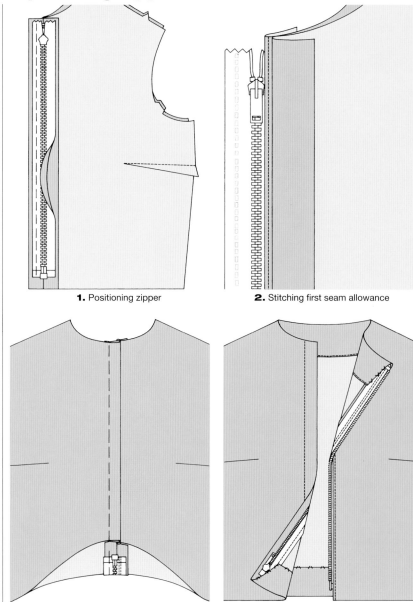

1. Positioning zipper

2. Stitching first seam allowance

3. Hand basting before topstitching

4. Finishing

A separating zipper should be sewn in before facings or hems are in place.

1. Machine-baste placket seam closed. Press open and seam-finish if necessary. **Position the closed zipper** face down on seam allowances, with zipper teeth centered over the seam and bottom stop at bottom of opening. Keeping tab turned up, machine-baste right-hand tape to seam allowance from bottom to top.

2. Turn zipper face up, forming a fold in the seam allowance. Bring the fold close to, but not over, the zipper teeth; pin if necessary. Change to a zipper foot, positioned to the left of needle. Stitch along the edge of the fold through all thicknesses.

3. Turn garment right side up and spread as flat as possible. Starting at the bottom of the placket, **hand-baste** up the length of the zipper, through garment, seam allowance, and zipper tape, about ½ in (1.25 cm) from the seamline. This should place basting close to stitching guideline on tape. Position zipper foot to right of needle; top-stitch close to basting. Remove hand basting.

4. Open zipper placket by removing basting from seam. Apply any facings, hems, or linings to garment, and slipstitch any edges near the zipper so that they will not be caught in zipper teeth during wear.

Bench cushion cover

Fabric: Texo Print, Enschedde (Netherlands)

Fabrics
Cotton decorating fabrics, heavy canvas, water-resistant synthetic blends

Amount
For a cushion size $38 \times 18 \times 2^1/_2$ in $(98 \times 45 \times 6$ cm):
$2^3/_8$ yd (2.2 m) of 54/56 in (140 cm) -width fabric

Notions
1 zipper, 39 in (1 m)

Pattern pieces
1 Upper panel
2 Lower panel
Bench cushions can be made from various materials. If they are going to be used outdoors, choose a fabric that can withstand a rain shower. Either a polyester cushion or a latex foam cushion is suitable for a garden bench. Less sensitive but durable fabric can be used for cushions on indoor benches in kitchens, bedrooms and living rooms.

These instructions would serve for making removable covers for sofa or chair cushions or sectionals. Including a zipper in the cover provides a neater fit and allows easy removal for laundering. The zipper is located inconspicuously at the lower rear edge of the cushion.

Cutting

● The cover consists of two pieces, one forming the bottom and the other forming the top and sides of the cushion. Each can be cut according to the actual cushion size, as follows:

For a cushion with dimensions of $38 \times 18 \times 2^{1}/_{2}$ in ($97 \times 45 \times 6$ cm): Upper panel: Length consists of the cushion length plus twice the cushion depth plus two seam allowances of $^{1}/_{2}$ in (1.25 cm): 44 in (112 cm).

Width consists of cushion width plus twice cushion depth plus two seam allowances: 24 in (61 cm).

Lower panel: Size is the exact length and width of the cushion plus $^{1}/_{2}$ in (1.25 cm) seam allowances on four sides: 39×19 in (100×48 cm). Finish raw edges of panels with a zigzag stitch or serger.

Sewing instructions

● On the wrong side of the upper panel, mark the rectangular outline of the cushion clearly with pencil lines 3 in (8 cm) in from each edge. Use a ruler and right-angled triangle for accuracy (Fig. 1).

● With right sides together, pin one long edge of the lower panel to a long edge of the upper panel between its marked lines. Stitch both end portions of this seam with $^{1}/_{2}$ in (1.25 cm) seam allowance, leaving a long space open to accommodate the zipper (Fig. 2).

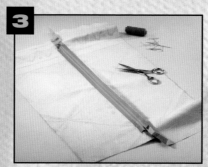

● Press seam open, pressing back the seam allowances along the zipper placket. Insert zipper in this opening (Figs. 3 & 4).

● Pin other pair of long edges together, so lower panel fits between markings on upper panel, and stitch seam.

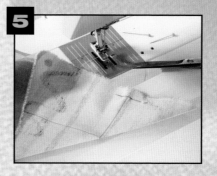

● **Corners:** With right sides together, fold the corners of the upper panel so the marked lines match, and pin (Fig. 5).
● Stitch along pencil marking at each corner, stopping at the lengthwise seams already sewn and reverse-stitching at both ends for strength.

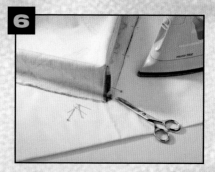

● Trim the seam allowances and corners.
● **End seams:** Open zipper slightly before this step.
● Match the ends of the two panels together and pin. Stitch both ends with $^{1}/_{2}$ in (1.25 cm) seam allowance, stopping and reversing at the corner seams (Fig. 6).
● Finish opening the zipper and turn cover right side out.

Types of zippers 284 · Uneven basting 70 · Reducing seam bulk 87

Fly-front zipper application

The fly-front zipper is the traditional zipper application for men's pants. It is often used on women's clothes as well, however, because it provides such a neat and durable closing. Traditionally, in women's clothes, the placket laps right over left as shown here; in men's garments, it laps left over right.

A special pants zipper is often recommended for use with this application. If a pants zipper is not suitable because of its weight, or the limited color range, a skirt zipper can be used. No matter what type of zipper you choose, it will probably require shortening; fly-front plackets are not as long as most other zipper plackets. See instructions at right. It is best to buy a pattern designed with a fly-front closing — it will supply all the necessary pattern pieces.

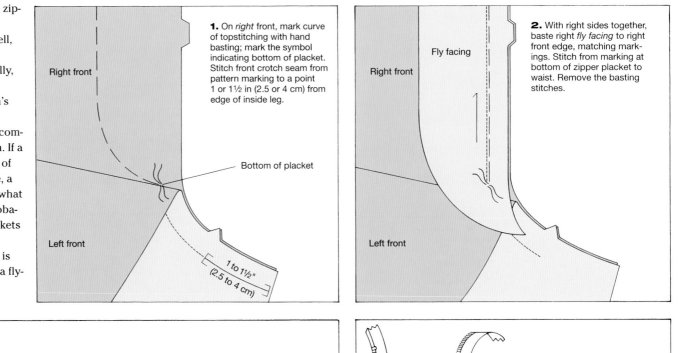

1. On *right* front, mark curve of topstitching with hand basting; mark the symbol indicating bottom of placket. Stitch front crotch seam from pattern marking to a point 1 or 1½ in (2.5 or 4 cm) from edge of inside leg.

Right front

Left front

Bottom of placket

1 to 1½"
(2.5 to 4 cm)

2. With right sides together, baste right *fly facing* to right front edge, matching markings. Stitch from marking at bottom of zipper placket to waist. Remove the basting stitches.

Fly facing

Right front

Left front

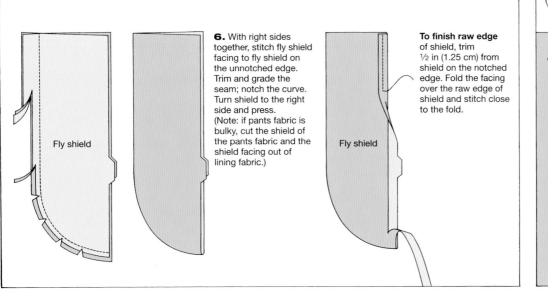

Fly shield

6. With right sides together, stitch fly shield facing to fly shield on the unnotched edge. Trim and grade the seam; notch the curve. Turn shield to the right side and press. (Note: if pants fabric is bulky, cut the shield of the pants fabric and the shield facing out of lining fabric.)

To finish raw edge of shield, trim ½ in (1.25 cm) from shield on the notched edge. Fold the facing over the raw edge of shield and stitch close to the fold.

Fly shield

7. Fold under and baste the edge of left pants from ¼ in (6 mm) beyond the seamline. Open zipper. Pin left front to zipper, next to ladder or chain, working from bottom to top. Baste in place. Close zipper to check positioning.

Left front

Bar tack 76

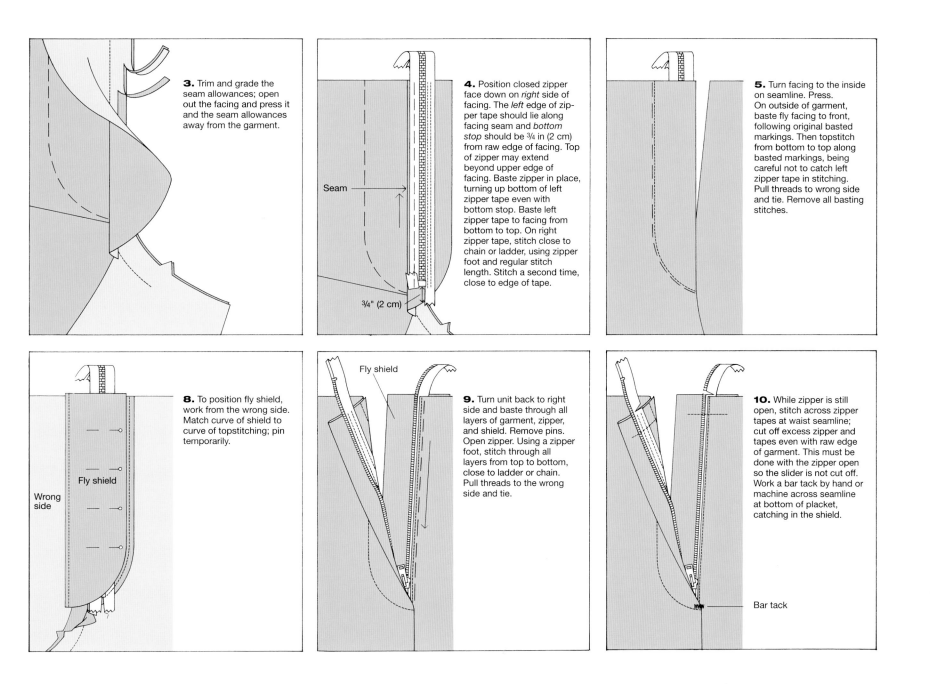

3. Trim and grade the seam allowances; open out the facing and press it and the seam allowances away from the garment.

4. Position closed zipper face down on *right* side of facing. The *left* edge of zipper tape should lie along facing seam and *bottom stop* should be ¾ in (2 cm) from raw edge of facing. Top of zipper may extend beyond upper edge of facing. Baste zipper in place, turning up bottom of left zipper tape even with bottom stop. Baste left zipper tape to facing from bottom to top. On right zipper tape, stitch close to chain or ladder, using zipper foot and regular stitch length. Stitch a second time, close to edge of tape.

Seam

¾" (2 cm)

5. Turn facing to the inside on seamline. Press. On outside of garment, baste fly facing to front, following original basted markings. Then topstitch from bottom to top along basted markings, being careful not to catch left zipper tape in stitching. Pull threads to wrong side and tie. Remove all basting stitches.

8. To position fly shield, work from the wrong side. Match curve of shield to curve of topstitching; pin temporarily.

Fly shield

Wrong side

9. Turn unit back to right side and baste through all layers of garment, zipper, and shield. Remove pins. Open zipper. Using a zipper foot, stitch through all layers from top to bottom, close to ladder or chain. Pull threads to the wrong side and tie.

Fly shield

10. While zipper is still open, stitch across zipper tapes at waist seamline; cut off excess zipper and tapes even with raw edge of garment. This must be done with the zipper open so the slider is not cut off. Work a bar tack by hand or machine across seamline at bottom of placket, catching in the shield.

Bar tack

Fly-front zipper application (men's pants)

A special pants zipper is used in the zipper application for men's pants (see illustration on p. 284). Different from the standard zipper, the pants zipper has a hook on the underside of the tab which locks into the teeth of the zipper. This prevents it from opening inadvertently. This type of zipper also has a formed band which fits better into a contoured placket.

Pants zippers are available with metal teeth and plastic teeth and come in lengths from 41 to 56 in (16 to 22 cm). They are applied in the same way as are zippers applied to straight front-fly plackets as shown on pages 294–295, but the placket laps left over right and the pattern pieces are cut out in the reverse way to those shown on pages 294–295.

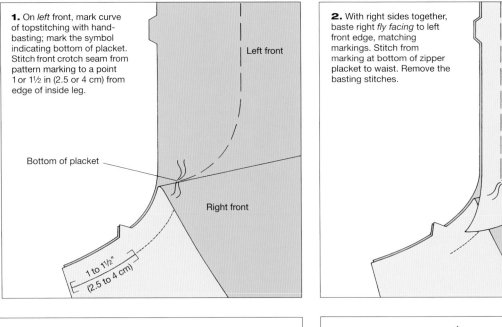

1. On *left* front, mark curve of topstitching with hand-basting; mark the symbol indicating bottom of placket. Stitch front crotch seam from pattern marking to a point 1 or 1½ in (2.5 or 4 cm) from edge of inside leg.

Bottom of placket

Left front

Right front

1 to 1½" (2.5 to 4 cm)

2. With right sides together, baste right *fly facing* to left front edge, matching markings. Stitch from marking at bottom of zipper placket to waist. Remove the basting stitches.

Fly facing

Left front

Right front

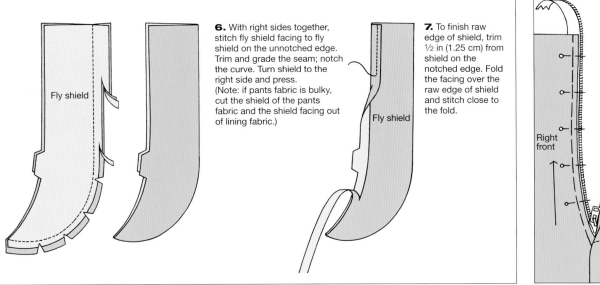

6. With right sides together, stitch fly shield facing to fly shield on the unnotched edge. Trim and grade the seam; notch the curve. Turn shield to the right side and press. (Note: if pants fabric is bulky, cut the shield of the pants fabric and the shield facing out of lining fabric.)

Fly shield

7. To finish raw edge of shield, trim ½ in (1.25 cm) from shield on the notched edge. Fold the facing over the raw edge of shield and stitch close to the fold.

Fly shield

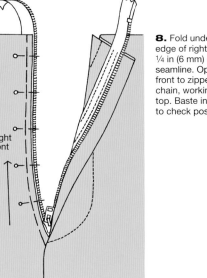

Right front

8. Fold under and baste the edge of right pants from ¼ in (6 mm) beyond the seamline. Open zipper. Pin right front to zipper, next to ladder or chain, working from bottom to top. Baste in place. Close zipper to check positioning.

Bar tack 76

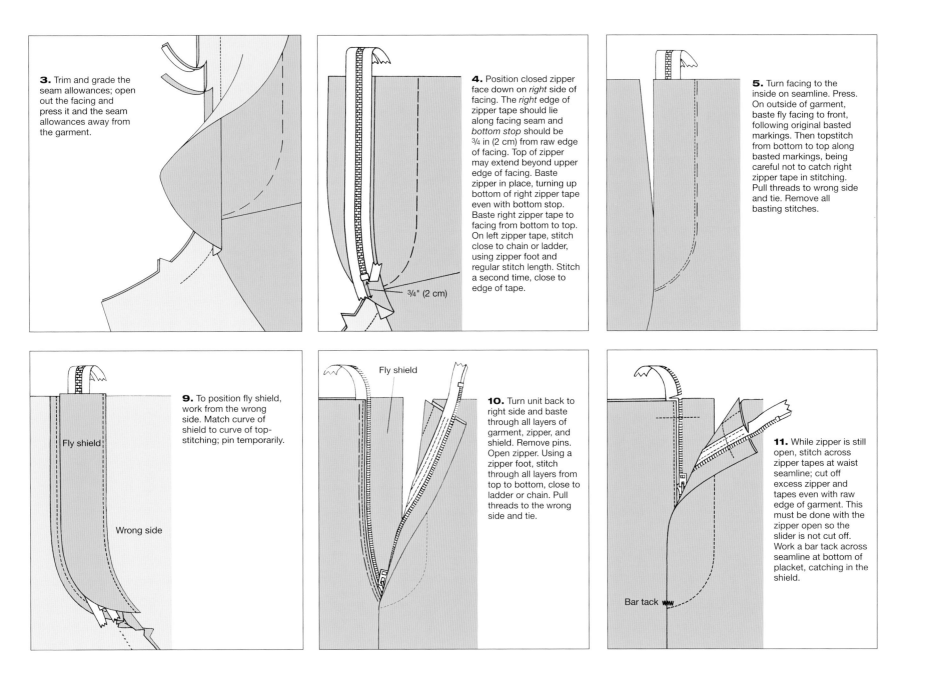

3. Trim and grade the seam allowances; open out the facing and press it and the seam allowances away from the garment.

4. Position closed zipper face down on *right* side of facing. The *right* edge of zipper tape should lie along facing seam and *bottom stop* should be ¾ in (2 cm) from raw edge of facing. Top of zipper may extend beyond upper edge of facing. Baste zipper in place, turning up bottom of right zipper tape even with bottom stop. Baste right zipper tape to facing from bottom to top. On left zipper tape, stitch close to chain or ladder, using zipper foot and regular stitch length. Stitch a second time, close to edge of tape.

¾" (2 cm)

5. Turn facing to the inside on seamline. Press. On outside of garment, baste fly facing to front, following original basted markings. Then topstitch from bottom to top along basted markings, being careful not to catch right zipper tape in stitching. Pull threads to wrong side and tie. Remove all basting stitches.

9. To position fly shield, work from the wrong side. Match curve of shield to curve of top-stitching; pin temporarily.

Fly shield

Wrong side

Fly shield

10. Turn unit back to right side and baste through all layers of garment, zipper, and shield. Remove pins. Open zipper. Using a zipper foot, stitch through all layers from top to bottom, close to ladder or chain. Pull threads to the wrong side and tie.

11. While zipper is still open, stitch across zipper tapes at waist seamline; cut off excess zipper and tapes even with raw edge of garment. This must be done with the zipper open so the slider is not cut off. Work a bar tack across seamline at bottom of placket, catching in the shield.

Bar tack

Even backstitch 72 · Flat catchstitch 81 · Tying thread ends 68 · Staystitching for knits 84

Zippers / Special applications — seam and pattern matching

When zippers are applied to a closed seam, as is usually the case, matching of plaids and other patterned fabrics is easily taken care of when the seam is basted before the zipper is inserted. If, however, a zipper is applied to an *open* seam, extra steps for matching will be required.

The method for matching diagonals can also be used to match garment seams, as well as to match a large print motif, such as a floral print. The fabric must, of course, be cut so that it is possible to match the stripe, plaid, or design at the seam.

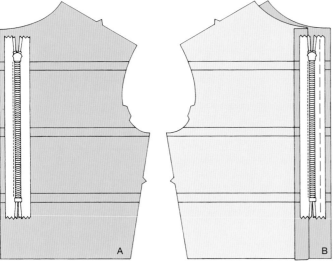

Plaids or stripes: Sew first side of the zipper in place, then close the zipper. Let the unstitched side of the zipper lie face down on outside of fabric (A). With a pencil, mark the zipper tape at each predominant cross bar or stripe. Then open the zipper and baste the second zipper tape in position, matching the marks on the tape to the plaid or stripe on the second side of the garment (B). Close the zipper and check on right side of garment for a precise match. If correct, open zipper and stitch second side; complete the installation.

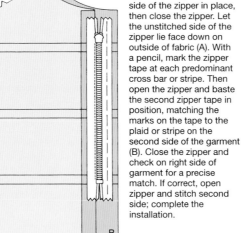

Yoke or waistline seam: Follow procedure at left for matching plaids or stripes, first trimming the cross-seam allowances to eliminate bulk.

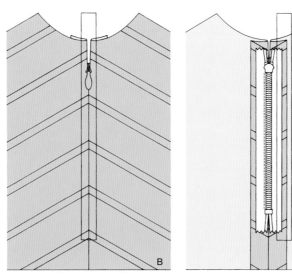

To match diagonals or large designs, stitch the first side of the zipper in place, then fold back fabric so that right side of zipper and fabric are both visible (A). Fold back seam allowance of unstitched side. Match second side to first side, taping in place temporarily (B). Turn fabric to wrong side and tape unstitched side of zipper tape to fabric seam allowance (C). Remove tape from face side of fabric. Open zipper; stitch the taped side of zipper; finish application.

Knits, leather, fake fur

Knits: Stabilize a zipper opening in a moderately stretchy knit by staystitching ½ in (1.25 cm) from the cut edges. In a very stretchy knit, stabilize both seam edges with woven seam binding. Stitch or fuse it to the wrong side ½ in (1.25 cm) from the cut edge.

Leather, suede, and vinyl: A centered application is recommended. Turn back the seam allowances on the seamline and glue them down to wrong side of garment. On outside of garment, hold the placket edges together with a length of masking tape. Use crosswise strips of tape to position zipper face down on seam allowances. Stitch on *inside* of garment from bottom to top, taking the same number of stitches across bottom of zipper on each side of seam. Pull thread ends to wrong side; tie.

High-pile fake fur: Use 1 in (2.5 cm) -wide grosgrain ribbon to form a smooth, flat facing between the zipper and fur fabric. First, clip the pile from the placket seam allowances. Cut the ribbon 1 in (2.5 cm) longer than the zipper. Edgestitch the ribbon to the right side of both seam allowances, aligning the ribbon edge with the seamline. Trim the fabric seam allowances underneath the ribbon to ¼ in (6 mm). Place the opened zipper face down on the ribbon with the bottom stop at the end of the opening and zipper teeth even with seamline; baste and stitch. Repeat for the other side. Turn the ribbon and zipper inside the garment along the seamline. Hand-backstitch the zipper tape and ribbon on the fur fabric *backing* only. Catchstitch the ribbon edge to the backing.

Running stitch 71 · Whipstitch 73 · Seam finishes 88–89 · Applying a waistline stay 186

Zippers in pleated skirts

When sewing a zipper into a pleated skirt, the two main objectives are to make the zipper as inconspicuous as possible and not interfere with the fold or hang of the pleats. Therefore, the positioning of the zipper seam must be considered when the pattern is laid out on the fabric. If the pleats are box or inverted, try to position the zipper seam down the center of the pleat *underfold*; then install the zipper with either the centered or invisible method. If the garment is knife pleated, position the seam where the pleat *backfold* will fall; then insert the zipper as shown and described at right.

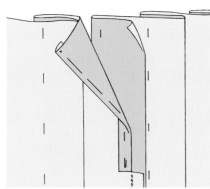

For knife pleats: 1. Stitch the zipper seam at the pleat backfold after the pleats have been formed. Leave the top part open for the zipper. Clip into the left seam allowance; turn it to the wrong side of the garment and baste in place, as shown above.

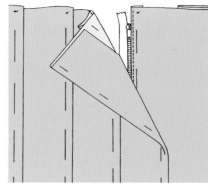

2. Turn garment to right side. Working with the open part of the seam, position closed zipper under basted seam allowance with the folded edge close to the teeth and top stop just below top seamline. Baste. Then, using a zipper foot, stitch close to fold.

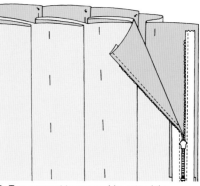

3. Turn garment to wrong side; extend the unclipped (right-hand) seam allowance. Place unstitched half of zipper face down on seam allowance with teeth ¼ in (6 mm) beyond seamline. Pin and baste. Open zipper and stitch to seam allowance only, not to top fold of pleat.

Zipper underlays and stays

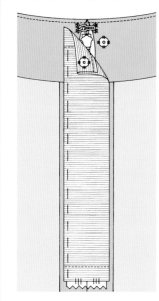

A ribbon underlay can be added to any zipper application after garment is completed. To make it, cut 1 in (2.5 cm) -wide grosgrain ribbon 1 in (2.5 cm) longer than zipper ladder. Fold under and finish top and bottom edges. Center over back of zipper, with top just above slider, and stitch to left seam allowance only. If attaching at a neck edge, hand-stitch, using a running stitch, to facing and then to seam allowance. Whipstitch across bottom to both seam allowances. Attach a snap fastener at the top of the ribbon as shown.

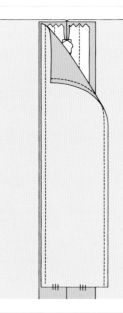

A fabric underlay is added to a skirt or pants before waistband is applied. (Waistband must be cut long enough to extend across entire width of underlay at top.) For underlay, cut a strip from garment fabric the length of the zipper tape and 2½ in (6 cm) wide. (For a self-facing, cut fabric 5 in [12.5 cm] wide and fold in half lengthwise.) Seam-finish raw edges. From wrong side, place underlay over zipper with top edge meeting the waistline edge and lengthwise edge even with the left seam edge. Pin, then stitch underlay to seam allowance only. To finish, whipstitch across the bottom to both seam allowances.

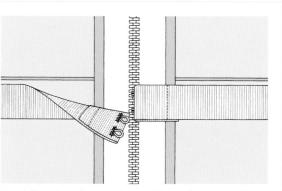

A waistline stay relieves strain on a zipper and makes it easier to close. To make, cut a length of grosgrain ribbon equal to the measurement of the garment at waistline plus 2 in (5 cm). Fold back ends ¾ in (2 cm) to finish, then turn raw edges under ¼ in (6 mm) and machine-stitch in place. Sew hooks and round eyes to ends. Position ribbon at waistline with ends at either side of zipper. Leaving 2 in (5 cm) free at each end, baste stay to waistline seam allowance if there is one; to seams and darts if there is not.

Buttonholes — types of buttonhole

All of the many buttonhole methods are variations of two basic types: worked and bound. The method you choose for a garment will depend on the design of that garment, the garment fabric, and your particular level of sewing ability.

Bound buttonholes are made by stitching strips or patches of fabric to the buttonhole location in any of several ways. The garment fabric is then cut as specified, and the strips or patches are turned to the wrong side, thus "binding" the edges of the opening.

Bound buttonholes are particularly suited to tailored garments, but are not recommended for sheer or delicate fabrics where the patch might show through or add bulk.

Machine-worked buttonholes consist of two parallel rows of zigzag stitches, and two ends finished with a bar tack as shown below. They can be made by using a special buttonhole attachment or built-in buttonhole capabilities. A machine-worked buttonhole is opened only after stitching is completed. These

buttonholes are used on most clothes today, such as sportswear, washable garments, children's clothes, and men's jackets.

Hand-worked buttonholes are made by edging a cut in the fabric with hand buttonhole stitches. The two ends can be finished with either a bar tack or a fan-shaped arrangement of stitches. Hand-worked buttonholes are used on men's jackets and women's tailored garments, and also sometimes on extremely delicate fabrics.

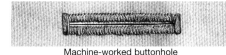
Bound buttonhole

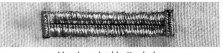
Machine-worked buttonhole

Hand-worked buttonhole

Determining and testing buttonhole length

It is important to make your buttonholes exactly the right length, so that they allow the button to pass through easily, yet hold the garment securely closed. The **length of the buttonhole opening** should equal the diameter of the button plus its height. On a bound buttonhole, this measurement will be the total length

of the buttonhole from end to end; on a worked buttonhole, however, because of the finishing at each end, you should add ⅛ in (3 mm) to the calculation for the actual length of the opening.

To check buttonhole length, make a slash in a scrap of the garment fabric equal to the length desired for

the buttonhole opening. If the button slips through easily, the length is correct. **Test the buttonhole method** on a scrap of fabric first including all the layers, such as interfacing and underlining, that will be present in the finished garment. Also, go through all construction steps when testing the technique.

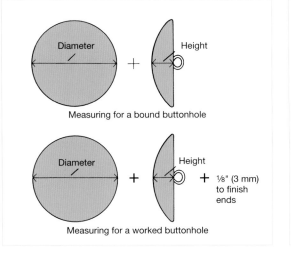

Measuring for a bound buttonhole

Measuring for a worked buttonhole

⅛" (3 mm) to finish ends

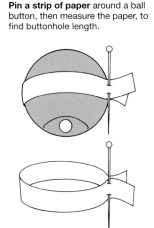

Pin a strip of paper around a ball button, then measure the paper, to find buttonhole length.

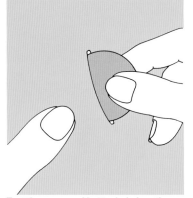

Test the proposed buttonhole length by slipping the button through a slash cut in a scrap of the garment fabric.

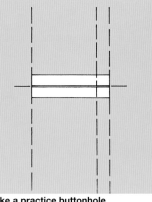

Make a practice buttonhole to test the technique, using all layers of fabric that will be in the final garment.

Fabric-marking methods 65 · Basic pattern alterations 36–46

Positioning buttonholes

Buttonholes in women's garments are placed on the right-hand side of a garment that closes at the front; if a garment closes at the back, the buttonholes go on the left-hand side. Buttonholes must be positioned on the garment in relation to the button placement line, which, in turn, is located according to the center line of the garment. The button placement line must be marked on each half of the garment so that the center lines of the garment will match when the garment is closed. The three key placement points for buttonholes are at the neck, the fullest part of the bust, and the waist. Additional buttonholes are evenly spaced between these points. The lowest buttonhole must always be above the bulk of the hem.

Horizontal buttonholes are the most secure, therefore used on most garments. When buttoned, the pull of the closure is absorbed by the end of the buttonhole, with very little distortion. These buttonholes are placed to extend ⅛ in (3 mm) beyond the button placement line.

Vertical buttonholes are often used with a narrow placket, such as a shirt band, or when there are many small buttons involved in closing the garment. They are placed directly on the button placement line, and the top of the buttonhole is ⅛ in (3 mm) above the mark for center of button.

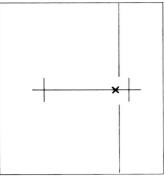

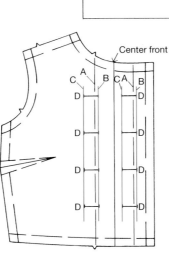

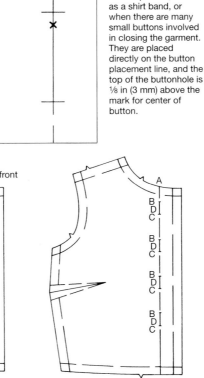

Markings for horizontal buttonholes:
Marking A is the button placement line of the garment; B and C mark the ends of the buttonhole (B is ⅛ in [3 mm] from button placement line); D marks the center of the buttonhole. These markings should all be transferred to the garment before the construction begins.

On **double-breasted** garments, the two rows of buttons must be equidistant from center line of garment. If buttons are to be 3 in (7.5 cm) from center line, locate the B line of the left-hand row of buttonholes 2⅞ in (7.2 cm) from center and the B line of the right-hand row 3⅛ in (7.8 cm) from center line. Mark remaining lines.

The markings for vertical buttonholes are placed directly on the button position line A. The D lines should be marked first, on top of the A line to prevent confusion between buttonholes and spaces. The B and C lines mark the ends of the buttonhole, with the B line placed ⅛ in (3 mm) above the mark for the button center.

Altering buttonhole positions

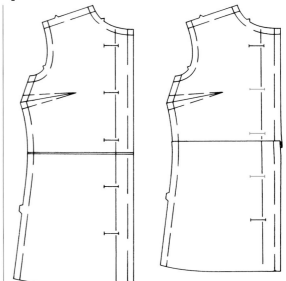

If a pattern with a button closing is altered lengthwise, the buttonholes must be re-spaced on the pattern itself after the alteration is complete. Shown above is the procedure for a shortened pattern; when one is lengthened, the procedure is reversed. In either case, a buttonhole may have to be added or subtracted for the sake of design. Remember the three key positioning points when re-spacing.

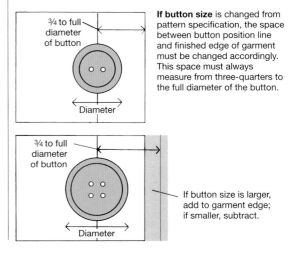

If button size is changed from pattern specification, the space between button position line and finished edge of garment must be changed accordingly. This space must always measure from three-quarters to the full diameter of the button.

If button size is larger, add to garment edge; if smaller, subtract.

Bound buttonholes — corded method

In this method, corded bias strips are used for the buttonhole lips. The cord produces soft, rounded edges instead of crisp ones, making this method particularly suitable for spongy fabrics that do not hold a sharp crease well, such as textured knits. The bias strip of each lip should be 1½ in (4 cm) wide, and the length of the buttonhole plus 1 in (2.5 cm). You will save time by cutting and sewing the lips for both sides of all the buttonholes at the same time. Use a cable cord or yarn that measures not more than ⅛ in (3 mm) in diameter. Make sure that the finished lips have body but not too much bulk.

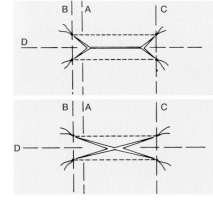

1. Fold bias piece, right side out, around the cable cord and pin the edges together to hold the cord in place. Stitch close to the cord, using a zipper foot. Cut into individual strips for buttonholes, each strip 1 in (2.5 cm) longer than width of buttonholes.

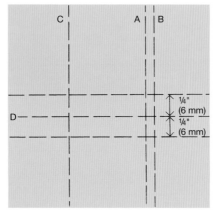

2. Thread-mark the four positioning lines on garment as described on p. 301. Baste additional marking lines ¼ in (6 mm) above end below the buttonhole position line. If the fabric is very heavy, baste these lines 5/16 in (8 mm) from the buttonhole positioning line.

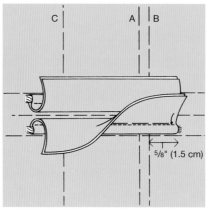

3. Center strips over marking on right side of garment so ends extend ⅝ in (1.5 cm) beyond lines for ends of buttonhole. Corded edges should lie along the outer ¼ in (6 mm) markings, with excess fabric of strips toward center of buttonhole. Baste each strip in place by hand.

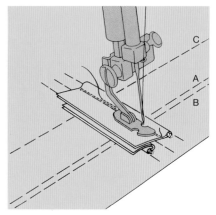

4. Attach zipper foot to machine. Lower needle through strip and garment precisely on the mark for end of buttonhole and just to the inside of the existing stitching. Stitch with a 20/1 mm stitch length, stopping at mark for other end. Repeat for remaining side.

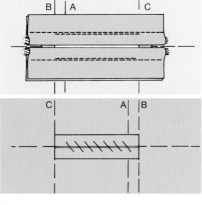

5. Bring thread ends to wrong side of garment and tie. Cut along center line of buttonhole to within ¼ in (6 mm) of each end, then cut diagonally into each corner. Or, cut directly from center into each corner. Do not cut through stitching.

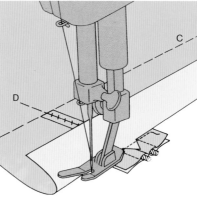

6. Remove the hand basting used to hold the strip to the garment. Turn strips through to wrong side and pull the triangular ends into place. Press as directed on page 308. From the right side of the garment, diagonal-baste lip edges together.

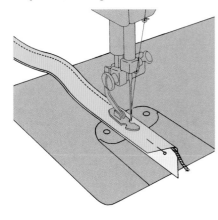

7. Attach the straight stitch presser foot. With the garment right side up, fold back enough fabric to expose one triangular end. Stitch back and forth across triangle several times to secure it to ends of strips. Repeat for other end of buttonhole.

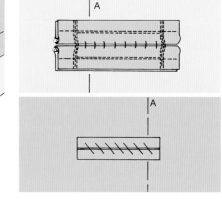

8. Remove all basted markings except center front markings. Trim strips to within ¼ in (6 mm) of the buttonhole stitching lines. Press the entire area. The diagonal basting stitches holding lips together should stay in until garment is finished.

Grain in fabric 56–57 · Hand-basting stitches 70–71

Patch method

The patch method involves making a rectangular opening the size of the buttonhole, with a patch of garment fabric as the facing. The patch facing is then folded so as to create the buttonhole lips. This method is a good choice for buttonholes in fabrics that are light to medium in weight, do not fray, but do retain a crease readily. For each buttonhole, cut a patch of fabric 2 in (5 cm) wide and 1 in (2.5 cm) longer than the buttonhole. To mark the center of the patch, fold it in half lengthwise and then finger-press the fold. Straight grain is preferred for the patch, although bias may be used.

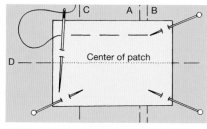

1. With right sides together, center patch over buttonhole markings, placing the crease of the patch along the buttonhole position line. Baste in place over markings.

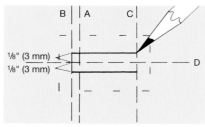

2. On wrong side mark lines ⅛ in (3 mm) above and below the buttonhole positioning lines. On heavy fabric, mark these lines ³⁄₁₆ to ¼ in (5 mm to 1.25 cm) away from positioning lines.

3. Using a 20/1 mm stitch length, stitch around the "box" made by the pencil markings and the buttonhole length markings. Begin on one of the long sides and pivot at the corners.

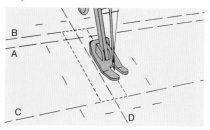

4. For an exact rectangle, take the same number of stitches (5 or 6) across each of the short sides. Overlap several stitches at the end. Remove hand basting and press.

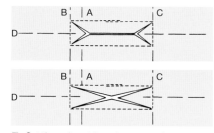

5. Cut through patch and garment along center to within ¼ in (6 mm) of the ends, then diagonally to corners. Or cut directly into the corners from the center. Do not cut stitching.

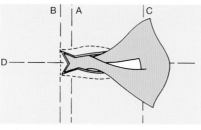

6. Gently turn patch through opening to wrong side of garment. A properly stitched opening will be a perfect rectangle. Pull on the ends to square the corners.

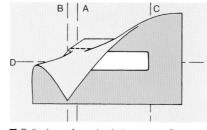

7. Roll edges of opening between your fingers until the seam is precisely on the edge of the opening. Press carefully so that none of the patch shows on the right side.

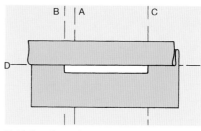

8. To form buttonhole lips, fold each long side of the patch over the opening so that the folds meet exactly in the center. For accuracy, fold along a true grain line.

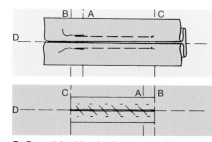

9. From right side, check accuracy of lips and manipulate them until exactly right. Baste along the center of each lip to hold the fold in place. Then diagonal-baste the lips together at their fold lines and press.

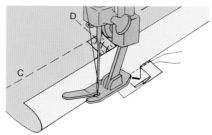

10. Place garment right side up on the machine. Flip back enough of the garment to expose one of the triangular ends, then stitch back and forth across both it and the patch. Repeat at the other end.

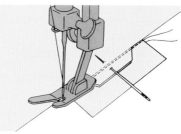

11. With the garment still right side up, turn it back to expose one of the horizontal seam allowances. Stitch through the seam allowance and the patch, just slightly inside the original stitching line. Repeat on other seam.

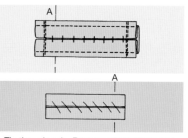

12. Tie thread ends. Remove all markings and basting except center front line. The diagonal basting holding the lips together should remain in place until the buttons are added. Trim patch to within ¼ in (6 mm) of machine stitching.

Grain in fabric 56–57 · Diagonal basting 70 · Slipstitch 80 · Machine-basting stitches 83

Simplified patch method

This buttonhole method is an ideal choice for a beginner sewer because both the positioning and the formation of the lips are done in one easy step.

Also, in this method, there is an easy way to check that the lips and stitching lines are properly located before the buttonhole is cut, which will virtually

ensure success. Because this method relies on machine-basted markings, it cannot be used on fabrics that are easily marred by a machine needle. Cut a

patch of fabric for each buttonhole that is 2 in (5 cm) wide and 1 in (2.5 cm) longer than the buttonhole, on either the bias or on the straight grain.

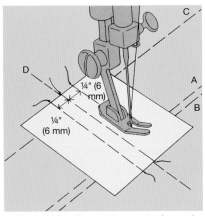

1. Placing right sides together, center the patch over the buttonhole markings on the garment. Machine-baste through center of patch along the buttonhole position line, then exactly ¼ in (6 mm) above and below this line.

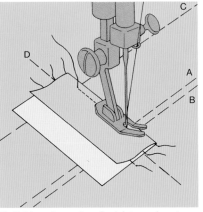

2. Fold one long edge of patch toward center on the ¼ in (6 mm) basted line and finger-press it in place. Using a 20/1 mm stitch length, sew precisely ⅛ in (3 mm) from fold; begin and end exactly on buttonhole length markings.

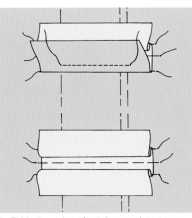

3. Fold other edge of patch toward center on ¼ in (6 mm) basted line. Finger-press it in place and stitch as above. The lips have now been formed and stitched in place. Press edges of lips away from center line of buttonhole.

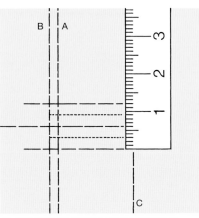

4. Five rows of stitching are now visible on wrong side of garment. Use a ruler to check that all five are precisely ⅛ in (3 mm) apart along their entire length. Re-stitch if necessary; tie thread ends. Remove machine basting.

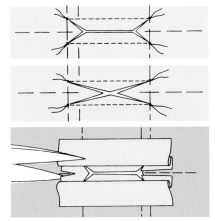

5. From wrong side, cut along center line to within ¼ in (6 mm) of ends. Then cut diagonally into corners. Or cut directly into corners from center. From the right side, cut through ends of patch so there are two strips.

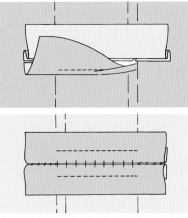

6. Carefully push the lips through the opening to the wrong side and press. Diagonal-baste them together. From wrong side, slipstitch the ends of the lip strips together on the fold lines, beyond buttonhole area.

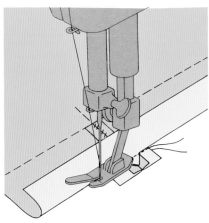

7. Place garment on the machine, right side up. Fold back just enough of the fabric to expose one tiny triangular end of the buttonhole. Stitch back and forth across this end, attaching it to strips. Repeat at other end.

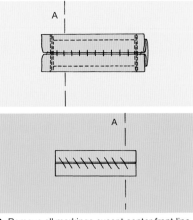

8. Remove all markings except center front line and press. Trim ends and sides of strips to within ¼ in (6 mm) of stitching lines. The diagonal basting holding lips together should stay in until garment is finished.

Tapestry needle 11 · Hand-basting stitches 70–71 · Tying thread ends 68

One-piece folded method

This method is suitable for light- to mediumweight fabrics that crease easily and do not fray. Like regular patch buttonholes, it involves a patch of fabric, but the lips are formed before the patch is attached to the garment. It ensures uniform lip widths and eliminates almost all bulk from the buttonhole area.

Buttonhole length + 1" (2.5 cm)

1. For each buttonhole, cut a patch of garment fabric 1 in (2.5 cm) wide and 1 in (2.5 cm) longer than the buttonhole. Cut patch on straight grain.

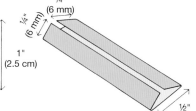

¼" (6 mm) ¼" (6 mm) 1" (2.5 cm) ½" (1.25 cm)

2. With wrong side inward, fold along edges so they touch. Baste through center of each fold; press. Patch is now ½ in (1.25 cm) wide; open side has two ¼ in (6 mm) sections.

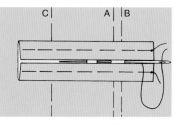

C A B

3. Center the patch, open side up, on the right side of the garment directly over the buttonhole markings. Baste the patch in place through the center.

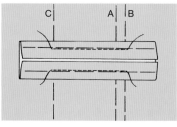

C A B

4. Selecting a 20/1 mm stitch length, stitch through exact center of each half of the patch, starting and stopping exactly on markings for end of buttonhole.

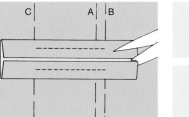

C A B

5. Pull thread ends to the wrong side of the garment and tie. Remove basting threads; press. Cut through the center of the patch to form two strips.

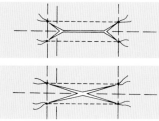

6. Turn to wrong side to cut into corners. Cut along center line and then into corners. Or cut directly into corners from center. Stop short of stitching.

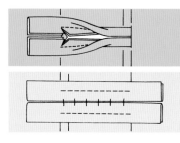

7. Carefully push the buttonhole strips through the opening to the wrong side. Pull on the ends of the strips to square off the corners of the rectangle. Baste the lips together diagonally from the right side of the garment. Press.

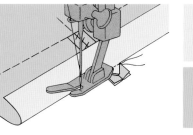

8. Place the garment right side up on the machine. Fold back enough fabric to expose one of the triangular buttonhole ends. Stitch back and forth across this triangle to secure it to the strips. Repeat at the other end.

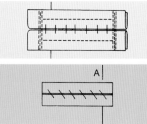

A

9. Remove all markings except center front line. Trim the edges of the buttonhole strips to within ¼ in (6 mm) of the ends of the buttonhole. Press. The diagonal basting should remain in place until the garment is completed.

One-piece tucked method

This method is the same as the one at left, except the lips are stitched before the patch is sewn to the garment. For each buttonhole, cut a patch 1½ in (4 cm) wide and 1 in (2.5 cm) longer than the buttonhole.

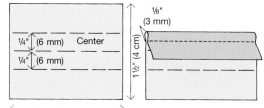

¼" (6 mm) Center ¼" (6 mm) ⅛" (3 mm) 1½" (4 cm)

Buttonhole length + 1" (2.5 cm)

Mark lengthwise center of patch; mark lines ¼ in (6 mm) above and below the center. Wrong sides together, fold patch on ¼ in (6 mm) lines. Press; stitch ⅛ in (3 mm) from folds. Proceed with Step 3, left.

Cording bound buttonholes

If the buttonhole lips seem limp and thin, draw wool or soft cord into the lips after they have been formed but **before** the triangular ends of the button-

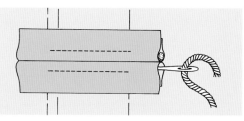

holes are stitched. The only buttonhole methods adaptable to this are the simplified patch and the one-piece folded and tucked methods.

Choose a wool or soft cord in a diameter that will just nicely plump the lips. If the garment fabric is washable, choose an acrylic wool. Use a loop turner or a blunt-pointed (tapestry) needle to pull the wool through the lips. Cut the wool even with ends of the patch strips, then stitch across the ends.

Uneven basting stitch 70 · Reducing seam bulk 87 · Lining fabrics 346–351

Two-piece piped method

In this procedure, a completely faced "window" is made in the garment, then the buttonhole lips are constructed and sewn in behind the "window." An advantage of the method is that the corners of the buttonhole, sometimes a troublesome area, can be made perfectly square before the lips are sewn in. It is an excellent choice for fabrics that tend to fray, because the raw edges of the garment are finished off early in construction. The lips in the finished buttonhole are slightly wider than in other buttonhole techniques, which makes it highly recommended for heavy, bulky fabrics.

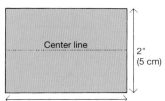

1. Cut a facing for the "window," 2 in (5 cm) wide and 1 in (2.5 cm) longer than buttonhole, from a sheer fabric, color-matched to garment fabric. Finger-press center crease.

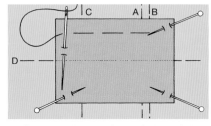

2. Center the sheer patch over the buttonhole markings on the right side of the garment. Carefully pin at each of the corners, then hand-baste in place.

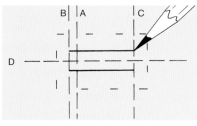

3. On the wrong side of the garment, pencil-mark lines 3/16 to 1/4 in (5 to 6 mm) above and below buttonhole positioning line. These lines and buttonhole end lines form a rectangle.

4. Using a 20/1 mm stitch length, stitch around the rectangle. For best results, start at the center of one long side, pivot at the corner, then stitch across the end.

5. Continue stitching, pivoting at corners and making sure that the same number of stitches are taken across each end. Overlap about four stitches at the starting point.

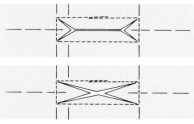

6. Next cut into corners. Cut through center of rectangle to within 1/4 in (6 mm) at each end, then into corners. Or cut directly into corners from center. Do not cut through stitching.

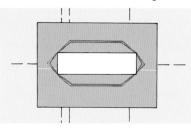

7. Push the patch through the opening to the wrong side of the garment. Square off the corners and press, making certain that none of the patch shows on the right side.

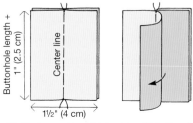

8. For lips, cut two fabric strips 1½ in (4 cm) wide and 1 in (2.5 cm) longer than buttonhole. Right sides together, machine-baste strips through center. Open out on basting, press flat.

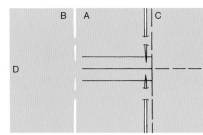

9. With the garment right side up, position the lips underneath the "window" so that the joining of the lips is aligned with the center of the buttonhole opening. Use fine needles instead of pins to hold lips in place so that presser foot can get next to the ends.

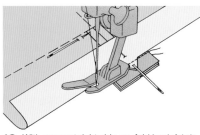

10. With garment right side up, fold back fabric on buttonhole end marking. The triangular end, and the ends of the sheer patch and the lips, will be exposed. Use a needle to pin triangle to other layers. Stitch triangle back and forth exactly on end of buttonhole.

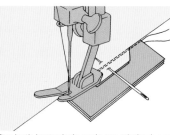

11. After both buttonhole ends are stitched, sew top and bottom to buttonhole lips. Use a needle to hold seam allowances of opening to the lips, and stitch through all layers as close as possible to the first stitching; take care to keep stitching straight.

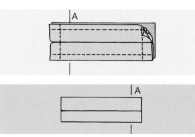

12. Trim and grade excess width of lips and patch so the layer nearest the garment is ½ in (1.25 cm) and the top layer ¼ in (6 mm) from the stitching. Remove all markings except center front line and press. Leave machine basting in center of lips until garment is complete.

Fabric-marking methods 65 · Even basting stitch 70 · Slipstitch 80 · Tying thread ends 68

In-seam method

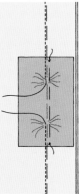

1. In-seam buttonholes are actually nothing but finished openings in a seam. Mark each end of the buttonhole opening, then baste the seam, going across the buttonhole opening. For each buttonhole, cut two stays made from lightweight fabric, 1 in (2.5 cm) wide and 1 in (2.5 cm) longer than the opening, and on the same grain. Center and baste a stay on each side of seam, over buttonhole markings.

2. Stitch the garment seam, interrupting the stitching at the buttonhole markings. Leave long thread ends at each end of the buttonhole. Pull thread ends to one side of the garment and tie them together.

3. Press seam open and trim stay so that it is slightly narrower than the seam allowances. If the buttonhole is in a horizontal seam that also runs through the facing, remember to leave a similar space in the facing. Make the opening in the facing the same way as the buttonhole, eliminating the stays. Then slipstitch facing and garment together.

Facing finishes

After bound buttonholes have been constructed, the interfacing is attached and the garment facing is ultimately sewn into the garment. The areas in the facing that lie behind the buttonholes must then be opened, finished off, and attached so that the button-hole is ready to be used. There are three principal methods for finishing a facing. Which method you choose depends mainly on the type of garment fabric but also on the amount of time you want to spend on the task. The **oval method** is a quick (cont'd on p. 308)

Oval method

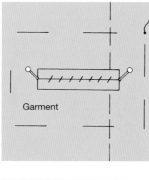

1. Position facing in garment exactly as it will be worn. Baste around each buttonhole through all the garment layers to hold the facing in place. Insert a straight pin from right side through the facing at each end of the buttonhole.

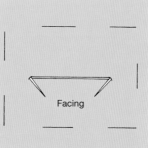

2. Working from the facing side, cut the facing between the two pins. This slash must not be longer than the buttonhole, and it should be on the straight grain if possible. Remove pins.

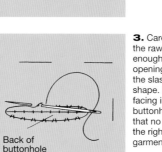

3. Carefully turn under the raw edges of the slash enough to clear the opening of the buttonhole; the slash will take an oval shape. Slipstitch the facing in place around the buttonhole, making sure that no stitches show on the right side of the garment. Remove basting.

Rectangle method

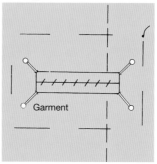

1. Position facing in garment exactly as it will be worn. From the right side, baste around each buttonhole through all garment layers. Insert a straight pin from the right side through the facing at each of the four corners of the buttonhole.

2. Working from the facing side, cut along the center of this pin-outlined area to within ¼ in (6 mm) of each end. Then cut diagonally to each of the four pins. Remove pins.

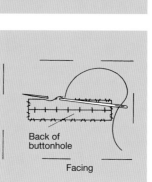

3. Turn under the raw edges so that the fold is even with the stitching on all four sides of the buttonhole. The slash will take a rectangular shape. Slipstitch the facing to the back of the buttonhole.

Pressing equipment 14 · Slipstitch 80 · Thread-marking 65

Facing finishes

and easy finish, and is a good choice for fabrics that fray easily because little handling is involved. The **rectangle method** is similar to the oval method except that the shape is more exacting and requires more manipulation. For this reason, this finish is recommended only for tightly woven fabrics that will not fray easily. The **windowpane method** can be used for all types of fabric. It is the neatest of all the facing finishes but requires more time in the execution than either of the other methods.

Windowpane method

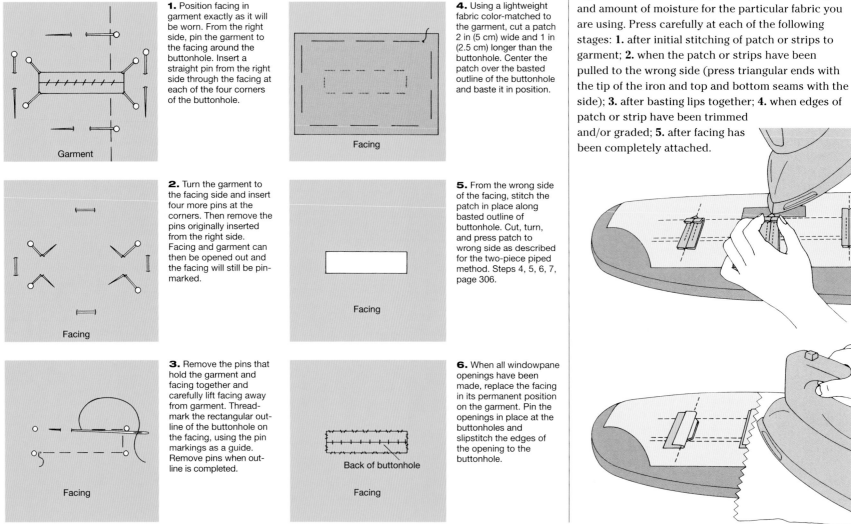

1. Position facing in garment exactly as it will be worn. From the right side, pin the garment to the facing around the buttonhole. Insert a straight pin from the right side through the facing at each of the four corners of the buttonhole.

Garment

2. Turn the garment to the facing side and insert four more pins at the corners. Then remove the pins originally inserted from the right side. Facing and garment can then be opened out and the facing will still be pin-marked.

Facing

3. Remove the pins that hold the garment and facing together and carefully lift facing away from garment. Thread-mark the rectangular outline of the buttonhole on the facing, using the pin markings as a guide. Remove pins when outline is completed.

Facing

4. Using a lightweight fabric color-matched to the garment, cut a patch 2 in (5 cm) wide and 1 in (2.5 cm) longer than the buttonhole. Center the patch over the basted outline of the buttonhole and baste it in position.

Facing

5. From the wrong side of the facing, stitch the patch in place along basted outline of buttonhole. Cut, turn, and press patch to wrong side as described for the two-piece piped method. Steps 4, 5, 6, 7, page 306.

Facing

6. When all windowpane openings have been made, replace the facing in its permanent position on the garment. Pin the openings in place at the buttonholes and slipstitch the edges of the opening to the buttonhole.

Back of buttonhole

Facing

Pressing during construction

Pressing during construction is essential for a well-made bound buttonhole. To avoid imprints or shine on the right side, place strips of brown paper between the patch or strips and the garment, and use a soft press cloth between the garment and the ironing board. Choose the proper temperature setting and amount of moisture for the particular fabric you are using. Press carefully at each of the following stages: **1.** after initial stitching of patch or strips to garment; **2.** when the patch or strips have been pulled to the wrong side (press triangular ends with the tip of the iron and top and bottom seams with the side); **3.** after basting lips together; **4.** when edges of patch or strip have been trimmed and/or graded; **5.** after facing has been completely attached.

Buttonholes for fur, leather, and similar materials

Real and fake furs, leathers, vinyls, and similar materials cannot accept regular bound buttonhole techniques, for several reasons. One reason is that usually they cannot be marked on the right side, because marking would damage the face of the material, as in leathers, or the markings would not show, as in deep pile furs. Other considerations are the bulk inherent

in some of these materials, and the fact that self-material often cannot be used for the lips. The result of these special limitations is that bound buttonholes in these fabrics quite often do not look like regular bound buttonholes and are not made in the same way.

To mark for buttonholes in leather, fur, and similar materials, use chalk, pencil, or a felt-tip pen on the

back side of the material. Some leathers and vinyls can be marked with a tracing wheel. If a deep pile fur must be marked on the right side, use either T-pins or extra-long pins with colored-heads to do so. Cut the buttonholes in these materials with a sharp razor blade or a craft knife, using a metal ruler as a guide if needed.

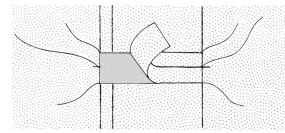

A false buttonhole, for real or fake leathers

A buttonhole for fur made with grosgrain lips

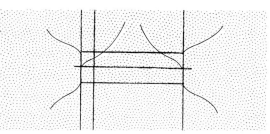

This fur buttonhole is merely a finished slit

False buttonholes for real and fake leathers

This is not a bound buttonhole in the true sense; it is actually two rectangles stitched to look like a buttonhole, with a slit in the center.
1. Apply a suitable interfacing and pencil-mark buttonhole (see p. 301). Draw additional lines ¼ in (6 mm) or ½ in (1.25 cm) above and below buttonhole position line.

2. Transferring of markings to the right side of fabric must be done carefully to avoid puncture marks from needles and pins that would show in the finished garment. Basted markings must be placed so that needle punctures will be hidden in the final stitching. This is done with three hand stitches, in this way: using

the pencil markings on the wrong side as a guide, take one basting stitch across each end and a third, longer stitch along the center of the buttonhole. Leave long thread ends on all stitches. This makes only six puncture marks, which then will be covered by machine stitches.

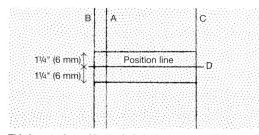

3. Remove the interfacing from within the rectangular buttonhole area carefully so as not to disturb the three long basting threads. To do this, trim out interfacing along the pencil marks for buttonhole sides and ends. To remove an iron-on interfacing, slit with a razor blade on markings, then apply a warm iron to the area to soften the adhesive.

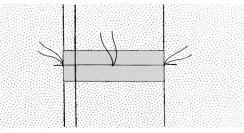

4. Now tie the thread ends together so that the thread markings on the right side of the garment are straight, taut, and secure. Before continuing with the buttonholes, apply the garment facing. Turn the facing to its permanent position, and anchor it securely in place, with either leather glue or topstitching, before stitching the buttonholes.

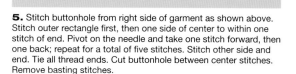

5. Stitch buttonhole from right side of garment as shown above. Stitch outer rectangle first, then one side of center to within one stitch of end. Pivot on the needle and take one stitch forward, then one back; repeat for a total of five stitches. Stitch other side and end. Tie all thread ends. Cut buttonhole between center stitches. Remove basting stitches.

Strip method for real and fake leathers

This is a true bound buttonhole, made in a way much like the strip method for fabric, except that several stitching steps are eliminated to avoid weakening the leather with excess needle punctures. Vinyls and leathers vary greatly in thickness and suppleness, which affects the width of the lips in the finished buttonhole. The thicker the material, the wider the lips. Use the guide, at the right, to select the correct width, then make a test buttonhole. The length of each strip should be 1 in (2.5 cm) greater than the length of the buttonhole to provide a ½ in (1.25 cm) extension on each end.

If garment facing is leather, use Step 6 to finish back of buttonhole; for fabric see pages 307–308.

Buttonhole width	Lip width	Strip width
¼ in (6 mm)	⅛ in (3 mm)	½ in (1.25 cm)
⅜ in (1 cm)	3/16 in (5 mm)	¾ in (2 cm)
½ in (1.25 cm)	¼ in (6 mm)	1 in (2.5 cm)

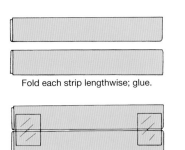

Fold each strip lengthwise; glue.

Tape strips together at ends.

1. Cut two strips for each buttonhole in the recommended width for the size of buttonhole you are making. Fold strips in half lengthwise, apply leather glue or rubber cement to wrong side and allow to dry, weighted if necessary. Abut the folded edges and tape together ½ in (1.25 cm) from ends.

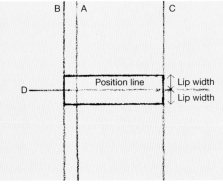

Position line
Lip width
Lip width

2. Mark the ends and the buttonhole position (center) line on the back of the fabric with chalk or a felt tip pen (see p. 301). Mark additional lines above and below the center line, making them the same distance from the center line as the recommended lip width.

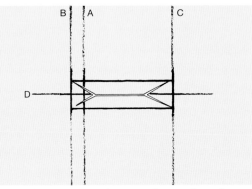

3. Draw additional lines into the corners from a point on the center line ½ in (1.25 cm) from each end. Using a razor blade or craft knife and metal ruler, cut along the center of the buttonhole to within ½ in (1.25 cm) of the ends, then cut diagonally into each of the four corners, following the marked lines.

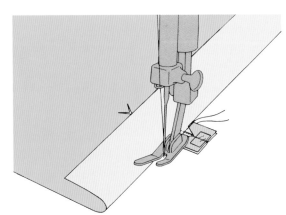

4. Center the buttonhole strips behind the cut, with the abutted edges of the lips exactly in the center of the buttonhole. With right side up, fold garment back to expose the end of the buttonhole. Turn out the little triangle so that it is on top of the strips and stitch exactly on the drawn line at the base of the triangle. Repeat at the other end.

5. Fold the garment down to expose one side of the buttonhole. Match the edge of the seam allowance of the slash to the edge of the buttonhole strips and stitch exactly on the marked line of the base of the seam allowance. Repeat on the other side of the buttonhole. Tie all thread ends; do not backstitch. Remove tape from strips.

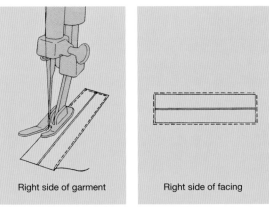

Right side of garment

Right side of facing

6. Apply interfacing, trimming it out of buttonhole area. Sew facing to garment. To finish the facing, stitch the lips to facing from the right side of the garment by sewing in the seam crevices that form the buttonhole rectangle. Tie all thread ends. Trim away the facing inside the stitching lines to open the buttonhole.

Leather sewing-needle 11 · Twill tape 12 · Backstitch 72 · Catchstitch basting 75 · Whipstitch 73 · Overhand stitch 73 · Slipstitch 80

Taped method for real and fake furs

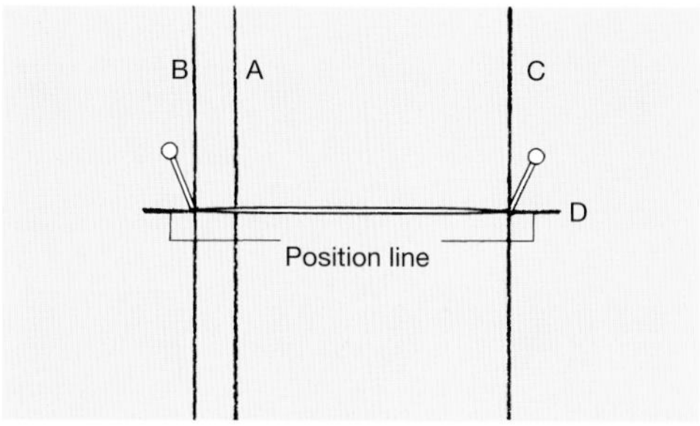

This easy buttonhole method for fur can also be used as a facing finish for the strip method described at right.

1. Using a pen or pencil, mark the buttonhole length and position lines on the wrong side of the material. Place a pin at mark for each end and cut between pins on buttonhole position line. Use a razor blade so that only the leather back, not the fur, is cut.

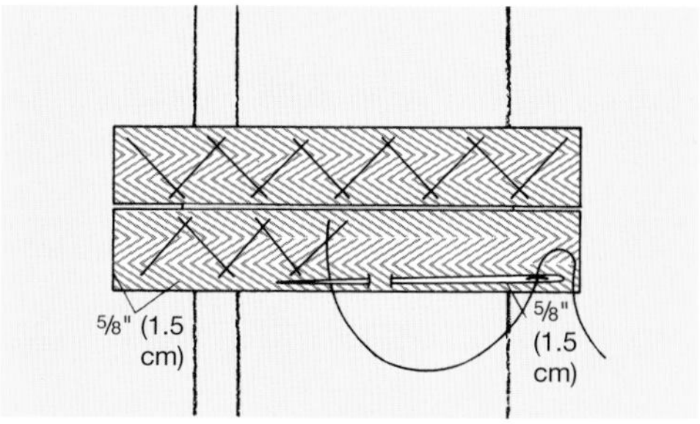

2. Cut four strips of ½ in (1.25 cm) twill tape for each buttonhole, each piece 1 in (2.5 cm) longer than the buttonhole. On the wrong side, center a strip of tape along one edge of slash, aligning edge of tape exactly to edge of slash. Catchstitch tape to skin. If a regular needle will not penetrate the skin, use a special wedge-shaped leather needle. Repeat on other edge.

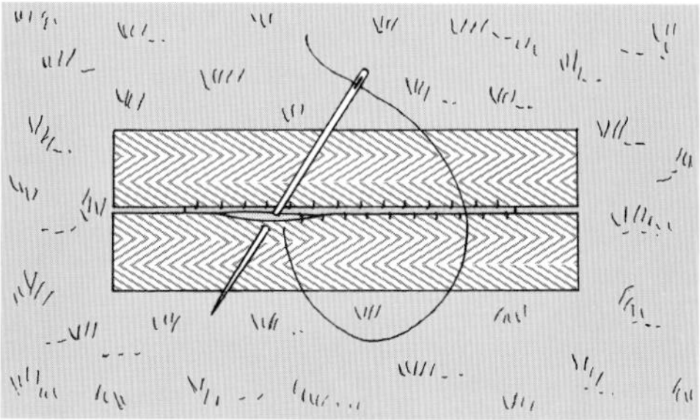

3. The remaining two pieces of twill tape are stitched on from the right side. Center them at slit in the same way as explained above. Sew edges of tape to buttonhole edges with a small overhand stitch. Push fur away from slit to ensure that it is not caught in stitching.

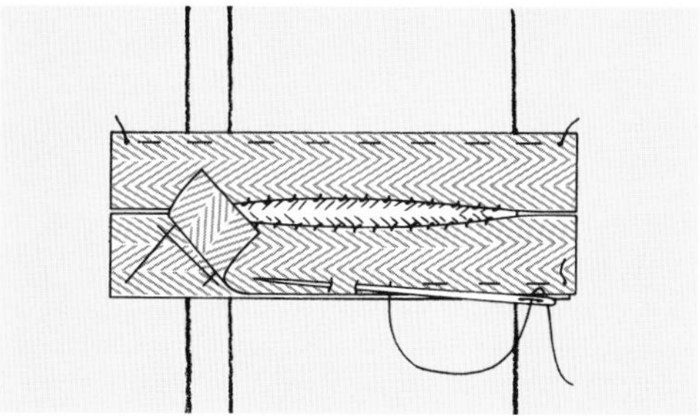

4. Turn both pieces of tape to the inside. Using a running stitch, secure these pieces to the corresponding catch-stitched tapes. This method may also be used for a facing finish. (An alternative facing finish involves simply slashing a marked opening in the facing and whip-stitching edges of slash to the back of the buttonhole.)

Strip method for real and fake furs

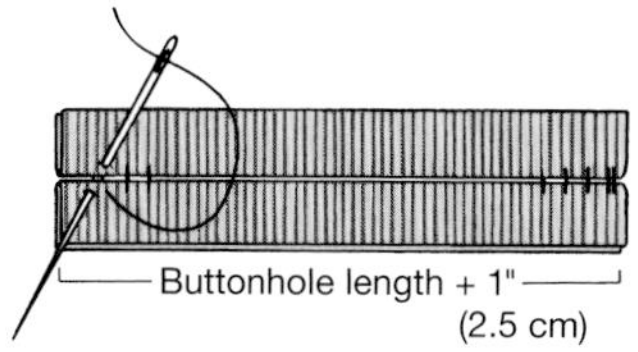

1. Mark buttonholes (see p. 301), drawing additional lines ⅛ in (3 mm) above and below the center line to extend beyond length lines. Cut two strips of grosgrain ribbon, of light or dark shade to match the fur, 1 in (2.5 cm) longer than the buttonhole. To form lips, fold pieces of ribbon in half and press. Whip-stitch strips together for ⅝ in (1.5 cm) at ends.

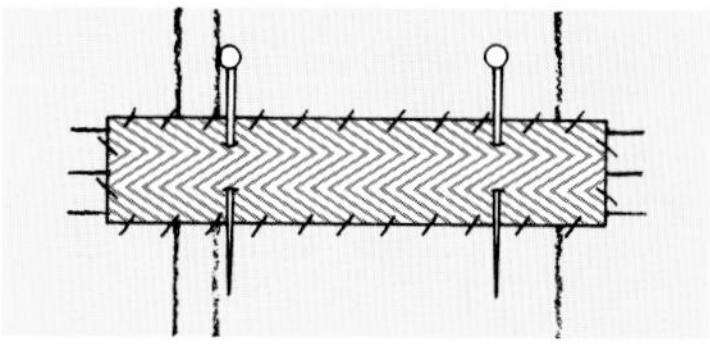

2. A stay of twill tape will keep material from stretching. Cut a strip of ½ in (1.25 cm) twill tape, 1 in (2.5 cm) longer than the buttonhole, and center it over the buttonhole marking. Whipstitch the tape edges to the garment, using a leather-point needle if needed. Place straight pins ⅝ in (1.5 cm) from each end of buttonhole to guide slashing.

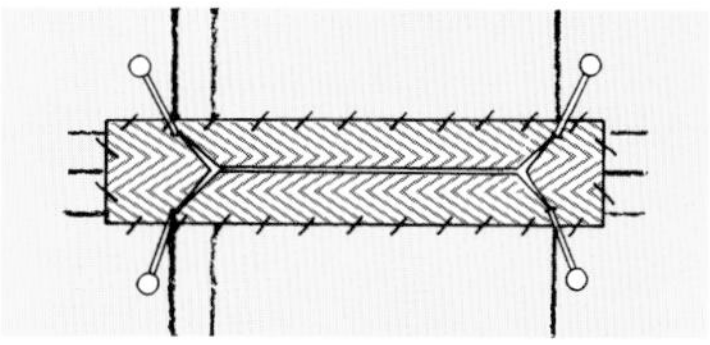

3. Slash through tape and fur between the pins, using a single-edge razor blade. Place a pin in each of the four corners of the buttonhole — exactly where the ⅛ in (3 mm) lines above and below center cross the buttonhole length lines. Slash diagonally into each corner.

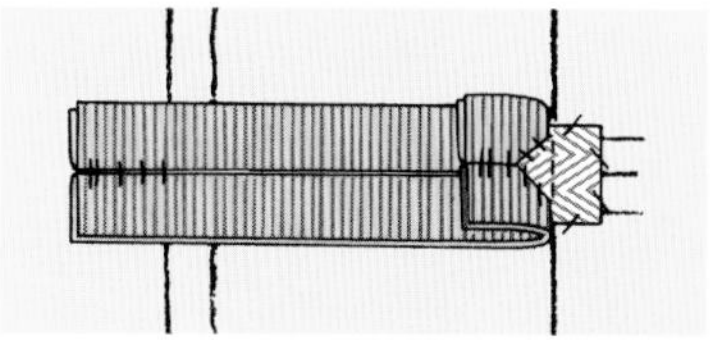

4. Carefully cut hair away from the buttonhole seam allowances formed by the slashing. Center the ribbon lips at the slash so that the opening in lips exactly matches the slit in the fur. Whipstitch edges of the little triangle at each end to the ribbon lips. Hand-backstitch across base of triangle.

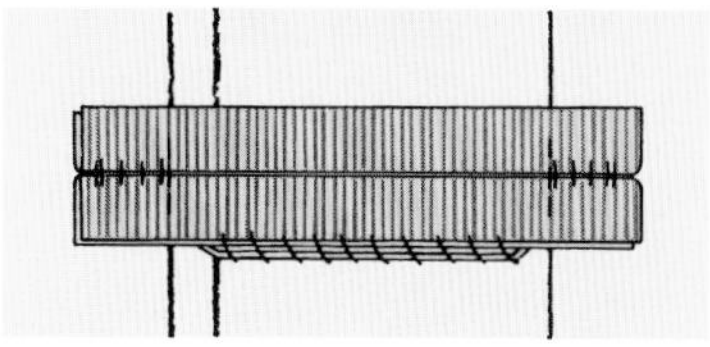

5. Match the edge of one seam allowance of slash to outside edge of the ribbon lip so that the sheared area lies against the ribbon. Whipstitch these edges together for the entire length of the buttonhole. Repeat on other seam allowances.

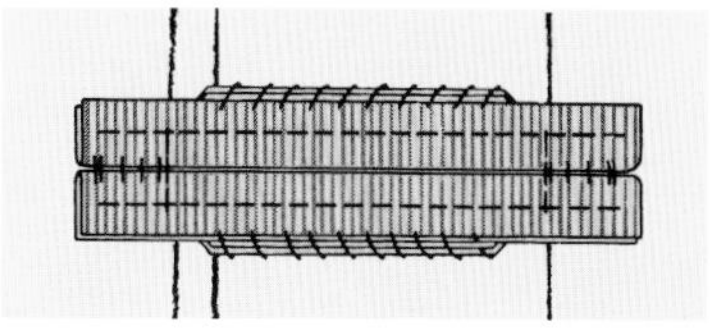

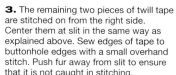

6. Stitch along each side of the opening, ⅛ in (3 mm) from the edge. Use a short machine stitch or a hand backstitch. To finish garment facing behind buttonhole, use the taped method at the left and slip-stitch facing opening to back of buttonhole.

Worked buttonholes — the two types

A worked buttonhole is a slit in the fabric that is finished with either hand or machine stitches. It has two sides equal in length to the buttonhole opening, and two ends finished with bar tacks (as illustrated at right) or with a fan-shaped arrangement of stitches (see p. 313). A worked buttonhole is stitched through all fabric layers, after interfacing and facing are in place; the colors of all the fabrics should match or blend to avoid a color clash at the cut edge.

There are two basic types of worked buttonholes:

hand-worked and machine-worked. A hand-worked buttonhole is slit first, then stitched; a machine-worked buttonhole is stitched, then slit.

Mark the fabric for worked buttonholes as described on page 301, Positioning buttonholes. The

Machine-worked buttonhole with bar-tacked ends

measurements for the actual buttonhole opening and for the stitched buttonhole are, however, different. The finished length of a worked buttonhole will equal the opening plus an extra ⅛ in (3 mm) for the stitches used to finish each end (see p. 300).

Hand-worked buttonhole with bar-tacked ends

Machine-worked buttonholes

There are various ways in which a machine-worked buttonhole may be made. The most common way is with **built-in buttonhole stitches** that are built into the sewing machine. By means of a few movements of a lever or turn of a dial, a buttonhole with finished ends is stitched quickly.

A second method of creating machine-worked buttonholes, but a method that is relatively rare today, makes use of a **special attachment** that clamps onto the needle bar and presser foot of the sewing

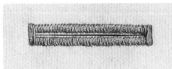

Rectangular buttonhole made with two widths of zigzag stitches, with fabric turned by hand.

Elastic buttonhole made with overedge stitch; suitable for stretch fabrics.

Reinforced buttonhole made with two rows of stitching for extra durability.

machine. This attachment moves the fabric in the buttonhole shape, while the machine does the zigzag stitching. The size of the buttonhole is limited by the capability of the attachment.

Most sewing machines on the market offer a range of built-in buttonholes to suit many different garments and fabric types. Consult your machine manual to determine which types of buttonholes are available on your machine.

A useful buttonhole which is offered by some machines is the elastic buttonhole. This type of buttonhole is made either with an overedge stitch or with a triple stretch stitch set to zigzag. Because this buttonhole is stretchable, it is suitable for knits and stretchy fabrics.

Whether or not your sewing machine offers the elastic buttonhole described above, it is essential to place a piece of interfacing between the fabric and the facing when you are working buttonholes on very stretchy fabric. The interfacing will act as a stay and prevent the buttonhole from stretching out of shape during use.

It is advisable to reinforce a machine-worked buttonhole when you are sewing a garment made of a heavy-duty fabric or a loosely woven fabric. It is also a good idea to reinforce the buttonhole when it is on an item of children's clothing. Simply stitch the

buttonhole twice with the same stitch. For a decorative effect, use the blind hemming stitch at satin stitch length for the second, reinforcement stitching.

It is always a good idea to practice making machine-worked buttonholes, through all of the fabric layers involved, on scrap fabric before beginning any buttonhole work on the garment. It is particularly advisable to practice this if you are not used to sewing with a machine.

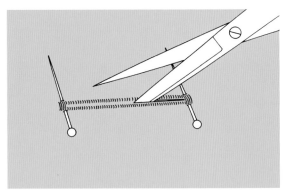

Machine-worked buttonholes are opened only after stitching is completed. Place pins at each end of the buttonhole opening to prevent cutting through the bar tacks. Cut the fabric slowly down the center of the buttonhole using a narrow, sharp, pair of scissors or a chisel-like buttonhole cutting tool.

Hand-worked buttonholes

Hand-worked buttonholes are made by cutting a slit in the fabric equal in length to the buttonhole opening, then stitching over the edges with a combination of buttonhole and blanket stitches. Horizontal buttonholes usually have a fan arrangement of stitches at the end where the button will rest and a straight bar tack at the other; a fan accommodates a button shank better. The tailored form of a horizontal buttonhole, the keyhole buttonhole, has an eyelet at the fanned end.

Vertical buttonholes are made like horizontals, except that both ends are finished either fanned or bar-tacked. Test the buttonhole through all layers of fabric that will be in the garment. Stitch with a single strand of buttonhole twist or regular sewing thread. (If you prefer a double strand of regular thread, take

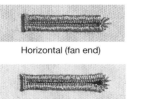

Horizontal (fan end)

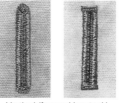

Horizontal (keyhole)

Vertical (fan and bar tack)

great care to pull up both strands uniformly with each stitch.) Stitch depth depends on fabric type and size of buttonhole. A deeper stitch is used on loosely woven fabrics and large buttonholes. Stitch depth must be considered when determining buttonhole length as it affects the buttonhole ends as well as the edges.

Keep stitches closely spaced and uniform when working buttonholes; do not pull them too tight. Fasten stitching on wrong side by running thread under a few completed stitches. Remove markings only after all buttonholes are completed. To start a new thread, come up through the last purl, and continue stitching.

Fan-end buttonholes worked by hand

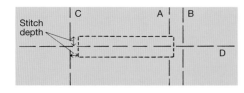

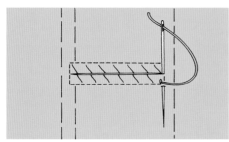

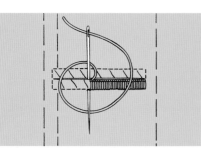

Horizontal (shown) and vertical buttonholes are alike, except ends of verticals are finished the same way.

1. Make stitch depth 1/16 to 1/8 in (2 to 3 mm). Mark position lines. Using 20/1 mm stitch length, stitch a rectangle that is a stitch depth away from center line and end markings.

2. Cut along the buttonhole position line from one end of the rectangle to the other. Overcast raw edges of slit by hand, using a thread color that matches the fabric. Turn the buttonhole in such a way that the end to be fanned is to the left. Take a short backstitch at opposite end between slit and machine stitching to fasten thread for hand stitching.

3. Working from right to left with the needle pointing toward you, insert the needle from underneath, with point coming out at the machine stitching. For first and each succeeding stitch, loop thread from previous stitch around to left and down to right, under the point of the needle. Pull needle through fabric, then away from you, to place the purl on the cut edge.

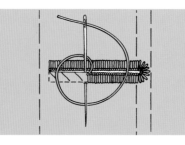

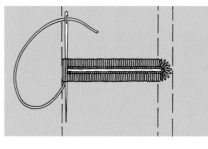

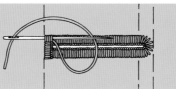

4. Take successive stitches very close together, continuing until that entire side is covered. Then fan the stitches around the end, turning the buttonhole as you work. Take 5 to 8 stitches around the fan, keeping them an even depth. When fan end is completely stitched, continue along the second side.

5. Stitch along second side until other end of the opening is reached. Then insert the needle down into the purl of the first stitch to the wrong side of the buttonhole; bring needle out just below the last stitch, at outer edge of buttonhole. Take several long stitches close together across the width of the two rows of buttonhole stitches to form the base for the bar tack.

6. Working with point of needle toward buttonhole and beginning at one end of the bar tack, insert needle into fabric under long stitches. Keep thread from previous stitch under needle point; draw up stitch. Continue, completely covering long stitches. Secure on wrong side.

Thread chart 12 · Awl 13 · Blanket stitch 78 · Overcast stitch 77

Keyhole buttonholes worked by hand

A tailored worked buttonhole, or keyhole buttonhole, is similar to the horizontal hand-worked buttonhole (see p. 313). The difference is an eyelet, or enlarged resting place for the button shank, at one end instead of a fan arrangement of stitches. By providing more room for the shank, the eyelet ensures the buttonhole will not be distorted when the garment is buttoned. This makes the tailored buttonhole the best choice for men's jackets and other finely tailored garments. Keep in mind that buttonholes on a man's coat or jacket are placed on the opposite side of that used for women's garments. Use a single strand of buttonhole twist or heavy-duty thread for buttonhole stitches. For a professional touch, cord a tailored worked buttonhole; filler can be heavy-duty thread, buttonhole twist, or fine string.

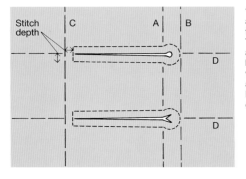

1. Machine-stitch at 20/1 mm stitch length around the buttonhole the stitch depth away from the buttonhole position line and ends. There are two ways to open the buttonhole and eyelet: Use an awl to punch the eyelet hole, then cut along the position line to within ⅛ in (3 mm) of the other end; or cut along position line to within ⅛ in (3 mm) of keyhole end of opening, then cut two tiny diagonal slashes to stitches.

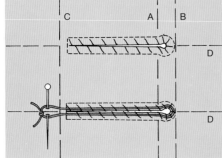

2. Overcast the edges of the slash by hand. If the buttonhole is to be corded, cut a length of cord and knot it to fit loosely around the buttonhole. Place the cord around the buttonhole so that the knot is at the end that will be bar-tacked; secure with pins. Overcast as above, enclosing the cord in the stitching.

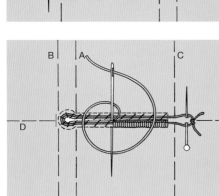

3. Work the buttonhole stitches with the keyhole opening at the left when work begins. Use the machine stitching as a guide for stitch depth. For each stitch, make sure thread from the needle eye goes around and under needle point. To form a purl on the edge, draw the needle straight up. Place stitches close together so that the edge is covered with purls.

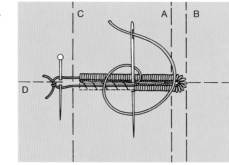

4. Continue the buttonhole stitches around the keyhole, keeping the purls close together along the edge. To form a smooth line, the stitches may have to be fanned slightly apart around the curve. Turn the buttonhole as work progresses and cover cut edge completely with buttonhole stitches.

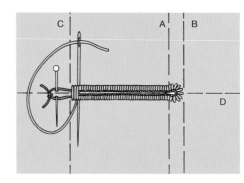

5. To make a bar tack at the unfinished end, take several long stitches across the end to equal the combined width of the rows of buttonhole stitches. Work blanket stitches across these long stitches, catching in fabric underneath, and keeping thread from previous stitch under the point of the needle with each new stitch.

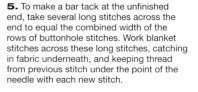

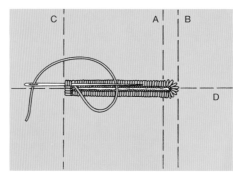

6. Cover long stitches completely with blanket stitches. When finished, fasten the thread on the underside. Pull slightly on the tied ends of the cording so that the buttonhole looks smooth and taut. Tie a new knot if necessary. Cut off excess cord; tuck knot into bar tack.

Whipstitch 73 · Uneven slipstitch 81 · Cutting bias strips 262–263

Fabric closures — button loops

Button loops can often be substituted for buttonholes, provided that loops are compatible with the overall styling of the garment. They are particularly useful for fabrics such as lace, where handling should be minimal. Although any type of button can be used, ball buttons fit best. Loops may be set into the seam at the opening edge of the garment or may be part of an intricate, decorative shape called a frog, sewn in place on the outside of the finished garment. Frogs are most frequently used in pairs, one frog containing the button loop and the frog opposite sewn under the button, usually the Chinese ball type (see p. 319).

Because loops go at the edge of the garment, the pattern may need slight adjustment before fabric is cut. First, cut the side of garment to which the buttons will be sewn according to the pattern. Mark center line of the side to which loops will be sewn, add ⅝ in (1.5 cm) for seam allowance, and draw a new cutting line at this spot. Adjust facing in the same way. (This adjustment eliminates any overlap.) Always make a test loop to see how fabric works into tubing and to determine proper loop size. Sew a button onto a fabric scrap to make sure loop will slip easily but also fit snugly over the button, as it must if it is to hold garment edges securely closed. Also check tubing diameter to ensure it is suitable for the button size.

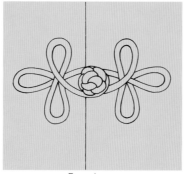

Frog closure

Button loop closure

How to make tubing

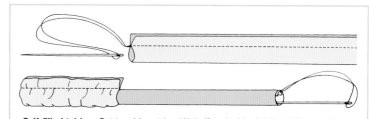

Self-filled tubing: Cut true bias strips 1⅛ in (3 cm) wide; fold in half lengthwise, right sides together. Stitch ¼ in (6 mm) from fold, stretching bias slightly; do not trim seam allowances. Thread a bodkin or large needle with a length of heavy-duty thread. Fasten thread at seam at one end of tubing, then insert needle, eye first, into tube and work it through to other end. Gradually turn all the tubing to the right side. This can be accomplished by pulling on thread and feeding seam allowances into tube.

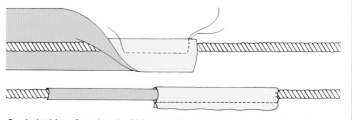

Corded tubing: Cut a length of bias equal in width to the diameter of cord being used plus 1 in (2.5 cm). Cut cord twice as long as bias. Fold the fabric around one-half of the length of the cord, right sides together. Using a zipper foot, stitch across end of bias that is at center of cording, then stitch down long edge close to cord, stretching bias slightly. Trim seam allowances. To turn right side out, simply draw enclosed cord out of tube; free end will go into tube automatically. Trim off excess cord, including stitched end.

How to make frogs

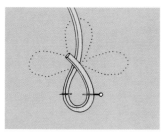

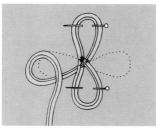

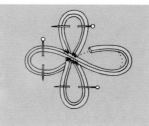

1. Draw the design for frog on paper. Place end of tubing at center of the design, leaving a ¼ in (6 mm) end.

2. Pin the tubing to paper, following design and keeping seam up. Conceal first end on wrong side of frog.

3. Whipstitch the crossing securely, making sure that stitches and ends do not show on right side.

4. Remove frog from paper and place it face up on garment with button loop extending over the edge. Then slipstitch to garment from underside. Make another frog for button and attach at button position.

Making button loops

Button loops are used on cuffs of sleeves, as well as at the front or back of blouses and dresses as the main garment closing. Though loops are most often made of self-fabric tubing, soutache braid also can be used.

If you are substituting button loops for some other type of closure, adjust your pattern as instructed on page 315. You also will need to make a diagram to establish the spacing and size of the button loops (see the step-by-step instructions).

When making your paper diagram, you must decide whether the button loops will be applied individually or in a continuous row. The choice depends on the fabric weight and desired spacing. Use single loops when the buttons are large, or if the loops are to be spaced some distance apart. Continuous loops are advisable when buttons are small. The smaller the buttons, the closer together they should be to close the garment effectively.

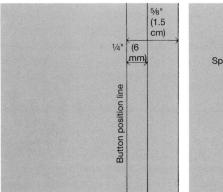

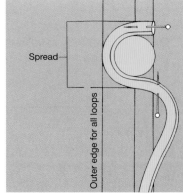

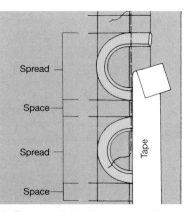

1. Making the paper diagram: On a strip of paper, draw a line ⅝ in (1.5 cm) from the edge to represent the button position line (the line on which the buttons will be sewn). Draw a second line ¼ in (6 mm) from the first, into the seam allowance. This is where the ends of each loop should be placed for either application.

2. Place exact center of button on position line and lay the tubing around it, with seam side up. Pin the end of the tubing at the ¼ in (6 mm) line, then pin again below the button where tubing meets the ¼ in (6 mm) line. Mark at the edge of tubing above and below button; this is the spread (top-to-bottom spacing). Mark outer edge.

3. To make individual loops, mark entire length of placket, indicating spread of each loop and space between loops. Place tubing on guide and mark it at both places where it crosses ¼ in (6 mm) line to determine tubing length needed for each loop. Position loops on guide, tape in place. Machine-baste.

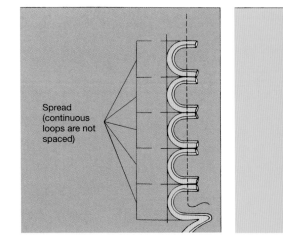

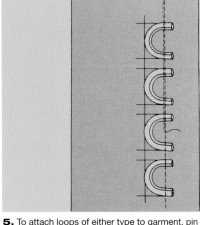

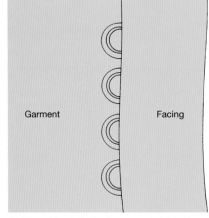

4. For continuous loops, determine the loop size as with individual loops; prepare a paper guide marked with seamline and lines for loop formation. (Omit the spaces between the loops.) Place tubing on paper guide, turning it at ¼ in (6 mm) marks in seam allowance. Trim or clip at turns so the loops lie flat and close together. Tape loops in place, then machine-baste.

5. To attach loops of either type to garment, pin paper guide to appropriate side of garment on right side of fabric, matching ⅝ in (1.5 cm) line to seamline of garment. Remove tape and machine-baste next to first machine-basted line. Stitch carefully, making certain that the machine goes over the tubing without skipping. Then carefully tear the paper away.

6. Pin and baste facing to garment, right sides together. Loops will be between facing and garment. Then, from garment side (so you can use the previous stitching as a guide), stitch on the seamline. This will conceal the previous rows of basting. Use the "top feed" assist if your sewing machine has it. Grade seam allowances; turn facing to inside.

7. Trim and grade seam allowances. Fold the facing to the inside along seamline. Understitch, then press. Loops will extend beyond the garment edge. Lap this side of garment over opposite side, carefully matching finished edge to the button position line on the button side. Mark button locations, then sew buttons to garment at correct positions.

Thread 12 · Buttons 13 · Marking buttonholes 301

Attaching buttons — placement

Mark button positions when the garment is nearly completed and after the buttonholes or button loops are made. Although the button position line should be marked at the beginning of construction and button location can be tentatively marked, the location should be finally determined when buttonholes are finished. Lap buttonhole side of garment over button side as garment will be worn, matching center front or center back lines; pin securely between buttonholes.

To establish button position for *horizontal* buttonholes, place pin at end nearest the finished garment edge; for *vertical* buttonholes, place below the top of the buttonhole opening (see illustration at right). Carefully lift buttonhole over pin and re-fasten the pin securely at proper location. Center button at pin mark, directly on center line, and sew in place according to type of button you are using. In double-breasted garments, layers must be smooth and flat before positioning pins.

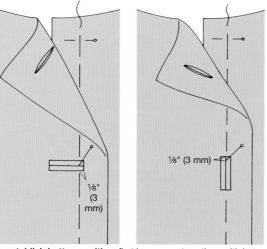

To establish button position, first lap garment sections with buttonholes on top and match up center lines. Push a pin through buttonhole ⅛ in (3 mm) from end to locate place for button.

Thread / needle choices

Buttons can be attached with any of several thread types, depending on the weight of the fabric. With **fine fabrics,** use spun polyester thread or a general-purpose sewing thread compatible with the fiber content of the fabric. For **light- to mediumweight fabrics,** use silk buttonhole twist or a general-purpose thread compatible with the fiber content of the fabric. For **heavy fabrics,** use silk buttonhole twist, heavy-duty thread, or button and carpet thread. Use nylon fishing line or dental floss for metal-shank buttons.

Use a single thread strand; double tends to knot. Waxing strengthens thread and smooths its glide through the fabric (especially recommended for silk twist). To wax, pass thread across a white wax candle or through a container of beeswax. The needle should be long enough to reach easily through the several thicknesses of button and fabric, but the diameter should not be greater than the holes in the button.

Shank buttons

There are two basic types of buttons: shank buttons and sew-through buttons. Shank buttons are those that have a little "neck," or shank, with a hole in it, on the lower side. The shank allows the button to rest on top of the buttonhole instead of crowding to the inside and distorting the buttonhole. The shank button is especially recommended for closures in garments made with heavy and bulky fabrics. If garment fabric is very bulky, as in a coat, it may be necessary to make an additional shank of thread below the regular shank to allow enough space for the buttonhole to fit under the button.

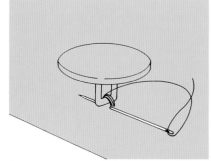

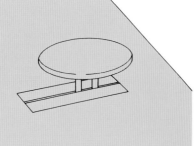

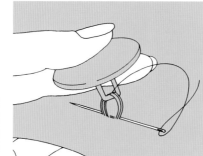

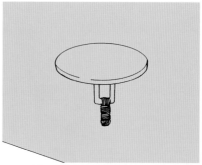

To sew a shank button onto fabric that is not very thick, first take enough small stitches through the fabric and the shank to make the button secure. Then position the button so that threads are parallel to the opening edge and the shank aligns with the buttonhole. This will keep the shank from spreading the buttonhole open. Fasten the thread between garment and facing with several stitches. Buttons used only as decoration are also sewn this way.

To make an additional thread shank, first take a few stitches where button is to be placed on the garment's right side. Holding forefinger between button and garment (this keeps the two apart until the button is secure), bring thread several times through shank and back into fabric. On last stitch, bring thread through button only, then wind thread tightly around stitches to form thread shank. Fasten securely on underside.

Sew-through buttons

A sew-through button has either two or four holes through which the button is sewn to the garment. When sewn flat, this button can be used as a closure only for very thin, lightweight fabrics, or as a decorative button. If a thread shank is added, the button can also be used to close heavy or bulky fabrics. The shank permits the closure to fasten smoothly and keeps the fabric from pulling unevenly around the buttons. The shank length should equal the garment thickness at the buttonhole plus ⅛ in (3 mm) for movement.

Buttons with four holes can be sewn on in a number of ways. Use thread in a color that contrasts with the button and treat the four holes as a grid for different arrangements of stitches. The thread can be worked through the holes to form a cross, a square, a feather or leaf shape, or two parallel lines. If the holes are large enough, narrow ribbon, braid, or cord can be used. (An eyelet may need to be worked in garment.) Run ribbon or braid through the holes in button and tie in a knot on wrong side of garment or on top of button.

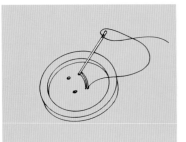

To sew button flat to a garment, take several small stitches at mark for the button location, then center button over marking and sew in place through holes in button. Fasten stitches on wrong side or between garment and facing.

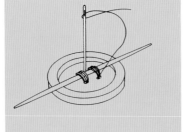

To make a thread shank, secure thread at button mark, then bring needle up through one hole in button. Lay a pin, matchstick, or toothpick across the top of the button. Take needle down through second hole (and up through third then down through

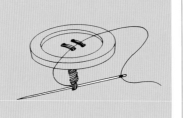

fourth, if a four-hole button); make about six stitches. Remove pin or stick, lift button away from fabric so stitches are taut, and wind the thread firmly around the stitches to make the shank. Backstitch into shank to secure.

Sewing on buttons by machine

A zigzag sewing machine can be used to sew on sew-through buttons. Check machine manual for exact instructions. A four-hole button may need to be sewn with two separate stitchings.

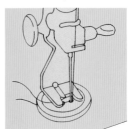

A button foot is included in some machine accessory boxes (some machines do not need special feet for sewing on buttons). The button foot holds the button in place while the needle stitches from side to side. Stitch width must equal the space between the holes in the button.

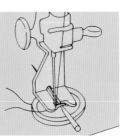

Some machines have button feet with adjustable shank guides. If your machine does not have such an attachment, push a machine needle into the groove on the ordinary button foot. The stitches pass over the shaft of this needle and form a shank. The thicker the needle shaft, the longer the shank.

Reinforcing buttons

Reinforcing buttons are useful at points of great strain and on garments of heavy materials. By taking the stress which is otherwise be on the fabric, they keep top buttons from tearing it.

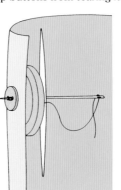

To add a reinforcing button, follow the steps for attaching a sew-through button with a shank, additionally placing a small flat button on inside of the garment directly under outer button. Sew as usual through all sets of holes (buttons should have same number of holes). On last stitch, bring needle through hole of top button only and complete shank. (If fabric is delicate, substitute a doubled square of fabric or seam binding for the small button.)

Alternative thread shank method

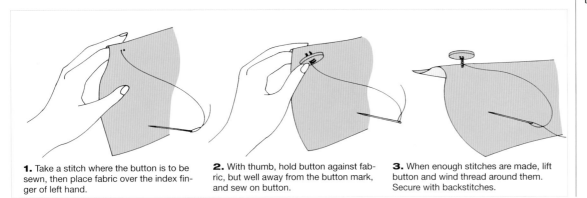

1. Take a stitch where the button is to be sewn, then place fabric over the index finger of left hand.

2. With thumb, hold button against fabric, but well away from the button mark, and sew on button.

3. When enough stitches are made, lift button and wind thread around them. Secure with backstitches.

Thread 12 · Buttons 13 · Running stitch 71 · Backstitch 72

Making buttons — fabric buttons

Use fabric buttons made to match the garment when suitable ready-made buttons cannot be found. There are many kits available for making such buttons. Covered buttons can also be made using plastic or bone rings, sold at notions counters.

1. Select a ring of the diameter required for the finished button. Cut a circle of fabric slightly less than twice the diameter of the ring.

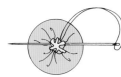

2. Using a double thread, sew around fabric circle, with a small running stitch, placing stitches close to edge. Leave thread and needle attached to fabric at the end of stitching.

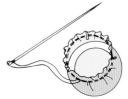

3. Place the ring in center of fabric circle. Gather the fabric around the ring by pulling on the needle and thread until the hand stitches bring the cut edges of fabric together.

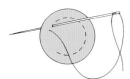

4. Secure the gathered-up fabric around ring by pulling up hand stitches tightly. Fasten with several short backstitches.

5. Decorate button by taking small backstitches around and close to ring, through both fabric layers. Use buttonhole twist. Attach button to garment with a thread shank.

Leather buttons

Leather buttons can be made using commercial cover-your-own kits. The easiest forms to cover are those with prongs all around the inside of the rim. Almost any type of leather, even fairly thick kinds, can be used. This is a practical way to use scraps and remnants.

1. Use the pattern in kit to cut a circle of leather for each button.

2. Center button front on wrong side of leather; shape leather over button, hooking it underneath small prongs on inside of rim. Work across the diameter of button, securing edges opposite one another.

3. When all excess leather is turned to the inside of the button, place button back over button front. Make sure that all cut edges are between button front and back, and that the leather is stretched smoothly over the front.

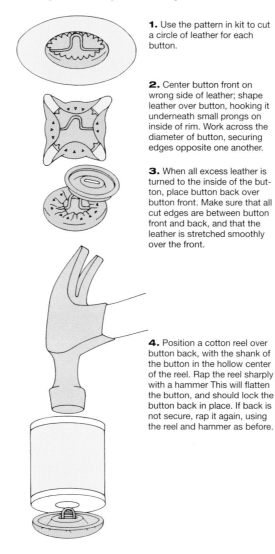

4. Position a cotton reel over button back, with the shank of the button in the hollow center of the reel. Rap the reel sharply with a hammer. This will flatten the button, and should lock the button back in place. If back is not secure, rap it again, using the reel and hammer as before.

Chinese ball buttons

Chinese ball buttons can be made with ready-made cord or braid, or your own tubing (p. 315). Make a test button, keeping size of tubing proportionate to button size: use 3⁄16 in (5 mm) tubing for a 1⁄2 in (1.25 cm) button; 3⁄8 in (1 cm) tubing for a 1 in (2.5 cm) button.

1. Pin one end of tubing securely to a piece of paper. Loop the cord once as shown.

2. Loop a second time over first loop, then go under end. Keep seam of tubing down at all times as you work.

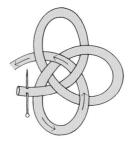

3. Loop a third time, weaving through the first two loops. Take care that the tubing does not get twisted at any point in either looping or weaving.

4. Gradually tighten up on loops, easing them into a ball shape. Trim the ends of the tubing and sew them flat to the underside of the button.

Hooks and eyes 13 · Whipstitch 73 · Blanket stitch 78

Hooks and eyes — types and uses

Hooks and eyes are small but comparatively strong fasteners. Though they are most often applied at single points of a garment opening, such as a waistband, they can also be used to fasten an entire opening.

There are several types of hooks and eyes, each designed to serve a particular purpose. General-purpose hooks and eyes are the smallest and are used primarily as supplementary fasteners such as at the top of a zipper placket. This type ranges in size from fine (0) to heavy (3) and are mainly finished in either black or nickel. Special-purpose hooks and eyes, such as those for coats, are larger and heavier, and so can withstand more strain. Covered fasteners can be used where a less conspicuous application is desired. You can buy these ready-made or make them yourself. You can also make your own thread eye using the blanket stitch method described below.

As a general rule of thumb, the straight eye is used on lapped edges, the round eye for abutted edges.

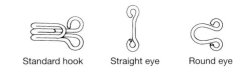

Standard hook   Straight eye   Round eye

Attaching hooks and eyes

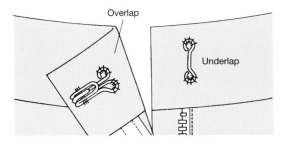

Overlap

Underlap

With lapped edges, the hook is sewn on the inside of the garment, the eye on the outside. Place *hook* on the underside of overlap, about ⅛ in (3 mm) from the edge. Whipstitch over each hole. Pass needle and thread through fabric to end of hook; whipstitch around end to hold it flat against garment. Mark on the outside of the underlap where the end of the hook falls — this is the position for the eye. Hold *straight eye* in place and whipstitch over one hole. Pass needle and thread through fabric and whipstitch other hole.

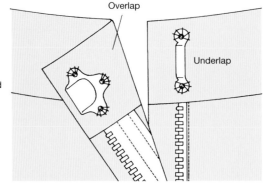

Overlap

Underlap

For use on waistbands of skirts or pants, special hook and eye sets are available. They are strong and flat, and designed so that the hook cannot easily slide off the eye. They can be used only for lapped edges. Position and sew on the hook and eye as for a lapped application of a standard hook and eye (end of hook need not be secured).

Thread eyes

A thread eye is a substitute for the metal eye. It is less conspicuous than a metal eye. There are two ways to form a thread eye: **1. the blanket stitch method** (the stronger of the two) and **2. the thread chain method.** For both methods, use a single or double strand of

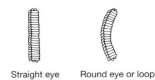

Straight eye   Round eye or loop

heavy-duty thread or buttonhole twist in a color that matches the fabric.

A *straight eye* should be as long as the space between its two placement marks.

Blanket stitch method

1. Sew hook to one edge of the garment by the lapped method (see above). Close the placket and mark beginning and end positions for eye on other edge.

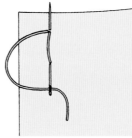

2. Insert the needle into the fabric at one mark and bring it up at the other mark. Take 2 or 3 more stitches in the same way; secure. (If the eye is round, let the thread curve into the intended size.)

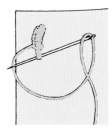

3. Being careful not to catch the fabric, cover all of the strands of thread with closely spaced blanket stitches. When finished, bring needle and thread to the underside and secure stitching.

Awl 13 · Hooks and eyes 13 · Whipstitch 73 · Seaming pile fabrics 99

Hooks and eyes on fur garments

Large, covered hooks and eyes are sometimes used as fasteners for fur garments. Because of the difficulty of hand sewing through furs, a special lapped method is used for attaching hooks and eyes. The hooks are inserted into the seamline of the overlapping edge, and the ends of the eyes passed through punctures to the underside of the opposite edge. (If garment has no overlap, both hooks and eyes can be inserted into the seamlines.) Underlining or interfacing the garment opening will facilitate the sewing of hooks and eyes. Do not machine understitch the seamlines; instead, hand understitch after attaching the hooks and eyes.

Attaching the hooks

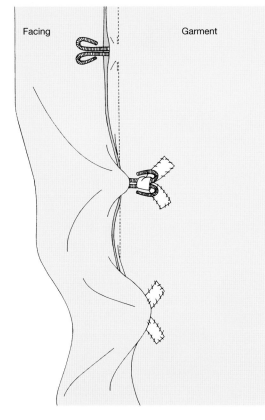

Hooks in fur garments extend out from the seamline of the overlapping garment edge. Before stitching this seam, mark on the seamline the position of each hook. When stitching, leave a ¼ in (6 mm) opening at each mark. Then proceed as follows.

1. Working from the wrong side of the garment, open out the facing. With the curve of the hook toward the facing, insert the hook through a ¼ in (6 mm) opening and allow curve of hook to wrap around to right side of facing.

2. Pass a 3 in (7.5 cm) length of ¼ in (6 mm) twill tape under the stem of the hook. Cross the tape ends, then pull on them to bring the stem of the hook to the garment. Pin tape ends to garment and whipstitch in place. Make sure that hand stitches do not show on the finished side of the garment.

3. Repeat Steps 1 and 2 for each hook. Then secure the facing to the twill tape, using small, close whipstitches.

Attaching the eyes

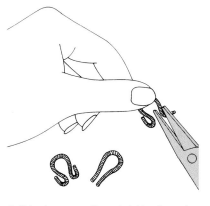

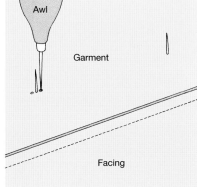

1. Using long-nose pliers, straighten the ends of each eye. This prepares the ends so that they can be passed through to the inside of the garment and then sewn in place.

2. Pin-mark the position for each eye on the underlap. From garment inside, pierce garment ¼ in (6 mm) to each side of each pin. If necessary, hand-finish holes (make eyelets).

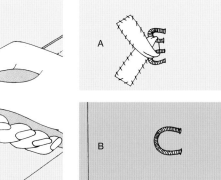

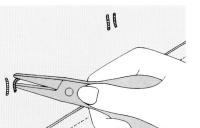

3. Insert ends of each eye into holes until just enough of the eye remains on right side of the garment for the hook to catch. Using the long-nose pliers, reshape ends of each eye to form open loops.

4. Pass a 3 in (7.5 cm) length of ¼ in (6 mm) twill tape under the stem of the eye and cross the ends. Pin the tape to the garment and whipstitch in place (A), making sure the stitches do not show on the finished side (B).

Snap fasteners 13 · Running stitch 71 · Whipstitch 73

Snap fasteners — basic application

Snap fasteners have less holding power than hooks and eyes. General-purpose metal snaps range in size from fine to heavy; finishes are either nickel or black. Clear plastic snap fasteners are also available. Fabric-covered snap fasteners can be purchased but you can also make them yourself (see instructions at far right). They are useful on garments such as jackets, as they are not apparent when the garment is worn.

The no-sew snap is a strong fastener that is cleated into the garment fabric. This type also comes in heavy-duty forms for use on overalls and canvas or leather, and with decorative tops. See packages for instructions.

Special applications

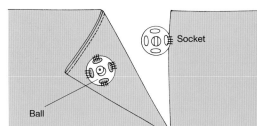

An extended snap fastener is used on abutted garment edges. Attach ball half of snap to underside of one garment edge. Position socket half at the other garment edge; whipstitch over only one of the holes to secure socket to edge.

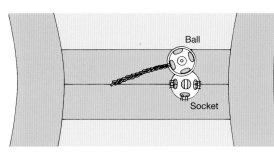

Lingerie strap guards are attached to underside of a shoulder seam. Sew socket of snap fastener to seam, ¾ in (2 cm) from the center of shoulder, toward neck edge. For a *thread chain guard* (above), start chain about 1½ in (4 cm) from snap socket. Form a 1½ in (4 cm) chain (p. 320). Take a few whipstitches over one hole

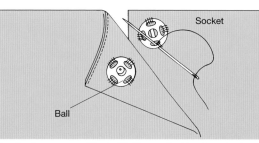

To attach a snap, position ball half on underside of overlap far enough in from edge so it will not show; whipstitch over each hole. Rub chalk on ball, then transfer to right side of underlap, in order to locate proper position of socket half. Position socket half to align with ball; whipstitch over each hole.

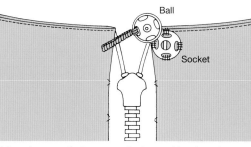

A hanging snap fastener can also be used for abutted garment edges. Attach socket half to underside of one garment edge. To attach the ball half to the other edge, use the blanket stitch method for forming a thread eye (p. 320).

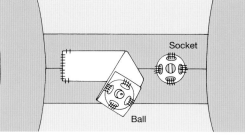

of a ball half of snap; pass needle and thread through chain and fasten in garment. For a tape guard (above), use a 2¼ in (6 cm) length of tape. Turn under one end ¼ in (6 mm); whipstitch to garment 1½ in (4 cm) from snap socket. Turn under free end of tape ⅝ in (1.5 cm) and sew ball half to underside.

Covering snap fasteners

To cover snap fasteners yourself, choose large snaps and a lightweight fabric that is color-matched to the garment. Cover following the instructions below, then attach the fastener to the garment. To keep the fabric covering from fraying, lightly coat the edges with clear nail polish or a commercial anti-fray solution before sewing to garment.

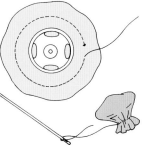

1. For each snap half, cut out a circle of fabric twice the diameter of the snap. Place small running stitches around and close to edge of fabric. Place snap half face down on fabric and draw up on stitches.

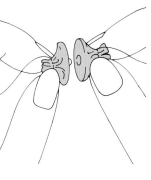

2. Push covered ball half into covered socket half — this will cut the fabric and expose the ball.

3. Pull the snap apart. Draw stitches up tightly and secure. Trim excess fabric on the underside; whipstitch over edges if necessary (A). Attach snap to garment (B).

Tape fasteners — types and uses

Tape fasteners are made in three types: **snap, hook and eye,** and **hook and loop.** Tapes are practical for cushion covers and loose covers, for children's clothing, and for such items as quilt covers, because they permit easy removal for laundering.

Uses and applications differ, so it is difficult to specify rules about fabric allowances for finishing edges. If a pattern calls for a tape fastener, the allowances will be given. When you determine for yourself how to cut fabric pieces, as with loose covers, these allowances are your decision. Allow, for example, a double seam allowance for the underlap in a lapped application.

Top and bottom edges of tape fasteners are usually caught into cross-seams and need no further finishing. Never let metal parts of any fastener extend into seams.

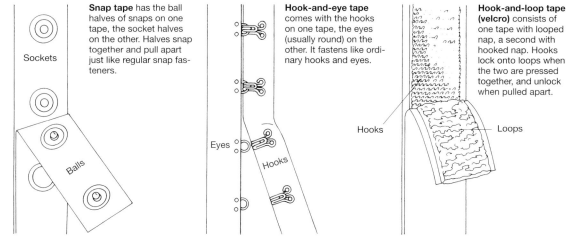

Snap tape has the ball halves of snaps on one tape, the socket halves on the other. Halves snap together and pull apart just like regular snap fasteners.

Sockets · Balls

Hook-and-eye tape comes with the hooks on one tape, the eyes (usually round) on the other. It fastens like ordinary hooks and eyes.

Eyes · Hooks

Hook-and-loop tape (velcro) consists of one tape with looped nap, a second with hooked nap. Hooks lock onto loops when the two are pressed together, and unlock when pulled apart.

Hooks · Loops

Applying tape fasteners

Overlap · Underlap

Overlap · Underlap

Snap tape requires a lapped application because of the way the ball half must enter the socket half. Both garment edges should be wider than the tapes; for greater strength, cut a double-width seam allowance for the underlap. Position the socket tape on underlap and stitch around all edges through all layers. Place ball tape on underside of overlap, align ball halves with sockets, and stitch around all edges through all layers. For a less obvious application, stitch ball tape to underlayer of overlap, fold edge under, and stitch along free edge through all layers.

Hook-and-eye tape calls for a centered application because hooks and eyes must abut to be fastened. As with snap fastener tape, both garment edges should be wider than the tapes. To apply, position hook tape on the underlayer of one edge, with hooks along fold. Stitch through both layers around each hook. Fold edge and stitch through all layers along the free edge (make sure needle does not hit hooks). Stitch eye half to the opposite edge in the same way, aligning eyes with hooks and positioning eyes just beyond fold. Again, make sure that the needle does not hit the metal parts of the fastener.

Hook-and-loop tape must be lapped for the two halves to fasten. Because the hooks and loops lock on contact, application to an open seam is best; this lets them stay separate during application. Garment edges should be wider than the tapes; for extra strength, cut a double-width seam allowance for the underlap. Position the hook tape on underlap; stitch around all of the edges through all layers. Align and position the loop tape on overlap; stitch through all layers. For a less obvious application, stitch the loop tape to underlayer of overlap, fold the edge under, and stitch along the free edge.

CHAPTER 10

TAILORING

Using tailoring techniques to create a garment requires more than the usual amount of time, attention to detail, and patience. Your efforts will be well rewarded by a long-lasting garment that fits perfectly.

Tailoring basics

To many, "tailoring" suggests sewing meant only for "experts." Yet, tailoring is just a refinement of standard sewing procedures, aimed at building *permanent* shape into a garment. Classic tailoring does, however, require more than the usual amount of detail work, including padstitching lapels and the under collar, lining, precise fitting, and emphasis of figure lines.

Advance considerations

A successful tailored garment begins long before a stitch is sewed — with an understanding of pressing methods, fabric choices, and the special fitting requirements of tailored styles.

Pressing equipment

An ironing board and a steam iron are, of course, standard equipment; in addition to these, a tailor's ham is needed to press shaped areas. Although a sleeve board is not absolutely necessary, it can be very useful during tailoring. Other valuable pressing aids include the seam roll and press mitt (see p. 14). When pressing the right side of fabric, always use a press cloth to prevent fabric shine. To produce additional steam, use a dampened cloth, but allow that pressed area to dry before handling. Avoid pressing seams so flat that their edges mark through to the right side of the fabric.

Selecting a pattern

When selecting a pattern for a tailored garment, choose one that suits your style and matches the other items in your wardrobe, as you will be investing many hours of work in your tailored garment. If possible, select a pattern designed for tailoring; that way, all the necessary pattern pieces, such as separate under collar and lining, will be included.

Selecting garment fabric

After choosing your pattern, select a fabric that is appropriate for the style. You may want to consult the pattern envelope for fabric recommendations. Keep in mind that wools and wool blends shape and mold well when pressed and are thus excellent choices for tailoring. Other suitable fabrics include firmly woven linens, double knits, and heavy silks. Limp fabrics cannot generally be molded or shaped and so are poor choices. When purchasing fabric, be aware of fabric nap (print or pile), if any, and buy yardage (meterage) accordingly.

Selecting underlying fabrics

To give the tailored garment adequate body, and to maintain its shape, the garment fabric must be used in combination with various underlying fabrics. These fabrics include **underlining, interfacing,** and **lining;** interlining is sometimes used for additional warmth. Each of three underlying fabrics must be carefully selected so that when they are combined, the garment will look natural and not be unduly stiff. (See p. 24.)

Underlining is attached to the wrong side of the garment fabric before the garment units are connected. The underlining helps maintain the shape of the garment as well as supplying additional strength and durability. However, the use of underlining is rare today. Although most underlinings are lightweight, they can still vary in fiber content and in the type of finish (soft, medium, or crisp). Select the one that is most complementary to the garment fabric and is similar in color; also consider its care compatibility.

Interfacing provides support and shape in designated areas such as collar, lapels, upper back, and hemline. Interfacings are available in different weights, fiber contents, forms (woven and nonwoven), type (fusible and sew-in), and degrees of crispness. For tailoring, a woven hair canvas is often best, as it shapes well. Select a hair canvas of a suitable weight for the garment and of good quality (usually with a high goat hair content and a balanced weave of even-sized warp and weft yarns).

Lining, the last fabric layer to be attached, conceals the inner construction of the garment to give a clean finish on the inside. The lining lies next to the skin, so a smooth, silky fabric is usually recommended. Linings are available in different fiber contents and in a range of weights from light to heavy. Choose a lining that is of a proper weight and is compatible, in care requirements, with the other fabrics; it should also be sturdy enough to withstand normal garment wear. Since the lining is usually visible, its color should match or be coordinated with the garment fabric.

Pattern alterations

As in all construction situations, the patterns for a tailored garment must be altered to size before fabrics are cut; major changes are difficult to make after a garment is cut and sewed, so flat pattern alterations are critical. For more specific information, turn to the section on Basic pattern alterations. When comparing pattern and figure measurements, remember that the minimum ease required in a tailored jacket is slightly more than in a standard dress, and the minimum ease in a coat is slightly more than in a jacket; take into consideration, also, the designed-in fullness of your particular garment style. If you are in serious doubt as to the fit of your garment, take the time to make up a test garment, then transfer all the alterations made on that garment onto the flat pattern.

Patterns for interfacing

Pattern pieces for interfacing vary from pattern to pattern. Some provide only a partial front and back interfacing; others may supply pattern pieces with seam allowances already trimmed; still others specify use of the same pattern piece for cutting both facing and interfacing. To give support and shape across the chest area and upper back of the tailored garment, full front and back interfacing pieces are recommended. If your pattern does not contain such interfacing pieces, make up your own from the main pattern pieces. Follow the directions below after you have made the basic pattern alterations, then transfer all markings to the new pattern. For a knit, use a two-piece interfacing across the back, as described on page 337.

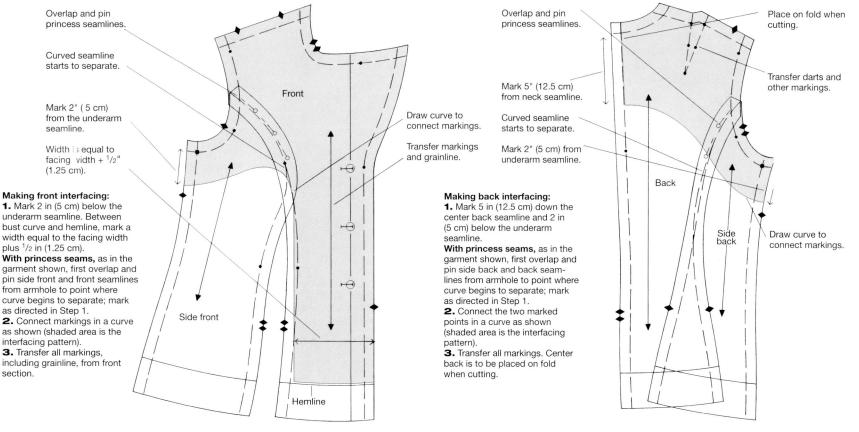

Overlap and pin princess seamlines.

Curved seamline starts to separate.

Mark 2" (5 cm) from the underarm seamline.

Width is equal to facing width + 1/2" (1.25 cm).

Front

Draw curve to connect markings.

Transfer markings and grainline.

Making front interfacing:
1. Mark 2 in (5 cm) below the underarm seamline. Between bust curve and hemline, mark a width equal to the facing width plus 1/2 in (1.25 cm).
With princess seams, as in the garment shown, first overlap and pin side front and front seamlines from armhole to point where curve begins to separate; mark as directed in Step 1.
2. Connect markings in a curve as shown (shaded area is the interfacing pattern).
3. Transfer all markings, including grainline, from front section.

Side front

Hemline

Overlap and pin princess seamlines.

Mark 5" (12.5 cm) from neck seamline.

Curved seamline starts to separate.

Mark 2" (5 cm) from underarm seamline.

Place on fold when cutting.

Transfer darts and other markings.

Back

Side back

Draw curve to connect markings.

Making back interfacing:
1. Mark 5 in (12.5 cm) down the center back seamline and 2 in (5 cm) below the underarm seamline.
With princess seams, as in the garment shown, first overlap and pin side back and back seamlines from armhole to point where curve begins to separate; mark as directed in Step 1.
2. Connect the two marked points in a curve as shown (shaded area is the interfacing pattern).
3. Transfer all markings. Center back is to be placed on fold when cutting.

TAILORING

Cutting

Before cutting, prepare the fabric as described in the Cutting section, straightening and re-aligning the fabric ends, and preshrinking the garment and underlining fabrics if necessary. If using wool, preshrink it by thoroughly steam-pressing the fabric. Work on small sections at a time, keeping grainlines straight.

Lay the pattern pieces out according to the pattern instructions. As a precaution, leave 1 in (2.5 cm) seam allowances on all side seams as you cut (see illustration); do the same when cutting underlining. Cut out the interfacing and lining pieces.

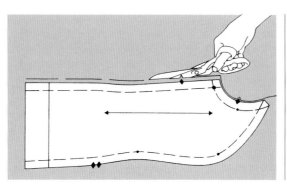

Marking

Markings for all garment pieces must be carefully transferred to each fabric layer. The recommended methods of marking, and the markings most likely to be transferred to garment fabric, underlining, and interfacing, are shown below. Note that the marking methods most often used in tailoring include tailor's tacks and thread tracings as well as tracing paper and wheel (see Fabric-marking methods).

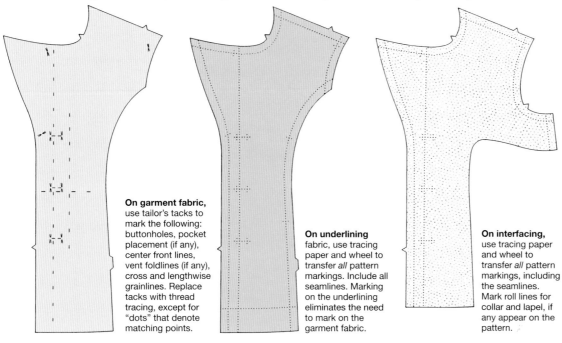

On garment fabric, use tailor's tacks to mark the following: buttonholes, pocket placement (if any), center front lines, vent foldlines (if any), cross and lengthwise grainlines. Replace tacks with thread tracing, except for "dots" that denote matching points.

On underlining fabric, use tracing paper and wheel to transfer *all* pattern markings. Include all seamlines. Marking on the underlining eliminates the need to mark on the garment fabric.

On interfacing, use tracing paper and wheel to transfer *all* pattern markings, including the seamlines. Mark roll lines for collar and lapel, if any appear on the pattern.

Basting underlining to fabric

If underlining is being used, the two layers of fabric are then basted together (see below) so they can be handled as one (see Underlinings). Note that, for easier comprehension, the diagonal basting threads have been eliminated in drawings that follow.

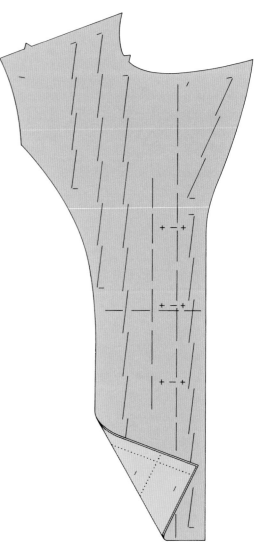

Hand basting stitches 70–71 · Darts 101–103

Underlining

There are two methods of underlining a garment. In the first, the two fabric layers (underlining fabric and garment fabric) are always treated as one layer. In the second method, the two fabrics are handled separately up to construction of darts, then handled as one.

With either method, the underlining must be repositioned in relation to the face fabric before garment sections are seamed. This is because a garment, on

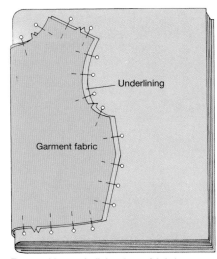

To reposition underlining, baste fabric layers together down center or one edge. Wrap fabrics around a thick magazine with underlining next to magazine. Smooth out fabrics; pin together, as they fall, along the edges.

the body, is cylindrical; the underlining, which will lie closer to the body, must be made into a slightly smaller cylinder than the one formed by the outer fabric. After repositioning, trim excess underlining, then mark new underlining seamlines (use sewing gauge and chalk) to align with garment fabric seamlines.

Method 1: Treating two layers as one

Of the two underlining methods, the technique shown and described below, in which garment and underlining fabrics are treated as one throughout, is used more often. The underlining layer will reinforce all construction details, including darts, and will prevent them from showing through to the outside of the garment.

1. Cut out entire garment from the garment fabric. It is not necessary to transfer pattern markings to garment fabric; the underlining fabric will be marked and it will be uppermost during garment construction.

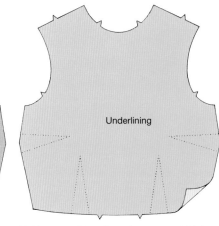

2. Remove pattern pieces from garment fabric sections. Decide which garment sections will be underlined and pin those pattern pieces to the underlining fabric. Cut out; transfer all pattern markings to the right side.

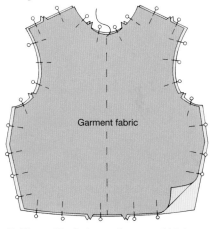

3. Wrong sides facing, center garment fabric over underlining. Baste fabrics together — down center of wide sections, along one edge of narrow pieces. Align basting with spine of magazine and reposition underlining (see left).

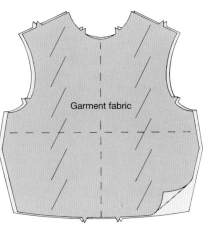

4. Remove fabric layers from magazine. With garment fabric uppermost, baste across center, then diagonal-baste a few rows within section. Remove pins; trim underlining at edges; mark new seamlines to match those on face fabric.

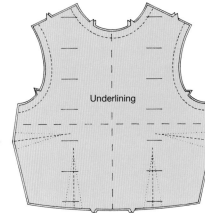

5. With underlining fabric uppermost, stay-stitch, where necessary, through both fabric layers. Machine-baste, through both fabrics, down the center of each dart, starting 2 to 3 stitches beyond the point of each dart.

6. Fold each dart along its center. Match, pin, baste, and stitch each dart; remove hand basting and the machine basting that extends beyond dart points. Press each dart flat, then in the proper direction (see Darts).

Method 2: Handling layers separately

In this method, the garment and under-lining fabric layers are handled and sewn separately from the marking and staystitching stage up to dart construction. The separately prepared layers are then basted together and handled as a single layer. The underlining layer will reinforce and prevent the *seams,* but not the *darts,* from showing through to the outside. Underlining this way will give the inside of the garment a more finished look than will the method shown on page 329.

1. While pattern is still pinned to the cut garment fabric sections, transfer all the pattern markings to the wrong side. Method of marking will depend on the fabric (see Fabric-marking methods). Bodice above was marked with a tracing wheel.

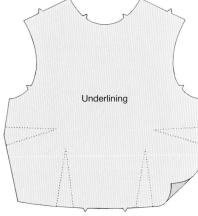

2. Remove pattern pieces from marked garment sections. Decide which garment sections are to be underlined and pin these pattern pieces to the underlining fabric. Cut out; transfer all pattern markings to the wrong side.

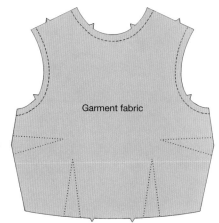

3. So that the edges will not stretch during han-dling, staystitch along the edges of each garment fabric section where necessary. Place stitching just inside the seamline and stitch directionally (see Directional stitching).

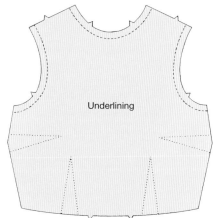

4. Also staystitch underlining sections as necessary to keep their edges from stretching in handling. Machine settings may need adjustment, since underlining fabric is usually lighter in weight than face fabric.

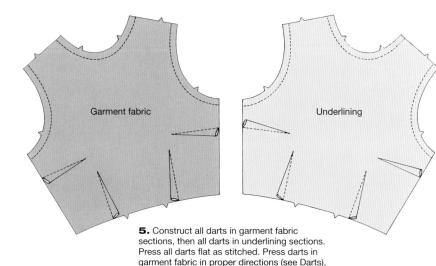

5. Construct all darts in garment fabric sections, then all darts in underlining sections. Press all darts flat as stitched. Press darts in garment fabric in proper directions (see Darts), corresponding darts in underlining fabric in opposite directions.

6. Wrong sides facing, center garment fabric over underlining. Baste fabrics together — down center of wide sections, along one edge of narrow pieces. Align basting with spine of magazine and reposition underlining (see p. 329).

7. Remove garment sections from magazine. With garment fabric uppermost, baste across center, then diagonal-baste a few rows within section. Remove pins; trim away excess underlining; mark new underlining seamlines.

Fitting shell 47 · Uneven basting stitch 70 · Running stitch 71 · Staystitching 84

Preparation for first fitting

Proper fit is all-important to the look of your tailored garment; to obtain this fit, your garment will go through not one but a number of fittings along the way. The first fitting is probably the most important one. It is at this point that the general fit of the garment is checked and roll lines on the collar and lapels are established. To prepare for this fitting, all darts and internal seams are first basted. If possible, the clipping of any seam allowance should be avoided until the seam is permanently stitched. The interfacings are in place, and the main sections then basted together. Before starting this preparation, staystitch the necklines of each garment section (see Staystitching). If a test garment has already been made and fitted, this first fitting is usually not necessary; simply proceed with construction after making needed alterations.

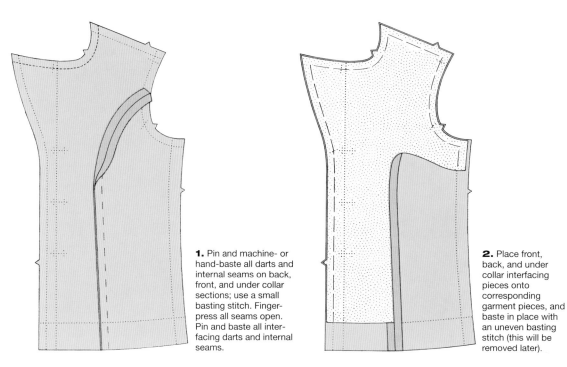

1. Pin and machine- or hand-baste all darts and internal seams on back, front, and under collar sections; use a small basting stitch. Finger-press all seams open. Pin and baste all interfacing darts and internal seams.

2. Place front, back, and under collar interfacing pieces onto corresponding garment pieces, and baste in place with an uneven basting stitch (this will be removed later).

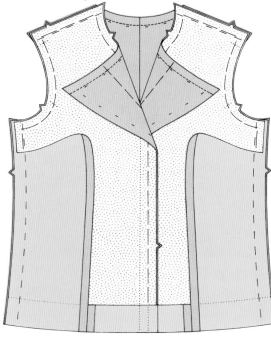

3. With right sides together, pin and baste front sections to back at shoulder and side seams. Finger-press seams open.

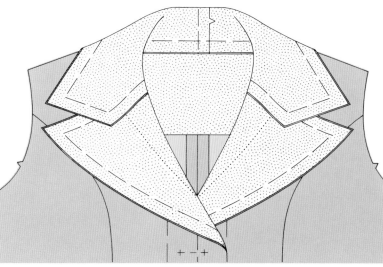

4. Lap right side of under collar over wrong side of garment neckline, matching markings and aligning seamlines; pin in place, starting from center back and working toward center front. Baste on seamline through all thicknesses.

First fitting

Most of the necessary adjustments should be noted during the first fitting of the garment shell; the garment seams at that stage are only basted together, and alterations can be easily made. To get an accurate fit, the garment shell should ideally be worn by the person for whom it is intended, with another person checking for fitting details. If the completed garment is to be worn with another piece of clothing, such as a blouse, that should also be worn during the fitting. If fitting on the real model is not possible, the next best choice is a dress form in the proper size.

Place the garment shell on the model, and adjust the garment so the shoulder seams are lying squarely on the shoulder line. If shoulder pads are to be used, position them in the garment. Align the center lines on each front section and pin the front opening together. Roll back the lapels and under collar so they are lying smoothly. Pin the hemline up so the length and proportion of the garment can be checked.

Examine the fit of the garment: Is there ample ease around the bust, waist, and hip areas? Are the darts or princess seams properly positioned over the bust? Are the lengthwise and crosswise grains straight? Are such details as buttonholes, pockets, and flaps marked at flattering positions? Now check the roll of the lapel and collar: Is the collar stand at a comfortable height? Does the fall of the under collar cover the neck seam-line? If the lapel/collar fit is satisfactory, pin-mark the roll lines on both under collar and lapels.

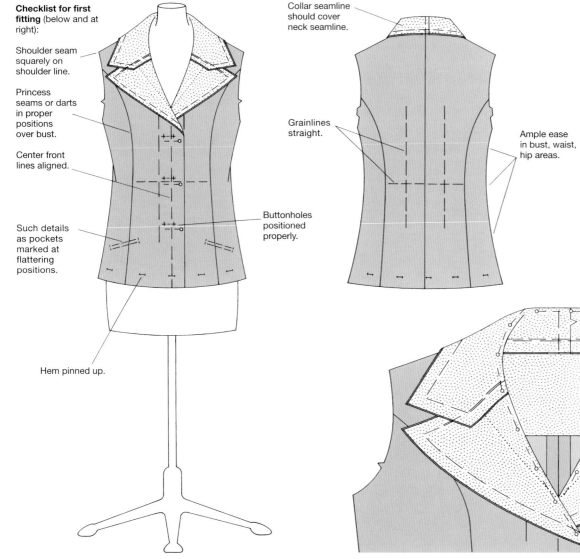

Checklist for first fitting (below and at right):

Shoulder seam squarely on shoulder line.

Princess seams or darts in proper positions over bust.

Center front lines aligned.

Such details as pockets marked at flattering positions.

Hem pinned up.

Collar seamline should cover neck seamline.

Grainlines straight.

Ample ease in bust, waist, hip areas.

Buttonholes positioned properly.

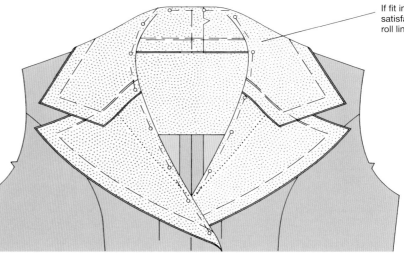

If fit in lapel/collar area is satisfactory, pin-mark the roll lines.

Pressing equipment 14 · Flat catchstitch 81 · Princess seams, Darts 100–103 · Pockets 234–251 · Bound buttonholes 300–311

Construction procedure

When the garment shell has been fitted, remove the bastings and separate the main sections. Remove the interfacing pieces as well and thread-trace the pinned roll line markings onto them. If alterations are needed, make all necessary changes on the garment and interfacing units; once these are completed, the permanent construction of the tailored garment can begin.

To start construction, complete all internal seams within the main garment sections (see below), and all darts as well. To eliminate bulk from each dart, slash through its center to within ¹/₂ to 1 in (1. 25 to 2.5 cm)

of its point, and press dart open over a tailor's ham. To keep the dart flat, catchstitch its raw edges to the underlining (see right).

Apply interfacings to the garment while the front and back sections are still separate. Carefully padstitch the lapels and under collar, and apply preshrunk ¹/₄ in (6 mm) twill tape to designated seams on the front sections to help prevent stretching and to define lapel and roll lines. After the main sections are joined, stitch the under collar to the assembled unit, and, lastly, attach the upper collar/facing unit.

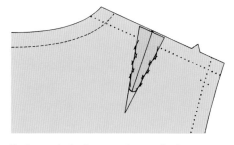

Darts are slashed open and pressed; edges are then catchstitched flat to underlining, if used.

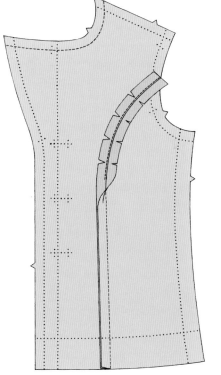

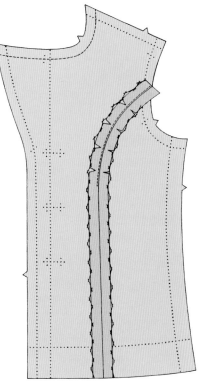

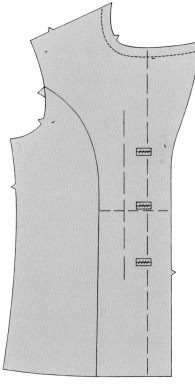

1. With right sides of fabric always together, match, pin, and stitch all the internal seams and darts on both the front and back sections. (Clip and notch princess seams if the garment has them.) Press each seam flat, then press it open over a tailor's ham.

2. Finish darts as described at the top of the page. To ensure that internal seams lie flat, catchstitch their seam allowances to the underlining; take care that the stitches do not catch the garment fabric below. Re-press each dart and seam over a tailor's ham.

3. At this point in the process, make bound buttonholes on the garment front, following the appropriate instructions in the Buttonhole section. At this same stage, construct pockets, if the garment is to have them, following instructions in the section on Pockets.

Padding stitch 71 · Flat catchstitch 81 · Darts in interfacing 106

Interfacing — applying front interfacing

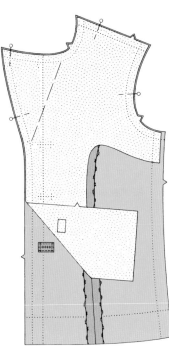

1. Construct any darts that appear on front interfacings. Position and pin front interfacing pieces onto front garment sections. On right front section only, check whether buttonhole markings on interfacing are lying exactly over bound buttonholes on garment; cut out rectangular openings on the interfacing, following the buttonhole markings.

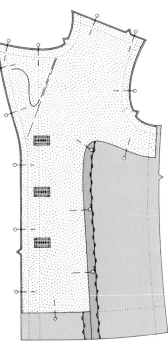

2. Pull raw edges of bound buttonholes through cut openings in interfacing. Baste through all fabric layers along the thread-traced roll line. Remove the thread tracing.

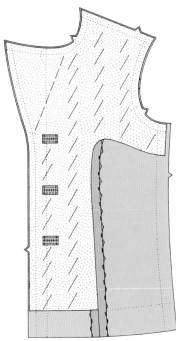

3. Hold interfacing in place, using a large parallel padstitch outside the lapel area. If using underlining, catch only the under-lining fabric, and do not stitch into any seam allowances.

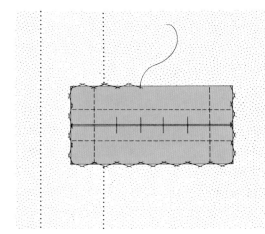

4. To secure the raw edges of bound buttonholes, catchstitch them to the interfacing.

5. Fill in lapel area with short chevron padstitching; catch only a yarn or two of the garment fabric below. Start at the roll line and shape the lapel, rolling it over your hand as shown. Do not padstitch into any of the seam allowances.

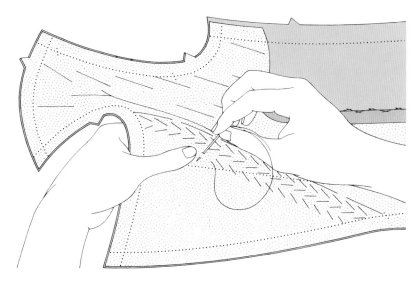

Pressing equipment 14 · Whipstitch 73 · Flat catchstitch 81

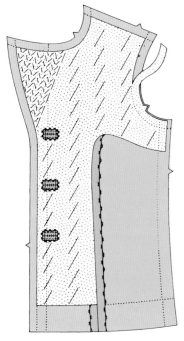

6. Trim away interfacing seam allowances from the front opening, upper lapel, neck, shoulder, armhole, and the side seam edges.

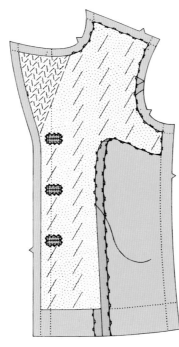

7. Catchstitch the trimmed interfacing edges along the neck, shoulder, armhole, and side seams to the underlining or fabric; catchstitch inner edges of the interfacing as well.

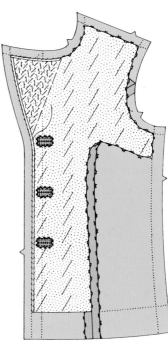

8. To stay seamlines along front opening and upper lapel edges, pin preshrunk $1/4$ in (6 mm) twill tape onto the garment with one edge against the seamline; cut the tape ends so that they meet rather than overlap. Whipstitch both tape edges to interfacing.

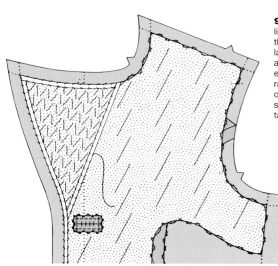

9. To stay the lapel roll line, pin the twill tape onto the garment, outside the lapel area with one edge along the roll line. Cut tape ends so that they meet rather than overlap the other taped edges. Whip-stitch both edges of the tape to the interfacing.

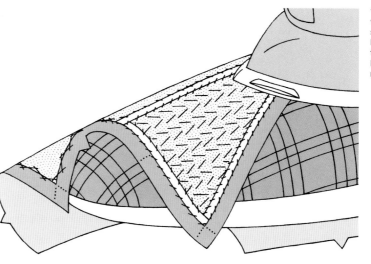

10. Position the lapel, wrong side up, over a seam roll or tailor's ham, and steam-press to shape and set the lapel roll. Let dry in rolled position.

Darts in interfacing 106 · Parallel padding stitch 71 · Flat catchstitch 81

Applying back interfacing

Back interfacing provides the necessary support for the upper back and underarm of a tailored garment. You can apply back interfacing by one of two methods. The first utilizes a one-piece interfacing (see p. 327 for instructions on making its pattern) and is the method most often used, especially if the tailoring fabric is woven. Unlike the front interfacing, the one-piece back interfacing does not require fine padstitching, only long parallel padstitches to hold the inter-

facing in place. The second method, using a two-piece interfacing, is ideal for knit fabrics; the two interfacing pieces are not secured with long padstitches and so are free to give with the movement of the knit fabric.

Darts in the back interfacing, like those in the front, are handled in a special way so that much of their bulk is eliminated. The lapped method, shown at right, is one such way. Directions for this and other methods are given in the section on Interfacing.

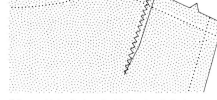

A lapped interfacing dart helps to eliminate some bulk in the dart area.

One-piece method

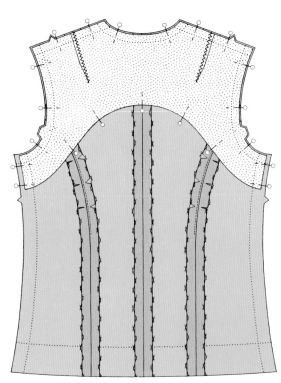

1. Construct all darts that occur on the interfacing unit. Position the interfacing on the wrong side of the garment, matching all of the markings. Pin around the edges.

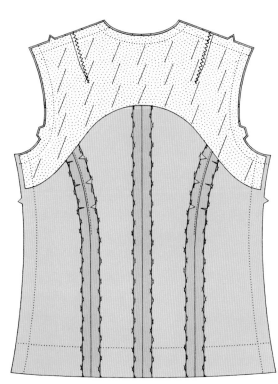

2. Secure the interfacing to the garment, using long parallel padstitches (see p. 71); do not padstitch into any of the seam allowances.

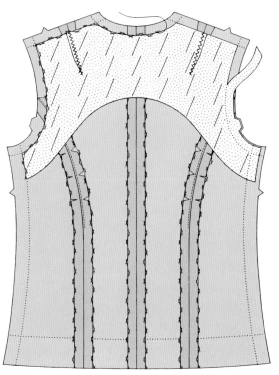

3. Trim away all of the interfacing seam allowances along the neck, shoulder, armhole, and side seam edges. Catchstitch the cut edges to the garment seam allowances.

Uneven basting stitch 70 · Flat catchstitch 81

Two-piece method

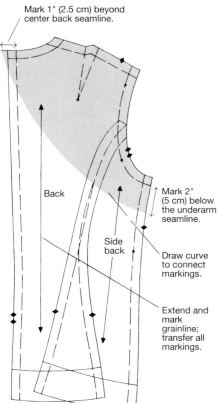

Mark 1" (2.5 cm) beyond center back seamline.

Back

Mark 2" (5 cm) below the underarm seamline.

Side back

Draw curve to connect markings.

Extend and mark grainline; transfer all markings.

To make a back interfacing pattern:
1. Mark 1" (2.5 cm) beyond the center back seam on pattern.
2. Mark 2" (5 cm) below underarm seamline.
3. Draw a curve connecting the two points (shaded area is interfacing).
If garment has princess seams, as shown, first overlap and pin side back and back seamlines from armhole to point where curve begins to separate; mark as directed.
4. Transfer all markings. Extend and mark the grainline.

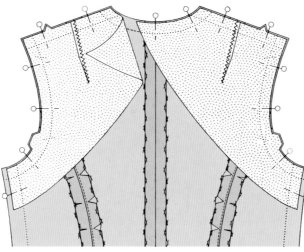

1. Construct darts on back interfacing units. Position and pin the interfacing units to wrong side of garment, matching markings. Edges at center back should overlap.

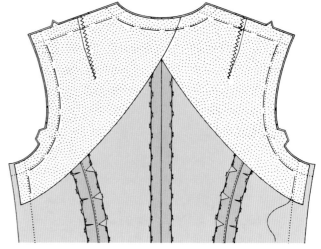

2. Secure interfacing to garment, using an uneven basting stitch, around the neck, shoulder, armhole, and side seam edges; place basting within garment side of seamline.

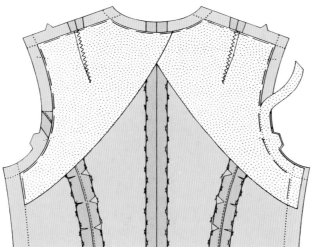

3. Trim away all interfacing seam allowances along the neck, shoulder, armhole, and side seam edges. Be careful not to pull or shift the interfacing while working.

4. Catchstitch trimmed edges to garment seam allowances; remove the bastings. The back interfacing is now secured in place but is still allowed some give across the back.

Applying interfacing to under collar

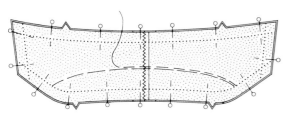

1. Complete under collar seam; press open. Thread-trace roll line on interfacing units. Join interfacing units with an abutted or lapped seam. Pin interfacing to wrong side of under collar. Baste the two together along the roll line.

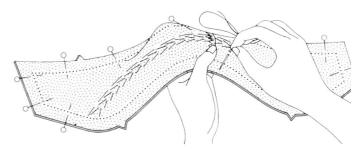

2. Remove thread tracing. Fill in the *stand* area with short chevron padstitching; catch only a yarn or two of garment fabric below. Start at roll line and shape under collar over your hand as shown; do not padstitch into any seam allowance.

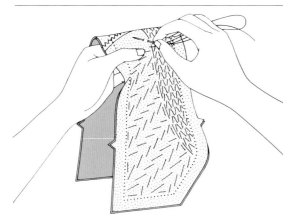

3. Using a slightly longer chevron padstitch, fill in *fall* area of under collar, following the grainline of the interfacing. Shape the under collar over your hand as shown, and do not padstitch into any seam allowances.

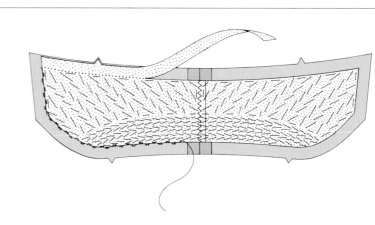

4. Remove basting along roll line. Carefully trim away all interfacing seam allowances. Catchstitch trimmed interfacing edges.

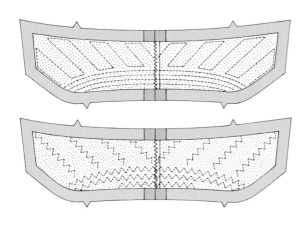

Padstitching can be done by machine to save time, using a straight or a zigzag stitch as shown (see Machine stitches, p. 83). However, the shaping quality of an under collar pad-stitched by machine is not as satisfactory as when padstitching is done by hand.

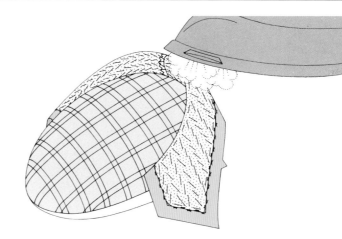

5. Pin under collar to tailor's ham as shown, and steam-press along roll to set its shape. If under collar is not to be used immediately, do not store it away flat. Instead, maintain the shape by pinning the under collar over a rolled-up towel or leaving it pinned to the ham.

Pressing equipment 14 · Flat catchstitch 81 · Staystitching 84 · Reducing seam bulk 87 · Seams finishes 88–89

Assembling garment — attaching under collar to garment

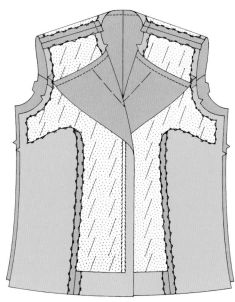

1. Before the under collar can be attached, the front and back garment sections must be stitched together. With right sides facing, match, pin, and stitch back to front sections at shoulder seamlines. Press seams flat, then open. Catch-stitch seam allowances to the interfacing below. Side seams have been left unstitched to facilitate subsequent steps in collar construction.

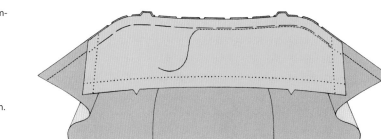

2. With right sides together, match and pin under collar to garment along neck seamline; clip garment seam allowance if necessary for collar to fit smoothly. Stitch with garment side up, securing stitches at both ends of seamline crossing. Press seam flat.

3. Trim stitched seam allowances to ⅜ in (1 cm); diagonally trim cross seams. Finger-press seams open. Clip garment seam allowance and notch the under collar seam allowance as necessary until they both lie flat. Press seam open over a tailor's ham.

Attaching upper collar to facing

1. Staystitch neck seam-lines on front and back facing units. With right sides together, match and pin front and back facings together along shoulder seamlines. Press seams flat, then open. Trim seam allowances to half width. If fabric tends to ravel easily, apply a seam finish to outer edges of the facing.

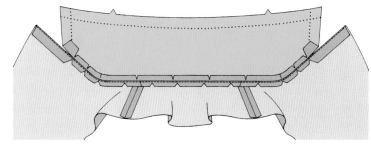

2. With right sides together, match and pin upper collar to facing along neck seamline; clip facing seam allowance if necessary for collar to fit smoothly. Stitch with facing side up, secur-ing stitches at both ends of seamline crossing. Press the seam flat.

3. Trim stitched seam allowances. Diagonally trim cross-seam allowances. Finger-press seam open; clip facing seam allowance and notch upper collar seam allowance as neces-sary until they both lie flat. Press the seam open over a tailor's ham.

Blunting cornered seams 86

Attaching upper collar unit to under collar and garment

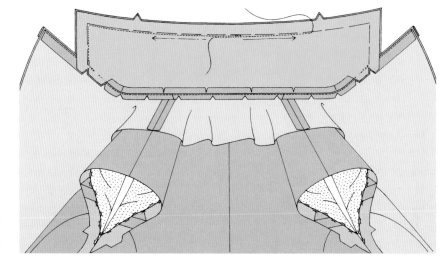

1. With right sides together, accurately match and pin upper collar to under collar. If necessary, ease in upper collar to fit. Baste in place; at the seamline junction of collar and lapel, turn down neckline seam allowances on upper and under collars so that they are not caught in the stitching.

2. Stitch as basted, starting at center of collar. Stitch around collar, reinforcing stitches at corners and stitching across corners to blunt them (see Seams). Secure stitches at junction of collar and lapel. Stitch remaining half of collars together in the same way; overlap a few stitches at the beginning. Press seam flat.

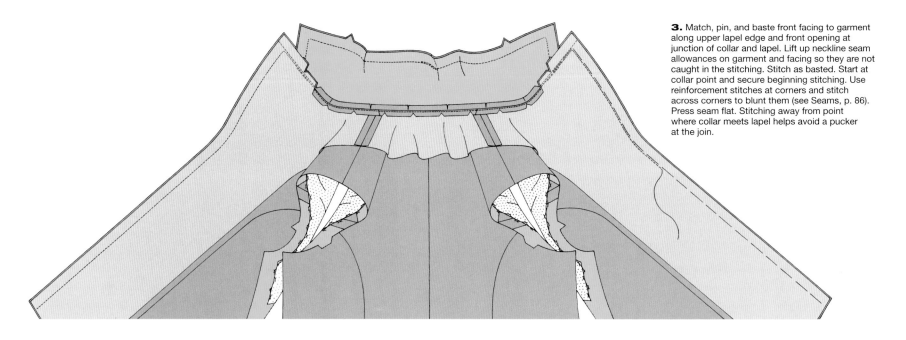

3. Match, pin, and baste front facing to garment along upper lapel edge and front opening at junction of collar and lapel. Lift up neckline seam allowances on garment and facing so they are not caught in the stitching. Stitch as basted. Start at collar point and secure beginning stitching. Use reinforcement stitches at corners and stitch across corners to blunt them (see Seams, p. 86). Press seam flat. Stitching away from point where collar meets lapel helps avoid a pucker at the join.

Pressing equipment 14 · Diagonal basting 70 · Backstitch 72 · Flat catchstitch 81 · Reducing seam bulk 87

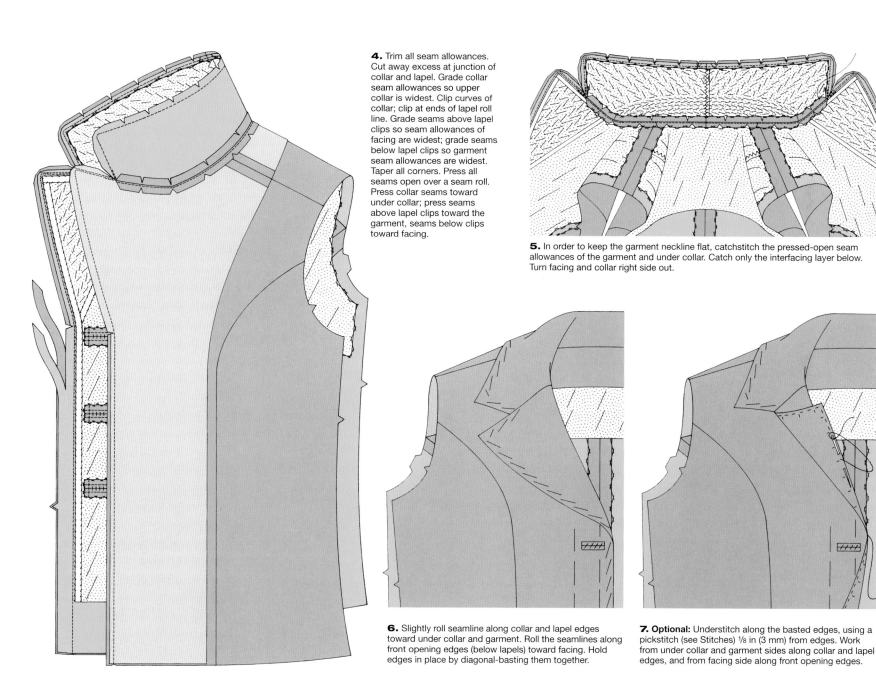

4. Trim all seam allowances. Cut away excess at junction of collar and lapel. Grade collar seam allowances so upper collar is widest. Clip curves of collar; clip at ends of lapel roll line. Grade seams above lapel clips so seam allowances of facing are widest; grade seams below lapel clips so garment seam allowances are widest. Taper all corners. Press all seams open over a seam roll. Press collar seams toward under collar; press seams above lapel clips toward the garment, seams below clips toward facing.

5. In order to keep the garment neckline flat, catchstitch the pressed-open seam allowances of the garment and under collar. Catch only the interfacing layer below. Turn facing and collar right side out.

6. Slightly roll seamline along collar and lapel edges toward under collar and garment. Roll the seamlines along front opening edges (below lapels) toward facing. Hold edges in place by diagonal-basting them together.

7. Optional: Understitch along the basted edges, using a pickstitch (see Stitches) ⅛ in (3 mm) from edges. Work from under collar and garment sides along collar and lapel edges, and from facing side along front opening edges.

TAILORING

Plain-stitch 75 · Bound buttonholes 300–311

Completion of collar and lapel

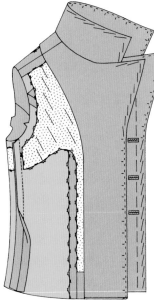

1. Before collar and lapel can be completed, side seams must be stitched so garment can be tried on. With right sides together, match, pin, and baste front to back along side seams. Stitch, then press seams flat. If garment was cut with 1 in (2.5 cm) seam allowances, trim them to ⅝ in (1.5 cm). Press the seams open.

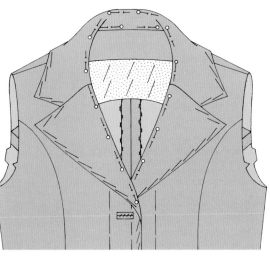

2. Place garment on model. Roll back collar and lapels, and allow them to fall smoothly into place. Hold them in position by pinning along the roll lines and just above back neck seamline. Remove garment.

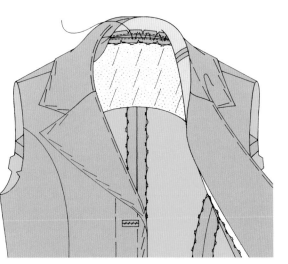

3. Baste along the pinned roll lines of collar and lapels. Lift up back neck facing and, using plain-stitch tacks, stitch facing and garment neck seamlines together as they have fallen in the pinning, not necessarily with seams directly on top of one another.

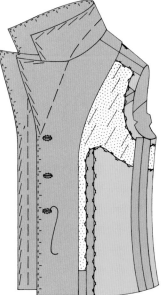
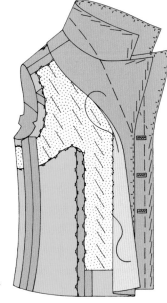

4. On buttonhole side of front opening, complete underside of bound buttonholes as shown at far left (see Bound buttonholes pp. 307–308). To hold the facing in place on opposite side of garment front, turn facing back 2 in (5 cm) from finished edge, and secure facing to interfacing with plain-stitch tacks between first and last button markings (see left). If last button and buttonhole are less than a double hem width from hemline, take these steps after hem is completed.

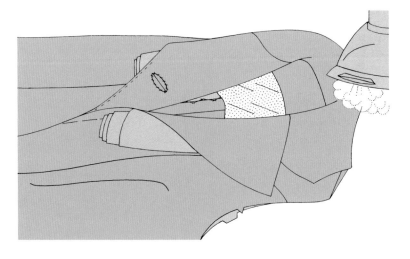

5. Remove all unnecessary bastings, and press front openings of garment. Place a rolled-up towel under collar and lapels for support, then pass a steaming iron over the garment, holding it close enough for the steam to set the roll of collar and lapels. Let dry.

Whipstitch 73 · Set-in sleeves 216–217

Sleeves

Sleeve procedures in a tailored garment are similar to those for standard garments so it is a good idea to review the Sleeve chapter before constructing tailored sleeves. One difference is extra shape-building steps. A **sleeve heading,** for example, usually made from a rectangular piece of lamb's wool, is sewed to the sleeve's upper seamline to support and smooth out the sleeve cap. A **shoulder pad** will help define the shoulder line.

Set-in sleeves in tailored garments are usually shaped according to one of three basic pattern types: 1. standard one-piece sleeve with an underarm seam;

2. two-piece sleeve with seams along the front and back of the arm; and 3. a variation of the one-piece sleeve in which the seam is at the back of the arm (see below). Most tailored sleeves are of the second and third types, as their seam positions give a better fit.

An optional step, to sharpen line definition around the sleeve, is to tape the armhole. This is done before the sleeve is inserted, by pinning and basting twill tape over the armhole seamline, easing the garment in slightly as you do. Because taping causes armhole fit to be closer, it is not recommended for coats.

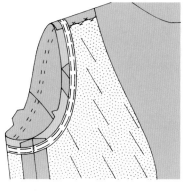

To tape armhole, cut ¼ in (6 mm) twill tape ½ in (1.25 cm) shorter than armhole circumference; center and pin tape over seamline; ease in garment so tape ends meet. Baste along both edges of tape. Whipstitch ends together. Insert sleeve as shown.

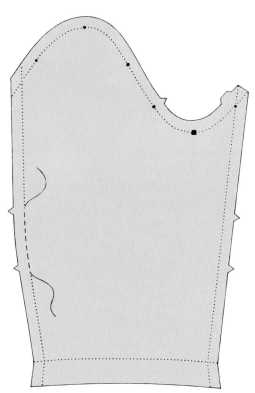

1. If sleeve is designed with elbow ease, complete the darts or place a row of easestitching within designated markings on the seamline, as pattern requires.

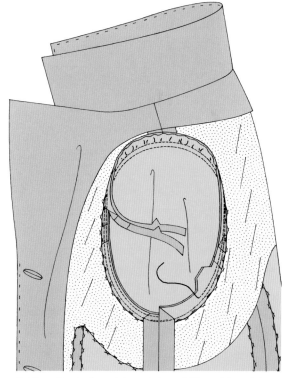

2. Right sides together, complete sleeve seam. Press flat, then open. Place two easestitching rows within seam allowance of cap, between front and back notches.

3. Pin and baste sleeve into armhole, matching notches, dots, shoulder and underarm points. If sleeve fit is satisfactory, stitch in permanently. Finish seam allowance with second row of stitching; trim close to second stitching line.

Running stitch 71 · Whipstitch 73

Sleeve heading

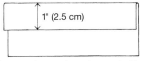

1. Sleeve headings can be purchased or made. To make sleeve heading, cut a 3 × 5 in (7.5 × 12.5 cm) piece of lamb's wool, flannel, or polyester fleece; make a 1 in (2.5 cm) fold on long side.

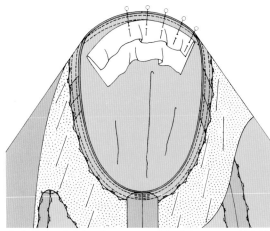

2. Center and pin heading to wrong side of sleeve cap with fold against seamline, wider half of heading against sleeve.

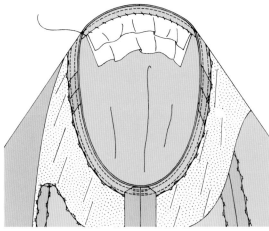

3. Whipstitch fold of sleeve heading to sleeve seamline. Heading now supports and rounds out sleeve cap.

Shoulder pads

Shoulder pads may be needed in a tailored garment to help maintain the shoulder line. They are also useful for de-emphasizing such figure characteristics as rounded shoulders and uneven shoulder heights. Thicknesses of pads can vary, depending on their purpose; select one that does the job without distorting the garment's natural shape. Shoulder pads like that shown below can be purchased in various shapes, or made for a more exact fit. To make a shoulder pad pattern, overlap shoulder seams on front and back pattern pieces; pin

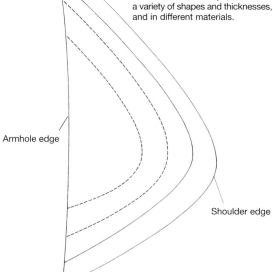

A purchased shoulder pad of the type shown here, sometimes called a *shoulder shape,* comes in a variety of shapes and thicknesses, and in different materials.

Armhole edge

Shoulder edge

any darts or seams extending into shoulder seam or armhole. Draw pad shape as shown upper right: connect armhole curve between front and back notches, gradually extending curve ⅜ in (1 cm) out at shoulder line. Draw shoulder curve with its top edge 1 in (2.5 cm) from neckline. Use pattern to cut out graduated layers of polyester fleece. Stitch layers together. Note that pads extend farther down the jacket back than front.

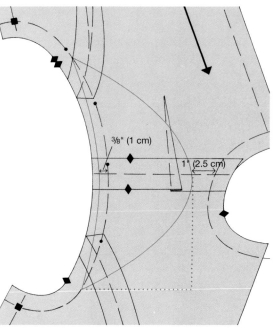

To make shoulder pads, draw shoulder pad shape as shown. For a hollow-chested person, square off the front portion of the pad, as indicated by the dotted lines.

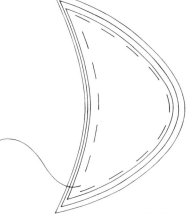

For each pad, cut the graduated layers of polyester fleece; hold layers together with long running stitches.

Catchstitch basting 75 · Single cross-stitch 75 · Interfaced hems 257

Inserting shoulder pads

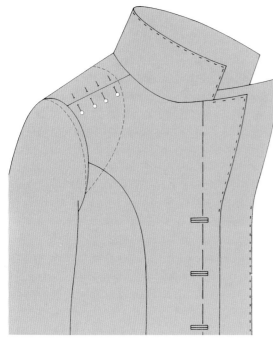

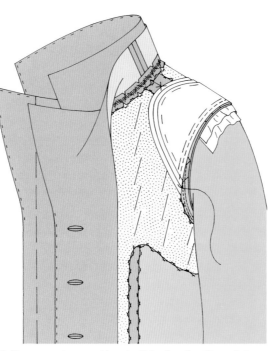

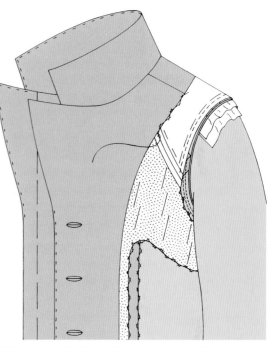

1. Place garment on model; insert pad and adjust its position as shown, with top edge extending ⅜ in (1 cm) from armhole seamline. Pin pad in place along shoulder line, and remove garment.

2. Turn garment wrong side out; stitch edge of pad to armhole seam allowance with a running stitch. Flip up facing, and tack shoulder end of pad to shoulder seam allowances.

3. To complete shoulder pad application, bring facing down, then pin and catchstitch the upper portion of the front facing to the top layer of the shoulder pad.

Hemming tailored garments

As a rule, the hem of a tailored garment is interfaced to give body to the area and to help maintain the hem's shape along the lower edge. The interfacing in the completed hem usually extends past the finished edge; this distributes the bulk and has the effect of "grading" the two layers. The interfacing is generally positioned so it goes over the hemline, producing a softly rounded crease; in a man's tailored jacket, the interfacing stops at the hemline so that the crease at the bottom edge will be sharp. When the hem is completed, all bastings are removed from the garment. Before attaching the lining, have the entire garment steam-pressed if possible, to permanently set all seams.

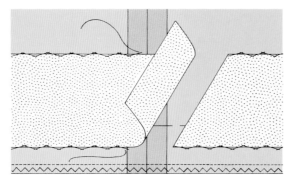

1. To hem garment, thread-trace hemline, and apply a seam finish to the raw edge. Catchstitch interfacing to underlining.

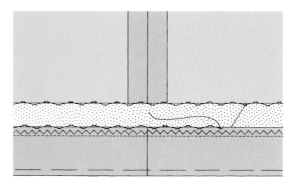

2. Fold hem up along hemline marking and baste along the folded edge. Catchstitch free edge of hem to interfacing.

Lining

Lining is the last fabric layer to be added to the tailored garment. It should fit smoothly within the garment, providing a neat inside finish. As a rule, the lining is constructed from a smooth fabric that complements the outer fabric layer. Any alterations in the garment also should be made in the lining. For sufficient ease for body movement without strain on lining seams, there is usually a vertical pleat down the back of the lining and a fold at the bottom of the sleeve and at the garment hem. If the pattern does not supply lining pieces, these can easily be made up from the main garment patterns. Instructions for preparing front and back lining sections are given at right; the sleeve lining can be cut from the sleeve pattern piece. In classic tailoring, the lining is generally hand-sewed to the garment, though it can also be attached partly by machine. Press lightly to protect lining from getting a worn look. For additional warmth, install interlining (see pp. 350–351).

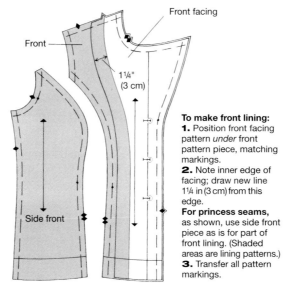
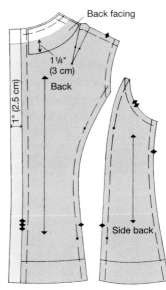

Front facing

Front

Back facing

Back

1¼" (3 cm)

1¼" (3 cm)

1" (2.5 cm)

Side front

Side back

To make front lining:
1. Position front facing pattern *under* front pattern piece, matching markings.
2. Note inner edge of facing; draw new line 1¼ in (3 cm) from this edge.
For princess seams, as shown, use side front piece as is for part of front lining. (Shaded areas are lining patterns.)
3. Transfer all pattern markings.

To make back lining:
1. Tape a strip of tissue paper to pattern's back edge.
2. Position back facing *under* back pattern piece.
3. Mark 1 in (2.5 cm) beyond pattern's center back edge (not seamline) to allow for pleat. If garment does not have a center back seam, mark 1 in (2.5 cm) beyond center back foldline.
4. Note inner edge of facing; draw new line 1¼ in (3 cm) from this edge.
For princess seams, as shown, use side back piece as is for part of back lining. (Shaded areas are the lining pieces.)
5. Transfer all pattern markings.

Joining main lining pieces

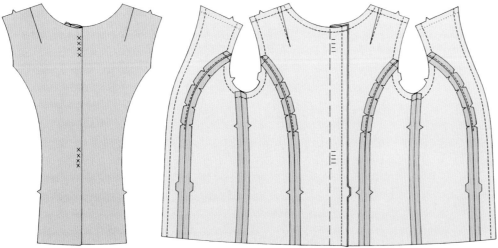
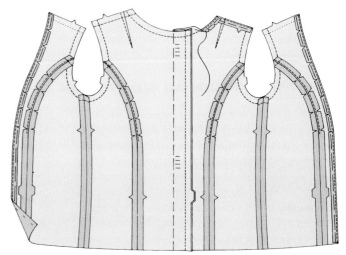

1. Stitch darts (and back seam, if any). Baste up the back pleat; press to one side; tack through all layers with cross stitches below neckline and at waistline.

2. Place a row of stitching inside the seamlines of the front opening, back shoulder, neck and armhole edges (staystitching can serve for this stitching line). Complete internal seams and side seams. Press seams flat, then open; clip and notch the seam allowances as necessary.

3. The seam allowances on all the stitched raw edges, except for the armhole edges, should be turned and pressed to the wrong side. Clip and notch the seam allowances as necessary so that they lie flat. Then baste the turned edges in place.

Running stitch 71 · Uneven slipstitch 81

Attaching lining to garment by hand

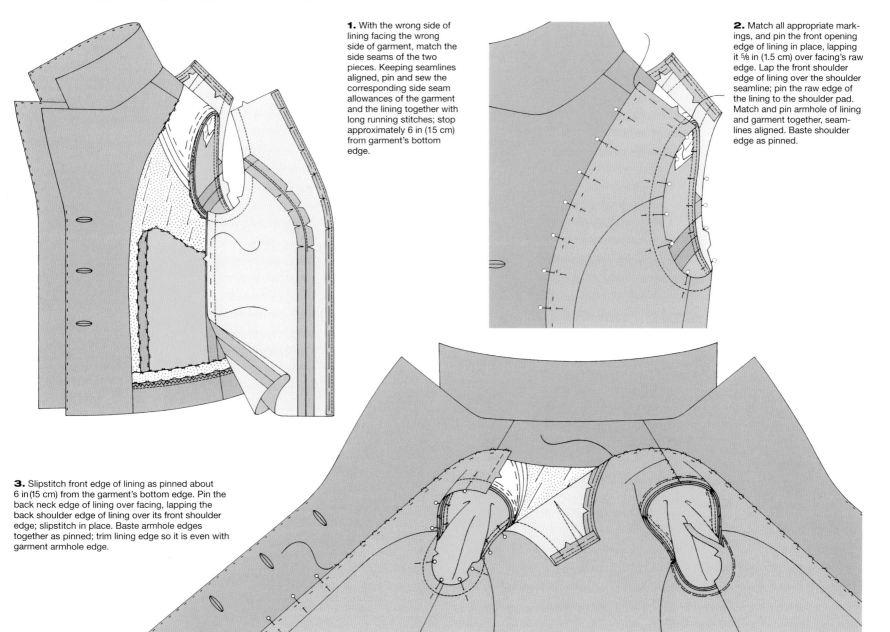

1. With the wrong side of lining facing the wrong side of garment, match the side seams of the two pieces. Keeping seamlines aligned, pin and sew the corresponding side seam allowances of the garment and the lining together with long running stitches; stop approximately 6 in (15 cm) from garment's bottom edge.

2. Match all appropriate markings, and pin the front opening edge of lining in place, lapping it ⅝ in (1.5 cm) over facing's raw edge. Lap the front shoulder edge of lining over the shoulder seamline; pin the raw edge of the lining to the shoulder pad. Match and pin armhole of lining and garment together, seamlines aligned. Baste shoulder edge as pinned.

3. Slipstitch front edge of lining as pinned about 6 in (15 cm) from the garment's bottom edge. Pin the back neck edge of lining over facing, lapping the back shoulder edge of lining over its front shoulder edge; slipstitch in place. Baste armhole edges together as pinned; trim lining edge so it is even with garment armhole edge.

Even basting stitch 70 · Running stitch 71 · Staystitching 84

Sleeve lining

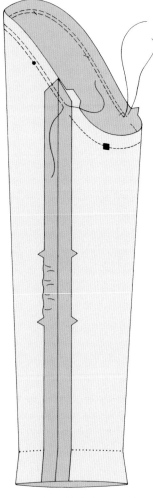

1. With the right side facing, complete sleeve seam; press open. Place two rows of easestitching within seam allowances of cap, between front and back notches. Staystitch sleeve underarm between same two notches.

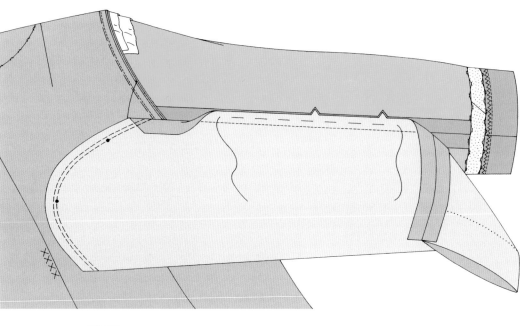

2. Turn both garment and sleeve lining wrong side out. Match and pin corresponding sleeves of lining garment together along seam allowances. Hold the seam allowances together with a long running stitch, stopping about 4 in (10 cm) from bottom edge of garment sleeve.

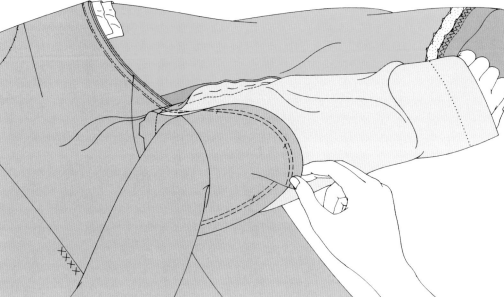

3. Slip arm all the way through the sleeve lining and grasp the bottom of the garment sleeve. Pull the lining back and over the garment sleeve.

Uneven slipstitch   81 · Hemming a lining   259

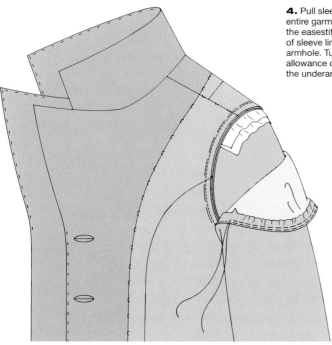

4. Pull sleeve lining up and over entire garment sleeve. Draw up the easestitching threads so cap of sleeve lining fits around the armhole. Turn under seam allowance of sleeve lining, clipping the underarm curve as necessary.

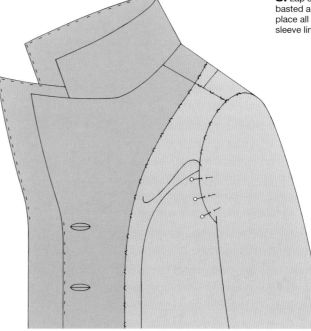

5. Lap sleeve lining over the basted armhole line, and pin in place all around. Slipstitch sleeve lining as pinned.

Hemming methods for linings

The lining hem can be completed by one of two methods. The first is used most often at the bottom edges of jackets and sleeves; in this procedure, the lining is attached to the garment hem and a fold created for greater wearing ease. The second method is used principally at the bottom edge of coats; here the lining is separately hemmed and secured to the garment with French tacks. Refer to the chapter on Hems for detailed directions for both methods. Before beginning either method, place the garment wrong side out on a model, and pin lining to garment 6 in (15 cm) above hemline.

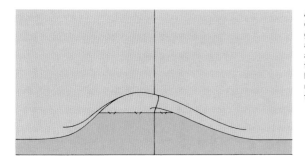

An attached lining is completely secured to the garment hem, with a small fold at the bottom to provide additional wearing ease within the lining. This is called a jump hem. Such hems are most often used at the bottom edges of tailored jackets and sleeves.

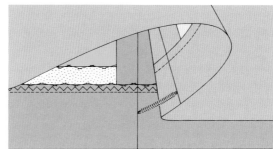

A free hanging lining is hemmed separately from the garment, then secured to the garment at each seam with French tacks. Free-hanging linings are most often used at the bottom of tailored coats.

Diagonal basting 70 · Staystitching 84 · Lapped darts 106 · Fastenings 320–323

Interlining

For additional warmth in a tailored garment, a layer of fabric known as an interlining can be applied between the lining and the constructed garment. Popular interlining fabrics are described on page 351. Because the interlining contributes extra bulk, more wearing ease must be allowed when adjusting the garment and lining patterns. The interlining is usually cut without a back pleat. In working with interlining, each section is basted to its corresponding lining section; both are then handled as one layer. To help reduce bulk, the interlining is cut off at the hemline and excess seam allowances are then trimmed away where possible.

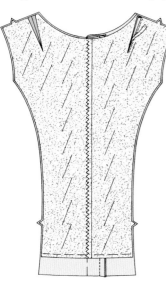

1. Before basting sections of interlining to corresponding lining pieces, prepare back pleat in lining as described on page 346. If garment has a center back seam, join the back section of interlining with a lapped seam as shown. Then position and pin interlining pieces to wrong side of lining; diagonal-baste the layers together, handling them as you would the garment fabric and underlining (see p. 328). Pin and stitch all darts. Slash darts open, and trim interlining close to stitching; press darts open.

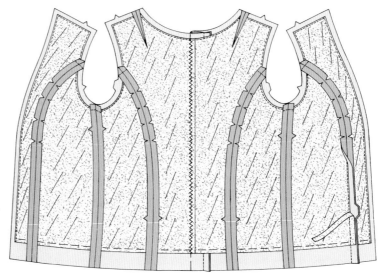

2. Baste around each interlined lining piece to keep the raw edges of the two layers from shifting. Then place a row of stitching inside the seamlines of the front opening, front and back shoulders, neck and armhole edges; trim interlining seam allowances close to the stitching. With right sides together, complete all internal seams within front and back sections. Then join front to back along side seams. Press each seam flat, trim interlining seam allowances close to stitching line, and press seams open. Remove basting. Proceed with lining construction (see p. 346).

Professional touches

Certain finishing touches can give your tailored garment a professional look. Buttons, for example, are important accessories if they are carefully coordinated with the garment. If snaps are used, buy or make the covered kind. Such visible items should be positioned properly and sewn on neatly and securely.

Weights at the hemline, either the chain or drapery type, help maintain the hang of the garment. Chain weights, used most often in tailored jackets, are sewed under the lining hem fold. Drapery weights are placed in small "pockets," which are sewed to seams and openings before the garment is hemmed; they work best in tailored coats. Any weight you use should hold the garment in place without distorting its line.

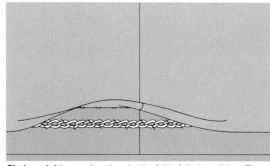

Chain weights are placed under the fold of the hem lining. They can be used either around the entire garment or along sections of it. To install, position the chain flat against the garment hem and secure it in place with a whipstitch every 2 in (5 cm) on each side of chain.

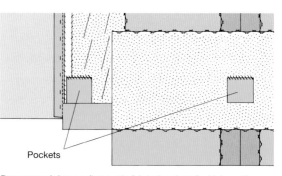

Pockets

Drapery weights are first put in fabric "pockets," which are then sewed to the garment. To make pockets, cut rectangles of fabric. Fold each in half; seam two sides; turn. Drop in the weight and stitch the pocket across the top. Whipstitch pockets to seams and front opening.

Hand-basting stitches 70–71 · Catchstitch basting 75 · Lapped darts 106

Interlining (cont'd.)

Interlinings should be lightweight but not thick; they should not add undue bulk or dimension to a garment. The most familiar interlining choices are lamb's wool, polyester fleece, flannel, flannelette, and brushed cotton. Other fabrics can serve the same purposes. Among these are felt, some pajama and nightwear fabrics, and thin blanket fabrics. Then there are the fabrics sold and handled as linings that also work as interlinings. Examples are quilted, insulated, and fleece-backed linings.

An interlining's care requirements should match those of the rest of the garment, although interlined garments are best dry-cleaned.

Choose a color that will not show through to the outside of the garment.

Before interlining a garment, make sure there is adequate wearing ease to accommodate the added thickness; keep this ease in mind while fitting the garment. Because of the ease problem, sleeves are not usually interlined; they can be if ease is sufficient. Use the lining pattern pieces to cut out the interlining.

There are two methods of interlining. The first is to **apply the interlining to the lining,** as shown at left, in a way similar to the underlining method on page 329. Then apply lining to the garment. The other method is to **apply the interlining to the garment** as shown below and then line the garment.

Applying interlining to lining

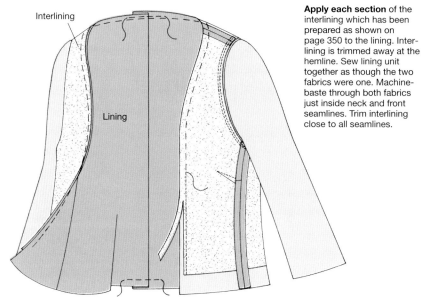

Interlining

Lining

Apply each section of the interlining which has been prepared as shown on page 350 to the lining. Interlining is trimmed away at the hemline. Sew lining unit together as though the two fabrics were one. Machine-baste through both fabrics just inside neck and front seamlines. Trim interlining close to all seamlines.

Applying interlining to garment

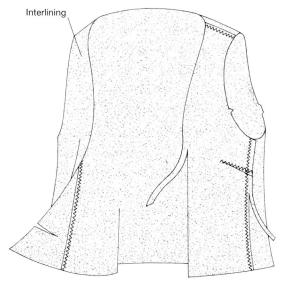

Interlining

1. Stitch the interlining sections together, lapping seams and darts (see p. 106). Trim away the interlining along the lower edge to a depth that is equal to twice the width of the garment's hem. Trim away the neck and front seam allowances.

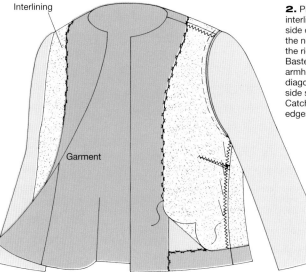

Interlining

Garment

2. Pin and match the interlining unit to the wrong side of the garment, lapping the neck and front edges over the right side of the facing. Baste unit to garment inside armhole seamlines, trim, then diagonal-baste to garment side seam allowances. Catchstitch neck and front edges to facing.

Seam ripper 10 · Waistline seam 184 · Zippers 285–291

Alterations

It is often the case that purchased garments don't fit quite perfectly and have to be altered. Also, figures change and, as a result, garments can become too tight or too loose and alteration is required.

It is definitely worthwhile to alter garments that have been worn but are in good condition or newly purchased garments that need to fit better. In most cases, you can make these alterations yourself. You have to know the basic techniques of sewing and a few additional tips.

When the alteration called for is a large one, it is best to take the entire garment apart, change the pattern (see also Basic pattern alterations pp. 36–46), and then sew the garment pieces back together. Always try on the proposed alterations before sewing.

A garment is too tight

Is a dress, jacket, blouse, or coat too tight?
1. When a dress, coat, jacket or blouse with buttons pulls a little bit, first try moving the buttons. Put the garment on and pin it closed through the buttonholes so that the garment no longer pulls. If the buttons do not have to be moved more than ³⁄₈ in (1 cm), mark each new button position with tailor's chalk. Always keep the new position for each button the same distance to the old position. Then, remove the buttons and sew them by hand or machine onto the new chalk-marked positions.

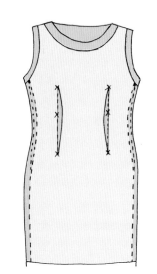

2. If the garment still pulls, the darts, when present, should be made smaller or released and the stitching threads removed. After you have released the darts, press carefully. Opening up darts is not recommended when the fabric is very thin or smooth and the old stitch-holes will be visible. If you are not sure, test this by releasing a small section of the hem.

3. Another method is to increase the garment on the sides. First, check to see whether or not the seam allowance is wide enough to allow for letting out the seams. If it is, divide the increase between the two side seams and mark the new seam line. Sew the new seam before releasing the old one with a seam ripper. When there is a zipper in a side seam, you will need to open up the old seam first and remove the zipper and old stitching thread. Then sew in the zipper again (see pp. 286–291).

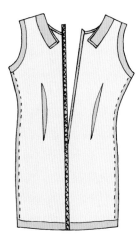

4. When the dress has a center seam in the front and back, you can let out the dress at these seams using the same method as for opening up the dress at the side seams. Also, you can open up the center seams and then add a decorative border, a method which lends itself to children's garments especially.

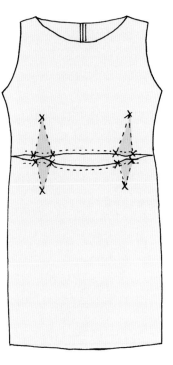

5. If the dress or coat consists of an upper and lower section and has darts, it is often sufficient to release the waistline seam at the front and then release the darts as shown above. Carefully press the darts open. Close the waistline seam.

6. If this is not sufficient, measure how many inches (centimeters) the dress has to be let out. Then release the waistline seam and distribute the increase evenly between the darts, side seams, and/or center seams on both the upper and lower sections. Mark the new seams and stitch. Release the old seams and remove the old thread. Then close the waistline seam (see p. 184), making sure that the darts and the seams match up. If there is a zipper, proceed as in Step 3.

Bands 12 · Waistbands 194–201 · Sewing on buttons 317–319

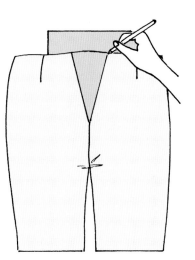

A garment is too large

Is a pair of pants or skirt too tight?

1. If the pants or skirt has a waistband, this should first be removed as should the zipper, if one is present.

2. If the pants or skirt does not need to be let out very much, it is often sufficient to release the back or front center seam and let out the seam allowances as required.

3. If this is not enough decrease, release darts when present and either reduce their size or open out entirely as required.

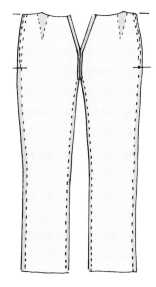

4. In addition, or as an alternative, release the pants or skirt side seams 5–6 in (12–15 cm) and, if the seam allowances are wide enough, mark a new seamline along the outside of the old one. Stitch the new seamline, then release the old one. Remove the old stitches. Press the new seam allowances open.

5. A piece of wedge-shaped fabric can also be used. Release the back center seam 6 in (15 cm) or more, then put on the pants or skirt. Determine how wide the opening needs to be. Place a piece of tracing paper under the opening. Draw an outline of the extension piece onto it and trace the extension onto a piece of fabric. Add a seam allowance of ⅝ in (1.5 cm). Cut it out. Place the new piece, right sides together, onto the seam edges, stitch, and press.

6. Re-attach the waistband. If it is now too short, release the back center seam of the waistband and let it out or cut it at center back and add a piece of fabric as wide as the top width of the wedge plus seam allowance, and sew on.

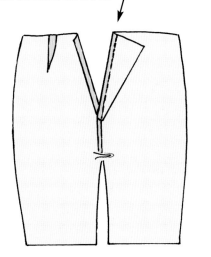

7. If the pants or skirt still needs letting out, release the side seams and let out the seam allowance.

Is a dress, jacket, blouse, or coat too large?

1. Occasionally, it is sufficient to purchase a matching belt.

2. If the garment has buttons and does not need to be taken in very much, it is often sufficient to move in the buttons from the edge ⅝ in to ¾ in (1 to 2 cm).

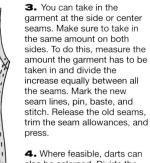

3. You can take in the garment at the side or center seams. Make sure to take in the same amount on both sides. To do this, measure the amount the garment has to be taken in and divide the increase equally between all the seams. Mark the new seam lines, pin, baste, and stitch. Release the old seams, trim the seam allowances, and press.

4. Where feasible, darts can also be enlarged. Divide the increase between the two darts. Mark the new size for each dart, baste, and stitch. Then release the old dart seams.

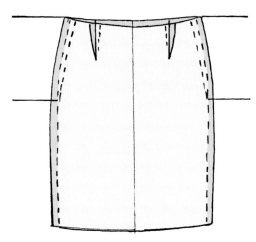

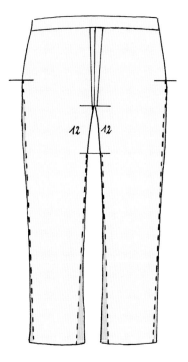

A garment is too long

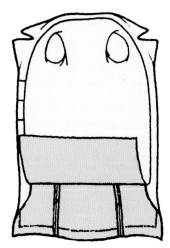

Is a skirt or pants too loose?

1. If a skirt or pants is too loose at the waist or hips, try on the garment and pin the excess width together on both sides.

2. If there is a waistband or a side zipper, separate it from the garment.

3. Measure to determine how much the skirt or pants need to be taken in for a good fit. Divide the increase between the side seams and, if needed, the darts, and pin.

4. Try on the garment again to make sure it fits well and that the basic shape has not been altered. Make any necessary adjustments. Then baste the seams and the darts, if you have taken in these as well.

5. Cut open the old seams and darts, remove the thread, and press well. Then stitch along the basting lines. If you have removed the zipper, restitch it in. If the zipper is no longer working well or is somewhat worn, this is a good time to sew in a new one.

6. Finally, measure to determine how much the waistband has to be taken in to match the altered garment, take it in accordingly, and then sew it back onto the garment.

7. If the pants legs are too loose below the hips, pin the excess width and, using a ruler and chalk, mark the new seam lines from hip level to hem. Take same amount of each seam.

8. Stitch the new side seam along the marked line. Release the old seams and trim back to the former seam allowance width. Finish the edges.

9. If the pants are too loose around the hips, start taking in width as high up as possible.

10. A pleated skirt is taken in by making the pleat widths deeper. Measure the amount the skirt has to be reduced in size. Count the number of pleats, then divide the reduction amount between all the pleats to determine by how much each pleat will need to be narrowed. Release the waistband and any sewn-in pleating lines.

11. Narrow the pleats, baste, and press. See pages 110–113 for detailed instructions on pleating.

Is your lined jacket or a lined coat too long?

1. At the bottom of the garment, release the lining from the facings about 6 in (15 cm) high.

2. Release the jacket or coat hem, and press well. Shorten the hem as required, and baste. Repeat this with the lining. Trim the interfacing. Sew seam as shown on page 255, then re-attach the lining to the garment hem as shown on page 351.

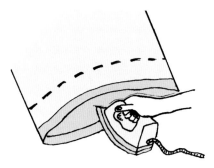

To shorten and press a skirt

1. Mark the new length using a hem marker or yard stick (meter rule) and pins. Place the pins or marks every 2 in (5 cm).

2. Release the hem, and press well. Cut the garment to the desired length, making sure to leave enough seam allowance. Hem as shown on pages 254–255.

Pleats 110–119 · Belt carriers 199 · Zippers 285–291 · Attaching a hem to lining 349

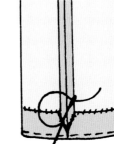

Do you need to shorten and press a pleated or patterned skirt?
1. Pleated skirts and some patterned skirts, such as those with border prints, must be shortened at the waist, not at the hem.

2. Measure to determine how much the skirt has to be shortened. Separate the waistline and the zipper. Mark the reduction amount on the top of the skirt. Iron the pleats carefully and cut off the reduction amount. Make sure to leave enough seam allowance.

3. Release the zipper placket seam and shorten the zipper to match the reduction measurement or insert a new but shorter zipper. Re-attach the waistband.

Is a lined coat sleeve too long?
1. Try on the jacket or coat and mark the reduction amount with pins. Carefully remove the garment and baste along the pin line.

4. Turn up the lining of the garment. Next, turn up the hem sleeve at the marked line. Open the sleeve seam to let it spread to fit (shown above) since otherwise the hem will most likely be too narrow. Trim the edges of the sleeves and lining, making sure to leave enough seam allowance. Then hem the sleeves as shown on page 255. Hem the lining as shown on page 349.

3. If pants legs or sleeves are tapered, open the seams in the hem to let it spread to fit, as shown above. Hem the pants legs or coat or jacket sleeves as shown on page 255.

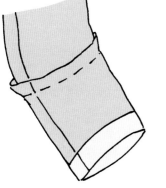

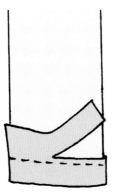

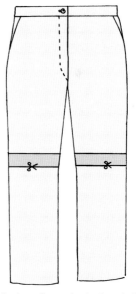

2. Turn the sleeve inside out and attach the lining to the sleeve with a few tacking stitches so that it cannot slip.

3. Open up the coat fabric and lining hem and press.

Are pants, an unlined jacket, or a coat sleeve too long?
1. Try on the garment and mark the reduction amount. Release the seam and press well.

2. Turn up the pants legs or the sleeves on the new marked line and cut off the extra fabric. Finish the edges (see pp. 88–91).

How to make shorts or Bermuda shorts out of pants
1. Try on the pants. Determine the length of the shorts and mark with pins or chalk. If desired, fold a cuff.

2. Cut off the excess fabric at the marked line, leaving enough seam allowance. Sew the hem as described on page 255. Sew on the cuff, if you have decided to add one, as shown on page 276.

3. Left-over fabric can be used for a belt, belt carriers, or pockets.

Faced hems 262–263 · Enclosing a hem edge 265 · Zippers 285–291

A garment is too short

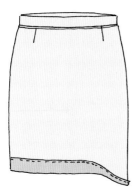

Lengthening a skirt hem

1. Lengthening skirts makes especially good sense for children's clothes. If the upper garment body still fits but the skirt is too short or if the garment is a one-piece dress, it is lengthened at the hem. If there is enough seam allowance left, release the hem, press, and then hem as shown on page 255. To remove a persistent hem crease, press using a cloth dampened in diluted white vinegar.

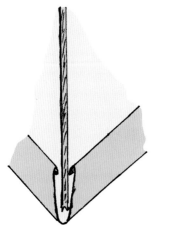

2. If there is too little seam allowance left to turn up, sew a faced hem as shown on pages 262–263.

3. If there is no seam allowance left, attach a band of other fabric to the edge of the hem. This can be the same color or a contrasting color to the garment or a matching pattern (see Enclosing a hem edge, p. 265).

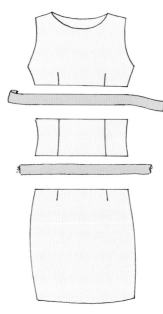

Lengthening a dress with a decorative band

1. Another, less common, method of lengthening a dress is by sewing-in a decorative band or by sewing on a flounce, lace, or trim.

2. To sew in a decorative band, cut through the dress in one or more places as shown above. Right sides together, pin the decorative band or bands to the edges, baste, and sew.

3. If this is not sufficient, release the hem and press. Right sides together, pin the flounce, lace, or trim onto the skirt edge and pin. Baste and sew.

Lengthening a dress with a waistband join and adjusting the zipper length to match

1. If the dress consists of both an upper and lower section, the dress can be lengthened at the waist. Measure to determine how much longer the dress should be. Then release the waistline seam and the zipper in the back or side.

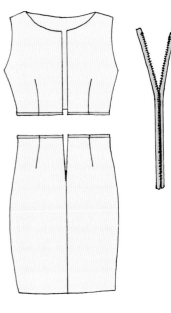

2. If the seam allowances at the upper bodice and the skirt are wide enough, pin the two sections together, reducing the seam allowance as needed. Then baste and stitch the new waistline seam.

3. Adjust the zipper placket opening to fit the zipper, or buy a longer zipper.

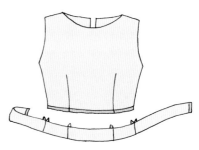

4. If the seam allowances are too narrow, a band of other fabric or trim can be inserted at the waistline. (Cont'd.)

Bands 12 · Hand stitches 68 · Machine stitches 83 · Pants cuffs 276

5. Cut the band wide enough for the increase plus seam allowances.

6. Make seams in the bands to correspond to the garment's seams and darts.

7. Right sides together, baste the band first onto the upper garment and then onto the skirt. Try on the garment. If it fits properly, stitch the seams.

8. An elasticized band can also be used instead of a fabric band. Separate the upper garment from the skirt and sew in the elasticized band. (See p. 207.)

Is a skirt too short?
Skirts can be lengthened in the same way as shorts. Alternatively, you can lengthen as you would a dress (p. 356) by adding matching lace, trim, or flounces, or by sewing in bands of fabric.

Inserting a new zipper in pants

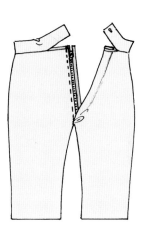

1. Remove the old zipper. You will also need to release the waistband seam to the left and right of the zipper placket about 1½ in (4 cm).

2. Pin the new zipper to the base of the crotch. Baste in place. Close to check positioning. Stitch on both sides close to chain.

3. On outside of garment, baste fly facing to front, following original basted markings. From bottom to top, topstitch along basted markings, being careful not to catch the opposite zipper tape in stitching. Work a bar tack across seamline at bottom of placket (see also p. 295 and p. 297).

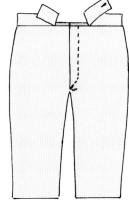

Sewing on a patch

1. When a pants knee has worn through, the quickest and easiest repair method is to purchase an iron-on patch and iron it to the outside of the pants over the knee area. You can also use scraps of fabric and bond them to the garment using fusible web. After fusing, stitch around the edges of the patch with a decorative machine or hand stitch. To use machine stitching, you will need to release one of the leg seams in the area of the patch.

2. To sew a patch onto a worn or torn area, first cut away the damaged areas. Then cut the worn spot into a square; clip ¼ in (6 mm) into each corner; press edges under ¼ in (6 mm) all around. The patch should be slightly larger than the hole and should match the garment fabric and pattern. Place the the patch under hole, matching the grain or design. Sew the right sides of the folded edges of the hole onto the patch using a slipstitch.

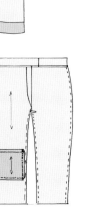

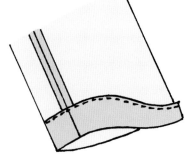

Is a pair of pants too short?
1. Release the hem and cuffs and press out the creases. If there were cuffs, use them for the extra length needed and hem as shown on page 255. If no cuffs, add a bias facing to lower edge and turn it to inside.

2. If the hem is too narrow to allow the hem or cuffs to be let down, sew in a band or binding. For further instructions on how to do this, see pages 262–263.

CHAPTER 11

PATCHWORK AND QUILTING

Unique projects can be made
doing patchwork — placing
together pieces of fabric,
usually variously colored,
as in a mosaic.
The patchwork technique
is often used along
with quilting in quilt-making.
Together, they can result
in decorative bedcovers
and wall hangings for your home.

Patchwork vest

Fabrics: Drews, Künzelsau (Germany)

Fabrics

For vest front and facings: firm cotton, suede cloth
For lining: lining satin

Amount

For size 40: Cotton: ½ yd (40 cm) beige; ½ yd (40 cm) light red; ½ yd (40 cm) mustard; ¾ yd (0.7 m) burgundy each of 58/60 in (150 cm) -width fabric
Satin: 1 yd (0.9 m) of 58/60 in (150 cm) -width fabric

Notions

⅞ yd (0.90 m) mediumweight interfacing, 28 in (70 cm) -width
1 belt buckle for ¾ in (2 cm) -wide belt
4 buttons, ¾ in (18 mm) diameter

Pattern pieces

Cotton, burgundy:
1 Front facing – cut 2
Satin:
2 Vest front lining – cut 2
3 Vest back – cut 2 full backs
4 Tab, short – cut 1
5 Tab, long – cut 1
Cardboard template for patchwork:
6 Vest front – cut 2
Burda pattern 3403 was modified for this vest. Wash the fabric before cutting to preshrink it and in case it fades.
Tip: If you have little sewing experience, it is a good idea to make the patchwork design first and then estimate the fabric amounts using the cardboard template.

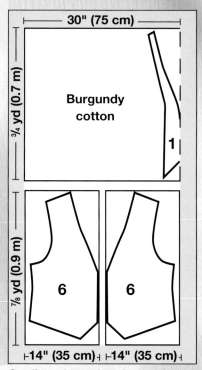

30" (75 cm)
¾ yd (0.7 m)
Burgundy cotton
1
⅞ yd (0.9 m)
6 **6**
14" (35 cm) 14" (35 cm)

Cardboard template for patchwork

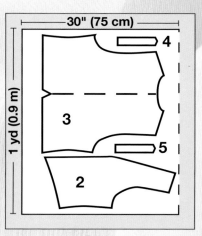

30" (75 cm)
1 yd (0.9 m)
4
3
5
2

Satin

Patchwork is the technique of connecting single small pieces of fabric of various colors and patterns to create a larger unit. Some patchwork patterns are simple while others are quite complicated and intricate. Patchwork can be sewn by hand or by machine.

The simplest patchwork is made with blocks of the same size and shape, as in this vest. Two or more colors can be cleverly arranged to result in interesting patterns.

Most patchwork patterns use geometric shapes. More complex patchwork is called block patchwork because the fabric pieces are arranged in individual blocks that together create larger units (see p. 367).

Beginners should start with simple patterns composed of a limited number of pieces. It is easier to copy a pattern than to create one.

The fabrics in the patchwork should all be of similar weight, texture, and care requirements. Not only is it easier to work with similar fabrics but also the finished product will look better. Mediumweight, uniformly woven fabrics work best for patchwork. If all the pieces require the same kind of fabric care, the whole piece can be either washed or dry-cleaned.

Creating a mock-up of your patchwork design before buying the fabrics will allow you to experiment with various colors and color arrangements.

Once you have decided on the pattern, determine the exact size of the blocks and make a template. You then can use the template to estimate the total amount of each fabric or color needed. If you are unsure whether or not the colors will match, buy only small quantities of fabric and make a sample piece.

This vest is made using a patchwork with rectangles. They are all made of the same fabric, in four colors.

Sewing tools
● You can use dressmaker's shears to cut the blocks, but a rotary cutter is preferred by most quilters. These come in several sizes: larger for heavy fabric and multiple layers, and smaller for lighter fabric and more intricate shapes. Rotary cutters must

be used with a special cutting mat; most have useful grid markings on them.
● A quilting ruler with angle marks or a right-angled triangle is useful for measuring the template. You will also need a measuring tape, thin cardboard, and a marking pencil.
● Choose thread that matches the main fabric for stitching the blocks together.

Patchwork
● The front panels of the vest are made of patchwork.

● Copy the pattern piece for the vest front, including the seam allowances, onto cardboard and cut out. Draw the rectangles (4 x 1½ in [10 x 4 cm]) on the template and determine the color arrangement You can use colored markers or small pieces of fabric to do this (Fig. 1).

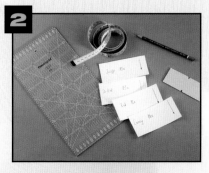

● Make a rectangle template out of cardboard and cut a notch in the center of each of the long sides. Place this *marking* template on top of the cardboard and add ¼ in (6 mm) on all sides. This is the *cutting* template.
● Cut one cutting template for each color. Write the color and number of rectangles to be cut on each template (Fig. 2).

● Cut out the required number of blocks of each fabric color.
● Place the marking template on the pieces of fabric and mark the seam allowances (Fig. 3).

● **Chain piecing:** This is a timesaving method of sewing the patchwork pieces together. Place the pieces together in pairs according to the design. Use the width of the front vest piece as a guideline. Then stitch the pairs together, one after the other, without clipping threads between them. You will need to raise the presser foot between blocks. Leave a small gap between pairs of blocks to facilitate thread cutting (Fig. 4).

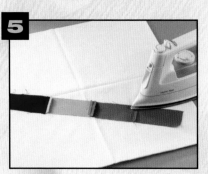

● Clip the connecting threads between the pairs. Trim thread ends.

● Press open the seam allowances (Fig. 5).

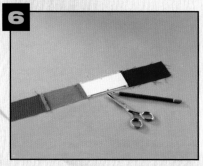

● Place the marking template on the fabric rectangles and mark the center on the lengthwise edges (Fig. 6).
● Pin two rows together staggered so that the center marks match the vertical seams of the row below.
● Stitch the rows together. Remove pins and press the seam allowances

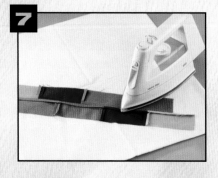

open. Leave the seam allowances unfinished. Do not trim the excess fabric on the ends (Fig. 7).

● Continue in the same way, adding the blocks according to the design.
● Prepare the second vest front piece as a mirrored image of the first.
● Carefully press both vest front pieces on the wrong side.

● Place vest front pieces wrong sides together, matching blocks, and baste along the edges (Fig. 8).
● Pin the vest front pattern piece template to the patchwork fabric and cut (the template includes seam allowances). Remove the template (Fig. 9).

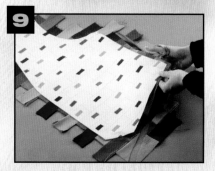

Vest sewing instructions
Cutting the pattern pieces:
Cut the back piece and the front pieces from the satin as shown. Cut the tabs.
● Cut the front facings from the burgundy cotton.
● Cut interfacing for the tabs and front facing and fuse to the wrong sides of the tabs and front facing.
● Place the facings, right sides together, on the right and left lining front pieces. Stitch together to create a complete front piece.
● Press the seam allowances toward the facing (Fig. 10).
● Fold the short tab in half lengthwise, right sides together. Baste and stitch at ¼ in (6 mm). Turn right side out and press.

● Sew the long tab in the same way, leaving about ¼ in (6 mm) seam allowance on one end. Trim corners.
● Turn in the other end of the long tab and pin to the marked position on the vest back.

● Pin the short tab to the marked position on the vest back, also turning in the end (Fig. 11).
● Stitch a square and crisscrossing onto the pinned tab ends (Fig. 12).

● Fold the open end of the short tab under and stitch.
● Pull the tab through the buckle and turn under about 1¼ in (3 cm) from the buckle. Stitch close to the edge (Fig. 13).

● Lay the lining front pieces on the patchwork front pieces, right sides together. Stitch together from shoulder point around front and lower edge to side seam.
● Place the armhole edges right sides together, and stitch.
● Do not stitch the shoulder and sides seams.
● Clip the corners and curves.
● Carefully press both pieces and turn right side out.
● Place the two back layers right sides together. Pin and stitch the neck edge, the armholes, and the hem edge, leaving a 6 in (15 cm) opening in the latter for turning right side out. Secure thread ends.

● Do not stitch the side seams. Keep the back piece wrong side out (Fig. 14).

● Press all seams on the front and back pieces.
● Slide the fronts through the open side seams of the back, right sides together.
● Pin shoulder edges together, baste, and stitch. Press.
● Stitch together the open side seams.
● Turn the vest right side out through the opening on the back hem edge (Fig. 15). Stitch the opening closed by hand. Press the vest.

● Make buttonholes on the left front edge on the marked positions with the machine or by hand. The buttonholes should be the size of the buttons plus ⅛ in (3 mm).

● Mark the positions for the buttons on the right front edge and sew on the buttons.

Baby blanket

Fabrics
Cotton, cotton blends, silk

Amount
For one blanket 32×32 in (80×80 cm):
32 in (80 cm) blue fabric, 1¼ yd (1.1 m)
white fabric, both in 54/56 in
(140 cm) -width

Notions
⅞ yd (80 cm) quilt batting

Pattern pieces
1 Backing, white
2 Triangles, white – cut 4
3 Rhombi, white – cut 8
4 Border, blue – cut 4
5 Rhombi, blue – cut 8
6 Triangles, large, blue – cut 4
7 Triangles, small, blue – cut 8
Rhombi are diamond-shaped
equal-sided parallelograms.

Wash the fabric before cutting to
allow for shrinkage and fading.
Quilt batting is available in a variety
of thicknesses. The thinner the
batting, the easier it is to work with.
This baby blanket uses ⅜ in (1 cm)
-thickness batting, quilted between
two layers of fabric.

The History of Quilting

When one thinks of quilting today, the colorful and attractive quilts made by pioneer women in the United States and Canada come to mind.

The quilting technique did not originate in North America, however. Although the origins of quilting are not known for certain, there are examples of this sewing technique from ancient Egypt: a quilted blanket has been found that dates back to around 980 B.C., as has a quilted garment on a carved figure of a Pharaoh dating as far back as 3400 B.C. Quilted fabrics have also been discovered in archeological excavation sites in China.

Then, quilting was not for decoration as much as it was a practical solution to a common problem — trying to keep warm in cold weather. It allowed insulating material to be placed between multiple layers of fabric.

Quilted pieces of clothing have been known to exist in Europe since the Middle Ages, believed to have been brought there by the crusaders in the late 11th century. Jackets sewn from several fabric layers not only protected one from the cold but also from arrows and truncheons. Quilted clothing was worn under suits of armor for comfort and as protection from the elements; it sometimes even replaced the armor itself.

Quilted bedding was introduced to Europe by the Romans. In fact, the word "quilt" comes from the Latin *culcita,* meaning a stuffed sack, though it came into the English language from the French word *cuilte.* The oldest known example of quilted bedding is a shroud of a Scythian duke who died around the last millennium. The shroud was lined with batting and quilted, and it displayed rhombi that were arranged around a spiral-shaped center. Fighting animals were depicted on its colorful borders.

In Japan, quilted bedding took the form of the Yogi, which proved the best protection against wind and cold. These quilts were the large and heavily padded version of the kimono. Filled with cotton batting, they were held together with plain, straight seams with white stitches and were used as mattresses as well as blankets.

In the 15th century, the wealthy in Europe kept themselves warm with quilts filled with wool, wool batting, and down feathers. Those who could afford to, fended off extreme cold temperatures with quilted clothing, curtains, and tapestries. Near the end of the 16th century, beds were regularly outfitted with feather beds, pillows, and quilted blankets.

Patchwork, a sewing technique distinct from but often closely associated with quilting, was also being practiced in many cultures at this time. With woven cloth considered a luxury, every scrap was put to use. The result was small, various-colored pieces of fabric sewn together, either to make a "new" piece of cloth or to mend clothing or bedding.

The tradition of quilting in the United States and Canada

Quilting and patchwork were a way for North American pioneer women to pass the time on the long winter evenings. But these sewing techniques also created the warm blankets necessary to fight the bitter cold. Usually, several women would sit together and sew a quilt — the precursor of the quilting bee. They used scraps of leftover fabric, old clothing, or reusable pieces of worn bed linens for the top layer, and dried leaves, rags, old blankets, cotton, and other insulating materials as batting. Plain-colored cotton fabric was used for the backing. To prevent the batting from slipping, they connected the layers with regular stitching or knots.

For the top layer, the women would cut various shapes, often geometric, out of their fabric scraps, arranging them together to make a pattern. This was called patch working. Sometimes appliqués were sewn on top or added later for decoration. Many different patterns were created in this way — the Amish quilt, the Flying Geese quilt, and the Wind Mill quilt, to name just a few. By the 1820s, quilting bees were well established.

For years, quilts were considered a sign of poverty and were threatened with becoming a thing of the past. It wasn't until the 1970s that they were "rediscovered." Today, quilts are cherished by many.

Quilting today

These days, quilts serve more of a decorative purpose than a practical one. They are used primarily as bedspreads, rather than as blankets for warmth. The more elaborate ones are considered "art quilts" and often are hung on the wall for display. These quilts are expensive and many eventually find their way into museums. Quilts are seldom sewn by hand anymore; sewing machines have proven much more efficient. New types of cutting tools have also made quilt production easier.

The baby blanket made in this project is constructed of two layers of fabric, with a layer of batting in between, all quilted together. You can use your own fabric remnants or buy them from a fabric store. Then it is up to you, and to your degree of experience, to select a simple or a more complicated quilt pattern.

Sewing tools and quilting accessories

You will find it much easier to quilt if you use the proper tools.

● A rotary cutter works best for cutting triangles and other pieces. Rotary cutters come in various sizes: larger sizes, for cutting through several layers, and smaller sizes, for cutting one layer or cutting curves. Cut the patches on a cutting mat that has several grid patterns and a scale of measurement (Fig. 1). You can also cut with scissors.

● You will also need a quilting ruler with angle marks, and a fabric-marking pen, sewing chalk, or a pencil. Make certain that the markings will wash out; experiment on a test piece of fabric before beginning the quilt. A special fabric eraser will also come in handy.

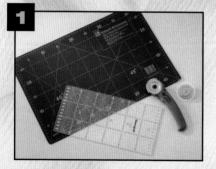

● Use brightly colored cotton thread to baste the quilt layers. The actual quilting should be done with special quilting thread, also made of cotton. Safety pins are essential for basting, as are long thin pins, or quilting pins.

● In addition to a pair of sewing scissors, you will need embroidery scissors or a seam ripper to cut threads, and also a pair of paper scissors for cutting the templates out of cardboard. Three other tools you will need are a tape measure, a ruler, and a thimble (Fig. 2).

● A basic sewing machine with plain, straight-stitch functions is sufficient for machine quilting. Look in your machine's instruction manual or ask

staff at a specialty-sewing store to determine which presser foot to use for quilting. The choice of needle size and type will depend on the fabric and batting you are using.

● And, finally, it is important to have a good steam iron and an ironing board.

Cutting

One of the most appealing things about quilting is the wide variety of patterns and designs possible. This baby blanket's quilt block — the patterned square of fabric that is repeated or alternated with plain blocks to form the quilt's design — is a patchwork pattern of blue and white triangles, squares, and rhombi. The quilt's border is made with blue fabric.

● Cut all pieces with ¼ in (7 mm) seam allowance.

Large triangles: $6\frac{5}{8} \times 6\frac{5}{8} \times 9\frac{5}{8}$ in ($17.5 \times 17.5 \times 24.5$ cm);

small triangles: $6\frac{5}{8} \times 6\frac{5}{8} \times 5\frac{1}{4}$ in ($17.5 \times 12.5 \times 13$ cm);

squares: 5 in (12.5 cm) side length;

rhombi: $5\frac{1}{4}$ in (13 cm) wide, 9×5 in (23×13 cm) long;

border strips: 4.5 in (11.5 cm) wide, $23\frac{1}{2} \times 26$ in (60×66 cm) long.

● The quilt backing is made of the white fabric. Cut a 32 in (80 cm) square piece of fabric, adding the seam allowances.

● Cut selvages off the fabric and discard.

● Draw the template design on graph paper (Fig. 3). Transfer the five pattern pieces with a seam allowance of ¼ to ⅜ in (6 to 8 mm) onto cardboard and cut out (Fig. 4).

● Cut the number of pattern pieces needed. Place the fabric on the cutting mat in one or more layers; cut with the rotary cutter through all layers. The cut should be exact, otherwise the pieces cannot be connected precisely. Take care to follow the grain of the fabric (Fig. 5).

Sewing instructions

● Stitch the border strips together. Make sure that the thread tension is set correctly so that the fabric does not gather. Choose a stitch length of 12 to 15 stitches per inch (a stitch length of about 2 mm).

● Keep the seam allowances of the corner pieces open (Fig. 6).

Chain piecing: The time-saving method for sewing the small fabric pieces together is called chain piecing. Place the pieces together in pairs according to the design. Stitch the patch pairs together one after the other without clipping threads between pairs (Fig. 7). Then clip the

connecting thread between the pairs with small scissors or a seam ripper; cut the threads at the seam allowance (Fig. 8).

● The seam allowances of the pairs should be pressed to one side. When using two colors, make sure the seam

allowance is pressed toward the darker color so that the darker color does not show through to the right

side. Smooth the seam out from the right side. Press the seam gently with a steam iron so the seam allowances do not show through (Fig. 9).

● Add additional pieces by chain piecing to create ever-larger units. Once you have connected the units together, stitch on the border strips. All seams should be stitched completely from one end of the seam

allowance to the next. If you make a mistake, you will have to re-cut and re-sew the whole unit.

● Carefully smooth out and press each seam.

● Press the whole block again. Cut off any remaining threads, as they might potentially show through to the right side.

● Place the quilt top on the batting, smooth out, and check to make sure

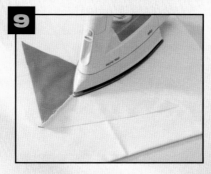

they are the same size. Cut the batting to fit if necessary.

● Pin the batting and quilt top together (Fig. 10).

● Baste together, starting in the middle. This important step prevents the fabric from slipping during quilting. The two pieces can also be connected with safety pins. The quilt top should be smooth and not over-stretched; it will stretch during quilting.

Hand quilting: Quilting can be done by hand or with a sewing machine.

● When quilting by hand, use a thimble and wax the thread. Quilting threads are pre-waxed, but you will find that stitching is much easier if you wax thread again.

● Knot the thread at the end before starting a quilting seam. Insert the

needle from above, through both layers. Pull the thread with a short tug so that the knot is in the batting

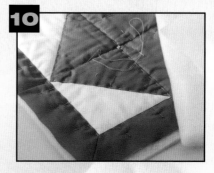

layer, where it is ideally placed. If the knot can be pulled through all the layers, begin again with a bigger knot. If the knot is too large, try to tie it tighter.

● Cut off any extra thread at the end of the knot.

● Carefully quilt along the edges of the patches with small, even running stitches. Make certain that both layers are caught.

● At the end of a quilting line, make a knot, with the needle still threaded, on the top of the quilt. Make one more stitch, then push the needle up through the batting. Give the thread a careful tug so that the the knot slips through to the batting layer.

Quilting with a sewing machine: Start in the middle of the quilt. Roll

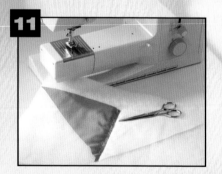

up the left half and keep it next to the presser foot while sewing the right half. The right half should be lying flat and not hanging off the table.

● Set the stitch length at 2 to 2.5 mm; keep the thread tension low. Choose an adjustable guide bar for the presser foot; this will ensure that every quilting line is stitched straight.

● It is a good idea to test the settings on a sample piece first (Fig. 11).

● Secure the fabric with the presser foot and stretch gently.

● There are three ways to quilt:

1. Quilt along the seam line or directly next to it (Fig. 12). This is called in-

the-ditch quilting.

2. Quilt parallel to the left and the right of the seam lines at a constant distance from the seam (Fig. 13). This is called grid quilting.

3. Quilt 1/16 in (1 to 2 mm) from the seam line on one side only (Fig. 14).

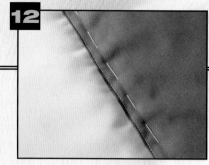

This is called outline quilting or contour quilting. This project is made using this method.

● Place the quilting seams so that interruptions in stitching are as

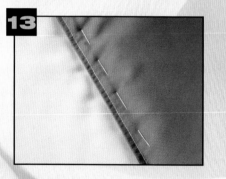

infrequent as possible.

● Sew slowly, stretching the fabric gently so that the seam is placed as accurately as possible. Avoid gathering the fabric.

● Quilt from the middle outward. Sew the long seams first, then the shorter ones, leaving the quilting lines along the border strip until later.

● Do not secure the seams with backstitching. Leave the threads long

and pull the bobbin thread up, then tie the top and bobbin threads together by hand on the wrong side.

● If a quilting seam is not straight, remove the entire seam and begin

again.

● Place the quilt top and backing right sides together, and stitch the edges, leaving an opening of about 8 in (20 cm). Turn the quilted blanket right side out through this opening and finish the open edge by hand with a fine slipstitch.

● Quilt the seam around the border strips through all three layers.

Patterns for quilting

There are myriad possibilities when combining design and color in a quilt. The colorful patchwork quilt shown being worked on at right was made using the Ohio Star pattern. Like the baby blanket, it is composed of squares and triangles. The distinguishing characteristics of the Ohio Star are the small squares made up of triangles. The blocks have the same patterns and the same colors; however, the colors are arranged differently within the blocks. The blocks are connected using grids. Decorative hand quilting can be seen on the grid strips.

You can design a pattern yourself, make a template, and then transfer it to the fabric with a marker.

Quilts are traditionally finished with a border strip of fabric around the outer edges. Both the baby blanket featured in this project and the Ohio Star quilt shown at right has such a border. Modern quilt designs often have no border.

If you do not yet feel confident enough to attempt a more complicated quilt project, you may want to consider taking a quilting course to improve your skills. Quilting classes are becoming an increasingly popular offering at community schools. Many communities also have quilting guilds.

A great variety of sewing terms are used in this book. Many are common terms and do not need explanation. Others, however, have special meanings in sewing. To help you better understand the tips, guidelines, and diagrams used in this book and to serve as a quick reference, certain terms are defined below. (The index will refer you to sections of the book in which terms are explained fully.) Definitions for some terms which describe the constructions of fabrics have also been included below.

Appliqué
Pieces cut from various materials, such as fabric, felt, and leather, which are then sewn onto garments, pillows, or other items to create a decorative effect.

Bar tack
A reinforcement tack used at points of strain. Bar tacks can be made by hand or by machine.

Basket weave
A variation of the plain weave in which paired or multiple yarns are used in the alternating pattern. The yarns are laid side by side without being twisted together. This makes the basket weave looser, less stable, often less durable than ordinary plain weaves.

Basting
Also known as tacking, used to temporarily hold together two or more fabric layers during both fitting and construction.

Bias
All fabric has a bias, which is determined as follows: Selvage is formed along each lengthwise edge. Lengthwise grain parallels the selvage; crosswise grain is perpendicular to it. The bias is any diagonal that intersects these grains; true bias is at a 45° angle to any straight edge when grains are perpendicular.

Blind hemming
A stitching technique used for joining fabric together so that the seam is invisible from the right side of the fabric.

Casing
A tube of fabric that is sewn in order to hold, or encase, elastic or a drawstring. Casings are most often used at the wrist, at the waist, and, in sportswear, at the legs.

Clipping
A technique that involves cutting slits into the seam allowance of convex, or *outward,* curves to permit the edges of the seam to spread and lie smooth. Great care needs to be taken during clipping not to cut the seam stitching.

Cording *see* **Piping**

Dart
A triangular shape sewn onto a flat piece of fabric, allowing the fabric to conform to the contours of a body.

Dobby weave
A patterned structure, usually geometric in form, produced by a special attachment (dobby) on a plain-weave loom. The dobby raises and lowers certain warp yarns so that warp and weft interlace in a constantly changing pattern. The most familiar pattern is the diamond shape.

Double knit
Produced by two yarn-and-needle sets working simultaneously. Double knits have firm body and limited stretch capacity. Depending on the design, the face and back may be alike or different. Some complex double knits resemble the woven dobby and jacquard patterns.

Easing
Making a larger piece of fabric fit with a smaller piece so that both can be sewn into the same seam. Through this process, you are at the same time allowing for extra room in the garment where it is needed, such as at the back shoulder. Collars are often eased onto the neckline seam. When a large amount of fabric needs to be reduced in size to fit a seam, the technique of gathering is used.

Fabric finishes
Various finishes may be applied by the manufacturer in order to change the performance, look, or feel of a fabric. A water-repellent finish is one of the most common types; it wards off stains as well as moisture. The finish used, if any, may affect fabric care and is usually indicated on the fabric bolt label.

Fabric marking
Transferring seam lines, darts, and other important pattern notations to the fabric before it is cut, using various marking methods. The most common marking method is to use dressmaker's tracing paper and a tracing wheel.

Facing
A piece of fabric that is used to finish the unhemmed or unfinished edges of a garment.

Felting
A process in which moisture, heat, and pressure are applied to short fibers, interlocking them in a matted layer. Wool is the primary fiber in felt fabric because it tends naturally to mat. Felts do not unravel and can be cut or blocked to any shape. They do, however, shrink when dampened and they tear easily.

Filament yarn
A long, smooth strand unreeled from a silkworm's cocoon or extruded from a chemical solution

(the source of synthetic fibers). Filament yarn may take the form of a monofilament (single strand), multifilaments (two or more strands twisted together), or staples (cut lengths to be made into spun yarn).

Finishing
Protecting the edges of a seam allowance or a piece of fabric so that it does not fray. This can be done either with hand stitches or machine stitches or, depending on the type of fabric and where the edge is to be located in a garment, with pinking shears.

French cuff
A cuff that is cut double the width of a standard cuff so that it can be folded back onto itself, exposing the facing.

Fusing
Similar to felting except that it employs a bonding agent to hold the fibers (usually cotton or rayon) together. The product can be a non-woven fabric of the type used for interfacing, or it can be a web, which is itself a fusible bonding agent.

Gathering
Gathering fabric into a smaller, predetermined area along one or more stitching lines. Fabric is gathered most often at the waistline, cuffs, or yoke, and to make ruffles.

Grading
A technique that involves cutting seam allowances to different widths. Usually seams are graded when they form an edge or are enclosed.

Grain
Indicates the direction of the yarn in fabric. The lengthwise grain usually runs vertically, from shoulder to hem. The crosswise grain usually runs horizontally and has more give.

Gusset
A small fabric piece, often diamond-shaped or triangular, that is inserted into a slashed opening. Gussets provide ease for a comfortable fit. They are often used in kimono sleeves.

Herringbone weave
A variation of the twill weave in which the diagonal ridges switch direction to form a zigzag pattern. The design is more pronounced when contrasting colors are used for the ridges.

Inseam
The seam on the inside of the leg of a garment.

Interfacing
A layer of fabric that supports, shapes, and stabilizes many areas and edges of a garment, especially collars, cuffs, waistbands, plackets, and flaps. It comes in many types and weights.

Interlining
A layer of fabric usually placed inside the body of a jacket or coat, sometimes the sleeves, in order to provide extra warmth without bulk.

Jacquard weave
A patterned complex weave. By means of a jacquard attachment, warp and weft yarns can be controlled individually to create an intricate design. Jacquard fabrics are usually expensive because of the elaborate loom preparation. Damask, tapestry, and brocade are types of jacquard weaves.

Jersey knit
A single construction in which all loops are pulled to the back of the fabric. The face is smooth, and it exhibits lengthwise vertical rows (wales); on the reverse side, there are horizontal rows of half-circles, characteristic of the purl stitch. Plain knits stretch more in width than in length.

Kimono sleeve
A sleeve that is cut as an extension of the main bodice of the garment rather than being cut out separately and set in. It is considered the easiest sleeve form to construct.

Knit band
A band of stretchy woven fabric that is mainly applied to sleeve edges or necklines. The application technique depends on the stretch of the garment fabric.

Lapped cuff
A cuff that has one end projecting from the placket edge.

Leno weave
An open-mesh structure produced by a leno attachment on the loom. The leno continuously changes the position of the warp yarns so that they become twisted in a figure-of-eight fashion around the filling yarns. Also called gauze weave.

Lining
A layer of fabric, sewn inside coats, jackets, dresses, skirts, and pants. Most often made from a relatively slippery fabric, it covers construction details and makes garments easier to put on and take off.

Master pattern
A pattern based on your own figure measurements, often made before beginning to sew a garment with expensive fabric. The basis for a master pattern is a fitting shell, sometimes referred to as a muslin. The fitting shell is sewn using a basic pattern such as for a dress or blouse. It is adjusted to fit your figure perfectly. The adjustments are then transferred to the master pattern.

Mitering
The diagonal joining of two edges at a corner, used to finish corners at garment edges. The join may be stitched or simply folded in place.

Notching

A technique that involves cutting wedges from the seam allowance of concave, or *inward,* curves. The space opened up by the removal of the fabric wedges lets the edge of the seam draw in.

Outlet

Extra fabric allowance in pants, which is usually added to the center back seam and the top of the front inseam.

Outseam

The seam that falls along the outside of the leg (the side seam).

Overlock machine

Also called a serger, this machine does not replace a conventional machine but complements it. Overlocking is a quick way of finishing seams and hem edges as it cuts and neatens in one operation. It is also used to sew two fabrics together — cutting, seaming, and oversewing in one operation.

Overtacking

Three or four hand stitches in the same spot, used to hold two pieces of fabric together.

Padding stitch

A stitch used primarily to attach interfacing to the outer fabric. Padding stitches can help form and control shape in garment sections or simply hold the interfacing in place.

Permanent press

A common fabric finish. The fabric is specially heat-treated so that it wrinkles less during wear and laundering.

Pile weave

A woven fabric construction in which an extra filling or warp yarn is added to a basic plain or twill weave. By means of thick wires, the additional yarn is drawn into loops on the fabric surface. These loops can be cut as for plush, sheared as for velvet, or left in loop form as for terry cloth.

Piping

Made out of bias strips that are folded and stitched. The strips can be of any type of material, from light fabric to leather. Piping is flat, while cording is filled with a length of cable cord and therefore rounded. Both are used to decorate garments, especially the edges of pockets, and for buttonholes.

Placket

A type of garment opening. Plackets are found at skirt waistlines, sleeve cuffs, on dresses, and at necklines on skirts and pants.

Plain weave

The simplest of the weave constructions, in which each filling yarn goes alternately over and under each warp yarn. Sturdiness varies with the strength of the yarns and compactness of the

weave structure. Plain weave is the basis for most prints.

Ply yarn

Consists of two or more spun yarns twisted together; the number of strands is usually indicated by the terms 2 ply, 3 ply, and so forth. When the combined yarns are different in thickness or degree of twist, the result is a novelty yarn, such as slub or bouclé.

Purl knit

A single construction in which loops are pulled in alternate rows to the front and back of the knit, causing a purl stitch to appear on both sides of the fabric. Purl knits have nearly the same amount of stretch lengthwise and crosswise.

Raglan sleeve

A type of sleeve that is made separately, then attached to the garment by a seam running diagonally down from the front neckline to the underarm, and up to the back neckline.

Raschel knit

Encompasses a wide range of fabrics, from fine nets to piles. The most typical raschel pattern has an open, lacy structure with alternating thick and thin yarns. Any yarn type is suitable, including metallic and glass.

Release

To open up stitches as needed.

Rib

Also known as wale. In knit fabrics, a lengthwise row of loops.

Rib knit

A single construction with rows of plain and purl knit arranged so that the face and the reverse sides are identical. Rib knits have expansive stretch and strong recovery in the crosswise direction, which makes them especially suitable for cuffs and waistbands.

Rib weave

A variation of the plain weave in which the fine yarns are alternated with coarse yarns, or single with multiple yarns. The alternating thicknesses may be parallel or at right angles, producing a ridged or corded effect. Durability is limited because the yarns are exposed to friction.

Ruffle

A strip of fabric cut or handled in such a way as to create fullness.

Satin weave

A basic structure in which a warp yarn passes over four to eight weft yarns in a staggered pattern similar to that of twill. Yarns exposed on the surface, called floats, give satin its characteristic sheen.

Seam allowance

The amount of fabric between the stitching or seamline and the fabric edge.

Selvage
A firmly woven strip formed along each lengthwise edge of finished fabric.

Shirring
Multiple rows of gathering, used as a decorative way of controlling fullness in fabric over a comparatively wide span.

Shirt cuff
A cuff that is constructed and applied to the sleeve after the placket opening is made at the sleeve edge. It is sewn with its ends aligned to the underlap and the overlap edges of the shirt placket.

Smocking
Fabric folds decoratively stitched together at regular intervals to create a patterned effect.

Spun yarn
Yarn made of staples (short fiber lengths) twisted together into a continuous strand. The strand may contain one fiber type, or two or more fibers blended during spinning. The smoothest and strongest spun yarns are those made from longer staples that have been given a high degree of twist.

Stay
A tape that serves to strengthen a seam and prevent it from stretching. It is added mainly to waistline seams. Since the aim is to add stability to a waistline, the stay should be made of a non-stretch fabric such as twill or hem tape.

Staystitching
A row of directional stitching placed just inside certain seamlines to prevent them from stretching out of shape during handling and garment construction. Curved or angled seams, such as at a neckline or armhole, are the most important ones to staystitch.

Straightening fabric ends
The first step taken with every fabric so that it can be folded evenly and also checked for grain alignment. It is done either by tearing, drawing a thread, or cutting the fabric on a prominent line. The method chosen depends on the type of fabric being straightened.

Swivel weave
A weave in which an extra filling yarn is added to form a circle or other figure on the surface of a basic weave. Each swivel yarn is carried on the wrong side of the fabric from one design to the next, then cut when the fabric is completed. Dotted swiss is one type of swivel weave.

Textured yarn
A synthetic filament that has undergone special treatments to give its surface a coiled, crimped, curled, or looped shape. Some textured yarns are the basis of woven stretch fabrics; others, the basis of fabrics with qualities of softness or bulk closely resembling those of natural fibers.

Topstitching
Machine stitches done from the right side of a garment for either a decorative effect or for functional reasons, or sometimes for both at the same time. Topstitching gives a garment a more tailored look.

Tracing
Transferring pattern notations onto the fabric before it is cut, using dressmaker's tracing paper and a tracing wheel.

Tricot knit
A knit with fine ribs on the face, flat herringbone courses on the back. Can be single-, double-, or triple-warp construction. Technical differences are not visible, but they do affect performance. Double- and triple-warp tricots are run-proof; single-warp is not. Tricots are usually made from fine cotton or synthetic yarn. They have a soft, draping quality and are suitable for linings, casual wear, lingerie, and dresses.

Trimming
A technique that involves cutting away some of the seam allowances when the full width of the seam allowances interfere with the fit or with further garment construction.

Tuck
A stitched fold of fabric that is most often decorative but can also be used in shaping a garment.

Twill weave
A basic structure in which weft yarn passes over at least two, but not more than four, warp yarns. On each successive line, the weft moves one step to the right or left, forming a diagonal ridge; the steeper the ridge, the stronger the fabric. As a rule, twills are more durable than plain weaves. Denim and gabardine are examples of twill weaves.

Underlining
A layer of lightweight fabric sewn into many types of garments to reinforce seams and other areas. It can provide opaqueness, hide the inner construction of the garment, inhibit stretching, and act as a buffer layer on which to catch hems and fasten inner stitching.

Understitching
A line of straight stitching, either by hand or machine, applied along certain seamlines such as neckline facing seams. Its purpose is to keep the facing and seam allowances lying flat in a particular direction.

Warp
The lengthwise yarns on a loom.

Weft
The crosswise yarns on a loom.

The Reader's Digest Association would like to acknowledge the following people, institutions, and companies who have contributed to and assisted in the creation of this book:

American Society of Testing and Materials (ASTM): 25

Verlag Aenne Burda, Offenburg, Germany: 28, 29, 30, 32, 33

Illustrations
Monika Hopfensitz 94, 104, 118, 124, 130, 146, 164, 172, 192, 198, 208, 222, 240, 268, 292, 358, 364
Reinhard Mutschler 92, 98, 104, 118, 124, 130, 146, 164, 172, 192, 198, 208, 214, 222, 234, 240, 268, 292, 326, 358, 364

Photography
DOUG HALL, Toronto, Canada: 1–2, 8–9, 26–27

WERKSTATT FOTOGRAFIE Neumann & Zörlein: 1, 6, 7,10–13, 14 l, 16–24, 66–67, 68, 93, 105, 119, 125, 131, 136–137, 147, 165–167, 173, 182–183, 193, 199, 205, 209, 212–213, 223, 232–233, 241–243, 252–253, 261, 269, 279, 282–283, 284, 293, 324–325, 358–359, 361–363, 367–369
G. M. Pfaff AG, Karlsruhe, Germany: 14 lr, 15
Rowenta-Werke, Offenbach, Germany: 14 lr, 14 mr

Additional Acknowledgments
The following companies kindly provided fabrics and other materials:

A. Berger OHG, Stuttgart; Bouvelle, La Tour-Du-Pin; Brennet AG, Bad Säckingen; Gebrüder Colsman GmbH & Co., Essen; Cortex, Marcy L'Etoile, Créations Sonetex, Paris, Freudenberg Faservliesstoffe KG, Weinheim; Gaenslen + Völter Tuchfabrik, Metzingen; M. Grabher GmbH & Co. KG, A-Hard; Hans-Christoph Hertel textilagentur, Herrenberg-Gültstein; Inter-Jersey GmbH & Co. KH, Burladingen; Jabouley, St-André Le Gaz; Lauffenmühle GmbH, Lauchringen; Nadel und Faden, Stuttgart-Bad Cannstatt; P + E Festartikel GmbH, Sobernheim; Pierre Rocle, Tarare; Prym Consumer, Stolberg; Seiden-Import H. Meier & Co. GmbH, Bremen; Verlag Aenne Burda GmbH & Co. KG, Offenburg; C. F. Weiss Kammgarnweberei, Helmbrechts.

Photos on pages 130, 192, and 292 were taken at La Maison, Nürtingen, Germany.